A Londoner, Tom Barling has worked for the national press, in advertising, as an art director and a TV producer. For many years he ran his own production company producing commercials and animated films, mostly for the American market. His previous novels include *The Olympic Sleeper, Goodbye Piccadilly, Bikini Red North, Terminate with Prejudice, The Smoke* and *God is an Executioner*.

Also by Tom Barling

THE SMOKE
GOD IS AN EXECUTIONER

and published by Corgi Books

SMOKE DRAGON

Tom Barling

CORGI BOOKS

SMOKE DRAGON
A CORGI BOOK 0 552 13253 5

First publication in Great Britain

PRINTING HISTORY

Corgi edition published 1988

This book is set in 10/11 Plantin

Corgi Books are published by Transworld Publishers Ltd.,
61–63 Uxbridge Road, Ealing, London W5 5SA, in Australia by
Transworld Publishers (Australia) Pty. Ltd., 15–23 Helles Avenue,
Moorebank, NSW 2170, and in New Zealand by Transworld Publishers
(N.Z.) Ltd., Cnr. Moselle and Waipareira Avenues, Henderson,
Auckland.

Printed and bound in Great Britain by
Cox & Wyman Ltd., Reading, Berks.

For my parents
John D
and Travis McGee

PROLOGUE

It rained even harder when the black umbrellas and the last funeral limousine had hurried away. The CID photographers were back at West End Central and the rabbi had returned to Golders Green. Smoke from the crematorium furnace scudded with the wind, and the sky greyed into evening. Only then did Charlie Dance emerge from the dripping conifers. He crossed the sodden turf to look at the wreaths around the memorial tree and read the bronze plaque below it.

ARCHIE OGLE   QUEENIE OGLE
1891 – 1964   1903 – 1965
They Sleep With The Angels

Now Queenie's ashes mingled with her husband's in the same urn. She had survived him by eleven short months and slipped away without complaint. She had died smiling, and Charlie gave odds she was smiling yet. With her beside him, Archie would have to stop chasing the more nubile angels.

Charlie bared his head and tried to feel something.

Dead leaves swirled to paste themselves against his legs and distant thunder lit the muddy horizon with sheets of brilliant light, rumbling low like a soft bass voice. He picked up a clod of brown clay and the rain turned it to slurry in his hand. He tried to mourn and could only see them alive, not turned to sludge like the mud oozing through his fingers. Queenie looking for bargains at the sales when she could buy the whole store. Archie back in the Rolls, waiting for

Charlie to fix him a stiff brandy and soda. They weren't here right now, that was all. Busy elsewhere.

Charlie crouched to wipe his hands on the grass. Lifted his face to the weeping sky to talk into the smashing rain. Knowing loss without feeling it.

'I'm still holding the cobbles for you, Arch. Queenie's probably telling you that right now. Giving you the heavy verbals. And you with all eternity to listen in.'

Charlie slopped rain from his hat. Shook it from his eyes.

'The old days are deader than you are. The heavy chaps don't live in the manors no more. Wear suits. Commute in from Weybridge and Esher like they was regular city-types. Carry briefcases and plan their tickles like they was at board meetings. You wouldn't like it, Arch. All too different for you. Right, Queenie?'

Charlie felt for cigarettes he didn't have. It was too wet to smoke anyway. Lightning sizzled across the grass and left vapour behind. The closing darkness smelled of raw earth.

'And you left me with a war, old son. Your Chinese Triads ain't as yellow as you painted them. You thought you had them in your pocket. Would have been the other way round in time. Their polite smiles don't go no deeper than the fronts of their faces. And there's more to their way of cobbles-fighting than handing out tasty whacks and surprises. A lot more. Just standing still around them means learning new tricks. I'm even learning their lingo. You're well out of it, Arch. Me, I've got nowhere else to go.'

Charlie listened to muted thunder.

'No I ain't going soft. Just telling you, is all. Keep plucking that old harp, Arch. See you around, eh? From down here.'

Charlie walked away to climb the wrought-iron gates and sit in the white Rolls. Sodbonce passed him a lit Player and drove back to Soho without a word. There was more than rain on Charlie's face.

BOOK ONE

CHAPTER ONE

Cho Sun cleared Heathrow Customs at dawn and took a black cab to London in a fierce thunderstorm. Hurricane Zelda had crossed the Atlantic to die in Europe; a bad omen that made Cho Sun glad he had consulted the soothsayer at Rennie's Mill after his last kill.

Braving the long busride from Hong Kong to the stink of the old Nationalist village had been worth the effort.

The ivory fortune sticks had fallen true in the booth off Don Tan Alley. The number seven had repeated itself seven times, and the prayer-roll of rice paper had burned clean with a straight plume of white smoke. Casting bone dice from a leather cup, Cho Sun saw his future shape itself on the green baize table. Seven bamboo *chops* had surrounded a single red dragon, and four amber snakes formed an eye of luck. Such a forecast was rare, and coming in the eighth month of the Year of the Snake was all the more remarkable. Even the old soothsayer had been impressed enough to burn half the fee dollars Cho Sun had paid him. Scattered around the village when the swallows returned in the spring, the ashes would keep the crops free of malevolent spirits. Until then, the luck belonged to Cho Sun of the Dragon T'ang; and on the strength of the forecast, Cho Sun flew to London to kill again for the Sichuen Brotherhood.

Cho Sun paid the black cab off in Shaftesbury Avenue and stood in the rain as it swished away, letting the alien city come to him in its own time. The rain smelled of soot and sulphur. Water gushed from a broken downpipe, and

11

an early bus ground towards Piccadilly Circus. A corporation dustcart chewed on garbage as Cho Sun followed it down Lower Wardour Street, and ruffled pigeons watched him as he turned into Gerrard Street.

There were other eyes on Cho Sun, and light flashed on bright steel as a dark figure stepped back into shadow. Without hurry, Cho Sun hid his bag behind a dustbin and crossed the road with his collar up, just another waiter on his way home from a night shift. He reached the doorway where the man hid and stopped. There was a sighing grunt. An arm shot out at his face, the fist hooked in a double phoenix. Cho Sun ducked, broke the wrist with an upward palm chop, and straight-armed a killing blow to the throat with pinpoint accuracy. Stale wine gusted at him as the head snapped to one side. Air bubbled in a crushed oesophagus and the man sat heavily, shooting his legs into the light. A surgical shoe jerked with nerves, and the steel leg-brace Cho Sun had taken for a weapon grated against the marble step.

Then Cho Sun saw the man's face. The bloated jowls of an alcoholic. The eyes as empty as dirty windows. The gaping mouth that huffed sounds instead of words. Boxes of matches falling from a palsied hand that begged for life instead of charity.

Appalled by his mistake, Cho Sun stayed with the old derelict until he died; checked the empty street for witnesses, and strolled back the way he had come, hating to waste his art on a creature of such little worth. When he had retrieved his bag, he scratched at a shop door and was let into a dark passage by the deaf man who expected him. Joe Yellow welcomed his uncle with sign language and lipread Cho Sun's response. The door closed on Cho Sun's back, and the pigeons came down to feed around the dead man's feet. By the time a street cleaner found the body and called the police, Cho Sun was sound asleep in a darkened room overlooking the Queen's Theatre.

*   *   *

Charlie Dance used Arnie Clover's overdue gambling debt to pay off a City of London detective for suppressing evidence, and had breakfast in Leather Lane with Sodbonce and Nasty Nostrils before strolling to Grand Buildings in Northumberland Avenue where the man from Hamburg had offices. He and the German date-stamped forged documents of origination for an arms cargo leaving Rotterdam for Cape Town, and Big Ben struck eleven as Charlie crossed Trafalgar Square against a spiteful wind. Outside the National Gallery a pavement artist worked on a chalk portrait of Admiral Nelson, and if Pencils Peachey noticed Charlie's shadow he gave no sign.

Pencils was a dumpling in three overcoats. His blob of a nose grew from a moon of a face, and white hair shocked out from his battered homburg. Amongst his drawings of the famous and popular was a chalk rendering of a pound note in shades of pale and brilliant green, one corner folded over to shadow the Queen's face; a precaution against prosecution for forgery. Pencils drew for the general public by day, but at night he was the best engraver the Royal Mint had never employed.

Charlie dropped a hundred pounds in Pencils' hat and told him the man from Hamburg was well pleased with his work as he reached for cigarettes he still didn't have.

Pencils' grin bared a lot of gum and two lonely eyeteeth.

'Old Pencils done the business, then?'

'Oh blimey yeah.'

Charlie refused a roll-up from Pencils' greasy tin and pocketed the envelope he was palmed. Traffic brawled into the square from the Strand as he said: 'What's this, sunshine?'

Pencils looked old and knowing.

'The best snide you'll ever clock, Chas. Right down to the metal strip and the watermark. Consecutive numbers, and the paper would fool the chief cashier in Threadneedle Street.'

Charlie watched a guide usher tourists into the National Gallery. The dip following them in saw Charlie and sauntered away as if he'd remembered a previous appointment.

Pencils laughed and blew his nose on a chalky rag.

'You do have an effect on people, Chas. We'd all be Persil-white if you was the law.'

Charlie thought better of smiling and said: 'Just don't need some twopenny villain getting his collar felt around me, is all. Who's printing these plates of yours?'

'Councillor Desmond. With him on the council, ain't nobody gonna turn his print works over, right?'

Charlie blew on his hands.

'Believe what you like. Been a lot of years since the fat boy in red came down my chimney. Have you passed any of this stuff?'

'Got Gerry Fox on that. Best passer in the Smoke. He's changing the snide for honest readies and paying the good stuff through his phoney charity accounts. Good as gold is Gerry.'

'You say.' Charlie knew 'Major' Gerry Fox. He'd specialised in impersonating officers during his National Service in Malaya and Hong Kong, and had sold tons of Naafi supplies to the Chinese before the army caught up with him. Now he impersonated anybody, and had enough aliases to fill a telephone directory.

'You in, Chas?'

'Not with Fox on the strength. He'll pocket your fingers on the first handshake. You'll end up drawing with your teeth.'

Pencils mumbled and gave Nelson's epaulettes gold highlights.

'Speak up, Pencils.'

Pencils looked defiant. 'Already shook hands, didn't I? With Gerry *and* Councillor Desmond.'

'That's me out. Think I'll take a squint at the Canneloni's before lunch.' Charlie started up the gallery steps.

Pencils' laugh would have shattered glass.

'Shows what you know, *Mr* Dance. Canneloni's pasta. *Canaletto's* the painter.'

'Watch your fingers, Pencils. See you.'

'But it's my best work, Chas. The very best. Even old Ironfoot Jack said so, and he was a great judge of snide, God bless his memory.'

Charlie turned on the steps.

'How long has old Jack been past tense?'

'Cockcrow this morning. Somebody flattened his gizzard. The law had me identify his mortals. Him rooming with me made me the closest thing he had to next of kin. His throat was caved-in horrible.'

Charlie pointed a gloved finger.

'All the more reason for you to pick your friends with care. Right?'

'You'll be at the funeral, Chas?'

'Not at any funeral. Put me down for a bit of a wreath.'

Charlie left Pencils with the wind for company, and the old forger started a portrait of Emma Hamilton.

'You may not go to funerals, Charlie, but you've by God caused a few,' he said softly.

Major Gerry Fox had a red moustache, pale blue eyes, and cheeks like boiled babies. His cheesecutter was tilted at a military angle, and he wore a small tea rose in his lapel. His briefcase contained cheque books and paying-in slips for thirty-eight different charity accounts, and two hundred forged ten-pound notes.

Kentish Town was thin traffic and thinner drizzle when he had Rosie Bottoms park outside Barclays Bank in the High Street.

'Bang on schedule, young Bottoms,' Fox said. 'Just two more banks and we'll stop for a spot of luncheon.'

Lunch for Fox would be several large pink gins and the passing of forged tenners. He would even lose pound wagers

15

on the dart board to get nine straight notes in exchange for a snide ten. Rosie would stay in the Humber with his mother's sandwiches and a motoring magazine, preferring the wonders of disc-brakes and fuel injection to beer and confidence trickery.

'What ever you say, Major.'

A ginger ferret with a riot of acne for a face, Rosie Bottoms had just finished five years of Borstal training for persistently joyriding in stolen cars. Rosie could hotwire any vehicle in four seconds flat, and had gone down for stealing a police Rover as the crew sealed off a road accident with hazard cones. The chase had ended when Rosie demolished the Rover, a garden wall, and twenty yards of ornamental hedging. To Rosie, speed was all, and brakes were an optional extra.

To keep Rosie off the streets at night, Fox had bought him a Scalectrix racing circuit with bridges and chicanes, ensuring that he drove himself to sleep far from the temptation of unlocked Cortinas.

Fox banked several hundred pounds, and Mr Salmon the manager called him 'Colonel Pastmaster' when he ushered Fox into his office. Salmon always deferred to clients he thought above him socially, and the names Fox had dropped over the previous weeks impressed him no end. He believed 'Pastmaster' to be on nodding acquaintance with several minor royals, that his charities enjoyed the patronage of half of Mayfair, and joyfully assumed he was not a complete stranger to the palace itself. Cheques signed by the peerage were promptly honoured, so there was no reason for Salmon to doubt their authenticity. He was not to know that Fox merely paid money to himself using a small number of his many pseudonyms.

Every quarter, Fox transferred all but his working capital to a numbered Swiss bank account Salmon believed funded the construction of a children's clinic on Lake Geneva. The 'clinic' was just a hole in the ground and a folder of

16

impressive-looking drawings Pencils had drawn up from the *Architects' Journal*. The money was hived off through paper companies and swelled a single account in Kuala Lumpar.

Salmon beamed across his pristine desk.

'The balance of your account has all but doubled this past month, my dear Colonel. You must be very pleased.'

Fox looked both shocked and modest.

'Not *my* account, old chap. I am merely the instrument of the generosity of others, a mere tool. It is the dear ladies who so jealously guard their anonymity we should praise. And only in the privacy of these four walls as is their wish. Are we the kind of men who would betray their trust by blabbing their names?'

'Naturally not. Nothing could be farther from my mind,' Salmon lied, wishing he could trumpet Pastmaster's patrons to his wife's circle in Hampstead Village. Make them swallow crow with their coffee and canapes. Have them beg him to chair one of their paltry committees.

Sighing inwardly, Salmon talked through cash projections for the coming month, authorised a telex transfer of funds to a paper company in Zurich, and bowed Fox out of his office.

Fox changed clothes as Rosie drove him to the Camden Town branch of the National Westminster Bank, and he was Father Leo Fallon from the Merciful Brethren of the Rosie Cross, Rhodesia, when he shook hands with the manager.

Detective Sergeant Brian Bulstrode cursed the leaking seal above his driving seat as he fell in behind the Humber. Four hours of surveillance with a wet crotch and no cigarettes was not how he had planned to spend his rest day. Commander Lemmon's five a.m. call had put paid to that. Instead of a late breakfast of sex with Deidre the air-hostess, a slow afternoon of fishing at Highbury Ponds, and more Deidre after a movie at the Finsbury Park Astoria, Bulstrode trailed bloody Gerry Fox. And all because Detective

Constable Payne had broken his clavicle in Switzerland. Just how he managed to get hit by a speeding Peugeot while sitting in a ski-lift was a mystery Bulstrode had no time to fathom. His immediate concern was to keep Fox in sight.

He was three cars back when the Humber accelerated to cross the Camden Road intersection on amber. Bulstrode shot a red light to stay close, and parked outside the Mother Red Cap just as Fox entered the bank as a priest.

'Naughty.' Bulstrode got a clear shot with his Pentax and logged the time in his notebook. Opened his empty Player's pack for the twentieth time and died for a smoke. Saw Bottoms leave the Humber, and risked following him into a tobacconists to buy a pack of full-strength Capstans as Rosie pawed the magazine rack. He even asked Rosie for a light on the pavement outside. Rosie shared his matches without looking up from his Ford handbook. When Rosie was back in the Humber, Bulstrode flashed his warrant card at the tobacconist and inspected the fifth tenner Rosie had passed that morning. Genuine it looked, and genuine it may have been, but Bulstrode was interested to know how an unemployed juvenile offender like Bottoms got his hands on so many. He was thinking about that and his first cigarette of the day when he walked back past the bank.

A hurrying figure slammed into him, and a briefcase spun through the air to burst open on the wet pavement. Money, cheque books and papers exploded into the air with the priest scrabbling to retrieve it all. Bulstrode lost his cigarette and trod on as much as he could as he pretended to help, gathered up paying-in books to read off the names, and knew he had Fox dead to rights. He offered Fox what he held, and as the phoney priest reached out, a handcuff circled his wrist.

'Gerry, my son,' said Bulstrode, 'You're nicked.'

Fox looked Bulstrode straight in the eye, and in the tones of the pulpit, said: 'And fuck you mightily, my son.'

Bulstrode cautioned Fox. Jerked a thumb at Rosie and

said: 'And let's have your choirboy to make up the set, eh, Gerry?'

'When was I ever violent, Buller?'

'Just see *he* isn't.'

Fox smiled a pale smile.

'No chance of a large pinkers before we go, is there?'

'No chance. See if I can't smuggle you one in after you've been charged.'

Fox dragged his feet past the saloon bar of the Mother Red Cap. Sighed, and rapped on the Humber to bring Rosie's nose up from his handbook. 'The law, young Bottoms,' he said, reaching to open the door with his unshackled hand.

Rosie didn't even blink. He made a Le Mans start with smoking tyres. U-turned on a sixpence, shaved the nose of a bus as he crossed the taxi rank, and went the wrong way up Parkway at sixty. He side-swiped a lorry, speed-wobbled up the pavement, and jumped a roadworks trench. Workmen scattered as the Humber ripped up a barrier of striped poles and tried to climb a stack of sewage pipes before flipping on its side in a shower of steam and sparks. The boot burst open and paper parcels of money spread across the road. Rosie banged out through the sunshine roof, bounced a couple of times, and came up running with a parcel under each arm.

When he had disappeared, Fox asked Bulstrode for a cigarette.

'Never knew the boy had it in him,' he said.

'Trap three out of Harringay,' Bulstrode agreed.

They sat in the Q-car until the traffic police arrived to sort out the chaos.

Rosie sprinted into Regent's Park and caught his breath on a swing in the children's playground. The parcels were heavy, but they had to be valuable or the major wouldn't have kept them under lock and key. With just pigeons and

19

a stray dog for company, Rosie risked tearing one open. The money was green and mint, and packed in blocks of a hundred, with eighty blocks to a package. And he had two. Doing the sums on his fingers, Rosie realised he was a fugitive with one hundred and sixty thousand pounds in his lap.

Rosie gnawed a skinned knuckle. Wondered what his mother would say when he wasn't home for his tea, and the filth arrived to upset her seven cats. The portrait of his late father on the mantel would get an earache from her scolding. No wonder he'd chucked himself in the canal when Rosie was only eight weeks old.

One hundred and sixty thousand pounds.

That was a Rolls, a Ferrari, and a souped-up Mini to drag-race in. Saveloys and chips every night. A pint and a Castella after. Speedway and the Destruction Derby any time he liked. Enough money to see Marion Clockworthy's bedroom wallpaper. Flushed and scared, Rosie Bottoms thought like a millionaire until he heard a police car bell up Parkway. Then he just ran.

Pounding through the dripping trees, he came to the South Entrance to the London Zoo. He bought a ticket on impulse, and wandered about without really seeing the animals. His head hurt, the keepers looked too much like coppers, and the big cats scared him. He bought an ice-cream and got it all over his face. Tried a hot dog and couldn't keep it down. Then he found the aquarium, and went inside to lose himself in the darkness with the cruising fish. He felt much better when he came out empty-handed an hour later.

With all that money stached, he could give the elbow to conmen like Gerry Fox and buy himself into a real firm. Make a deal with the likes of Charlie Dance, just a name to Rosie, but a top face in villainy. With Charlie Dance at his elbow, Rosie could make people call him Ernie like they should. When it got dark enough he would go to Soho.

Rosie fell asleep watching the gazelles, and dreamed he was the great Fangio.

Joe Yellow took Cho Sun food and a manilla envelope, and waited to be of service to his illustrious uncle.

Cho Sun ignored him, still angry with himself for killing a worthless beggar. He had many ways of killing with his bare hands, and only used weapons when there was no alternative. To calm himself he thought back to the perfect kill he had made in the Walled City north-east of Kowloon. For sixty years it had been a criminal stronghold, had never come under British jurisdiction, and none of the undercover agents sent in by the Hong Kong Police had left the old Chinese fort alive.

Dressed in the rags of an illegal immigrant from mainland China, Cho Sun had gone in at night. To earn enough rice to stay alive, he used his bicycle to carry dunny cans of human waste to the middens outside the walls. He slept in the open outside the hotel where his target lived in luxury surrounded by armed guards, and brooded over ways of making the kill without noise. His target showed himself every evening when he tended the rare blooms on his fifth floor balcony. An easy shot with a bow, an easier one with a rifle, but Cho Sun was above such crudity. The solution to the problem when it came was breathtakingly simple.

Every night for two weeks, Cho Sun climbed the sheer face of the building to carefully weaken the balcony floor, climbed back down, and slept in the filthy gutter under a tarpaulin. On the fifteenth night his target fell to his death, impacting with his orchids a bare yard from where Cho Sun feigned sleep. Beaten back when he tried to help carry the dead man back inside, Cho Sun cursed the blows and rode his bicycle back to Kowloon.

Cho sighed as he found peace. There was no need to tell the Sichuen Dragon of his recent mistake. It was of no consequence.

Joe Yellow bowed low. Burning to let his fingers speak. Cho Sun read his thoughts and spoke in perfect Mandarin.

'There *is* much danger here, Xian Tu, my nephew. Not only from the rival Snake Society of the Fook family, but also from within our own Dragon Brotherhood. The local chapter has lost face with the Sichuen Dragon, my very presence here proves that. So, in order to regain face, they must succeed where I fail. Is that not so?'

Joe Yellow's fingers said: *Yes, Uncle.*

'And how then must they achieve this thing, Nephew?'

By moving before you are ready. They do not possess your great skills, so cannot appreciate them. They will use the hatchet against the Snakes. Then come smiling with gifts of greeting.

Cho Sun's bony face remained impassive. During sleep he had become a thinking stone. His eyes rolled to white, he'd sought enlightenment in the dark corners of his mind. The smell of wrongness was stronger than the odours of this alien city. Sent here by the Sichuen Dragon, he was the Dragon, and should have been greeted as such. Yet there was no gift of rice and sandals. No show of dutiful honour.

'Did the Brotherhood tell you they would honour me after I had rested, Nephew? When I was clear-eyed and strong?'

They said those things, Uncle.

'And lied in the name of hospitality. The gifts should have been left at my door even if I slept a thousand years. You see?'

No, Uncle.

Cho Sun's smile was ugly.

'Tonight they will make me a paper Dragon with their hatchets. Tomorrow they will come with gifts to gloat at my shame. They must be very sure of themselves, but will they succeed, son of my sister?'

I do not know.

'A fool, however honest, remains a fool, Nephew.'

I am a green wand. Too young for wisdom.

Pleased, Cho Sun nodded.

'Then let your wand bend with the wind of your enemies. When their breath is spent, you spring upright again.'

I hear you, Uncle.

When the dark comes, we will be darker. Shadows upon shadows.'

I hear.

'Now look at me. Look closely.'

Joe Yellow stared at the man on the narrow cot. Saw the mesmeric eyes fill the room with vapour. Cho Sun could have been a fish pedlar or a menial in a one-wok café. Could have been thin, frail, or wiry. His face melted to become many people. Old and young, wise and stupid; ugly and attractive. Every face unmemorable once it had been replaced by another. Cho Sun was truly a Shadow Warrior. Invisible without disappearing. The more Joe Yellow looked the less he saw, and he was relieved to be told to stand outside the claustrophobic room until he was called.

Cho Sun dressed in black before opening the manilla envelope. Inside were photographs of two men, and their details were written on several sheets of rice paper. The first man was Aman Lee Fook of the Snake T'ang. A man of great cunning who brought refined opiates back to poison the British, just as they had enslaved many thousands of Chinese during the Opium Wars of the previous century. If Fook had not been an enemy, Cho Sun might well have admired him.

The second man was a long-nosed white with knowing slate eyes and black hair. A lean face with good cheekbones and a smile that left the eyes untouched. He and Aman Lee Fook were to die with the marks of a thousand cuts on their bodies.

Rare anger brought Cho Sun off the cot in a liquid surge. He scattered the contents of the manilla as he whirled and countered invisible opponents with fluid arm and leg blocks, working off his fury with silent venom until he regained control. Then, breathing hard, he lay back on the cot to empty his mind of emotion.

Bringing death to a target with supreme grace was Cho Sun's only criterion. He was revolted by the irrevocable command to mutilate these men as though he were some dogfaced hatchet man from the alleys of Kowloon. There was beauty in a single ruby of blood marking the forehead of a corpse still reaching for a peach, neither his expression or his dress disturbed by the killing thrust. Any butcher could dismember a man and cover himself with gore, but it took a master of stealth to kill without leaving a mark.

Cho Sun stared at the ceiling light until an oblong of shining bromide caught his eye. The portrait of the man with slate eyes had lodged in the corner of the room at head height, and it stared back with such an air of game cynicism, a chord was struck in Cho Sun's mind. True, the eyes were round and European, but as they held his, Cho Sun recognised a kindred spirit.

Wondering why he had not noticed this at first glance, Cho Sun found the man's details and committed them to memory. When he had analysed the bald truth behind the cramped Mandarin script, Cho Sun knew he had found a worthy opponent. He would kill this man with honour and make the thousand cuts after death. That way, all parties would be satisfied, not least of all Cho Sun himself.

Lying back to wait for night, Cho Sun smiled at Charlie Dance as he thought of ways to outwit the enemies inside his own Tong.

Commander Theo Lemmon thought about Sod's Law driving to Kentish Town. It put DC Payne in a Swiss hospital and cost Bulstrode his rest day, but it had also got Gerry Fox nicely fitted up for passing snide. A case of Sod's Law sodomising itself. Bulstrode was a lucky copper, and had shown sense enough to involve the local law instead of bringing Fox back to West End Central for interrogation. There was far too much inter-divisional rivalry, and the more the police squabbled amongst themselves, the better the heavy villains liked it.

Holmes Road Police Station smelled of wet paint and damp uniforms. Lemmon was shuffled through the chain of command to the chief inspector, and after a chat over lukewarm tea and the evidence, Lemmon used the judas hole in the Number 2 Interview room. The green and cream room was windowless, had chairs and a table, and a rattling radiator. Gerry Fox toyed with his last cigar, and Bulstrode chewed on a Capstan, saying: '. . . half a million of funny money in the boot of your Humber, and you dunno how it got there? That *is* your story?'

'As I've said a dozen times. As my solicitor will confirm once I'm allowed the statutory phone call.'

'No being nice to you, is there?'

'*Nice* would be the large pinkers you promised me, Buller.'

'After you're formally charged, I said. Maybe, I said.'

'Ifs, buts and maybes.' Fox decided to sulk.

'We've got you surrounded, Gerry son. Passing snide ain't enough for you, is it? Had to impersonate an African vicar, a retired colonel from the Coldstreams, not to mention convincing that Highgate bank manager you're a member of the aristocracy – a blood royal no less. Thirty-seven phoney accounts for unlisted charities. Your prints all over the parcels of snide from your Humber. Three bank managers who'll identify you under three different and dodgy aliases. It'll all stand up in court, Gerry my son, so go the whole hog, why not? Cough the whole lot like a good little chicken? Where the paper came from. Who done the printing. Not forgetting who engraved the plates. Make it all as neat as ninepence.'

Fox shrugged. 'Can't help, old lad. Sorry.'

'So it's all down to young Rosie Bottoms, is it? That snotnosed little turk gulled a smooth operator like you, right? He collected you in the Humber this morning, and you maintain the snide must have already been in the car, that it?'

'Can't comment on that, old boy. Wasn't there, d'you see.'

'No, you was off saving souls in Swazi-sodding-land. Taking the salute at Horseguards Parade 'cause Her Majesty had the sniffles. Which was it, I forget?'

'Breakfasting at my digs in Holloway, actually. As my landlady will no doubt confirm.'

Bulstrode lit a fresh cigarette from his stub.

'Has she donated to your charities?'

Fox smiled faintly and shook his head.

'No. Nice try, old chap.'

Bulstrode pointed a heavy finger.

'One more "old boy, old chap" out of you, and I'll interview you the hard way. Tickle your moustache with my knee.'

'My brief loves police violence, Buller. A black eye on a client looks so spectacular in court. Certain acquittal.'

'Not this time, Gerry.' Bulstrode pushed his chair back and banged on the door. 'I'll be back with a senior officer to charge you. Then you can call your solicitor, and bail will be opposed by the Director of Public Prosecutions. Forgery still comes close to treason in this country.'

Fox shrugged and lit his cigar with a flourish.

'Run along then. I'll be out by opening time this evening.'

Lemmon opened the door from the outside and took the chair Bulstrode had warmed for him. Smiled his avuncular smile at Fox and blew Player smoke into his face. Made the chair creak when he settled himself, and turned his hat on a forefinger as Fox lost his confidence.

'No way to talk to one of my lads, Gerry,' he said softly.

'Damned puppy threatened me, Mr Lemmon.'

'Did you, Buller?'

'Not as I remember, guv.'

'No witnesses were there, Gerry?'

26

'No witnesses,' Fox sighed through Havana smoke.

'Do we get a cough then, Gerry? Tell old Uncle Theo so he can offer that in mitigation of sentence in court?'

'Absolutely not.'

'You're sure now?'

'Certain. Adamant even.'

Lemmon's sigh paled Fox's effort to insignificance.

'That leaves me no choice. Empty your pockets and take your clothes off for a full strip search.'

Fox's cheeks turned to chalk.

'I know what you brutal bastards can do to my anal canal with a finger-stall and an endoscope. I insist on a doctor being present.'

Lemmon smiled gently.

'Of course there'll be a doctor present. And your brief. *And* a police photographer. Pretty little thing she is. Name of Felicity. She'll get a great close-up of your bottle.'

'A woman?' said Fox.

'So's the duty doctor, isn't she, Buller?'

'Yessir. Dr Jasmine Persad. From Calcutta originally.'

Lemmon got to his feet to stretch lazily.

'Outside, Buller. Let's leave Gerry to contemplate all that female pulchritude.'

In the passage, Lemmon just smiled and turned his hat. Fox's anger was a muffled scream of rage.

'He'll cough it all now, Buller.'

'What was all that Felicity and women doctors, guv?'

Lemmon's smile widened to show his molars.

'Major Gerry Fox is a latent homo – hates women anywhere near him. That's why he likes to work with young chaps. Never lays a finger, just likes them around. We wheel our Felicity in with her box-Brownie, and he'll fall over himself to talk.'

'Who is this Felicity?'

'Any WPC in plain clothes will do. And another one with a stethoscope and a white coat. The younger and prettier the better. Better get a constable in there before Gerry hangs himself with his old school tie.'

Bulstrode shook his head.

'And I thought I was devious. Fancy a cuppa in the canteen while he sweats, guv?'

'When the pubs are open and you're buying, Buller?'

Fox sobbed openly when the duty constable went in to guard him. An hour later, he began talking to a police stenographer with a grey moustache as Lemmon patted his shoulder.

Cho Sun was just another Chinaman when Joe Yellow walked him through Soho in evening drizzle. He tried British beer in the Nellie Dean, played pinball at the Golden Goose, and watched the strippers in St Anne's Court. In Wardour Street he checked out the Lotus House and Fu Yong's, found the Troubadour and the Mandrake without Joe Yellow's help, and sipped lemon tea in the Nosh Bar across the road from Charlie Dance's Windmill Street office. At no time were he and his nephew followed, which made Cho Sun gnaw his lip instead of his salt beef sandwich. The wrongness of it all was as oppressive as the weather.

Cho Sun threw up in the toilet to keep his reflexes tuned, and sat by the window to watch the street through a hole rubbed in the condensation.

A youth he had seen twice before tried the door of Charlie's office, stood back to stare up at the darkened windows, and went away. When the boy came back fifteen minutes later, Cho Sun told Joe Yellow to follow him, and trailed them both, keeping to the shadows.

Rosie Bottoms was tired and soaked through. He missed his racing circuit and wanted his tea. Only fear of the law and his mother's slipper kept him going. After drawing a blank at the Windmill Street office he toured the pubs and clubs looking for Charlie Dance.

The Maltese barman at the Blue Posts just shrugged, the barmaid at the Pelican told him to take his spotty face out of it, and an alky street trader outside Isow's tried to borrow a fiver. Rosie was about to give up when he remembered Solly Evergreen the kosher butcher in Berwick Street market. Solly knew everybody, and Rosie had been mates with his son in Borstal. The shop was closed when Rosie scratched at the window, and Solly stopped sweeping sawdust to let him in.

'Don't tell me. You've got trouble, and you want what?'

'I got this message for Charlie Dance, Sol.'

Solly leaned on his broom.

'Some message you could have for that low-life. Charlie ain't nice people, Rosie. The man's too heavy to be a *mensch*. Go home, go away. You want money, I'll give you money. But much it won't be.'

Rosie persisted and Solly sighed at the ceiling.

'How do they find me? Only the *meshugginahs* Solly gets. Listen, Charlie Dance you won't find tonight. You know why, boykin? It's the big fight tonight. A sell-out at the Albert Hall. TV and everything. Trooper Wells is going twelve rounds with the Brixton *schwartzer*. That Congo Billy Devon, that's what. Me, I got 5-1 on the black boy. Now *that's* a gamble.'

'I'll go there then.'

'And waste good shoe leather? You know how much law will be there – maybe waiting for you? Half the Met, you *schmuck*. Better you wait. Better I make a call. Here, sweep while Solly dials. I should do everything myself?'

Rosie had the floor spotless when Solly came back to lean on the counter.

'Maybe you should work here, keep out of mischief, boykin. How much trouble you got?'

'I done this blag with—'

'I asked how much, not what. Let me sleep nights. I

ain't got enough trouble with a son who likes second storey windows better than butchering? OK, boy-fool, you go to the Lotus House in Wardour. Maybe eleven, maybe midnight, Charlie goes there. But boykin, I don't tell you, eh?'

'You'll earn out of this, Sol, I swear . . .'

Solly looked at his ceiling and didn't see Joe Yellow read his lips before backing away through the market stalls.

'Another Rockerfeller. He don't even shave yet. Go away, go . . .'

Rosie went outside with four long hours to kill.

CHAPTER TWO

'Drink your champagne. Fidget.'

Charlie Dance slapped Vinnie Castle's hand away from his blindfold as Sodbonce took the Rolls into the Piccadilly underpass.

'The bubbles tickle, and surprises get up my nose.'

Vinnie scratched the upholstery where his left leg had been. The surgeons had saved his right leg, but walking with an artificial limb was still a sometime thing for the future. The Troys had gone down for thirty years, but taking a shotgun to Vinnie hadn't earned a single mention during their Old Bailey trial. Charlie blessed Vinnie's sneeze and tucked a car blanket around his waist.

Vinnie lost his brilliant white smile.

'Don't mother me, Chas. Blaming yourself won't bring my pin back. And over is over, right?'

'Nothing's over until I say so.' Charlie tapped Sodbonce for a lit Player, his grey eyes flinty.

Vinnie's grin was white and wide.

'Not everything, Chas. If I knuckled under you wouldn't keep me around. I'm the still small voice you listen to. Ain't nobody else left. They got my leg, not my brains, so do me a favour and let me wipe my own backside.'

'For that, you get to lose at poker tonight.'

'Depends who's sitting in, Chas. If it's that Chinaman of yours I'm in for a killing. The man gambles, he don't play what he's holding.'

'Fook ain't that bad.' Charlie dribbled smoke.

'You *let* him win.'

'Take a clever man to prove that, Vin.'

'Clever it ain't. Stands out a sea-mile to anybody with half an eye. Think I don't know you let your pile drift to his corner and let me take it back? Way of buttering my parsnips, is it?'

'Give your imagination and my ears a rest.'

'Who else is sitting in?'

'Should have blindfolded your mouth.'

'I'd use sign-language. Come on, who else?'

'A couple of the chaps. Chappie August. Micky Raven maybe.'

Vinnie's lower face sobered. If Charlie was talking to Fulham, something was in the air, and it didn't take a genius to work out what. With the Troys and Connie Harold doing heavy bird, there was a power vacuum in Bethnal Green and Camberwell. If Micky Raven moved east, he'd have the West End territory surrounded, and there was no love lost between the Dance and Raven firms.

'Ain't just poker, then?' Vinnie said as the Rolls purred to a halt outside the Albert Hall.

'When is it ever just poker?' Charlie lifted Vinnie into his wheelchair and guided him through the crowds. Carried him up the main stairs as if he weighed nothing and wheeled him down to the ringside, nodding at faces he knew in the crowd. Two City of London coppers went behind their programmes, and three whores from Soho blew kisses as Vinnie tried to work out where he was.

'Not more Shakespeare is it, Chas? I've had culture up to my collar-stud.'

'When did you ever smell good cigars at Shakespeare, Vin?'

'Now *is* the winter of my discontent,' Vinnie said. Puzzled.

Charlie locked his wheelchair off behind a timekeeper, took his own seat beside Chappie August the boxing promoter, and whipped the blindfold away. Vinnie blinked and grinned at the smoke and noise. He saw the boxing programme in his lap and said: 'You hound. You told me the Pope himself couldn't get tickets.'

'Nor he could. And it's tradition to lie to a man on his birthday. Happy returns, Vin.' Charlie shook August's hand. 'Who's taking the fix tonight, then?'

'Not so loud, you kidder.'

Charlie rolled his shoulders. 'Who's kidding?'

Chappie August was a pink man with silver hair and a green cigar long enough to trip the referee. Seated he was imposing. Standing in Cuban heels he was barely five feet tall. The blonde with him was all cleavage and long black silk legs that continually crossed and recrossed themselves. She wasn't Mrs August, who was divorcing Chappie through the American courts; an exercise in futility he paid for with a smile, knowing his assets were safe in the Cayman Islands.

'This one answers to Binkie,' Chappie whispered. 'Thinks she's a starlet, and being with me will get her picture in the papers. Fat hope with my cigar along. That's all the press boys wanna point their Speed Graphics at, right? But she does the three-card trick in my four-poster, so who am I to disillusion?'

'That gets it said in a hurry.'

Charlie refused a Havana in favour of one of Vinnie's Rothmans.

Chappie's cigar rolled itself to the corner of his mouth. 'When did poetry promote likely lads into contenders? The boy I want you to watch comes out of the blue corner in the third bout. Boy's got class, Charlie. Stand on me, he's maybe another Trooper Wells when we smooth the edges. Buy a piece of him now, you got millions coming.'

Charlie's smile was vague. Fifteen years before, he had gone three rounds with one of August's young hopefuls at Marshall Street Baths. Held him up for two, danced through the third, and decked him on the bell to make him look game. August's gratitude had stopped at a ten pound note slipped into Charlie's glove. The young hopeful had gone on to earn August a fortune.

'So who's holding this one up? Another berk like me?' Chappie bit on his cigar and looked shocked.

'That was then. It was business. You earned, I earned, so who got hurt?'

'Your young hopeful the next time out. Had his gumshield rammed down his throat with most of his teeth. You bribed the Boxing Federation doctor to turn a blind eye. Had Doc Rudge take the teeth out of the kid's gullet with forceps down in Spitalfields. Had double vision when he drove himself off Hammersmith Bridge. You have to remember it all, Chappie. You don't, there's some face who will. If this new boy of yours is tasty, I'll tell you.'

Chappie got pinker.

'Would I tell porkies to a *face*? My word on it, Charlie.'

'Your *word*?'

'My word *now*. Not back *then*. When we all had the arse out of our trousers and scratched lice instead of a living. *Now*.'

Charlie feigned relief. 'That,' he said, 'makes all the diff.'

'Course it does.' August turned to pat Binkie's thigh.

Vinnie leaned in with: 'Does he understand irony, Chas?'

'Thinks that's some kind of scrap metal.'

'You'll see, Charlie,' August said, pawing the blonde.

'Oh blimey yeah.'

A recorded fanfare brought two flyweights into the ring. They put on a display of speed, and the kid from Fulham took the Belfast boy out five seconds into the fourth. Vinnie said it was a foregone conclusion and bet Charlie fifty sovereigns that the lightweight in the red corner would take the next bout. Charlie took the wager 'to make the birthday boy happy', and was out fifty pounds by the end of the second round.

The crowd liked the decision enough to buzz as the

cruiserweight contest got started with a fresh referee. Billed as Tony Hackney, August's boy was a rangy blond with a long reach who gave several pounds away to the freckled Scot he was matched against. With clean features and good shoulders, he looked fast against the dogged efficiency of the Glasgow boy. Round one was a lot of sparring as they got each other's measure, the seconds did a lot of talking and towelling in the break, and round two saw the Scot using his shoulder to hit low on the ropes when the ref was unsighted. The crowd saw, and catcalls and whistles echoed around the domed Victorian ceiling as the blond snaked away to deliver some solid looking rights.

Charlie sat low in his chair and ignored August's elbow. Watched the Scot maul and smother where the blond ducked and weaved and kept his temper, using all the ring there was to keep his distance. On the bell he took a glove-rake to the right eye, and it was puffed and angry when he come out for the third. From then on he punished the Scot with hard combinations to the head and torso, forcing the Scot to use the ropes to cover and slip away. A crossing right to the Scot's temple travelled five inches. His head snapped back, and as his heels went down on the canvas, a straight left sat him on the deck looking dreary.

Charlie blocked August's elbow as the Scot climbed the ropes, and the ref was giving him a standing count when the bell went. By then the crowd knew who they liked, and there was genuine applause amongst the yells and whistles. August almost lit his cigar in the excitement. He squeezed Binkie's thigh hard enough to make her squeal and didn't notice.

'How's that for chopped liver,' August purred. 'What a darling.'

'He's got something, Chas.' Vinnie passed a lit cigarette.

'Ain't measles,' Charlie said, wanting a cold beer.

'We're out of the bargain basement now, Charlie. Each round puts us closer to penthouse prices,' August laughed.

Charlie shrugged. Watched the red corner work on the Scot. Saw his eyes clear and turn sullen, even more dangerous now he had been humiliated. Knew Tony Hackney would learn about professional fouls the hard way if he allowed the Scot to get in close. A deliberate clash of heads could turn the contest around in a split second. Vinnie wanted double or quits on the outcome, and Charlie told him to save his money for the main bout as the bell opened round three. 'If this goes the distance, I'm a Mandarin,' he said.

The Scot came out playing dizzy. Went into a clinch and bored Hackney into a neutral corner. Got two low ones in before the ref parted them. Kept in close and used his superior weight to wear Hackney down. Charlie saw him use his thumb and grind his head across the blond boy's mouth on the ref's blind side. Then it was a clumsy waltz to the bell, and Hackney's right eye was almost closed when he spat his gumshield into a second's hand.

Rounds four and five were much the same, and the crowd booed and hissed and turned ugly. Hackney took more punishment in the sixth, and was on the ropes with the Scot working on his ribs when he found a short hook from somewhere, and put the Scot back on his heels again. The Scot didn't see the sucker punch that turned him in a half circle, or the two short lefts that staggered him the width of the ring. He draped an arm over the ropes and went down on one knee, grinning at nothing. Raised an arm as though in victory, and went down on his face to lie very still. The crowd was on its feet counting in time with the referee's arm, and roared when Hackney was chaired around the ring.

'What d'you say to them apples, Mr Dance?' August crowed.

'Thirst-making.' Charlie wheeled Vinnie up to the Opera Bar as if nothing had happened. Sodbonce had the drinks set up in the corner, and over a gin and tonic Vinnie asked Charlie what he really thought. 'Handy,' Charlie admitted.

'But no chance with that management. Chappie promotes Chappie, not the fighters on his string. He buys and sells them like used cars. He had an orchard, he'd sell the trees and steal the apples back.'

'Don't get that, Chas,' said Sodbonce.

'Don't mean nothing is why, Soddy,' Charlie explained.

Vinnie knew different. Everything Charlie Dance said meant something, if only to himself. Vinnie had a second drink to kill the itch in his missing leg and hoped the poker game with Micky Raven would be on neutral turf. Vinnie no longer took chances. He had burned up a lot of ammunition becoming proficient with the Mauser he kept under his blanket beside the plastic bag his waste fluids decanted into. He would never be a proud father, but he planned to live to be an old man.

Vinnie was still in a brown study when he was wheeled back to watch the main event of the night, and doubled his winnings when Charlie took Congo Billy Devon to beat Trooper Wells. Trooper stopped the black boy in the eighth with a cut eye you could stick three fingers into. Charlie refused August's invitation back to the dressing rooms to pop some bubbly with the champ because he had to feed the 'birthday boy', and would see Chappie later at the Troubadour to relieve him of some of his winnings. August went away with Binkie, and Sodbonce drove Vinnie and Charlie to Wardour Street through squalls of driving sleet.

It was too cold for snow.

Sleet smeared the lights of Cromwell Road as Aman Lee Fook allowed Wind to settle his bow tie and call his car to the front of the hotel. Wind had pleased him on the golden bed before his bath, her long black hair a tent over them both. Climaxed him with the butterfly strokes of hands and mouth and two strings of ivory pleasure beads, freeing him from the carnal plane to contemplate matters of the mind.

Wind was fifteen and had been with Fook for three

months. Soon he would send her back to Hong Kong and replace her with another. Fook could not afford to become too attached to any of the young flowers who cared for his physical needs. The head of the Snake T'ang was above such human frailty. Wind's family had been well paid for her services, a handsome enough dowry for her to marry well if she so chose. Many such girls took husbands and retired into respectability. Others contracted themselves to one of the great pleasure houses for the three years it took to earn their complete independence, and started their own houses under the protection of the Snake T'ang.

But never again were they allowed into the presence of the Supreme Snake, Aman Lee Fook, and to mention his name in public was a capital offence. Only one flower had even been so unwise. Fook's Killing Shadows had cut out her tongue and burned it before her eyes. And sewed her into wet hides that contracted about her like the coils of a serpent as they slowly dried, crushing her to death with infinite slowness, a fitting end to a treacherous flower.

Fook hoped that would not happen to Wind as he took the lift down to the lobby and was escorted to his car by two of his Killing Shadows. The drive to Soho was a long snarl of slow traffic, and Fook used the time to think. The illegal importation of hard drugs into Britain had gone well until the beginning of September, the previous month. Then four of his best couriers had disappeared along with their consignments in Formosa and Singapore. On the heels of that had come a greater blow. A large consignment of pure Laosian heroin concealed in containers of racehorse sperm had been seized by the Hong Kong Customs who admitted they had acted on 'information received from an anonymous source'. Losing the heroin itself was a minor nuisance, but discovering who had informed was not. Only a trusted handful of men had known about the shipment, and they were all ranking members of the brotherhood. None of the missing couriers knew, and even if put to the question under torture, could have told their inquisitors nothing of value. Fook needed to move with extreme caution if he was to purge the brotherhood without weakening it unnecessarily. The Snake needed every man if he was to crush the rival Dragon T'ang of Sichuen.

The Dragons had already established themselves in London and Manchester, and Aman Lee Fook knew they had placed a price of many millions of yen on his head. There had been attempts on Fook's life in the past, but the blood money remained unclaimed. Fook bore a sickle-shaped scar on his chin where an assassin had struck him a glancing blow with a morning-star. Fook had remained conscious long enough to burn the poison out with a hot iron before it reached his heart. Luck and a strong constitution had pulled him through. There were no known antidotes to some of the ninja poisons they coated their weapons with, and some killed silently within a matter of seconds.

Now he had proof positive there was a traitor within the Snake, Fook planned to be doubly careful about his personal safety. He had already planned to move from the Cromwell Road hotel suite Charlie Dance had put as his disposal, and had chosen a house in Hampstead for its walled garden and unrestricted view of the heath. He would leave there infrequently, always by a different route, having set up several 'safe' houses on the way should he need to break his journey.

The Daimler made the turn into Wardour Street, and Fook hurried into the Lotus House with his collar up against the freezing sleet.

Across the way, Rosie Bottoms stamped his feet to keep warm, unaware that Cho Sun and Joe Yellow watched him watching. They had seen Charlie Dance wheel Vinnie Castle into the restaurant through the side entrance in St Anne's Court when Rosie had not; and their patience, like their eyesight, was infinitely superior to his.

Rosie dreamed of playing hide the sausage with Marion Clockworthy. Eating plates of hot chips with his face against her plump white thighs in front of a roaring fire with his racing cars doing fast circuits. The smell of her Woolworth's perfume blending with the vinegar on his lips. He spat phlegm and shook with cold.

Bulstrode sat in the snug of The Elephant and let his snout gild gold and paint lilies, building his squib of information into an epic of De Millean proportions. Billy Black had been a useful second-storey man until age and vertigo reduced him to listening at keyholes to scrape a living. Billy asked for twenty and a large brandy, got five and a small bitter, and went away quite happy. Bulstrode finished his pint and joined Lemmon in the leaking Q-car parked across the road from a printing works on the canal near Camden Lock.

Lemmon finished the *Evening Standard* crossword with a flourish and envied the lager on Bulstrode's breath.

'Anything, Buller?'

Bulstrode bit a yawn in half.

'Councillor Desmond ain't just a champion of the people, guv. His print works handles all the Labour Party stuff, point-of-sale material for breweries and advertising agencies. Laminating and quality five-colour offset. Silk-screen, you name it. So busy, he has three eight-hour shifts round the clock, seven days a week. Got that from one of the day-shift machine minders for a pint. He says there's never any overtime though, and he don't know none of the night shift.'

'Say on.' Lemmon looked interested.

'Says the night-shift even use different machines on the top floor, and use their own paper store. It's kept locked, and our friend Councillor Desmond keeps the key on his watchchain when it ain't in the safe. My man says they must be handling security bonds or something. Got vague about then, and I didn't push it.'

Lemmon waved smoke from his face.

'And could mean two day shifts for the legitimate – a night shift for the snide and clandestine.'

'Smacks of it, guv. But we'll need more than a suss and the word of a villain like Fox. Our squad's too thin on the ground to handle it alone. We'll need at least twenty uniforms and a couple of dog-handlers.'

'And an iron-clad warrant if the Treasury's involved. And needing uniforms means using Holmes Road or King's Cross nicks to draw our manpower. That's a lot of bodies to keep from opening their clacks.'

'Both nicks have got more holes than a laddered fishnet stocking.'

'Are all your similes sexually based, Buller?'

'If you'd seen what I had to elbow tonight, you'd know why, guv.'

'More to life than air hostesses.'

'Ain't married, guv. Wouldn't know.'

'What did your snout come up with?' Lemmon didn't know the names of Bulstrode's informants, each copper had his own and kept their identities a secret.

'Says the place is never empty. Got right up his nose did that. He'd cased the joint before high places gave him the shivers. Reckoned it was worth petering the safe for all them wages, even with a straight drop of eighty-some feet into the canal.'

'Not dreaming or pulling his own pudden, was he?'

'I've boiled down what he told me, guv. He told it with a cast of thousands. He did say there's a way in over the roof if you ain't into nosebleeds. All the ground floor doors are steel-faced and double-bolted. Have to pull 'em off their hinges with a land-rover and chains.'

Lemmon looked at his watch and knew he'd missed last orders.

'Find out who the Safety Officer is at Holmes Road. Get into his files and see what security arrangements he made with the good councillor. The morning will do for that. Let's have another dig at Gerry Fox and snort a quiet bevy in a club on the way home. I think better over a late scotch.'

Bulstrode woke up the engine and drove back to the West End through bouncing sleet.

Fook accepted a bowl of green tea when it had been tasted and his Killing Shadows had checked out the Lotus House. He sat with Charlie to watch Vinnie being fed noodles by the two Eurasian girls Chinese Cyril had laid on for the evening. Sodbonce took a lot of Polaroids, careful not to get Fook in frame as Charlie had ordered, knowing he'd lose more than his camera if he got it wrong. Charlie would break his neck if Fook's 'Happi Coats' didn't. Nasty Nostrils had locked horns with one of them when he was pissed on Bacardi and all his horses had gone down at Redcar, and had ended up the other side of the room with his arm hanging all wrong. The Happi Coat had reset his arm as fast as he'd dislocated it, but Nasty still rolled his shoulder when one of them came within spitting distance of him.

'Like fighting elastic with a rubber hammer,' he'd grumbled. 'You have some if you reckon it's funny, Soddy.' Sodbonce had declined. Seeing eighteen stone of muscle fly twelve feet was all the lesson he needed.

'Good to see Vinnie enjoy,' said Fook.

Charlie let a prawn cracker melt on his tongue.

'With another op coming up, he deserves to. He look well to you?'

Fook shrugged.

'He uses the pain to build his spirit. He has a foot in both worlds, that makes him strong in the mind. He will walk again, but his mind will always run. No man is a cripple if his mind is clear.'

'That gets it said.' Charlie smiled for the camera. 'Raven's agreed to play poker. Stalled for a week and suddenly said "yes".'

'Too suddenly?'

'Always a possibility.'

'Can this thing be talked out?'

'Won't know without trying, will we? What can it cost but air? And what's the alternative?'

Fook smiled and sipped tea.

'Three questions with a thousand answers, Charlie. We have many people in the docks. They will not come to heel if there is indecision. The Chinese don't like choice, it makes them unsure of things.'

'Not so different to the voting public anywhere.'

'Democracy is a Western concept. Better to tell them what to think and when to think it. They obey, and things are better.'

'If you say so, Aman.'

'You say otherwise, Charlie?'

'I deal with the possible, ain't that enough?'

'For you perhaps.'

Charlie snapped his fingers for a cigarette and refilled Fook's bowl with tea. Chinese Cyril lit him up, and he blew smoke away down the table. Reading Fook was like making out invisible writing with closed eyes. Nothing in the darkness but the swirl of liver spots. He passed Fook the envelope Pencils Peachey had palmed him that morning.

'Tell me which one's the forgery,' he said.

Fook fanned the notes, touched them with his fingertips, held them up to the light one by one and smelled the ink as he crackled the paper.

'All or none. They are very good.'

'Good enough to pass in Hong Kong?'

'How many?'

'I'm told a million, could be more or less.'

'You've said "yes" to this?'

'I've said nothing to this.'

'As always.' Fook pursed his lips. Smiled his meaningless smile.

Charlie yawned smoke and put the forged notes away.

'Now, Charlie?' said Chinese Cyril. Hovering. His father may have been an English sailor, but he was as yellow and fat as an overfed canary. His suit hung off him in billows, and his chins hid his collar and the knot of his tie. The fingers of his right hand were covered in rings of gold and jade. Cyril had wrestled all over the world, and liked his wealth where he could see it. The concept of investing his money instead of wearing it baffled him.

'Now's good,' said Charlie.

Cyril clapped his hands and the lights dimmed. A spot-light picked out the chef as he wheeled a huge cake from the kitchen. Covered in lit candles, the cake shone like precious metal. Vinnie grinned at Charlie as everybody but Fook chorused 'happy birthday' to the sound of Chinese strings. The Eurasian girls kissed Vinnie for the camera, and the lights came back on for 'he's a jolly good fellow' and three cheers. Vinnie was handed a sword to make the first cut, and insisted on standing to do it. The girls supported him as he plunged the blade home, and his sallow cheeks were flushed when he sat down.

Charlie kneeled beside him for another Polaroid.

'How'd you get the cake to look gold, Chas?' Vinnie asked.

'Had it gilded at Goldsmith's Hall. Seems the Tudor kings went in for all that old toffee when they showed off to visiting royalty. Figured gold-leaf was good for the diges-tion. Their gingerbread men was gilded too. Ginger spice coming all the way from India or China made it as precious as gold in them days, so they covered the best with the best. Eat hearty, your majesty.'

'Charlie, Charlie . . .' Vinnie was lost for words.

'You want Soddy to snap you looking that wet? Eat.'

Fook caught the flash of unguarded affection in Dance's eyes. Saw it as a weakness that could be of use if exploited the right way. A possible weapon for the uncertain future.

44

Charlie Dance was an indispensable ally at present, but that may not always be the case. Occidentals such as he must be considered expendable in the great scheme of things. There was no room for unwarranted sentiment in the coils of the eternal Snake.

Fook smiled as Charlie sat beside him.

'Such generosity is only fitting when honouring the loyal, Charlie.'

'Yeah?'

Fook found himself looking into eyes as cold as slate.

'All kids like what shines. But a cake only tastes of cake, whatever you cover it with.'

'True.'

Fook's face was yellow bone as he hid behind his smile. Shocked that Dance could still surprise him, he kept his expression bland. Saw again the naked force that had first attracted him to his man as the iron eyes locked with his without staring. Then they blinked and softened and looked away to bring Chinese Cyril to the table.

'Coffee with the cake, and have the cars round front in fifteen minutes. You done us proud, Cyril.'

Cyril beamed and went off shouting orders.

'Anything for you, Aman?'

'Nothing.'

'Yeah, enough's enough,' Charlie said softly.

Fook wondered what that meant as he sipped the last of his tea. Knew Micky Raven had better be holding good cards when he bet against Charlie Dance. Very good cards indeed.

Gerry Fox had got sleepy and irritable in his cell, and even a smuggled slug of unpinked gin couldn't engage his mouth to his brain. He added nothing, detracted nothing, and was just a used-up old poser in need of eight straight hours. Commander Lemmon called it a day and pointed his Jaguar towards Soho with Bulstrode's Q-car close behind. They parked in Archer Street amongst the Rolls and Cadillacs, and went down to the lower bar of the Troubadour for scotches on the house.

The usual crowd of toms, pimps and suitcase traders looked hard into their drinks and talked about last trains home, early nights, how the wife/tart/husband was waiting up, and blimey was that the time? as they smelled the filth and made for the street. Lemmon and Bulstrode made the club manager join them at a table away from his office telephone, and had him tell his staff the bar phone was out of order. No point in frightening fresh custom away with wild calls, now was there?

Franco Mella had managed the club for three years for his Maltese uncle George, and ran straight tables for high rollers with hot money on the upper floors. Illegal though that was, it suited the law to know where the action was without driving it further underground. And being neutral turf, the heavy faces met there to settle differences; arrange territories and concessions, agree on fines or punishment for the out of order or downright naughty, and shook hands knowing they had a three mile head start when they returned to their home manors. Although the Troubadour was on Dance turf, that's how he liked it. And it worked.

Lemmon got Franco talking about the Trooper Wells – Congo Billy Devon fight, and watched sweat glisten as the clock ticked towards 1 a.m. Something was in the wind, and Bulstrode caught it too. They ordered a second round as Franco described the fourth round, and settled in to see what happened. By round seven, Franco looked as if he'd taken a shower inside his suit. That was when Micky Raven's party walked in and seemed oddly pleased to see the law on the premises. Micky even sent drinks over as he back-slapped his two minders, Big Alphonse and Rupert Baer.

Lemmon watered his scotch out of sight and sat glued to his chair.

Bulstrode forgot his air hostess and went along for the ride.

The lights of Wardour Street bled into the shadows of St Anne's Court and turned the puddles to pools of golden sodium. Fook's Killing Shadows guarded the Rolls and the Daimler as Sodbonce and Nasty Nostrils watched the alley behind.

Sodbonce got a nod from the Happi Coats and passed it inside.

'Clear, Chas.'

Charlie let Fook out ahead of him, patted Chinese Cyril's face for a job well done, and swung Vinnie into the alley without jarring his chair. Vinnie had the remains of his cake in a box on his lap. Red dye from his party hat ran down his forehead, and he sang softly, buoyed up by three flagons of white wine.

> *Indicate the route to my abode*
> *Mmmm fatigued ann I wanna turn innn*
> *Had a little bevy sixty minutes ago*
> *Annn iss penetrated to my craniummm*
> *Nooo madder where I perambulate . . .*

'That wheelchair's gotta nasty squeak, Chas,' Sodbonce said.

> *'Over land or sea or effervescent liquid . . .'*

'Hold it down, Vin. Think of the pigeons.'

Vinnie shushed loudly behind a raised finger.

'Lovely pigeons gotta sleep . . . 'night pidgy-pidgys . . .'

'That's my birthday boy.' Charlie saw Fook had stopped dead.

Had gone into a defensive crouch as he hissed and backed.

'Aman?' Charlie was stuck behind the wheelchair. Soddy and Nasty were watching their rear. Laughing at Vinnie. The Happi Coats were facing the wrong way. Coming at Fook, arms raised in threat postures. Steel came out of a sleeve to swing at Fook's head. Striking home with the chop of a cloven cabbage. The hatchet chimed as it struck sparks from the alley wall. Fook staggered to genuflect with disordered hair. Took a glancing blow to the shoulder and kicked out at the second man. Fell back into Vinnie's lap, smashing the cake box.

'Fair shakes, Fookie-old-wookie . . . S'my cakey-fun-wakey . . .'

Charlie heard Sodbonce grunt as he was hit. Heard Nasty open a forehead against brickwork. Heard rubber soles squeak on the flags and splash through puddles behind him. Saw more black figures come in from Wardour Street. The shine of hatchets and the gleam of slitted almond eyes. Fook sprawling across Vinnie with dark claret spurting from his scalp.

'We're fucking dead 'ere,' said Nasty. Using his boot.

Charlie heaved Fook from Vinnie's lap and threw him against the closing restaurant door. Sensed his dazed fury as he pushed the door wide to see more men coming through the tables as Chinese Cyril went into a wrestler's defensive crouch, his face a blanched lemon.

Then Charlie was too busy to look any more. A cleaver opened his temple and skated off his shoulder, paring flesh. He punched the outstretched arm hard. Forced the elbow the wrong way and heard bone splinter. The cleaver clattered from dead fingers, and Charlie hooked the head away with a short left. Pushed the wheelchair through a sudden gap with all his strength as Vinnie lolled and sang 'Wakey-wakey-for-cakey', careening through lithe black figures to cannon into the side of the white Rolls. Sprawled on slick paving as the wheelchair overturned. His scream of agony nails on a blackboard that chopped off when he fainted.

Charlie punched thin air as his target left the ground to sail over his head. A heel exploded against the side of his neck and he fell with whiplash, slapping his palms against the paving to save his face. Thought: I only nailed one and there are hundreds . . .

Felt a kick lift him and turn his stomach to fire. Rolled as he sensed the downward chop of a hatchet and felt it slice his shoulder-pad away. Caught an exposed scrotum with his heel and watched a man come down on his knees with a black zero for a mouth. Grappled for the hatchet and tore it away, wondering what the hell to do with the bloody thing. Fighting with blades was for Malts and Eyeties and these bastards . . .

That was somehow funny, but Sodbonce holding his stomach wasn't. He'd slid down the wall and looked to be holding a pound of raw offal in his hands. Except it was spilling out of his open waistcoat and turning his shirt a very dark red. Nasty Nostrils was banging a head against another head, but there was something metallic growing out of his ribcage and his face was bled meat with eyes like wet holes. Eyes like that stared from iced fish on marble slabs in Berwick Street Market.

Charlie tried to rise and couldn't. The Chinese he'd kicked was across him now, and didn't move. There was something crazy going on and Charlie tasted blood in his mouth as he tried to make sense of anything that occurred to him.

Men in black were going down all around him. A small shadow was in amongst them. Tiny hands darting like a chameleon's tongue. Legs whirling into head and groin. A soundless ballet. A dancer whose mere touch stiffened faces and sent bodies away in loose sprawls. Christ, but he was beautiful. A thin wraith in a baggy overcoat two-sizes too big for him. An old trilby too greasy to beg coppers with. But under that, and inside the flowing coat, was a steel and rubber machine that destroyed with a simple flick.

Men ran and blades dropped to the cobbles. There was just poor Soddy and Nasty in the alley with Charlie and the limp Chinese pinning him down. Glass smashed inside the Lotus House and then that stopped.

Charlie lay still to fight manic laughter. Wanted to go to Vinnie and couldn't just manage it at the moment. He thought slanted black eyes shadowed by a battered trilby stared at him as his pulse was felt. Blinked, and they were gone. Then there was another face that was spotty and freckled and had a runny nose.

'If you're Charlie Dance I gotta have words. Is now a good time if you're him?'

'I'm him,' Charlie said, feeling the laughter bubble.

'I'm Rosie. Rosie Bottoms. You can call me Ernie.'

'Well, Ernie Rosie Bottoms. You can get this tart off me for a start. Get me on my feet.'

The spotty face glowed in the yellow sodium light.

'That mean I'm on the firm?'

The world tilted upright to laughter, but it was a sadder, darker place.

The bar phone jangled like a whore dunning a trick.

Bulstrode reached it before Mickey Raven and said: 'Yeah?'

There were pips and the money dropped.

'This you, Micky?'

'Yeah.'

'Them chinks done the business. Hair teeth and bleeding eyebrows all over Wardour Street.'

'Any law nosing?' Bulstrode asked.

'Who hung around? Dance got it hard and fast, is all.'

'Hang on,' Bulstrode passed the phone to Raven whose face had turned to hating chalk. 'For you,' he said.

Raven depressed the tines to kill the connection. Blew smoke in Bulstrode's face.

'Wrong number,' he said, his eyes drilling holes.

Bulstrode reacted without thought. Slammed the receiver across the bridge of Raven's nose. Driving him back into Rupert and Alphonse.

'And my hand slipped. We all make mistakes, right?'

Raven pinched bleeding nostrils. Held Rupert and Alphonse back with his free hand. Said: 'We'll drink to that big truth, Buller. You can't refuse a bevy from one fuck-up to another. Can you, eh?'

Bulstrode tasted slime. Lemmon took the phone and laid it gently to rest in its cradle. Handed Raven a bar towel and edged Bulstrode down the bar with his superior bulk.

'Got something to drink to, have we, Micky?' he asked in his soft West Country burr. 'One funny phonecall enough to push the boat out, is it?'

Raven snorted into the towel. Banged the mahogany for service.

'Who's had a call? Not me. Right, lads?'

Rupert said: 'Only the copper.' And Alphonse agreed with: 'Seen it with me own eyes, didn't I?'

'What did you see, Franco?' Raven asked Mella.

'About the same, Micky.'

Raven dabbed blood spots from his white dress shirt.

'There you are then. Large ones here, barman. Best in the house for our friends the filth.'

'Another time, Micky.' Lemmon asked Bulstrode what had come down the telephone. Listened, and without a change of expression, swept the fresh drinks from the bar with his forearm. 'Now we've all had an accident tonight. Evens things up, wouldn't you say, Micky?'

'Seems like, Mr Lemmon. You could well be right.'

Raven watched Lemmon and Bulstrode walk away through broken glass. The swing doors batted to and fro, and the street door gently slammed. Two cars revved and drove away, leaving silence for Rupert and Alphonse to talk hard, fast and heavy into until Raven hit the bar with his fist.

'Shut it, you pair of defectives. Get out there and earn your corn. See what the full SP is. Dance is handshaking them Triads, not me. But who's in the frame with the law if he's all the way down, eh? Me.'

Raven turned his back until Rupert and Alphonse had left. Snatched a bottle and poured himself a stiff Black Label. Stared at himself in the mirrored backbar. Saw the thinning widow's peak cut into his high forehead. The grey flashes over his long ears. Scarred brows lowered over small white eyes with colourless pupils. High cheekbones and hollow cheeks that needed shaving twice a day. The big teeth bared in a wide mouth above a cleft chin. The fear nobody else could see.

If Charlie boy's finished, I've got the East End sewn up, he thought. *No contest. But if he ain't, Charlie won't come looking for me with just his finger . . .*

'Best he's dead,' he muttered. 'Best he's with old Archie in the big blue beyond . . .'

The Maltese waiter retreated to the end of the bar and Franco Mella locked himself in his office, knowing the phone would ring.

Wardour Street was already sealed off when Lemmon and Bulstrode parked outside the secure perimeter. Two ambulances waited to be loaded, radios squawked on officers' lapels, torches played over the bodies and blood in St Anne's Court, and the Lotus House was in darkness. Hatchets and a Mauser pistol were being photographed in situ before being bagged and tagged and taken away for forensic tests. Lemmon found Dillman and the new man Taggart taking notes in a doorway, and had Dillman give him his first impressions while Bulstrode went off to locate Chinese Cyril, the named keyholder to the restaurant.

'We've got two dead Chinese males lying up there by the door to Black Mary's crib. Broken necks, it looks like, and their clothes stripped off. Whoever smacked them did it with more force than I've ever seen before. Turned their bloody heads around.'

Taggart chimed in with: 'Apart from old Ironfoot Jack.'

Lemmon and Dillman blinked at him.

'Sorry to interrupt, Sir, Dillman mate. But you did say I should attend all the autopsies I could. For the experience, and to get over the dry heaves. Well, I was at Jack's . . .'

'And?'

'His neck was whacked out of true, just like them. Worser maybe.'

Lemmon nodded as if he understood. Wondered what kind of a word 'worser' was, and told Dillman to continue.

'I figure there were more than a dozen assailants, Guv. The alley was covered with wet prints when we arrived. Most of them dried out in the wind, but we'll lift a few of the muddier ones okay. And get good latent dabs off the ironwear if they didn't wear gloves.'

Dillman took a breath. Pointed his pencil into the shadows.

'Our old chummy Sodbonce Carver is back there too. The ambulance crew's working on him now, trying to stuff his vitals back behind his belt buckle. Them pig-stickers opened him all the way up and then some. Touch and go if he'll make it to the theatre, let alone survive an op. Got a uniform standing by in case he says something, but I doubt he will.'

Lemmon steeled himself for what was coming next. Taggart cleared his nose between pinched fingers.

Dillman said: 'And one of the uniforms found Nasty Nostrils O'Donovan trying to crawl out into Dean Street. A good half a yard of butcher's knife through his kidneys and half his right hand gone. Found his fingers by Soddy. He'd leaked most of his eight pints of O-type the length of St Anne's Court, so he's iffy-to-critical too.'

Dillman closed his notebook with a snap.

Lemmon waited.

'That's *it*?'

'Guv?'

'Nobody else? No Charlie Dance?'

'Not that we saw, Guv, no. His Roller's nowhere around neither. There is that Daimler sitting there, but it's not one registered to the Dance firm. We've got them all on file.'

'Check the plates out anyway.'

'And the wheelchair?' said Taggart.

'Wheelchair? What bloody wheelchair?'

'That bloody . . . that one, Sir. Leaned up against the Lotus House door. With the blanket and the box.'

'And inside the box?' Lemmon was almost afraid to ask.

'A cake, Sir. A broken golden cake.'

Bulstrode was suddenly there. Nodding and hard eyed.

'Vinnie Castle's birthday. I'd know that wheelchair anywhere. Somebody gonna tell me something, or what?'

Bulstrode had been a regular visitor when Castle was shotgunned into hospital. Had grown close.

Lemmon patted his shoulder.

'Vinnie's not here, Buller.'

'But he was, Guv. He was . . .'

Bulstrode lit a cigarette with palsied hands. Flicked the match over the Daimler and stared at something only he could see.

'Find Vinnie, you'll find Charlie.'

Lemmon nodded at the Lotus House.

'More reason for us to take a goodly squint inside Exhibit A. Did you find Chinese Cyril?'

'Sent a mobile to his house, but ten-to-one he ain't home. There's claret all over the floor in there. And Cyril won't want to come up with answers.'

'You saw that through the windows?'

'Didn't have to, Guv. The door's open.'

Dillman looked startled. 'They told me different.'

'Bloody uniforms,' Lemmon swore. 'Let's get in there and count the fat lady's tattoos. But tread carefully, lads. Leave the forensic boys a clear field.'

He took Taggart's torch and followed the beam into the Lotus House to find the house lights. There were no more bodies. Just blood spatters and trampled linen, overturned furniture and a lot of unwashed crockery. But there were fingerprints on the wine glasses, cigarette stubs for saliva tests, and crumbs of golden cake on some of the plates. More than enough to be going on with.

None of Lemmon's squad slept that night.

CHAPTER THREE

Doc Rudge's breath smelled of old books as he leaned in to inspect Charlie's gashed deltoid. He had used delicate butterfly stitches to close the cut on Charlie's temple, but this hole was in need of all his skill.

Vinnie lay sedated on the observation couch, and Fook looked like a morose buddha with his scalp shaved and sutured. Rosie Bottoms had his nose in a Rolls-Royce catalogue, his eyes as shiny as the art paper it was printed on. He'd driven the Silver Cloud like a low-flying jet, and made Spitalfields in minutes.

Charlie bit on a snarl as Rudge used needles and surgical gut to gather the lips of his shoulder wound.

'*Now* d'you want the local anaesthetic I offered?'

'No is no, Doc. Stuff makes you dozy.'

'Miles to go and promises to keep, huh? No matter that Vinnie should be back at Stoke Mandaville soonest. Or that the *Chinoise* there should have X-rays. An old man I am, St Thomas's I ain't.'

'You'll do me, Doc.'

'And them? Heads ain't cabbages. Bangs on the skull need special care. Be a hero for your ownself, Charlie, but your friends? They should be allowed what's best, eh?'

'Tonight you. Tomorrow, Harley Street.'

'It's some terrific tomorrow that never comes.' Rudge swabbed welling blood from exposed bone. Teased tissue into place, pleased with his embroidery.

Charlie used the wall clock to re-establish his sense of time and place. Fought the mist fogging his mind. The manic laughter had died away in whimpers. The red hand sweeping off seconds was too slow to measure his heartbeat. Black figures came at him from every angle until he shrugged them away.

'Be still. You ain't got enough holes in you?'

'Sew, you quack.'

'It's your bad mouth I should stitch.'

Charlie used the rhythmic bite of the needle to stay alert. *In, draw through, loop. In, draw through, loop . . .*

Told himself again and again that leaving Soddy and Nasty for the police had been expedient. That they needed the best emergency care to make it, not old Rudge's make do and mend. Micky Raven came into his mind. Micky shaking hands with black Dragons.

I get a Fook, you get a Dragon, that it, Micky . . .?

'This you won't like, Charlie.' Rudge had found a splinter of steel imbedded in bone. 'Ready?'

'As I'll ever be.'

Pain made Charlie grin. The clock fuzzed as the probe went in. The room revolved as hot marbles were plunged into bone marrow. Metal chinked in a kidney dish. The sound of a hatchet striking brick.

'Now we clean.'

Rudge fed antibiotic implants into the wound. Held Charlie erect until his balance came back. The mad bastard wouldn't even lie down for treatment. Sat perched on the edge of the table staring at the clock as if it was the answer to something. Thought: *Miles to go and promises to keep* . . . Sucked the surgical mask in against his face as he got the bleeding clamped off. Working finer than he ever had to sew the artery back together. Released the clamps and watched the blood turn the white tube blue. Closed up and covered his work with a sterile white dressing, knowing it was the best work he had ever done. Hoping it was enough.

Charlie rolled to his feet with ridged muscles standing out

like an anatomy lesson as he tested his equilibrium. The floor stayed under his feet and the walls remained steady as he drew Fook's attention without a word, making him talk.

'The Dragons were clever if crude. They overcame my Killing Shadows and took their places. Very fast, Charlie, too fast. It was well done, and there are no words to explain how I knew in time. Only their smell was different. That small thing was enough, and came almost too late to save us. I owe you a life, my friend. Mine. Your men must have fought well to turn things our way.'

Fook spoke in careful Cantonese to exclude Bottoms and Rudge, and Charlie knew enough to understand. He was also very sure that Fook hadn't seen the man in the flowing overcoat and greasy trilby. Wasn't certain he had himself, until he remembered the yellow face staring down into his. A face he could pass in the street a thousand times and not know it.

Charlie said nothing about it. Found Vinnie's Rothman's and smoked as he let Bottoms tell his story, killing time until Matt and Froggy arrived with fresh clothes. There was something in the boot of the Rolls they had to take care of before Charlie kept his appointment to play poker. He had phoned Franco at the Troubadour to say he would be along.

The Turkish Baths below the Russell Hotel was empty but for two effeminate men sleeping off their massage in curtained booths and the duty masseur dozing in his cubicle. Cho Sun and Joe Yellow had the steam room to themselves as they sweated the night from their bones, talking in sign-language and Mandarin.

Joe Yellow's fingers said: *This green wand would know something, Uncle.*

'Ask your question, Nephew.'

You broke the Dragons without killing when they deserved to die. You saved the Snake and the roundeyed Dance when you could have killed them with ease. You allowed the half-Chinese Cyril to see your face when you took the Dragons from his back. And the women who were there. They saw. You looked into the face of the roundeyed Dance before we left. I understand none of these things.

Cho Sun bared small white teeth and slapped his shoulders to make the sweat flow. Brought his legs up into the lotus position to feel the hot Edwardian tiles against his hams.

'An obedient hawk flies to the kill when his hood is lifted. Is that not what the young Dragons did? Do you kill a good hawk for taking a pigeon on the wing when that is what he is born to do? To kill what he is directed at? The master pointed and they followed. They are blameless, it is the one who pointed who bears the guilt.'

Joe Yellow nodded through ball-bearings of perspiration.

'The Snake and Dance had to live through this night. I will write when their time comes, not the council here, *me*. They have failed, so I cannot. You see?'

Yes.

'The Snake did not see me when I turned the hatchets away, so why should Chinese Cyril or the women remember what they thought they saw? They saw shadows and their own fear, that is all. And I saw what I only *thought* I knew when I looked into Dance's round eyes. A photograph is a flat thing with no heart. The living face tells all as nothing else can. Seeing is knowledge, the greatest weapon of all.'

Joe Yellow followed Cho Sun to the cold pool and plunged in after him. Floundered in icy green water tasting of chlorine with iron hoops turning his lungs solid. Kicked to the surface to gasp as Cho Sun flipped himself from the pool using his fingertips. Joe struck out for the side with a clumsy dog-paddle and was hauled out on to the tiled surround as if he were as light as a rice-ball.

'You are a drowned stone when you swim, Nephew.'

The water hates my ears, Uncle. I lose my balance and walking is not easy. And I hear the sea inside my head for days afterwards. Strange for a man with dead ear drums.

'You were stupid to follow me blindly.'

And as guilty as the young Dragons for following the master's finger?

Cho Sun bared teeth and gum. Threw back his head and barked. He was laughing.

'You have no guilt, Nephew. But you have guile.'

Joe Yellow heard surf pound up a pebbled beach and wondered why his back was slapped on the way to the changing rooms. Truly, his uncle was a strange man.

Smithfield Market was a brawl of lorries and hurrying meat porters, and nobody gave the white Rolls a second glance. There was no such thing as a poor butcher, and class wheels were a common sight amongst the barrows and sides of beef.

Froggy Farrell drove, and Matt Mandrell had the sawn-off shotguns in a holdall on his lap. Froggy had dressed over his pyjamas, and Matt hadn't shaved for the week he'd spent in bed with Asian flu. Neither man was in the best of moods, and the news about Soddy and Nasty made them savage.

The Rolls swung into the outer yard of Stripes Flynn's cold store, drove on to an elevated platform, and dropped eighty feet into the crackling cold of permafrost. Passing through row upon row of frozen carcases, the Rolls halted in an empty section used for fletching hides. Matt closed and locked the steel shutters, threw Froggy a shotgun, and opened the boot.

The Chinese came out in a forward roll, using the kicks of the emperor's horse to give him space. A walnut stock slammed across his jaw. A boot ground his face into the concrete, and a double-barrel took the air out of him with a savage stab to the crotch. Rolled on his back, he was stripped naked and his wrists and ankles were wired together hard enough to cut into his flesh. Hung upside down from a meat hook, he silently called upon his ancestors to make him brave. He bit his mouth to shreds as he was beaten with brass stair rods. His already swollen genitals grew to the size and colour of aubergines, and he passed out with his own blood running down his body into his mouth.

Icy water smashed into his face to bring him back, and he knew he wouldn't last long when the blood and water froze on his skin. A good thing, because he would die in silence.

Then they hosed him down with hot water, dried him and wrapped him in horse blankets to bring his body temperature back to normal. Left him hanging there, and began to clean the bloody upholstery of the car, whistling as they worked.

Ho Fatt of the Dragon T'ang knew despair as his head turned in slow circles bare inches from the frozen concrete floor. Only dying well would make him a man again, and he wanted that very badly.

'Feeling lucky, Micky?'

The question swung Raven's spine to the bar.

People had invaded the Troubadour. Chappie August hung between Binkie and Trooper Wells, the long green cigar smoking into his glassy eyes. Trooper's seconds were armed with methuselahs of vintage Krug, and Tommy Badell the trainer wore Wells' Lonsdale Belt around his neck like a chain of office. Some girls they'd picked up in Shepherd Market kissed everybody in sight, and Trooper's wife Hettie found a quiet corner to knit in when she'd dumped a huge bouquet of prime blooms in a champagne bucket. Big Alphonse and Rupert Baer came out of the gents at a run, and were swamped by the crush of laughing bodies.

'Gonna take you with a three high tonight,' August leered.

Raven shook Trooper's hand.

'Heard you were good tonight, Champ. Would have been there, but you know how it is.'

'Congo Billy wished he'd stayed home too,' August slurred.

Trooper sipped a small lager.

61

'Congo was game all the way. Won't have nothing said against the man. Had to work on that eye of his, or he'd be coming at me yet. A good strong boy. Like hitting iron chocolate when I hammered his ribs.'

Raven kept an eye on the door. Saw Rupert and Alphonse station themselves either side, watching for Charlie.

'Does Congo earn a re-match, Troop?'

Wells shook his head.

'My Hettie says "no", and she's the governor outside the ring. Hanging up my gloves, ain't I? Always fancied a nice restaurant, and could be me and Chinese Cyril'll work something out now his lease is up in Wardour Street. My name out in front should mean something for a few years yet, eh?'

Raven thumbed his tender nose.

'A lot of years. Put me down for a table on the opening night.'

August hiccuped into Binkie's bosom.

'Can't retire, Troop. Got miles in you yet. Gotta contract with yours truly, and there's millions of money to be made out there with your name over the marquee. You leave Hettie to me, I'll handle her.'

Trooper's mouth grew hard lines as he laid August over the bar with a shrug.

'You'll handle nothing, Chappie son. You give my Hettie the heavy finger you'll do my brain in. Have to put you on the ropes, wouldn't I?'

August paled and his eyes swam like yolks in white sauce.

'Sleep on it, Troop . . . Sleep on it . . .'

Wells's crumpled face darkened with a hard shake.

'Decided, ain't I?'

August held his stomach and broke wind.

'Ate something. Better point my primate at the porcelain.'

He staggered away, bouncing off people and tables.

Binkie wrinkled her snub nose.

'Smells like he swallowed a dead dog,' she said prettily,

leaning to show her bosom to non-existent photographers. She could have been made of wax for all the notice Wells and Raven took.

'Watch his fountain pen in the clinches, Champ. He'll tie you up in litigation for years, he puts his bog of a mind to it.'

Wells' smile made him boyish.

'Just what Chas Dance said moons back when I used his lawyer. Ain't a sixpence in my name. All in Hettie's, and she'll knit and nod and let Chappie chew crow before she'll drop a stitch.'

'Just so's you know he'll come at you ugly and sudden.'

'You and Chas grind the same organ, Micky. But old Troop's seen the elephant and the fat lady. I didn't take on all-comers in fairground booths without learning a few wrinkles. Had a hundred some fights the first summer. Fought half of 'em with a broken hand. And got set on team-handed in the car park if I smacked the local bully-boys too hard. Durham miners don't give up a purse without they let you know about it. And them Taffies out of Tiger Bay ain't smiling losers neither. I've punched my knuckles raw to put a bit of bacon on the table for me and my Het. She stuck through all them hard years, and now she's earned her tiara and mink. You think me and her'll have it grabbed off by a dwarf on the end of a ten-foot cigar? Ain't likely.'

Raven thought otherwise but said nothing. Just the mention of Charlie Dance made his stomach flutter, his hand reach for a drink. He made a fist on the bar and left the Black Label bottle where it was. Hated being sober in a crowd of drunks and knew he had to be. His bladder wanted to burst, so he followed August to the toilets.

Chappie was draped over a basin sluicing his face. Wiped drool from his chin as Raven used a stall to relieve himself.

'No gratitude left, no loyalty,' he droned. 'Made that man a mountain of poppy, now he wanns a sodding café selling heathen nosh. Where's the justice, eh, Micky? Where's the "anything you say, Mr August, Sir", eh? Gone with the wind, that's where. Well different when they're hungry. When they're unknown cobbles-fighters. Then it's road work and elbowing the women, and "You're the boss, Mr August". First sip of champagne and *wallop* – they're wearing camelhair coats and elbowing good old Chappie for some frizzy blonde with legs up to her earlobes. And screaming over the small print of the contract when it says plain as day they have to repay the expenses I laid out to put them onna map.'

Chappie swayed into Raven to breath into his face. Raven pushed him away. Hard enough to slam his head against the wall-tiles. Chappie looked bemused and slid down the wall like a melted pink frog.

Raven zipped up and washed his hands. Patted his hair smooth in the mirror and gave August a long look of disgust.

'Trooper shook your hand, Chappie, and it stayed shook. You're pissed and pissed-off because you laid your dough off on Congo Billy Devon. Thought old Troop'd waltz for a few rounds and take a gentle dive. Put the odds up for the re-match and then give Billy a hiding. Got it well wrong, didn't you?'

August's hands could find no purchase on the glazed tiles.

'You don't know that . . . Know nothing of the kind . . .'

'Don't I? You had Arnie Clover lay the bets off for you, right? But Arnie was into me for a lot of dough already. Had to come to me and bubble straight because his marker's worthless without my say-so. It was that or lose his toenails the hard way. You can only steal from a greedy man, Chappie. Means you stole for yourself, don't it?'

'Thassa dirty, rotten . . . who told you that load of . . .'

Raven banged out into the passage and strode into silence.

The party spirit had died, and everybody stood in a loose semi-circle facing the main door to the club. Froggy Farrell and Matt Mandrell pointed rolled raincoats at Alphonse and

Rupert, and Charlie Dance just stood there with street cold coming off his clothes and nothing showing in his face.

There was just the clack of Hettie's needles.

'There you are then, Micky.'

Raven swallowed air.

Felt a hole open up around him as people sidled away.

Told himself it was no time to get rubber knees or yellow up like a jaundiced Chinaman. That was for little boys and twopenny tarts. Not Micky Raven.

'Looks like it, Chas.'

A hard bubble of wind bloated Raven's gut and his nose throbbed as he walked towards Dance and the rolled rain-coats. The carpet went on for miles and seemed to snatch like an unmown lawn. His feet were too small for his shoes, and he had the crazy idea his clothes would melt and leave him naked when heavy buckshot tore into his shrunken penis. He got within an arm's length of Dance and offered a hand as cold and steady as monumental marble.

'Heard you was served bad suey tonight, Chas.'

Charlie kept his hands in his pockets.

'That so?'

'Yeah, an anonymous on the blower.'

'Two of my faces got food poisoning. That what you heard?'

'Something similar. Trouble is, the anonymous call got blown into the filth's ear by mistake. Lemmon's lad Buller, as it happens. Got a way of picking up telephones before they ring. Nothing anybody could do. The anonymous told him, he told me.'

'Just like that.'

'Exactly like that. My hand on it.'

Charlie extracted a fist and crushed knuckles until Raven squeezed back. Their hands locked, they stared at each other. Then Charlie looked through Raven's skull at the rest of the bar.

'That how it was, Rupert son?'

'Yeah.' Rupert saw the raincoats swing into Raven's midriff. Waited for a flashing roar to hurl Raven away towards the toilets, and added: 'Who went down, Chas?'

'Soddy and Nasty. Hatchet job. A lot of claret, Rupe.'

'Fucking shame. God's honest.'

'I'll tell 'em you said so when their bellies have knit back. Funny how overcoats worry about overcoats, even if they're on different firms, eh, Micky?'

Raven had nothing to say. He thought he might have nodded.

Charlie's eyes brushed Baer's face.

'That it, Rupe?'

'Micky told it gospel. The law had the telephone surrounded. We was bevying with the filth when you got done, so where's the need for shooters?'

Charlie smiled at nothing.

'Shooters. It's a good man who speaks up for the face who coughs the weekly readies, Micky. He got X-ray vision you reckon?'

Raven hooked his free thumb into a waistcoat pocket.

'It's been said.'

Charlie looked at the sweat leaking from Alphonse's moustache. Saw how it glistened on his bald patch.

'You saying anything, Al?'

'Only it's a cold old night, and I'm standing in a draught.'

Raven's stomach muscles ached from being tensed. He just had to make light of things before he strangulated a hernia. Said: 'Al grew through his hair. Makes him susceptible to chills.'

Charlie nodded. Jerked a thumb at Froggy and Matt.

'Got something to warm you up. Show 'em, lads.'

Froggy and Matt shook the raincoats away. Light flashed on green bottles with engraved labels and gold-foil caps, and the popping champagne corks were as loud as shotguns.

'Bang-fucking-bang,' said Froggy.

Matt just leered.

Charlie knuckled Raven's chin with: 'Glasses, Micky. Before the bubbly runs into the carpet.'

Raven felt the club swim. Wanted to laugh and vomit.

'I could smack you for that, Charlie. Really get the hump.'

Charlie's face was an empty winter beach.

'Only with the right cards, Micky. Keep that in mind.'

He left Raven standing there with damp underwear. Walked away to shake Trooper Wells' hand and kiss Hettie's cheek as the conversation stumbled awake to grow frantic with released tension.

Baer couldn't believe it. 'He done us with bubbles, Micky. Had us passing blood with two bottles of piss and air.'

Big Alphonse wiped his naked scalp with a horny palm.

'You are playing him, Micky? You gotta give him some stick with the pasteboards. Plain got to.'

Raven saw things with such clarity he could actually see the perspiration well inside Alphonse's enlarged pores. The tiny silver hairs sprouting from his rumpled ears. The blue sheen on the whites of his widened eyes.

'How much you carrying for me, Rupe?' he asked quietly.

Baer thought, using his fingers.

'Five grand in readies. Two thousand in markers from Arnie Clover. And Chappie August's cheque to Arnie Clover for his bet on Trooper going down to Congo Billy. With that you got twenty-seven thousand. A lot of heavy poppy.'

Raven kneaded his stomach.

'Have to do,' he said.

'This I gotta see,' said Big Alphonse.

Raven's look was ice on ice.

'Can't can you? You being such a close mate of Soddy Carver and Nasty O'Donovan. Needing to be at their bedside with flowers and a sorry expression, eh?'

'Forgot, didn't I?'

Baer looked at anyone but Raven. Wanted to see the poker too much to blow it with a wrong look or a sudden stupid word. Saw Froggy and Matt retrieve their raincoats and hold the door open.

'Want a lift then, Al?' said Froggy. 'Happens we're going that way. Can drop you off.'

Raven's laugh was flatter than unleavened bread.

'Leave the poppy and the markers, Rupe. Go with Al. Can't break up a matched set, can I?'

Baer protested with: 'Stuff it, Micky . . .'

'You said *what*, Rupe?'

'Said "Stuff it". Meant well different. Meant I'd call in if anything breaks either way, didn't I?'

'There's a loyal overcoat.'

'Try to please, don't I?'

Baer crowded out after the others and complained all the way up to the street. Raven refused champagne at the bar when Franco said Johnny the Builder was ready to deal for the house in the top room. August sent Binkie away with taxi fare, and Trooper said he'd sit in for an hour. Charlie took a bottle of Irish from the shelf, and Raven ordered club soda before taking Trooper out of the bar.

'He laid hands on me, you know that, Chas?' August whispered. 'Put an egg on the back of my head. Feel.'

'And grease up the cards?'

Charlie left August to manage the stairs on his own, in no mood to pander to the self-pity of a drunk.

The steel door of the underground fletching room opened, and a torchbeam seared Ho Fatt's eyes. Patent shoes and the skirt of a heavy overcoat showed in the spill of light. Breath clouded in the freezing air, and the circling shoes left black prints in the frost. Then the beam stayed on his face, and the voice of the Supreme Snake talked at Ho Fatt as though he were already a dead thing of no value.

The short monologue promised exquisite agony as he

lingered between this world and whatever lay beyond the last dark door. Suspended in limbo, his body would be cut away until only his mind was left. Then he would want to pass through the last door enough to allow his tongue to betray his T'ang. Only then would he be allowed the eternal darkness of total release.

The torch went out and the steel door closed.

Ho Fatt hung in timeless darkness. Without light or sound he was nothing, and the real world was a slowly fading dream. Only the radiant pain was real.

Johnny the Builder shuffled and dealt the fiftieth hand of the evening, skimming the cards in perfect lines before the players. Each time August had lost a decent pot he'd asked for a change of cards, and Johnny had just broken the seal on a fourth deck of casino bicycles. Raven played straight percentages as if his seat hadn't warmed, and Charlie was a Sphinx wrapped in smoke and silence, the cut on his temple darkening as the bruising came out. Trooper Wells had enjoyed the early luck, and he had over fifteen hundred pounds of August's money in front of him. Johnny finished the deal and said August's pair of showing queens should open the betting with: 'The fat ladies to talk.'

'The fat ladies go fifty sovs.'

August fanned tenners without a flicker, and when everybody matched the ante, raised another hundred. Johnny folded for the house, Charlie stood pat, and Raven raised a further fifty to make Trooper throw in his cards with a wry smile. Nobody wanted to draw, meaning there were good hands around the table, and Johnny said: 'Back to the fat ladies to bet.'

'Two hundred sovs,' August said.

Charlie threw his money in, and Raven raised the pot by a thousand.

'Twelve hundred to you, Chappie.'

'Eight hundred cash, my marker for four more.'

69

Charlie shook his head.

'No paper-hanging. Cash.'

'I'm good for it.'

'You say,' said Raven. 'Bet what you're wearing or pick up your marbles and go home to Binkie. You want an hour to get back with the money, OK.'

'I ain't heard that from the house,' August said moodily.

Johnny scratched a liver spot on a brown knuckle.

'You have now. Unless the company says different.'

Raven sipped a club soda.

'This company don't. You, Chas?'

'Not this chair.'

'Come off it, Dance. You'd take my signature on a bus ticket if this was the Philadelphia House. So what's so flaming different here?'

'That's business, this is personal. We ain't punters against the house here.'

'Nor boy scouts betting matches against woggles around the bloody camp fire,' Raven said. 'Bet or fade.'

'My marker's good.'

Johnny sighed through Piccadilly smoke.

'And we're good for the hour it takes to get the money. Don't play little boys with the chaps, there's a good lad.'

'Tell them I'm solid, Troop?' August appealed.

Wells spread his palms.

'How? I've folded.'

'Then I'll cover the pot.'

Johnny picked tobacco from his tongue.

'With only eight hundred? Not on, is it?'

'Then the house takes a personal cheque.'

'If Franco swallows it, OK.' Johnny reached for the house phone.

'Save your dialling finger for pleasure,' Raven said. 'He won't.'

Johnny watched him unfold August's cheque to Arnie Clover.

'I'm already wearing twenty grand's worth of your promises, Chappie. And I've got this feeling it's naughty enough to come back marked "Refer to Drawer".'

August wiped off his mouth with his eyes all the way open.

'What's this then? The hanging tree? Suddenly Chappie ain't a face?'

Raven's laugh was unpleasant.

'When was you ever a face? You could live long enough to take in God's washing – put the sun out with a damp thumb, but a face you'll never be.'

August changed colour like a fat chameleon.

'Nobody says that to Chappie August and . . .'

Raven's face turned taut and white.

'And, Chappie? And *what*?'

'Stays in my good books . . .'

Raven glanced at Dance.

'You hearing this, Chas?'

'But not believing it. Threats, Chappie? And that cheque wouldn't be the dough Arnie Clover figured to pay me with, would it?'

Charlie's soft question raised Raven's eyebrows.

'Arnie's into you too?'

'Yeah, Arnie's had a bad season. A shame if he thought to get out from under with Chappie's rubber money. How do we play this then, August? Do we all take a package tour down to the Caymans to get paid out? You don't have a solitary sou in the Smoke, and I'm laying nine-to-two-on you've got yourself a one-way airline ticket in your sky to go visit the islands at first light.'

August's jowls were the grey of crusted whey. A plump hand went to the lump on the back of his head, and he conjured brothers for it in his mind. Somewhere in his repertoire were the right silver words, but they wouldn't slide on to his thick tongue.

'Nothing's ever the way it looks, chaps,' he said.

Raven turned the cheque like a soiled flag.

'Looking at you I can believe it,' he said.

Trooper looked from Raven to Dance and across at Johnny's perfect poker face. Spread his square hands on the baize and pushed his chair back.

'Tonight's purse weren't written in invisible ink, was it, Chappie? Can't have my Hettie dropping her purls and plains from worry. So just hook your wallet out and show Troop there ain't no flying Red Rover in there.'

'Do I look sui-flaming-cidal, you dumb pug?' August flashed.

Trooper grabbed silk lapels and pulled August up at him.

'Do I look convinced?'

'Leave it out, Troop,' said Raven.

Charlie blew smoke down the table.

'Keep your hands in your pockets, Champ. In the ring you're the business, but laying a glove on offal like that out here on the cobbles puts you well out of order.'

Wells shook August, flushing him up.

'I'm hearing you, but it's him showing me the elephant.'

'In this company, Chappie?' Charlie asked.

'On my sainted mother's life, Chas . . .'

'Listen to it,' Raven sneered. 'His sainted mother. An Airedale bitch dropped you at Battersea Dog's Home one foggy Christmas, you hound.'

Charlie spoke as if he and Wells were alone.

'Put it down, Champ. Take your Hettie home. I'll see you get what's coming to you.'

Trooper dropped August into his chair. Picked up his winnings and knuckled his chin. Said: 'Your word's all it takes, Chas,' and padded away without looking back.

Nothing was said until Johnny lit cigarettes and passed one to Dance with: 'This a game of poker or a cobbles knees-up?'

Raven hooked a thumb at August.

'The bet's still with this tart.'

72

August smoothed his ruffled front and looked contrite.

'Thirty days is all I need, Micky, Charlie. Then that kite'll sail through Barclay's like a Derby winner. And what's thirty days to you? Nothing.'

'You make thirty days sound like dodgy Judas silver, you goat,' said Raven. 'Twenty grand earns more than lumps and few weeks in traction. More like a permanent spanking.'

'Micky, Micky, this is Chappie you're talking to, not some baby punter betting a snide florin on an outsider. Lemmee play out this hand, square the pot, then we'll talk dough, not whackings.'

'Betting with what, you toerag? Chocolate buttons from Santa's waistcoat?'

'My word and what's backing these queens.'

'Nothing back of them tarts but your gut, you chancer.'

August swelled in his chair with wounded dignity.

'Chappie August Enterprises is backing these queens.'

'Comedian,' Raven snapped. 'A rusty Remington in a rented office full of dead flies? Your meal ticket just walked out the door in case you hadn't noticed. What else have you got but not a lot?'

'Forget Trooper. I got contracts worth a dozen of him. Two fights in Madison Square Gardens for a start. The TV rights alone are enough to sweat up your money finger. Don't short change me, Micky.'

Raven thought about laughing. Changed his mind, and leaned over to slap August's face several times. Leaned back and waved the cheque.

'You ain't worth the paper you're printed on.'

Charlie breathed something through his Piccadilly. Eased a long ash into a dish and waited.

'You what?' said Raven.

'I said I'll have some.'

'Of his porkies?'

'Every pie has a crust, Micky.'

'No time for chuckles, Charlie. This tart stays, pays, and takes his lumps. Job fucking done.'

Charlie shrugged and sent flame into his shoulder. Rubbed his pounding temple and fought overwhelming exhaustion.

'Twenty grand in cash for Chappie's cheque sets you square. Also buys me whatever I want out of August Enterprises, excluding any outstanding debts. You both agree to that, and we'll play this hand as a straight show of cards.'

Raven bit on his signet ring, calculating odds.

'Let me get this straight in my loafbone: You'll pay me twenty grand for this cheque. If I win, I keep the twenty, take the pot and Chappie's marker for four hundred.'

'That's about it.'

'And if this tart wins?'

'Chappie wins he get the pot, his marker, and a new partner. You off his back, and his rubber kite torn up.'

Raven looked down at Charlie's hand.

'With two small hearts showing.'

Charlie made smoke with a nod. Wanted an Irish and knew he'd see treble after one sip. Raven and August were muddy blurs, and Johnny was a thin shadow with a ruby bobbing on his lower lip.

'You getting this, *tart*?' Raven asked August.

'And an apology for my corner,' Chappie said.

'For what?'

'For two unwarranted smackings is for what. For Chappie's pride.'

Johnny pulled at his thin brown nose and smoothed his thinner hair. Made his chair creak when he folded his arms.

'Pride ain't even a two-high in this game,' he said. 'Cut what you want any way you want, chaps. Just so's the house gets its ten per cent in cash. Not in sodding apologies.'

'I mean it,' said August.

'He says he means it,' Charlie said as the room swam.

Raven almost laughed. Cracked knuckle bones. Shook his head at the room as if it was a goldfish bowl cutting off his air.

'Am I dreaming, or what? Show me the money, Chas. That I know is real. He's doing my brain in with his "apologies for my corner".'

Charlie pushed a neat pile of fifties across for Raven to count. Took August's cheque and laid it on the pot.

'He wins, he'll get a proper sorry,' Raven said.

Johnny wiped a smile away with a lean hand.

'Let's see what's behind them fat ladies, Mr August.'

August turned three jacks to make a full house.

'Look and weep,' he crowed.

Raven's laugh was as hard as halitosis as he showed his cards out of turn.

'Weep nothing. Kings over tens. A bigger house than Maxie Miller pulled at the Stepney Empire.'

August shuddered, paled, and slapped a chubby hand to his shirtfront. Looked at Charlie, who looked back, showing nothing.

'Happens there's three in this game, Micky,' Johnny said.

'So have him show us his low flush.'

'Two pairs,' said Charlie. 'But they're all threes.'

Raven tore his cards across, his smile as dead as his eyes. Without shifting position or changing expression, he hit August full in the mouth, throwing him and his chair to the floor. Said, 'Sorry, ain't I?'

August blew air and lay still, and Johnny pushed the pot at Charlie with a solemn wink.

'Prefer my poker with more cards and less temper,' he said with sly humour. 'But when was it ever a perfect world?'

Charlie forged a smile through pink fuzz.

'Take for the house, and adopt a ton for y'self. See you soon, eh?'

'Soon as you like, Chas. Night, Micky.'

'Be lucky,' said Raven. 'Don't trip on nothing on your way out. Carpet's got a lump in it.'

Charlie tidied the money and put it away. Turned the cheque to confetti and let it drift to the floor. Stubbed his cigarette and leaked a last thin blue stream at Raven. Watched the man from Fulham think, brows hard down over pale eyes.

Micky Raven looked shrewd, hard and forty, and was. West London had been in his pocket for twelve years, the local law collected regular brown envelopes from a pub in King's Road, and Archie Ogle had been best man at his wedding when Micky only minded the bookies he now owned. Now he had more legitimate fronts than a breastless girl had padded cups, ran his girls like a drill sergeant, and his pinball machines pinged up millions from Southend to Skegness. The Raphael brothers handled his porn circuit and some Paddington hotels, and he had Alphonse and Rupert to marshal the heavy muscle. His manor was a tight little kingdom, and he could afford to sit back to watch the mini-skirts promenade past his boutiques if that was his pleasure, but there was an itch behind his eyeballs, and his thin mouth had the jut of a man hungry for new and exotic tastes.

Charlie had seen that look before.

'Still hungry for new turf, Micky?'

Raven's look was lazily insolent. A Porsche dealer kicking the tyres of a used trade-in.

'Ain't that why we're here?'

'As it so happens.'

'You look a bit used-up, Chas. Another time maybe.'

'Can't tell a crook by his cover. Hard territory east of the City. Ain't nobody held it for long.'

'Everywhere's hard. Like me.'

'Some harder than others.'

Raven showed contempt.

'Can see that from here, can't I?'

Charlie smashed throats in his mind. Popped eyeballs like petit-pois with his face in repose.

'Already a couple of Bethnal Green families who figure they fit Tommy Troy's boots now he's doing serious porridge with brother Jesse. Then there's the Chinks, a few hungry Maltese, not to mention the Cypriots and the Asians.'

'Where's your mouth leading, Charlie? Get it said.'

'New turf takes money, muscle, and a lot of hard. A lot of things you maybe don't have.'

'Weren't me got chopped and sueyed tonight. So who's got the sick firm? You or me?'

Charlie saw fire inside his head. Saw Raven as a smear of flesh tones in jiggling spots of light. Wanted to lie down and stay down. Until Soddy's stomach came at him like endless coils of slick rubber hose. And Nasty staggered in circles with a butcher's knife growing out of his ticket pocket.

'You could be walking into a lot of the same, Micky.'

'Walking blindfold ain't in my nature.'

'Heard that said before.'

'Now you're hearing it from me.'

'Hearing ain't proving, Micky.'

'That's as maybe, and nothing to do with nothing.'

Charlie's mild smile had nothing to do with his eyes.

'Go with God, Micky.'

'Meaning fucking what?'

'Meaning you got my blessing. You want the East End, have it.'

'Ain't yours to give, sunbeam.'

'Nor yours to take, neither.'

Raven stood to stretch kinks from his back. Looked down at August and across at Dance. Laughed his crisp laugh and pointed a long finger over a fist.

'You're a great one for standing aside. Just at first. Then your overcoats and snouts are suddenly everywhere. You holding the door open makes me nervous.'

Charlie wanted to snap the pointed finger off. Feed it into a pencil-sharpener. Saw balloons swell and burst, swell and burst.

'As it should be. A nervous man stays healthy. He don't get a swagger to his walk. Get loud in public and figure to kick his way under every table. My turf's right here, Micky. A small island between Fulham, Camden Town and Bethnal Green. Just don't plan to have no tidal waves coming at me. Get my meaning?'

'Enough to think it's worth a handshake.'

'So long as we play with a straight deck without jokers or wild deuces.'

'Always have. Didn't I with Archie? Why should it change?'

'Maybe it's the East End air. Or the bends in the river. Does strange things to a man's word. Happened to others before you, and they all ended up sad, sick and sorry for themselves.'

The long finger stabbed again.

'That was *them*. This is *me*.'

'I heard them. Now I'm hearing you.'

'And I'm seeing you behind them rolled raincoats.'

'Makes my point. We'll give it six months. See how it goes.'

Charlie offered his hand.

Raven stared at it.

'You shaking for them Chinks of yours?'

'They shake for me in Hong Kong. Why not.'

'Why not is simple. You don't have a lot of yellow brethren down in dockland. They do. They come at me wholesale or packets of three, it's you I'll come looking for, Charlie.'

'I won't be hard to find.'

Raven gripped Dance's palm. Saw the grey pupils veil.

'Nor you won't,' he said, wondering if he was seeing pain or the first cracks of defeat.

Out in Archer Street, Raven raised his collar against pre-dawn chill. Looked back at the upper window where light showed through a chink in the velvet curtain. Heard a phone ring deep inside the Troubadour, and knew it was more bad news for Charlie Dance. That did nothing to lighten his mood, and he had a headful of curves when he drove home. All with sharp edges that spun his morbid thoughts into a splitting migraine.

The gaming room had shrunk to shadows and stale smoke.

The four threes were victorious oblongs beside a worthless deuce, and Raven's hand was a scatter of decapitated royalty. August was a rumpled sprawl outside the spill of the bin light, and Charlie's thoughts were minnows braving cold currents of doubt.

Warm ooze pasted his shirt to his back when he climbed all the way to his feet. Raven's last handshake had torn something open. The green baize table was a soft lawn he wanted to lie down on. He used the house phone to bring Franco running, had him carry August down to the Rolls. The stairs went down a long, long way. The landings bobbed on nauseous swell, and the banister rails were sponge under his sweating palms.

Then he was outside, and the snapping cold stole his breath. The quickening sky was awash with muted greys and pinks. Franco said he was choked Nasty hadn't made it, and hoped Soddy got lucky as he laid August in the back of the Rolls and opened the driver's door. Charlie patted Franco's face with limp saveloys hanging from a bloody cuff. Drove west along Shaftesbury Avenue to Piccadilly Circus.

Eros fired an empty bow at Swan & Edgars. The neon signs were tawdry winks above swirling litter. Junkies huddled outside the all-night chemists with National Health prescriptions, and a pair of derelicts with a bottle of biddy hurried to find a hot-air vent at the back of the Piccadilly Hotel.

The Rolls found its way up Park Lane and into Edgware

Road with Charlie hanging onto the wheel. The traffic lights glared green all the way, and Charlie made the turn into Sussex Place with one hand. Locked August into the car, and went up the front steps of a Georgian house like an old man. Leaned on the bell for as long as it took for the door to open. There was a panelled hall with animal heads and pampas grass in Chinese urns. A lot of white gloss and brown nubbed carpet. Furniture polished to glass, and a passage that went uphill in a fast tilt.

Sam the Spade caught him as he fell, and Charlie glimpsed long bare legs and a swirl of silk coming down the stairs. Black hair being swept back from a wayward nose, and a mouth without lipgloss making an O of concern.

'Just passing through, Margot,' he mumbled before his face sagged against a hard black thigh.

Then there was a lot of nothing smelling of Attar of Roses.

CHAPTER FOUR

Joe Yellow spent the night drowning in violent water, and awoke with the ocean for company. Nausea dogged him, and yawning only changed the pitch of the incoming waves. Atlantic breakers boomed against his mastoid bones when he dressed. He shaved meagre stubble with sea-surge lapping his sodden inner ear, took Cho Sun breakfast with the care of a two-bottle drunk, and tramped through undertow when he ushered the Council of Seven into the cloy of oriental provisions.

They wrinkled their noses at the crowded racks of rusted Dexion shelves, and looked startled when Joe's fingers told them not to go to the anteroom of the council chamber. A lean, mousing cat gave them a bored feral stare and went back to sleep on a carton of canned seaweed, her night's catch a still grey row on the concrete floor. The big one known as Pu had his cousin present Joe Yellow with the gifts for his uncle. Joe backed through a hanging curtain and left them with the stink and the purring cat.

Pu rolled thick shoulders. Kept his coarse features bland. The longer Cho Sun kept the council waiting, the greater the respect the envoy allowed them to show the Sichuen Dragon. It was fitting, and there was no loss of face. The hatchet attack on the Supreme Snake had been a near disaster, but Pu planned to describe it in glowing terms; confident he could control the man from Hong Kong as readily as he manipulated the council. What was Cho Sun but an old Shadow Warrior sent by an even older Dragon?

After two years in London, Pu knew more than this old nobody could ever learn. Veneration for men with years was all very well, but this was a changed world that had outgrown such feudal concepts. Pu was the future, and it was only a matter of time before his star rose high enough to place him at the right hand of the Dragon himself. The spy Pu had placed deep inside the coils of the rival Snake had proved invaluable. Nobody had ever achieved so much, and with careful planning, Pu meant to conjoin the two most powerful tongs under his leadership. He would please this Cho Sun with flattery and presents, continue as he meant to, without interference.

'I see you,' a cold voice said.

Not from before the hanging curtain, but off in the shadowed racks of bean curds and chicken feet. The outer door had been bolted and triple-locked. There was no other way into the storeroom. Pu had designed the security system himself. There was a barred skylight, but that meant cutting through steel bars and a drop of forty feet without a rope. The skylight was closed, the bars in place.

How then? Pu swallowed a brief gnaw of disquiet. Turned to face a small man with a face that told him nothing. Dressed in black cotton, Cho Sun sat on a crate of green figs. Not wearing the traditional robes and sandals – a deliberate insult he seemed to enjoy. But he wore the bloodstone ring, and if he chose to receive the brotherhood in a stinking storeroom, there was nothing Pu or the others could do about it.

Cho Sun stopped them bowing. Another break with tradition.

'Which of you speaks?' he asked.

Pu bobbed his head. Seethed inwardly.

'This unworthy one has that honour, Env—'

Cho Sun clapped his hands. Cut Pu off.

'No flowery rhetoric. No ceremony. You dispensed with

that privilege yesterday. I dispense with it today. Your disrespect was noted.'

'Your decision can only be respected, Envoy.'

'A small beginning,' Cho Sun snapped. 'Do you dream, Pu? I dreamed last night, and was shown a black thing. Was it put into my head like your worm of disrespect? Or did I truly see what happened to the north of this place?'

Jolted, Pu hid surprise behind a marshmallow smile. Steepled fingers under his chin and bowed low.

'You wear the Dragon Ring, Cho Sun. It makes you all-knowing, and I am prostrated with admiration. It sent spies into the night like eyes. Long-eared bats that shared their enhanced senses with you, enabling you to see more than this one ever could. Since the Dragon's Envoy alone knows what he was shown, he would honour us by sharing what it was he dreamed.'

Clever, Cho Sun thought. Said, 'My dream showed me an old snake cornered by dragons too young to make fire, but full of misguided mischief. They lost their advantage of numbers when the old snake summoned white dogs to savage the young dragons. It was a bitter thing to see them defeated by foreign mongrels. So, did I see truth in the night, or was the dream a lying worm? Put into my head by those who would blind the Dragon's eyes with black images?'

'You dreamed well, Cho Sun. But the dreaming eyes you saw through must have been clouded by the fatigue of travel. Our dragons were full grown. They killed two snakes with cunning. Cut down three white longnosed dogs before cutting into the brain of the Supreme Snake himself. But those of our dragons who returned spoke of a sudden dark wind that came at them from behind. Stole their victory away with magical cunning and black mist. They were defeated with honour, for none of them were trained to fight the night wind itself.'

Blowfly, thought Cho Sun. *Dung beetle. Trapped in resin*

83

for ten thousand centuries you would make a handsome scarab, Pu Fatt. 'You pass on the words of dishonoured men as if they can be believed. Are you naive? Is your brain an addled egg? Those who did not come back would tell it different, I think. And I saw no dead dragons in my dream.'

Pu spread huge yellow palms.

'Who spoke of deaths, Envoy?'

'A worm lives in your mouth. Your tongue is a worm.'

'I am clumsy, Envoy. My poor words confuse. Perhaps we should speak further when you are better rested. The dream world robs a man of sleep when he most needs it. Flying away from the sun can do that too, I understand. With your permission, we will withdraw. Come again when you are—'

'Now!'

Tired of Pu's hairless face and false contrition, his calm insolence, Cho Sun angled the bloodstone ring at the skylight he had dropped through with soundless ease. The stone flamed to paint Pu's face crimson. Closed his eyes to a squint.

'No more shadow plays with words. How many died?'

Pu felt strangled. The red fire was inside his head. The stink of fish and curds made breathing hard. Heard himself stammer as if he had been stripped of maturity.

'We . . . lost one mmman. Only one. My ownnn brother, Ennnvoy. . . If he is not dead, he isss witha ennnemmmy . . . But Ho Fatt will die in silencccce . . . I swearrrr . . .'

The crimson light died. Pu took a shuddering breath. Blinked at Cho Sun through green afterburn. The small man's laugh was like water on stone. A cold tinkle.

'You *swear*? On what? Your own head?'

Pu needed air. Time to think. Knew Cho Sun had trapped him. Wild honey swallowing a hornet.

'On my head and honour I swear this,' he said.

'The Dragon hears you. I hear you. And we will remember.'

Pu fell back to stand with the others as Cho Sun walked along the line to smell their fear. Pu smelled of funk and sandalwood. The others gave off the sweet odour of wine lees left too long in the barrel. Cho let them feel his anger without the need of words. If they believed in black winds, let them, it merely meant they had not placed him at the fight in St Anne's Court. He curbed the corrupt pleasure his absolute mastery over these men gave him. Let them drown in such weakness, it was not for him. The Snake had a live Dragon, and that was a serious matter. Perhaps he should have brought the unconscious man away with him, but how else would he have made Pu offer his neck for the axe? And the council wouldn't dare to act without his approval in the future. He had made the right decision.

Cho Sun dismissed the seven men. They trooped out into Gerrard Street, and Cho Sun smiled his ugly smile when Joe Yellow had locked them out. His nephew looked like a bad sailor in heavy swell.

'Bring your face here.'

Joe Yellow almost fell trying to bow. Felt a hand steady his elbow. A thumb probed his ears and neck, and hard fingers flicked his temples. The sea crashed, boiled away, and hissed into silence.

Joe's fingers spelled out gratitude.

'What good are you without the ability to walk? You have much to do, Nephew. It is ironic, but to save the honour of the T'ang, I must also save Pu Fatt's neck.'

Cho Sun threw back his head to bray, and Joe Yellow saw the laugh he could not hear. It was wonderful.

The sign on the scuffed brown door read: *Command Room. Enter on Green Light Only.* But the bulb had been dead for three years, and nobody had thought to replace it. Inside, a single window overlooked a tiled well and an identical window the grey of a formal sock. There were five steel desks and two typewriters. Some swivel chairs that didn't, filing cabinets and metal waste baskets, old black telephones on long threadbare cords, and a pinboard thick with official notices nobody read. Nicotine and grime had dulled the cream walls to the rind of mature cheddar, and a flyblown Marilyn Monroe calendar wore a Groucho Marx moustache. Taggart typed reports with his tongue out, and Bulstrode bit the head from a Mars bar. A legal adviser from the Department of Public Prosecutions read Major Gerry Fox's signed statement, and a man from the Treasury studied forged notes at the window with DCI Egan of the Fraud Squad.

Commander Lemmon sipped overboiled canteen tea through a sugar cube and worried about his marriage. Wondered if it was just another casualty of antisocial hours and the grinding plod of turning scraps of physical and circumstantial evidence into watertight indictments the courts could convict on. Decided it all came down to an equation of means, averages and percentages. Forty-three per cent of all criminal prosecutions were successful, and fifty-nine per cent of all coppers' marriages foundered; proving once again that the villains won by a convincingly high average.

Breakfast with Elizabeth had been a hurried affair with no small talk. She was boning up for a post-graduate degree in something grand, eloquent and highflown like *Semantics and Dialectics: Their Effect on Cheese Production in the Low Countries during the Dutch Reformation*. At least, that's what it had sounded like through the munch of slimming biscuits dunked in unmilked tea. Lemmon had rushed through a shave and a change of clothes, worried about the thirsty Lobelias in the greenhouse, and sat down to runny eggs Elizabeth had underboiled with her nose in a paperback primer. A few words, a hurried kiss and a doorslam later, he had the kitchen to himself. Nothing to do but stare out at the sodden lawn and brush away the crumbs she'd left on his cheek.

Even her scent had smelled of Academia. Burned book-marks and boiled heretics. A mulch of moribund scholars. The smell of her new enthusiasm for culture, and his inability to relate to her circle of new friends. The sincere beards and intellectual tweeds on the men. Homespun kaftans and psychedelic prints on the women. Silly cocktails and carrot wine as they enthused over Joyce and Milton and medieval pottery with the verve they had once expended on crash diets and bonsai trees.

Too often it seemed, he'd blundered into a living room vibrant with talk and Brahms and Jazz and Mozart, when all he wanted was an armchair and a fireside drink to take the pavement out of his feet. Elizabeth with bright welcomes and snuggles just for him. Putting on her sleepy face and smiling yawns when she wanted to be taken upstairs for languid or fierce interchanges of breast and mouth and thigh. Rapid fruition and mumbly talk, or hanging forever on the abyss of climax like cautious tomcats circling a queen in succulent heat. The joint crash into bottomless salve and soundless sleep.

Now he came home to Elizabeth asleep, the counterpane heaped with working volumes. Elizabeth writing margin notes in his office under the stairs, too engrossed to share a nightcap. And worst of all, the notes telling him she was at Damien's, Celia's, the bloody Wentworth's; or attending some lecture with dinner out afterwards, and to be a dear and eat up the lovely cold collation under foil in the fridge . . .

Lemmon made a fist. Let a Player burn between white knuckles. Half-heard the Treasury man tut and marvel over the genuine paper and the foil strip as Bulstrode hit a waste bin with an empty chocolate wrapper. Taggart answered a phone mid-ring to tell Payne he hoped he wasn't reversing the charges from Zurich to take the royal piss. And, 'No, sunshine,' with heavy sarcasm. 'Not a lot happening, as it happens. Only three homicides on our patch. Not counting the late Ironfoot Jack, and an iffy suicide at Tottenham Court Road Underground Station. And your bloody paperwork to do. What d'you mean, which platform? The eastbound Central Line, as if it mattered, you berk.' Taggart told Bulstrode that Payne was flying his broken collarbone home for rest and ruddy recuperation.

'He can bloody rest and recuperate manning the phones here,' Bulstrode said around a finger of Kit Kat. 'Tell him.'

Taggart told him. Egan of the Fraud Squad sucked his briar and emptied the goo-trap with a long blow. Droned on about another year of dodgy antiques and funny money before lecturing to promotional classes at Bramshill Police College. Sounded what he was, a time-server more interested in retirement with a fat pension than taking collars.

Lemmon had twenty minutes before the autopsy on the two Chinese. Needed to hurry things along, but the DPP lawyer still turned pages of statement under a hovering biro, and Elizabeth wasn't a romantic novel he could earmark and set aside. But how was he to curb her hunger for culture? Pull down all the dreaming spires? Raid every university common room between Edinburgh and Brighton for illegal cannabis smokers? Bang up all the professors and burn all the books like some lovesick Hitler?

Elizabeth having an affair would have been different. Have focus. He'd have a lover to chase around the bedroom and out through the hollihocks. Corner him in Lover's Lane with his trousers down and take a five-iron to his shiny red sports car. Shove a meaty fist through his tennis rackets and show Elizabeth he was the better man by proving the smooth bastard had defrauded the local cricket club by selling them an outfield of undrainable bog. Wag a moral finger as a penitent Elizabeth turned the smooth bastard in herself . . .

'What?' said Lemmon.

'You said something about a purple sunset, Sir.' Taggart had finished putting fleas in Payne's ear.

'No, Tag,' Bulstrode corrected. 'The Guv said: ''The

happy couple sailed into a purple sunset''. Right, Guv?'

Egan and the Treasury man had turned from the window. The DPP lawyer stared with his ballpoint raised. Lemmon held his chin. Found a patch of stubble he'd missed with the razor. The runny eggs still lining his throat.

'I *said*,' he said, 'there are a couple of prime suspects we need to make this enquiry a total wrap. Fox gives chapter and verse on Bottoms and Peachey in his statement.'

'At length,' said the DPP lawyer. 'Fox is a classic wriggler. An apologist who'd bring down the temple to save his neck. Not the best kind of Crown witness, were we to offer him some measure of immunity and use him in such a fashion.'

Lemmon felt his gorge rise with the eggs.

'Immunity, my posterior. I don't care if Fox claims the Bethlehem Virgin as his mother, and bleeds pedal stigmata every Easter Monday. We've got him bang to rights, and he's long overdue for some heavy porridge. You're here to make certain the heavy Latin doesn't trip itself up, Lewis. I'm not having Fox going free over some piddling legal technicality. He's in the bag, the printer, forger, plates and paper are not. This meeting is to make sure it's a complete collar. That printing works has to be raided within the next twenty-four hours. Tops. Egan has the manpower, I don't. Mr Bank of England there has the clout to make the top judiciary jump through hoops with one call to the Home Secretary. And you, Lewis, can go straight to the DPP himself. I'll produce Bottoms and Peachey on a plate, but you high-powered citizens have to do the rest.'

'I see,' said the DPP lawyer.

The Treasury man rubbed his nose with a thoughtful 'Yes, indeed.'

Egan worried a cardigan button. Made his pipe gurgle and said: 'Now then, Theo, old compatriot. No need for outbursts. There are channels, you know. And being Thursday, the weekend's almost upon us. Softly, softly, catchee monkey, eh?'

Lemmon showed contempt with a snort of smoke.

'Softly, softly, catchee cold on the links. Burying balls in a sandtrap more like. What's your handicap, Egan? Mine appears to be you. And before you colour up like some goosed typist, I'm recording this point: Holmes Road nick has more holes than your golf course. Too many on the take, as you well know, so how long d'you think it'll take some bent CID with a yen for the horses to make the right phonecall? Blow this case out from under us. Action This Day, as Churchill would say. Not Monday, after you've lost your balls.'

Egan looked at the walls for inspiration or allies, and found none. The Treasury man flaked paint from the window frame, and the DPP lawyer clicked his pen. Tucked the statement into his briefcase, put his pen away, and went to the door, searching for an exit line.

'You know I'm right, Lewis,' Lemmon said.

'Yes, and as abrasive as Egyptian underwear. I'll breathe in the right ears, Commander. As I'm sure Mr Slade of the Treasury will. Coming, Slade?'

The Treasury man consulted his watch and nodded.

'Right there,' he said. 'One look at these pretties, and the Director will choke on his quail's eggs. I may have these samples of the forger's art, may I not, Mr Lemmon?'

'Sign this and this,' said Bulstrode. 'Thanks. Now you can do what you like, they're yours. Don't get picked up passing them, eh, squire?'

Slade and Lewis left the brown door to close itself, and Egan shrugged into his jacket and overcoat. Got his pipe tangled in his scarf, and gave Lemmon a look of thoughtful hatred. Pointed his briar and chose his words carefully in front of Bulstrode and Taggart.

'One day, Theo,' he said in hard Northern brogue. 'You'll go just too far with your personal remarks about fellow officers. Wind your neck out just far enough, you'll see . . .'

Lemmon was too tired to pull Egan's ears or pinch his cheek.

'And one day, Egan, you'll stop being a Toytown copper. Go all the way to the touchline with the ball. Good day, Detective Chief Inspector. Watch the bunker on the fourth hole. Don't get sand in your navel.'

The self-closer stopped Egan slamming out, and Bulstrode had to laugh aloud.

'Sorry, Guv. Slipped out. You want me at the autopsy? Or does Taggart harden his stomach yet again?'

Lemmon scrubbed his moon of a face with a tired palm.

'I want you two out there pulling old Pencils in. Then you find Rosie and his two bundles of forged poppy. Dillman's turning stones for Chinese Cyril, and then there's Mr Dance to interview. Give old Pencils a bath before you put him in the dirty cell we save for the vagrants. And catch up with me when you can.'

'Be lucky, Guv.'

Lemmon left, setting his hat square.

Bulstrode finished his chocolate and licked his fingers.

'Fit then, Tag?'

'Mr Lemmon looks worn out. Should take some leave.'

'And sit in an empty house on his lonesome?'

'What, trouble at the old homestead?'

Bulstrode gave Taggart a hard look.

'Nobody said nothing, right? Nobody.'

'Nor they did,' said Taggart. 'Deaf, dumb and blind, ain't I?'

'And learning fast. Let's give the cobbles a leathering.'

The fat Turk called Stavros had locked Rosie Bottoms in the attic room with, 'Charlie say you stay here,' leered, and plodded down several flights of stairs to his bed above the pornographic bookshop in John Adam Street. Sleeping on the hard cot for eight hours had been no problem, but after a greasy breakfast and a trip to the first floor lavatory, the attic room became a cell. A boring box with a view of rooftops and raincloud, and bundled magazines Rosie leafed through for something to do.

There were no cut-away drawings of engines or formula cars. No champions sprayed champagne from winner's rostrums or made spectacular spin-offs at Indiannapolis. There were strange titles like *Spank, Leather Ladies, Passion Pose*, and *International Skin*, and girls from Sweden and the Philippines, from Thailand and the Caribbean islands, showed their all with less than a pocket handkerchief between them. They lounged on beds, bared themselves on beaches, and emerged from surf with staring nipples. They posed in fleshy tangles of three, and formed gymnastic pyramids with studs sporting erections like Garand rifles. Nubile nurses with bare rumps played doctor with men too tanned and muscular to have suffered a head cold. Schoolgirl nymphets looking at the wrong side of thirty caned naughty old sir over his desk, and muscles and mammaries simulated orgies on phoney grass under studio lamps. Breasts bigger than Rosie's head bulged from double-page spreads, underwear frothed, walnut nipples peeped from unzipped leather, buttocks formed double moons, and erectile men threatened pouting lips with hugely swollen members. Skin romped with skin, limbs of black granite locked with globes of female pink, and close shots of pubis and penis had the spiky look of mating hedgehogs. Frozen in harsh and clinical details for the sexually inadequate, nothing was left to the imagination, and the virginal Rosie felt the walls come in at him.

There was no room to pace, and Marion Clockworthy was a weighty stir in his loins. He heard her giggle as she hung washing on the line and he watched through the fence. Showed the backs of her dimpled knees as she stretched to peg a sheet. Let the wind take her housecoat to give him a glimpse of lumpy breasts under thin cotton printed with teddy bears. Rewrapped herself to retrieve a fallen peg so the round bulk of her backside had a centre pleat. Her giggle finding him in a jungle of green beans, his knees deep in herbaceous border. Until his mother took him inside to break a wooden ladle over his head . . .

For five crisp pounds she'd take him into the coal shed. For a box of cream fondants she'd let him run a hand over the outside of her knickers, hadn't she?

'Definitely,' Rosie said aloud, beyond the stimulation of mere photogravure. A quick nip into the zoo, call her from a public phonebox, and meet her on the allotments where there were lots of sheds with flimsy doors and lots of warm sacking to lie on. He could hide out there, have her bring him food and racing magazines. Better than an attic with that Stavros holding the key like some Borstal screw. And that Charlie Dance was a cold geezer, for all he had a Rolls and a gold watch, and overcoats who took his nod as a royal command. That Froggy and that Matt had called him Rosie when they thought to call him anything at all. For a new tenner that Marion Clockworthy would call him Ernie as he rolled her out of whatever was under that housecoat. Definitely. The front of the adjacent building was scaffolded, he had a good head for heights, and hadn't Solly Evergreen's boy Denzil showed him the basics of the rooftop trade? Easy. Just let his groin settle down, and he was away.

The sash was stiff enough to break a fingernail, and Rosie worked it open sucking his thumb. The parapet was thick with pigeon guano he scaled off with a magazine before edging out. There was just him and the sky, the sooty brickwork of Charing Cross Station, and the permanent shadows of John Adam Street way below his boots. He got a heel to the scaffold board and nodded to a man tiling the roof. Ducked through a window where a carpenter erected new timber studding, went down the stairs to the street, and crossed the Strand in a lull in the traffic. In Trafalgar Square, he realised he had no money to take the Underground, and hoped the stiff walk would relieve the pain of sexual frustration. The thin rain had sent the tourists scattering, and the pigeons had the fountains to themselves. A uniformed copper took shelter in the portico of St Martin's in the Fields, and Rosie pretended to watch the pavement artist outside the National Gallery until he'd wandered away down William IV Street.

'You throw a good shadow, son. Sling a coin, or sling your hook,' the chalky old man said as drizzle spotted his Lord Nelson.

'Would if I had one, wouldn't I? Could use an earner m'self.'

'You and the workhouse donkey both. Shove off, you're making the street untidy.'

Rosie was too jumpy to be pushed.

'And you don't, you old tosser?'

'I fought in two world wars for rubbish like you. Got medals.'

'The junk shops are full of 'em. Any one you like for a tanner. And ain't nobody in the whole British Army has the Italian Star *and* the Burma Star. I got uncles who fought, mate, so I know junk shop tat from your actuals.'

'Mind your mouth, mother's boy.'

'Mother's nothing. If you was anything, you was a Conchie. Or a G.O.D. from the Grand Order of Deserters.'

'Put 'em up,' came at Rosie on a gust of sour breath, and unbelievably, the old man was trying to rise on unsteady legs with clenched fists and more than wine in his milky eyes.

'Steady on, dad.' Rosie looked for the copper. The best way to retreat.

'I'll give you sodding *dad* . . .'

Rosie ducked a lunge and caught the old man as he fell. Chalk smeared his leather jacket as a hobnailed boot hacked at his shins.

'Bleeding *dad*, you whore's melt . . .'

'Watch it, you geriatric nutter. Flaming hell on wheels . . .'

Rosie's ankle turned white hot from a hard rake of studs.

'Laugh *that* off while I turn your nuts to hundreds and bleeding thousands . . .'

A chalky knee caught Rosie square in the crotch. Blinded by hot tears and knives of nausea under his tongue, Rosie fell backwards. Held agony that had been uncomfortable desire just seconds before. Smacked the kerb with the back of his head and didn't know what to hold next. Somebody hauled the old man off him, and there was soft upholstery under his quivering buttocks.

'We *had* to pick a day Pencils fell off the waggon.'

'One old man full of biddy, Tag? Where's your Hendon training?'

'In Hendon. Come off it, Pencils, you're nicked.'

'I'm a veteran. What's the charge, eh, eh, eh . . .?'

'Absent without leave. Defacing Council property. Just get in the car.'

'Not with you, sailor. Not with nobody ain't a Redcap . . .'

The suspension bounced Rosie into a curl as a flail of arms and legs and chalk dust was thrown in beside him. The door slammed and Rosie gagged on old sweat and cheap wine. Squealed in high register when horny palms took him by the throat. There was a low curse, a soft click of dentures as a fist crossed Pencils' jaw, and Rosie was left to cuddle himself.

Bulstrode tutted as he pulled out into traffic.

'He had it coming, Buller. A bloody handful.'

'You got my vote, Tag. When thieves fall out, eh?'

'I know this old tosser. He identified Ironfoot's mortals. You telling me he's a master forger?'

'Wouldn't tell you the time if I wound Big Ben m'self. Mr Lemmon wants them, Uncle Theo gets them. Job done, Mr Taggart.'

'Good mind to put 'em in the same cell. Let 'em bash each other sensible.'

'That,' said Bulstrode, 'ain't half a bad notion. Could

learn a lot, they start bunnying together . . .'

Rosie let the real tears come. Finding out what was under Marion Clockworthy's housecoat amongst the cabbages and leeks was no longer in the stars. He should have stuck to Fangio.

The white carousel had no horses or riders, and its pristine canopy ignored the rain at the windows. White roses proliferated around cornices and mirrors that shone without reflections. The bed was as firm as a young woman, and the pillows under his hot face matched a tangle of white satin sheets. A hanging arm fingered the cream down of a Persian carpet, and the thing gnawing his shoulder had a tight shell of padded bandages. There were girlish flounces and bows on the lamps and furniture, and furled brocade made soft falls around the carved bedposts. As delicate as iced sugar, fluffier than a pedigree kitten, and whiter than the soul of a saint; the room screamed virginal virtue. Faggot purity in designer whites for a woman no longer young.

Charlie knew he was Charlie. Knew there were things he should be up and doing instead of lying supine in a silent star's boudoir on Sunset Boulevard. Looked for a bald German butler burying a very dead chimp amongst drooping gum trees in an overgrown garden where deader leaves formed drifts in an empty swimming pool. Used pain to shrug the last shreds of hallucination away. He was real, his body had been sandbagged by experts, and he needed to do more than sprawl in luxurious glue gaping at scintillant knives.

He got the good shoulder under him. A hip sighed across satin, and a leg dropped a heel to the floor. He was still wondering what to do next when Attar of Roses came in a cloud. A slender arm went under his rubber neck, a pill was fingered on to his tongue and washed down by the coldest and clearest water ever to come from a mountain spring. He wanted more water. All the water there was.

What dribbled down his chin cooled his naked crotch. Something medicinal hit him hard and he floated on a lake of peace.

'You're a mother to me,' he said.

'The doctor said they acted instantaneously. He prescribes them for women in labour.'

The voice was as brown as nicotine. As feminine as lace. The mouth shone with wet-look lipstick, and very blue oval eyes showed now the black hair had been scraped back and teased into glossy curls. The eccentric nose curved as pertly as ever, and Margot Sadler's earrings were small cornucopias of diamonds. The silk trouser suit seemed to melt into the rich bedding Charlie had rumpled in fitful sleep. He wanted to rumple her. Wanted to bite at her with a sardonic chuckle, just as she sniped at guests who bored or tested her patience with suburban mores.

'Had to be your interior decorator was a pastry chef before he wriggled into cerise pants and learned to mince on shiny floors cooing at pastels. Veddy wedding cake. Veddy, veddy dry martini.'

'Not your kind of room, ducks. No beerstains or sawdust. No decor here that smacks of early barmaid.'

Charlie tried a frown but it came unglued. Bad things were coming out of the walls of his mind to show in his eyes. Blood on blood on blood . . .

'Too early for the dailies. The early evenings . . .'

'Lie still, sport. Count slowly to a hundred backwards. Those potent little pills make one garrulous, and we don't want you babbling, do we? You told dear Sam what you wanted done, and you know Sam. On it like zip. I could pin you through the thorax for not coming to see me. Were I that kind of woman, I'd pump you whilst you're doped to the gills. Find out just why my bed has been just that, a bed. Something to drop into after a grinding day doing the country auctions. But I'm not, and I won't.'

97

'Gooo ole Margo . . .' Charlie heard echoes behind his teeth.

'Hush, my dear, it'll all come back.'

Charlie bore down on his mind. Tensed it like a lazy muscle.

'You got gooo ol' Sam to play bedtime with . . .'

It wasn't what he meant to say. Sam the Spade was black and camp and preferred Empire furniture to sex.

Margot arched a high brow. Looked down her wayward nose.

'Sam, as you very well know, is my business partner. You gave him to me for Christmas last year. He was just out of some dreary northern prison, and I could have killed you for foisting him on me. When he'd seen there wasn't a single key in the house, that his bedroom opened on to the garden, and there were fresh flowers in his very own vase, we had a lovely breakdown together. Wept and honked and cried through acres of tissues. I tamed him, he taught me; and now we're a real force in the antiques world. I lock horns with the Bond Street sweeties, Sam growls at the cobbles cowboys who promote stained pine as genuine rosewood. And with him on my arm even the ghetto bloods tip their hats when we work Brixton market.'

'All girls together, huh?'

Margot saying 'crap' in her crystal accent made laughter bubble.

The sugary white room bleached and dimmed to ivory. Folded in on itself like a closing pop-up book and turned normal. In focus with up definitely up, and down where it ought to be. Charlie's mental clock was wound down. Dead. He needed a real timepiece. Even one with Mickey Mouse nodding to a clockwork tick as his yellow gloves pointed to childish numerals. There was a carriage clock on the mantel way over the far side of the room. Ten days march away across rugs the white of burning sand. Asking the time came out as: 'Ain't Beau Geste . . .'

Margot looked 'crap' without saying it.

'You could well have joined the French Foreign Legion for all the attention you've paid me these past months. Damn and damn and apologies. Not to you, Charlie Dance. To me. I promised myself I wouldn't nag the man who gave my life back to me.'

Margot had conjured her late husband's ghost. Bastard Malcolm whose paid assassin murdered two innocent women because Charlie destroyed his dream of a criminal empire. Had confessed as much to Margo in a terror tantrum, and paid the ultimate price in three countries. 'Drowned' in Buenos Aires and executed at the Tower of London, his pickled head had been buried where Dotty and Ingrid had died, on the road to Zeerust in South Africa.

Charlie patted a silk thigh with a Plasticine hand.

'Don't sweat it. Could eat.'

'I told that doctor you wouldn't curl up for forty-eight hours with your thumb in your mouth. I thought two myself. You've already missed breakfast, luncheon and dinner. How does supper sound?'

Charlie swore long and loud, too weak to make fists.

'Thanks for the testimonial.'

'Not you I'm cussing, you daft, lovely old pudding. It's me. I should have held on long enough . . .' *For what? What was out there?*

'I watched you sleep with all that sad anger in your face. And I bribed a perfectly respectable doctor to forget he ever saw you. I am utterly shameless where you're concerned, you bastard.'

'Those ain't tears, toffee nose?'

'These old things? Just sky juice, you impossible thug.'

'Does that knot of wire round your wrist tell the time?'

'Only if I'm wearing contact lenses. The face is smaller than your IQ. And before you ask, I am *not* having emotional vapours.'

'One of us is.'

Charlie's shoulder glowed with sullen pain. Behind a distant door, courtesy of the good doctor's magic pills. He could do serious hurt to a wet paper napkin if Margot worked it over first. Remembered sending Sam the Spade out with messages and money. The key to the Rolls. Instructions. No details, but they'd come. *They'd better*.

'Pickles and cheese. Fresh bread. Crusty. Not supermarket pap wrapped in plastic tasting of soggy yuk.'

'We *are* feeling macho. I'll feed you solids if you articulate your other leg to the floor and get it to support the bulk of you. Otherwise it's a bowl of nourishing broth on a tray right here, my lad.'

'You,' said Charlie, 'are definitely on, old love.'

Time tripped, and there was a rubber sway across soft Persian sand. A passage that elbowed his elbows. A bright kitchen with teak units and golden wood. Copper pans and jelly moulds on a hessian wall like baronial armoury. Pulses and pasta in Italian glassware. Angular modern chairs around a scrubbed pine table. Lamps that cast soft pools of light. The food came in attractive ceramic bowls. Elegant taste treats for a jaded palate.

'Ain't lost your touch with the culinary arts. What's funny?'

'You, you oaf. Slipping three-guinea phrases between the gawd blind mes. A mass of contradictions, aren't you?'

'Ain't everybody? People only hear how things are said, not the words themselves. Get yourself a class accent and talk drivel, there's some clowns who'll think you just delivered the Gettysburg Address.'

Margot brushed hair from Charlie's face.

'My Cockney Lincoln. Are you staying, or am I a convenient bus stop between bedrooms?'

'All sex with you, ain't it?'

'I can hardly discuss your real destination, can I? Or what you plan to do there. I saw the early news. Doesn't take much to know you've got . . . trouble . . .'

'Again. You left out "again". But it's in them clever blue eyes. In them worry lines you try to paint out with cosmetics.'

'Now he throws my age in my face.'

'Age lives in faces. For everyone. You can keep your body trim and supple, but the old boat tells the tale unless you have it lifted so high your navel gives you a cleft chin.'

'Brutal. Even for you, Charlie dear.'

Margot laced black coffee with Irish whisky. Passed Charlie a Carnaby Street mug to hold. Bright Art Deco colours on cheap glaze. Lit two cocktail Sobranie and passed one across.

Charlie let it bob in his mouth. Leaked Turkish smoke through the pink and gold cigarette and said, 'You have to see deeper than the wear and tear, Margot. See the person under the dogeared wrapping. I can see you for what you are, why can't you?'

'Because I'm not you. I've been seventeen for thirty years. A hard habit to break. The thicker the panstick, the finer the silks. A kitten knows it's cute chasing its tail. Then it's a cat and becomes haughty. Old women chase their tails through beauty parlours trying like mad to be kittens for ever. They'll pay fortunes to some effete scissor-wielder for a basic crimp and buttered lies. I once met an old Gaiety Girl who'd been one of C.B. Cochran's young ladies. She was ninety, and as simian as an old monkey. She said she should have died young because she was an ephemeron. A bug that lives for a single day, and dies in flight reaching for the sun. I see her point.'

'You a bloody moth, or a person?'

'Both, you male dodo.'

Charlie leered through smoke. Felt the room slip to port.

'And I'd like to play on the swings and have a catapult. Live with Red Indians and never wash behind my ears. But I ain't Peter Bedpan, and you have to grow up like Wendy Darling did. You can't be bloody Tinkerbell.'

'And I don't see myself as your maiden aunt, either.'

'That, Margot, you ain't.'

Charlie saw the kitchen as blobs of watercolour smudged by rain. Margo bit a soft red lip that invited Charlie to cool his face against its carmine fullness. The pink Sobranie was a finger dragging his mouth into a yawn.

'And I wish I didn't adore you so.'

'You adore you, rich people, and richer things. You and class have been together too long to swap ormolu for brass. You like the bits of me you can see. Not the deep dark stuff you close your eyes to. We're competent in bed together, but when the main event's over, you lie there wishing I was Eton and Harrow instead of whelks and mean streets.'

Margot's expression could have been anything from furious to sad. She was a blur to Charlie, but her tone gave him a clue, her laugh was as false as a scenic flat in a theatre wing.

'Keep them off-balance, eh, Charles? Bed-soft and willing, and smart enough not to be overly clever with the dominant male. There's nothing so painfully moral as the working class man faced with a lady who knows her own mind and has a healthy attitude to the carnal. He ups and mutters, and gets his elbow to a bar to drown his fears in bitter beer. You're a fraud, Charles, you know full well I see you as you are. Why can't you see you as I do? And I quote a self-confessed expert.'

'Go play with your hoop, you like circular arguments so much.'

'Margot one, Charlie nil. I can say I love you aloud with trumpets, what can you allow yourself to admit, Mr Dance?'

Charlie had a mouthful of smoke and nowhere to blow it. There were too many dark alleys in his mind to beat Margot at her own game.

'Is it hot or cold in here? I smell like the inside of a tram-driver's glove. Need a shave. Too many holes in my face, and my sweat stings. You look about twelve in this

102

light, and the walls keep going soft. Christ . . .'

Margot was rising in slow motion. A hand to her mouth. Charlie lost the pink cigarette holding her off.

'Gotta run where the kittens are. And old ladies have nice smiles and flowered hats. Smell of oil of wintergreen and let us kids play in the rain in our Sunday best shoes . . . Wear the backside from our trousers on the big playground slide . . . Bloody pills. Told Rudge no pills. Don't go with thinking and Irish whiskey. Four threes, Mickey. You have to eat up the whole world, go ahead . . . Like you best when you ain't shoving your age up my nostrils . . . Margot . . .'

The Carnaby Street mug rolled, and Charlie reared away from a pond of black coffee. Margot had him wrapped in something quilted. Massaged his neck and got iced liquid into him. Sponged his face and slaked his thirst. Held him as he muttered disjointed nonsense about Raven and Triads and Soddy's erupting stomach. And Nasty dying to protect his back as a dancing yellow gnome kicked faces like a deadly Nureyev. Leaving bodies on cobbles and Nasty's fingers jerking in a puddle as Nasty staggered away to find somewhere quiet to die . . .

Then the night went quiet, and Charlie was coherent when Sam the Spade let himself in with his own key.

The Chinese doctor wore an MCC tie, many years, and had been Westernised by twenty-five years in Harley Street. He clucked over Aman Lee Fook's sutures with the directness only the very young or the very old can express openly without fear of retribution. But on the matter of his thinking Wind pretty but thin, and Fook far too self-important, he wisely held his tongue.

'Hai, Warlord,' he scolded. 'A poultice of herbs and cobwebs under rice paper would have left your scalp unblemished by scars. You should have come to me first. My hands and silver needles can see into your skull as well as any X-ray machine. Do you possess a radio?'

'Yes, physician. Why do you ask?'

'The Test scores. England plays the Australians in Perth. I am curious to see if our batsmen are up to their bowling.'

'*Our* batsmen?'

'We all live in two worlds, Warlord. Hold still whilst these leeches take the blood from your eyes. The physicians of the Great Emperor were trepanning skulls before the Ancient Egyptians had raised the first stone of a single pyramid, did you know that? But where are those two great cultures now? Swept away by barbarians and internal weakness. Had we Chinese played cricket, there might still be emperors in Peking, not these political bandits, these Hos and Maos. When the Great Khan, Genghis, conquered our land, he sat under willows to drink green tea. The British shape the willow into cricket bats for their gentlemen to make cuts to fine leg. There is the great difference.'

'You babble.'

'Perhaps, but your headache is gone, eh?'

Fook was surprised to find it had, and it showed in his face.

'Acupuncture leaves no scars, Warlord. And a gorged leech leaves no mark when it drops off. If only the British practised medicine the way they play cricket. Ah, it saddens me. Eat nothing tomorrow, and sleep alone for four nights. Let plain boiled rice and jasmine tea purge your system until the fourth day. Then I'll remove the stitches and bleed you again. This pretty child needs rest too, I will give her a sleeping potion. On the fifth day, you can come together again.'

Fook felt nothing as the leeches were removed and dropped into a japanned pot. A salve was smeared on his cheekbones, and the doctor was finished.

'There is another service you can do me, Physician,' he said. 'It is a short car journey away, and you can listen to the cricket on the radio as we travel. You have scalpels?'

'I have knives, Warlord. But they are . . .'

'Sharp?'

'As the edge of green bamboo.'

'I will dress. Wait here,' Fook ordered, shedding his robe.

Joe Yellow had pointed out Stripes Flynn's old store in late afternoon gloom, and left Cho Sun to wait for dark.

Cho Sun made himself inconspicuous by joining a pair of meths drinkers at a bonfire until it was time, left his coat and hat under some pallets, and climbed into the liftshaft. Let his fingers and toes find their way down through the girders and oily cables, moving as fast as he could before the cold stiffened his fingers and joints. Opening the wire doors on the bottom level without sound took patient care, and it was long minutes before he dropped amongst frozen sides of beef hung in long aisles. The childhood Buddhist in him was offended by the smell of animal blood, and too thick for him to smell his way.

He slipped past a group of joking butchers clouding the air with white breath, and took the time to massage his limbs before leaving their cheerfully traded epithets behind, going on into sub-zero temperatures in nothing but thin black cotton. The next three chambers were unlit, and Cho Sun walked on the outer edges of his rope-soled shoes to leave no prints in the permafrost. He reached closed steel doors and felt for the lock, careful not to press too hard and leave his skin behind on the frozen surface. Letting touch act as his eyes, he traced the outline of the lock with the ball of his thumb, and formed a picture of levers and tumblers in his mind. Then, using a piece of tensile wire with tiny barbs along its length, he made contact with the combination, and gave the wire a smooth jerk. The sprung lock snapped open, and Cho Sun listened for alarms. There was nothing but his calm breath in the cold silence. He worked the iron handle, let himself into the fletching room, and locked the door behind him.

Cho Sun could see Ho Fatt hanging from the hook as

clearly as if the room were floodlit. His nose and ears told him where the Dragon hung, and he walked to within three feet of Ho Fatt, knowing the man was aware of his presence.

'Well, brother of Pu,' he said. 'I see your disgrace. Even without brother moon to light my eyes.'

'It is night?'

'Even so.' Cho Sun brought out a phial of water. Held it close to Ho Fatt's face. 'You are thirsty enough for the last drink before the Great Door? Have you the courage?'

Ho Fatt cleared gum from his throat. Made the wire creak against the hook. 'If you swear you are not a Snake. On your honour as a Shadow Warrior. I have.'

'I swear, brother of Pu. Your honour and mine are greater than his. Drink.'

'Yessss . . .'

Cho Sun put the stopper in the corner of Ho Fatt's mouth. Fed the phial between his lips, and listened to the water pour into his throat. There was a pause. An intake of breath. Then Ho Fatt bit through the phial and stopper. Chewed on glass, and swallowed the shards without a whimper. Sighed again, and hung silently.

'May the Great Door open quickly, Ho Fatt.'

Cho Sun bowed three times. Set himself, and drove a single pheonix into Ho Fatt's midriff. Bowed again, and went back the way he had come.

The butchers had gone off shift, and Cho Sun worked his way up the liftshaft in total darkness. He was halfway to the top when the cables jerked into motion with an electric whine. The cage came down the shaft with inexorable speed, and Cho Sun was swept from his perch into freezing blackness.

The heat of Margot's kitchen melted the snowflakes on Sam the Spade's head as he gulped tea from a flowered breakfast cup. Charlie chewed on a red Sobranie and let him talk.

'First off, I dumped August at his hotel. Got that Binkie

woman outta bed, and she took him in like he was washing sent back dirty. Told me fortune without tealeaves until I waved your dough at her. Then she put her bosom and her bad mouth away, let me go through old Chappie's stuff without no demur. Got all dimply and saccharine, told me I was a good-looking black boy in need of some loving. There's old Chappie whooping up Technicolor yawns in the toilet and wanting to die, and she's giving me the business. Tawdry ain't in it, Chas.'

Charlie just grunted.

'I turned up Chappie's travel folder, his single ticket to the Caymans, and some bank books. Showed that Binkie the ticket, and she exploded like Guy Fawkes Night. Would have got her nails into Chappie's face if he hadn't locked hisself inna bathroom. Said the Caymans ain't Cannes Film Festival, and she weren't no Canvey Island bint to be left onna pier when the coach went back to London. Man, she blew like Etna. Got weepy and spitting angry and quiet, and gave me the office keys. Told me where all the contracts was, put a dent inna bathroom door, packed and went. I left Chappie his ticket, sent the bank books and key round to J.C. Hatton, and went looking for Chinese Cyril.'

Charlie threw in another grunt and Margot filled Sam's cup.

'Found him at Trooper Wells'. Got a six-inch cut up his arm, and was holding wool for Hettie to ball up. Chinese said he'd go to his brother's in Manchester until the filth went away. I told him "No" like you said. Told him to take a ferry to Paris and play tourist until you said otherwise. Gave the OK nod when Troop said he'd take care of the Lotus House for him.'

'I'll drop by and square Troop,' Charlie said.

Sam sipped scalding tea. Shook his brown head.

'No need. Troop figures he owed you already, and him and Cyril is gonna be partners, so no sweat. You better know the filth picked up old Pencils and some kid outside the

National. Got them at West End Central. Got that squib over a pie and a beer at the French Horn. One of the newsvendors who work the square saw the whole thing. Said he knew the kid on account he runs with Denzil Evergreen, Solly's kid. Rosie somesuch name. You know him, Chas?'

Charlie nodded. 'I'll spank that Stavros. What else?'

'Swung the wheels down to Camden Town and cased that print works. It's a fortress, Chas. There's a way in over the roof, but taking a heavy team in'd mean they'd all have to be mountain goats. And you want 'chinery brung out, 's'gotta come through the front door. And transport's a three aspirin headache. I mean, some of them presses *weigh*, y'know?'

'But can you do it?'

Sam shrugged. Blew on his tea. Rubbed the scar on his flat nose. Grinned like a toothpaste ad.

'With enough poppy – a week's planning. Four years in Wormwood Scrubs and most of a year in antiques, ain't exactly honed my acumen, Charlie man.'

'Tonight.'

'This is tonight.'

'Tonight, tonight. Counting this as the wee hours of today.'

Margo came away from the cooker in a surge.

'Now just one minute . . .'

Charlie held up a hand. 'I'm only borrowing our Sam, ain't taking him permanent. So hold your water, girl. Well?'

Sam looked thoughtful. Stared at Charlie as if he was an auctioneer knocking the Elgin Marbles down to a manufacturer of garden gnomes. Let Margot huff into rigid silence. Said, 'You really need this, Charlie?'

'Like a blood transfusion, Sam.'

'When you call in, you really call in, Charlie.'

Charlie lit a blue Sobranie from his red stub. Said nothing.

'Oh, God,' said Margot. 'He's wearing his stoic martyr's face. Leonides the Spartan holding Thermopylae. Hercules against the seven-headed Hydra.'

'More like Noddy potty-training without Big Ears,' Charlie said.

Sam scrubbed his woolly mop with a creamy palm.

'I'll need your best overcoats, and a lot of heavy poppy, like now. Your firm's a bit thin on the ground for this with Soddy and . . .'

'You can have Froggy and Matt. You need more bodies, I'll get you Pimlico Johnny and Ollie Oliphant. They'll drive anything with wheels up a one-in-one gradient. Enough?'

'And three grand in readies.'

'OK. Get the dough from Vinnie Castle, but you don't tell him nothing from nothing. Just I said to give you the dough.'

'Still taking care, eh, Charlie? Man, makes me almost wish I was on your strength permanent. Don't look that way, Margot darlin'. Just Sam telling the man here him straight enough to be an honorary Negro. Well, shuteye time for this nigger. Get some y'self, Charlie man. Can see the wall through your pale face.'

Charlie made smoke through a theatrical yawn.

'Yeah. The sparrows can have the rest of the morning. Got a heavy day myself. Auntie Margot's taking her favourite face to the zoo.'

Margot snorted at the 'Auntie'. 'In the first snows of winter? Are you quite mad?'

'As it happens,' said Charlie. 'As it happens . . .'

And Sam's face melted like hot chocolate as Charlie dozed off.

There was slamming impact and shock.

Nothing for a long silent infinity of bare moments.

Then sound.

The electric hum of closing circuits, the whip of oiled cables. The crunch of tyres on frosted boards, the purr of a limousine drawing away overhead. Light bled into the pit to show him his twisted limbs, and it was too early for pain. Polluted man-made snow cushioned him, and maverick nerves jerked a cold crab against his numbed face. It was his right hand, the fingers grotesquely splayed. He could feel the heel of his dislocated leg pressing against his spine, and the floor of the lift cage was near enough to touch.

Cho Sun told his right hand to move, but the wrist and fingers were broken, and they began to blacken and swell as he watched. He thought down his left arm. It came out of the powdered brown snow, made a bridge, and turned Cho Sun on his side.

The pain came then, and Cho Sun blanked it off with a supreme effort of will. His loyal left arm took the dead leg by the ankle and pushed it away down his body, ignoring the grate of bone against socket. Sitting up took a long time, and his sweat froze on his face as he straightened the leg out ahead of him. It was broken below the knee, and he tore a sleeve from his tunic to bind it tightly. Then he had to rest, and he listened to raised voices echo through the vaulted chambers. Two men speaking Mandarin. An old reed with an English accent, and a deep bass used to command.

'. . . Don't ask this, Warlord,' said the Reed.

'You wish to join this offal on a hook, Physician?'

'In the name of pity . . . No.'

'You are certain he is dead?'

'By his own hand, yes. And not too long ago. It is difficult in this temperature to ascertain just when . . .'

'A pity.'

'A barbarous end. He ate broken glass. Swung himself against the wall to bring about massive internal bleeding. It would not have been an easy death.'

'As is the way of our kind.'

'Yesss . . .' The Reed's sigh was an echoing plaint of regret.

'You know what now has to be done.'

'I would rather you did not ask this of me.'

110

'Who *asks*? Use your knives. Or shall one of my Shadows use them on you?'

'No, I will take the head for you.'

Cho Sun leaned in the snowlined pit and bared his teeth. Pu Fatt was about to receive a lacquered box. He would have to pay heavy tribute for the rest of his brother's corpse if he was to return all the bones to China for burial. The loss of face was almost immeasurable, and Cho Sun laughed without sound. Even if he were to die in this shaft, Pu Fatt was finished. Others would have to be sent to replace the dishonoured Council of Seven.

Cho Sun wormed his way to the side of the shaft. Used his teeth and one good hand to tear the rest of his tunic into a sling that would bear his weight. When the cage went up the shaft, he planned to go up with it. Time and cold were his enemies as he made knot after knot, and his body began to lose all feeling . . .

CHAPTER FIVE

DC Bulstrode missed Sam the Spade by minutes when he walked up two flights to the outer office of Ogle Enterprises in Windmill Street. Armchair Doris hammered a portable Olympia with deft fingers, thin grey hair pinned under a red pixie hood, swollen feet stuffed into fluffy carpet slippers. Her ample hips swamped the modern swivel under her, and she looked as out of place amongst the chrome and plastic and rubber plants as a broken couch in a furniture showroom.

Bulstrode blew on the back of her neck and made her jumble the keys when he thrust a bouquet of chrysanthemums against her pug nose. Said, 'Time Charlie Dance sprung for a new electric typewriter, Doris my darling.'

'My favourite filth. And flowers,' Doris said. 'Don't want no truck with them fangled things. Ain't safe. Leak 'tricity, and give you headaches. Known fact that. 'S'why half the typists in London look constipated.'

'Get away. Is he in?'

'Depends who "he" is, dunnit?'

Bulstrode wagged a Capstan before lighting it.

'Can't get past you, can I? Chas won't be, Vinnie might, right?'

'Daisies or no daisies, don't wind me up. Ain't no clock.'

'Who's winding?' Bulstrode did his best to look innocent.

Doris's attempt at a Mayfair accent came out as, 'Ooh shull high say's callin'?'

'Glubb Pasha and the Camel Corps, who else?'

'Wind, wind, wind. A regular gramophone.'

'And my needle's stuck in your groove, you sexy dumpling.'

Doris looked sad when she depressed a switch on the PBX.

'I've had more male members than the Hallé Orchestra's got band parts, and you have to come along thirty years too late.'

'No timing, me,' Bulstrode agreed.

Doris asked an extension if it was in to the law today. Listened, and asked: 'You official, or friendly?'

'D'you see a warrant?'

'Friendly. Bribed me with half of Interflora. Shameless is right. The man says go on in.'

Bulstrode pushed through an electrically released sound-proofed door into deep carpet and oiled teak. Archie's portrait hung in pride of place above the desk. Still draped in black crepe, the photograph had been hand-tinted with great skill. The face glowed with life, unlike Vinnie Castle's when he told Bulstrode he had exactly eleven minutes.

'Playing in goal for Fulham, are we?' Bulstrode sank into upholstered black hide.

'They've already got a one-legged keeper. The car's coming to take me to Stoke Mandeville. You want what?'

'You to claim some lost property, is all.'

'Right after they get through cutting, OK?'

'Thought you'd need your wheelchair, Vin.'

'You can bring it on visiting day.'

'Not this time, Vin. Not with three dead and one on the critical I can't. You have to come in, you and Mr Dance. I'd rather it was voluntary, but any way will do. And don't tell me your clever old lawyer J.C. Hatton'd have you out with a *habeas corpus* before we'd burned through our first interview ciggie. We'd still have the right to keep you for twenty-four hours "helping the filth with their enquiries", right?'

'I hear you. That your plan, Buller?'

Bulstrode shredded his Capstan with asbestos fingers. Killed sparks on his thumb with a quick lick, and came out of the chair fast. Leaned over the desk and took Vinnie's chin in his big left hand.

'Look at you. You're half-dead now, you clown. You wanna join Archie the hard way? Like Nasty has? Like Soddy will, most like? How do I get through to you? Charlie Dance is taking you down the shittiest road there is. Drugs and Triads make an evil crow to swallow, my son. Don't have me taking my hat off when your coffin passes. I wouldn't like that one particle, you slow-witted armpit.'

Vinnie's squeezed smile was distorted and wan.

'We both need a settling Scotch, Buller.'

'You are fucking *right*.'

'Pour two. No wheels, remember?'

'You're getting a lot of mileage out of one leg.'

'Have to, don't I?'

'Have to, don't I?' Bulstrode echoed heavily. Gave Vinnie his face back and opened cupboards until he found the bottles. Poured a stiff Glen Grant and drank it down. Poured two more and forgot to hand one across.

'Cheers.' Vinnie held out a hand. 'That mine, is it?'

'Eh? Yeah. And why the Mauser, Vin?'

Vinnie didn't choke. He just shrugged.

'Some kind of German dog, ain't it?'

'With nine rounds up the spout. Your dabs all over the rotten thing. Came over as soon as forensic verified. You carrying a shooter. Uncle Theo'll eat you sideways when he finds out.'

'He's gonna find out then.'

'You saying something I should slap you for?'

'Just asking, is all.'

Bulstrode peeled a cuff from his watch.

'About now, I'd say. Dillman won't keep that to himself for longer than he has to. Tell Charlie to come in. You too.

114

There's no way round this bastard. Not for any of us. Tell me your side of what occurred 'tween you and the bloody Chinks now, and I'll do what stalling I can so you can get your op over and done.'

'All of it. Straight?'

'Straight down the roller-coaster. No Dodgems.'

'Better chase that with another. You ain't gonna like it.'

'Just get it said, you tart.'

'I got pissed on my birthday. Saw the Wells-Devon fight. Had some Chinky-Chinese at Cyril's. Cut my cake and had some hot rice wine. Hit the street, the cold air hit me, out like a light.'

'You are definitely pulling my pisser.'

Vinnie got his elbows under his drink. Whirled the golden liquid and stared deep into Bulstrode's angry eyes. Shook his head very, very slowly.

'You think I wouldn't have used that Mauser with Charlie knee-deep in Happi Coats if I wasn't under the total influence? You want it dead straight, you got it. Just listen. I ain't blind, and neither is Chas. You try quoting me, and I'll buy another shooter and come looking for you. They take the other leg and both arms, I'll still come looking. Give me a nod this is just you and me, and I'll go on.'

Bulstrode looked into his drink, back at Castle, and sounded old when he said, 'I'm gonna regret this, but OK.'

Relief brought a smile to Castle's mouth. A brief, bright shadow of his former sunny nature.

'This ain't Charlie's road. It's Archie's. He's still loyal to the man, and I'm still loyal to Chas. Once Charlie can get shot of the mindless idiocy Archie shook hands on with the Chinks, he will. But, he does it too quick, gets crude with them yellow faces, we all get demised faster than fast. The firm sinks, and the law has a party in celebration. But you'll have another power vacuum like in the East End right now. Small firms trying to take over what's left. Except the Chinks'll have the whole bloody network to expand at will, and when they close ranks, you won't get anywhere near them. You and the law will have nothing but blue serge fingers up your darkest aperture. The Triads'll piss all over you, Buller. And just about every flower-power kid with a vein in his forearm. You getting this?'

Bulstrode vibrated with disbelief.

'Suddenly the Dance firm's a committee of moral vigilantes? That what you're promoting full-frontal? To *me*?'

Castle looked as weary as a ten-trick whore.

'Do I talk on, or button it?'

Bulstrode wiped a suffused face. Nodded with clenched teeth. Watched Castle light a Perfectos Finos and toss the box across. Caught it and lit one for himself.

'So, I'm listening.'

'Like you and Lemmon did last time? Like you lot just *had* to see the Troys in the dock at the Old Bailey when Charlie told you to let them and the Harolds blow each other's faces off? Save the taxpayer's money, because a bullet's cheaper than ten short minutes of wigs and gowns and heavy Latin. Like then, Buller? Or are you really listening?'

'These ain't cauliflowers on the side of my head.'

'Then it's simple for you, hard for us. Book motorists and nick drunk drivers. Make yourselves busy and look the other way. This ain't your war, and ain't mine neither. It's theirs, the Triads. We've got sucked in on the edge of it, is all. Like a bystander takes a ricochet. All right, before you say anything, we ain't innocents. But we can duck and dive and get things done whilst you're still licking your pencil over your notebook. It'll get handled, right?'

'You say,' said Bulstrode. 'I see your mouth flapping, but all I can hear is Charlie Dance. Don't work me the three-card trick. Not me.'

'All right, don't say I didn't warn you, Buller. Get to some of the Hong Kong police who transfer over here. Have them mark your card about the Chinese Tongs. They ain't smiling waiters bowing over the chicken and almonds, they're well different. Can you punch through a brick wall without barking a knuckle? They can. They can hook a man's heart out with their bare hands, mister. Kill with the heel of a palm, and climb into your suit with you still in it.'

The PBX warbled, and Vinnie Castle sat back in the huge leather chair like a lost waif, his face as yellow as a smoker's finger. Waved a thin hand.

'My car. Does it take me to hospital, or do I have it drop us at West End Central?'

'Emotional blackmail from a twopenny villain, and I'm falling for it. This Scotch or LSD? Don't tell me, I don't wanna know. Couldn't find you, could I? Couldn't have, haven't started looking, have I? But when I do, no arguments, Vin.'

'Fair enough, old friend.'

'We ain't mates. Never were. Just, well . . . I dunno, do I?'

'Yes you do. Hard having feelings and a warrant card.'

Bulstrode pointed a furious finger.

'Enough of *that* tart's parlour. There's a fence right here between us. A mile thick, a mile high. Only the long arm of the law can reach over it. I'll feel your collar when and if I have to. That clear, is it?'

'Finish the bottle, Buller. I'll see you . . . if I'm lucky.'

'Going downstairs on your elbows, are you? Or is old Armchair giving you a piggy-back? Get your arm around my shoulder. Let's get you under the anaesthetic before you have me passing snide – or pulling a bloody shooter on the Home Secretary.'

Bulstrode lifted Castle and carried the frail figure down to the hired limousine. Watched the Bentley pull into the brawl of Piccadilly Circus with snow settling on his hat brim.

'Like a bundle of straw,' he said in a sick whisper. 'More fat on a chip and two broomhandles . . .'

Thinking of wasting diseases he wouldn't name, Bulstrode

tramped through slush to the nearest bar with snowflakes melting against his flushed face. Blind to the stares of the people he blundered into.

Regent's Park was a black and white postcard. The may trees were naked black skeletons against the building drifts, and wore fat white bouquets on their upper boughs. The Georgian crown properties on the outer circle blushed rose in the pink light, and the sky was dull iron clotted with lazy grey cloud. Traffic crept through a chill fall of fresh snow, and black ice formed a crust on the uncleared pavements.

Margot paid the taxi off at the North Entrance, hired an orange wheelchair, and pushed Charlie into the zoo despite the CLOSED TO THE PUBLIC sign above the ticket booth. She got Charlie down the slope to the aquarium, and helped him up the steps like an aged relative. Went back for the wheelchair, and wheeled him through the dark to watch turtles swim in green water.

'They weep when they lay their eggs,' Margot said.

'Make good soup too. How'd you work the oracle and get us in?'

'I'm an honorary fellow. Would you like to see the new elephant house my cheque book helped to build?'

'Another time.'

'Yes, I'm a great lover of wild life. Probably why I'm so fond of you. We have the place to ourselves.'

'Keep your big blue eyes peeled, girl.'

Charlie levered himself out of the chair and went through a door that opened onto the passage behind the display tanks. Leaned against a sweating wall as aeration filters hissed in the humid closeness. Heard the slap of fins as a fish surfaced. The scrub of a hard broom on concrete. Got his feet moving, and found Rosie's parcels behind a cistern of bubbling seawater. Carrying them back to Margot was a long plod. He kept them on his lap under the blanket Margot tucked around him, and got his breath back as he was lectured on rays and shark, floral gardens of anemones, and stately scorpion fish. Fever sweated Charlie up and he needed air, a drink.

They were on their way to the fellows' restaurant when Fraud Squad busies moved in on the aquarium with sniffer dogs. Rosie Bottoms had talked.

Lemmon took the phone from Dillman, and a briar bubbled in his ear as Egan said: 'You'll be distressed to know, I am sure, that your precious Ernest Bottoms put his illiterate signature to a pack of lies. There was nothing at the zoo, and means you've had eight of my best men frightening fish and society officials for damn all. I'd have another word with that young man if I were you, Commander. I'll let you have a copy of my report. To clarify things, inter-departmentally, as it were.'

Lemmon refused to swallow the honeyed poison dripping from Egan's tongue. Said agreeably, 'You do that, old compatriot. And the raid on Chalk Farm? How's that coming along?'

Egan's teeth snapped against his pipestem.

'I and my command are naturally doing all we can to assist the Treasury in this matter. Let's just hope it isn't another empty building. My lads have seen the elephants at the zoo, so I imagine they'll take another disappointment with equanimity, should it be necessary. Patient they are, but the mere mention of your name does lengthen their faces.'

Lemmon heard Egan's lips part with a sucking pop. Imagined him smiling as yellowed dentures bit off pungent smoke.

'I'm grateful for their co-operation. And heartsick the snow has ruined their golfing weekend.'

'Regards to your wife, Commander. A most attractive woman . . .'

Egan cleared down on what might have been a laugh. Lemmon slammed the phone into its cradle and ignored

119

Dillman's shy glance of surprise. Glared at the fat flakes of snow floating down the tiled well outside the window. Elizabeth had stayed out all night and had left no note of explanation. Reformation cheese production had made way for extramarital sex. Was it Damien, the potter with bad breath? That dry stick Wentworth with his nervous twitch and hands like thin scrolls of vellum? Not that limp effeminate with yellow bangs and a passion for 16th Century verse?

'Something funny, Guv?' Dillman asked.

'Nothing you'd appreciate, Dildo. Put Bottoms and Peachey up in the Interview Room at once.'

'Now? Together?'

'And have Gerry Fox brought up. He can be the meat in their sandwich.'

Puzzled, Dillman reached for the internal phone. Lemmon hadn't reacted at all to Vinnie Castle's latents on the Mauser pistol. Wondering if he witnessed the downhill start of a nervous breakdown, Dillman dialled 11, and wished Bulstrode hadn't buggered off on one of his mysterious errands. When Lemmon sank into introversion, Bulstrode was the only one who could handle him.

Joe Yellow opened the shop door and stopped dead.

Knew with sick certainty why Cho Sun's bed had not been slept in.

The lacquered box was a carmine scream in the snow, and there wasn't a footprint within fifteen feet of it. The ceremonial knots told Joe what had to be inside, and with due reverence, he took the box into the storeroom. With Cho Sun dead, Joe's life expectancy had shrunk to the length of the finger Pu Fatt chose his executioner with. He waited for the trembling to stop before he looked at the head of his newest ancestor.

The mousing cat purred against his legs as he worked the knots loose and slowly lifted the lid. A sweat ball dripped from his nose to mark the red satin lining, and his violent and silent caper of relief sent the cat streaking for the topmost shelves. Cans crashed on concrete like falling armour. Joe heard nothing. His eyes glittered as he patted Ho Fatt's dead cheek, sudden hope in his constricted chest. He closed the box and retied the long silken cords, carried the box to the council chamber, and left it on the circular table before Pu Fatt's chair.

There were eight short hours to go before the council met on Cho Sun's orders. Joe Yellow went to his room to pace and think. If his uncle still lived, something bad had happened to him. If the Snakes had him, his last journey to the Great Door would be a long one. If he was dead, another box would come. Either way, Joe Yellow was dead the moment Pu Fatt saw Cho Sun's empty chair. Pu and the council would blame Cho Sun for the abortive attempt on the Supreme Snake's life. The loss of Ho Fatt. Without Cho Sun to contradict their clever lies, the Sichuen Dragon would have to make a show of believing them.

And what could a deaf mute do? Joe Yellow tried to think like his uncle. Chewed the finger from one of his gloves, slapped his stupid forehead and grinned. Pulled a shred of grey wool from an eyetooth, and found the revolver a drunk Sinn Feiner had sold him in Portobello Road. Loaded the clumsy Webley with soft-nosed shells he'd rubbed with garlic, wrapped a rope around his waist, and fed a throwing knife up his sleeve. He was no Shadow Warrior, but he could die like one, he decided.

Fear feeds on fear, green wand, he saw his uncle say as he made his way to Smithfield Market through whirling snow. The city was at a standstill, and the gravel lorries were out salting the main roads to keep them open. Joe kept to the back streets, his hands cutting and pecking the air. He was talking to himself.

There was the diesel thump of nausea.

Careless sewage workers had held a long wake in his mouth and cremated the corpse on his tongue. The funeral pyre had gutted the vault of his throat, and wet volcanic ash mummified his raw gums. Every hair on his head was a spike of living fire in his scalp, and a tone-deaf sadist beat marimba rhythms against the thin eggshell of his skull. One small cough would reduce the roof of his mouth to smoking rubble, and his eyeballs had been scoured by hot Martian sands. Death was too much to hope for. Salvation was lying quiet, and trying not to see unspeakable things in amoebic soup behind his eyelids. A red biddy hangover reduced global nuclear war to nothing but a kindergarten spitting contest. Only a delirious alcoholic knew greater horrors in the rubber room of his mind.

A steel door crashed light and stamping heels into his cell. Keys like singing lances clashed in battle on a metal ring.

'On your feet and out!' bawled a screw. Loud enough to split granite, topple mountains, and part Biblical waters for the fleeing hosts of Israel. And softer, but still thunderous, 'C'mon, dad. Let's have you upright, eh?'

The hand on his shoulder dug into jellied muscle. His face slid into his lap as melted glop, and his head revolved in sixteen different directions with the twanging dischords of a dropped piano. His mouth tasted of middens and boiled horse, and the Sargasso weed in his throat bred wriggles of bile for him to gulp around.

'Lemmee die,' he said reasonably. Wondered if his dentures had dissolved in a lake of cheap wine along with his leg bones. His socks were full of old veins and marrow, and his arms hung off his broken shoulders like dead boughs. 'Bury me, you bastards . . .' he pleaded with a sighing gust of noxious breath.

The screw was hauling him off the cot with his face averted.

'If that's your tongue, I wouldn't put it back. Spit the bastard out. I've smelled a few derelicts, Pencils old son, but your breath'd give terminal halitosis a bad name.'

Pencils hated knowing who he was. Owning a name was too much of a responsibility. Went with self-disgust and denied him anonymity.

In a tiled room with plumbing and a badly silvered mirror he was given soap and a safety-razor. The shakes came as he tried scraping at white bristle, and small pink mouse eyes peered back at him from the flaking glass. He got yellow soap in his mouth, and carbolic joined the other foul tastes. He buried his head in tepid water, belched with his face submerged, ridding himself of humid internal gas. Drew a sour comment from the screw, and was taken up an internal staircase that jogged his eyeballs in swimming dance with every step.

There was a brown and cream room with hard chairs and an ugly table. A boy with livid acne and a red mop of hair was trying to climb the wall to get away from Pencils. He set the overhead light swinging as he was brought down from the ceiling by another screw who slammed him into a chair and held him there.

'Who's that bleeding twot?' Pencils asked without much real interest. 'Give the silly tart a sugar tit and shut his bleeding clack . . .'

Pencils dropped off to sleep and was bullied awake. Lemmon and Dillman showed him his old steel box of engraving tools. Zinc proofing plates and etching acids. The copper engraving plates mounted on ebony blocks he'd kept hidden under the floor boards. The dental wax and dies he used for sovereigns, and had all but forgotten about. The beautiful working drawings he was immoderately proud of and would have boasted about if he wasn't captured by the filth. Said they must have been old Ironfoot Jack's, nothing to do with him. Was shown Rosie Bottoms again and honestly didn't know him, God's truth, gents. Was shown forensic evidence that proved he'd handled every item in his forger's weasel. They even had his dabs on the cloth

123

he wiped his inky hands on when hand-proofing between cutting operations. Showed him the traces of blackboard chalk that matched him to his clothes, his clothes to his tools.

A Treasury man enthused over his craftsmanship. Told Pencils he was a genius on the sinister side of the legal blanket, and Pencils had enough heraldic terminology to know he was being called a naughty bastard. Found himself wanting to talk to keep the horrors from oozing out of the cream walls to feed on his exposed nerve-endings. The lower border turned liquid to lap his feet with a tide of sucking ordure. If he talked nice to the Treasury man, maybe he could turn the tide back, force the rotting images back behind the painted wall. Then Pencils saw bleeding Major Gerry Fox between two uniforms in the passage, and his mouth closed with a snap. Knew Charlie Dance had been right about the no-good grassing bastard. And Councillor Desmond would fall apart like fresh halva under interrogation. But they'd get nothing from Patrick Cadogan Peachey.

Pencils broke wind with violent relish. A long blast that turned the air green, the language blue. Cleared the room, and let him fall asleep across the ugly table.

Held on the minor charge of causing a public affray whilst under the influence, Pencils was put back into the dirty cell to sweat through nightmare things eating his face. His whimpers went unheard as the snow deadened all sound.

Bulstrode woke up in a white womb with a crick in his neck. He fed himself a Capstan as the wipers cleared the windscreen and the heater pumped meagre warmth over his frozen feet. Early snow had come with the dusk, and Chalk Farm was a bleak vista of dark buildings with white hats and smoking chimneys. The afternoon fall of soft fat flakes had become vicious swirls of powdered snow that smeared to grey crystals when the wipers batted them aside.

Bulstrode wiped condensation away with a shiver. Deidre's flatmate had been cool on the phone. Said Deidre had flown to Bahrain, would be away for a month, and she'd leave a message he'd called. A plain girl who studied economics with the aid of an astrological chart, she was not a reliable ally. Her unhealthy affection for Deidre was only matched by her dislike of mankind, and DC Brian Bulstrode headed her shit list of undesirables. The car radio played 'The House of The Rising Sun' by the Animals, and Bulstrode retuned to hear a newscaster tell of blizzards from the Solent to the Wash. The M1 was closed, and there was a multiple pile-up on the A4 near Reading. Motorists were advised not to travel unless strictly necessary, and Bulstrode decided he ought to include himself in that number after a last look round.

Parked on the hump-backed canal bridge, he had a good view of the immediate area. He used his binoculars to pick out the unmarked Fraud Squad cars sheltering under the railway viaduct. Cigarettes glowed through the windows, and thin trails of exhaust showed they had their heaters full on. The print works was a gaunt Victorian fret surrounded by virgin snow, and there were only two cars in the parking lot. Lights from the top floor were reflected in the dark waters of the Regent's Park Canal. Six-foot drifts covered the towpath, and the black waters were as still as a fresh coat of ebony gloss. Icicles hung from the closed lock gates, and ice formed a thin crust on the blanket of water inside the lock itself. If Egan's men were content to maintain surveillance until the weather improved, Bulstrode was the last man in the world to disagree with them. Best to go in when a full shift was working and nab the lot, including the noble councillor, whose XJ6 was safely garaged outside his house in Hampstead.

Bulstrode decided he couldn't face his empty flat alone. Flicked his heads at the unmarked cars under the viaduct, and crossed the bridge for a warming Scotch or several in

125

the Lock Tavern. Missed seeing a narrowboat chug down the canal from Little Venice to moor up out of sight of the Fraud Squad behind the print works.

Councillor Desmond's Italian shoes had lost their shine in the long, sliding walk down the hill to Hampstead Underground Station. Not used to being a pedestrian ploughing through deep snow, he was breathless when he bought a return ticket to Warwick Avenue, and took the stairs down to the platform rather than use the lift.

The man holding a kettle of boiling water over his wife's head had carefully explained what Desmond must do. The one stroking his daughter's hair had said nothing, but the steam-iron he held close to her cheek reinforced what the other man had said. Any deviation from their directive meant the permanent disfigurement of his family, and it was made clear that he would be watched every foot of the way.

There were few people on the down train, and Desmond saw nobody who looked like a hardened criminal. A woman with a poodle on her lap did give him long looks, but she got off at Belsize Park, and Desmond had the carriage to himself all the way to King's Cross where he changed trains. At Baker Street he changed again, and waited for his connection with a crowd of drunken Australians. The train smelled of wet footwear and wetter raincoats. He strap-hung in the packed carriage, smelling his own perspiration as his sheepskin gave off the odour of goat. The close atmosphere was as oppressive as a dirty blanket, and he had to stop himself panting open-mouthed.

His wife had told the silent man where her jewels were, where the wallsafe was, offered her wedding ring to get the hot iron away from her daughter's face. Offered herself in the end. Let her gown open at the front to show her full breasts, still fragrant from the bath she had left to answer the door. Let them see her long legs and the ripe curve of her thighs. The golden and tufted triangle of her mount

of venus. Promised them all the things she had denied
Desmond in her bed. Things she would do for both men
in the glare of electric light if they would just let her nine-
year-old daughter run out into the night.

Councillor Desmond came out of morbid reverie with
a start.

Had to push through the Australians as the doors began
to close at Warwick Avenue. Got onto the platform with
his coat half off his back as their loathsome jeers rolled into
the tunnel with an electric whine. Had to sit on a bench
to swallow heartbeats and hold back vomit.

Her daughter, Fiona had said. Not *our* daughter. *Hers*.

He hated her for that. Despised himself for marrying a
younger woman so late in life. Thought how different
she had been before their wedding made all the society
magazines. Brought him alive sexually in the most out-
landish places. Bonked his brains out in parked cars and
on the frozen turf of Hampstead Heath. On an hotel balcony
with French rain running off his buttocks. Until she had
her own Mercedes. A handsome and irrevocable settlement.
Charge accounts at all the big stores, and the finest house
on the prestigious Cherry Tree Estate. Then she was just
a cool and expensive decoration on his arm at civic functions.

He should never have agreed to separate bedrooms, even
with an interconnecting dressing room. Called himself a
vain and foolish man with an ice-queen of a wife whose
expensive tastes his legitimate business could not hope
to finance indefinitely.

Desmond remembered all the sleepless nights knowing
she was the other side of a thin wall. Lying awake until
powerful sleeping draughts gave him a few hours of blessed
oblivion. Worrying about the huge monthly bills. His
standing in the political arena if his business crashed. If he
really had fathered the girl he called his daughter. Taking
the necessary but illegal steps to keep his business afloat.
How much longer the presses would have to remain on his

premises before he could ship them abroad with the men who worked them. All those long afternoons Fiona had never adequately explained away. The dewy look on her that had nothing to do with her circle of bridge-playing matrons. The worsening of her chronic 'condition', and her insistence on sleeping alone as her 'doctor' had ordered. A Harley Street charlatan who'd write any damned prescription for enough guineas.

Christ, Desmond thought, *it's been four bloody years of locked bedroom doors and celibacy. For me, but not for Fiona.*

Ever since that specious charmer Barrymore had returned from somewhere abroad to haunt their dinner table night after night. Until Desmond had lost his rag over the sorbet and ordered Barrymore out of his house. Sorbet between the courses to freshen the palate, yet another ludicrous fancy Fiona had imposed on their household. Like the racks of furs down her side of the dressing room. The mausoleum of dead leopard and mink and sable that went into summer store every June 1, to be replaced by new organdies and lace, water-silks and fine satins she wore to race meetings and 'bridge' afternoons. The drawers full of sheer under-wear he would fondle when she was out somewhere with someone.

A train hammered into the station. A blast of stale air plastered sopping hair to his scalp. He knew he looked ridiculous when his thinning hair was wet. He should have worn a hat. He needed to move. He needed another moment on the bench with his thoughts.

'Bridge' was Barrymore, and Barrymore was 'bridge'.

And Councillor Desmond, who wanted to be His Honour The Mayor, had known that black truth for a very long time. Almost since the moment it had started. Had never found the courage to undress the suppurating wound and look at it. Until now. Now, when she could be on her bed with the talking man and his silent partner. Doing what she did for Barrymore, but with the desperate finesse of a female

128

defending her young. Her pale rump in the air and her mouth busy. Strange hands on the papery fineness of her hips and back. Doing it and doing it with her upper lip misted with effort. Pumping ever downward with liquid ease. Pushing perfect breasts against anoraks dark and damp . . .

Desmond could face it all now. Come to terms with his folly.

Now that boiling water threatened to destroy her pale beauty. Scald her face to the bone. Turn the fine grain of her cheeks to ridges and weals of bubbled unsightly tissue. Blind those violet eyes. Blister the moist and succulent mouth that had lied and lied and lied . . .

Move, he told himself.

Desmond took the emergency stairs. Climbed the echoing steel spiral with its foul graffiti and discarded rubbish crushed to brown pulp by commuters' feet. His chest was tight. Breathing hurt, and there was a nagging pain in his left arm. All he had to do was have someone call the police. Let the talking man and his silent partner destroy Fiona's looks. Then she would be his. No more waking nights. No more Barrymore. But Desmond would have no use for a disfigured wife. Without her beauty she was nothing to him. Could not be displayed on his arm at political functions like the radiant totem she was. That lucky dog Desmond and his sparkling wife.

And little May was his daughter, blood ties or no. Even if bastard Barrymore had impregnated Fiona during some sordid hotel afternoon before he was posted abroad. May was Desmond's. Legally, morally, and by the unbreakable bonds of paternal and filial affection. He got all her huggles and cuddles and kisses without buying them with gifts. May held his hand and sat on his lap for stories because she wanted to. Turned away when mummy gave her goodnight pecks on her way out to dinner, not liking the powder and paint that hid her daytime face.

Mine, he told himself. *Truly mine.*

Cold air brought his head up.

Knives of cutting draught.

He was in the ticket hall and had trouble finding his ticket. Had it torn in half by a sleepy Negro, and went out into the snow rubbing his left arm. Skidded on the icy crust. Felt his sweat freeze on his jowls as he rested against a cabinet of bright posters that warned against spitting and assaulting railway staff.

Lurched off in the direction he had been told to go. Passed tall villas in need of decoration and repair that were let out as rooms for the obscure and nondescript. Brushed against overgrown hedges heavy with snow, old ironwork spearing out of crumbling garden walls. The snow was up to his knees in places, and had worked up inside his sodden trousers. His shoes squelched and threatened to part at the seams.

He was in a wide crescent, and railings circled a canal basin where moored boats were long white ghosts under tarpaulin shrouds. Desmond lumbered to a halt. Stood there wild with fear. The talking man had told to get here, and here he was. Alone.

Councillor Desmond. A sixty-year-old-man with insomnia and a serious weight problem. A man used to comfort, to having people fawn when he raised a finger for service. An after-dinner speaker with a reputation for drollery and a firm handclasp. A lucky man with a successful business and a rosy political future, a stunning young wife and an affectionate daughter. A man to watch, to envy.

Except he was a fat man lost in snow, not knowing what to do next.

A hand took his elbow. A flashlight showed him where to tread. He was taken through a gate in railings. Out across a gangplank, and down into the relative warmth of a long saloon crowded with muffled men. Sat down, he was given a glass of hot rum and lemon. A masked man with black knuckles clinked his glass against Desmond's, and Desmond felt the narrowboat begin to move without engine-noise.

The man with black fingers and a Caribbean-Oxford accent said, 'We're using poles to get under weigh. No need waking up the neighbours, eh, Councillor?'

A man about Desmond's build fed wood into an iron stove. Winked a blue eye at Desmond through ribbed wool and said, 'Seeing as how we borrowed it without bothering the owner.'

There were quiet snorts of laughter. Then nobody had anything to say, and the boat crept down the waterway in total silence.

Desmond had to ask before his chest burst.

'Please, my wife and daughter? They're . . . safe?'

A black finger touched his chin.

'So long as you behave.'

Desmond sipped his rum as his pores leaked fear.

A bulldozer had heaped snow against the outer wall of Stripes Flynn's cold store, and Joe Yellow used it as a ramp to reach the top of the wall and drop quietly into the swept cobbled yard. A chiller lorry was parked near the elevator shaft, and a man fitted snow-chains to the wheels. Joe hit him behind the ear with the Webley because he couldn't think of another way to neutralise him. The man went down with a roll-up still burning in his mouth. Joe doused the butt in snow and put the man into the cab of the lorry when he had made sure he hadn't swallowed his tongue. Covered him with the blanket lying on the seat with a thermos, took the keys from the ignition and locked him in. Apologised with his fingers, and went down to the lowest level on the open cage.

Some men in bloody overalls and aprons opened and closed their mouths at Joe when he stepped out at them. But Joe knew little cockney and fewer expletives. He just showed them the Webley was loaded by shooting a hole in a carcass. When their arms lifted as high as they would go, Joe herded them into a meat locker and threw the bolt on them. If they continued to swear in complaint or bang on the walls, Joe had no idea. He explored the five chambers, and retraced his steps when he found nothing but hanging meat. Even the fletching room was empty, and meant Ho Fatt's corpse was somewhere else.

Back at the liftshaft, Joe again did his best to think like his uncle. Cho Sun would have come down the shaft, there was no other way in, and if the Snakes had not taken him elsewhere, he was still down here somewhere. Joe peered up the shaft and saw nothing but shadows and girders and cables. Looked at the cage. Climbed into it and checked it out. It was just a cage with nowhere to hide. He lay on his stomach to peer over the side, but the pit was too dark for him to make out detail. He stepped out of the cage and looked at it again from the outside. It was still only a cage.

The back of his neck went cold and tight. He felt his backhair stand out from the nape of his neck. He wiped a glove across his dry mouth. Reached out slowly, and pressed the control to send the cage three feet up the shaft. Held his breath.

Hanging down from the support bars was a ragged black bundle. A thin arm hung down, and didn't swing when the cage jerked to a halt. It was as stiff as the arm of a plaster mannequin. Was the wrong colour to be a living arm. Had the look of a badly bruised chicken carcass.

Joe leaned out over the shaft to touch it, but it hung just out of reach. If he lowered the cage into the pit and jumped down there, he would have no way of getting out again. The seemingly insoluble problem creased his face, and he wanted to weep, to let the bitterness out of his constricted throat. Drum his heels until Cho Sun or somebody as clever told him what to do. He punched his stupid forehead as his fingers spelled out what had to be done. Simple.

Joe's fingers told the unconscious Cho Sun to please wait.

Joe walked right down to the end of the first aisle of beef carcasses. Took a deep breath and put all his weight against the last side of beef. Pushed as hard as he could to overcome inertia. Felt the meat move and bump against the next carcass, then that too moved. Then Joe had the whole line moving, and he ran them forward as fast as he could. Then there were carcasses falling off the end of the rail, skidding on the ice and falling into the pit, filling it.

Panting with exertion and pride, Joe walked out across a platform of frozen beef, and took Cho Sun into his arms very gently. Felt for the big artery in the cold neck for the bump of a pulse and found nothing. Then he took off his pebble glasses and held a thick lens against the half-opened mouth. The mist there was the merest bloom, but it was enough.

Joe took Cho Sun up to the surface with the Webley pointed ahead of them. The yard was just as he had left it, and the man he had hit lay in the same position. Joe borrowed his blanket and his thermos. Wrapped Cho Sun up and poured hot tea into his mouth until it stopped coming back at him. Chafed the frozen wrists until the lids flickered under the film of ice.

Joe capered in falling snow. Wrapped Cho Sun in straw and cardboard to keep him warm. Laid him on a meat barrow and blew the lock from the yard gate with two shots. Wheeled Cho Sun out into the market, and started to trot towards Soho. Some porters called after him from a cafe near the Blackfriar's exit, but Joe Yellow kept going. Nothing would stop him now. Nothing.

The snow drifted with solemn majesty. White confetti at a winter wedding.

Sam the Spade started the donkey engine a hundred yards downstream from the Little Venice Basin, gave the tiller to Ollie Oliphant, and sent Matt and Pimlico forward to run out the portable lifting gear. Ollie took the bends wide and watched the narrowboat's trim as the long steel rods ran out to dip the bow lower in the water, and Sam brought concrete slabs along from the waist to weight the stern. He worked alone because Froggy stayed in the saloon with Councillor Desmond, keeping his hands warm and supple in the event that there were locks at the print works Desmond had no keys for. Sam brought Matt and Pimlico back into the cockpit to help with the trim, nobody was needed forward until they'd cleared the last road bridge.

Despite the cold, Sam began to enjoy himself. Haggling over the heavy plant with Irish Dermot in Kilburn had made a welcome change from shaving guineas from whatnot stands, stuffed animal heads, and Georgian silver with antique dealers in Bath or Chelmsford. Charlie calling in his favour had got the old adrenalin flowing like never before, and working against the clock with what amounted to a scratch team exhilarated, where in the past it would have turned his stomach ulcer acid.

The terraces of the Zoological Gardens came up on the right, and the blocks of private flats off to the left showed no lights. There was no traffic on the perimeter road, and there were no birds in the stark aluminium triangle of the Snowdon Aviary. The park was a hard patchwork of bald trees and gentle blue-white undulations of virgin snow, spotted here and there by the small brilliance of gas standards. It was hard to visualise the park in summer bloom, alive with children and prams and barking dogs.

Sam told the lads to finish their cigarettes and to leave their hipflasks of rum unswigged as the narrowboat came into the straight and open stretch backing St Margaret's Grove. Ollie got her close enough to the east bank for Pimlico to jump ashore. Pim hit clean and rolled upright with a wave. Went over a low garden wall where he had parked Irish Dermot's caterpillar crane, patted the FOR SALE sign a hopeful estate agent had nailed to the Victorian brick, and disappeared.

Ollie turned the bow into midstream and lined up for the long bend that curved into the roadbridge tunnel below

Gilbey's Distillery. He closed the throttle, and helped Sam and Matt pole through to the open water beyond. Eased the throttle open to bring them in sight of Camden Lock and to drive them into the lee of the printing works. Let the engine putter into silence with the rudder hard astarboard. With a light bump, the narrowboat came in against the towpath, and Matt went ashore to tie up to the mooring eyes he'd sunk there that afternoon.

Clockwork, Sam thought, checking his watch. *On the button.*

He connected a steel hawser to the crosstrees of the lifting gear, and used the hand winch to raise and swing it against the side of the building, as Matt and Ollie used kingpins to lock off the sections as they rose. The topmost arm went in against the large central window with a soft thump of its rubber buffer, Sam put the winch to neutral, dropped the locking arm, and made two turns to set the hawser on perfect tension, and it was done.

Sam called Froggy and Desmond on deck. Froggy went up the central rungs of the lifting gear like a squat gibbon, and was working on the window before Desmond realised where he was. He blinked up at the soles of Froggy's shoes and the drifting flakes, and the pain in his arm was the dull throb of a poisoned tooth. His left shoe had split, and the cold began to freeze his soaked trousers. He watched the black thumb jerk twice before he got the message.

'Up there?' he said with hoarse disbelief. 'Me?'

'After you, Councillor,' said Sam, counting off seconds in his head. Matt was priming the hydraulics and watching the gauge with care. The lifting gear had to take five tons and drop it on the deck without a bump. There would be no chance of a second try. Dropped too fast, the press would take the narrowboat to the bottom of the canal as if it had negative bouyancy. Sam had explained it with care, and Matt was imbued with respect for the mechanics involved.

He was also keen not to be pulped by an inanimate chunk of machinery.

'You was told to behave, fatface,' Matt hissed. 'Be-bleeding-have.'

Desmond reached for the first rung with his right hand. Let his left arm hang as he started to climb. His split shoe slipped on the cold metal, and he kicked it off. It went into the canal with a soft plop, and he didn't need Sam to tell him not to look down. He climbed like an automaton, tasting rum as it tried to come back. But to have disgorged it would have been impolite. Would have upset the man with black knuckles who was in behind him, stopping Desmond from falling after his ruined shoe. Desmond was grateful for that, and might well have said so. Thought of little May waiting for a bedtime story as he was helped through the window the security officer from Holmes Road police station had said needed no alarm. Knew he couldn't disabuse the man or claim a substantial insurance rebate, and took the men where they wanted to go. Behaving like mad despite the savage pains in his arm and chest.

Then they were gone, and let him rest. The skeleton printing crew were locked in the now empty paper store, the press had gone out of the window, and the precious plates had followed it in the man with black knuckles' overcoat pocket.

Desmond ignored the shouts from the paper store. The snow coming in through the open window. May waited on the end of her bed in a nightgown sewn with oriental fish, anxious to hear about the Swiss Family Robinson.

Desmond fell on the stairs, and again on the bottom landing. There was an odd lemony fuzz to the edges of his peripheral vision, and the front door was ten times heavier than it should have been. It closed on his belly and tore a hole in his sheepskin when he fell out onto the front steps. Crossing the parking lot, the snow was much colder under his left foot, and looking to see why that should be pitched him onto his side in the snow. Now both arms hurt, and he thought he would save getting up for later. May wouldn't mind waiting, she was daddy's bestest girl in alla world . . .

Bulstrode mooned over Deidre browning her limbs under an Arabian sun until he sank the second Scotch and ordered a small bitter chaser. The barman watched television, and two old domino players snapped their tiles and dentures at each other, playing a grudge match that probably started before the pub was built around them. Bulstrode looked at the bar. His half-pint had doubled in size and had a large malt to keep it company.

'Where'd you come from, lovely boys?' he asked the drinks.

'Them two down the bar.' The barman rang up change, his face tilted at wavering electronic images. 'Bloody weather's ruining the film. John Wayne's wearing three hats and five noses.'

'Get to fight ten times as many Indians then.'

Bulstrode raised his pint at two Fraud Squad men who'd come in to take sustenance. They grinned like conspirators from the House of Montagu greeting a servant of the Capulets when Bulstrode joined them. Commanders and Detective Inspectors may fight to the death, but DCs were members of a different club. Johnson said he was Johnson, and the ugly one was Graves. Graves said he was the brainy one, and old Johnson had the bigger feet and a shorter shadow. They both knew Bulstrode was Bulstrode, agreed the weather was a bastard, and didn't object if Bulstrode sequestered his pension to buy another round. They agreed to smoke Gold Flake because the pub didn't carry their brands, and let Bulstrode pay for them too. They all said 'cheers', and got on the outside of that round so Graves could prove he didn't keep his pennies in a Jewish sporran, and wasn't as mean as having a Welsh granny might imply. Bandying slighting ethnic humour between them, the three detectives weighed each other up, and decided they could share straight talk.

'Our Mr Egan, God rot him, hates your guv'nor,' said Graves.

'Hates everybody,' said Johnson.

'Mutual, my sons,' said Bulstrode. 'My Uncle Theo says your Mister lost his balls in the rough. The ones he plays with now has *Dunlop* stamped on 'em.'

Johnson nodded into his drink. Blew smoke, and watched it emerge from the glass as a neat blue ring.

'And our master golfer reckons your uncle got his command pips kissing arse in Whitehall. Sod all gov'nors. Ain't human once they trade cobbles crime for a desk-shaped beer belly.'

'Does something to your brain, promotion.' Graves flipped a beer mat and caught it neatly. 'You go up in this job, they do something to your head. Can't find your old mates with a road map.'

'You could try being a civilian.'

'Cabbing or being a hotel doorman?' said Johnson.

'There's the army.' Bulstrode made himself shiver at the thought.

'That's for soldiers.' Graves watched three John Waynes hit three Lee Marvins with a triple roundhouse. 'Money's in pop music. There's one kid I used to bang up regular for juvenile naughties. Now he bangs a guitar in a lot of echo and drives a Rolls Royce. Pays out more in parking fines than I take home in my brown envelope. Is this snide caper worth catching cold over, Buller?'

'And amoebic dysentry, my old compatriot.'

'Egan's dripped that one at you, has he?' said Johnson.

'A couple or three times. Stand on me, podners. There's gold in them thar print works. Chummy Desmond's been doing the naughties down in the old corral.'

'Got a tasty wife – from the snaps we was shown. Should have been issued with Russian snow-gear to work in this

138

weather. Me and old Johnson here is susceptible to colds.'

'Eleven o'clock closing around here, is it?' Johnson asked.

Bulstrode nodded. 'Another lovely hour of paupering ourselves.'

'Not for us, Buller. One quick round, and then we spell Collis and Dalton for their bevy. Scotch and chaser, lads?'

'S'long as you chase Scotch with Scotch,' said Graves.

'Triples, barman.' Johnson laid a damp note on the bar. 'Even the Queen's beer vouchers are wet. Know what me and the boy idiot here was doing before we got roped in on this? Tracing the owners of rare books some prawn had been punting round the antique dealers. All nicked from university libraries. Lovely quiet libraries with chairs and central heating. Boring, but dry.'

'Beat the fluff outta sitting in a damp Q-car,' said Graves.

'There's a hole you can see the moon through over my driving seat,' said Bulstrode.

'You've got a driving seat?' Johnson rolled his eyes. 'I sit on a beer crate. Change gears with a ballpoint pen. He sits in the back in a broken pram. Holds up the rear axle with a kid's magnet.'

Bulstrode snorted, Graves chuckled, and all three of them laughed loud enough to turn the barman away from Hollywood gunfire. Even the domino players turned to glare.

A harried man pushed into the bar in a flurry of snow. He had copper written all over him.

'Outside,' he said.

'That's Collis,' said Graves. 'Five more minutes, Collis.'

'Tell that to Egan. Now, you dollop. Got a live one in the snow. Our friend the councillor. Heart attack we reckon.'

'You radioed in?' Johnson swallowed his drink on the way out.

'And an ambulance,' Collis led the way across the road in an ungainly run. 'He came out of nowhere. Suddenly, there he was sitting in the snow.'

'No Jaguar?' Bulstrode jumped a rut and black ice broke under his heel.

'He's a shield. Tell him,' Graves told Collis.

'Nothing, like I said. He was just bloody there. Only one set of tracks coming out, nothing going in.'

The four detectives hurried down the mews and into the parking lot where the other Fraud Squad men stood around a hump in the snow. One of them had laid his overcoat over the hump and held a fat face away from the slush. Bulstrode recognised Desmond's drawl despite the slur in his speech. He also recognised a coronary when he saw one.

'. . . Have to get home before the talking man uses the boiling water . . . I behaved . . . a gentleman because of the kettle . . . Had black hands and said "behave" . . . just behave . . . May's waiting for her story . . . Swiss . . .'

'Save your breath, Sir. The ambulance is coming.'

'Better move, or he's gonna turn up his toes.'

Desmond mumbled through a twisted mouth, one side of his face frozen in a leer. Mentioned a narrowboat. May's nightgown. Going in through a window and losing his shoe.

Bulstrode followed the erratic footsteps to the front of the print works with Graves and Johnson on his heels. Took the stairs to the top floor and looked down at the canal through a sashless window. There were scuffs in the snow below, and the canal was a back slash between white banks.

'You thinking what I'm thinking?' said Johnson.

'They used a barge, yeah. Couldn't have gone east without you hearing them use the lock gates, right?'

'Can't go further than Little Venice to the west. What's that, a mile and a bit?'

Bulstrode flicked his Gold Flake stub down into the water.

'I'm taking the towpath. You wanna try by road, go ahead.'

Graves shouted. He'd found the printers in the paper store.

'My guv'nor'll bite right through his pipestem.'

Bulstrode made for the stairs wishing he was armed. Johnson told Graves to stay put and clattered down after Bulstrode. An hour later they found the abandoned narrowboat on the far side of the canal, and the FOR SALE sign above it was some kind of a miserable joke.

It was after midnight when the snowman on the roof sat up and blinked down into Gerrard Street. Cleaned its pebble glasses, banged snow from its hat and shoulders, and became Joe Yellow on the roof above the council chamber. Pu Fatt and the others had been gone over an hour, but Joe had learned to take no chances. He hauled himself back along the ropes he had tied off to the chimney stack, rolled over the pitch, and let himself slide down the other side until the rope brought him up short with a jerk. He kicked an icicle from the gutter, and it speared down into the enclosed yard to shatter on the cobbles. Snow avalanched as Joe let himself down over the eave and swung in through the bathroom window he had left propped open. He gave the rope a tug to free the deadman's hitch, rolled it up and threw it into the bath. Quaking with cold, fear and anger, he shook his Webley at the dark hallway. Would have just pointed it if he could control his hand better. Found he had nothing but shadows for company, and went down to the store where he had Cho Sun hidden behind cases of soya sauce.

Pu Fatt may be clever, but he would never have thought of looking for Cho Sun right under his treacherous nose. The cat had curled up on Cho Sun's chest with a mouse it had brought as tribute, and Joe let it stay where it was. A cat was good luck, and its body warmth could only help his unconscious uncle. He was gravely injured, and Joe Yellow had to get him to a doctor who could be trusted. Joe had splinted the broken leg and set the wrist and fingers, but knew nothing about the extent of the internal damage, or how to physic a torn hip joint.

Joe heated soup on a spirit stove and was feeding it to Cho Sun when his wrist was gripped. The bruised mouth made words and dribbled soup. One bright eye looked at Joe's fingers, willing them to talk. Watched the council meeting come alive in Joe's eloquent hands. The decisions they had reached being summed up by Pu Fatt with:

'Then we are agreed: Cho Sun's madness brought about the death of my brother Ho. I must pay tribute for the bones, but it is the dragon's own envoy who is culpable. The reason for his banishment and eventual execution – the liquidation of his nephew, the wordless one. The Sichuen Dragon must honour us for our actions – has no option but to put his power behind us when my spy leads the Supreme Snake into our trap. When Aman Lee Fook is dead, the Dragon will absorb the Snake, become a single and all-powerful T'ang. I shall send Cho Sun's head in tribute to the old Sichuen Dragon, and it will kill him with one poisoned look. Then it will be Pu Fatt who mounts the Dragon Throne, and you of the brotherhood will be more powerful than you have ever dreamed.'

Joe Yellow's hands fell silent, and he watched Cho Sun's mouth shape careful words. Tell his shocked nephew where he wanted to be taken.

There? Is your mind clear, Uncle?

Cho Sun held Joe Yellow's wrist until he agreed.

Sam the Spade found Charlie reading Xenophon's *Persian Expedition* in Margot's wedding cake bed. Margot slept in a loose curl on the couch, still nuzzling the *Country Life* she'd been leafing through. Sam perched on the bed and accepted a cocktail Sobranie Charlie lit for him.

'Good read, is it?' he said, drawing flame and making smoke.

'Just another war story.'

'You do wear 'em out, Chas.'

'Margot's had a busy day. Had to walk to Baker Street

before we pulled a cab. You look pleased with y'self.'

Sam laid the engraved plates on white satin with a verbal fanfare.

'Tarrah . . .'

Charlie turned one in the spill of the bedside lamp.

'This is a fifty. Looks like they were about to come up in the world.'

'Saw a friend of yours tonight. Young Buller. There was a canal between us, so I didn't shake hands. Threw his hat in the water, and his language was a bit on the ripe side. Ollie and Pim were well away with the press in the lorry by then, so I left him there giving the fish hard verbals. Had Froggy drop me off in Edgeware Road, and here I am. Froggy and Matt have taken the paper to a lock-up garage I keep in Lavender Hill. It's there any time you want it.'

'Now I owe you one, my Brixton brother.'

'Bite your tongue, whitey. I want patronage, I'll apply for an Arts Council grant. We're square, and nobody owes anybody a brass farthing.'

'Keep it down, cocker. Let nursie get her rest, eh?'

'Don't make me feel like some coon just dropped out of a bunch of bananas, then.' Sam scrubbed his flat nose with a brown hand.

'Nothing was meant, Sam.'

Sam grinned, annoyed with himself and the chip he thought he'd shrugged from his shoulder long ago. Knowing he'd confused direct cockney thanks from a friend for an imagined racial slur, he slapped Charlie's knee in apology.

'I know it. Put it down as after-tickle nerves, Chas. A bit like post-coital depression, y'know? You come off a job, and there's all these glands jumping like monkeys on a stick. Adrenalin surging like you've just found the ultimate wave. Surfed right through the eye like a champion, and there's nobody there to witness it. Just an empty beach to walk up. No applause.'

Charlie clapped quietly. Eyes closed against smoke from his cigarette.

'Sam Surfer for President. Brass bands, cheers and flying flags. Now get a good drink down your scrag, you'll be asleep before your head hits the pillow. Wake up ready to take the antique world with one hand tied.'

'Candle-snuffers just *won't* seem the same.'

Charlie pushed the engraved plates down the bed.

'Lose these beauties somewhere safe for me.'

'No problem, my man.'

Sam went away to be just another shadow in the silent house, and Charlie thought about Xenophon and his Greek hoplites fighting their way home from a lost war fought for a dead king. The enemy had let them leave the field with their weapons and their honour intact, and Charlie envied them as he wished Margot would slide in beside him. Give Charlie the comfort of home and hearth that the clever Greek general and his soldiers had fought so long and hard to reach over three thousand years before.

Charlie turned off the light. Finished his Sobranie and listened to the silence the snow had made all the more silent. Somehow, the quiet made London as alien as ancient Armenia must have seemed to Xenophon the Athenian, and Charlie was a stranger in his own town as his spinning thoughts drifted him into borderline sleep.

Then Margot was there. Long legs twined with his, her breath warm on his chest. Bringing them both sexual salve with gentle urgency and a twisting pelvis. And much later, everything was back in perspective as she snuggled in sleep across his thighs. Soft hair tumbled across his flat stomach, her musk and perfume a friend in the dark.

Ready for whatever waited for him, Charlie slept without dreaming, and when Margot awoke, he was gone.

CHAPTER SIX

The telephone was ringing when Charlie Dance let himself into his apartment, and Stripes Flynn started yelling the moment Charlie put the receiver to his ear. Editing out the ripe expletives, Charlie heard that a skinny Happi Coat short on words had shot a dead cow, waved a shooter at Stripes' butchers, and locked them in a freezer unit to catch double pneumonia. Had turned fifty sides of prime Scotch beef to catmeat by heaving them down the liftshaft. That Donny Waddle was still seeing stars in duplicate after a smack behind the ear when he was minding his own business fitting snow-chains. His tea-flask had been half-inched, and that some shooter had made a right mess of the yard gate locks. Some of the market porters had seen some Chink with glasses like bottletops running a trolley off, and what was Charlie gonna do about that box of monkey's, pray?

Charlie felt for cigarettes and hoped his cleaning lady would be in soon. Aggie Ince lived with a Woodbine in her mouth.

'You're the upright tax-paying citizen, Stripes. Invest twopence in a call to the law.' Charlie broke the connection as Stripes gobbled like one of his Christmas turkeys. He put a call in to Stoke Mandeville Hospital to confirm that Vinnie Castle was due in surgery that afternoon, and called the Cromwell Road hotel to have Wind tell him Fook had already left. The University College Hospital would give no information on Soddy's condition over the phone. Too many reporters had said they were relatives. Charlie rang off without leaving a name, and took an incoming call.

145

Armchair Doris said the heavy filth had just tramped through the Windmill Street offices. Dumped and trampled the contents of the desk drawers and looked for clues under the carpet. Made the usual mess and went away saying they'd be back. Yes, it was West End Central, and Lemmon and Bulstrode hadn't been friendly. Doris could still see the flash of Dillman's camera when she blinked, and she didn't like the new one, Taggart. And don't be prawn, Charlie love, how could she take the rest of the day off with all that cleaning staring at her? Made her head itch just looking at it. Humming in anticipation of hours of hoovering, lavender polish and Windolene, Doris rang off.

Wondering why retired whores became obsessively house-proud, Charlie tried to keep his shoulder-dressing dry under the shower. Dripped suds on the carpet when Margot came on the line to make angry-relieved noises at him. Wanted a return bout the moment she and Sam got back from the Bath Antiques Fair, and mewed happily when Charlie promised her the best of three rounds without Marquess of Queensbury rules. He had rinsed off and towelled his hair dry when the doorman used the housephone to say Aggie was on her way up, and was Charlie expecting two Chinese gentlemen? Thinking Fook had made good time from West London, Charlie said to have them wait two minutes before using the lift. Got into some clothes, and started a Cona of coffee bubbling. Recharged the shrimp hopper in his tank of tropical marines, and made a mental note to strip down the charcoal filter as Aggie let herself in.

Aggie had a pyrotechnic coughing fit with clamped thighs and crossed legs in the lobby. Said, 'Blood silly habit,' and, 'Only bit of pleasure I got, ain't it?' And just as predictably, puffed another Woodbine alight with, 'That's better . . .'

The widow of Bottles Ince, Aggie consoled herself with Woodbines and religion. Bottles had made a shotgun withdrawal from a Canning Town bank; and with three constables in hot pursuit, had crossed a railway viaduct to lose a head-butting contest with a goods train. Aggie had buried the bits with a picture of Bottles pinned to the pillow where his head would have rested; turned to God for solace, and foresworn shoplifting as her chosen career. Now she was a pillar of the church, and only drank milk stout when the weather got to her legs. Aggie left the front door ajar, skimmed her Woodbines at Charlie as she passed, and started the washing-machine on her way to vacuum the bedroom.

On his way to meet Fook at the lift, Charlie was turned around by the telephone. He grunted into it as he struck a match one-handed. Heard Fook say he was using his carphone because of the traffic-jam between Marble Arch and Piccadilly. Charlie said something about holding on as the front door opened wide enough to judder against the jamb. Watched a wheelchair come in ahead of a thin Chinese and a black Webley revolver. Listened to Fook being impatient with distant squawks.

The Hoover hummed, the washing-machine gurgled, Aggie coughed ash, and the aquarium bubbled. Charlie just stood there holding the phone. Until the match burned his fingers.

Commander Lemmon stood in the brown slush of Windmill Street to light a Player before crossing to the Nosh Bar for a lemon tea and a salt-beef on rye. Vandalising Dance's offices had left him flat. As depressed as though he'd just seduced a friend's wife. Lemmon was an emotional swan, he'd mated for life. He sent Dillman to put the returned Payne to work on the office paperwork, told Taggart to make himself scarce, and let Bulstrode share his moody silence. What could be talked about needed no words, and Lemmon's private grief was just that; private.

Looking for Chinese Cyril, they'd found Trooper Wells. The heavyweight champion of Great Britain up to his elbows in suds, washing dishes at the Lotus House. Enthusing about the perfect rice-batter for butterfly prawns instead of roadwork and finishing an opponent inside the distance. And no Charlie Dance, only poor old Armchair Doris to growl at. Dance hadn't been at his Pimlico flat at 6 a.m. Nor in his Savoy suite at 6.45. None of the hotel staff in Cromwell Road had seen him for days, and a phonecall north had established he wasn't in residence at the inn near Stoke Mandeville Hospital. If the bastard had a new bolthole, none of the squad's many snouts knew about it.

For all Lemmon knew, Dance could be holed up with Elizabeth. Both of them mugging up for a master's degree in extra-marital sex. At it like knives on an historic fourposter Good Queen Bess had used during one of her Royal Frogressions. Playing perfumed gardens to the sound of sackbutts and harpsichords. Adopting every lewd posture ever carved on the walls of the temples at Ankor Wat, cuckolding Uncle Theo with limber enthusiasm. Awarding each other merit badges for posture, style and aggression . . .

Lemmon finished his sandwich without tasting a thing, and called himself a moral coward. He should have woken Elizabeth to ask where the hell she'd been the night before. But she'd looked so peaceful lying there with the book she'd used to send her off. The collected works of some poet he'd never heard of. In the original Spanish yet. Being an ignoramus in one language was bad enough, but now Elizabeth read in Dutch, French and bloody Spanish, he was a dumb copper in most of Continental Europe as well.

'Your car's here, Guv,' Bulstrode said.

'Who's what?'

'It's here. Your car.'

Lemmon came back to the snow and the taste of dill. Remembered the appointment he'd made at New Scotland Yard. Reached for his wallet to find that Bulstrode had already paid.

'How's your Spanish, Buller?'

'About as good as my French. Lousy.'

148

'No Chinese dialects, then?'

'Only enough to read the menu in English, Guv.'

Lemmon pushed Bulstrode into the street. Ducked him into the official Daimler. 'Have I got a treat for you,' he grunted. 'You know where, driver.'

'Yessir.'

Bulstrode played guessing games for a living, so he wasn't tempted to ask where they were going. The first rule of survival in the CID: Never Look Surprised At Anything. Ever. And being chauffered anywhere for any reason had to be better than walking the streets any day. He watched Lemmon chew a knuckle and kept his own face pleasantly neutral.

If total surprise has a brother, it is panic. If panic has a colour, it is the black of lunar night. The bore of the Webley was an ebony full stop in Charlie's mind. A manic cannonball scattering thoughts like skittles, it turned composure to a mindless goldfish gape. Dropped the mental jaw as whole images exploded into irrelevant jewels of detail. Grey-nosed shells in black chambers. A saffron knuckle turning white inside a trigger guard. Enlarged eyeballs behind thick lenses. Aggie murdering 'Secret Love' to the nasal whine of her electric fluff-eater. The sting of fire eating a small hole in the dermis of one thumb. Yelling hard to take the pain away and away.

Making the reaction natural.

The spiteful surprise that sends the right arm into spasm and jerks it off somewhere, taking the enlarged eyeballs with it for the merest fraction of a millisecond. The ugly Webley swaying aside to point where the eyes darted for that finite infinity. Coming back with a wrist-snap to where the nice white shirt was a clean target. Except that it had blurred left in a feint, and the Webley swung to overcompensate. Pointed itself off at clown fish darting from stinging tendrils to feed on jerking shrimp. Was held down and away by a clamping hand as a hard shoulder expressed into the pit of the gut. Imploded ribs. Collapsed lungs to expel air and a soundless bawl of pain. Sent legs up in a flail, the head and one side of the neck into a hard skirting board. Banged the spine against hard pine and rucked carpet. The Webley left worthless yellow fingers in a snatch, popped a knuckle as it tore away, and there was just sprawling with the ceiling a hover of sickened white fuzz.

Charlie slowed time to normal and broke the revolver to empty shells into a steady palm. Hit the Chinese with glasses in the chest with the useless gun, and looked at the man in the wheelchair for the first time. Reached a wooden match from a brass dispenser, and lit the Woodbine. Blew smoke like blue spit as he calmed himself all the way down. Still ready to maim or kill if he had to.

The unmemorable face looked back at him. Oiled vellum on scraped bone. Every pit in the grainy skin popping out balls of tart sweat with the faint cling of an odour more at home in a geriatric ward for the terminally ill. The dull eyes had life in them. Just. Small amber flecks in the syrupy blobs of brown pupil. Filmed by pain and fever, like the protective membrane of a predatory bird that wouldn't blink away for a bright-eyed kill, the eyes watched Charlie. Gave nothing, asked nothing. Charlie intuitively knowing who he must be was enough, and Cho Sun let his lids droop with the ghost of an ugly smile.

Joe Yellow's hands asked if he could try to get up, but Charlie was on the telephone again with his back turned. The Webley hit the floor with a thud, and Joe let it lie there. Uncle Cho had been proved right yet again.

Joe got his glasses back over his ears and lipread through upfalls of nausea. Watched imperatives form in spurts of cigarette smoke as the long-nosed Dance told whoever was out there what he wanted. There were several calls before Joe was hiked to his feet and made to wheel his uncle into an empty apartment down the hall. There was central heating and a soft bed, and nothing to do but sponge the sweat from his uncle's face. Everything else was being taken care of.

New Scotland Yard was a liner beached on soiled snow. The architects had made Victoria even duller with their unimaginative box of glass, concrete, aluminium and blue plastic panels. The whirling sign whirled in the cramped courtyard, and security was tight when Lemmon and Bulstrode were issued passes. Escorted to a small cinema, they shook hands with a wry Scot called Stannard with ten years of policing Hong Kong under his belt. He showed them his 16mm film of arrests in street markets, surveillance footage of suspects dealing through car windows, in doorways, or glimpsed on highrise balconies through a long lens. He put unpronounceable names to faces like sleek seals; untouchables with no police convictions who ran the colony's black economy without soiling their hands. There were plenty of eager young men to push tabs, supply girls, or float corpses out into the harbour in return for enough Hong Kong dollars. To underline Stannard's point, there were shots of bodies coming out of murky water between bobbing sampans.

Bulstrode counted forty-three as he sat low in a steam-formed plywood chair that had earned a Design Award sticker for the precious clown who'd slapped it together. Somebody who burned joss sticks and sat on grubby cushions blasted by rock with a fat roach in his mouth. Said what was currently trendy, and had graduated from mother's knee to the floor without bothering with what usually came between. He-she-it surely knew nothing about the dimensions of a copper's posterior, or how to accommodate footballing thighs.

The screen showed knockout Chinese girls escorting male tourists, feeding them food, or dancing close under paper lanterns. A pair of wonderful legs showing an acre of thigh

151

through a split silk skirt. A tumble of lustrous black hair, a trim waist, and arms spread on oily concrete. Hands rolled her over, and her face wasn't so nice. Bloated by the ligature around her throat, and blackened by lividity, it was barely human. The swollen tongue poked from a ball of putrid lard, and the eyes and nose were bare foetal scratches on corruption. A ficky-fick girl who's annoyed her masters, and Stannard hadn't needed to say, 'Iron-stomach time' in his studied Edinburgh accent. The rest were equally unpleasant, and Bulstrode would have liked a cup of tea to go with his diet of full-strength Capstans. Life in the British colony on the coast of mainland China seemed to be cheaper than the imitation luxury goods sold in the markets.

Bulstrode learned there were nine main families operating in Hong Kong, that they had been around as long as the Great Wall itself, and would probably last until the last Imperial brick crumbled to dust. Most of them could be identified, but as Stannard said, knowing who they were and what they did, wasn't proof. Not one had been brought to trial, and like most normal people, managed to die in bed of old age. There had not been an all-out Tong war since the late thirties, and even then, with hundreds dying in the streets, only one family head had lost his life.

Stannard had some colour footage of the martial arts performed by members of the police force. Men punched, chopped and elbowed through brick, tile, and blocks of hardwood. Leaped and parried with balletic grace, jumped, countered and kicked with blurring speed. Bowed politely when they were through, and sat on rubber mats looking hot and breathless.

None of it did anything for Bulstrode or Lemmon, and that made Stannard turn up the house lights to smile. A sandy-haired man with yellow lashes and a raw Highland complexion, he was a showman who hid his real freaks behind the final curtain. The last reel came out of a locked briefcase, and as Stannard laced it into the projector, he said: 'When Hitler was almost killed by a bomb, he had the conspirators involved slowly hanged on piano-wire. Cheered himself up on wet evenings by screening their death agonies for his inner circle of intimates. It ran for almost half an hour. I'm no necrophile like crazy Adolph, but I like to remind myself of what's out there, *if* I ever have the stomach to return. It's not every copper who gets himself on the wrong end of an execution order.'

Lemmon stood to rub his cramped backside.

'Bloody chairs were built by some sadistic pervert. Come on, Mac. You don't plan to leave it there, do you? Show us your Black Museum travelogue, make that cryptic comment, and breeze us out of here with nothing but frozen arses from these bum-killing buttock-clamps?'

'Right,' said Bulstrode. 'Piano-wire garrots would go down well with a Nazi suffering from uncontrollable farting. Can't see what that ghoulie-loony-tunes has to do with Mr Stannard and the Chinese Mafia, though. Bad hats come in all colours, shapes and sizes. And there ain't nothing pongier or uglier than a floater that's been in the water for a month or more. So what's in your horror movie, Sir, that's gonna make two hairy-arsed coppers go all unnecessary at the kneebones? With respect, that is.'

'Is yon laddie always so direct, Theo?' Stannard asked mildly.

'Too much protein,' said Lemmon. 'Come *on*, Mac!'

'Just the bare bones, then,' Stannard lit a Tom Thumb cigar and tried one of the chairs for size. 'One of the Crown Colony's main problems, as you're both doubtlessly aware, is illegal immigration from the Chinese mainland. Thousands every week, from grandfathers to babes in arms. All looking for the good life. Usually, we leave border security to the army. But for once we, that is *I*, had rock-solid information about a shipment of opium base coming across. Got it from a man they later crucified, but that's rather beside the point.'

153

'They?' said Lemmon.

'The Tongs, the Triads. *Them*. Nailed him to a cross and flayed him alive. Covered the poor wretch in naptha and tar, and turned him into a human torch.' Something unreadable showed in Stannard's eyes, the set of his mouth. Gone in a moment. He was Mr Mild again. A Scot with a temper like an underground peat fire. Smouldering right there under your feet unseen. You could walk across without feeling a trace of heat through your shoes. But break through the crust and you were a lost cinder in eternal fire.

'Mac?' Lemmon jogged.

'Aye . . . They were bringing it across whilst a massive influx of illegal immigrants stretched the army patrols to breaking point. For a week, the border had been overly quiet, so it became obvious that somebody was massing the immigrants for a concerted push. Holding them back as a perfect cover for a small baggage train of poison poppy. But this time, I knew where, and had a platoon of the 9th Gurkhas to back my people up. It's bad country up there in places, just bog and the mangrove swamps, and those Nepalese soldiers were just the ticket for that kind of terrain. They got in amongst those Tong bastards and created merry hell.'

'Not something I read in the *Telegraph*, Mac.'

'Nor would you. It was *in* Chinese territory, man. Not our side of the border at all. Inside the Socialist Democratic Republic itself. We were behind the lines, and nobody was going to publicise that, eh? Use your common-sense, man. Not us or the Chinese, but they allowed it to happen all the same. We deep-sixed tons of the filth, *and* every bloody Tong member along with it. By St Andrew, that was a fight and a half.'

Bulstrode stirred uneasily. Crossed a cramped leg. Knew he had yet another story he wouldn't be telling his grandchildren in retirement.

'We took eighteen heads in the mangroves. Stuck 'em on

poles and left them there, and none of us with so much as a scratch. Must have put the shit-traffickers back a decade, and the loss of face was worth another century. Aye, they wanted my head all right.'

'And?' Lemmon prompted. Sensing another silence.

'They posted me all over Hong Kong. Every public wall bore my name and the price, nothing more. But it was enough. I was as good as dead.'

'Except you ain't,' said Bulstrode, adding, 'Sir.'

'Not for want of trying, young Buller. They caught me at night about a month later. Sent one man. He hit me once in the side. Took a kidney with his bare hand, and left me for dead. Almost was too.' Stannard's voice had got dreamy. A recitation from the Book of the Dead by a man who'd been there and back. 'It was the night I was due to fly out by RAF transport. Our security people were smothering the place, but he got in and got to me. I remember the shock of being punched. Came awake to darkness and swimming in my own blood. Passed right out trying to hold myself together. Next thing I knew it was three weeks later. A military hospital in Kuala Lumpar, I think. Then Malta. They had me on one of the very first dialysis machines. Said I'd saved my own life by putting my fist in the hole. Showed me my obituary in the Hong Kong newspapers, and one of the wall-posters daubed with pig's blood. Told me to keep them as souvenirs. And I did until I got home, then I burned them on the compost heap with my old identity. Goodbye to all that, eh?'

Stannard cut the lights and started the projector, and his cigar smoke writhed in flickering leader numbers. There were no titles. A man in black threw a punch at a naked male cadaver hung from a tripod in what looked like an autopsy room. Filmed in slow motion, his fist went into the ribcage, turned at the wrist, and withdrew an internal organ squeezing out between the fingers.

'Kidney,' Stannard murmured.

There were other bodies and other organs being ripped out with the same brutal efficiency. It went on too long and far too slowly for both Lemmon and Bulstrode, and they were glad when the lights came up.

'Where in . . . where did you get hold of that . . . *stuff*, Mac?'

Stannard started the rewind.

'Japanese footage circa World War II. Made for the military high command, we think. Sorry about the quality, that was a slash dupe of a slash dupe. Nippon used specialists like that behind the British and American lines. Thank God for the atomic bomb, eh? If we'd have had to take the Japanese islands, they're the sweeties we'd have come up against. What price the SAS now, eh, Theo?'

Lemmon said, 'There's a bar down the street. Any street. And inside are a lot of drinks with my name on them. Coming, Mac?'

'When you lose a kidney, you don't drink, Theo. Not even the Highland dew itself.'

'I'll have one for you, Mr Stannard,' said Bulstrode. 'Would you mind if I shook your hand, Sir?'

'An apology for scepticism, or d'you think luck rubs off, laddie?'

'A bit of both, to be honest, Sir.'

Stannard wore his Mr Mild expression as Bulstrode pumped his arm.

'There is another reel I could have borrowed. In colour. A rare piece in a private collection, and from a Chinese source. Using convicted criminals as live targets. But on reflection, I thought not. Something best left to the scholar and the archivist, eh?' he smiled.

Stannard was still smiling when Bulstrode and Lemmon left him with the empty white screen and the uncomfortable chairs. The chauffeur took them to the Nell Gwynne where the bar was dark and the drinks were club measures.

* * *

Charlie offered Fook the floral chair and told his two Happi Coats not to tap the aquarium glass. Fish weren't toys. Their faces blanked when Fook raised a finger, and they stood behind him to look at nothing an inch above Charlie's head.

'I'll have them wait outside if they displease you, Charlie. But that would cause them loss of face after . . .'

'They're a matched set. Leave 'em.' Charlie thought about the private ambulance coming to collect the man in the next apartment. 'Don't want them cluttering up the corridor. Giving my neighbours hard looks. They're humpty enough after the filth handed out the dawn frighteners this morning.'

Fook looked thoughtful. 'The police will come back?'

'Not without I know about it. You're here about Micky Raven, not the filth.'

The seawater tank made a bright halo around Fook's shaved scalp. His face hated Charlie's abrupt suddenness without showing anything. 'And to see a good friend.'

Charlie rolled one of Aggie's Woodbines in his fingers. Lit it looking out of the window at the forecourt below. Saw nothing of interest, and sat in his Conran recliner to face Fook.

'You're seeing me. I told Micky Raven OK. For six months.'

Fook stiffened without moving a muscle.

'That requires an explanation.'

'For the obvious? Why?'

'I want your reasons.'

'Which are bleeding legion. As you know.'

'I will hear them all the same.'

Charlie snorted smoke. 'I grow hair on my tongue talking. The long-nose does his party-piece in logic, and you decide to throw pennies or use the hook, eh?'

'Sound reasoning can always be expressed. Only mistakes are difficult to match to the right words.'

'Straight from the deltoid: I've got a war. You've got a war. We don't need another one. That's it.'

'I do not agree.'

'Try this for size, you hardhead. The East End ain't for us. Not this year. Maybe never. I don't tell you how to operate in Hong Kong. Here, you pay me the same compliment.'

Fook smoothed a trouser crease and put a thumb to his chin.

'We discussed the East End. The need to control the docks. You agreed to it, and I hold you to that.'

'How, Aman? I promised you the possible. Your race is supposed to be the one with infinite patience, so let's see some. Micky Raven is walking into trouble. Let him. Six months will see the truth of that, and I plan to sit back and watch it happen. That, is *it*.'

'No,' said Fook. 'That is not it. You are not a coward, yet you play the part with conviction. Why?'

'Caution ain't cowardice. Know that, cocker.'

'Then there is a reason I cannot see.'

'You bet there is.'

'And that is?'

'*You*,' Charlie said with quiet force, 'won't like it.'

'I'll hear it, all the same.'

'Because you lied to me.'

'Fook's eyes were dead glass beads. His mouth hardly moved.

'I should kill you for that,' he said with venom.

Charlie's laugh surprised him. Brought his head up. Charlie was through being pushed, he radiated uncaring anger.

'Go ahead. Do I get to finish my cigarette?' Charlie's grin was insolent, and he winked at the Happi Coats.

'You dare to say I . . . lied . . .?'

'Spit it out, my old warlord. Only a word. Opposite to the truth is all. A sin of omission. You lied without opening

158

your trap. And I know because a little bird whispered. Flew right out of the Willow Pattern and gave idiot Charlie the good news. And about what? I hear you thinking . . .'

Charlie leaned forward. Unsmiling. Pointed his cigarette into Fook's face.

'. . . About four missing drug couriers for a start. Ring a bell, do they? And how about a half-ton of refined heroin snatched by the Hong Kong Customs? Horse hidden in a canister of what makes little horses ought to have worked, but didn't. Now why would that be, eh? Why don't you tell idiot Charlie?'

Fook's show of fury died stillborn. He thought in silence. It was as if his suit had hardened around him, leaving him relaxed. The soft core of an exoskeleton.

Charlie lit a second Woodbine from his stub. Let the silence lengthen. It was Fook's and he was welcome to it. Made three smoke-rings and watched them curl to nothing. Would have whistled if he'd remembered an apt tune.

Fook used rapid Cantonese, and his Happi Coats went into the spare bedroom, leaving him alone with Charlie.

'You heard this . . . how?'

'Oh, you *do* talk? I know, and that's enough.'

'How do you know?'

'That the Snake Tong has grown one mouth too many? That you're in the deep nasties until you've found out who it is? A little dragon told me. I also know the Dragon Tong's got itself big trouble. Why they whacked at us the other night, and why we're still walking around. Put your house in order, Aman. Maybe then you can tell me how to run my firm. Too many wild cards in your deck, and somebody ain't dealing straight.'

Fook stood to look down at Charlie. Menace in his stillness.

'I must move against the East End. There is no choice.'

Charlie shrugged.

'Then it's without me, old son. The Pool of London is

159

just about dead. All the big freight companies have moved to the coast, and it's a rotting desert down there. And going the distance for no prize money is a good-hiding to nothing. You do this, we're divorced.'

Fook smoothed a white cuff. Nodded.

'I owed you a life. The debt is paid.'

Charlie's laugh was a sudden snort of smoky cynicism.

'And we're square, eh? Except I'd have gone off a bridge long ago if you hadn't needed me. Now you figure you don't, but it serves your purpose to leave me be. "Why" is for me to figure out in a quiet moment. Not that I can sleep that easy. You still might take it into your head to lose me permanent if I become a nuisance as well as a bloody supernumerary. OK, I'm warned, and I return the warning. You shake hands with Micky Raven, we're on different sides and all bets are off. Fair?'

Fook smoothed his second cuff. Nodded again.

'Eminently fair.'

The Happi Coats materialised as if summoned by extrasensory command. Stood flanking the Supreme Snake to stare directly at Charlie, who knew he had the speed to get to Fook before they got a killing blow in. Wondered if that thought coloured Fook's thinking, and decided it didn't. The lift came up the shaft, and a trolley banged against the aluminium door as it was wheeled out into the corridor.

'Must be this way,' somebody said. 'Yeah, 3A, 3B . . .'

Charlie leaked a thin trail of smoke.

'Bloke next door,' he said. 'Coronary case. Slip out now, eh, Aman? No need to hand him another scare he can't handle. We'll not shake hands.'

'This should not have happened, Charlie. But life is a series of endings. There will be others.'

'Yeah,' Charlie agreed, looking off at his clown fish as if he were alone. 'Oh blimey yeah . . .'

When he looked away to find the ashtray, he was alone. He strolled to the window to watch Fook being driven away.

Heard the lift come back up and take the hospital gurney down. Saw Cho Sun lifted into the ambulance and Joe Yellow climb in beside him. Then the ambulance sped away, and there was just the empty street to stare at.

'I kept it going as long as I could, Archie.' Charlie's breath pearled the window pane. 'Choosing enemies is easier than picking friends you can trust.'

Ten minutes later, Charlie walked towards Soho, knowing he would never return to his apartment. It was a wrench he had shrugged off by the time he flagged a taxi.

'There you are, Guv.'

Dillman found Lemmon and Bulstrode at the Nell Gwynne. Lemmon had three Player's burning in the ashtray, and Bulstrode tried to make his beer glass throw up smoke rings when he blew into it.

'Dildo the detective,' Bulstrode said.

Dillman accepted a bitter he didn't want, and Lemmon draped a meaty arm over his shoulder with: 'How goes the battle, Pistol? Does the noble Henry prevail on Flanders Field this day? Does the Dauphin weep in defeat?'

Dillman ate an inch from his beer to save his suit from stains.

'Fraud Squad, in the person of Egan the Golfer, has the serious sulks.'

'Like Achilles before Troy. Say on, sweet messenger,' said Lemmon.

'Egan has fleas in both ears from the Treasury and the DPP. They didn't like him losing all that snide evidence from Desmond's print works. And with Desmond paralysed and speechless from a stroke, he'll get nothing more there. Mrs Desmond threw her lawyer at Egan, and has moved out of the ancestral home with her daughter for parts unknown. But Fox, Bottoms, and old Pencils go for trial at the Old Bailey as soon as there's a hole in the lists.'

Lemmon took his arm back. Iced his whisky and swirled the glass.

'A lamprey, a minnow, and a chalky old flounder. Better than not a lot. And you, my Lord Dillman, how went your quest for the chalice of truth?'

Dillman was shown eight fingers when he mouthed 'How many?' at Bulstrode. 'Me, Guv? Sent Taggart to watch Dance's flat. Looked in on Sodbonce at the UCH. Not a well lad, that one. Had his condition described to me as "comfortable as can be expected", and you know what that means. Asked for his personal effects, and it was like looking through an uncooked black pudding. The bag was soaked in his claret. Hooked out some happy snaps. Think you ought to take a long squint at them.'

Lemmon and Bulstrode peered at the bloodstained Polaroids Dillman laid on the bar. Vinnie Castle cut a golden cake, smiled beside Charlie Dance, was kissed by a couple of Eurasian girls, and toasted the camera with a bowl of rice wine.

'Happy birthday,' said Lemmon. 'So? So what?'

Dillman tapped a figure on the edge of two prints.

'Him. The Chinese connection.'

Bulstrode's thumb turned a print.

'I've seen him somewhere. You've seen him, Guv. Today . . .'

Lemmon shed alcohol like a swimmer breaking through surf.

'Mac's picture show.'

Dillman lost his unwanted beer in a plastic potplant.

'I've got one of two names for him from Alien Registration. He's either Chiang Chu something, or—'

'Aman Lee Fook,' Bulstrode finished for him.

'On the bottom,' Lemmon agreed.

'Wasn't the Bamboo Tong, was it, Guv?'

'Snake, Buller. Snake.'

Dillman groaned at the discoloured ceiling.

162

'How do they do it? I chase all over – they sip grog and get messages out of the ether.'

Lemmon turned Dillman to face him.

'Valuable police work there, Dildo. Confirmation of a suspect's identity before it's asked for? I call that clairvoyant, Buller.'

'The man's a miracle, Guv. Walks on water. Does conjuring tricks with wine and fishes. But his glass is empty.'

'And eight or several behind. Facilitate a refill.'

'You're the guv, Guv. Barmaid, a lemonade and two straws.'

Lemmon peeled off a note. Slapped it on the bar.

'On me, Dildo. A man's drink here. Scotch for my noble laird.'

Groaning inwardly, Dillman held the double whisky, grateful when Taggart arrived to say he'd tailed Dance's taxi to Soho. Dance had gone into a Berwick Street cafe and was still there.

'Be gentle with him,' Lemmon told Bulstrode. 'Don't break it over his head like a bottle.'

'No, Tag. Dance went in and kept going. Straight out the back and into Duck Lane. After that, who knows . . .'

Lemmon and Bulstrode collapsed over their drinks, stifling laughter. Taggart's poleaxed expression made Dillman break into a smile, then he too bowed over himself to let the laughter come. Taggart ordered himself a lager and nuzzled it looking at the Polaroids.

'Chinese are very popular in Pimlico,' he said. 'Think Dance runs a take-away for 'em. Heathen junk food must be poison though, saw two yellow monkeys took away by ambulance.'

'Yeah? Never?' Bulstrode wiped away a tear. 'Well, there's a thing. Good heavens.'

'So you ain't interested. Froze my tockers off for nothing.'

'Don't get sniffy, Tag. You don't laugh, there's only tears.' Bulstrode looked and sounded strangled.

Taggart tried a weak grin. 'So I'll learn, and you don't want the number of the ambulance. But seeing that particular face coming out of Dance's block of flats, I thought . . .'

'Which particular face?' Lemmon asked, snorting into a handkerchief.

'Him. In the pictures. Difficult with all them beetroot stains, but it's him all right.'

'Point,' Lemmon ordered, and watched Taggart tap Aman Lee Fook on the nose. Caught Bulstrode's eye, and came off the bar rolling his shoulders. 'Finish your drinks, lads,' he said. 'No hurry, you've got ten long seconds . . .'

Dillman abused the potplant for the second time and was the first one outside.

DC Payne was waiting for them in the Command Room when they got back, and nobody made jokes about his arm being in a sling, or asked him to ski down to the canteen for a tray of teas. Payne didn't notice, he had more than enough on his mind. Lemmon had one arm out of his coat when Payne said, 'Somebody just kidnapped your Chinese cadavers, Sir. Walked into the mortuary like regular undertakers and drove them off in a hearse. And the same thing happened to Nasty Donovan's corpse. Same bald-faced MO. Who do we inform about that, for crying out loud?'

Lemmon's coat slid to the floor unnoticed, and Bulstrode trod on it as his jaw dropped.

'That,' said Taggart, 'is fucking sick.'

Nobody else had anything to say for a long time.

Night was coming on, and the frozen Victorian necropolis of Highgate Cemetery was blooded by a dying sunset. The gatekeeper's lodge was unmanned when the hearse parked alongside to offload three coffins. Lifted over the gate, they were carried down a curving path into the shadows of pious monuments to a glorious afterlife. Pitted stone angels offered

164

gilded wreaths to the greater beyond above the leaden cloud, or lay weeping on mossy rocks carved with unfashionable names from the previous century. Icicles hung from the marble canopy of a dead knight, and the marble face of the Hertzog family mausoleum was overgrown by frosted ivy.

Bolt-cutters took care of the chain holding the iron gates closed, and the coffins were carried inside and laid to rest behind the lead and marble caskets on their solid stone bier. Heaped over with dead leaves, the coffins disappeared in the detritus of decades. The gates were closed, the chain repaired, and the pallbearers trudged back to the hearse for a cigarette and a warm.

Ollie Oliphant drove back down the hill, skirted the DETOUR sign he'd placed there on the way up, and let four of his passengers off at Tufnell Park Station to make their own way home. Then he drove Charlie to the Ford they'd left in Oak Village, and took the hearse back to Kilburn.

Charlie waited until Ollie's tail-lights had disappeared, checked his fishing bag in the back of the van, and drove to Fulham, taking his time.

A warm westerly heralded a thaw.

Lemmon closed his front door with his back, almost too tired to shed his coat. The familiar hall with its solid old furniture was lit by the brass lamp on the oak escritoire, and there was a single red rose where Elizabeth usually left her notes. He stared at it, a suspicious dog that had flushed a heliotrope rabbit. A single red rose went with Spanish verse and bonking to Handel's Messiah!

Lemmon hung his coat next to his wife's sheepskin and a man's raincoat. A Gannex with plain lining he'd never seen before. His stomach growled, and the Nell Gwynne whiskies were a dead swale on his tongue. He had to face the owner of the sporty coat with fresh breath, and he went into the downstairs bathroom to use Colgate and Listerine, brush his hair and splash his face with cold water. He left his cutthroat razor where it was, and heard muted violins in the living room. Andy Williams, 'Moon River', and seduction. The vague sandalwood smell of Elizabeth's favourite perfume, the expensive stuff she only dabbed between her breasts on those special nights he had almost forgotten about. The bathroom mirror and tiles were still misted from the bath she'd taken, and Lemmon knew Mr Gannex was in for the luckiest night of his life if he lived to enjoy it. Lemmon went up to the bedroom and snapped on the light. The bed was turned down but empty. So it was a romp on the living room carpet for lucky Mr Gannex. Lemmon went back down the stairs and threw open the living room door.

A lit candelabra pointed phallic wax fingers of light at the flickering ceiling, and the banked coal fire crackled cheerfully. The record had changed to the Swingle Singers doodling with Bach, and champagne stood in an ice bucket by salvers of canapes and fancy cheese biscuits. Elizabeth lay in a nest of plump cushions with the firelight dancing in her hair and on her sleeping face. She wore peach silk pyjamas he'd never seen before, and the plunging V neckline showed a lot of creamy bosom. One peach slipper had fallen off, and her toenails were shining pink shells.

Commander Theodore Lemmon was the only man in the room, and when he perched on the couch, he saw the framed diploma lying beside him. In amongst the heraldic mantling and illuminated calligraphy was his wife's name and the honours she'd been awarded. Lemmon forced himself not to put his fist through it as one drowsy brown eye opened, and long lashes batted slowly.

'Am I not a clever girl?' Elizabeth yawned.

'A very clever girl.'

Elizabeth licked her shining pink lips.

'But incredibly vain, my darling. And so anxious to show off to you, I traded on the good offices of others to gather it to my rapacious heart. You are married to a scheming and shameless harpie.'

'Am I?'

'Most certainly. Am I forgiven?'

'For what, exactly?'

'For rushing off without a word. For dashing off to Cambridge in filthy weather. Getting a flat tyre, and getting the teensiest dink in the door when I skidded into that ditch. I didn't actually turn all the way over, but I did get bounced silly. This sweet man in a cottage let me use his phone, and an even sweeter AA man moved several universes to get me towed out of the ditch. I'd banged my head rather, you see, and had awfully wobbly legs. They could have put me up in some dreadful rooming house and got me a doctor, but with my skirt torn open to the waist, a trillion ladders in my stockings, and my coat and shoes ruined by mud and slush, well, I wasn't going to be seen dead amongst a lot of sleazy travelling salesmen in some absolutely grotesque commercial hotel without you there to take care . . .'

'You were hurt?'

'. . . With a chair against the door all night, and facing one of those foul and greasy breakfasts those places serve, well, naturally I thought of darling Bunny . . .'

'*Elizabeth* . . .'

'Well, since I'd already rather imposed on Bunny Halliday to winkle my diploma out of those slowcoach university people – he's terribly well in with all those bursars and deans and such, and even though he was somewhat shocked by my effrontery, he was, nevertheless, sweetness itself . . .'

'Elizabeth, will you please slow . . .'

'. . . And even though it *was* a thousand years past midnight, and I had rather woken him from a deep sleep, he just wouldn't hear of me *not* staying with him. Well, I was rather weepy and sorry for myself. So the nice AA man took me out to the Halliday mansion which is just enormous, had a lovely warming brandy before he went back on patrol,

167

and left me there. Bunny's housekeeper made me this enormous supper because I was absolutely ravenously starved, and when I'd demolished that and a bumper five-star brandy, I was desperately whacked. Bunny sent me off to sleep in a bed the size of several royal barges, and that was me until the morning.'

'But you did see a doctor . . .'

'I'm *telling* you, darling. The nice doctor came after a lovely breakfast in bed. Said I was a fine, fit and lucky girl with just the teensiest scalp abrasion. Bunny must have pulled strings, because the garage brought my car back as good as new except for that tiny dink. The housekeeper had done wonders with my suit, so I poodled off to Cambridge behind a snow-plough. Bought these pyjamas and some new stockings. Collected my diploma, had it framed by this bearded chap in a side street, had a giggly luncheon with Bunny and some donnish woman he's currently sparking, and drove home very, very carefully. Fell into bed, and only this morning realised I hadn't called you or anything. Probably the bang on the head and Bunny's luncheon, but I *did* call your office this afternoon, and young Payne sounded awfully off, Theo, so I told him to forget I'd called, and decided you deserved one of our old evenings. Do say you're surprised and pleased, darling, and that I'm forgiven . . .?'

'Yes, I am surprised.'

'How lovely. Have I been awful to live with these last months?'

'Awful.'

'Well, it's over and finished, and I feel better for it. Selfish but necessary. You do understand?'

'I'm glad for you.'

'Truly, Theo? Bunny said you'd be proud. I think there's more than a little envy there, about us.'

'Is there?'

'Oh, yes. He's got all those titles and that huge house

168

to rattle around in, but you can't cuddle up to bricks and mortar, can you?'

'Not readily, no.'

'Not like us.'

'Not at all like us . . . I saw a . . . forget it. Doesn't matter.'

Elizabeth sat up. Embraced her knees and wiggled her toes.

'The Gannex,' she said. 'Do you like it?'

'Like it?'

'I have my diploma and pyjamas, you deserve a present for patience above and beyond the call of matrimonial duty. So, one Gannex.'

'Ah.'

'Should I have wrapped it up like Christmas? I thought it better if I didn't . . .'

'Quite right. A splendid garment like that should not be boxed.'

'And there's champagne. And things on biscuits. To make up a little for all those lonely fridge meals.'

'And candles and firelight.'

'And snuggles. After the duck in aspic.'

'Why after?'

'Has it been that long? You look quite red in the face.'

'Longer. The blush goes all the way down to my friend.'

'Little dicky is big dicky? How delicious. I hope he's in fine fettle, I have plans for him. But I don't want your tummy rumbling in the middle of a climactic cadenza, so first you eat.'

'Henry VIII did both at once. Couched a lance *and* ate a capon.'

Elizabeth grinned and patted Lemmon's thigh.

'Bet he fell off his horse a lot.'

'Is it possible on horseback, I wonder?'

Elizabeth held Lemmon's face.

'My darling man, if you want to do it at the top of a

human pyramid juggling plates, that's just fine with me.'

'Mr Gannex wants to be inside his wife for as long and as deeply as possible. No frills. Perhaps the second or third times we could ring the changes. But right now, I want you out of that tailored piece of arousement so I can really look at you.'

'Why, Theo Lemmon, you positively smoulder.'

'Guilty.'

'There are only two tiny bows between us. Shall I declare the fete open, or will you?'

'Silly question. Come here.'

'Yes, master . . .'

Later, naked in rest, Elizabeth said, 'You know, you look decidedly uncopperish with your trousers around one ankle and firelight on your bare bottom. Are you ready for the duck now?'

'I don't think my erect friend will let me get close enough to the table to eat.'

'Mmmm. Are you threatening me with that appendage?'

'His idea. I'm appended to him.'

'Role reversal. Pitiful.'

'And uncomfortable, madam.'

'How rotten. Lie back and think of Scotland Yard.'

Lemmon was straddled by firm thighs, and Elizabeth bore down on him with liquid surges, her breasts in soft dance on his chest. Weeks of doubt and frustration fled down the second road of fulfilment, and all the angry colours were washed to nothing as he was ridden to a wild climax in the glow of burning anthracite.

He dozed for a while, and found Elizabeth carving the bird without a stitch on. They made love over the kitchen table with the silverware chinking to the steady thump of their thighs, and then picnicked on the floor like children with giggles and enormous appetites.

Micky Raven yawned at the screen as a big girl in something

flimsy answered a cardboard door to a plumber with a bag of tools and a ready smile. She took him into a bathroom set where the tap leaked and a window-cleaner polished a window-shaped hole in the painted backdrop. The plumber winked at the window-cleaner, the window-cleaner winked back, and the big girl pointed at her leaking tap with a show of plump cleavage and a waggling rump. The cameraman gave her breasts a lingering close-up and panned across to her plumper backside. The plumber spread his tools, and the big girl passed him a spanner with a witless smile. Then she passed him a wrench, and the plumber handed her something that wasn't, and she looked vapidly coy without letting it go. The plumber leaned over to see better, and fell through the painted hole. His bucket of water soaked all of them, they took off their overalls with the big girl's help, and the big girl came out of her flimsy tulle without appreciable argument. Then she was holding two erect somethings that earned another loving close-up, and her breasts were being shared by two pairs of hands.

'Boys meet girl, boys bonk girl,' Raven said. 'Ain't nobody got an original idea left?'

'Got her clothes off, didn't she,' said Big Alphonse.

'About as exciting as missing the last bus,' Raven yawned. 'My clientele want something better, they ain't just a row of dirty raincoats wristing it over eight-mill rubbish in some cellar club. They want class filth. I want class filth. I'll have to send this batch up north to the beer and skittles clubs. Them I don't need to bother about.'

'Thought it was artistic − with the water,' Alphonse said around a thick ham sandwich.

'Picasso it ain't − dumb you are, Al.'

A wedge of light bleached the big girl's face as the viewing-room door opened, and Raven told whoever it was to close it fast. The darkness came back, the big girl used her tongue on a pair of fleshy helmets.

'Two at once is different,' said Alphonse.

'So is doing it with donkeys, you prawn. And the Romans was doing that in AD frozen-to-death. Still do in Cairo cabarets.'

'Well, they're Arabs, ain't they?' Alphonse drank from a can of Long Life and belched comfortably. Had his elbow jogged by somebody sitting heavily behind him, and wiped beer from his lap with: 'You been taking clumsy lessons, Rupe?'

Raven peered through the projection beam.

'You got my Castellas then, Rupe?'

Rupert Baer snorted through blocked nostrils.

'Dropped 'em, didn't I?' he muttered. 'Your change went all over the pavement, Mick.'

'Course you did. Now hand 'em over.' Raven stiff-fingered Baer's chest.

'I'm telling you,' Rupert sounded wearily patient. 'Dropped the offing-pot. There's this shooter talking to my right lug, Right? And on the end of the shooter is the fist that decked me. Down and bloody spark-oh. Never saw it, and I'm dead sorry, ain't I? Now I've got a head like a bucket, and the tasty end of a twelve-bore digging me in the headbone, right? And I ain't about to try looking back to see who it is. I ain't that interested in knowing, right? If the man had wanted to shake hands nice, he wouldn't have come out of nowhere all of a sodding-sudden, now would he?'

Raven could see nothing but glare.

'You are getting up my anal canal, Rupe,' he snarled.

Rupert edged his sigh with tired fury.

'And *that* makes me about as sorry as I can get. *Right*? Now I've told you gospel what's going on. All I'm hoping for is a nice quiet doss when the man with the shooter takes himself off out of it. Hoping he leaves my swede in one piece on the end of my neck.'

Alphonse stopped wiping his trousers. Left his hands in view.

'We've got company, Micky. Evening, Mr Dance.'

Raven groaned. 'Leave it out, the pair of you . . .'

Big Alphonse prodded Raven's shoulder. Nodded off at Charlie in the gloom.

'The man's there, Micky. With a pump-action Remington nosing Rupe's ear. That's one cartridge up the spout, four in the magazine. More than enough for all of us. Think you'd better talk to the man.'

'You'd better be there, Dance,' Raven said, blinded.

'I'm here.'

'And you couldn't just knock and say, "hello"?'

'Not the way things are, no.'

'Who declared war? Nothing inna papers.'

'They report news – don't make it. Wanted you to be the first to know, Micky. What's coming your way'll come just this sudden. No time for printing posters. I'm saying my piece, then I'm out of it.'

'Can't print my obituary without I get buried, Charlie.' Raven thought he heard a sigh in the darkness. Sensed a shrug.

'That could happen. What I'm telling you.'

'Do me a fucking favour,' Raven sneered.

'The man is,' Rupert said. 'I'm listening. Al's listening. Only one who ain't is you. And the shooter ain't eating *your* earhole.'

'S'right,' said Alphonse. 'Yeah . . .'

'So I'm listening,' said Raven.

'I was wrong about handshaking for my Chinks, Micky. "Sorry" don't cover that, so I won't bother. They want the East End enough to get a divorce from me and mine. You get in their way, they'll come after you hot and heavy. If that's your pleasure, fine with me. Just know I'm out of it, whatever comes off. You got two options: make nice with them, or get your knee in first.'

Raven stood with suddenness, and the big girl's mouth seemed to eat his face.

'Hold water. I thought them yellow monkeys never walked away from an ex-partner without leaving him nailed to the wall. How come you ain't wearing a three-nail Easter present?'

'Took out some insurance. The kind the man from the Pru don't sell. I came to say my piece, and it's said.'

Raven's face bawled from a huge pink phallus.

'Too easy, Dance. Too flaming pat by half. It smells. Stinks. Last week's catmeat out inna sun. I get Charlie Dance's warning, right? Say: "What a lovely geezer, warning me like that. What a chum." And I turn my back, and there's a knife in it. I wouldn't trust your word if you was first-cousin to a churchful of plaster saints. I'm smiling at you, and them Tong bastards are grinding my balls for noodles. You slimy get – coming in here with all that smarm. Hoping I'll swallow your old toffee while your Fu Man Chus are picking my bones.'

'Fuck it, Micky . . .' Alphonse groaned.

'Shut it, you tart. Or are you making one with Dance against me?'

Alphonse came out of his seat to cover his face with pubic hair.

'Nice fucking talk. All I'm saying . . .'

Raven pushed him away. Bared his shirtfront.

'Take your best shot, Dance,' he roared as a big blue eye rolled in ecstacy on his chest. 'Trigger me, you cheap nebish.'

'He won't,' Rupert snorted.

'Because he's as yellow as his chinky-Chinese.'

'Because he's gone.' Rupert used a handkerchief to wipe his bloody nose. 'Went when you was raving.'

'Who's fucking raving. Get after him.'

Alphonse laughed with derision. Sat beside Rupert.

'You gotta be joking. Let's have a look there, Rupe . . .'

'I'll live,' said Rupert. 'If Micky learns to listen for once.'

'Fucking revolution, is it? Have to do every bleeding thing

myself.' Raven kicked down the aisle and opened the door. Looked out at peeling paint and pornographic posters. Listened to the pub below turning out with the usual chorus of drunken farewells. The slam of car doors and revving engines. Shook his head and pinched his lower lip. 'Wish I had that clever bastard's timing. Could be any one of those pissed nightingales out there. Just another face inna crowd. Clever, clever . . .'

'You calmed down a bit sharpish,' said Big Alphonse. 'A minute gone, you was pointing your head at Mars.'

Raven cut the air with a hand.

'That was then. Had you two deadheads well convinced. Have to get a decent lock on that door. And a peephole.'

The film faded out and black leader clattered in the gate.

'Now he's going for cheaper insurance,' said Alphonse. 'You understanding any of this, Rupe?'

'Can't even see straight. That big tart had ten tits.'

Raven stood over both men. Smiling.

'You want a glass of hot milk and bed, or are you man enough for a nice ride out in Uncle Mick's motor, young Rupert?'

Baer stared at him. 'Going where?'

'Gerrard Street for fried prawn balls, you prawn. If Dance is out, we're definitely in. Get the Raphael brothers and the lads on the blower. Tell 'em to meet us there. Got to see a man about a merger.'

Baer continued to stare.

'Just walk in there, order some sweet-and-sour, and shake hands as a side-order of: "By the way, Emperor Ming, I'm your new partner"?' With the Tongs? Christ, Micky, you don't even know who they are.'

Raven pinched Baer's bruised cheek.

'But Chinese Cyril does. And Chinese Cyril owes big dough to Arnie Clover. And who does Arnie Clover owe even bigger dough to?'

Baer pointed a mute finger at Raven.

'Yes, my beamish boy. Me.'

Big Alphonse drained his beer and crushed the can.

'Cyril pissed off to Paris.'

'Didn't though, did he? Couldn't stay away from the Lotus House. Even with Trooper Wells running it for him. He's been tucked up at Troop's place all along. And Troop being a mate, he'll get Cyril to meet us without thinking twice.'

'Shooters, Micky?' Alphonse asked, dialling the Raphael's number.

'Only out of sight. See you at the car.'

Raven went out into the King's Road to heat up his Princess. When he finally drove east, an anonymous Ford van fell in behind, and Charlie trailed Raven's firm into Soho. He watched Raven meet the Raphael brothers in the Lotus House, then parked in Duck Lane to talk things through with himself.

'Fook and Raven playing four legs in a bed means they got an army to put on the streets, Archie. Me, I've got two hospital cases, three soldiers I can trust, a deaf Chinaman, and a bent Shadow Warrior who fell off the shelf before I got him. Have to do, won't it?'

And smiling, Charlie drove to Sussex Place to break into Margot's town house.

BOOK TWO

CHAPTER SEVEN

The slow thaw had slicked Trafalgar Square with ice-melt puddles to further dispirit the pigeons, and Landseer's lions shone like seals in the watery sunlight as Lemmon's chauffeur changed lanes to speed down St James's. Lemmon wore Elizabeth's fading rose as a buttonhole, and his suit had creases sharp enough to peel fruit. Saluted by a commissionaire, Lemmon strode into the Reform Club as though he belonged there. A porter took him up the marble staircase and ushered him into the member's library.

Inside, there was more marble, an open fire, and a stately clock on the huge mantel. Leather editions in gleaming bookcases, a few busts of ancient politicos, and the smell of confidence. A crystal chandelier took up most of the ceiling, and there were decanters of port and old madeira on a table. Feeling like the new boy coming before the head, Lemmon stopped himself shining his toecaps on the back of his trousers. Didn't shout 'Shop', or blow a raspberry.

'Theo, my dear old chap.'

Bunny Halliday emerged from the depths of a footman's chair to shake hands and draw Lemmon nearer the fire. Even rounder and pinker than ever, Bunny wore his best conspirator's smile as he poured two glasses of vintage Dow's and sat Lemmon in a huge leather settle. Saw the rose and dimpled up as though he were privy to a state secret.

'Came out of your hothouse, Elizabeth told me,' Lemmon said.

'A very rare woman.'

'So she keeps telling me, Bunny.'

'As she should. How's that bang on her head?'

'Makes her dottier, even though it was a week ago. And I should pull your nose for spoiling her.'

'She was a damsel lost in a blizzard. What could I do?'

'Just what you did. I'm talking about pulling strings in academia.'

Bunny's smile hid his eyes behind pink lids like shy stones.

'What you so sneeringly term as my "Grace and Favour" manoeuvres. The world spins, we all spin with it. You've been too long amongst the disagreeable criminal elements, Theo. You have the seniority, so why not leave the ethnic minorities to kill themselves off? There are many doors I could—'

'Splendid port, Bunny. Splendid,' Lemmon boomed theatrically.

'Answer the question, you emotional socialist.'

'The moment you come out into the open.'

'I?'

'You.'

'Ah.'

'Well?'

'What was the question? My memory . . .'

'Is perfect. Total recall. You never forget a birthday, or how many favours you're owed or owe. What's for luncheon, Bunny? I'm ready for the nosebag.'

'You have a crude stance, but you fence well.'

'You taught me, remember? And you've given me the clue I needed. Why I've been summoned to this last bastion of dead empire.'

'Really?' Bunny purred. 'Am I that transparent?'

'Only when you mean to be. You said "ethnic minorities". That leads us neatly to our small Chinese community, does it not?'

'Very good, Theo. Very, very good. You improve. More port?'

Lemmon laughed aloud and liked the sound of it.

'The only move to the left that isn't considered political in this den of dodos.'

Bunny poured with care. 'The very last of this vintage. I hope I'm not sharing it with a retarded cloth cap palate.'

'No, my tastebuds are Tory. I've missed squabbling with you.'

'Is that what we're doing? I did wonder.'

'No you didn't. Has my Elizabeth been lobbying behind my back? Truth now, Bunny.'

Halliday looked up with a blank face. Hard eyes brittle.

'Absolutely not, you munchkin. Nor would I allow it were she to try. You malign your friend and your wife, sir. Now answer this: Just how bad is this Triad-Tong-drugs-thing?'

'Right now? Contained. But for how much longer I couldn't say. Dunno.'

'But you see the shadowy hand of your favourite villain in there? The ubiquitous Dance?'

Lemmon refused a cigar in favour of a Player.

'Easy to see him everywhere, and I'm not overly paranoiac. But yes, he's connected to one of our Chinese groups. And don't ask for details, I don't prattle, Bunny. I can place him at the scene of a triple murder, but the evidence is only circumstantial. Not enough to issue warrants for arrest. That's one monkey we will catch with the old Chinese slowly-slowly. Not by going into court like Dick III, "scarce half made up".'

'An allusion to the Tudor view of Richard Crouchback, Theo? My, my, Elizabeth has sent you back to your books in a big way, hasn't she?'

'You won't see me reading Don Quixote in the original Spanish.'

Bunny looked puzzled. His raised eyebrow drew only silence.

181

'The new so-called "Drug Culture" has come hard and fast, Theo,' he said. 'Is government doing enough to curb its spread?'

'Ask them.'

'You'd like to see the police with wider powers?'

'To achieve what? Undercover task forces with national powers might turn some clammy stones. But unless coppers have the same rights of search and seizure as the Customs and Excise boys, and *they* are as well-trained as they ought to be, drugs will come here in larger and larger quantities. We have more seaboard than you can hopefully police. Heathrow is the largest and busiest airport in the world. Day trips to the Continent could see half a ton coming through Customs in carrier-bags every day. Right now, we're ten years behind the American experience, but these things have an unfortunate habit of accelerating. The philosophy of even the brightest is: don't knock it unless you've tried it. I see us having the same giant-sized headache as Uncle Sam inside five years. Maybe sooner. "Anything goes" is the philosophy, and to experiment with speed and horse and LSD is the new national disease amongst the young.'

Bunny nodded over his port.

'I tend to agree. If this Tong thing were . . . neutralised fast? Would that change things?'

'In the short term? Maybe. In the long term? No. The market's there, and there's too much easy-big-money to be made for the farmers and the pushers. And the big boys are untouchable. They make millions without even seeing the stuff. Political clout could dry the stuff up at source. Use the big stick to beat the Third World over the head, there's maybe a chance.'

'Left-handed grants to the poppy-growers of Turkey and Pakistan? Compensate them for growing less lucrative crops? Already in the pipeline, thanks to our cousins across the Atlantic pond. But they do have a good deal more spare cash than us church mice in Europe.'

182

'Your part of the ship, admiral. Not mine.'

Halliday pointed a manicured finger.

'Yours is the dirtier end of the stick. Retail to consumer.'

'Pusher and user, Bunny.'

'Just so. It's already in the universities. I hate the thought.'

'Any kid with boiled brains, scabs on his arms, and a permanently snotty nose, is an ugly sight. Doesn't matter who his daddy is, and I am *not* being socialistic. Just realistic. Come and see some of the kids who didn't make it out of their first acid trip, you'll know what I mean. They climb walls that aren't there. Pick holes in their faces because their skin is too tight on their faces. Half their brains have flown to the stars and got lost in transit, and what's left sits there screaming without making a sound. And the bastards who do that to the young should hang high, Bunny. Dealing shit for profit should earn the capital charge, because it's murder. Nothing else.'

'Capital punishment is a dead issue with this government in power. I need to know what can be done on the streets.'

'Honestly?'

'Naturally.'

'Nothing. And don't hand me that "Come now," look, Bunny. That's right, damn it. Until the public has the will to turn away from using the stuff, we just sweep up what's left of the bonfire. When school teachers light up a joint marking homework, ain't much a copper can do. Except bang up the few we catch for the lightest of light sentences. The bench doesn't know what it's up against. Probation orders and medical reports have their place, but to me, it's just another way of shuffling the problem sideways. Nobody wants to grasp the drugs nettle, Bunny. Nobody. They make sighs of distress and turn to the racing results.'

Halliday leaned back in his chair. Spoke over his shoulder.

'You hear that, Bill? From one of your best chaps.'

183

Lemmon watched the well-known face come around the wing of an overstuffed chair to stare at him. Faded blue eyes taking him in over the top of half-glasses. The white hair slightly dishevelled. The smile shy and warm. The voice plummy.

'And he talks sense,' said the Shadow Home Secretary. He folded his copy of *The Times* and stood, taller than he looked on television. 'Listen to him, Bunny. Anything I can do, you know where I am.' And laughing like an amused school prefect, he went out, closing the door.

Bunny poured the last of the port.

'You, my lad,' he said, 'have earned your luncheon.'

'I thought we drank port after the nosebag,' Lemmon said. Dazed.

'Rules are there to be broken, remember?'

'By those who make them.'

'Haven't you just been arguing the opposite with not a little passion, Theo? Now, how about repatriation as a weapon?'

Lemmon found himself blinking.

'What? Oh, the Chinese. Most of them are British subjects.'

'Not necessarily. Assumed identities and suchlike. But that's for the paper-pushers. You hand me the ammunition, Theo, and we'll ship the rascals back home to Uncle Mao. How d'you think that regime would receive our unwanted Triads?'

'With a trial and a rope.'

'Exactly.'

Bunny's smile was bland and fond. Until Lemmon looked into his granite pupils. They were as uncompromising as shards of wet kerb.

'Shall we dine?' Halliday asked politely.

When Doc Rudge had removed the last of his stitches, Charlie spent an hour in Grand Buildings with the man from

Hamburg, and emerged paper-richer by £260,000. The arms shipment had reached Colonel De Wit in Cape Town without a hitch, and a further order for Centurion tank parts and Bloodhound missiles had been placed. The commission for that would be a cool million. Charlie tipped his hat as he passed the South African embassy, a building he'd never been in, and scattered pigeons crossing to wait for Froggy Farrell outside the National Gallery.

Nobody had taken over Pencil Peachey's pitch, but years of ingrained chalk still tinted the paving flags. According to the Lincoln's Inn lawyers Charlie had hired to defend Pencils at the Old Bailey, the old forger would probably die in prison unless there were technically legal flaws in the prosecution's case.

Froggy brought the white Rolls into the kerb, drove Charlie to the University College Hospital, and parked amongst the 'snips', 'bargains', and 'offers of the week' in Warren Street. Soon to be swept away by massive redevelopment, it was still the bustling hub of the dodgy used-car trade.

The Feathers public house was the motor traders' official watering hole, and every street corner was an outdoor office where, for cash money and no questions asked, rare automotive esoterica was to be had in any quantity. From reconditioned wet-cell batteries, Packard running boards, and Indian-silver imitation Spirits of Ecstacy, to 'genuine' vintage radiators without makers nameplates or added purchase-tax. Nod, wink.

Every shop, doorway, upper floor and basement, housed accessory factors, shady insurance brokers, or hire-purchase agents with usurious rates of interest for the uncreditworthy and gullible.

Specialists with picaresque talents supplied wound-back milometers, doctored riddled bodywork with metallic putty, sold precisely-worn tyres to match the 'mileage' of any vehicle, and fast shellac 'blow' resprays that turned rusted

185

kerb-leaners into showroom champions until spotting rain brought out the blisters.

A small deposit and a signature bought years of trouble. Rash complaints to salesmen about failed big-ends, fractured chassis, sheered steering columns, blown paint or collapsed suspensions earned the same weary shrug and, 'Hard cheese there, squire. No-warranty vehicle, ain't it? Should have read the small print.' And the gypped punter found himself shoulder-deep in unsmiling gentry with no concept of charity. Invited to withdraw with his head unpunched, the sadder and wiser owner truly understood the meaning of 'buyer beware'.

To the police, it was a civil matter. To the legal profession, a lost cause. Go home. Knock it out to another green mug, ha, ha. Swallow the loss and use good old London Transport. Experience comes expensive, my old son.

Froggy lowered the electric window to smoke, and large men in barathea and camelhair skimmed envelopes into his lap with varying degrees of bad grace, automatically offsetting the 'overhead' against the next wheel-hungry idiot willing to put himself into debt until the Second Coming. A man without an envelope leaned in to talk in a low voice as Froggy nodded through his third Gold Flake, and went away with money in exchange for information. The Dance firm also had 'overheads'. Charlie came back and told Froggy to take the North Circular out to the Southend Road to shake any tails, and sat back with a closed face as Froggy passed on what the man from Fulham had told him.

'Micky Raven's been busy, Weasel says. Says he's done a deal with that Fook. Given him the waterfront for whatever, so long as Raven gets his dibs from the longshoremen – still a lot of bent gear coming out through the dock gates – and's supplying a ring of muscle for some sort of meet between the Snakes and the Dragons. Wanna exchange gifts, Weasel said, and threw in a bit of a laugh. Said there ain't no love lost, but both firms wanna keep things nice.

Some Chinky ritual thing, and if Micky plays referee, ought to go off without a hitch. They ain't set a venue yet, Weasel'll get on the blower soon as he knows. Said Micky's been sniffing around the footer clubs though, and that oughtta give us more than a clue on what's occurring. That make sense t'you, Chas?'

'Some. That it?'

'Not for three hundred notes it ain't. Seems there's a bit of a groundswell of aggro from the small East End family firms. Don't like Raven moving in on 'em worth a cold carrot. They might take a pop at the Raven mob, but they are penny packets of sherbert up against a wholesaler, ain't they? Least, that's what Weasel reckons.'

'What Weasel reckons ain't worth the poppy from six motor forecourts. What else?'

'Could be three of the family firms are making a merger to have a serious pop at Raven's mob. There was a meet of the Crosbys, the Tates, and the Finns. The Tates had it away after a lot of words, but the Crosbys and Tates shook hands. The word is, the Tates'll be back when they've simmered sensible. Them three families get cosied up, old Micky's got aggro by the bucket. Ain't none of them averse to packing heavy shooters for a simple night out at the flicks, Chas. They'll kneecap a granny for a florin and the change of a pound.'

Charlie agreed with a sombre nod.

'Has Raven tried to split 'em? Get 'em on his side?'

'Weasel says not. Says Micky figures that as a waste of a handshake. Figures one Raphael brother with a pea-shooter's worth a hatful of Tates, Finns and Crosbys any slow Tuesday.'

'On Fulham turf, maybe. In Bethnal Green? Another story, Frog.'

Froggy kept silent until the Crooked Billet roundabout, then lit Charlie a cigarette and asked about Sodbonce.

'He didn't know me, Frog. All drugged-up, oxygen tent,

187

and tubes up every orifice. More internal complications than a Mensa questionnaire. Took the senior quack aside for some straight talk. Soddy's punctured bowel leaked a lot of nasties into what's left of his innards. The quack had a lot of fancy words for blood-poisoning and the virus that's eating the clever bit of his brain. Seems a massive loss of claret starved Soddy's bonce of oxygen for maybe too long. What's left at the end of next week might not be our Soddy. Could be a cabbage with a sloppy grin. Or a useless dollop without the nouse to wipe off his own drool. A three-year-old incontinent that has to be sat on the pan like he'd never been a man. If that's the story, I hope he don't make it past Friday.'

'This get passed around amongst the lads, Chas?'

Froggy lost a couple of weaving tipper-lorries, overhauled a coach draped in football colours, and left it behind with a smooth surge of acceleration.

'Ollie Oliphant does the fast coaching, Frog.'

'Had to get it out some way, Chas.'

Froggy shook with sudden ague. The Rolls dropped back to a steady fifty through Woodford.

'Sorry, Chas. Just came over me.'

'Feelings are a bastard, Frog. You don't have 'em, you're dead. Have too many, you get your friends dead.'

'Do I clue the lads about Soddy?'

'No.'

'That's a lot of saying nothing, Chas.'

'Button it or walk. No room on this firm for bleeding hearts. Last time that happened, three got dead, two still feel buckshot when it rains, and you earned a boat like a ploughed field.'

Froggy shivered, remembering.

'That's me convinced. It's buttoned, Chas.'

'Uh-*huh*!' Charlie grunted.

Froggy took the Rolls past a flagpole factory and into open fields where seagulls hovered in mottled scud. Beyond

188

Battlebridge, Charlie directed Froggy down a long avenue of elms to a grey-brick Victorian sanatorium with modern annexes. There was a folly on an island across a lake, and swans sailed in armada under willows. It was too cold for the wheelchair patients, and some ornamental ducks had the sloping lawns to themselves.

Told to wait, Froggy waited, and Charlie pushed through double-doors into convected heat and gleaming tiles to shake hands with Dr Ben Bunch. As swarthy as a thin Arab, Bunch had a lazy smile and wore tinted glasses to hide his comedian's eyes. Without them, his patients refused to take him seriously. Appointed to the post of Senior Medical Director when Charlie bought the place as a memorial to Archie, Ben Bunch was the only member of staff Charlie had kept on. Now there was a small but well-equipped wing given over to cancer research funded by selling off Archie's Mafeking Street development to a consortium of City smoothies for petro-dollars.

Ben Bunch knew full-well what Charlie was, and couldn't have cared less. Any new medical toy he needed arrived without demur. No waiting in line with his colleagues in the public sector for MOH hand-outs. He was actually conducting the kind of research they only read about in the *Lancet*, and if that meant having a marble bust of a man named Ogle in his foyer, what the hell. Charlie's finance had made him a front-runner. In five years, Ben Bunch would be in California on a research budget with more zeros behind the big numbers than Nagumo used over Pearl Harbor one ignominious Sunday.

Bunch talked as he walked Charlie through the secure ward where alcoholics and addicts with generous families underwent detoxification whilst being purred at by staff, decor, and psychologically soothing music. Silent fish swam in tanks amongst bowering greenery, and the barred private rooms were quiet havens without sharp edges or drab institutional colours.

Bunch said, 'I own to being awed speechless by our guest in Suite D, Charles. The man possesses the most extra-ordinary recuperative powers I've ever seen. Not only has he shrugged off viral-pneumonia and the onset of pleurisy in under a week, but has recovered his muscle-tone with a regime of exercise totally new to me. Even with his hip and leg immobilised in traction, and lying as still as a board, he puts single muscles into controlled spasm at will. They come up out of his skinny limbs like tubes of liquid mercury. An astonishing phenomenon.'

'Where's your professional detachment, Ben.'

'At the laundry with my socks when you bring me three-ring circuses. He's nothing like our usual cases, the one-dimensional personalities swamped by fatalism. I look into their eyes and see my own reflection staring back from empty glass rooms. And the blame for their addiction never ever rests with themselves. Some are pitifully forthright about it. Others are sly or whining. But they all maintain they are the victims of *Them*. *They* gave me the bottle, the thirst, the pill, the tab. The need for the addictive crutch. The need for inexorable retreat from the great grey kingdom of *Them*. They stole all the self-regard needed—'

'Yes, Ben. No, Ben. Heard it all before, Ben. Can my Chinaman talk? I *know* you can.'

Bunch smiled lazily. His eyes laughed behind tinted lenses.

'The noble benefactor chides the good physician. Cho Sun talks in Mandarin, Joe Yellow translates it into sign-language for Mutton Jeff, and Mutton tells us, if it's relevant. Mostly Mutton writes notes for you. Did you know the deaf and dumb language was universal?'

Charlie said nothing as he watched an old alcoholic use an aluminium walker to inch down the ward. He'd brought Mutton Jeff to Essex for just that reason. Mutton had been born profoundly deaf, but dumb he wasn't, in either sense of the word.

Bunch unlocked a heavy door and held it closed.

'Will my exotic guests be the cause of bitter tears, Charles?'

'Nothing comes for free, Ben.'

'My mistake for asking. You could have lied, damn you.'

Charlie nodded down the ward at the torpid patients.

'That remark makes you like them, don't it, Ben? Hiding from reality in the safe womb of self-delusion.'

Bunch made a face. 'I never want you as a patient. Too much like playing chess with a man-trap.'

'Just give me my Chinaman back in one piece, and you can shoot radium at crab cells to your heart's content.'

Bunch let Charlie through into cool greens.

'Ring the bell when you want to be let out. I'll be keeping a firm upper lip in my office. D'you want ice in your Irish?'

'Another time, Ben.'

'No wonder doctors are solitary drinkers,' Bunch grumbled.

'You could always book yourself into one of your own wards, Ben,' Charlie said as the self-closer shut Bunch out.

An hour later, Charlie walked out with a scroll of elaborate Mandarin addressed to Aman Lee Fook, the Supreme Snake, and read Mutton Jeff's copious notes on the road to Stoke Mandeville.

'Whaddya mean . . . *no*?'

Micky Raven glared at Chinese Cyril across a bald penalty area. Chinese Cyril was a stubborn fat man in houndstooth and pinstripes. Raven was gaunt and furious in sheepskin and smart gaberdine. A faded club flag flapped from a tall mast against rolling cloud, and hard winds sang dirges in the shadowed stands.

'They plain won't wear it, Micky.'

'Meaning *you* won't buy it. You working for Dance or me?'

'I can't sell them this venue. Not even with free balloons and five flavours of ice cream.'

191

'Craven Cottage ain't good enough, that it? Whadda they want, Wembley Arena?'

Cyril toed the mud and a clod stuck to his shoe.

'Wembley'd take an army. I feel naked out here, how'd you think they'd feel?'

Raven's arms embraced the whole ground.

'That's the bleeding beauty of it. 20,000 screaming fans can't be wrong. They come every Saturday to see ninety minutes of professional fouls. Ain't a single fan that's unsighted. See every kick and elbow the ref misses, so how bad? We're up in the stands with the heavy weaponry, and they're down here in plain sight. We start Fook's mob from one end. We start Pu Fatt's mob from the other end. They meet inna middle. Make nice noises and do the business. Say teddah, back off, and go home from different exits. Any humpty-naughty Chink gets popped, no messing. Down he goes bleeding like a horse. Knowing that, they all gotta play the white man, right?'

'No. You wear the shooters, they wear nothing but trust. You put yourself down here. Would you wear it?'

'We do it at night. Floodlit. How bad?'

'No!'

'Whaddya mean, *no*?'

'Where I came in.'

Cyril waddled away across scarred turf. Sat on the trainer's bench and shook his head at the dark tiers of seats. Put a shine on his oxfords with a handkerchief and wondered where Raven's street-sense had gone. Being floodlit in the middle of an empty stadium with Raven holding all the aces was something Fook would never swallow.

Raven stood over Cyril to use a hard forefinger.

'I ain't taking "No", Chinese.'

Cyril sighed. Fed himself a stick of gum. Showed his fear with rapid jaw movements.

'If I try putting this in their laps they'll feed me my ears.

And what if some other shooter got in behind *you*, Micky? What could Charlie do from up there with a shooter? Yeah, you may well look over your shoulder. They'd be fairground ducks with nowhere to run. I feel naked just thinking about it.'

Raven kicked an advertising fascia.

'Don't throw Chas Dance at *me*, Chinese. I'm here because he walked. I've still got my balls, his leaked out of his backside long back. I'll come up with what's needed, don't you fret.'

'In two short days? Good, Micky. That's t'riffic, 'cause I don't wanna get dead. Owing you heavy dough has put me in the middle, and I've paid you back in sweat twice already. Them Tongs get the hump, won't just be big elbows they hand out. They bake people in pies and feed them to their grieving relatives. Take my old mother a full year to scoff me down with gravy and potatoes. Your kids got big appetites, Micky?'

Raven hissed and Cyril just smiled when he was hauled to his feet by his lapels.

'Go ahead,' he said, swallowing fear with his gum. 'Give me a whacking. I'd rather take what you hand out than have them bake me under a crust.'

'You yellow tart.'

'Whatever you say, Micky. Put me in the critical ward. Do me a favour. Just so long as I don't have to try selling them this humpty old idea. Saturday's only three nights away, counting—'

Raven threw Cyril away from him. Sprawled him on gravel. Pointed a hating finger down at the placid fat face.

'I'll get back to you at Troop's. Be there.'

Cyril lay still as Raven stalked away through the player's entrance. Sat up to watch the Raphael brothers lead Big Alphonse and Rupert Baer down the back stairs of the North Stand. Climbed nimbly to his feet when they'd gone, dusted himself down and lost his smile. Wore his

193

fear like an extra layer of fat as he found his own way out of the football ground.

'Should have gone to Paris, Charlie,' he said, unlocking his Cortina. 'Should have listened . . .'

There were get-well cards and flowers, bottles of squash and fruit. The clipboard chart read: Patient UD/100394 CASTLE Vincent E, but the hospital bed was empty. The pillows were plumped, the hanging bar hung silent, and the covers were tucked hard enough to bounce coins. The patients on either side slept, and the screens were drawn around a double-amputee. The rest of the ward was bare springs and rolled mattresses. Empty wheelchairs formed rows under the portico outside the window, and there was winter sun in the distant hills.

Charlie thumbed the panic button. Held it down.

Heard the buzzer drone and listened to vague nothings bruise a hard silence. The measured tread of soft shoes coming down an interminable corridor with slow professional haste. The hush and brush of a woman's stride.

The nurse was wholesome, plain, and too young to be motherly, but she was working on it. She had cropped waves of chestnut hair, large amber eyes, and a mouth as plump as her cheeks. She took the buzzer from Charlie's hand and looked up at him gravely. Saw the slow tic in his right cheek and the knobs of muscle working along his jawline.

'I think,' she said, 'you'd better come this way.'

Charlie's voice was as remote as Alpha Centauri.

'Where is he?'

'This way, hmmm?'

Smart enough not to move concrete, she walked off pointing ahead of her, making Charlie match her unhurried pace. They left the ward and crossed a paved and planted area. Walked up a slope between glass walls to a small gymnasium permeated by the sweet-sour sweat of atrophied muscles being worked back to life. There were walking-frames and wallbars, parallel bars and men in white coats giving encouragement to the disabled. A paraplegic in a wheelchair pumped iron against a stopwatch. An armless boy reached for coloured pyramids with a metal armature and his tongue out. A legless man swarmed up a rope on arms like knotted serpents, and there was a lounging group in robes and dressing-gowns smiling at Charlie as if they knew something he didn't. The wholesome nurse just looked pleasant as she took Charlie across the satin hardwood floor. The loungers parted, and there was a rubber mat marked out in feet and inches between hand-bars. Two men in white started a patient down the long walk, pacing him outside the bars.

He steadied himself with stiff fingers. Raised his hands from the bars, swayed onto his good leg, and swung his artificial limb forward. Eased his weight onto it, swivelled at the hip, and scraped his good leg ahead of him to take a second painful step. Paused, swayed for balance, and began again. The dark eyes glowed with inner determination, the neck tendons corded, and the spread fingers fluttered. Sweat stood out from the thin face, and Charlie had trouble swallowing.

The steel and plastic foot thumped when it landed, squeaked on rubber when it turned with the swivelling hip. Inches became feet, feet became yards, as the painful progression brought Vinie closer and closer to where Charlie stood. The robes' and dressing-gowns' murmured encouragement was a soft sea urging him ever forward. The legless man hung from his ropes to watch, and the paraplegic forgot his stopwatch.

Vinnie's eyes were hooked into Charlie's face as he thumped and scraped and squeaked the full fifteen yards, stepped out onto the hardwood floor, and stood erect to grin his very white grin. There were quiet 'bravos' and light applause, and the attendants lowered Vinnie into his wheelchair. Took his artificial limb off and inspected his stump for abrasions. Made low and pleased noises, and drifted away with the crowd.

Charlie had trouble with lumps where words were born.

Sparrows squabbled in the eaves and weak sunlight made patterns on the blonde flooring. Vinnie lit cigarettes and flicked one across. Drew smoke all the way down and streamed it from both nostrils.

'You kept that a dirty, dark secret,' Charlie dredged up from somewhere deep and painful.

Vinnie's nod was tired but happy.

'Had to. You'd have been here smothering me if you'd known. Not out there, doing the business. This way, you saw the opening night, not the fall-abouts at dress rehearsal. But I could use a push back to the ward.'

Charlie kicked off the brake and took the handles.

'That's me, a unidexter's labourer. How long before you star in *Come Dancing*?'

'Take over from Victor Silvester on Monday. When're you gonna start talking to me again, Chas?'

'About what?'

'Anything. Everything. You've kept me at arm's-length for months. Wrapped me in cotton-wool. Think I don't know you're trying to go it on your lonesome-ownsome? Had to keep my ear to the ground somehow, so I had a couple of the lads come see me on the QT. You kept me well out of that snide caper you had Sam the Spade handle for you. Now you've put Fook in bed with Raven after the shortest honeymoon in history. Given them the East End pie on a plate. If that's your pleasure, fine, but I do have one question.'

Charlie turned a bend in the passage. Stopped the wheel-chair to watch clouds chase their own shadows across the valley towards the setting sun. Dropped his long stub in a sandtray and turned Vinnie to face him.

'Just one? You?'

'For now, yeah.'

'Make it a goodun.'

'It is. Who pays for Nasty and Soddy? And when?'

'That's two questions.'

'You got answers?'

'Life ain't a sixpenny romance, Vin. The Masked Avenger has his clever scriptwriter to knock his straw men down for him. Get him out of tight spots in a single bound. You're angling to know if I'm going off half-cocked to kick heads and break mothers' hearts.'

'Am I?' Vinnie ate a yawn. Rubbed his tender stump. 'Maybe . . .'

'Maybe nothing.'

'Then *talk* to me, damn it.'

'They feeding you enough? Look thin.'

Vinnie paled with sudden insight.

'Where are you, Charlie?'

'On the Road to Morocco with Crosby and Hope.'

Vinnie fought a wave of lassitude. Blinked to stay awake.

'I'm seeing something new, ain't I? You can see all the dealt cards, but you won't make the killing raise. You won't even call or ante. Why? Something's holding you all the way back.'

Charlie's face was unreadable.

'What pills are you popping, Vin? You'll see snakes inna wallpaper next.'

'Or the truth.'

'That old stuff? That fifteen yards jangled your brain.'

Vinnie sighted along his cigarette. Jabbed it forward. Awe in his voice.

'What got to you, Charlie? You ain't scared of nobody. Not God or taxes or little green men. Gotta be you're scared *for* somebody. For a *lot* of somebodies, for Chrissakes. That's bloody it.'

'That's bloody what?'

Vinnie stifled another yawn. Sat back with inverted eyes.

'Scared for me and the whole bloody firm. Well, well . . .'

Charlie turned. Glared out at silver light with more lumps crowding his throat. Thick cloud had rolled around the sun like a dark fist, and beams of metallic light speared down from knuckles of cumulus. Turned the brooding hills to petrified saurians. The river to a soft twist of dancing sequins.

'Don't like getting fond of things, Vin. They have this bad habit of getting lost. Getting dead. Anything gets close to me, gets hurt. Gets . . . gone. So, how I feel is how I feel. Nothing to be done about that. Just day following night, is all. Can't keep people inna vault like family heirlooms. But I can keep them away from me. Well away and safe. I'll have to do the business for Nasty and Soddy, but it won't bring nobody back to sup a pint or smell the daisies. Knock down one domino, you have to knock down the whole boxful. And the world's full of . . .'

Charlie stopped midsentence. Turned slowly. Vinnie's mouth had dropped open. His head lay against his shoulder, and his cigarette still smoked in his hand. Charlie dogged the butt under his heel and stood in the dusk to watch him sleep.

'Some father confessor you are,' he grunted. He wrapped the rug around Vinnie's thighs and tousled his damp hair. Took a Player from Vinnie's pack, and was turning it in his fingers when the wholesome nurse came to take her patient back to bed.

'We've had a hard but successful day,' she said, wheeling Vinnie away.

Charlie watched them go. Looked for matches he didn't carry.

'My day tomorrow,' he said, and took the unlit Player back to Froggy and the white Rolls.

On the way back to London, Armchair Doris came on the carphone to give Charlie an urgent message from Trooper Wells. Charlie told Froggy to make for Enfield, thinking of dominos with Chinese faces.

Enfield was a lot of nice houses trying to be a village in

198

the middle of suburban sprawl. There were neat lawns, Tudoresque frontages, and grass verges. Sodium lamps on concrete poles hadn't yet replaced the old cast-iron gas standards.

Hettie Wells answered the door to say Trooper was at the Lotus House, and for Charlie to get comfortable whilst she made coffee in her best china. She went off to the kitchen with Froggy offering to wash dishes for a sandwich, and Charlie pushed into the living room. It was a fussy clutter of glass ornaments and boxing trophies. Gas logs sent phoney flames up a chimney from a Georgian fireplace. Heavy furniture in orange brocade squabbled with the incredibly crimson carpet, and the violently patterned wallpaper was as busy as a traffic accident. Chinese Cyril sat in a floral chair with a face as jaundiced as a tungsten bulb, and forgot to shake hands.

Charlie found cigarettes in a carved box and struck a long wooden match on a brass elephant's serrated trunk. Sat by the fire and said, 'This why I didn't get a postcard of the Moulin Rouge?'

Cyril spread hands heavy with gold rings.

'You don't have to spank me, Chas. There's others who'll do that for you. Free, gratis, and smiling.'

Charlie lit a dry Rothmans and blew stale smoke.

'Raven got to you through Troop, them being mates. Now you're in the middle of the Snakes and Dragons. I could cry, you moron. Even if it does sound like a kids' boardgame.'

'You already know that? How?'

'Same way I know the moon ain't best gorgonzola. Same way I know this ain't tobacco I'm burning. I smoke this I'm dead, You, my son, are in a worse hole. Can't stub your troubles out.'

Cyril watched Charlie smear the cigarette to shreds.

'You know about the meet, then?'

'Not the where or when I don't.'

Cyril wiped his wet forehead. Looked at his damp palms.

'That's the crux of it, Chas. No venue. This is Thursday night. Fook wants the meet for Saturday. Some clever date on the Chinese calendar that's lucky, if you're into all that astrology tonk. And Micky only wanted to hold the meet at Fulham football ground. Him and his in the stands with shooters – Fook and Fatt down there on the pitch as naked as Godiva. Can you see them noshing that down like hot noodles? Course you can't. And that's me burning incense with the ancestors, ain't it?'

'So, you want what?'

'Fucking out, don't I? How about it, Chas? Ain't you got a packing-case about my size? A nice long sea-trip to somewhere?'

'Can't oblige, can I?'

'You ain't noing me? Not me.'

'You gave the big no to Raven's venue, but you ain't passed that item on to Fook or the other face.'

'You gotta crystal ball, or what?'

Charlie tapped his temple.

'Grey cells. The answer's as simple as you are. Get 'em a venue. Then pick up your marbles and walk away smartish.'

'Where do I get *that* wholesale? Woolworth's? Christ, Chas.'

'From me. Where else?'

Cyril stared. Wiped his face and left it as wet as before. Used his sleeve and soaked it.

'Look at me. I could water a lawn.'

'Or a grave.'

Cyril thumbed moisture from his eyes and groaned.

'How can I use a venue you hand me? Apart from each other, you're the kiddy they're constipated about. The bogeyman from the bog. Look, I trust you, Chas. Straight I do. But how can I trust you down that road?'

Charlie shrugged at the awful wallpaper.

'Ill have a cup of Hettie's tea, then. Leave you to it.'

'You can't just . . . *go*!'

200

Charlie's smile was a white knife. His eyes stones.

'Like you didn't go to Paris, Chinese?'

'So, I didn't listen. So break my legs.'

Charlie stayed silent. Waited.

Cyril stood. Looked at the ceiling and Trooper's trophies. Slumped back in his chair and revolved his hands on his wrists.

'This time I'm listening. *Really* listening.'

'With both ears pricked? Your brain sitting up like Rover? Not jumping about like the fleas on his back?'

'I've said, haven't I?'

'Right. Can you dog-paddle more than twenty-five yards?'

'Swam the mile at school. Can still stay under for four minutes. Got lungs like a whale.'

'Then I'll give you one guarantee, Chinese. I won't be within five miles of the place. That settle your feathers?'

Cyril tried a smile and liked it enough to keep it.

'Now *that*,' he said. '*That* stops my gut bubbling. Talk to me, Chas.'

Charlie laid it out in five short minutes, and had finished when Hettie brought coffee, tea, and dainty sandwiches with the crusts cut off. Cyril got in amongst them like a starving yellow dog, making Hettie cluck.

'First solids I've seen him take in a week, Chas. What have you said to the old prawn?'

'Just boys' talk, Het.'

'Don't try selling *me* Tower Bridge,' Hettie sniffed. 'Drink your tea before it gets cold.'

Charlie sipped stewed Typhoo, wanting an Irish and his bed.

'Whatever you say, Het . . .'

Cyril took sandwiches to the telephone and dialled Raven's hideaway at Fulham Reach. Talked with his mouth full, and didn't notice Charlie slip away.

Lemmon passed Bulstrode the port whilst Mac Stannard

inhaled a third helping of strawberry flan, and kissed Elizabeth goodnight when she excused herself. At the door she mouthed, 'Don't stay up all night', winked with a lewd pout, and went upstairs to exchange a modest black sheath for peach pyjamas. The smell of sandalwood haunted Lemmon as he forced himself back to irregular police work. Stannard had confirmed Fook's identity from Sodbonce's Polaroids, and had brought photographs of the Council of Seven for Lemmon's files.

They sat around the fire with their drinks. Stannard wondered why he was still a confirmed bachelor when there were meals like that in the world, and Bulstrode agreed that a diet of tinned pilchards and frozen peas was a hard price to pay for freedom. Lemmon murmured something polite and said, 'Just how do we nail these monkeys to the mast, Mac?'

'By due legal process, d'you mean, Theo?'

'By any means. Short of shooting them myself.'

Stannard raised a rusty brow over his iced soda water.

'And old Mac had Mr Clean pegged as an honest finikin of a copper. The devil drives, so needs must, eh?'

'Needs definitely must, Mac.'

'Aye, well, that minds me of a similar cleft stick I had my posterior in. Before I shook the dust for Hong Kong. I'd surveilled a Glasgow house for a week. Knew there were shooters in there. Knew there was a bank job planned, but I hadn't the clout to get a search warrant. The super was pulling me off the next day, and I was one desperate young copper. Had nothing to lose, so, I made two fast phonecalls. One to the local nick saying there was an affray outside the house I was watching. Made it sound good by panting like a scared civilian, and smashing a bottle against the wall. Then I called the bad bastards inside the house. Put on my thickest Gorbals accent. Aye. Told them to shift their sporrans fast, the police were on their way to raid the place. Worked as smooth as alabaster. My gang of beauties came out toting their hardware in cricket bags. I arrested two on the pavement, and had a third in an arm-lock when the marias turned up. They got the other two after a car chase. I nipped into the house, scooped up all the evidence I needed, fed it into one of the cricket bags, and let the uniforms "find" it down at the station. Never was credited for that collar, but I got five bad bastards off the streets, nonetheless. The super guessed what I'd done, but there was nought he could do about it. Except ream me out and make it very plain I was in a dead end on the force. And that suited me. Aye.'

'You tackled five armed nutters on your own?' Bulstrode asked.

Stannard's peat eyes darkened and crinkled to slits.

'I "arrested" the first two from behind. With my truncheon, laddie. And the third bastard never made children after I was through with him. You think I was born yesterday? I gave them no chance.'

'That's me told.' Bulstrode buried his nose in his glass.

'And that anecdote tells us what?' Lemmon said.

Stannard shrugged. Looked at his half-hunter.

'Is that the time? I'm lecturing at nine a.m.'

'Come on, Mac.'

Stannard put his watch away.

'The devil drives, *you* direct traffic. Young Buller there sees my point.'

'Do I, Sir?'

Stannard pointed a stubby finger.

'At your age, I'd have had a goodly stab at it, laddie. That makes one of us smart – the other more stupid than he needs to be. Ach, you get one of your own in amongst them. Plant a snout, or buy one of theirs. How d'you think we were tipped off about that heroin in the shipment of horse sperm? And how did we manage to see four of their couriers face-down in some dark alleys? We bought the information. Passed it on to some local pirates. Let them do the rest.

203

They kept half the heroin for services rendered. It's the way things are done over there in the colony.'

Lemmon refused a Capstan and Bulstrode lit up alone.

'This ain't the colony, Sir. We'd earn the big elbow like you did in Glasgow if we tried that.'

Stannard pinched his mouth with thumb and forefinger.

'I could say you were a little young to be thinking about your pension, laddie. But I won't, eh? Don't even let your belly growl at old Mac. You set a small thief to catch a bigger bandit. Smash the network like you would the legs of a spider. One at a time, working in towards the fat body. Use small men too weak to move outside their own territory. Let them poach from the big boys just the once. The worst that can happen is, they try to grab off the next chunk of bandit country. That leads to a bloody local feud, and they forget all else. The fight itself becomes all important. You've got what you want from the bastards, so you let them gobble each other up. Now d'you see where I'm driving, laddie buck?'

'On all cylinders, sir. Except the devil wouldn't drive with you as a passenger. Wouldn't dare turn his back. No disrespect, Mr Stannard.'

'None taken. You learn fast. You've got local villains ready to play with fire. Give 'em a box of matches and stand back. I would.'

Bulstrode blew smoke through his fist. Gnawed a knuckle. Went back to sitting opposite Vinnie Castle in Windmill Street. Heard again the specious morality Vinnie attributed to bloody Charlie Dance. How he'd laughed in Vinnie's face. How he despised himself for already having one foot in the gutter. Wondered how little it would take to muddy the other shoe as Lemmon said:

'You've got a mouth inside the Snake Tong, Mac? Actually inside?'

'Aye. He'll die the millionaire I'll never live to be. If he lives to collect.'

'Sounds a big if.'

'Aye. My guess is, he'll last to the New Year. Shouldn't have told you otherwise. And no, before you ask, we can't get him out, even if he wanted to. If we lifted him, they'd cut his heart out inside a week. But that'd save the colony money. Nobody pays a debt to a dead man, do they?'

Lemmon lit the cigarette he'd refused.

'And the good servant Stannard saves his masters bawbees and groats wherever he can. If the mouth's talking to you for a huge remuneration, what's to stop him selling to another Tong?'

'Nothing. Probably does.'

'To the Dragons? To this Pu Fatt fellow.'

'Aye, why not?'

'Get me to this informant of yours, Mac.'

Stannard found pictures in the fire. Shook his head.

'You wouldn't care to whisper a name?'

'I would not.'

'I need it, Mac.'

'And die with a morning-star in your throat? Be your age.'

'Give me something, Mac.'

'Advice, maybe.'

'I've had enough of that to last me—'

'Shut *up*, Theo.' Stannard got to his feet and drained his soda water. 'I've sung enough for my supper. Be like the baby bandits, stick to your own patch. I only lost a kidney. You they'd cut into Oxo cubes. Pass my regards to your wife. Are you going my way, young Buller? I came without my car.'

'Drop you anywhere, Sir.' Bulstrode finished his drink and said he'd see Lemmon at the office in the morning. He and Stannard talked until the dawn came up, and parted with a degree of understanding.

When they'd gone, Lemmon climbed the stairs to shower, and made a poor job of pleasing his wife. Elizabeth lay awake in the darkness and listened to him mutter in his

205

sleep. She had neglected him for far too long, and she planned to ferret his problems out at the earliest opportunity. Sometimes, listening was more efficacious than all the peach pyjamas in the world.

Micky Raven actually allowed Chinese Cyril to make his pitch without interruption. Said warmly, 'I'll buy that brahma bull of a crack, Chinese. And they'll go along with it, both Tongs? Nice one. You're at Troop's? Stay by the phone.'

Raven lit a cheroot. Admired the naked Eurasian girl on the bed under mirrors and a poster of a woman with a fifty-inch bosom. The black girl in the silver G-string hummed something ethnic from the Caribbean as she mixed cocktails at the small bar. Raven could personally vouch for them both being prime rib. And enthusiastic, a pleasant change from the usual dull cattle on his string. They had walked in to his office that afternoon after working cruise ships for a season. Offered their services with free samples. And with Chinese Cyril coming up with a tasty plan, Raven could smell roses around his door.

'You want the finale now, Mr Micky?' said the Eurasian girl. 'Me and Ebony gal make you the white meat in our sandwich.' Her smile showed a sliver of purple gum and a great many small white teeth.

'Put yourself back inna packet, Zuzu.' Raven dialled the Enfield number, got a yawning Hettie who put Cyril on. 'Just checking you're where you should be, Chinese. See you tomorrow.'

'Now, Micky man?'

Raven took a gin-fizz from Ebony. Rubbed a tender nostril with a sigh of regret.

'No time, girls. The Raphaels will fix you somewhere to stay until I decide which circuit you work. No Shepherd Market for you two lollipops. But get this – no naughty girl-to-girl stuff. Not on my firm.'

Ebony pointed her breasts like naval shells. Dry-spat at the fifty-inch bosom.

'We'me *straight*, white stuff.'

The rest of her speech was the vile rot of the charnal house.

Raven hid his surprise at such vehemence.

'You want proof?' Zuzu asked.

'Beaten by the clock. Gotta have it away home to my everloving. Where's my clothes?'

Raven finished his drink as the girls dressed him. Walked to his car and looked down the Thames towards the brewery.

'Two riverboats as a venue. Bloody genius, that. And I thought old Chinese Cyril was all rubbery chicken and no nouse.'

He drove home looking for flaws.

There weren't any.

Froggy was parking in Beak Street when the carphone rang. He listened with his face hardening, and handed the receiver to Charlie without a word.

'Chas, lovely boy?' Armchair Doris was close to tears. 'We lost Soddy, love. Matt says he went peaceful . . . in his sleep . . .'

'Full board meeting tomorrow morning. Pass the word, Doris.'

'Yes, Charlie . . .'

Froggy watched Charlie's eyes invert as he cradled the phone. Felt a flock of geese walk over his grave. Knowing full well what that look meant. Somebody had bought themselves a war.

CHAPTER EIGHT

The last Saturday of October was born in mist.

Mellowed by warm haze and pale autumnal shadow, it was a rare golden island in the darkening winter tides from Siberia. Soft falls of crisp copper leaves littered the emerald lawns, and the river spiked the balding trees with erratic brilliance.

The motherly nurse had wheeled Vinnie Castle into the sunny lee of the horse-chestnuts to doze or read the morning away before lunch and an afternoon of controlled strengthening exercises. His stump ached and the letter he'd started to Charlie Dance was a scatter of balled pages around his chair. He'd sat at this selfsame spot the day before when Sam and Margot brought fruit, magazines, and the news about Sodbonce. Then it had been damp and sunless, and he'd fallen between the parallel bars after they'd gone. His fists still ached from hammering the hard rubber mat in frustration, surprising nobody but himself by his outburst. Left alone to get over it in his own time, Vinnie had slept until the night-nurse brought hot sweet tea and her holiday snaps of Knossus in Crete. She talked about bull dancing and paying a pound for a Coke in the same breath, but she was company to kill the wee small hours with. Gave him time to marshal all the unformed thoughts he needed to make a cogent whole for Charlie. To somehow explain, and the result was a lot of scribble on wasted Basildon Bond.

'Keep Britain Tidy, you toerag.'

Bulstrode stood where Sam and Margot had the day before. Chewed on a Capstan and loosened his tie.

Vinnie squinted up at him, closing his writing pad.

'Why ain't you watching Spurs kick nine bells out of Liverpool? Or Arsenal at home to Chelsea? Even watching Fulham limp through ninety minutes is a better waste of time than coming to watch me doing not a lot, Buller.'

'Nice to feel wanted. I'll waste my day off any way I fancy, my feisty cock sparrow. The drive here was worth seeing your ugly face. Nice to see a bit of sun for a change.' Bulstrode gathered the discarded notepaper and dropped it into a wastebasket a ball at a time. Sat on a green bench with his jacket off. The warrant poking from his inside pocket was as white as a flag of surrender.

Vinnie pointed his chin at it.

'That my invitation to a private room in one of Her Majesty's houses of correction, or what?'

'Too nice a day to hurry, Vin. See how the water looks like bits of broken glass through them elms down there? Or bits of silver paper catching the light? Lovely country this. Best inna world. Not the sort of day to be locked in, is it?'

'Your twopence. Your imagery. Your bloody move.'

Bulstrode's expression was as lazy as the puffballs of cloud.

'We never have played chess, have we? Ought to have, I'd like to see what you'd do against a Yugoslav sacrifice in the King's Indian defence with you taking White.'

'Chess is for old men, or young men with thin blood. Clever fencing in black and white – no colour; as arid as the desert air. Play Charlie, he's thirty moves ahead in any game.'

Bulstrode leaned back to stare into pale blue haze.

'Thought his game was Chinese Checkers these days. And he ain't been making himself that visible around the manors, has he? Must be on the night-shift. He was here Thursday though. Saw his John Henry in the visitor's book. Where's he got the bodies buried, Vin?'

'Still your brass farthing, Buller.'

Bulstrode could have been talking to an invisible sky god.

'Micky Raven likes them at blood temperature. With nice round girly bits and willing ways. Photogenic rather than dead. Can't see him collecting cadavers like chess pawns, even though Chas got him well cosied up with the Tongs. Riding old Micky for a fall, is he? Yeah, I'd say so, it's his way, ain't it? Play out the rope and then pull it back hard enough to snap the old neckbone. He gets Micky to offer crowd-control to both sides when they make the exchange of bones and tribute. They buy it so the ceremonial ain't in any way tainted by either side playing fast and loose, and go home well happy. Except somehow that don't quite happen. They get disappointed, and Micky is up to his collarbone in a midden of shit. Makes sense to me, Vin.'

'That's one of us happy. You been at the magic mushrooms, or you been tripping on LSD?' Vinnie heard himself sneer as he raced to keep up with Bulstrode's dreamy delivery. 'That, or you took my ad—'

'Your *advice*, Vin. That's right. What I did. But you shouldn't bite your words off like that. Bad for the throat. Yeah, I've had long chats with a face who knows your Tongs from Hong Kong. A very erudite geezer. Filled in a lot of gaps in my knowledge, and that leaves me with all these questions I was too ignorant to ask before. Like: where the bodies are? Like: where's the meet? Like: what happens to you when it all goes nasty? You, old Armchair, ordinary faces like Matt and Froggy? What happened to Nasty's mortals? And what's gonna happen to Sodbonce's corpse if we don't guard it night and day? Those sorts of conundrums, Vinnie my son.'

Vinnie fumbled a cocktail Sobranie alight. Blew Turkish smoke down at his lap. 'Hope you've got answers. Me, I don't understand the questions.'

Bulstrode gazed at the sky. Hands behind his head.

'Not surprised,' he said. 'He's kept you well in the dark,

has Mr Dance, and you hate it. Charlie's right hand, and you don't know the talk from mutter. Sunning your one and a half legs like the end of the world ain't a spit and a jump down the motorway. Charlie Dance off doing what Charlie Dance does best – leaving you and the others staked out for the tiger like biblical goats.'

Vinnie flicked the pink cigarette away, and it lay on the lush grass like a severed finger. Saw Charlie in the dusk trying to talk as Vinnie sank into exhausted sleep.

'That's what he was trying to get at . . .'

Bulstrode turned his head. The unlit Capstan pasted to his lip.

'Who was?'

'The jolly green giant. You wouldn't know him.'

'Try me.'

'Like you're trying me? Stroll on, Buller.'

'And now you're *smiling*? Giving half of Buckinghamshire the fat Cheshire Cat with enough teeth for two grown men? Wipe it off, it's obscene.'

'You put it there, Buller. You'd cheer up a corpse.'

'There's three of *them* I'd like back for burial, Mr Castle.'

'That's your fur coat. You scratch it.'

Vinnie ignored the pain in his stump. The terminal itch in his missing foot. Charlie had been through all the gears circling the problem, but Sodbonce dying had put him into overdrive. He *was* scared for everybody but himself. Vinnie selected a red Sobranie and the gold band glowed as he screwed it into his mouth.

'Where'd you get them tart's parlour fags? Like kids crayons.'

'An admirer. Jealous?'

'Smell like Solomon's brothel.'

'Or a remand cell, Buller? That what you've in mind for me?

'Safer than here, son.'

211

'If I'm nicked, where're the uniforms to back up the warrant?'

'In the car. Or the canteen, And who's nicked? Protective custody, right?'

Vinnie's smile was genuine.

'Play that on a stringless banjo. Once I'm protected, there's a Mauser pistol you want explained. *Right*?'

'That's well down the road. Forget it.'

'Have *you*?'

'Not what you might call *exactly*, no.'

'So that's the charge I'm collared on if I tell you where to put your protective custody.'

'You telling me that?'

'Who else gets your baby-sitting service? Armchair? Matt? Froggy? Ollie Oliphant or Pimlico Parsons? Soddy's mortals? How far are you going with this farce?'

'All the way, Vin. Everybody we can scoop. The whole squad's out.'

'And Charlie? Him too?'

Bulstrode laid a flame to his Capstan and leaned to light the red Sobranie. Folded his arms behind his neck and watched the hard sparkle through the elms.

'More like diamonds than cheap glitter, come to think of it,' he said in a long stream of smoke. 'Don't you think?'

'You know what I think, filth.'

'I know what you think, yeah. You've kicked me in the balls, put the boot in when I knee the cobbles, and then got nasty about it. Only trouble is, you wouldn't even do that if you had two feet to use on my tender young body.'

'That gun's worth no more than two years suspended, and you know it.'

'Still a collar. Show the top brass I'm a boy to watch.'

'Elephant doody, Bulstrode. You figure to leave Chas out there on his own. Hoping he comes well unstuck. Hoping he'll go down and dirty, and maybe bring Raven and them

212

yellow jobs out into the open where your boy scouts can have an easy pop at them. Jelly on a plate.'

'Good here, ain't it?' Bulstrode said comfortably.

'You couldn't arrest a bloody dead man.'

'You wanna give me Charlie, Vin?'

'In your ear I do.'

'That's it then,' said Bulstrode. 'Out of my hands. You want a push to the car?'

The man from Hamburg was buying steel for the Indian Government when Charlie arrived; five miles of an axed railway spur in Wales, and a metallurgist's analysis lay beside the client's specifications on his huge desk. He waved Charlie into a chair with an Irish, closed the deal in halting Hindi, and poured himself a schnapps.

'Next year, they'll need steam rolling stock. We should be buying it in now, Charlie. What British Railways put into museums or sell as scrap, they run as a passenger service.'

Dusty sunlight made his hairless scalp shine as his small fat mouth tasted yet more profit. Charlie crossed a leg and made a negative face.

'When we've closed the arms deal with De Wit you can buy all the train sets you like. It'll take you that long to get straight export licenses. Too many train-spotting vicars talking preservation of heritage to take chances, Herman.'

The man from Hamburg wrote himself an *aide memoire* to that effect.

'You could make millions as an honest broker, Charlie. Give up your other . . . business.'

'And die of boredom. You got something for me?'

'Arrived yesterday. Very small, very expensive.'

'To the power of ten, Herman? Am I paying for quality, or you not liking being so close to the stuff?'

Herman laced thick fingers on his blotter.

'To be honest, both. I am not like the other *herrenvolk*,

213

passing as Austrian or Swiss. If I convince Special Branch I am no nazi, I automatically become an agent of the Muscovites. In Bolivia, in Cape Town, I am a German expatriate. Here, I'm a bloody kraut. Even the Israelis treat me better. They are the true realists.'

Charlie swallowed Irish. Refused a smoke.

'And if you had to choose between love and profit?'

Herman wagged an unlaced finger.

'You know my weakness. What is hatred, but a small surcharge? I will get your samples.'

Charlie watched him grunt as he folded over his belly to open a safe. The folds at the back of his thick neck pinked up as he straightened and turned with a small complimentary airline bag given free to first-class travellers. He sat with another grunt, unzipped the bag and laid the black devices in front of Charlie with extreme care. The plastic explosive was in three grey slabs and looked like dirty uncooked dough. The contact switches were the size of dice, the wires were thin filaments of plasticated copper, and the priming needles were similar to rounds of ·38 ammunition.

'With this equippage,' Herman said in his overly precise English. 'You could blow a red London bus to Galveston, Texas. A four-storey house to nothing larger than a sixpence. But I don't have to practise my salesmanship on such as you, my friend. It is exactly what you asked for.'

Charlie spun a timer on its axis. Watched it revolve to a halt.

'Only one pop at this, *friend*.'

'The reason I've supplied double the number of needles. One might fail; a million to one chance, but two? Never. I am usually an incurious man, but here in the London that hates me, it pays me to be cautious. When should I make certain I am surrounded by impartial witnesses to vouch for my whereabouts?'

Charlie eased the plastic slabs into an overcoat pocket. The rest into his waistcoat and jacket.

214

'Tonight might be a good time to get soup in your lap at the Savoy. Calling the head waiter a dumkopf usually turns heads. Dine about eight and tread on some toes on the dance floor.'

Herman looked genuinely shocked. Slapped a meaty palm to his meatier forehead.

'The Savoy? But I am known there. No, no, it will have to be Claridges.'

'Same meat, different gravy.'

Charlie took the stairs to the street. Strolled through the subway to Charing Cross and John Adam Street. Stavros bolted him in and waved his arms a lot, his sweat stale with funk. The heavy filth had turned him over that morning without a smile. Stavros had Armchair Doris safe in a back room, but Lemmon had Froggy in an armlock and had impounded the white Rolls.

'What I do, Mr Charlie? What?'

'Steal a teabag. Put the kettle on, what else?'

'You iron, Mr Charlie. You stone. You harder than that man on Nelson's column. You . . .'

'Thirsty. Get that gas lit.'

Stavros waddled away and Charlie stood surrounded by pornography.

Thinking.

Aman Lee Fook left the ornate scroll on his desk, walked away from Pu Fatt's honeyed words, and drew damask curtains to admire his view of Hampstead Heath. The house commanded the high crossroads, secure behind a walled garden and heavily scrolled iron gates. The Whitestone Pond was a still mirror reflecting the bronze fret of beech, and the Vale of Health fell east into pale morning mist. The Spaniard's Inn was a white clapboard pennant in the coppery oaks above Bishop's Avenue and the playing fields of Highgate School. Kenwood speared the northern horizon with pine, oak, and elm, and russet folds of grass, bracken,

215

and beechmast rolled west to the neatness of Hampstead Garden Suburb. Beyond, the sheer upward thrust of Muswell Hill was a ghostly pyramid pastelled by winter haze.

Fook felt Wind at his side without turning. Jasmine scented her thick hair as he fondled the shining weight of it, running his hand to where it fell to her waist. Felt his fingers tingle with static from the hundred brushstrokes of her morning toilet. Dug his fingers deep to add the sensually tactile to the stimulus of natural beauty. Used it to push the words of Pu Fatt away and away, spinning them down to a distant image caught in the single jewelled facet of a crystal prism. Small words from a man who would be great. A man who feared losing face because he must pay tribute to a rival T'ang for his brother's bones. Rather would he bargain, trade body for body, to save his foolish pride.

Pu Fatt had no substance. Beneath the eloquent phrases was an emptiness of spirit, a void the man filled with vapid egotism. His core was nothing but superheated vapour that would turn to water when cooled, but it could scald the unwary hand reaching to lift his boiled pot from the fire of life. Fook wanted his hands on the fat throat. To take bamboo flaying knives to his bloated carcass. Watch his ribs being opened into a bloody spread eagle for Fook to take the living heart . . .

There was a low hissing. Wind's face was scraped bone. Fook's fist had twisted in her thick hair to cause her agony. Even though Fook could do what he would with her, he had never willingly hurt the girl, and wished he could show contrition without losing face. The thought made him laugh inwardly; he was as trapped by feudal concepts as his enemy, and he stroked Wind's disordered hair with a gentle palm. A single tear had formed on her cheek, and he took it on a fingertip and licked it away. Tasted salt. There was no need for words to show his profound regret. The simple mime said it all.

Back at his desk, he dismissed Wind and studied the

scroll. An exchange of bones *was* more honourable than accepting gold as tribute. Even thinking like a base merchant, two bodies for one was not an ungenerous arrangement, weighing heavily in Fook's favour. The man Raven had finally come up with a suitable point of exchange, and Fook would have the opportunity of studying Pu Fatt across a narrow stretch of water. There was no reason to delay further. He, Fook, the Supreme Snake, would accept the terms of settlement. All that was now required was a suitably drafted reply, and he drew a writing tablet towards him to compose it in the correct form and metre. His words of fire would reduce Pu Fatt's formal language to guttering embers – to spitballs hissing to nothing on the hearthstone of his blazing eloquence. And when he had made a fair copy, he would have his messenger deliver it a bare hour before Pu Fatt was due to embark from Westminster Pier. The wait would open his pores to let some of the fat out of his belly.

Smiling, Fook wrote with serene confidence.

'Uncle Theo working the weekend? What's the charge, then?'

'Sit *down*, Oliphant.'

'And you calm it, bear's breath.'

Ollie Oliphant resisted being pushed into a chair. Shot his cuffs at Dillman and sat as if he wanted to. Crossed a knee, and looked around the Command Room like a Punch and Judy man checking his puppets.

Lemmon looked his most avuncular behind his scarred desk. Payne typed one-handed by the window, and the new man Taggart shared his notebook with Dillman. Ollie saw Froggy, Pimlico and Matt sitting in a row beside him, and two empty chairs showed the filth expected a couple more collars. Ollie hid a worried smile lighting a Pall Mall he didn't really want.

'Anybody made the one phonecall yet?' Ollie asked nobody in particular.

'Speak when you're spoken to,' Taggart snapped.

'Listen to Oliver Twist whistle for more.' Ollie gave Froggy the gentle elbow. 'See they ain't collared the *real* desperado, Frog.'

'Chas?' Froggy mouthed behind a hand.

'No, you pilchard. Old Armchair. Hear she does a naughty line in green shield stamps. Shocking, Frog, shocking.'

Froggy accepted a Pall Mall. 'Desperate old bat. I'm being spanked for parking on a double yellow line. Only thing I was driving was my size nine wide-fitting suedes.'

Ollie leaned out to skim his cigarettes. 'And you, Pim?'

'Wearing pyjamas in bed. Owning a canary without a license. Who knows with this bunch of comedians?'

Matt looked down at his shoes.

'Got a stand ticket for Highbury this afternoon. Drinks inna director's bar with the players after the match. They pulled *me* for obstructing traffic. Know where I was? Weeding me mother's bit of garden. She caught that Dillman a right crack with her spade, though. Didn't know the old lady knew such language.'

Ollie flicked ash over Taggart's shoe.

'So, nobody's phoned the brief. Had words with J.C. Hatton.'

Froggy jerked a thumb at Commander Lemmon.

'The *führer* there reckons the lines are dead. The GPO playing silly buggers.'

Ollie smiled at Lemmon. Tutted through smoke.

'That chestnut's got hair on it. The GPO working a Saturday? Any Saturday? Rarer than duck's eggs hatching Derby winners. Now whaddaya say, Mr Lemmon? Let's cut the heavy kid and talk to the adults in the crowd?'

Lemmon wreathed himself in smoke. Smiled at a framed photograph of his wife. Said nothing in patient silence.

'Waiting for a full house before he does Hamlet,' Matt told his shoes. 'The Student Prince ain't here. You see Bulstrode doing a chorus of 'The Road to Mandalay'?

Gotta be because he's on the road to Stoke Mandeville.'

Ollie kicked himself for not working that one out for himself. Vinnie and old Armchair made a full set. Lemmon hadn't split the firm up to sweat them solo in separate interview rooms, so he was happy just pulling them off the street. Leaving Charlie Dance on his lonesome ownsome. Lemmon was either fishing in hope, or he had the Dance firm by the short and curlies. The only way to play this game was to sit it out, give nothing away.

'Got a thirst on me like Lot's wife,' Pimlico said.

'Don't break my heart,' Matt sighed. 'All them free drinks at Highbury going begging for want of me and an empty glass. That's one hangover I won't get to stick in my scrapbook. Tragic.'

Ollie nudged Froggy into Matt and Pimlico to draw their eyes.

'A good thirst needs building, lads. It's a known fact you get all the old dregs supping at lunchtime. Evening tipples are favourite. You've got a man's swallow, and the new barrels are on tap. None of your ullage dosed with aspirin and lemonade. Just your best sparkling ale. My old dad was a publican for thirty years, so you're hearing it from someone ain't the north end of a drayman's horse.'

'Bloody know-all, ain't you, Oliphant?' Taggart sneered.

Ollie's smile dimpled. He loved a new copper feeling his way with bluster, and this one was tailored for his brand of honed wit.

'Yeah, you'd be a boy who knows his lemonade, Taggart. Too much man for me, sonny. A sip of warm sarsaparilla, I'm on my back for a sweetheart like you. Ask Uncle Theo to give us a nice empty cell to romp in. We could play hide the sausage, and mine wins prizes. Come out through the top of your boy scout hat if I got in behind you. Wanna play, *Lemonade*?'

Taggart blushed beetroot and trembled like an aspen.

Ollie blew him a wet kiss. Needling Taggart over the edge.

219

'My sister's got a mouth like that,' he said. 'Only her moustache spoils it a bit. But what a goer. Roll your shirt up your back and count your ribs with a tuning fork. Leave you on the mattress in little pink bubbles. Take a week before they all went pop. All yours for a few copper coins. You can have us both for ten shillings cash money. Tell you what, *Lemonade—*'

Lemmon rapped his desk.

'Game, set and match, Oliphant. Taggart, a tray of teas from the canteen. Now.'

Taggart went away down the passage and sent flinty echoes up the stairwell. The lift whined in the shaft and pigeons cooed from the coping outside the window.

'No sense of the humorous, the young filth,' Ollie sighed.

'He'll learn,' said Lemmon.

'Not before we all die of boredom.'

'Bored you won't be,' Lemmon promised.

'Afternoon all.' Bulstrode wheeled Vinnie Castle into the Command Room as if on cue.

'And sounds a long one.' Ollie counted his cigarettes. Rationing himself.

'Bang goes Highbury,' Matt told his brogues.

'And my pint.' Pimlico figured Charlie had set things up the night before because he knew this might happen. Pimlico nursed the uncomfortable thought like a grudge.

Wondering.

Fook's messenger arrived at Leicester Square at dusk. The cold air was welcome after the stuffy train packed with Liverpool supporters coming west to celebrate. The news-vendors had abandoned their pitches for a pint and a warm, and the buskers worked the cinema queues like a Royal Command Performance. He took a turn around the square to see if he was tailed, the scroll addressed to Pu Fatt snug inside his quilted jacket. He made sure with a second circuit, ducked through the Swiss Centre, and made his way up

Lower Wardour Street. To run this errand had less honour than protecting the Supreme Snake, and he thought he could get to Greenwich Pier before Fook if he was both quick and cautious.

Fifty yards from Gerrard Street, he melted into a shop doorway to check his rear and the way ahead. Two youths shared a joint in the entrance to the Whisky-a-Go-Go, and a huddle of derelicts shared a communal bottle outside a sex-aid shop on the corner. One was a gross woman with a rusty perambulator, and her terrier slept with twitching legs, chasing rabbits in a canine dream. She fed wine to the man she held up against the wall. Dribbled it down his chin as he swore in feeble monotone. That made the woman laugh, and her pink bedroom slippers were gay shouts of vivid colour, in direct contrast to her drab hat and greasy topcoat. She would have a bad smell, he knew, and the men would beg if he lingered near them for too long.

Fook's messenger made his move. Crossed the road to turn the corner, giving the drunks a wide berth. The woman lurched out to maul his sleeve. Begged for money in a low whine. He shrugged her off, pushing her back against the old pram. The dog woke up to growl. Got his teeth into the messenger's trouser cuff and set his legs to hold him. The messenger brought up his free foot to make a killing stamp as the man came off the wall too fast for an alcoholic. The bottle went into his ribs with a twisting stab, and the messenger gasped for air too solid to inhale. His killing stamp turned to water as he recognised the hard slate eyes. Going down on one knee, his arms crossed in the crab defence as a chopping palm took him in the side of the neck. Blood exploded from his ear, and the dog pulled him off balance, aborting the killing kick he aimed up into Charlie's scrotum. A fist mashed his throat, and he registered the death-blow as spangles of rushing nothing.

The pavement came up at his dying face in a long loop of discordant sound that chopped off as he was caught under the armpits. Heaved into the perambulator, his legs were folded against his chest, and a blanket smelling of dog stole the last of his breath. Bundles of old clothes were piled over the body, and Armchair Doris wheeled it away to the waste ground behind St Anne's church.

Charlie passed the bottle to the real drunks. Gave them enough money to keep them mindless for a week, and wove down Gerrard Street to feign sleep outside an oriental provisions store. He was there an hour later, and Pu Fatt ignored him as he left for Westminster Pier in a car driven by Chinese Cyril. When Charlie was sure they would not turn back, he used Joe Yellow's keys to let himself into the store. Stood in darkness with a cat sniffing his shoes.

Listening.

Then he went to work, one ear cocked for the squeak of Armchair Doris's borrowed perambulator.

The radio snapped, 'Talk to me,' in Raven's voice.

Chinese Cyril sent 'Wait', and waited himself.

The dragons were coming ashore after searching the pleasure-boat, and Pu Fatt stood apart with the tribute casket. It was slack tide, and a lazy slop rolled about the landing stage. The Houses of Parliament showed lights for an all-night session, and the rising moon had a hard silver halo.

To Chinese Cyril that meant nothing, to Pu Fatt it was the omen of good fortune predicted by his astrologer. The captain of the *Princess Alexandra* knew it meant snow or a hard frost, and was impatient to leave. Being well-paid was handsome, but this whole business smelled, and he wanted it over and done with.

If two daft Chinamen wanted to meet in mid-river to exchange boxes and put a nice earner in his pocket, fine; but he didn't want to manoeuvre on a turning tide. The Thames could get naughty when it wanted to, and heaving-to alongside the *Princess Mary* halfway between Westminster

222

and Greenwich was a risky old business if you didn't know which end was up. The cross-currents could whirl you down to Woolwich and shove your nose into the foreshore bend before you could kiss your ticket goodbye. And all this security was getting right up his bloody fingernails.

Pu Fatt sent his men up to the car. 'We leave now,' he said.

The dragons would drive to Greenwich and be there when Pu came ashore, just as Fook's shadows would come to Westminster by road.

'About time.' The captain went up to the bridge as his boys stood by the lines.

Cyril told Raven to wait again as the radio huffed expletives.

'We? But I thought—'

'You go with me,' said Pu. 'Someone must go between the Snake and the Dragon. You are the herald. Tell them that.'

'You get that, Micky?' Cyril asked the radio.

'In spades. I've got a nod from my man, so come ahead.'

'In the middle again,' Cyril grumbled to himself, plodding after Pu Fatt. From the wide bow he watched Westminster Pier go astern, his stomach turning acid. No wonder Charles asked him if he could swim. He might well have to.

The council chamber was as Joe Yellow described it.

Hanging lanterns casting pink light, seven chairs around a circular table. Seven Sacred Wind Dragons defending the Heavenly Sky Gates on one wall. The magnificent teak door inlaid with ebony and ivory, and the secret way behind a hanging silk drape sewn with ornate ideograms. A rich Chinese carpet worth a grand a square inch, and tall bronze incense stands stinking of the stuff although unlit. The air was as pungent as an unopened tomb.

Charlie carried the corpse up from the store and sat it in Pu Fatt's chair. Arranged the limbs naturally. Gave the dead

223

mouth a cigarette, the grey trilby a rakish tilt. Laid the cold hands on the arms of the chair, and made a perfect spear of the handkerchief in the breast pocket.

Was standing back to take a last critical look when he felt the slight draught on the back of his neck. The hiss of silk falling back into place. Sensed the silent footfall behind him, and went down on bended knees to make a low swivelling turn. The blow that would have broken his neck hit air, and the hard grunt of effort made a damp explosion near his forehead.

Charlie ducked and feinted and moved.

Glimpsed a turning thigh before it glanced off his skull to make a chair jump into the table. Dug a savage left into a crotch as it leapt away. A punch that skated instead of crippling. Took a mantis chop to his barely healed shoulder and parried a like blow to his ear. Hooked a right into a muscular chest. Slammed the young dragon into hopping retreat and came up on his toes.

Saw a face from St Anne's Court without a hatchet to wield. The hatred and contempt was there; the fanaticism. The need to inflict pain for its own sake. Saw again Soddy holding bloody tripe. Nasty wandering away to die like a gentleman, no trouble to his friends.

The dragon blurred. Spun at Charlie in a flurry of blows.

Charlie let him come. Countered scorpion stings on blocking forearms. Took the scrape of a phoenix along his jaw. Jumped in with a feinting block and smothered the kick of the emperor's horse between the scissor of rib and arm. Trapped the extended ham. Put a twisting lock against the joint and punched down to dislocate the kneecap. Heard it pop and had an elbow numbed by a scything hornet.

The dragon wormed free and staggered. Charlie bowed and rose. Put a hip into a rising crotch. Felt the softness there grind on bone and burst. Saw the slanted eyes open in shock. Stepped across the falling dragon to kneedrop the supine face. Mashed nose cartilage. Stood away and measured a short kick to the knotted jaw.

The snap of the fracturing bone was the brittle crush of cereal.

Charlie made sure of his man with a heel to the throat. Sagged against the table to catch his breath. The Chinese stared at a hanging lantern without seeing it, a dying nerve tapping an index finger on the carpet. When that stopped, there was just Charlie's breathing in the stuffy chamber. He looked at the dead man in Pu's chair. Winked and said he hoped the ringside seat was to his liking. Shed fatigue, checked his watch, and connected the circuits he'd laid. Hauled the Chinese into the passage behind the drapes, and went below to wait for Pu Fatt. Armchair Doris would make the terrier bark when the car drew up, then wait for Charlie in the Bedford truck parked behind St Anne's church.

The cat watched Charlie wait from the top shelf. Purring.

Chinese Cyril caught the warp thrown from the *Princess Mary* and tied it off to a stern bollard. As both craft used their engines to keep station, he ran to secure the forward line. Both craft cut their throttles and sawed on the ropes as they settled in the slack seaward ebb. The captain of the *Princess Alexandra* told Cyril: 'Your Charlie Chans have got ten minutes. Then we let go, no arguments.'

Cyril pointed a finger over a fist.

'And if I say we go sooner, we go.'

'Suits me.' The captain shut himself in his wheelhouse.

The wind brought the rich smell of the old spice warehouses, and the full moon silvered the river swell with slick runs of mercury.

Fook had stationed himself amidships on the *Princess Mary*, and his mourning robe was a hard white scream against the dark upperworks. Cyril called Pu Fatt, and he emerged from the unlit saloon in a long white robe, the full sleeves trimmed with gold. Walked along to the waist to

225

stare across at Fook. They both bowed low and stayed low, and Pu Fatt said, 'Begin.'

Cyril gabbled the words drummed into him on the trip downriver. Got through the formal address to both parties with a couple of minor stumbles, and heard their grunts of acceptance with relief. Bowed to both men when they straightened again, and took the tribute casket from Pu Fatt. Crossed to the *Princess Mary* and laid it on the deck at Fook's feet. Rolled away the prayer shawl draping it, and opened the lid to show Fook the sovereigns inside. Wished he had a good handful of them to back the fast ponies as he straightened to receive the funerary casket on Pu Fatt's behalf.

Fook's 'No!' was a spit of venom.

Cyril stood back. Let his hands fall, startled and repelled by Fook's contorted face. The man had the look of a spitting cobra, and spittle gummed his working mouth. Many of the words he used were lost in hiss, but his hatred made his meaning clear. Then Pu Fatt was bellowing back in gutter Cantonese.

'Who lies, you flyblown turd? This is what was agreed, you crawling dung-beetle. Bones for bones? What bones? Your words are toads, your spit is urine. There is your gold, midden roach. Take it. Take your usurer's coin.'

As they traded insults, Cyril backed along the thwarts. Caught a heel against a stanchion chain, and sprawled to clap his head on an aisle seat. Cradling his head, he kicked himself away to the stern of the *Princess Mary*.

'Here are your bones, tongue of a sodomite!'

Fook held the funerary casket high. Braced his arms, and threw it over the side.

Pu Fatt's cry was a tear in rich cambric.

Cyril's overcoat snagged on a deck-bit, and the warp holding the stern to the *Princess Alexandra*'s bow burned the back of his neck. He fumbled to free the knots. Yelled to attract the captain of the *Princess Alexandra*, but saw he was mesmerised by the screaming match. The casket hit the water, bobbed, and turned in the quickening seaward race. Floating away towards the open sea, it trailed its prayer shawl like a fanciful tail.

Pu Fatt had thrown himself at the rail. Drew himself along it, following the course of the box holding his brother's bones.

'And *this*, king of ordure!'

Fook took up the casket of sovereigns. Drew Pu Fatt's attention, and saw him flinch as the casket was held above Fook's head. Saw fear as Pu Fatt forgot the bones that had been so precious to him bare moments before. Kept his hold on the casket with a supreme effort when he realised what Pu Fatt had done. Hurled the booby-trapped box away from him, aiming for Pu Fatt. The casket turned in the air to shower the decks with coins, struck the rail near the shrinking Pu Fatt, skidded away along the gunwhale, and went into the river just feet from the *Princess Alexandra*'s bow. Turned over and sank.

Pu Fatt threw himself flat.

Cyril had the warp free. He ducked along the port side of the saloon to stay away from Fook. Shouted to the skipper to make weigh as he pounded past the wheelhouse. Heard the engines growl as he fell over the bowline, and lost a nail trying to free it from the bollard. The *Princess Mary* was yawing, opening a gap between the two vessels, all the strain on the warp Cyril was trying to release.

There was a dull *whump* that threw the deck up at him. Canting with slow deliberation, the deck took a steep list, and bowled Cyril away to slam him into the port rail. Hanging there, he saw the river rise in a great grey hump. It burst open to throw great white streamers into the moonlight, and muddy orange spits of fire grew into spirals of stinking smoke. Water fell in a solid wall across the *Princess Mary*, the bow warp parted as sound cannoned Cyril's ears, and a scour of boiling water washed him overboard.

There was cold and silence. He was in undertow that wanted his heavy camelhair coat, his shoes and him. The pain in his chest was too much air in his lungs, and he unlocked his jaw enough to stream some away. Somehow he was out of the clinging folds, had kicked off his shoes. Found good air to dribble out slowly, and let natural bouyancy take him up and up and up . . .

He was in moonlight and lapping water. Coughing scum and treading water. Widening ripples rode over his shoulders, surfed around his face. A ball of thinning smoke drifted downriver, and the riding lights of both pleasure-craft were receding glow worms. There was just Cyril and the river, and the outgoing tide took him east into sudden undertow. He struck out for the north foreshore and made no headway, the tide had him, and there was no fighting it. Cyril lay on his back and went with the flow, wondering if he'd drown before dying of hypothermia. Thought he had enough fat to keep him afloat and warm, and hoped the current would turn him into one of the river bends . . .

'What occurred, for Chrissake?'

Aman Lee Fook shrugged Raven and his question aside. Stepped ashore giving orders in Mandarin. Balled up the ruined mourning robe and threw it to one of his men as Raven blocked his path.

'Talk, mister. Where's Cyril? We heard the bang.'

Fook struggled to think in English. The words came out all bitten off.

'Back there. Dead. Who knows? Take care of the boat driver. He has a radio. You want the river police here?'

Raven told Big Alphonse to use knuckles or fivers to make the captain see sense. Sent Rupert to make sure he did. Said, 'The fat dragon pulled a flanker, that it? Would you let me search him and his box of tricks? No. And that puts us right here. Fucking nowhere.'

Fook's face was suffused saffron streaked with mud.

'A bomb in the tribute. I . . . finish it. Tonight. In Gerrard Street.'

Raven showed hard palms. Used his height to dwarf Fook.

'Alone, you ain't got the clout. It's on Dance's turf too. You want a war there, you've got the dragons *and* Dance. Without me and mine, you go down. All the way down.'

Fook sneered with glittering eyes.

'You want . . . bargain.'

'I want just that. I make one with you all the way, you go all the way inna East End with me. You never cross East India Dock Road without I say so. You back me when I give the local families a real serious spanking.'

The dragon has a thousand heads, you know this? You cut off a head now, you're children's children will still be dragon slayers. You can swear this?'

Raven bared teeth, not really understanding. Thought Fook was giving out adult fairy tales because he was shaken stupid by the near miss with ten pounds of gelignite.

'You want Micky Raven's word, you got it. You want the fat man's head on a stick, we'll give it to you.'

'Tonight. Now.'

Raven snapped fingers and Vito Raphael slapped a sawn-off in his hand. 'You just bought yourself a war.'

'We do it,' Fook said simply.

Charlie heard the terrier bark as tyres squealed against the kerb. He coaxed the cat from her shelf, and stroked her as he waited. Armchair Doris wheeled her perambulator away, and Pu Fatt crossed the pavement to throw his shoulder against the storeroom door. Charlie swung it open and dropped the cat at Pu Fatt's feet, tripping him. Pu Fatt stumbled against a shelf and the cat streaked away down Gerrard Street. Too furious to make more of it, Pu Fatt made for the stairs to the council chamber with his dragons on his heels. When they had gone through the hanging curtain, Charlie let himself out, closing the door very quietly. Dropped the filthy hat and coat into a dustbin, and strolled after Doris. Humming.

The undertow was a great wet mouth.

Swallowed by a savage eddy of cross-current, Chinese Cyril was drawn deep into choking, polluted water. The falling tide had scoured silt from the rising mudbanks, and Cyril tasted rotted mulch as he was bowled over in fouled turmoil. His foot touched sucking mud, and he had the presence of mind not to kick out at it, knowing it would have held him down until he drowned. His head boomed against iron, and he surfaced in the swill of a rusting lighter buoy. There was no purchase for his fingers on the slimy surfaces, and he was swept on in the turbulent central channel with the distant river banks skimming past as fast as a man could run.

Cyril struck out to keep his head above water, and his arm hit something hard and angular. Swept into it by the turning overfalls, he grasped it and hung on. Folds of sodden material pasted themselves to his face, and he tore them away to draw breath. Saw Chinese characters before the prayer shawl was swirled away, and held on to the box, knowing he kept company with Ho Fatt's bones. Together, he and the casket went into the Woolwich reach and the deeper waters beyond, and Cyril could see himself breakfasting on cockles in Canvey Island. If he lived.

Pu Fatt's ears still rang from the explosion.

Silencing the captain of the *Princess Alexandra* had been a simple matter of offering him the sovereigns scattered on the bow deck. Apart from a bent rail and some chipped paint, there had been no other damage to the pleasure-craft. The dragons had merely reinforced the point with their slow, hard looks when they boarded at Greenwich. With the *Princess Mary* beating upriver against the tide, there was no doubt in Pu Fatt's mind that he would be back in Soho before Fook docked at Westminster Pier. But he must still think and act quickly.

The Supreme Snake had survived the bomb despite the astrologer's confident prediction to the contrary, and that meant Pu Fatt must address himself to the pressing matter of survival. Using the sacred ceremony of exchange to work murder, Pu had made himself outcast and, only the dragons who'd sworn fealty to his person would still obey him. The rest of the council would already be planning to throw themselves on the mercy of the Sichuen Dragon. Pu Fatt could see them pointing him out as the sole author of the recent disasters. How different it would have been if the assassination attempt had been successful. Pu Fatt could easily have made them believe Fook had died by his own hand trying to kill him, for a corpse could not have borne witness against his word. Nor could the halfbreed if he had also died in the blast.

The car made a fast turn into Gerrard Street. Pu Fatt wiped river mud from his face and left the car to shoulder the storeroom door. Tripped over Joe Yellow's cat and booted it into the street. If it returned, he would kill it with slow strangulation. Post the corpse to the deaf man's mother. A small pleasure that must wait.

Ripping aside the hanging curtain, Pu Fatt took the stairs at a run, calling his men to hurry. They must all cross to the Irish Republic, fly from Dublin to the Continent, and make their way to Hong Kong from there. It was an escape route Pu Fatt had plotted for such an unlikely eventuality as this, and it was imperative he had the ear of the Sichuen Dragon before the rest of the council.

He pushed into the council chamber and stopped dead. First smelling the sweet corruption of human flesh, then seeing the man sitting in his chair. The unlit cigarette pointing from a twisted smile that was the sardonic rictus of death. The milky eyes staring sightlessly.

Pu Fatt took a step back to cannon into the dragons piling in behind him. Jogged forward, Pu Fatt slapped his palms on the circular table, and was trading looks with Nasty Nostrils' corpse when the storeroom blew itself apart. Heat and blast came up the stairs in a boil of acrid yellow smoke. Created a vacuum on the landing, and sucking one of the dragons into the fire, slammed the teak door closed. The secondary contacts completed their circuit, and Nasty Nostrils rose to embrace Pu Fatt before they were both blown through the roof as splinters of bone and spinning gobbets of flesh.

'A black rat. Hide the shooters.'

Micky Raven braked as a motorcycle cop flagged him down on the turn into Lower Wardour Street. A fire-engine came in from Shaftesbury Avenue, mounted the pavement and roared off towards Gerrard Street, its bell drowning the cop's directions.

'Do what, constable?' Raven asked, seeing hoses and firemen all over the intersection.

'There's a fire. Probably a gas-leak. You'll have to turn back. Do you need directions to make a detour?'

'No, ta. Just going for a Chinese. Looks bad.'

'Bad enough. I'd settle for an Indian or an Italian.'

Dark smoke rolled over the roofs and down the street. A tall column of flame licked the stars.

'Good advice. Thanks, constable.' Raven made a three-point turn and drove towards Cambridge Circus. 'The war started without us, Mr Fook. That was no gas-leak. That, my old mandarin, was Charlie Dance. Stake my kids' lives on it.'

'Temper, temper,' said Vito Raphael.

His brother Mimi laughed softly.

Fook was a clay idol between Alphonse and Rupert. Only his eyes lived through the mask of dried mud. He glanced back to see that his men followed in the Daimler and said: 'Then we find him.'

232

Raven met his eyes in the driving mirror.

'Charlie you want fingered?'

'Is there a choice now?'

Raven grinned at the Raphael brothers and made the turn towards Pimlico. 'You call 'em, we'll play 'em,' he said, leaving tyre-stripes on the roundabout.

Cyril held on as the tide sloshed around his knees. The foreshore was firm under his feet, and he shook with reaction as he embraced the slimy piling. He had been there a long time, and he wasn't really certain how. He remembered crawling over a mudflat into shallows with the casket pushed ahead of him. Going into the deep channel below a sewer outlet that had steamed and stank as he swam across it, then a long, sliding slog through muddy shallows to this old jetty. Now he was cold, exhausted, and bloody angry. He'd never lost his temper in fifteen years of wrestling the dirtiest of them, but being washed up like a piece of old driftwood after being left to drown was enough to make St Francis pluck live doves and make them walk home from Assisi. Cyril was wilder than any joker.

He worked his way up the beach to the high-water mark, and hid the casket in the pilings where it wouldn't get washed away. Then, slapping circulation back into his legs and ribs, he climbed to the road and looked for a car to borrow. He had to walk a long way before he found a residential area with a spare Morris Minor.

The first fire-engines were arriving when Charlie climbed into the lorry. He patted Armchair's head and told her not to weep, it was how Nasty would have wanted it.

'You know that, do you?'

'He said as much.'

'And who's crying? A smut in me eye is all.'

'Did you get shot of the dog and the pram?'

'Give 'em back to Humpty Hilda with a good drink for her trouble. And I ain't crying, right?'

'Fine. Shift over, I'll drive.'

'You won't. You'll get some rest, now then.'

'Doris, this is a ten-tonner.'

'And what was I motoring about in for the ARP in 1940? Eh? A bleeding tricycle? One of these, sonny, and bigger. Think I ain't seen or touched bodies before, neither? Ask Johnny the Builder about the flats in Charing Cross Road taking a direct hit. Took us the best part of two days to get the bodies out. And a lot of them wasn't all in one piece, neither. Carting Nasty and the Chink about was nothing compared to what I've seen. There was more to my war than lying on my back for Yanks, Charlie Dance. I done my bit and got a medal for it. The king, God bless 'im, pinned it on me himself.'

'You showed me, remember? The picture of you and him at the palace?'

'Well, don't tell me I'm crying when it's just smut.'

'You've got the wheel, Doris.'

Armchair Doris sniffed mightily. Reversed in a clash of gears, and drove north along Wardour Street in second. She was driving smoothly by Camden Town, and said nothing more until they were motoring through Belsize Park.

'Charlie . . .?'

'Yes, Doris love?'

'I will have a cry . . . later.'

'You and me both, love.'

'And for Soddy.'

'Him too.'

'You get the bastards, Charlie. Promise me that.'

'They won't shoot this horse for trying, love.'

'Up the hill to Whitestone Pond?'

'Yeah . . .'

'We'll do 'em in the eye, Charlie. You'll see,' said Doris.

* * *

234

Vito Raphael showed the doorman his sawn-off, took his pass-key and threw it to Mimi. Drove the butt into the doorman's gut and used it on the back of his head when he hit the floor with his face. Was rolling him under the reception desk when Big Alphonse said Vito could have just told the poor bastard to sit tight without cracking his headbone for no good reason. Vito said that made Alphonse the new doorman while the adults were busy upstairs, him being soft in the head and heart. Took the stairs with Mimi and the Killing Shadows, leaving the small lift for Raven, Fook and Rupert Baer. Alphonse caught Rupert's eye before the door slid closed, and they silently agreed the Raphaels were no-good bastards. Handing out spankings to civilians was definitely out of order, and the Raphael's were known as nutters long before they swapped tag-wrestling for running tarts and carrying shooters. There was a big difference between doing the business and hurting people for the charge it gave, and the Raphaels were hiding behind a door when God handed out nice lessons. Alphonse plugged all the phones into the Talking Clock and broke off the master key. Made sure the doorman hadn't swallowed his tongue, and sat astride him to watch the street.

Vito and Mimi were either side of flat 3A when the lift reached the third floor. They had let the Happi Coats out through the emergency exit and onto the balcony of Dance's apartment. With them covering the windows, the occupants were bottled up. Mimi used the pass-key to open the front door and held it closed until Raven gave the nod. Pushed it wide, and he and Vito went in low. Threw themselves to the floor and covered the living room where a lot of people in chairs stopped banging tambourines and singing in cracked falsetto. Raven kicked out at both sawn-offs, pointing them off to the sides of the lobby. Walked forward hiding his shotgun under his coat as an old lady with a blue rinse blew a last flat on an ocarina.

'Glory be, sinners.'

235

Raven watched Aggie Ince do a jig, spilling Woodbine ash down her best black dress as she laugh-coughed-laughed. She pointed past Raven at Fook, trying to get her breath back.

'What,' said Raven, fighting back anger. 'What *is* all this load of Salvation Army gone wrong?'

'And a true heathen to hear the Lord's words,' Aggie gasped. 'Yellow as a packet of custard powder and stiff with ignorance of His ways. Seen you with Charlie, didn't I? Used to come here before Chas had me move in. Got an Irish name. Eamonn, right? Here, girls, get the sausage rolls out. Feed the rascals, they'll hear the Lord's word better on full stomachs.'

Raven saw the Happi Coats coming through the windows, dropping silently to the floor. Aggie had his arm, was dragging him into a press of white-haired women smelling of lavender.

'You're Bottles' old woman,' Raven said. Blinking.

'Before the Lord sent a train to knock sense into him, yeah. And I know *you*, Micky Raven. One of the devil's toerags ripe for some uplift. And them Raphaels too. Don't go creeping out, Vito, Mimi. A couple or three hymns wouldn't do neither of you no harm at all. And your Irish Chinaman. *And* his ignorant savages what don't know the difference between doors and windows. Chas Dance might of liked them sort of surprises, but not Aggie Ince when she's holding her Ladies' Church Guild Meeting. Now, it's sit and listen, or me and the girls use our hatpins on your backsides.'

Rupert was the first to laugh. The Raphaels managed stiff grins, but Fook just stared when Raven threw back his head to bray at the ceiling and say a nice cup of tea would go down very nicely.

Dillman passed Lemmon the phone as the flyblown clock ticked to 10.05 p.m. There were paper cups all over the floor, and Olli shared his last cigarette with Froggy and Matt. Vinnie had fallen asleep in his wheelchair, and non-smoking Pimlico tore a folded *Evening Standard* into lines of paper dollies. Bulstrode chewed gum to freshen his mouth, and Taggart played a listless game of chess with Payne. They all listened to Lemmon say 'Yes', and 'I see', and 'Thanks for calling', before he rang off to stare at the wall.

Ollie bet Froggy it was Lemmon's bookie giving him the bad news, and Matt said it was his missus saying his dinner was cinders, his slippers were in the fridge.

'Those of you who want to, are free to leave,' Lemmon said, sounding bored.

'He mean us?' Ollie asked Dillman. Got a shrug in reply, and went to lean on Lemmon's desk. 'That was a bit supersonic. You want to give us that at walking speed?'

'The door's over there. Leave, *if* you want to.'

'If? What's the "if" for? Sounds iffy.'

'You tell me.'

Ollie pointed at the phone.

'Wasn't me got the clever call. You know what we have to guess, that it?'

Lemmon's smile was anything but sincere.

'Goodnight, Mr Oliphant,' he said.

Ollie grinned and frowned. Wagged a finger.

'You're playing piano with the lid down. Which hand has the toffee. Pulling our puddens, laughing up your sleeve. Except you ain't laughing. You know something we don't, and it's got right up your nose. And us being here puts us well in the clear with the perfect alibi. That don't sit right with you, but you figure there's an angle you can play once we walk through that door. Right?'

Pimlico stood and dropped the shredded newspaper.

'That's me in the nearest pub, then.'

'And me,' Matt said. 'Coming, Frog?'

'Dunno, do I? Wanna see which way Ollie and Vinnie vote.'

'Vinnie ain't even awake,' Pimlico snapped.

Vinnie opened one eye.

'Who ain't? Keep going down that road, Ollie.'

Ollie blew a last smoke ring. Flicked ash near Lemmon's ashtray.

'That's two of us seeing round corners. Three, counting Frog. And suddenly, this kiddy is frightened of the dark. You, Vin?'

Vinnie fed himself a last black Sobranie.

'Am I the only one who's been hearing fire-engines? Must be a hell of a fire, and there was a bit of a bang about an hour ago. Put them two together, what've you got? Some Gerrard Street Charlie Chans burning the roast pig, or what?'

'He's asking you, Uncle Theo,' Ollie said.

Pimlico sat down with: 'I drink too much any way.'

Lemmon said nothing with bridged fingers.

Vinnie lit himself up looking at Bulstrode.

'Am I included in the invitation to walk, Buller?'

'Guv?' Bulstrode asked Lemmon.

'Why should a gas-leak stop him?' Lemmon yawned.

'That gets it said.' Vinnie wheeled himself up to Lemmon's desk and lifted the phone. 'Now this thing's working, you won't mind if I make my one telephone call, will you? Like to the *Daily Mirror* to ask them what's happening out there. Me being a loyal reader and all. Or are you gonna tell us about your big fat "if"?'

'Me?' said Lemmon. 'I'm a copper, not a newshound.'

'Where's all this going?' Matt asked anybody.

'Ask Vinnie,' Froggy said. 'He's read the script.'

'My birthday cake getting blood on it,' Vinnie said.

Ollie sat down very slowly.

'Now I *am* frightened of the dark. I claim police protection, Mr Lemmon. I've been receiving these threatening phonecalls, stones chucked through my windows, like that.'

'That's a complete fabrication,' Taggart blurted.

'You wanna prove that, *Lemonade*?' Ollie said, unsmiling.

238

'Ain't in the mood for a baby cop talking over a big breakfast. If I dot you one I get a cell for the night. Think on that.'

Vinnie's laugh was humourless. 'Hit him for me, Ollie. I'll plead guilty to common assault. It is a cold old night for being on the streets.'

'Why me?' Taggart bleated. 'Why bloody me . . .?'

'I'll do the honours, Vin,' Pimlico volunteered. 'Be worth doing fourteen days to shut his clack.'

'Maybe we should toss for it?' Matt said, making fists. 'Turn this shithole copshop into a disaster area. I owe some lumps for missing Highbury.'

Payne put the cover over his typewriter. Put his hornrims in his desk drawer and wheeled his swivel and his back to the wall. Bulstrode just rolled his shoulders, and Taggart stood behind Lemmon. Vinnie held the phone like a weapon.

'Well?' he asked Lemmon.

'It seems we have some guests for the night, Buller. Ask them what they'd like to plead guilty to, sign them in, and allocate the cells.'

Vinnie dialled out. 'I'll just tell J.C. Hatton where we all are. All right if he bails us out in the morning, Mr Lemmon?'

'At his own convenience by all means, Mr Castle.'

'Best to keep things nice and neat,' Vinnie said. Thinking, *and the Dance firm in one piece until Charlie needs us. There'll be blood on the moon before this night's much older.* 'Hello, J.C.? Vinnie Castle here . . .'

Lemmon's broad wink at Bulstrode confused Taggart and Payne. Dillman laid his lead sash-weight back on his desk, puffing his cheeks. Matt pleaded guilty to riding a bicycle without lights when Vinnie finished his call to Hatton, and Froggy decided that drunk and disorderly had a ring to it. Vinnie said that would do him too, and Pimlico and Ollie went along with him. Bulstrode took them all down to the

239

cells and came back to ask Lemmon who had called him.

'Bomb Squad,' Lemmon said. 'They're prepared to treat it as a gas-leak for the time being, but they know there have to be more bodies inside once the fire's under control. They've scraped a couple off the pavement, and one of them was dead long before the explosion. You in the mood to view the deceased, Buller?'

'One way of rounding off a dull Saturday night, Guv.'

Lemmon sent the rest of the squad home to get some sleep. Coughed a cigarette alight and dogged it. Squeezed tired and swollen eyes and gave Bulstrode a long smouldering look.

'What's the betting we'll be seeing at least one familiar face?'

'Evens,' said Bulstrode. 'Somebody had to be hiding those bodies somewhere. And if the Tongs are chucking bombs around, could be our Mr Stannard is right about letting them play with matches.'

'But whose matches?'

Bulstrode got his coat and held the door open, shaking his head.

Fook tasted Aggie Ince's tea and seedy cake long after leaving Pimlico, and the subsequent search of the Sutton Place house had been a waste of time. Dance and the woman had been out, and the black man had died hard, saying nothing. That had surprised Fook, he had always thought of negroes as feckless eaters of watermelon who shuffled to bongo rhythms muggled by white rum and lust. This one hadn't passed out until his thumbnails joined his fingernails on the floor. They were using pliers on his teeth when his heart gave out. If nothing else had come out of the short encounter, Fook had revised his opinion of African men. Any lesson, however learned, was valuable.

The black man's death had made the Raphaels vicious. They kicked the body until the chair it was tied to smashed into mahogany kindling. As if the black man had cheated them of something. Raven had turned away to study a sentimental Victorian canvas of girls in white making daisy-chains by a river; bored rather than squeamish, just as Fook himself had been. Coagulated blood had spattered the white dresses, freckled the deft, plump fingers. Raven had stopped the Raphaels with: 'Need muzzles, the pair of you,' and told them to burn every stitch including their boots when they got home. Rupert and Alphonse would ransack the upper rooms for valuables and money to be dumped in the river. Give the filth a motive if the dead coon was found.

'Why if?' Fook had questioned.

'Depends who finds him, right? If it's Charlie, matey there'll just go missing. If it's that class tart of his, there'll be law all over. Your basic motivation, ain't it?' Raven had said, being tidy. A park-keeper sweeping dead leaves from his immoral lawn. 'Give Dance something to occupy his mind, losing the black meat. That's if we don't find the bastard tonight, that is. Best you go home now. It's us who'll flush him if he's still inna Smoke.'

Fook made the turn at the Whitehouse Pond and used the dash control to open the electric gates, swung into the drive and sent his men ahead of him into the darkened house. Stood by the Daimler smelling wrongness in the promise of fog drifting sullenly from Highgate. A first-floor window went up, his name was called with hushed urgency. Fook did not turn immediately, he squared his thin shoulders and watched the pond across the way ripple with snakes of reflected sodium, beyond surprise.

Wind would have left the porch light burning if all was well, set on a timer, it needed to be reset every fifteen minutes, and she would not have overlooked that basic precaution. The carved stone arch and portico was shadow upon shadow. Heavy tyre tracks had scarred the gravel drive, and the turning vehicle had churned soil and leaf-mulch from the naked flower beds. Going inside meant

Fook might find Wind lifeless. He wouldn't have left her alone if there had been any other choice, and he hoped she had died clean without disfigurement.

Fook climbed the main staircase and went to look at the men lying on his study carpet. The two men who died in St Anne's Court were as ripe as flyblown pork, and there was mould on their shrouds. The messenger he had sent to Gerrard Street still had the scroll of acceptance inside his coat, and the death blows welting his face and neck were livid. He would have died quickly. The note pinned to his collar had been typed on Fook's own machine and read:

FOUND THEM IN GERRARD STREET. C.

'Where is the woman?' Fook did not say *my* woman as he tore the note to shreds.

'In her room, Lord. Unhurt and unblemished. She says she was taken from behind by a long-nosed woman. She smelled her. Tape was used to bind her, there are no bruises.'

Fook released a long 'Aaaah' without realising it. The man could have been reporting on the condition of his porcelain collection. The vase is unchipped, Lord. The glaze is perfect. A thing Fook owned was intact; a valuable thing, but a thing nonetheless.

Fook stood before the open fire. Charlie Dance lurked in every shadow, was every creaking floorboard. He hummed in the central-heating, and his laugh mocked with the chimney's updraught. His grey eyes were ash flakes between the burning logs in the fire basket. He had walked through the electronic defences like smoke. Done the same thing in Gerrard Street whilst Pu Fatt broke faith on the Thames. As elusive as fog curling against a window.

Fook could not warm his frozen hands, more than delayed reaction to the explosion making him tremble. Once Dance had found the black man's body he would come again. This time for Fook himself. The thought did not exhilarate as

242

it might once have done. Now it chilled like the morbid English winter. Was as deep in his bones as the damp mists of old age. Raven's mad dogs would not find Dance tonight, or any other night. He could be out in the trees and fog now, coming silently through the stiff winter grass with the tread of a cat. Fook's hands shook in the firelight as his men awaited his orders, refusing to wrinkle their noses at the stench of death in the presence of the Supreme Snake.

Fook laced his hands in the small of his back and told them what must be done. Speedily and without haste. There was nothing dishonourable in a strategic retreat, he told himself, nothing at all . . .

CHAPTER NINE

Charlie dropped from the ten-tonner in the Edgware Road, and Doris drove it back to Irish Dermot's yard in Kilburn. She slept little with her swollen veins, and she would catch the night-bus home after a nice joy-ride along the Harrow Road.

Charlie went to the all-night cafe in Church Street for a quiet think amongst strangers. He sat over stewed tea amongst donkey-jackets and accents from Mayo, Donegal and Belfast; motorbike yobs on a diet of pinball, Coke and crudity; derelicts nursing empty cups, and old women who preferred company to the solitude of unheated homes.

Ignored after the initial silent appraisal, Charlie was left alone with his thoughts.

If Fook acted true to form, he'd bury his head and go after the docks in tandem with Micky Raven's firm. But if they weren't seriously divorced by the end of the six months he'd stipulated, Charlie planned to be very surprised. Those two had about as much chance of making a marriage as a pangolin and a lake of Martian plankton, even if they did manage to finger-tame the local East End families.

The Tates, Crosbys and Finns were as territorial as Bedouins defending their waterholes; they shot first – asked if you were really thirsty afterwards. To make them see sense, Fook would have to kill them first. Tread on one adder, he'd wake up the whole snakepit, and the three families were related to half of Essex. The Finns alone could boast a thousand uncles and cousins amongst the Romanies who worked the fairgrounds and circuses touring the British Isles. Put a serious hole in a Finn, and you were knee-deep in pikeys, diddys and gyppos very anxious to swap ten holes for one. Those hard bastards would kill over a look or a spilled pint; even over a losing bet on a horse, and still cut a woman's nose for attracting the wrong kind of attention.

Charlie lit a crumpled Player and called for a bacon sandwich. Half-listened to the excitement caused by a late arrival. He was skinny, unshaven, and wore a plastic mac over two overcoats.

'. . . I'm telling yer, gospel straight. Seen it with me own eyes, coming here for a cuppa from a tasty little earner down never-mind-where. Won a few quid too, but that's none of your never mind. There's this woman in curlers screaming up the street for the law. In a right two-and-eight. Turns out she's seen lights on in this house, the door wide open. Knows the woman who lives there's away, so, she calls down the hall and hears nothing. Goes in to black her nose like, finds this dead geezer onna floor. Right there onna carpet. Been done proper, tied up and everything. Had a right kicking.'

'Where's this, but in your imagination?' asked a totter in a trilby.

'Look inna papers t'morrah, yer don't adam-and-eve me. Be bloody headlines I shouldn't wonder. Bigguns. Her in curlers was hollering outside one of them big houses they didn't pull down for flats over in Sussex Place. This woman in antiques lives there with this black ponce. Big black geezer talks lahdie-Oxford. Was him her in curlers found, wannit? Right there onna floor.'

'And you, being honest, dialled 999.'

'What, me with my form and lights going on all down the street? The minute the law steamed up, I done my famous running act. They don't call me "Not here" for nothing. They come, I'm gone . . .'

245

'That's you,' laughed the trilby. 'Not here, not there.'

'Let heroes have the aggro. I'll settle for a tea. Anybody sitting here, matey?'

'Help yourself.' Charlie toed a chair out from the table.

'Ain't you gonna eat that bacon sarnie?'

'Remembered I'm Jewish.' Charlie left coins by his plate and went away through the tables.

'Well I ain't. You should have seen this woman running up the street showing more than she had. Curlers dropping out of her head like . . .'

The cafe door cut the simile off, and Charlie walked towards Sussex Place. His mind busily blank.

The mortuary attendant sucked a hollow tooth as he laid pieces of charred anatomy out on steel tables, matching limbs to torsos with inspired guesswork. His latex gloves made his hands deader than the flesh and bone he manoeuvred into position, and the smell did not change his dedicated expression. He could have been at home by the fire with his cat purring as he worked on a thousand-piece jigsaw puzzle before a cup of soporific cocoa sent him off to his bed.

Probably made with formaldehyde, Bulstrode thought, *sweetened with rubbing alcohol and meths*. What had been Nasty Nostrils Donovan's head grinned with half a face and no top to his skull. There was an arm that might have been his, a foot still wearing a grey sock. The rest of the stuff in the bodybags was just seared whatever, and would need pathological tests to give them an owner's nametag. All Bulstrode and Lemmon knew for certain was, some ghoul had dressed the corpse in street clothes after death.

They stayed for as long as seemed necessary, then left to look at the gutted building in Gerrard Street.

The cellars were still too hot to approach, and the odd food can blew up with a snapping pop in the hot cave of fire. The roof had gone, and the upper floors had collapsed into falls of rubble and charred wooden joists. It would be days before patient sifting would yield up any real clue as to the cause of the explosion. A guess at this stage, however accurate, was an exercise in futility. Lemmon and Bulstrode were about to give up and leave when a call came over one of the radio-cars. Lemmon took it washed by red light from a fire-engine, and came back to Bulstrode looking thoughtful.

'Edgware Road CID,' he said. 'Tommy Fuller. Asked if we were interested in an extremely dead negro male killed during what looks like an armed burglary.'

'Are we, Guv?' Buller had visions of an acre of bed catching him as he fell.

'Seeing as how it's a fellow with form. A houseguest of one Mrs Margot Sadler, widow of this parish, I'd say we were. Just what she's doing with Samuel Coleridge Washington lying moribund on her best carpet is worth a few discreet questions, wouldn't you say?'

'Sam the Spade?'

'The very same, Buller.'

'And ain't she got real friendly with Chas Dance since her old man popped his clogs swimming down in Rio or someplace?'

Lemmon looked as if he'd just woken from a refreshing nap.

'Indeed, and we're invited to the wake as observers. Nice to know I've still got some friends left in the force. Did I ever tell you about Tommy Fuller? A rugby fanatic. Well, one night after a game in Cardiff, Tommy decided that nothing would do but that he had to have the flag from the Town Hall. Two of us got a ladder . . .' Telling the anecdote, Lemmon led Bulstrode to their Q-car and drove to Sussex Place.

The ambulance had gone away empty, and that made Sam dead. In no hurry to go anywhere as they took his

247

temperature with an anal thermometer and photographed him where he lay. Checked his skin for lividity, his blood for clotting, his muscles for onsetting rigor mortis to ascertain approximate time of death. Vacuumed the floor around the corpse, taken hair, lint, and dust samples. Checked all likely surfaces for latent prints, including Sam's own to eliminate him from their enquiries. Then, and only then, they'd draw their chalk lines, zip him into canvas, strap him to a stretcher, and take his body off to some basement smelling of chemicals for his second Calvary; the autopsy.

Charlie walked away like a bored neighbour, turned into the Edgware Road and found a doorway to stand in. A Q-car came down from the West End and slowed to make the turn. Charlie saw Lemmon at the wheel and Bulstrode yawning beside him before they were gone in a surge of acceleration. There were no cruising cabs. Charlie and the slowly changing traffic lights had the streets to themselves. He set out for the Savoy, walking off the manic compulsion to make for Hampstead or Fulham.

Knock down one domino, he reminded himself, *you have to knock the whole box down. Right, Arch?*

Keep walking Charlie. Keep walking . . .

The night porter let Charlie into the suite, and two fivers helped him to forget the whole thing. Charlie built himself a tall Irish and water in the chocolate and cream sitting room. Killed it with two long bites, and made a second weaker one to keep him company in the shower. Scrubbed clean, he toned himself under the cold jet, put on a black turtleneck, black Daks and socks, blacker Bally moccasins. Checked his fishing bag, his foreign currency, the perfectly forged passports, and took a third drink into the bedroom to watch Margot sleep.

She was an erotic tumble of limbs, pillows and fanned hair. Long thighs clamping a bolster took nocturnal comfort

248

from a surrogate lover of twill and down. Her small round breasts had large pink crests and erect nipples, and her skin shone with pale vitality. Her face was purged of waking artifice, and he could see how she must have looked touring the provinces as a Wildean Gwendoline, a Brontean Cathy. Before marriage to Bastard Malcolm twisted the generous mouth with cynicism and endowed her with an unquenchable thirst for mixed drinks. Charlie and widowhood had weaned her from the cocktail-shaker breakfast, and Margot the Maid inhabited the sleeping face whilst Margot the Sophisticated Scold practised withering Dorothy Parker lines in some darkened corner of subconsciousness.

Charlie drank deep. Margot the Maid was an illusion, it was the clever adult he needed to talk to. He blew on Margot's eyelids to bring her out of her Green Room dream into the cold, early hours of Sunday morning.

Her groan was mannish, her sinuous stretch feminine.

'You're early, or I'm dead and dreaming. Pinch me softly.'

'Plug your brain in. We have to talk.'

'Not without baskets of kisses and gallons of coffee.'

'That you, or a hangover lying there?'

'One teensy nightcap is hardly a debauch, darling. The night was dark and drear and needed uplift. A stinger for then, coffee for now.'

'We *talk* now. Room service comes later.'

'All black and saturnine he comes to my chamber. God!'

'Could be there's a reason.'

'Oh, Christ. Conundrums before coffee. Get in here and give a girl a warm.'

'Not now. Not in this room. Not in that bed.'

'Aaaah, yes. The couch of the deified. The Sainted Ingrid. The lost love of yesteryear. And for naughty Margot to soil the sheets of her sacred bed would be too, too sordid. Dead and gone, yet not forgotten by the man in black, black, black. I should weep bitter tears in her

249

shining memory, but not before I clean my teeth.'

Charlie sipped his drink. Took a long swallow. Showed nothing.

'Tell the bitch to take a walk, Mrs Sadler. Leave me with the decent half of what used to be a nice lady.'

Margot shook her hair forward to hide her face.

'Oops-a-buttercup. When I'm Mrs Sadler I'm in bad twubble. The baddest, worstest twubble . . .'

Charlie stood against the light. Said nothing.

Margot stopped fooling. Gave him a long grave look. Sat up and embraced her knees.

'I'm here, Charlie. The bitch has gone. She pops out when I'm not looking. Oh, Christ, but I'm a self-destructive idiot. Forgive me?'

'Forgive yourself. Sam's dead.'

'What?'

'That's right.'

'Charlie Dance, if you're . . . you're not, are you?'

'No.'

Margot sucked her thumb. Bit on the ball hard enough to blanche the knuckle. She saw Charlie through a swim of lurching shadow, and gummy bile rose in her throat. She swept from the bed and slammed into the bathroom. Made small hicking and drooling sounds. Tiny rips in thin sateen, wider and ·wider apart. The shower ran, then taps. She flushed plumbing and came back with combed hair, smelling of spearmint and Listerine. Sat holding the bolster with her knees together, cornflower eyes cloudy and attentive.

'How?' she asked.

'They beat him to death. Using him to find me.'

'Who, Charlie?'

'Best you don't know. I'm only guessing myself.'

'Hah,' Margot said. 'You? Guessing? Double hah. He was my friend, damn your eyes. I have to know who.'

'He had a bad heart.'

'Sam said as much. Made light of it, like everything. But

250

that's . . . that *was* Sam all over. But why, Charlie? And how did they find him in Chelmsford?'

'He wasn't in Chelmsford. He was at your house.'

Margot blew a damp stray curl away. Suppressed a shudder.

'But Sam wasn't supposed to go home. He was to stay up in Chelmsford. Meet me, meet us, in Hamburg on Monday. Why would he go back to Sussex Place? It makes no—'

'You tell me.'

'Tell you what, for heaven's sake?'

'That you maybe forgot something. A brooch. Spare knickers. Please, Sam, be a dear? Just drop by—'

'Bastard!'

Charlie stopped the slap a mere millimetre from his face. Held the slender wrist until Margot sagged, fighting tears.

'You didn't have to say that, Charlie. You *didn't*.'

'Didn't I? Think about it.'

'And you're so sinless, so pure? You weren't the prime cause—'

'You think I don't know that, lady?'

Charlie went into the sitting room to chink bottle to glass. Came back in a hunched prowl to slump in a wicker chair.

'And before you ask, Margot, he wasn't working for me. He got himself dead by being in the wrong place at the wrong time. And dying, he's done nobody any favours. Including the bastards who killed him.'

Margot didn't understand and said as much.

'You've got the heavy filth on your doorstep, love. And they don't ever go away. Once they've stopped asking what's missing in the way of valuables and tomfoolery, they'll end up wondering why you had a black ex-con lodging at your drum. And what really happened to your late husband.'

'I can handle that, Charlie. I swear.'

251

'You won't have to. You're going away and staying away.'

'Not without you, Charlie.'

Charlie may not have heard her. Light, slatted by the ornamental bathroom screen, tiger-striped his unseeing face.

'Tonight it was over. You got that? *Over*. I'd done the business. Cleaned up the mess, satisfied honour, given blood for bloody blood. All that old crack. Got us all off the hook. Then Sam plays the joker. The knave of spades. Walks into a house that should have been empty, and gets himself kicked to perdition. And that puts you, me, and mine, right back in shit alley. Fighting a war I thought was over. Finished.'

There was a hard, splintering crack. Glass shards flew to catch the spill of fretted light. The base of Charlie's glass hit the carpet, and blood wormed between his clenched fingers. He didn't seem to notice.

'Dear God!' Margot got a handtowel. Forced Charlie's hand open and used eyebrow tweezers to pick glass from his lacerated palm. 'Did he know, Charlie? Did Sam truly know? Not have to guess like I had to. Think, Charlie. Did he?'

'Armchair called him when the whole firm was at the meet. They all knew to stay out of it any way they could. Be in public places well away from . . . I even had the heavy filth doing favours without realising.'

Margot stopped the bleeding and taped the superficial wound. Took Charlie's face between her palms.

'You're only one man, Mr Dance. You can't think for everybody. Nobody could, not even you.'

Charlie looked through her face.

'So Sam proved.'

Margot fixed him a fresh drink, make him hold it.

'We'll go abroad. A holiday.'

Charlie changed the glass for the telephone. Asked for a Hampstead number and listened to it shrill unanswered.

An electronic shrew making Fook's farewells, and Charlie saw him watch Sam the Spade die.

'Christmas in St Tropez, Charlie.'

'Hong Kong,' Charlie said. Tasting it.

Fulham could wait.

Charlie talked in tropical heat as November sulked outside the window. He lounged in a green chair in a greener room where self-watering troughs of sables, palmettos and bonsai trees fringed the walls with miniature rain forests. Flowering yuccas in a central planter threw stems of waxed yellow blooms up at Growlite neon tubes, convinced it was summer in Mexico instead of winter in Essex. Ducted air stirred the liquid heat, condensation ran on the window, and Charlie's bald sketch of the previous night was translated into finger-sign by Mutton Jeff and Joe Yellow.

Cho Sun lay on a veridian couch. His chrome robe was worked with pale silk dragons, and the grey pallor had left his ageless face. When Charlie and the fingers fell silent, he stroked his chin at the ceiling, digesting what he had been told in silence.

Charlie thought about the three kinds of cigarettes in Ben Bunch's onyx box, the bottle of Irish on his desk. How the Hampstead house had been emptier than a widow's bed, and the rush to get Margot aboard the Harwich ferry to Ostend before he drove back to Battlebridge. His head pounded from lack of sleep, from the small talk in the smaller hours that had somehow led to exorcising Ingrid's ghost from the hotel bed.

How Margot had embraced his sudden and savage need with no thought for her own pleasure, thinking only of him as he sought elusive release. Surfing the fine line between the violent and sordid, he'd used her as he had no other woman. Lanced up into her soft cave in compulsive rushes, driven on by a gorged and swollen thing too hot and erect to feel any stimulus she might have offered. He rode behind it as it rode her; both of them reaching out, twining together, turning and twisting about to bring the monster home to flaccid tranquillity. But it was a thing apart; a gluttonous stranger that probed and reared without gently conjoining. His body was just a pumping engine, and he had bruised her breasts, shoulders and thighs with unthinking hands as he strained and bucked to free himself of the huge and erectile agony.

With a surge that lifted Margot bodily from the bed, he dug his nails into her rump to walk her around the room, her legs clamped around his waist as she bored down as hard as she dared. The manic tango ended when Charlie laid her back on the bed. Withdrew his insatiable member and stood away. Shaking and running with sour sweat, hair plastered flat, his fists clenching and unclenching, a wild and throttled mewing came from somewhere deep and untouchable inside him.

Charlie shifted in the green chair, still haunted by that sound.

Margot had soothed him with soft words in the darkness. Brought him back to the bed to wipe off his face and neck with a scented cloth packed with shaved ice. Squeezed fragrant and cooling essence over his chest and thighs. Took whisky into her mouth and dribbled it between his lips in a long, moist kiss. Eased him onto his back and worked her pecking mouth down his torso to his parted loins to find the risen crest with her peaty lips and tongue. Liquid butterfly strokes that drew off the sudden explosion of warm fluid to leave him drained and replete. Drifted him into a sleepless void of wonderful nothing that was timeless and peaceful.

Under the shower, in creamy strands of bubbling suds, Margot brought him back to life with simple, wordless contact, and Charlie had stroked her sodden hair, knowing the gift for what it was. He just couldn't use the words.

With Cho Sun's smooth Mandarin as a musical backdrop

to his thoughts, Charlie went back to the green room to find himself alone with the patiently watching Chinese. He flowed from his chair to bring the two men back to finish what had been started, but Cho Sun's voice stopped him midstride. In clear, but oddly accented English, he said: 'We are beyond the need of their poor services, Mr Dance.'

Charlie laid a hand to the blank steel door. Gave himself a moment to swallow surprise before going back to his chair. Saw the small hands make flicking parabolas in the air and caught the Gold Flake and Swans Cho Sun threw him. Lit up with: 'Like all Chinese cabinets, there's always one more secret drawer.'

'Come now, Mr Dance, are you so very different? Do you turn out your pockets for a complete stranger at the first meeting?'

'I get the point,' Charlie said in smoke.

'English is both a necessity and a curse in a British colony. I mainly use it to know what is being said without seeming to understand. You are perhaps the first long-nosed white I have ever wanted to talk to . . . directly.'

'You,' Charlie said, 'should play poker.'

'A Western game of chance, I believe.'

'Not played right it ain't.'

Cho Sun dismissed that as contradictory.

'Yet you enjoy taking long chances with longer odds. You are a complicated man, Mr Dance. You have as many facets as there are tiles in the wall game of Mah Jong. You must therefore know that courage and cunning are never nearly enough on their own to win or endure. There is the tyrannical element of luck, both good and bad.'

'Like your liftshaft. Like young Joe pulling you out.'

'And your black associate dying needlessly. Good luck is a golden apple. Bad luck is the maggot at it's core, hey?'

'One way of putting it.'

'Killing Pu Fatt with explosives was crude but clever.

255

Not your style at all. But will it have your police looking elsewhere for the culprit?'

'I shouldn't wonder.'

Cho Sun smiled his ugly smile.

'I see you hate absolutes, even in conversation. There are no simplistic blacks to counterpoint the totally white. Only the grey areas of "perhaps" and "possibly", hey?'

'This is all going somewhere?'

'Ha!' Cho Sun barked. 'There is your weakness. The need to find absolutism in others. You are too used to the lonely heights of command, so much so, that you forget you give yourself away each time you hand out an imperative. You expect me to give you my blessing – to allow you to die a headstrong fool in Hong Kong. But I will not allow it. There is your absolute imperative, Mr Dance, I tell you "no".'

Charlie walked around that thought and didn't laugh.

'You'll have to explain that, mister.'

'Only if you can listen without prejudice. Can you do that, or will a practical demonstration of your inadequacy become necessary?'

'I'm hearing you.'

'Not enough. You must *listen*. There is a great difference. The difference between a solid wall and an opened door.'

'All right, so I'm listening.'

A black cigar grew between Cho Sun's fingers. Smoking and lit. He drew on it and leaked smoke through a nostril. Streamed words with herbal fragrance.

'Words are nothing if you ignore their meaning, their intent. Truly listening is an art. One cannot absorb wisdom when the mind is closed as yours is. You see only revenge, you hear only the sound of fury. You have put those maggots in your own apple. Pinch off their heads, free your mind of the face of Fook. Forget the need to cut his head from his body. Even if you succeeded in that vain hope, which I doubt, the Snake Society would grow another head

256

instantly. And one man cannot kill an infinity of coils that have lived a thousand years.'

'Why not?'

'The question of a fool. An ignoramus. In the colony, you would be the hare, not the hawk. The Snake would stake you out on a mudflat in the mangroves – leave you for the land crabs. Fook would not even bother to watch you die, and the crabs would not feed on your eyes until you had putrefied. You are not ready to hunt in Hong Kong. You may never be ready. Can you come to terms with that truth, Mr Dance?'

Charlie was jolted out of his slouch. Cho Sun was making the kind of noises Charlie usually made to others. Hadn't he said as much to Micky Raven about his plans for the East End? He saw the uncomfortable parallels and shifted uneasily.

'You get it said, don't you?'

Cho Sun bridged fingertips. Steepled them under his chin to look at Charlie, giving nothing away.

'And you hear yourself in my words, hey?'

'You got that right.'

'Then you should be convinced, hey?'

'Should I? Maybe.'

'No, I have changed nothing. You still expect my help. You expect me to take you to the very heart of the coiling Snake. Turn you to vapour until you have your man by the throat, hey?'

Charlie couldn't deny that. But he wasn't happy seeing the images in Cho Sun's crystal ball. There were too many negatives, and he despised those who told him what they couldn't do instead of what was possible. 'You telling me you can't?' he asked.

'Cannot. Will not. Which would you say? There is a great difference.'

'A difference that means nothing if it still comes out as "no".'

257

'You lie to yourself, Mr Dance. You know different.'

Charlie knew he sounded dull. Dogged. There seemed no way out of Cho Sun's web of sly sarcasm. He palmed his face and found sweat there. Wanted to haul the complacent Chinese off his couch and bellow in his face. He picked at the chair fabric and burned his tongue on a second Gold Flake. Found himself laughing with the realisation that there had to be an exit from Cho Sun's maze. The clues were all there if he could only spot them.

'Then it's *will not*,' he said.

'Ahhhhh,' Cho Sun sighed. 'At last.'

Charlie leaned to point his Gold Flake.

'And means *you* ain't ready to go back, right? Ain't just me you don't have faith in. It's *you* can't cut the Chinese mustard.'

Cho Sun's hand hid his mouth. His eyes hid everything else.

'Could you touch the tip of my nose if I didn't want you to?'

'I could try.'

'And succeed?'

'You wouldn't make it easy for me.'

'On the contrary, Mr Dance. I will hide my hands in my knotted sleeves. Wear a blindfold. Wear chains and ropes and lie under the bedclothes. Fill my ears with flock.'

'You're that good, huh?'

'No, Mr Dance, you are that inept. Oh, I have a fair idea of your capabilities. Your dossier tells of killings with the knife, the revolver, the bare fist. You killed Fook's messenger with a bottle, one of Pu Fatt's dragons in unarmed combat. But that was here, not in Hong Kong. Here, you cut a formidable figure, there . . .' Cho Sun shrugged. 'You also forget that I am contracted to kill you. Only the Sichuen Dragon can release me from that duty. And it is only because I am charged with killing you and the Supreme Snake in tandem that we can sit together in

258

this room as friends. Were Fook here now, I should be obliged to honour the contract immediately. The horns of a true dilemma, wouldn't you say?'

'Ain't you forgetting something?'

'My coming to you for help? Of course not. But my personal *chop* on the assassination contract must take precedence. My warning you of that irrevocable fact is my poor way of repaying you.'

'Thanks, friend,' Charlie grunted.

Cho Sun's short bow was mocking.

'Why precipitate the inevitable? Why not let time and circumstance put us back on opposing sides, hey?'

Charlie punched his thigh. Seeing the fatal flaw in Cho Sun's logic.

'And that's *your* weakness, Cho, my old Sun. You believe in the inevitable, and there ain't no such animal. Life ain't written out in straight lines like totals in a ledger. It's more like interstellar space; all curves and orbits, not a straight line any-sodding-where. Even sunlight bends through refraction. So don't hand me all that tonky fatalism. All that, "What must be, will be". What man makes, man can change.'

'There is no precedent for changing the reality of our situation, Mr Dance.'

'Then we'd better create a precedent bloody fast. We don't, ain't but one of us leaving this room upright.'

Surprise painted crescents of white around Cho Sun's pupils.

'You're threatening me? You believe you can?'

'I told you. Poker ain't a game.'

'But you have nothing to confront me with. No weapons.'

'Sure of that, are you?'

'Try to touch my nose. End it here.'

Charlie just laughed. Flicked ash and shook his head.

'And give them the last laugh for free? Forget it. That'd make us both dead, and we'd be throwing our cards in before the bets are down. There's been no deal, no ante. Dead man's hands don't take the pot, mister, and I ain't cashing in without the Snake and the Dragon buy chips and draw pasteboard.'

'Your obscure symbolism means nothing to me.'

'Together, we're a winning hand. Apart, forget it.'

'You cannot believe that.'

'I'm saying it, ain't I?'

'Together we make what? A cripple and a conceited long-nose. Worse than nothing. Two nothings.'

'I'll take that bet in thousands.'

'This is no crude game of chance.'

'That's just exactly what it is. You can't see it, is all. Your honour says you have to fulfil your contract, but it don't say when. Ain't nothing in the rules to say you can't change the sequence of events. Give the cards a good long shuffle.'

Cho Sun's eyes dipped under his lids. Opened wide to glitter.

'I hear you,' he said.

'Would the Sichuen Dragon listen if you went to him? After the rest of the Council of Seven had reinforced Pu Fatt's lies to save their sorry necks? No, he'd believe them. Even if you had put Fook and me in the ground, he'd put a contract on you. Post you all over Hong Kong as a renegade. Where'd your honour be then? Maybe it's already too late, but ain't nothing that can't be changed.'

'Riddles,' Cho Sun hissed.

'No Sichuen Dragon, no contract, right?'

'It would die with him, that is true.'

'That's what happens then. You give the Sichuen Dragon to me.'

'The hare thinks he has teeth. Ridiculous.'

'As ridiculous as you sitting there, waiting to die dishonoured? Trying and failing is better than all your bloody fatalism, mister. And what's wrong with being underestimated?'

260

'They say the madman sees with total clarity at least once in his life,' Cho Sun said. 'That one divine moment . . .'

'That's me. A magic idiot. Well?'

Cho Sun said something in soft Mandarin. His hand cut the air in dismissal, chopped lazy channels through his cigar smoke. Charlie and the green room no longer existed for him. He looked deep inside himself at something only he could see.

Charlie got to his feet, dizzy with exhaustion.

'If the world was a quail's egg,' Cho Sun told himself, 'I could eat Asia without appeasing my hunger.'

Wondering what that meant, Charlie pressed the hidden bell and waited to be let out. Wanting a tall glass of Ben's good Irish whiskey.

J.C. Hatton dropped Vinne and Ollie, Matt, Froggy and Pimlico at the Oasis to swim themselves clean, and took their clothes to the Savoy to have them laundered and pressed. As last man out of the changing rooms, Vinnie had added his clothes to the pile with: 'Have these back in a trice, my man.'

'My lost Sunday morning getting you out of West End Central is rewarded by this?' Hatton had shot back. 'An unpaid valet to the riff-raff of Soho?'

'You had us bound over into your care, J.C. So, *take* care.'

Vinnie had hopped away to make a clean header into the deep end, striking out in a three-limbed dog-paddle as Ollie bombed down from the high board.

They were snapping towels at each other when Hatton got back, and were more than ready to drink his health at the Kemble's Head opposite Bow Street magistrate's court.

None of them spotted the black saloons circling the block, waiting for them to come out.

Warren Street was as deserted as Sunday closing could make it when Charlie parked for a quiet pint in the Feathers. A huddle of mechanics on Sunday overtime took a break for quick halves and free cold snacks, and the barmaid buried her nose in a *Sunday Pictorial* when she'd stabbed a double Irish from the optic and drawn a lager from the pump. Charlie added water to the whiskey and took his drinks to watch a man in overalls feed the one-armed bandit. The mechanics drank up and left, and the barmaid barely grunted when they made their goodbyes. She left their dirty glasses where they stood, more interested in scandal than service.

'She'll have to go,' said the man in overalls. 'Her *and* this robbing machine. She's about as lovely as a rusty bucket, and this pays out like a man with short arms and deep pockets.'

'No way to talk about one of my money boxes, Weasle.'

Weasle glanced at the barmaid. 'Make noises like a punter, Chas. She's got ears like a bat – face to match.' Louder he added: 'Gears grinding you say? Sounds like clutch trouble. I'll take a squint, but it'll cost you a good drink. Day of rest, ain't it?'

'The vehicle's right outside. Jumps out of second.'

'Nasty.'

The bandit took Weasle's last sixpence and he followed Charlie into chill mist to look under the Ford's bonnet.

'Who maintains this heap for you, Mothercare?'

'The Mormon Tabernacle Choir. What gives?'

'Have *you* got Fulham in an uproar. My maisonette's right over the mews where the Raphaels keep their motors, and they was coming and going the best part of the night. They don't bother to keep their voices down, neither, so I had a ringside seat to them slagging you from cocoa to breakfast. They was burning clothes in their incinerator and bandying your name like a shuttlecock, Chas. They've definitely marked you down as a fairground duck, so you better keep a handy shooter down your sock from now on.'

Charlie imitated the barmaid's grunt. 'And?'

'Discreet they ain't. That right about them and Sam the Spade?'

'You're telling me, remember?'

'They was crowing, so it is. I liked Sam, Chas, but a hero I ain't, and this is getting a bit on top of me. Whackings I can take, but the OK Corral with shooters is well out of order. Wasn't born in that brand of flameproof underwear, y'know?'

'So?'

'So it don't make no odds to me if you think the less of old Weasle. Sneers I can live with. Shooters, forget it. I'm looking for a long holiday after this, Chas.'

'Holidays need paying for.'

'You'll dig deep when you hear the rest. The Raphaels cracked a bottle of cooking brandy when Micky Raven dropped in with Rupert and Big Alphonse. Must have been threeish in the a.m. and there was a bit of a naughty between Rupert and Vito over being too heavy in Pimlico. Seems that Vito smacked some doorman a bit too hard when they was turning stones for you, and Alphonse backed Rupert when he said it wasn't called for. That got Mimi snarling like he does, and even Big Alphonse got out of his pram backing Rupert. Well, Micky put the hush on that by calling them all face to face. You know how tasty he can get when he's throwing a wobbly?'

Charlie nodded. Knowing.

'Micky had his bawl and scream and got their minds off their differences by boasting about these two new darlings he's got on his string now. Spade bird and a Eurasian. Said he ain't handing them over to the Raphaels they don't come to heel a bit. Then he says the whole Dance thing has to be finished clever and fast. The heavy Chinaman wouldn't play until you was all over and done, and anyway, Micky needed the decks clear for some huge bank tickle in the City. Straight, Chas, that's what he said. I see this as an earner for a long holiday inna country until this blows over, so I ain't gilding nothing. Promise.'

'For once I believe you.' Charlie thought fear must have turned Weasle honest. 'And?'

'Seems Micky's gotta inside man in some clearing bank. Can you believe that? An inside man knows all about deliveries of cash money for the Christmas rush. Means he's talking heavy money, right? Micky reckons the new schedules are coming in, and it'll be a certain Friday the heavy loot'll be aboard one certain dustbin. The dustbin is one of those new, heavy-armour delivery waggons. Know what I'm saying, Chas?'

'I've heard of 'em.'

'Well, you can't chainsaw through them bastards. You use gelly, you might just blow one on its side. Warp it all to hell and kill who's inside, but it don't put the money in your hands. Micky didn't actually *say* how he can get inside them things, but there ain't no doubt that he's got some clever scheme going for him. He never went into details, but he definitely made it sound like he could maybe pull the same trick twice before the heavy filth tumbled how it was done. By then, Micky Raven's stone-rich by millions, and nobody to pick up the bill but the insurance companies. And that's about all there is to that. They all went back to droning on about you being at the top of their shit list, and how Micky needed all that dough to grease a path in Bethnal Green. That I didn't make nothing of, so you'll have to sort that for yourself, right?'

'Never did cotton to your theories any way.'

'So Froggy was fond of saying.'

'Anything more said about the heavy Chinaman?'

'Only that he's staying well out of the Smoke until you're sorted final. Sorry, Chas, but that's what they said. They was all strung out from brandy and no shut-eye, and all they had in mind was to grab a few hours before hunting you and yours tooled-up with sawn-offs. They ain't coming at you smiling.'

Charlie lowered the bonnet with a gentle slam.

'I'll buy you that drink now.'

'If it's all the same to you, Chas . . .'

264

'Spit it out, Weasle.'

'Well, if I could just have me the dough. Like, you know . . .'

'And stay out of range?'

Weasle's wet eyes watered with sad sincerity.

'Sneer all you want, Chas. Hard looks don't break bones, right?'

'Nor they don't.' Charlie found an envelope in his inside pocket. Slapped it across his palm and flipped it at the man in overalls.

'Feels generous, Chas.' The wet eyes flooded.

'It'll keep you smiling to Easter, you don't feed it to the bandits.'

'Be . . . lucky, Chas.'

Charlie watched Weasle back away and walk rapidly towards the corner of Charlotte Street. A small and nondescript nobody in greasy blue twill, the cuffs of Weasle's trouser cuffs flapped inches above his broken shoes. When he turned from sight, the street seemed no emptier. Realising he had never known Weasle's real name, Charlie drove to Bow Street, needing a drink in company.

Vinnie had his wheelchair backed into the corner of the saloon bar, Pim and Ollie were showing the barman tricks with water, matches, upended glasses and beermats, and Froggy and Matt told Hatton the cleanest jokes they knew in an attempt to amuse him. Hatton convulsed them with the one about the whore, the American airman, and the park railings, and left them to have a quiet word with Vinnie.

'Like the dormitory of a reform school after lights out.'

'Not bad lads,' Vinnie said. 'Boisterous is all.'

Hatton pressed his hornrims against the bridge of his nose.

'One does need to be in the mood for their basic badinage though, eh? Look, Vincent, I do need to closet myself with Charles very soon. He's rather allowed business to slide these past weeks, and I cannot continue to prevaricate any longer. Have you seen him to really talk to recently?'

'Not a lot, no. Been a naughty old time, J.C..'

'I'm not totally unaware of the problems, Vincent. Archie left Charles too many loose ends. He has too many crosses to bear to cope in splendid isolation.'

Vinnie swirled a slice of lemon in warm tonic.

'He's got me playing Solitaire as much as you, y'know.'

'Then we must pool our resources, Vincent. Charles dropped all that Chappie August business in my lap, and I'm quite sure he has forgotten every last word on the subject. I've handed all the outstanding debtors – the odd squibs of tax and accountancy, but a boxing promoter I most assuredly am not. Can't we get August back from wherever it is he's hiding?'

Vinnie thought about an eel in a bucket being dynamited by Micky Raven. Trying to nail August down to straight talking without giving over half the firm's strength to keeping him alive and honest.

'Not without Charlie's say-so, no.'

'But we own fifty per cent of a stable of young pugilists, and there are training schedules and bouts to be arranged. Not least of these is an entire promotion at the Madison Square Gardens, and the fellows across the pond assume we can produce Trooper Wells for a non-title exhibition. Well, dear boy, the fact is we can't, and I am absolutely useless at negotiating with the Americans. For one thing, I understand no more than one word in three they speed at me over the telephone during the dead of night. But I do understand barely veiled threats when I hear them, and I do draw the line at their use of expletives as creative nouns. It has come to such a pass, my devoted secretary Miss Tupper has threatened to leave my employ.'

'She's been with you since The Flood.'

'Longer. A fifty-nine-year-old spinster may sound like sweet sixteen on the telephone, but she hates being called

"Cutes" whilst being propositioned by some foul-mouthed New Yorker.'

Vinnie hid a grin. 'I can see how she would. Maybe we should lend you old Armchair. She got medals in the war for Anglo-American relations.'

Hatton had the grace to smile.

'I may have to consider that as a serious proposal. But there are other matters arising. Most pressing is our contractual obligation to stage a preliminary series of bouts at a foreign venue before Madison Square Gardens. What our Mafia contacts call an "Oomph bomb" to start the publicity rolling. And Vincent, the US promoters are talking about half the purse money coming under the table as cash. Tax free cash. It was put with such bald crudity, that it is clear to me August conducted his business that way as a matter of course whilst handling Trooper Wells. So clear in fact, I find myself wondering how much of previous purses August siphoned off before the fighters themselves were paid. It would only take one boxer with a grudge to take himself off to the Inland Revenue with a story like that, and the ramifications could be legion. Once the tax boys start to investigate one's affairs there is no chance of them ever going away. There is no statute of limitations on tax evasion. The whole of Ogle Enterprises could come under the very closest of scrutiny, something I have avoided like the plague.'

Vinnie nodded with veiled eyes.

'Charlie won't stand still for that.'

'Exactly my point. Why I must see him as soon as possible.'

'OK, J.C., we'll get his attention together.'

'My relief is boundless. Let me get you another drink.'

'A nice weak gin and tonic.'

Hatton went to the bar and was taking a new note from his wallet when the window behind him blew in. Etched glass tore into the ceiling, and shotgun pellets cleared the top shelf of the backbar. The hanging light swung on its chain, shedding bursting bulbs and tatters of vellum lampshade. Holes appeared in the ceiling, and plaster drifted down in fine drifts of talc.

Ollie and Pim had gone over the counter without thinking, and broken bottles doused them with jets of spirits. Froggy had gone under a table, and Matt tripped over him trying to pull Hatton to the floor. Vinnie stayed where he was, wishing he had his Mauser, and Hatton just stood at the bar with his money in his hand, plaster turning his white hair grey and opaquing his hornrims.

The shots had been aimed high, and the lower part of the window was intact, obscuring the street. Engines roared and metal shrieked as vehicles collided in a scream of spinning tyres. A windscreen caved in, something bounced off a radiator, and engines roared away down Bow Street. A police whistle shrilled weakly and dribbled into silence. A last piece of window glass hit the floor, and a bottle gurgled itself empty. Then there was just the sound of beer dripping from the counter, and Froggy swearing in monotone.

'The same again, chaps?' Hatton said before fainting in a heap.

Charlie found Hatton's chauffeur polishing the green Mercedes outside the old *Daily Herald* building in Endell Street. A fussy ex-guardsman with a clipped manner, he told Charlie his employer entertained at the Kemble's Head. His tone suggested Hatton chose the oddest people to waste time with, and that it was just as well there were only twenty minutes to closing time. He would have preferred Hatton to sip from a pewter tankard in a beamed country inn with brass scuttles, geraniums in tubs, and a pub cat too aristocratic to shed hairs on the flowered carpet. Rubbing shoulders with the new gentry in stockbroker Surrey instead of compromising himself with dodgy oddments from the lower orders in sight and sound and smell of Covent Garden.

As if the very air would corrode his morality and the shining chrome trim of the new German car.

'So long as he drinks and you drive, you've got no complaints,' Charlie said. 'If it was the other way round, you'd be out of a job.'

'I never drink,' said the chauffeur. 'And it's just as well with the low standard of driving in the capital. Twice our machine has been shaved by two black Princesses. Twice, Mr Dance. I can't allow Mr Hatton's vehicle to be scratched by imbeciles.'

'Sunday drivers. Tourists probably.'

'Not with London plates. Not with their shocking turn of phrase. They actually swore at me when I threatened to take their numbers.'

'That right? Shame.' Charlie kept his lazy smile. Pulled his fishing bag from the back of the van and laid it on the passenger seat beside him. Drove down to the intersection with Long Acre and stopped with the engine running. A black Princess came down Long Acre, passed Charlie's Ford and made a meal of the turn into Bow Street. Slowed to a halt outside the Kemble's Head, and went on to the Opera House turn in a studied creep. A second Princess made the same manoeuvre moments later, and the faces inside stared at the pub with the same intensity. Micky Raven had the wheel and Vito Raphael stank up his face with a miniature cigar.

Charlie stayed where he was. Unzipped the fishing bag and laid his shotgun on the seat near his hand. Cocked the hammers and opened the offside window. Adjusted his rearview mirror and turned up his coat collar to hide his face. Opened an A-Z street guide as if he were lost, and waited for the first car to come around again.

The Princess rang the changes by running across into Neal Street, cut through a side turning, and came up to the Long Acre intersection behind Charlie's Ford. Charlie pulled out ahead of it to make a wide left and right turn, cut the

269

engine to fake a stall, blocking the narrow road and stopping the Princess right behind him. The Princess just sat there, and Charlie saw Mimi Raphael in the front beside Big Alphonse, both of them more interested in the Kemble's Head than the idiot stalled in front of them. Charlie stroked the shotgun and sat still, watching the second Princess idle down Long Acre to halt a car length behind the first. He started the engine, drove forward ten feet, slammed into reverse, and smoked his tyres on full throttle.

The first Princess seemed to leap at him, and he saw Mimi duck below the dash a moment before the impact threw Charlie back in his seat. The Ford bucked and the rear doors stove in with the crash of a dropped dinner service. Big Alphonse hit the windscreen with his face, and the bonnet sprang up to hide his opened swearing mouth. Charlie stiffarmed the shotgun through his opened side-window and fired both barrels through the pub window. Jumped forward in second, leaving his rear bumper locked to the Princess's buckled radiator. Braked hard, and reversed around the first Princess to meet the second car full tilt as it tried to pull out. A tyre burst and a rear door tore off completely. The silencer fell into the road in a roar of exhaust and scales of dried mud and rust, and Charlie found first gear to surge forward again.

The first Princess bored out to cut him off, and Charlie sent the Ford down along its side in a massive sideswipe. The heavier Princess lost some trim as it rocked on its suspension, and Charlie's Ford went over on two wheels, trying to flip on its side. Charlie fought the wheel, swung the Ford back onto four wheels, and wobbled away past the magistrate's court on flattened tyres. A hubcap bounced away, and Charlie glimpsed a constable come down the court steps to swing his truncheon at the windscreen before it starred and opaqued, leaving Charlie with no forward vision.

Charlie punched himself a peephole as he over-corrected for the Opera House turn. He ploughed into a row of dustbins and plastic garbage sacks, slewed left to strip rubber from his rear tyres, and came to a rocking halt with a racing engine. The constable had been flung away from the bonnet of the first Princess, and rolled in the gutter trying to blow his whistle. His lapel radio had torn away and was crushed under the spinning wheels of the accelerating Princess, driving blind with its bonnet up. Micky Raven had his head out of his side window and wore a bloody moustache. The Princess hit a rolling dustbin, and came to a sliding halt with it jammed between its offside wheel and its buckled mudguard. Raven was trying to reverse himself free when Charlie made the turn, and the faint trill of a police whistle followed him through the market to the piazza. There was no sign of pursuit as Charlie coaxed the dying Ford into Henrietta Street, and only the pigeons saw it cough itself to death outside Moss Bros.

Charlie was catching last orders in the Salisbury when the first police cars came down from West End Central, and he listened to an old busker's life story with his snugly zippered fishing bag on the floor at his feet.

The bitter tasted of perspiration, tired hops and too much adrenalin, and Charlie would have dropped off where he sat if the manager hadn't rang time on his ship's bell.

Commander Lemmon released a gaseous belch and bit through another antacid tablet, a martyr to massive indigestion. He had just bitten into a roast potato when the telephone rang, and chewed of it as a very angry Elizabeth told the Watch Commander at West End Central to forget there *was* a Commander Lemmon for at least forty-five minutes if he wished to avoid being scourged until death by unspeakable plagues of Biblical proportions. After that, Lemmon had gone through the motions of enjoying his Sunday luncheon, and was paying for it as he sat across from a young constable with scrapes, tapes and bandages on his hands and face. Constable Leonard Prebble's hand shook

271

as he sipped the hot, sweet tea Bulstrode had brought from the canteen, and Lemmon skimmed his written statement. It read:

I had stationed myself outside Bow Street magistrate's court in accordance with Inspector Harris's instructions to observe the Kemble's Head public house. It had been alleged that the landlord of the Kemble's Head was serving drinks after licensing hours, a serious violation if proved, and I was there to observe the comings and goings of his clientele. I had checked that the doors of the court were properly secured as was my habit when on foot patrol in that area, and was about to check the side entrance and windows when my attention was drawn by a yellow Ford Transit van that had stalled, blocking the north end of Bow Street and the road between Endell Street and Drury Lane. As I approached the said vehicle to offer assistance I noticed its dirty condition made the licence plates unreadable. The driver's face was also obscured by his collar and hat and his hunched posture. A black saloon I later identified as an Austin Princess had stopped behind the Ford and was unable to proceed forward. I also noted at that time a second black vehicle almost identical to the Austin Princess blocked by the same Ford. The Ford suddenly drove forward into Bow Street, halted just as abruptly, and reversed into the first Austin Princess causing damage to itself and the aforesaid vehicle. At the same time there was a double report that sounded like a car without a properly fitted silencer backfiring. The east-facing plate glass window of the Kemble's Head shattered, the glass flying mainly inward, causing me to believe the projectile(s) had emanated from an exterior source. I at first thought that debris from the collision must be the cause, but then I saw what appeared to be a double-barrelled weapon projecting from the offside window of the Ford Transit van. I had reached the pavement on the west side of Bow Street when the Ford Transit van moved forward a second time, halted in the previous abrupt manner, and reversed around the halted and damaged Princess to strike the second Princess as it attempted to manoeuvre into Bow Street by over-taking the first halted and damaged vehicle. The impact pushed the second Austin Princess across Long Acre to strike the front of the *Daily Herald* building near the entrance to the circulation department. The second Austin Princess damaged itself and the building fascia, and the passengers inside were attempting to kick their way out through the jammed doors when the Ford Transit van drove down along the side of the first Austin Princess, doing yet more damage to itself and the other vehicle. A rear door previously attached to the Ford Transit van fell onto the road surface as the Ford Transit travelled on two wheels toward me. I struck at the windscreen with my truncheon and managed to hit it, but the vehicle continued past me to strike a row of dustbins left at the roadside for the corporation refuse operatives to empty as they do during the latter part of Sunday evenings. I had been struck by the open rear door of the Ford as it passed me, and was precipitated into the road. As I was attempting to get to my feet to halt the progress of the now moving first Austin Princess I was struck again by the offside mudguard of that vehicle, and found that my lapel radio [Constable Prebble had obliterated 'Talking brooch'] had been torn away and been made inoperable. I was blowing my whistle for assistance when the first Austin Princess ran over my right hand. I was now in a state of shock and was attempting to follow the first Austin Princess when it was halted by a dustbin that was jammed under its front right mudguard. It reversed into me, knocking me down again. I struck my head on a kerbstone and lost sight of it for a moment. Dazed, I found a man in blue clothes and a

273

stocking mask holding a shortened weapon I took to be a 12-bore shotgun. He proceeded to point this at me and said: 'Stay down, cunty, or you will get dead without a pension.' He kicked my hand and my ankles to make certain I was lying in the gutter. Said: 'When we're off out of it you can blow your penny whistle till the moocows come home. But now shut it fast and lie doggo.' I did not reply to this as I was too dizzy to speak. The man in blue also had the bore of his weapon held to my chin, forcing my head back against the kerb. I heard a good deal of swearing before both vehicles were started up and driven away. The man in blue kicked me again and went away with one of the vehicles and I could not say which one for the nausea my injury was causing me. That is the incident as I recall it, except that I remember hearing people leaving the Kemble's Head in a hurry, and the landlord or one of his staff locking the doors and shouting for somebody to call the police. I then lost consciousness.

Lemmon looked across at Constable Prebble to see that he had fallen asleep.

'Not a bad move, you bloody idiotic young hero,' he said. And to Bulstrode: 'How long has he been on the force?'

'Eighteen months, Guv. A good strong lad, according to his file, but not too clever at the written exams.'

Lemmon got up, lighting a Player.

'We need Phds to face shooters unarmed now, do we? Is his testimony all we've got?'

'Apart from the fluff I got from the landlord of the Kemble's Head, yeah. He's the original brass monkey, that one. Adamant he knew none of the people in his public bar when the window mysteriously got itself broken. All strangers. He did remember one had white hair and a toffee accent, and another one might have been in a wheelchair. By the time we prove circumstantially it's possible Hatton

274

took the Dance firm there for a drink, they'll all have more clever alibis than my tomcat has girlfriends.'

Lemmon released a painful bubble of wind.

'Just keep plugging away, Buller. It's what we do best.'

'Forensic might get lucky with what's left of that Ford van.'

'Like a bloody tournament at Camelot, with cars instead of knights on horseback. And not a Chinese in sight. So who kicked the life from Sam the Spade, and why? Somebody looking for Charlie Dance? Who's got the dead needle with the Dance firm now, Buller? Or have the Chinese bought themselves new allies?'

Bulstrode fed himself a matchstick to chew.

'Might be a question of matching class motors to the right faces. Ain't Micky Raven partial to Princesses?'

'So who pulled his chain hard enough to drag him out of Fulham? Unless . . .'

'Unless he's steaming for the East End in a straight line, not caring who's in his way? That the road you're going down, Guv?'

'Question is: Is Micky Raven going down that road?'

The question hung between them like soiled linen until they went out into the dusk to find a quiet bar to fly fanciful theories in.

Night.

Charlie ran through dark galleries without forward motion.

Nails of doubt clawed his back, drew blood to scald his boiling spine. The sucking ground sapped his meagre strength, slowed him to a motionless sway as the surreal dream forest melted and changed and hid the answers he chased. They were flitting glow-worms somewhere ahead, always one turn beyond him in the changing yet changeless wherever. Cars smoked their tyres on distant tarmac roads, tore themselves apart with metallic screams in showers of smashing glass. Ethereal shotguns boomed like bitterns, and flying things twittered in Mandarin as they brushed his face with trailing wings of rotten offal. Yellow men padded about in stink and noise and disorder, and all the anywhere roads led nowhere. The hating faces of Fook and Raven hung in the branches, rotten pumpkins dripping slime on mourners at too many gravesides. The dead were burying the living, and Charlie saw himself as a patient shadow haunting thickets of black umbrellas. Vinnie and Margot were sucked into mire trying to reach him, and the hands of the living dead grew in swaying rows, a foul crop of grasping weeds. A cowled and faceless reaper scythed at them to fill a bottomless sack, but they scuttled away into the greater darkness of outer nothing where scaled dragons hunted them with long prehensile snouts, gulping them down like soft-shelled crabs.

Charlie's bellow of rage became a great wind that blew the trees to streamers of stinking smoke and a flood of green filth that swirled into a vortex to swallow Charlie's shouting face as porcelain rattled and tea was poured, and Armchair Doris was there, dressed in her best black.

'Drink that, lovely boy. Sleeping in the office, what next?'

'Tying my own shoelaces and going out with girls.' Charlie gulped hot, sweet tea. Wiped sweat from his unshaven face. 'You going to church?'

'Soddy's funeral. You ain't forgotten?'

Charlie looked out at morning drizzle and said he was sending a wreath.

'If you won't go, you won't. I'll mutter something appropriate.'

'I know it.'

Doris tapped the shotgun on the desk with a teaspoon.

'You was maybe expecting company last night?'

'Fell asleep cleaning it.'

'And pink elephants come wrapped in cellophane. Another cup? You'll need it.'

'Pour and tell me.'

'Got a deputation in the outer office. I said you'd maybe let them bend your ear after you'd wet your whistle. Seems you wasn't the only one had a busy weekend.'

Charlie took his tea into the washroom. Sluiced his face and lathered for a shave as Doris laid out a clean shirt and underwear. 'Who ate a big breakfast, then?' he asked, using his razor.

'The whole firm and J.C. Hatton. Ollie, Pim, Froggy, Matt . . . all of them.'

'And Vinnie?'

'Most of all Vinnie. Somebody put glass in their beer.'

'Happens, don't it?'

'Like rain at a funeral. Why cemeteries are so green. See I get planted in sunshine, there's a love.'

'In a hundred years maybe.'

'So, I'm cheered up. But they're well sulky, lovely boy.'

'Sulky-sulky, or humpty-sulky?'

'They're in black for the funeral, faces and moods to match. Hatton's bleating on about boxers, Vinnie's chain-smoking with his mouth all pinched up, and they all want a serious pop at the Raven firm. They want a home game before they play away. London's their manor, not Hong Kong.'

'You think they're right?'

'Don't matter what I think. *They* think they're right. And with their heads coming to a point, you'd better have it out with them before they blow stupid.'

Charlie buttoned his shirt and tied his tie. Stung his face with witch-hazel and sat at his desk.

'Open for business, Armchair.'

'You'll do it your way, whatever, lovely boy. But let 'em think they got something ticking under their haircuts.'

Doris opened the door, and Vinnie was wheeled in at the head of a shouting flood. Then they were all looking at the shotgun Charlie pointed across the desk.

'Sit, shut it, or walk,' Charlie said.

There was some milling about, then they were all in chairs, watching Charlie with hot eyes.

'You're treating us like little boys, Chas,' Pimlico said. 'Out of order, and you know it. We're being picked off one at a time, and we ain't standing still for it. Sam makes three, ain't none of us plans to be unlucky four.'

Charlie turned the shotgun on Pimlico with the hammers back. Let them fall with a double click and watched them all flinch.

'This got your heads down yesterday. All five of you would have walked into eternity without it.'

'You?' Vinnie's smoke went down the wrong way, and he choked as uneasy glances were exchanged.

'That's how it was.' Ollie spread himself in a chair and gave his jowls a rub. 'Had me up half the night wondering.'

Vinnie gave himself a fresh cigarette with: 'You got the floor, Chas. No more leaving us in the dark though, eh?'

There was a muted chorus of 'yeah', 'right', and 'no'.

Charlie drained his cup and spat a tealeaf into the saucer. Showed undisguised disgust.

'When was this a democracy, you daft tarts? You want debate, go to university. Today, you plant Soddy. He gets what he deserves, you lot getting legless after the coffin drops. Then you sober up and go to work. You want Raven's head, you'll have to earn it. Like men, not boys with muscles and shooters. Using your noddles.'

Charlie snapped fingers at Matt's sleepy expression.

'You got that?'

'He's got it, Chas,' said Froggy.

'You see it penetrates, Frog.'

'Always *me* gets the finger,' Matt grumbled. 'Deserving it don't make it right, do it.'

Froggy hit him with his hat.

'He gets there in the end, Chas. Like British Rail – late with apologies.'

That earned laughs and a lessening of tension.

278

Charlie gave Hatton a hard look.

'And you hold your water, J.C.. Working your mouth like a drowning goldfish won't move things along no quicker. You've had a taste of the sharp end – had to pick buckshot out of your gin. Now you know what the lads know, ain't no such thing as a friendly weapon. And you're in this war right up to your old club tie. You want to live, think. Got that?'

'Yes, Charles.'

'Right, ears cocked then. Business. Ollie and Pim. I want an armoured security vehicle. A dead ringer for the type they use at Doyle & Brandt's. I want it painted in their livery. And I mean perfecto. So kosher, you could park up in their compound overnight and they wouldn't blink twice. And that's what you'll maybe have to do, so botch it, and you're both well nicked. Get Irish Dermot onto building one, so photographs, plans, whatever it takes. And I want it parked near the City, and I do mean near. No more than ten minutes drive from Threadneedle Street.'

'That's a tall order,' said Ollie.

'Not many,' said Pimlico.

'You're tall fellows. And six sets of Doyle & Brandt uniforms. Found out where they're made and nick one. Have it copied at Manny Manson's shmutter shop in Marlborough Street, then get the original back where it came from. Then the canvas sacks they deliver money in. Fifty perfect copies, right down to the stencilling and the padlocks. Got that?'

Ollie tapped his temple.

'In the old computer, Chas. But—'

'Buts and maybes later. It'll all fall into place nearer the time. Froggy, wake Matt up and listen. Two police motorbikes and black rat uniforms. And if you can't ride one, learn. I want them fitted with radios that pick up the police bands, but I want at least one frequency nobody can cut into. You'll be carrying stripped-down shooters in the panniers. Get onto Horseface Flynn, he's got a tame gunsmith who'll do you a lovely job. But them shooters stay well locked up unless I nod different. You got that?'

Froggy said, 'Right.' Blinking. Matt just stared.

'And make sure they're City of London machines. Not Met ones.'

'Thought they was all the same,' Matt said.

'You want to pull fifteen long ones for being wrong?'

'Not likely I don't. City bikes, right.'

'They'll be kosher, Chas. What about warrant cards?'

'That's using your brain, Frog. Nice one. I want you two good enough to drink tea in the police canteen. You got the balls for that?'

'Do elephants?' Matt said.

Charlie winked at Vinnie.

'Now you, big brain. You find us a warehouse west of Marble Arch. Maybe Ladbroke Grove. Somewhere we can come and go without being overlooked. Suitable for printing presses. Use one of our gash paper companies as a front. J.C.'ll fix you up with all the headed paper and stuff. But don't bother getting telephones installed, just power for the presses. The place stays under your hat until I want to know about it, right?'

'Kid's stuff, Chas. But how does this nail Micky Raven?'

'It's his tickle we're taking over. He draws the twenty years, we walk with the dough. Could be as big as a certain mail train, could be bigger. A nice little Christmas bonus for all of us.'

'And laundering the money, Charles?' asked Hatton.

'In the Cayman Islands, using our Chappie August accounts.'

Hatton actually smiled. Cracked his knuckles as he thought profits.

'How stunningly devious. We need cash flow in that direction. One of the points I wanted to bring up with you.'

'Later. When do they fit you with your new artificial limb, Vin?'

'This week.'

'Good, you'll need it. You and J.C. are taking Chappie August to Hong Kong. You'll find him hiding out in a flat in the Edgware Road. Seems somebody put the block on him down in the Cayman Islands. Now he's hungry enough to do what you tell him.'

Hatton shook his head at that.

'But I'm a total ignoramus about professional pugilism.'

'You know contracts and international law. What Chappie don't know, Vinnie does, and I'm only a phonecall away. They'll set up the deal, find a suitable venue, and get our string of fighters over there to acclimatise. Find the right opponents to make the New York promoters happy. Maybe amongst the local Chinese, or get some Chinese Americans over. Make it a real international bill.'

'Very well, Charles.'

Vinnie looked as if Christmas had come early, but there had to be a catch. Charlie nailed his suspicions.

'No, I ain't keeping you out of harm's way. I need you to keep Chappie August on a short chain. He don't make a trip to the gents or buy a joss stick without you know about it. And take Chinese Cyril with you to handle the locals. He's wrestled all over the planet, and if anybody knows a good stadium, Cyril does. He'll jump at it now the lease is up on the Lotus House, and he needs dough to start a new place. And if you can talk Trooper Wells into going along as a trainer, adviser or whatever, do it. Make him a nice cash offer. Tell him he can take Hettie. Just get him on that plane with you.'

Vinnie's grin was wide and cynical.

'In the hopes that Troop'll maybe put on an exhibition and boost the gate and the TV coverage?'

Charlie slapped his forehead.

'Why didn't I think of that?'

'No idea.'

Charlie pushed his chair back. Put his feet up on his desk.

'Well?' he yawned. 'Any reason why you're all still here breathing my air?'

He was asleep before the soundproof door closed them out.

CHAPTER TEN

'Nice funeral,' Lemmon said as Margot Sadler refused a Player. 'You must have thought a lot of Mr Washington to go to such expense.'

Margot withered him with a look. Flicked a small silver lighter at a black Sobranie and streamed Turkish smoke at the Command Room ceiling.

'Sam was my friend, money doesn't come into it. You are impertinent to count the cost of grief in pounds, shillings and pence. And having your men drag me bodily away from the graveside before the last "amen" had faded was the act of an unfeeling barbarian.'

'I invited you to accompany me here, and you agreed.'

'Was there any choice? Would you rather have had me resist arrest whilst that poor woman, Sam's mother, looked on? They say society gets the kind of police force it deserves, and if that is so, then I grieve for the future of mankind. Three huge Myrmidons to take one frail woman into custody? How telling *that* is.'

'You are not under arrest. You are not in custody.'

'Then I am free to go.'

'Not just yet. You agreed to help the police in their enquiries. When you've done that to my satisfaction, you may leave, knowing yourself to be a good citizen.'

'Let none of us forget our civic duty, Inspector.'

'Commander, actually.'

'Of course. I remember the night you joined the upper echelons of the noble whores. You were quite sweet then.

Now, you are not. Tell me, do you still play acolyte to Bunny Halliday's bishop?'

Lemmon was stung enough to retaliate.

'And wasn't it you who abhorred your late husband's habit of entertaining criminals under your roof? It seems his bad habits did not die with him, but continue with you as the hostess.'

'Have a care, Commander. This cat still has claws, and I'll not listen to you impugn my reputation whilst playing tit-for-tat. Sam was killed during a burglary whilst I was out of the country, and I see little evidence of any effort on your part to apprehend his murderers.'

'Why should it be plural? D'you have evidence to that effect?'

'I read the newspapers. The insurance investigators talked of more than one assailant. If you wish me to help, you had best confine yourself to direct questions a feeble-minded woman such as myself may answer with simple affirmatives and negatives.'

'There is nothing feeble about your mind, Mrs Sadler.'

'You invite rudeness with remarks like that.'

'It's the masochist in me. I shall need proof of when you went abroad, where you stayed, who you met. A full accounting of your movements during the period in question, in fact.'

'You will find that information lodged with my solicitor. You merely have to telephone Mr Thrupp in Lincoln's Inn. He has been instructed to supply you with all relevant information, and is expecting your call.'

'That sounds rather thorough of you, Mrs Sadler. I wonder why you thought that necessary?'

'Obvious, surely. I have been in similar circumstances, as you no doubt recall, and I have learned to make provision for the unexpected twists of fate. You, like the insurance people, have your set ways of going about things. I have learned to pre-empt your, and their, needs. They like lists and photographs of items of insurable value, you want to know my movements during the time my house was ransacked and my house-guest was unlawfully killed. I have made careful provision, that is all. Mr Thrupp has my diary, my travel documents, hotel receipts, and other ephemera which place me in Hamburg and Paris. I thought that best, rather than both of us attempting to rely on my imperfect memory.'

Lemmon's expression hardened with his voice.

'Why so thorough?'

'Why not? It saves confusion in the long run, wouldn't you say?'

'Were you accompanied on this trip?'

'By whom? Mr Washington was to have joined me, but as you know, he was prevented from doing so.'

'Not Mr Dance, then?'

'Not Mr Dance, no.'

'That can be checked, verified.'

'I am sure it can, Commander.'

'Mr Washington was your business partner, I believe?'

'Yes.'

'You'll know where his private and business papers were kept?'

'I don't know that I do. He had his own interests apart from our joint ventures, and I was not privy to all his activities.'

'We believe he rented several lock-up garages. We have his keys, but no idea which locks they fit. It would be helpful to us to be able to locate these premises.'

'Why?'

'It may supply us with some clue as to the motive behind his death. A clever woman like you should see that.'

'Don't sneer at me, Commander, I really don't like being treated like a fool. The motive was robbery, pure and simple. You wish to search these premises you say Mr Washington rented for other reasons. Reasons I don't fully

285

understand, but I have the feeling you are pursuing a line of enquiry that has nothing at all to do with his death, or my involvement with him in the business sense of the word. But naturally, being a dutiful citizen, I will help you in any way I believe to be reasonable. Any information I may have for you will be passed on to you through Mr Thrupp.'

'You have a neat mind, Mrs Sadler.'

'Why should that surprise you? Not drinking does give one clarity, you know. The woman you met in Esher one Christmas long ago has been dead for some time. She died with my late husband.'

'So it would appear.'

'That,' said Margot, 'is at least one thing you do recognise as the truth.'

'Have I called you a liar?'

'Only obliquely. Now, I do have to get back to Sam's mother. She has no other friends or relatives to turn to. Can we terminate this . . . interview?'

'For the present.'

'Which means you plan to bring me back to this dismal building until you've quite wrung me dry. Do understand that I shall not come here on my own again. I shall be accompanied by my legal adviser.'

'Why d'you think that necessary, Mrs Sadler?'

'My dear Commander, wouldn't you were our positions reversed?'

'That would rather depend on how much I had to hide.'

'I hadn't thought of that, but then I'm not a working copper, am I?'

'Give my regards to Mr Dance.'

'When and if I see him.'

'He wasn't at the funeral.'

'Nor he was. I understand he has no liking for them.'

'An odd aversion, wouldn't you say?'

Margot peeled her cuff from her watch. Put on her long black gloves and smiled faintly through her black veil.

'Is it? I hate weddings and people from Fulham. And you are more than a trifle discomforted by the female of the species who might prove to be just a little too knowing. We all have our quirks, do we not, Commander?'

'Why Fulham?'

'Because it tries so hard to be Chelsea when it is nothing more than a piece of the East End that somehow got misplaced in West London. I'm surprised you hadn't noticed that. Perhaps you should walk the streets there with your Myrmidons at your heels, you'd be amazed at what comes crawling out of the brickwork at you. Ravens are only large black crows, but they will eat carrion.'

'The only ravens I know are at the Tower of London.'

'You're quite wrong, you know. Perhaps they commute between the East End and Fulham at the dead of night. I'm no ornithologist.'

'Perhaps not, but you are many things, aren't you, Mrs Sadler?'

'Once an actress, always an actress. A good memory for prepared speeches can sometimes prove useful, wouldn't you say?'

'Message received. We'll meet again, Mrs Sadler.'

'If you say so. I myself do not believe I'm going anywhere until I see myself coming back.'

Margot went out in a swirl of black fur and perfume, and Lemmon sat at his desk without moving as his Player burned itself out in the ashtray next to Margot's Sobranie.

'Arrogant moo, ain't she?' Bulstrode said, coming in from the small outer office where he had been listening over the intercom. 'You can hear Charlie Dance behind every word she says.'

Lemmon breathed a fresh Player alight.

'Move over Vinnie, the Dance firm has a new mouthpiece,' he said. 'Her claws were out at the very mention of Charlie Dance. More to those two than four legs in a bed.'

287

'Nobody gets that close to Chas Dance. Not even that cut-glass cow.'

Lemmon snorted with compressed lips.

'That's a losing bet, Buller. Her pointing us at Micky Raven puts her on the firm, my son. She just hasn't bothered to tell Charlie, that's all. Should be interesting when he finds out.'

'That's one fifteen-rounder that'll go the distance,' Bulstrode said. Grinning.

Lavender Hill sprawled in twilight.

Charlie strolled into a mews behind a new estate of tower blocks that had replaced a cheerful slum of worker's cottages. The local shops had been taken over by Asians, and a sudden influx of black families had changed the area completely. Okra, green plantains and yams had ousted cauliflowers and cabbages from the market stalls, and there were saris and kaftans where dungarees and workshirts had hung. The cinema showed X-rated sex films between bingo sessions, and the two pubs sold more Red Stripe than best bitter to immigrant customers attracted by jukebox sausa, striptease and low lights. The traditional pie and eel shop had become a plasticated hamburger house, and the old Jewish tailor's sold bright PVC garments and bold print shirts under the glare of tubular lights and stuttering neon.

Charlie found Sam's lock-up garage and let himself in with a wire pick. A single bare bulb showed him tea chests of china oddments, art deco figurines and lamps, Victorian prints in heavy frames that might one day come back into vogue. Makeshift shelving was stacked with mahogany and rosewood for refurbishing antique furniture, a collection of chisels and boxwood planes, boxes of old watch and clock movements, and the dust of recent neglect. The whole lot could have been worth a million pounds or ninepence, and would have seemed worthless to the local hounds.

Charlie thought like Sam for as long as it took him to find

Pencils Peachey's plates. They were in a carton under a layer of mint condition Lawson Hope cigarette cards. The surprise was a modern two-shot rimfire Derringer and a box of soft-nosed ·45 ammunition, and proved to Charlie you could be close to a man without really knowing him. Charlie slipped the gun and shells into his fishing bag with the plates, locked up and took a bus back to Windmill Street.

Armchair Doris took the plates to a warehouse in Ladbroke Grove, and the presses installed there rolled continuously for five days. During that time, Micky Raven couldn't make a phonecall or get a haircut without being observed or overheard. Lemmon's squad used their Post Office van and rooms overlooking Raven's offices, home, and cinema above the Raphael's pub. Using equipment supplied by the man from Hamburg, Charlie's telephone engineers wire-tapped the van; every word was relayed to Windmill Street by illegal cables, and by the end of a week, Charlie had enough information to make his move.

He chose to wait for the run up to the twelve days of Christmas.

Regent Street was decked in tinsel stars and illuminated snowflakes, selling Yuletide with cheerful commercial cynicism. By contrast, St James's was as grey as gruel, and the Christmas tree in the foyer of the Reform Club was as frivolous as a circus clown scrawled in the margin of a Latin primer by a homesick mother's boy. Bunny Halliday fed his headcold mulled wine in the library, and started snapping the moment Lemmon sat down.

'The name Lemmon is writ large in my small black book. In letters of blood on a page of fire. In short, my friend, you head my faeces list of the graceless, worthless, and mindless ingrates who've bitten the hand that feeds.'

'Seems I've been a busy boy without knowing it.'

'Shove your bloody impertinence, you disaster. I've been

289

trying to contact you for a week. Where in the blue blazes have you been?'

'Being a proper copper for a change.'

Halliday's snarl was glottal with phlegm.

'In Fulham of all places? Surveilling some pornographer with pretensions? It's simple, you've lost your mind.'

'Not me who's raving wildly enough to be committed, though.'

Halliday coughed into a large handkerchief. Blew his nose with tender care and stared at Lemmon with streaming eyes.

'Now you listen to me. My sources inform me the man Fook surfaced in Hong Kong to conduct a purge of Draconian proportion. The police reports read like the worst excesses of the Spanish Inquisition. I declined seeing the photographs of the victims, thank you very much. The written descriptions were graphic enough for my digestive tract. Unfortunately, one of the casualties was our very valuable informant. Whether he was executed as part of the general purge, or was found out, is not clear. But since he was fed his own tongue before being flayed alive, we assume he admitted his guilt under torture. I doubt that we'll ever get such splendid intelligence again.'

'I'd drink to the poor sod's memory. *If* I had a glass.'

'You've already courted disaster, don't gild the funerary lily with your wayward tongue.'

Lemmon rejected a dozen things he could have said. Gave himself a Player to breathe through and waited for Halliday to stop smothering coughs and sneezes in his sodden handkerchief. The coughs turned to wheezes, and petered out as a series of honks and sniffs.

'Christ, Bunny, why don't you take that temperature off to bed? Cuddle up with a bottle of VSOP and let the virus run its course? Beats hitting me over the head with liverish threats and temper over some supposed misdemeanour of mine. When you're better you can yell at me properly. I'll even hold your coat.'

290

Halliday found a fresh white handkerchief to mop streaming sockets. He was as pink-eyed as an albino coney.

'They'd give you shorter shrift at the Home Office.'

'So that's it. My friend the buffer state reams me out for my own good, not for his own benefit. Gosh, Uncle Bun, thanks.'

'You'd drown without my umbrella, Noah. Your leaky ark is beached on my Mount Ararat. And what was freely given, can as easily be confiscated.'

'My career ain't a bag of sweets, Bunny. So, before I'm sent down in disgrace for upsetting our masters, tell poor dumb Theo just how he's managed to immolate himself. It's not as if I'd set fire to the Home Secretary's old granny, is it?'

'Calmly beetling off in the middle of a multiple murder enquiry might have a *little* to do with it, wouldn't you say? And for what purpose? Why, to watch some grubby film-peddling whoremonger screen salacious footage. Does that strike you as the actions of a reasonable man? And has it not occurred to your malformed brain that your disgrace will doubtlessly reflect badly on myself?'

'Somebody's playing politics with my warrant card?'

'The penny drops. Light dawns.'

'Who?'

'Irrelevant, surely.'

'Not to me, and not to you it seems. You want me to justify my recent actions, so, and let me get this clear; so you can defend us both by using the importance of this covert operation as evidence of what? Justifiable digression?'

'Precisely.'

'Negative, my old son. One word of what I'm doing in the wrong ear – game, set and match.'

'You don't have a choice.'

'Everybody has a choice. I choose "forget it", Bunny. Tell *that* to your witchfinders.'

Halliday's sneeze spilled wine lees over his cuff. He dabbed at the stain, pinking up his third handkerchief.

'Suicide, Theo?' he asked through glue.

'The noble Romans all fell on their swords to avoid the disgrace of public trial. I'll just knock my brains out with my truncheon.'

'You are not the general of a private army, you dolt.'

'That's exactly what I am. And that's what I stay until this is over.'

'Or stopped by order of a higher court.'

Lemmon stared. Swallowed.

'They wouldn't.'

'Ah, but they would. Will.'

'But they don't know what I'm . . .'

'Precisely.'

Halliday pressed a bell and ordered brandies from the steward.

Lemmon stared out at grey buildings and greyer light.

Saw his squad crouched over their tape-recorders and cameras. Suffering cold and cramp and snatched convenience foods for rotten wages and mean expenses. Eavesdropping on lice parading as men for the greater glory of whom? Keeping the sewers from overflowing for superiors who treated them as numbered cyphers and were blithely indifferent to all but their own shining careers. Using dedicated coppers like Bulstrode and Dillman as disposable dressings on a continually weeping ulcer, to be discarded without thought or thanks when their absorbent powers were exhausted.

And here he was, their respected Uncle Theo, being brought to heel by his political master. A man who held no clearly defined post in Whitehall or New Scotland Yard, yet could pull strings within the Metropolitan Police with consummate ease. Using that creaking and outdated Victorian edifice as his own private playground, bending and breaking the rules in the deluded belief that results, however achieved, justified this total perversion of power.

Looking at Halliday with unscaled eyes, Lemmon saw a new truth. There were cracks in the shining veneer. There must have been a subtle power shift. It showed in his conjurer's face, as visible as a botched trick of legerdemain. The magician's egg had fallen from his sleeve to smear his chin with the yolk of failure. A sudden reversal of political fortune made him shrill and unsure of himself. His risen star was waning, and he needed to use Lemmon's operation as a lever to stop the door of success slamming on his foot. And it mattered nothing to Halliday that his loose crowing would jeopardise everything. He was a crippled tiger turned maneater to survive.

The drinks came and the steward left. Halliday fed a balloon of fine Napoleon brandy into Lemmon's hand, waiting for the light of reason to penetrate Lemmon's obdurate skull.

'Act the realist, Theo,' he said. 'And cheers.'

Lemmon rose like a somnambulist. Dashed the brandy into the log fire, heating the core to golden brilliance for an eye-searing second. Blue flame spat like furious cats and Lemmon sounded dreamy.

'The reality is this: Pu Fatt and his dragons are dead, courtesy of Charlie Dance. My knowing that deep in my craw does not mean I can prove it. Just a criminal doing the law and society a favour in his usual left-handed way. And we didn't chase Fook out of London, though I know you made it sound that way when you had one of your clandestine drinks in Whitehall. No, Mr Dance did that. And all because a negro you've never heard of was beaten to death. Murdered I suspect by Vito and Mimi Raphael. Did I say suspect? I know, Bunny, I bloody *know*. The Raphaels work for the man you dismiss as a small-time pornographer. Well, Micky Raven's that and a lot more besides. He's also in bed with Aman Lee Fook. And when Fook returns, as he surely will when he's finished dumping corpses in Hong Kong harbour, he and Raven will forge a drugs circuit that'll be unbreakable. And all you'll have to fight them with will be a bunch of time-serving whores who'd rather take early retirement or a fat bribe than get down to some honest coppering. You won't have me. You won't have my lads. That I promise you.'

'Calm down, Theo, there's a good—'

'Bloody calm down?'

Lemmon's hand found Halliday's mouth. Clamped it closed. Held it closed for several long heartbeats.

'The worm turns, Bunny. Now you just *listen*.'

Halliday nodded with wide eyes thick with cold and shock. Lemmon was a dangerous stranger in a friend's body. Capable of anything.

Lemmon took his hand away. Wiped mucus off on a napkin.

'I quit, Bunny. Resign. You've treated my squad as your own private army for too long, and now it's over. One day some visionary with clout will form a proper national force that can steamroller over the barriers of city and county, but there won't be a bastard like Bunny Halliday controlling it. You know what I've got, old son? Tape. Miles and miles of recording tape. The Raphaels condemning themselves in their own words. Admitting to murder as though it were a game they played. Got Raven's admission of his own culpability. But I can't use any of it, can I? Tape recordings are not admissible as evidence in a court of law in this enlightened society of ours. These animals have to be proven guilty before a judge and a jury. Before twelve citizens who haven't the faintest notion of which end is up unless the judge spells it out in words of one syllable. But that's the British way, isn't it? Having amateurs doing the work of professionals, and let the clever defence lawyers turn a copper's evidence into lies and nonsense. It doesn't matter that the copper may have gone up against shooters with nothing but balls and a truncheon. In court, he's a soft target for any glib whore in a powdered wig arguing his client's cause. You're that kind of an whore, Bunny. So in love with the sound of your own clever rhetoric, you no longer know the meaning of the words themselves.'

Halliday watched Lemmon pace and talk. Mesmerised by the quiet fury of a man pushed far too far.

'The only way I'll bring Dance or Raven to justice is to catch them right in the act. And I'm about to do that with Raven. At least I *was* going to do that. Now I won't, will I? Because you have to know the details. Have to breathe them into the rarified ears of the idiots who govern us. Have them pass it around as an amusing anecdote whilst telling each other what a splendid chap the Halliday fellow is. How, in the fullness of time, he will appear in the New Year's Honours List. Not a mere knighthood for our Bunny, the House of Lords for him, old chap. Then he can really operate, eh?'

Sweat stood out like trembling marbles on Lemmon's upper lip. A moustache of wet pearls. He leaned over Halliday, his hands on the arms of the leather chair.

'You whisper away, Bunny. Blurt it all out to your chums in high places – those who think that the definition of discretion is doing it in the dark under the bedclothes. Raven has an inside man at one of the major clearing banks. A man who orders the security vans to load up their vehicles with huge amounts of money. Millions of pounds. And Micky Raven needs that kind of money to build his new empire in the East End with his new Chinese partner. They plan to heist the security vehicle before it leaves the depot. To be aboard when the collections are made from the clearing banks. Ten in all, we think. Keep that money, and return to collect the mint notes earmarked for delivery. A sweet tickle that I planned to let go ahead – catch them all red-handed with their fingers in the till. And if they were to resist arrest using armed force, they would then save the taxpayers a goodly amount of money by avoiding the need

295

for a lengthy trial. All academic now, Bunny. All a complete waste of time. Congratulations, you whore, you've just made the world a rottener place to live in.'

Halliday could not speak. His nose ran and his eyes were wet blobs of frightened hatred. Lemmon stood away, lit a Player with a very steady hand. Drained of all emotion save mild disgust, he felt cleaner than he had in a long time.

'Save your threats, Bunny. I'm quite aware of what you'll do to me. Be as vindictive as you wish, me and Rhett Butler don't give a damn.'

In the street, Lemmon straightened his shoulders and walked away towards Piccadilly. His driver caught a glimpse of him striding into a biting wind, but by the time he had the car turned around, Lemmon was on a bus to Fulham.

Gone.

Charlie carried his tape-player down the side of a pleasant house in Dulwich Village, and found himself in a neat garden mulched down for the winter. Every tree and plant was labelled, and the lawn was as green as a mint banknote. The greenhouse was a miniature Crystal Palace the size of a small bungalow, and lovingly restored by the owner. Halogen lamps brightened the obscured glass walls, throwing leafy patterns out into the gathering dusk.

Charlie went inside to watch a middle-aged man pottering amongst blooms usually found in the hothouses of Kew Gardens. He wrote notes in a gardening ledger with his glasses on the end of his nose like the chief cashier he was. None of his plants straggled or sported dead leaves; like him, they were neat and well behaved, but grew with a quiet confidence he would never possess. Albert Penslow had never made branch manager despite long and dedicated service to a company that had long ago pegged him as a pen-pusher with no managerial spark. Recently widowed, and with no prospects of promotion, the unloved Penslow loved his garden and hated the bank for making his five years to retirement a barren and meaningless slog to nowhere. Micky Raven had done well to find him.

Charlie admired a jacaranda. 'Didn't know you could grow them in this climate.'

'Given the right conditions, anything will grow.'

Albert Penslow spoke before starting with surprise. A clerk disturbed by a precocious junior.

'That right?'

Penslow tried weighing Charlie up and couldn't. Proving he wasn't the man to refuse or approve overdrafts. 'You're trespassing.'

'So I am. Good to talk to a man who knows the law. Simplifies things.'

'You can't just enter private—'

'I just did, Albert.'

Charlie blew on a maidenhair fern to make it shiver. Tweaked a bowering palm to make it bob. Allowed Penslow to study him through pebble lenses. Said: 'Nasty to think what a bottle of paraquat would do to this lot, Albert my son. And wouldn't you miss it when the law tumbles you? This all here – you in a damp old cell where nothing grows but bars and steel doors.'

Penslow swayed against the potting bench.

'Who are you? How dare—'

'And they'd cancel your pension. You'd come out with nothing, to nothing. If you lived out the fifteen years the judge's slap your wrist with. The courts go hard on trusted servants of the bank who take home free samples. By the time you come out, there'd be strangers in this house. The sort who'd concrete over all this greenery, turn it into a nice four-car garage. And your wife's bits and pieces would go to auction with the rest of the furniture. You back on the streets with a record and nowhere to go. Not a rosy future, Albert.'

'Look, please, I don't understand – are you—?'

'Not the law, Albert.'

'Then . . .'

'And Micky Raven didn't send me, no.'

The name turned Penslow to sallow wax. A hollow man lost in rich foliage.

'I know all about you, Albert. Naughty old you, Micky Raven, the Raphaels and all that money. What's your share, Albert? A few nice grand?'

'Get out of my—'

'Don't be silly, Albert. I'm being friendly. Not like the heavy filth when they find your sticky fingers in the till. They never let up, and they'll gut you in the first twenty-four hours. And the disgrace, Albert. Albert the thief all over the papers and the TV. Your sister in Brighton would know, and her neighbours. They'd know down at the horticultural society. And they'd know in Fulham. And there's your real problem, Albert. Fulham. You don't think Micky Raven's gonna let the filth have you, eh?'

'He promised—' Penslow's delicate mouth clamped closed.

Charlie tutted in pity. Put his tape-machine on the bench and turned it on. There was ragged laughter, the tap of bottle to glass. 'Ain't happy about what, Vito?' a voice slurred. 'We'll get our inside man away sharpish like we said we would. Then you lose him, quiet, no noise.'

'That's . . .' Penslow whispered.

'Raven, yeah,' said Charlie.

The spool turned through background noise to Mimi saying, 'He'll go over the side lovely. Pop him in the ear, into a weighted sack. Pop. Gone. Fish food. Us inna clear . . .'

Charlie switched the voices off.

'There's twenty minutes of that. Ways of making you the late Albert Penslow. They have to make you dead, Albert. What can't speak, can't bubble to the law. That's you buried under your own compost heap. The end.'

Penslow took off his glasses, turned Charlie to fuzz. Replaced them shakily, fearing the unseen.

'Who . . . are you?'

'That depends on you, Albert.'

'Yes . . . I see that.'

'You can't back out, so the tickle's still on. What's needed is a way of keeping Micky and the law off your back, and you alive and without money troubles. Give me what I want, I'll give you that.'

Penslow toyed with a gardening fork. Saw the needle-sharp tines plunged into his back, and dropped it on the bench. Found a stool and sat with his knees drawn up to his chin. Gazed around at his collection of rare floribunda, his flame trees and dwarf hybrids, as shrunken and dessicated as one of his drying corms.

'I should have to leave all this, shouldn't I? Go far away and never come back. All I have is this, and Edith's memory.'

'Never's a long time, Albert. You could put this place into the care of the horticultural society. As a trust. Travel to Peru and do the research for that paper on rare mould disease you said you'd one day write. Really make something of the remaining years.'

'You *know* about that?'

'You've got a reputation, Albert.'

Charlie had Armchair Doris pump a gardening correspondent who used Mother's Club. As fey as his articles on flower arrangements, he'd researched Albert Penslow in exchange for a Brighton weekend with one of Kensington Kate's special fairies.

'But not in my professional life,' Penslow snarled with weak ferocity. 'The bank has used me so . . . *shabbily* for so very long.'

'Bastards. You want Peru, I'll give you safe passage. And a nice little pension that should see you round the world twice. Depends on how co-operative you can be.'

Penslow's sigh was bitter. 'There's always a price.'

'Like bank charges. Feeling sorry for yourself won't realise a lifetime's ambition.'

299

'Ah, a positive thinker. The bank said I never was. I saw my file, you know. They actually wrote of me—'

'Forget it. Send the bastards a postcard from South America. "Glad you ain't here".'

'Wouldn't *that* be something?'

'All you need is a stamp and a ballpoint.'

Charlie eased Penslow off his stool and towards the greenhouse door.

'What exactly *do* you want, Mr . . .?'

'Call me Theo. We go into the house. You make a nice cuppa tea, and we have a nice chat. You make the call our Micky's expecting, then we go over your travel arrangements. Couldn't be simpler, could it?'

'No, Theo,' Penslow said, carefully closing the door. 'That's my Albert.'

Deidre the air-hostess swam beside him in incredibly blue water, matching him stroke for languorous stroke, hair fanned out around her face like golden sea-grass. She was a voluptuous brown fish in submarine sunlight as she turned to embrace him, leaking bubbles from a pouting kiss he couldn't quite reach. There was too much undertow, and a phone refused to stop ringing as he drowned and drowned and drowned. Then Dillman's elbow took Bulstrode in the ribs, and he came awake with the phone being answered in his earphones. Vito Raphael bawled for Raven without covering the mouthpiece, and told Albert Penslow to hang on as Big Alphonse went off to shout down some stairs.

'Lovely manners, those boys.'

Dillman passed lit cigarettes to Payne and Bulstrode and chewed gum as he smoked himself, hoping this was finally the call that mattered. Taggart had gone off for more sandwiches and a crafty pint, and none of them remembered the last hot meal they'd enjoyed. It was bitterly cold in the Post Office van, and the air was thick with old smoke and their collective musk.

'That was some dream, Buller. Looked like the breast-stroke.'

'You'll never know, Dildo. You'll never know . . .'

Dillman grinned and Payne rubbed his broken clavicle. It didn't like the cold and he longed to steep it in a hot bath with an iced gin and tonic going misty from the steam. They all had their private dreams, and Dillman's was being fed steak and kidney pudding by a gorgeous Sloane Ranger with a long silver spoon and longer legs.

'I'm listening,' Raven said too close to the phone. Breathless from three flights of stairs.

'Friday morning,' said Penslow. 'The details will be sent on in the usual manner.'

'What usual manner?' Dillman asked, spilling ash on his dials.

'I get you,' said Raven. 'This Friday definite.'

Bulstrode leaned across to check the internal bug planted in the light socket above Raven's head. The needle jumped with the voices, recording at good gain. He switched across to the ones on the landings and in the cinema. All A-OK.

'Thank you,' said Penslow.

'No, thank *you*,' Raven laughed.

'Good night to you.'

'Yeah.' Raven broke the connection.

Bulstrode tuned to the inside bug as Dillman turned in his seat.

'What usual manner? Have we missed something?'

'What?' Bulstrode grunted as Taggart climbed into the van with his forage. 'Don't tell me, Tag. Sandwiches, right?'

Payne tapped a pen on his log.

'Every syllable's here. That was the first mention of "the usual manner".'

'Wrong,' said Taggart. 'Bread rolls. They'd run out of sliced loaves. But it's ham off the bone and fresh lettuce. She fancies me, that one.'

'Well? Is it a goer, or is it a goer?' Vito asked Raven.

'What d'you think?'

'Give us a break, Mr Raven,' Big Alphonse groaned. 'My undies are ruined as it is.'

'Yeah,' said Rupert.

Dillman said, 'Bread rolls are not the food of love, Tag. She can't fancy you that much.'

'Says you, Dildo. Left her saloon bar customers to serve me.'

'You and barmaids,' said Payne. 'Who else'd swallow your beery breath and get weak at the knees?'

'Barmaids with weak heads.' Bulstrode heard Raven make himself comfortable in an armchair with:

'It's a definite maybe for Friday.'

'What's all this maybe?' Mimi snorted.

'Always a maybe with a big tickle.'

'You holding something back, Micky?'

'No, Vito, I ain't. It all depends on the midweek demand for cash money. You know what Christmas shoppers are like – erratic. Saturday's always been the traditional day for boiling around the stores and elbowing your way up to snatch bargains at the counter, right? And that means a heavy draw at the bank on Friday. But if this new Thursday late-night shopping takes off, it changes the whole thing. Then there could be a big draw on the Wednesday, or even on the Thursday itself. We just have to be ready for which way the punters jump.'

'But you reckon *Friday*, that it?' Mimi asked, frustrated.

'It's a definite maybe, I told you.'

'Bloody riddles,' said Vito. 'Question: when's a goer not a goer? Answer: when it's a definite maybe. You sure you've got any of this right, Micky?'

'I certainly do, my son.'

'All *you* know is bloody maybe.'

'And it's enough,' said Raven. 'I'm going out for a pint. Stretch my legs.'

'Cave it, lads,' said Bulstrode. 'Raven's coming out. Shut that door and put them fags out. Keep it well stumm.'

The rear doors gaped and closed, letting in more street cold.

'Only me, lads,' said Lemmon. 'Uncle Theo's taking you all out to dinner. You remember plates and napkins, knives and forks? Fine wine in finer glasses?'

'Raven's coming out, Guv,' Bulstrode warned.

Lemmon waved an indolent palm.

'Let him pass. Never did like his table manners.'

They crouched in silence until Raven had gone by. He crossed the road and looked to be making for the Bald Eagle when he turned from sight.

Lemmon took Bulstrode's earphones. Turned off the tape recorders.

'Pull the plugs, Buller,' he said softly. 'As of now, we're all on indefinite leave.'

Nobody spoke. Their faces said it all.

'Nobbled,' said Lemmon. 'From a great height.'

'Not the fucking fickle finger, not again?' said Payne.

Bulstrode looked as though he'd taken three low punches and a haymaker. He stamped on his cigarette stub hard enough to rock the van. Worked his shoulders behind his grinding heel as though he mashed an enemy's face. Beyond speech.

'Again,' said Lemmon. 'Shall we up anchor on this brave red ship? Sail towards bright lights and fine cuisine? Talk of what might have been with stoic calm and philosophical insight?'

'I'd rather get pissed if it's all the same to you, Guv,' Taggart said. 'They let us get so close, then give you a parking-metre to guard. My mother warned me, but I didn't listen.'

'Mothers,' said Dillman. 'Are never wrong.'

'You really want us to walk, Guv?'

'Not walk, Buller. Drive.'

Bulstrode got behind the wheel and stripped the blinds from the windows. Blinked at the hard street lights and drove.

Anywhere.

Micky Raven fed coins into the public phone in the Bald Eagle and dialled a phonebox near Dulwich College. Heard the pips die as Albert Penslow answered. Said, 'You used the emergency code. What's gone wrong?'

Penslow could have been reading from a prompt as he assured Raven he was ensuring that nothing would go wrong. A special directive from head office meant tightened security during the critical Christmas period. There were radical changes in the scheduling of deliveries, and a change of routes through the City. He gave Raven the licence plate number of the target Doyle & Brandt vehicle, and the approximated delivery times for each branch.

Raven committed it all to memory; asked why Penslow hadn't given him all that earlier.

'Once a security officer, always a security officer, Michael. Are you so very certain of your own . . . arrangements?' Penslow rang off with a dry, nervous laugh.

Raven went for a long walk to clear his head. Albert Penslow wasn't the fool he'd taken him for. The pity of it was, he couldn't let Mimi and Vito lose the little twerp in the marshlands of Foulness before the robbery. Penslow had to be on duty until it was over.

Penslow hadn't the strength to push out of the phonebox. Charlie let him out and walked him back to his house on rubber legs.

'D'you know,' he said from his favourite chair. 'I rather enjoyed that. Rather like amateur dramatics, Theo.'

'Albert, you're a diamond,' Charlie said, liking the little twerp.

* * *

Lemmon's squad had Gennaro's Restaurant to themselves. The waiters only attended the long table when they were called; Italian discretion at its most wraithlike.

Dillman stirred his brandy with a breadstick, owlish with drink, and Payne's shoulder behaved as he drank gin and tonic from a goblet big enough to house tropical fish. Taggart had decorated his gateau with flags and cocktail cherries, and Lemmon smiled into a tumbler of whisky with four cigarettes burning. Only Bulstrode had picked at his food and drunk little. His brain and stomach churned in opposite directions, and there was nothing left to bring up. He sipped a Perrier water without hearing the brave jokes, too morose to even think about Deidre being home for the New Year. After C10 had done with him, they were quite likely to ship him off to the wilds of nowhere, or stew him through a protracted suspension.

Dillman planned to disappear into Gloucestershire where his sister's husband farmed, and Payne had enough savings to blow on a foreign holiday with sand and camels instead of ski-slopes. Taggart had no ideas, but he was working on it. Lemmon thought about his begonias and time with Elizabeth, waiting for Bulstrode to shrug off depression and fight back.

'You could get some fishing in, Buller,' he suggested.

'Out of season.'

'Sea fishing.'

'Wrong tides.'

Lemmon leaned in and sneered at him.

'Then get some books out of the library and shut yourself in to rot. Drown your liver in Scotch. Eat out of tins and never get out of bed. Forget to shave, to smile, to *think*. Give up, nobody's going to stop you giving your brain to the dustmen. They won't even charge you for taking it away.'

'Ain't me who resigned.'

'You get a nice long holiday out of it, you ingrate.

Pity to see it wasted in a wallow of morbid self-pity.'

'You got a better idea?'

'I've got a wife and begonias. What have you got?'

'A bloody warrant card and a lot of dead time.'

'Why waste a winning combination like that, then?'

'You saying something?' Bulstrode saw he wasn't the only one listening. Even boozed stupid, the squad looked for a way out of the seeming dead-end. Dillman discarded the ploughed fields of Gloucestershire, Taggart pushed his overdecorated pudding away, and Payne stopped blowing bubbles in his drink. They all stared at Lemmon as though he had risen from the tomb to show them life after death.

Dillman called for a gallon of black coffee, and Payne actually shared his cigarettes.

'Well, Guv?' said Bulstrode.

'All I've done is give you indefinite leave. What you do with it is your own affair. I am no longer a party to your various doings, brave lads. If you wish to conveniently lose those tape-recordings, fine with me. If you wish to spend your time and energies sightseeing in the City of London, all grist to my mill. What I don't know about I cannot pass on to those who would know, can I? Whilst I am under scrutiny by those above, they will show little interest in you. Later, of course, that would change. *Later*, being the operative word.'

Bulstrode frowned at Taggart with suspicion.

'I know these prunes enough to trust them. You I don't.'

Taggart belched into a napkin. 'Meaning we four have to trust each other from Hendon Central to Finchley Cemetery, right? One of us squeals, we're all dead coppers with dead careers.'

'I'd find the mouth that bubbled – see how long it could keep bubbling under ten fathoms of salt water.'

'And I'd hold Buller's coat,' Dillman said.

'I'd . . . me too,' Payne slurred. 'Definitely.'

Taggart's smile was sloppy as he put an elbow in his gateau.

'My feelings exactly.'

Lemmon rose ponderously, holding his wallet and a fifth cigarette.

'I shall pay for this repast, bid you adieu and adieu, and yet once more, adieu.'

Bulstrode found the brandy and poured himself a medicinal slug.

'Here's to crime,' he toasted.

'Pays our wages,' Taggart said, clinking glasses.

Dillman picked soggy breadstick out of his drink.

'One for all, and all for one,' he said.

'Me too,' slurred Payne. 'Definitely.'

Then they tackled the black coffee and started planning.

BOOK THREE

CHAPTER ELEVEN

At precisely 6.a.m., Friday 11th December, Ollie Oliphant and Pimlico Johnny Parsons showed their official identification to the gatekeeper at Doyle & Brandt's Maintenance Division in Whitechapel Road. They found the night manager very anxious to co-operate with two senior safety officers from the Heavy Goods Vehicle Licensing Bureau. He took them down to the maintenance bay where the offending vehicle was about to undergo a 3,000 mile service. Wasting no time, the two safety officers donned white coats with HGVLB roundels on the front patch pockets, pulled on rubber gloves, and talked in swift official jargon over their clipboards as they checked the vehicle over. A half hour later, Harris the night manager signed a five-page report of faults that declared the vehicle unroadworthy, and an official enquiry necessary. The vehicle was 'deregistered' and sealed with metal tags, and the two safety officers confiscated the licence plates and the rotor head. Made to understand that the faults lay in the design and manufacture of several mechanical parts, and did not reflect on the excellence of his staff's workmanship, Harris the night manager had no need to be overly concerned, but he would be well advised to keep the matter to himself until officially summoned to attend the enquiry.

Ollie and Pim then drove to their lock-up garage in Bethnal Green, fitted the licence plates to their vehicle, and loaded the sacks of forged money aboard. When they had changed into coveralls silk-screened with perfect replicas of Doyle & Brandt logos, Ollie locked Pim in with the money, and drove the armoured truck to Doyle & Brandt's Security Compound in Pudding Lane. The gatekeeper there had Ollie sign himself in, issued him with a temporary pass, and had a security officer escort the truck into the secure area where the traffic officer came out of his office to stare.

'What's that dustbin doing back here?' he said. 'Ruddy thing's been running sour ever since it went into service. I told Harris I wanted her running, not bodged and back here giving me ulcers.'

Ollie left the engine running and jumped out of the cab. Read the traffic officer's ID patch and winked at him.

'You know Harris, Mr Welbeck. If he ain't crawling to management, he's whacking out memos of complaint about us mechanics. I've just done nine straight hours on this heap of tin, and I know she's a bloody rogue. It's the transmission, you see. There's a bug in it somewhere, and we don't rip the whole lot out, she'll keep coming back to the shop.'

'And I'm a vehicle short,' said Welbeck. 'Good mind to put a flea in Harris's ear. A few home truths'

Ollie offered his Capstans and a light

'What's the point, Mr Welbeck? Only be a shouting match. Do what we do down the shop, get the memos flying. Bury him in paper. Get copies up to management. Tell you what, you seeming a decent bloke, how about I get some of ours sent over? You match your complaints to ours, got to be management takes notice, right?'

Welbeck looked suspicious.

'You ain't a union man, are you? I ain't getting myself in dutch with upstairs by taking the union line.'

'I pay my dues like a good comrade, but I'm strictly for Number One. My mother's eldest son, me. I've done three years under our Mr Harris, and I'm the only one left out of them that started with me down there. The union's done

312

nothing – management's done less. You don't think us mechanics down at maintenance *like* bodging when we're all skilled men, d'you? Letting you blokes up at the sharp end down? Madge, I tell my missus, they're bleeding heroes, them lads on the dustbins. Heroes, and they deserve having the best vehicles, not being sloughed off with what they get.'

Welbeck squared round shoulders. Sucked in a yard of paunch.

'Got the kettle on in the office. Fancy a wet?'

'Can't think of nothing nicer, Mr Welbeck. But to tell you the truth, I only brought this tin cow back to nurse her a bit. I know I shouldn't have done it, but I brought a spare rotor head along. Old Harris hates spares going out of the depot. But knowing how pressed you blokes are with Christmas coming up, I thought I'd have a tinker while I'm here. Then, if she does break down, won't be my head on the block, eh? And you'd have old Harris by the short and curlies for delivering an unserviceable vehicle.'

Welbeck liked that. Ollie drew him aside like a conspirator, even though they had the yard to themselves.

'I could even fix it so it won't bloody go. So long as it don't put your schedules out. Wouldn't want that. But if you could cope, how bad?'

'Harris right up the Congo without a canoe.'

'Has a ring to it.'

'You could do that, er . . .'

'Micky, Micky Raven,' Ollie said. 'Glad to know you, Mr Welbeck, and I can work anywhere. Just let me park the old tin cow with the other dustbins, and with her nose up against the wall, ain't nobody can see me, right?'

Welbeck looked around the yard.

'You'd have to be quick. Can't have you here when the dustbins load and roll.'

'Five short minutes, Mr Welbeck. She's either a goer, or a dead tin cow. Your choice.'

'Dead,' said Welbeck, whispering without need.

'Dead she is.'

'Over there in the secure compound. Just five minutes, mind.'

Ollie winked solemnly and climbed back behind the wheel.

'Trust me,' he said, and drove into the compound.

Four minutes later, he had a cup of Welbeck's tea with two rotor heads over his arm.

'Now, you say nothing, Mr Welbeck. I'll go back and make out my report. Come back in about two hours, and bring you a copy of it. You can make your own report and send it up with mine to management this afternoon. That ought to roast old Harris.'

Welbeck used his watch to make rapid calculations.

'It's coming up to seven-thirty now. You come back between half-nine and ten. We'll have cleared the yard by then.'

'Yeah, and means I can log up another couple of hours overtime. See you later, Mr Welbeck, and thanks for the tea.'

'Nine-forty, then,' said Welbeck. Pleased with his new ally.

It was 7.14 a.m. when Vito Raphael walked up the path of the cottage in Oak Village and put his shotgun against Barney Conran's chin, backed him into the kitchen where his wife made breakfast for their two children, and told Barney to finish dressing whilst his family went for a nice drive in the Bedford van parked outside. So long as Barney did as he was told, he'd see his family for supper. No point in acting brave because he wore a Doyle & Brandt uniform and looked like a real copper when he was only a glorified delivery boy. Vito called Mimi in Camden Town where he had a shotgun on the Tidyman family, told him the Bedford was on its way, and when Micky Raven had called him to

314

say the other two families were in the bag, Vito ripped the phone from the wall. Then Vito told Barney Conran what was expected of him, and made sure he left for work on time. Only then did Vito tear off his rubber clown mask and let himself out of the cottage. He caught the Broad Street train from Gospel Oak and arrived in the City at 7.50 a.m. Spitalfields Market was a short walk away, and Vito collected a big chiller truck from a meat wholesalers next to the police station without drawing any attention to himself. The drive along London Wall to St Paul's took him fourteen minutes, and he reached the old bell foundry in Distaff Lane ahead of schedule.

Micky Raven drove the Bedford van into Euston Station at 7.59 a.m. His ugly rubber mask made the children fretful and his cold voice chilled the women when he told them how to keep their husbands alive. The four women and three children were thoroughly cowed when they boarded the Manchester train, and sat in the Pullman car as directed, trying not to look for the men Micky Raven said would be watching them. The train pulled out at 8.05. Nobody pulled the communication cord or tried to alert the British Rail staff. Every male aboard seemed to be a criminal to the women as they went through the motions of breakfast to keep the children occupied.

In Manchester they would be told what to do next.

Bulstrode and Dillman kept their appointment with the managing director of Intercontinental Bankers Incorporated, and were shown into his penthouse office-suite at 8.02 a.m. He had fifteen minutes to spare before a critical board meeting, and was short of time and temper until Bulstrode explained why they were there in bald English. A tall ex-naval man with a silver Van Dyke and startling blue eyes, the MD listened without comment, delayed the meeting with clipped precision, and stared out at Farthingale Place

315

as he absorbed what he had been told. The long room could have been the bridge of a corvette, the vista of the City of London a frozen ocean of concrete and stone.

'You're both certain there *is* an inside man?' he asked Bulstrode.

'Yessir. No doubt at all. We don't know if he's an employee of the bank or of Doyle & Brandt's.'

'Academic since we own both operations. But you suspect one of my people is the culprit?'

'Yessir.'

'And you've had these suspicions for over two weeks. Yet you let me stew in ignorance. Have I that much right?'

'Yessir.' Bulstrode added nothing more. The MD could work out why for himself.

'Because coming to me earlier might have proved counter-productive. Possibly jeopardised your investigation.'

'Yessir.'

The MD buried a thumb in his beard.

'A narrow view, and one I'd expect from a policeman. I do not castigate, merely observe. It suits you CID fellows to catch these entrepreneurs in the criminal act, whilst the bank would prefer prevention to crude curative surgery. The obverse of my coin bears a very different imperative to yours.'

Bulstrode said nothing, and the MD turned with a raised didactic finger.

'*But*, I hear you argue, *then*, Mr Banker, you could never know for certain who your fifth columnist is. Knowing that assertion to be correct, and knowing also that any precipitive action by myself or any of my senior people might just have sent our Judas scurrying for cover, I therefore grudgingly concur with your opinion.'

Dillman said, 'We're gratified to know that, Sir.'

The MD's look made Dillman feel like a midshipman with an open fly.

'*Are* you, indeed? Never butter a man on the quarter-deck

of his own flagship, Mr Dillman. Your colleague has the
sense to go dumb when it suits. He also knows I have no
choice but to co-operate, and does not presume to labour
the point.'

Dillman thought murder and looked pleasant. Talking
to money was always a strain, and if the MD took it into
his head to call the City of London police, an alp of ordure
would hit a thousand fans.

'Yessir,' he said. Following Bulstrode's lead.

The MD talked down to Bulstrode.

'Whatever plans my Judas and your villains have con-
cocted cannot now be changed at this late hour. They, like
you, and now me, are locked into a ''commit'' mode. I do
not thank you for that, but I can learn to live with it. The
frightened man strikes his colours, this bank will not. The
money will be loaded aboard the armoured car as per
schedule, and the routes will remain unchanged. You people
must be responsible for your actions, just as Doyle & Brandt
must honour their contract. Money in circulation is a worthy
tool of commerce, hidden under granny's floorboards it is
merely worthless coloured paper. From this point onwards
my co-operation will be tacit, but it won't hurt to throw
a scare or two into my security people, eh?'

'How?' Dillman asked, adding a belated, 'Sir?'

'How? By having you meet them, of course. Nothing like
sudden confrontation to flush the Judas hare.'

'Oh,' said Dillman.

'Yessir,' said Bulstrode.

'And they can confirm the route the armoured vehicle will
take. Wouldn't do for you to be guarding the wrong place
at the wrong time, would it?'

Bulstrode pushed that nightmare aside with, 'Nossir.'

'Come. I never use lifts.'

Bulstrode and Dillman followed the MD along a marble
corridor to gallop down eleven flights of stairs to the
basement area where opulence gave way to starkly functional

austerity. The walls were burnished steel, and the black composition rubber floors absorbed sound with banker's discretion. The three great vaults had circular portals and were protected by light-beams and pressure sensors. The staff were all young trainees with the notable exception of the head security officer. He was small and seamed and genteely shabby, and when he saw the MD he shrank inside his clothes like a fearful acolyte seeing the fearful majesty of God in a cellar beneath the Sistine Chapel.

'Penslow,' boomed the MD. 'Police officers Bulstrode and Dillman. You will offer them every facility with your usual sterling efficiency and discretion.'

'My pleasure.' Penslow offered shy handshakes.

'We're being robbed today,' said the MD.

'Really?' said Penslow. 'We can't have that.'

Bulstrode dropped the limp hand with the gnawing suspicion that he and Dillman had been expected.

Bloody how? he wondered.

By 8.26 a.m. Welbeck the Traffic Officer knew it had definitely turned out to be one of those days. He had two crews out with flu, was an armoured truck light, so there was no back-up vehicle, and the crew of armoured truck DB101 had reported for work looking like death warmed up. Even cheery Barney Conran was so down in the mouth his chin nudged his knees. Tidyman, Ross and Cleaver were more morose than usual, and here was bloody Albert Penslow on an unscheduled inspection tour with two hard-faced CID men in tow.

On his usual bi-monthly visits to the Pudding Lane facility, Penslow did nothing but nitpick about the already stringent security at Doyle & Brandt. You'd think the man had invented the atomic clock the way his delivery schedules were timed to the precise minute, unlike the quarter-hourly approximations of the security firm's other clients. Penslow was a pygmy with a big stick, but Welbeck knew enough

318

to ingratiate himself with the smarmy little fart. Penslow represented the major shareholders who paid Doyle & Brandt handsomely to trundle their millions around the City of London clearing banks in dustbins on wheels. Not for Welbeck to rock the lucrative boat then, and keeping his ulcer quiet was the order of the day as he smiled and smiled until his jaw creaked.

Welbeck had day passes issued to Bulstrode and Dillman, and took them into his office to show them the master plan of the Pudding Lane complex with its underground vaults and the high-speed lift that brought the money up into the centre of the maximum-security inner compound. Even in the unlikely event of unauthorised personnel getting into the inner compound, they would be trapped there until released from outside. All the electronic controls were operated from the control tower on the north-east corner of the building. The only access to the inner compound was through a single set of electrically-operated steel gates, and these were further protected by alarms and automated shutters that dropped into place in under two seconds. Welbeck crowed a little as he explained all that, knowing Penslow had never been able to find a flaw anywhere. A man must take sly pleasure where he can.

Penslow bared his wristwatch at 8.32 a.m. with a tut of dismay.

'DB101 should already be loaded, Welbeck. My schedule stipulates that loading should take place one clear hour before departure. I and my masters made that a contractual obligation, as you are well aware.'

Welbeck willed a coronary on Penslow with a poisoned smile.

'Perhaps you'd like to watch the loading operation, gentlemen? By the time we reach the inner compound I'm sure they'll have brought the consignment of new banknotes up from the vault.'

319

'Let us hope so.' Penslow jotted a note in a small black book.

'How much is the consignment worth?' Bulstrode asked, sure he had Penslow's voice on tape, a piping falsetto to Raven's grating baritone.

'About two mill.' Welbeck held the door open.

'Two million, one hundred thousand and fifty eight pounds,' said Penslow. 'Precisely.'

'And you've a record of the serial numbers?'

'Naturally, Mr Bulstrode.'

Bulstrode and Dillman hung back to put space between them, Penslow and Welbeck. Dillman pointed a finger at Penslow's spine, his thumb cocked.

'Got to be that rooster's in on this with Raven. But are they coming in here after it?'

'Not likely, is it? Too much like a shooting gallery.'

Dillman turned his imaginary gun into crossed fingers.

'Hope you're right there, Buller.'

'You, me, *and* Tiny Tim.'

Bulstrode and Dillman opened their stride to gain on Penslow and Welbeck as they crossed windblown concrete to the inner compound. Welbeck nursed an ulcer and a grudge, but Penslow could have been returning a library book. The man was too cool by half, and Bulstrode wished he knew why.

Pimlico raised the trapdoor in the floor of the armoured vehicle at 8.34 a.m. After eighty-four minutes of breathing stale darkness, the cool and conditioned air blowing in to dry the sweat on his face was very welcome. He heard the electric hoist bring the money up from the vault on a trolley, and the slap of rubber soles as the crew of DB101 wheeled it across to load aboard their armoured vehicle. By lowering his head and shoulders through the trapdoor, Pimlico could see their boots a vehicle's width away, and know good old Ollie couldn't have parked closer without losing paint. He laid his tools to hand, listening to the drone of voices as he waited to make his move.

Welbeck's description of loading procedures was constantly interrupted by snotty asides from Albert Penslow. Pimlico grinned, the little twerp was keeping Welbeck flustered, just as Charlie had told him too, and the man certainly seemed to be enjoying his last official function for the bank he hated so much.

Then Dillman was suggesting they run a second dustbin as a decoy.

'A splendid notion.' Penslow kicked the rear wheel of the armoured car Pimlico lay in, barely rocking the suspension. 'We could use this vehicle here, Welbeck.'

'Ordinarily, yes, Mr Penslow,' said Welbeck.

'And just what is so extraordinary about today?'

Welbeck's ulcer complained audibly.

'It's a non-runner,' he mumbled.

'A horse-racing term is hardly fitting for this situation, Welbeck.'

Welbeck's stomach rumbled.

'You have a serviceable vehicle and an able crew. A schedule cannot be changed without twenty-four hours notice, Mr Penslow. If there is any doubt in your mind, you can always cancel the run. That's the usual procedure when faced with a serious security risk, and I'm not certain that you're not holding something back here. Doyle & Brandt isn't obliged to risk it's personnel if we have information—'

'Look here, Welbeck—'

'No, sir, I won't. If my crew doesn't want to volunteer for this run, you won't see me trying to change their minds.' Welbeck had dug his heels in. Was about to let management take the decision. By the time they'd put their guinea-pigging heads together and come up with a ruling it would be too late to make the run anyway. Stuff it.

'Forget the decoy,' said Bulstrode. 'We don't have the manpower to cover two trucks.'

'Something ain't kosher here, Mr Penslow. I'm taking this to management.'

'You'll do no such thing,' Penslow snapped. 'My instructions are clear, as these policemen will verify. The run will take place.'

'Not if the crew don't volunteer their services, it won't.'

Penslow drummed fingers on the side of Pimlico's truck.

'Very well, Welbeck. We will ask them. But this is hardly the place to discuss the matter.'

'There's my office if you prefer. But I still think—'

Barney Conran cleared his throat. Thought of his family at gunpoint.

'I can't speak for the other lads, but I'm willing to chance it.'

'And me,' said Tidyman.

'I won't have you being pressurised, lads, Barney. Let's go into it over a nice cuppa in my office,' said Welbeck. 'You wouldn't have any objection to *that*, would you, Mr Penslow?'

'How you spend your time in the forty-six minutes between now and the scheduled departure is entirely your own affair. I myself would be grateful for a hot drink.'

'This way, then.'

The group went away, the steel doors closed, and the main lights were replaced by the dull red glow of service lamps.

Pimlico rolled out onto concrete, wormed across to the loading bay in the left wall of DB101, and went to work with his custom-built tools. Ten minutes later, he had wriggled up inside the vehicle and opened the rear doors from the inside. Changing the money from one armoured car to the other took him thirteen more minutes, and he was bolted back inside his own truck long before the crew returned to take DB101 out at dead on 9.30 a.m.

Pimlico dozed, his head resting on canvas bags of unused banknotes.

*　　*　　*

Charlie Dance arrived at Bank Underground Station at 9.01 a.m. Unlike the rush-hour crowds of City office workers he was in no hurry, and he rested his fishing bag on the corner of Threadneedle Street to watch two motorcycle policemen direct traffic across the busy Cornhill-London Bridge intersection. Froggy and Matt looked well in their uniforms, and their immaculate machines were parked on the corner of Lombard Street. A young beat constable with white armbands took advantage of a lull in the traffic to cross from Poultry to explain that he was assigned to traffic duty there.

'Right, laddy.' Froggy showed off his sergeant's stripes and false military moustache. 'Just as well you came when you did. Me and Constable Dixon here are on special escort duty. We'll be coming back this way in a hurry, so you watch out for us and an armoured truck. The second we cross Cornhill going west, I want you to seal the road behind us for a good two minutes. And you let nothing, and I do mean nothing, get on our tails. Can't tell you more than that, but you seem a bright enough lad.'

The young constable glowed.

'Got you, Sarge. A Doyle & Brandt comes through here most every Friday. That the dustbin you're on about?'

'Very observant. Well done.'

Froggy threw a small salute, and he and Matt roared away down Lombard Street. Charlie wandered towards Cheapside, and the young copper thought about growing a moustache like the sergeant's. It was very handsome.

Dillman drew Bulstrode aside at 9.28 a.m.

'I smell very red herrings, Buller.'

'You and me both. Shoals of the crimson rascals.'

Bulstrode watched Barney Conran's crew board armoured car DB101. None of them were happy about making the run, yet nothing would persuade any of them to back down, despite Welbeck defying Penslow and offering to take the flak from 'upstairs'. They were sleepwalkers going through the motions, and whatever motivated them, it wasn't bravado. Barney Conran had needed the toilet twice, shrugged it off as flu symptoms, but his haunted eyes told a different story. And Albert Penslows chirpy manner struck dischords, playing the game as though he climbed the ladders and the police slid down the snakes. Bulstrode missed Lemmon's insight and wished he had more man-power. Wished he could slam Penslow in a cell until this was all over. Sweat him hard instead of allowing him to trot back to the bank.

Dillman had chewed his lips raw.

'Somebody's working the crew's strings. I smell coersion.'

'There's a switch coming, Dildo. Time we pulled one of our own.'

'With what? Us four idiots and two mobiles? Some army.'

'We leave Tag and Payne to bring up the rear in Mobile Two. You take Mobile One on your own.'

'And you're going where? On your holidays?'

'With them.' Bulstrode pointed at DB101. Patted his shoulder holster. 'Me and my brief inside should even up the surprises. And with Penslow back at the bank, ain't no way he can know about it.'

Dillman showed shock for a millisecond.

'A revolver against shotguns is spit against the apocalypse, you lunatic. At least take my Thompson.'

'Too much firepower in an enclosed space, Dildo. The inside of that dustbin is probably the safest place to be.'

'Famous last words, General Custer. Be lucky. Be careful.'

'My middle names, Dildo.'

Bulstrode jumped aboard DB101 to trade stares with Conran and Tidyman as the door slammed closed. Both men had a bilious look in the tungsten light, and Bulstrode hoped they wouldn't vomit as the truck jerked into motion. Bulstrode checked the load of his Smith & Wesson ·38, exuding confidence he didn't feel.

We're coming Raven, he thought. *Be there.*

Dillman raised Taggart and Payne on his Q-car radio. They responded with 'Mobile Two', listened to the change of plan without comment, and Dillman signed off when DB101 pulled out into Pudding Lane to take Upper Thames Street east. He was about to move off ahead of it when his passenger door opened and Lemmon sat in beside him.

'You may proceed, Dildo, and I will tell you a tale to gladden your heart. If you can listen attentively without taking your eyes off the road.'

'Sugar my porridge,' said Dildo, who never swore.

Lemmon talked about a midnight session at the Home Office, a lot of straight talk amongst a lot of very senior policemen, a directive that gave Lemmon very wide powers for a very short period, and put a certain Bunny Halliday firmly out to grass in the political wilderness. It kept Dillman nodding all the way to the first collection in Crutched Friars where absolutely nothing happened.

Charlie Dance walked past the old bell foundry in Distaff Lane without a second glance. The old wooden gates were locked closed and covered with faded and not so faded fly poster. The dirty windows stared, and a demolition contractor's shingle was nailed to the brickwork below a plaster bell set in a crumbling tower that had once had a gilded dome. The carved legend on the bell read: *Saml Beckhorn & Sons. Est AD 1832.*

The office block next door was a century younger and had once been a warehouse. It had been facelifted with a glassed lobby, modern Critall windows, and was for rent on a short lease before also being bulldozed for development. A green Mercedes was parked outside, and Hatton's chauffeur was too busy polishing chrome to see Charlie enter the building. Charlie heard Hatton being called 'Mr Weaver' by an estate agent as they argued terms somewhere on the first floor, and Charlie went down into the basement to lock himself into a storeroom until he heard Hatton and the estate agent leave. Then he took the stairs to the flat roof to look down into the yard of the old bell foundry.

A new chiller truck was parked on the cobbles below him, and was faced towards the rear gates leading out into Victoria Mews where Charlie knew there was nothing but hoardings bordering an empty building lot. The rear doors of the chiller truck were bolted open and the ramp was down. Vito Raphael read a newspaper leaning against the cab, and Mimi Raphael watched the gates leading out into Distaff Lane, a broken shotgun under her arm. There was no sign of Raven, Big Alphonse or Rupert Baer, but they wouldn't be far away.

Charlie unzipped his fishing bag and laid it on the parapet. There was plenty of time to assemble and load his ·30/30, from the look of the sky there could be a cloudburst, and he didn't want it rained on unnecessarily. He rummaged for a two-way radio and laid it beside his bag. Found Sam the Spade's Derringer and a pound bag of granulated sugar, put them in his overcoat pockets and checked out the fire escape leading down into the foundry yard. No problem. It was 9.39 a.m., and he had time to kill. He did it humming softly to himself.

Welbeck had stared at Ollie Oliphant for a full minute by 9.46 a.m.

'You called Harris *that*? A dictatorial inadequate with a power complex? *Harris*? Where does a mechanic learn words like that?'

Ollie scratched his false moustache with a gloved finger.

'Library books mostly. That phrase come out of one on Adolph Hitler. Got some beauties saved from a book on Mussolini.'

The radio-link to DB101 fuzzed from the wallspeaker, reporting its arrival at the second bank in Jewry Street without incident. Ollie watched Welbeck read his phoney memo to Harris the Whitechapel Night Manager a second time.

'How'd you get away with it, Micky?'

Ollie shrugged. Toyed with a rotor head lead.

'Nobody else can keep that rogue dustbin onna road, can they? Only me, right? I write memos and reports. Harris reads 'em, goes purple and has a yell. Tears 'em up, writes one of his own, and has me sign it. It's a game we play. Thing is, he don't know I keep copies. Got me a file a yard thick.'

Welbeck filled his kettle. Lit the gas and sat down again.

'They're a bit strong if they're all like this one, Micky.'

'That's as maybe. You don't want my file, ain't no skin off my spanner.' Ollie moved to take the report back.

Welbeck got to it first. Shut it in a drawer.

'Didn't say that. Now did I?'

Ollie winced at his wristwatch.

'Time I wasn't here. Harris won't pay overtime much after ten. Listen, Mr Welbeck, you have a think, eh? You want that file of mine, you give us a bell down at the yard. I ain't on shift again until next Wednesday, so leave it till then, eh? See, what Harris don't pay in overtime, I take in days off. Adds up too.'

'Sounds like you've got him coming and going, Micky.'

'I told you, it's a game. OK if I get the truck now?'

'After a nice cuppa.'

'Love to, but I can't give Harris no ammunition, now can I?' Ollie offered his hand. 'Excuse the gloves, acid burns.'

Welbeck shook hands warmly.

'I'll be in touch, Micky. You walk over to the inner compound. Time you get there, the tower'll have opened the gates.'

'DB101 leaving Jewry Street for Mincing Lane,' said the wallspeaker.

'Wednesday, Mr Welbeck. Don't forget.'

Welbeck dialled the tower and took a stomach powder as he waited for his tea to brew. DB101 was pulling up outside the Mincing Lane bank when Ollie drove Pimlico and over two million pounds out into Pudding Lane.

Wind threw spits of rain at the office windows, and Welbeck was glad he was in the warm. He took out the phoney memo to chuckle afresh, enjoying his fifth cup of hot, sweet tea.

'Mincing Lane branch,' said a bored girl telephonist.

Mickey Raven spoke briskly through a handkerchief.

'Traffic Control, Doyle & Brandt here. One of our units is making a collection at your branch right now. Please have one of the crew come to the telephone, this is most urgent.'

'One moment, Doyle & Brandt.'

Raven listened to dead air. Watched the long hand of his watch sweep off precious seconds. After some clicks a voice said: 'Conran here, Mr Welbeck.'

'Listen good if you want your family back. There's a change of plan. You pass up the Change Street collection. Pass the bank and keep going south. You cross Cannon Street and watch for the man with a newspaper. You got that? The man with the news—'

Conran butted in. Holding back hysteria.

'No, *you* sodding listen. Call it off. We're knee-deep in the filth.'

'You want your kids back without noses?'

'We're surrounded by the CID, you effing animal. Armed law, you got that? Effing shooters. There's even one aboard the dustbin.'

Raven's acid voice etched metal.

'Who bunnied? You?'

'Nobody talked. They *know*, is all. Effing Christ, listen—'

'The filth. How many?'

'Two cars. I dunno. There's this Bulstrode—'

Raven gripped the phone hard. Touched the bridge of his nose, still tender from the night Bulstrode hit him in the face with the bar phone at the Troubadour. *Things have a way of coming around*, he told himself.

'What?' said Conran.

'Tell your driver to watch for the man with the newspaper when he crosses Cannon Street. Go where he says.'

'But the filth—'

'We'll take care of the outside filth, Barney. *You* get to handle the rozzer inside the dustbin.'

'How, you mad basket? The man's got shoulders and a shooter. He don't never take his eyes off—'

'They're your kids.'

'But—'

'But nothing. Do it.'

Raven cut the connection and buffed the receiver with his handkerchief. Smiled at the old man in the Mincing Lane tobacco kiosk. Tipped him ten-shillings for being allowed to call his heavily pregnant wife and went outside. Barney Conran came out of the bank, talked to the driver of DB101 through the grilled side window, and climbed back aboard. Dillman and Lemmon were in the leading Q-car, and when DB101 followed them up the street, Raven calmly watched Taggart and Payne drive past.

To them, Raven was just another face in the crowd. He flagged a taxi in Fenchurch Street and had himself driven to Cannon Street where Rupert Baer and Big Alphonse were stationed in doorways. Raven's nod sent Alphonse off towards Change Street, and Raven strolled down into Distaff Lane like a man dawdling between appointments.

It was 10.11 a.m., and rain spotted the pavements.

Charlie went over the parapet when Micky Raven called Vito and Mimi under cover to share hot drinks from his vacuum flask. They lit up cigars in one of the side buildings, and Charlie went down the slippery fire escape on rubber soles.

The last flight was hooked up on a rusty chain, and there was an eight foot drop to the cobbles. Charlie went through the railed guard, got a hand to the edge of the iron landing and let himself swing into space. Hung there and listened to Vito worry about his low sugar levels. Let himself drop behind a row of bins filled with scrap metal, and crouched there as Raven told Mimi his brother was faddy about his diet.

'Gotta take care of the old bod, Micky. It's a temple,' said Vito.

'Well, yours has been desecrated by vandals,' said Raven.

'What's the time?' Mimi asked.

'Time you bought a watch.'

'Never carry nothing personal on a job, Micky. You know that.'

'You could have put more sugar in this tea,' Vito grumbled.

'Listen to the Tate & Lyle kid. Mr Cube himself.'

'Sugar's bad for you, bro,' Mimi said.

'Not with my metabolism. One of the doctors told me that when I was wrestling. Said it was a kind of diabetes us atheletes suffer from.'

Raven said something that made Mimi laugh, and Charlie crept across to the side of the chiller lorry. He used a pick on the locked petrol cap, taking his time.

'It's the excessive use of like, y'know, sweet things that's bad for you, right? Not ingesting it when you need it,' said Vito.

'Fucking ingesting? Listen to the hippocratic oath giving the long words an outing. You been reading the back of the aspirin bottle again, Vito?'

'What's wrong with words? Every sod uses them, right?'

'Only to get it said. Long words is for longer brains. You ain't qualified, Vito. Stick to shooters and bonking tarts, right, Mimi?'

'If you say so, Micky.'

'I say so.'

Charlie got the petrol cap off. Laid it on top of the tank and reached for the pound of sugar. The cap slid off. Made a tinny chime when it hit the cobbles and rolled under the lorry.

'Cats,' said Mimi.

'More like rats,' said Raven. 'Take a look, Vito.'

'Not with my low sugar levels, I ain't.'

Charlie froze against the cab with rain dripping off his hat.

'No sugar in your bottle, more like it.'

'Who can like rats?' Vito said.

Charlie kneeled to peer under the lorry.

Mimi laughed and said, 'There's a box of Bertie Bassett licorice allsorts in the cab I got for later. You can have a dip in them on your way to check on the rats, right?'

'Ain't much sugar in licorice.'

'There is in the hundreds and thousands they coat them with. All coloured sugar. Red and white and blue. Patriotic.'

'That's rich coming from an Eyetalian.'

'Born in this country, Micky. I ain't some pasta immigrant.'

Charlie could see the petrol cap and couldn't reach it.

'Don't wind me up, Mimi,' Vito said. 'They're there, are they?'

'A bag as big as your head, bro. Straight up.'

'Gimmee me shooter.'

'For what? That's all we need: you shooting at mice and waking up the filth. You're wearing boots, ain't you?'

Vito came outside grumbling. Charlie rolled under the lorry and watched his boots walk to the cab. Disappear when he jumped onto the running board, and jump back down as Vito tore at cellophane.

'Any rats?' said Raven.

'No,' Vito said without looking. 'And there ain't any sugared ones neither.'

'Life's a bastard,' Raven sneered.

331

Charlie scooped up the petrol cap and rolled out into rain as Vito went back inside to share the licorice allsorts. Poured sugar into the tank and replaced the locked cap. The rain smashed down into the yard, and puddles began to form as Charlie jumped for the edge of the fire escape and missed. He made it on the third attempt, and was hauling himself up when Vito started talking about the merits of a wheat-germ and carrot juice diet. That made Raven even more caustic, and Charlie could hear his sarcastic comments from the roof as he loaded his rifle.

Flurries of quartering rain made Dillman's windscreen wipers work hard as he led DB101 up Gracechurch Street to make the left turn into Cornhill. The stoplight glared red, and Lemmon cursed to save Dillman drawing on his restricted armoury of innocuous expletives. He was in no mood to hear 'Heaven's entrails' or bloody 'Golly gosh' for the umpteenth time.

'Rain and a traffic jam,' Dillman groaned. 'It's enough to take the shine out of your trousers.'

'Take heart, Dildo. The fun can't start without us.' Lemmon made certain his Browning automatic pistol didn't snag on his pocket. Went over the plans he had made in his mind.

After the collections from the Cheapside and Change Street banks, DB101 would double back through Cannon Street and Eastcheap Towers to make the final delivery to the head office in Farthingale Place. Lemmon was confident the Raven firm would strike there, and had the entire area surrounded by armed units of the Flying Squad. The pleasure of having Detective Chief Superintendent Saul Cotton hand over his men and vehicles without the chance to demur kept Lemmon buoyant despite three short hours of fitful sleep.

The lights turned green and nothing moved. Cornhill and Leadenhall Street was a solid mass of halted vehicles.

Dillman said, 'Mother of pearl', and refused one of Lemmon's Player's, his mouth too dry for tobacco.

There was a roar of motorcycle engines, and two black rats came out of nowhere to clear the intersection of traffic. They bullied the private cars into the kerb and waved DB101 and its escort out onto the crown of the road.

'Am I seing this?' Dillman asked.

'Move, Dildo, you frozen pilchard. They're waving you on, man. D'you really want a suspicious City of London traffic wally poking his nose through your quarter-light?'

'Nossir.'

Dillman swung left into Cornhill with DB101 on his rear bumper. Followed the police motorcycles down a magically opening path to the intersection where no less than nine roads converged. The copper on point-duty outside the Bank of England gave the black rats the high sign as they roared past, and waved Dillman on, giving him and DB101 the right of way through Poultry to Cheapside beyond.

With the grey bulk of DB101 blocking their rear-vision, Dillman and Lemmon didn't see the policeman on point-duty force Mobile Two to brake hard. Or the heated exchange that followed as Taggart and Payne showed their warrant cards just too late to stop a solid wall of traffic flowing across the intersection towards London Bridge.

Froggy used the high-frequency channel to report to Charlie, he and Matt keeping well ahead of Mobile One.

'Nice one,' said Charlie. 'See them safely to Change Street, then get back here to cover Victoria Mews, And no shooters – yet.'

'Roger,' said Froggy.

It was 10.19 a.m.

Rain drummed on the roof of DB101 as it pulled up outside the Cheapside bank. Ross and Cleaver left the cab to bring the money out of the bank, and Conran and Tidyman waited to haul it inside through the chute. Bulstrode spun his revolver into its holster and decided to bring things to a head before Conran and Tidyman fell apart.

'What's Raven got on you fellows?' he asked abruptly.

'Who?' Conran's face had too many hollows.

'So he didn't give you a name. But you know who I mean?'

'What's he on about, Tidy?'

'Dunno.' Tidyman looked nowhere and everywhere.

'Come off it, you clowns. You broke security back there in Mincing Lane, Barney. Ross or Cleaver should have taken that call from Doyle & Brandt. Assuming it *was* Doyle & Brandt. But you left the armoured car yourself. That call wasn't from Welbeck, he'd have used the radio link in the cab. Who whispered in your ear, Barney? Raven?'

'Don't know any Raven.'

'Then who whispered? A nameless friend?'

Conran tried not to gabble.

'In your ear, mister. I'm senior man on this crew. All security calls come to me. That's regulations, right, Tidy?'

'Right,' said Tidyman. Uneasy and pale.

'Lies beget lies, lads.' Bulstrode was about to nail them with his true suspicions when somebody thumped on the rear doors, and he heard Dillman call his name. 'Open up, Barney.'

Conran's sneer almost worked.

'That's a *real* breach of regulations, mister.'

'My responsibility. Open it.'

Conran used his keys and Bulstrode peered out at Dillman hunched in quickening rain.

'Tag just came on the radio. He and Payne are in the middle of a traffic jam you couldn't unravel with a crochet hook, would you believe. Some soppy copper took them for villains and decided to drown them in nine streams of traffic. You'll have to watch your own tail until they catch up, Buller.'

Bulstrode stared at the traffic jam behind him. Thought,

Some hopes of that this side of Christmas. Said, 'Can't we take a chance — whistle up our tame black rats to clear the way?'

'Mr Lemmon said not. Emphatically. Gotta go.'

'Lemmon? Hold up, Dildo.' Bulstrode was talking to an empty gutter. He slammed the self-locking steel door and stared out through the small grilled window as Conran and Tidyman hauled canvas sacks of coin out of the chute. The traffic seemed to brawl through dark waters, driving on sidelights in the gathering gloom. Uncle Theo may have turned up, but Bulstrode knew a lot of jokers were about to be played. He just had to break Conran and Tidyman down without further delay.

He turned away from the window and was slammed in the face by a heavy canvas bag of silver coin. There was the sound of a fist in sand. He felt his mouth numb and split open as goblins of light danced behind his thick eyelids. He got hold of blue serge that ripped out of his hand. Something heavy took him across the back of the neck and his knees hit the floor. There was a sickening spiral of whiplash and bile as he fell reaching for his revolver. Hit again, hot neon arrowed into his exploding brain and he didn't feel his face flop against crisp sacks of notes.

'Gonna be sick . . .sick . . .' Tidyman drooled.

'Think of the kids,' Conran screamed. 'The *kids*!'

'Sick . . . thinking of the . . . kids . . .'

'Empty the chute, you tart. The chute!'

'Sick . . .'

'Move.'

Conran held the heavy black revolver between thumb and forefinger as the truck lurched into motion, mesmerised by the thick worm of blood leaking from Bulstrode's ear. If it touched his foot he knew his heart would stop.

Dillman turned into Change Street at 10.32 a.m., two minutes behind Penslow's overtight schedule. The two motorcycle policemen made U-turns and roared off back

335

the way they had come without a backward glance. Nobody was sorry to see them go, least of all Commander Lemmon, who thought of them as 'two-wheeled bastards'.

'Your position and status, Mobile Two? Over?' Lemmon asked the radio.

Payne's voice crackled with more than static. Was underlined by swearing and tyre-squeal. 'Using the pavements to reach you, Mobile One. Feel like Ben Hur's co-driver. Estimate with you in two minutes. Over and out.'

'Bloody silly sodding uniformed dollops,' Taggart swore into the mike before Payne released the 'send' button.

Dillman pulled into the kerb, leaving enough room for DB101 to park directly outside the bank. 'Did Painful say pavements, Guv?'

'Who cares? So long as he gets here.'

Lemmon got his Browning to nestle more comfortably, and was lighting a fresh Player from his stub when a pedestrian with a rubber face smashed the windscreen with a heavy wrench. Lemmon raised his forearm to protect his face and eyes. Something metallic rolled in his lap, and he found himself choking on thick fumes. The interior of the car turned crimson and his crotch caught alight. Lemmon fell out through the passenger door as DB101 accelerated past, barely missing his kicking legs. Thick red fog rolled out of the Q-car, and Lemmon heard Dillman coughing hard enough to burst blood vessels. The bank alarm rang and traffic squealed to a halt as Lemmon scooped water from the gutter to douse his burning fly. More canisters made smoke, and there was nothing to see but rolling carmine stink.

Trying not to suffocate as he crawled after DB101 on hands and knees made of useless melted rubber, Lemmon wondered how he would explain his wound to Elizabeth, and that made him angry. He cleared the smoke and ran with tears streaming down his blackened face, forgetting he was over forty and no longer needed to prove himself.

Taggart swore like a Borstal inmate and drove at oncoming traffic on full heads, elbowing his horn. He had smoked his tyres leaving Cornhill, and swung left at Mansion House to enter Victoria Street on the wrong side of the road. Mounting the pavement to avoid a slowly turning lorry, Taggart knocked a street-sign out of true as he corrected the first of several speed-wobbles. When he took the Q-car across the Bread Street intersection, Payne knew he was going to die.

Taggart just swore and drove.

Never a good passenger, Payne rode with braced arms and legs and clenched buttocks. The strain on his barely-knit collar bone sent pain through his chest, and sweat popped out across the bridge of his nose. Watling Street was just a blur as the wipers batted through rain and diesel scum kicked up from the puddled road. Payne's larynx had failed. His mouth was just a hole he breathed through, and he knew he would die without the small comfort of a last whimper of protest. He couldn't even think of a prayer, let alone utter one.

The Q-car touched eighty as it raced towards Change Street where the traffic lights flicked from amber to red. Taggart would never find the brakes in time, and Payne's short career would end when Taggart buried their bonnet in the back of the newspaper truck ahead of them. Payne's last view of the world would be the red and yellow legend: *First With The News* THE EVENING NEWS.

Bloody pathetic.

Taggart stopped swearing. Said, 'Hold water, Canute', and braked stiff-legged.

The Q-car spun in its own length and the world made two crazy circles. Payne's nose bounced off the windscreen and whiplash turned his head in the wrong direction. His knees hit the dash as he was jack-knifed forward, and he saved his face with his elbows. Then there was a sort of quiet the wipers flicked through, and Payne was alive enough to pinch his bloody nostrils. Taggart had somehow managed to find space between the newspaper truck and a grey saloon, and had come to a sliding halt with his front wheels dead in line with the pedestrian crossing. His grin was all teeth when he winked across at Payne, and he was sorting out first gear as DB101 went across the intersection at speed. Payne decided he'd murder Taggart later as red smoke drifted down Change Street, and they both heard the bank alarm drilling holes in the driving rain. Then Dillman was retching into his radio-mike, trying to make words out of throat convulsions.

Taggart put his foot down. Made a racing turn, spinning his wheels on the slick cobbles and zebra stripes. Payne shouted directions as a running man came out of red smoke to flip over their bonnet. He made a lazy somersault and a lazier sprawl on the crossing. A rubber respirator hung from one ear as he tried to rise on wobbly legs, the familiar face blank with surprise. A monkey wrench and a smoke canister fell out of his clothes, and Taggart managed to brake before he ran over his long legs. Payne was out of the car without thinking, and Big Alphonse found himself looking up at a bloody nose and the bore of a ·38 Webley.

'Bleeding hooligans,' he muttered. 'My lawyer'll do you for dangerous driving.'

'Your toys, Al?' Taggart was there to retrieve the wrench and canister and handcuff Big Alphonse.

'Never seen 'em before.'

Taggart threw Alphonse across the backseat and sat back behind the wheel. Payne put his Webley to Alphonse's temple as Taggart followed DB101 down Change Street to the Cannon Street junction.

'You ain't charging me?' said Alphonse. 'You write

338

Dunlop up me back in rubber stripes, and you've got the nerve to prefer charges?'

Payne cautioned him, sniffing and swallowing blood.

None of them saw Lemmon pounding after the car at a dogged trot.

By 10.35 a.m. Rupert Baer felt he'd been seriously rained on for twenty-four slow Tuesdays instead of as many miserable minutes. Daft Rupert out in the heavy weather, loaded down with instructions and smoke-canisters like some mentally defective anarchist, whilst Micky Raven and the Raphael brothers were cuddled up to their shooters and schemes in the warm and dry.

'As usual,' Rupert sniffed through streaming mucus.

The newspaper under his donkey jacket had turned to pulp, just like his brain and the two Woodbines he'd tried to smoke, and he could definitely feel himself catching flu as his feet turned to stones inside his boots.

The fattest percentage of all the millions in the world would be of no bloody use to the *late* Rupert Baer, carried off in his prime by galloping pneumonia and terminal boredom. No tears for poor old Rupert if he snuffed his candle, a few wilted tulips and a thicker slice of the big poppy for Micky and Vito and bloody Mimi . . .

'About bleeding time.'

DB101 surged out of Change Street and stopped. Rupert waved his soggy *Daily Mirror*, flagging the armoured car across Cannon Street and into Distaff Lane. The driver's eyes seemed too big for his face, and too close together to see beyond the end of his nose.

'Come *on*, you wavering tart. The bleeding road's clear.'

Rupert stepped off the kerb ankle-deep in a muddy puddle. Pumped his arms so hard the *Daily Mirror* flew to pieces, leaving him with nothing but bits of margin to wave. But the driver saw the signal, found the right forward gear and raced the engine for traction. He drove at Rupert as if intent on running him down, saw at the last moment he had to make a hard left to enter Distaff Lane, and swerved past Rupert with bare inches to spare. Bumped over the pavement, scraped a bollard, and accelerated into Distaff Lane with Rupert telling him to keep going.

Rupert pulled the pins on two smoke canisters thinking of home and comfort and retirement from all this heavy and hard. He lobbed the first one far out into Cannon Street before he saw the muddy brown Q-car coming at him. It had crossed the intersection right on the tail of the armoured car, and wasn't going to stop for God, man, or villain. Rupert's second canister bounced off its roof, and he had a frozen glimpse of Taggart and Payne and the gun at Big Alphonse's head. As he jumped to save himself he realised Big Alphonse had somehow muffed it. Got it well bloody wrong. And that meant Raven pulling Alphonse's ears off if he tried bubbling to the filth to save his scrag. And Rupert didn't fancy sharing a cell with Alphonse's flatulence for a couple of decades, thank *you* very much.

Rupert smacked brickwork with his shoulder. Felt his boots skid on slick paving. Rammed his head into something that gave him multiple vision and morning sickness. Felt a hard jerk burst his buttons, and saw the sleeve of his donkey jacket fly away with the Q-car, snagged on a door handle like a ragged windsock. He'd been dragged without realising it, and had surfed to a halt millimetres from an iron lamppost that would have brained him.

Lying sprawled in dancing rain, Rupert heard somebody tell him to stay where he was. He was collared. Since the shouted command came back from the Q-car chasing DB101, Rupert decided that running in the opposite direction was a much better idea. He balled his ruined donkey jacket up, remembering not to leave it behind. Thinking straight was as hard as keeping a straight line, but he knew about not leaving the filth any clues. Not now the filth were pointing more than fingers at the firm. Then he remembered the filth already had his right sleeve, so they might as well have the rest of the bloody garment, and he was about to just throw it away when he saw a nice big drain swallowing rain by the gallon.

Rupert lifted the iron grating, dropped the jacket in, and watched it sink under the weight of the remaining smoke canisters. That took care of that, and Rupert thought he'd jog across to St Paul's Cathedral. Mingle with the tourists until he'd dried off enough to make his way back to Fulham where the bought-and-paid-for filth could start earning their brown envelopes. All Rupert had to do was hold his breath until he'd cleared the red smoke, and there he'd be – gone. Easy.

'Going somewhere, Rupert my old bear?'

Rupert got his eyes to behave long enough to see his luck had gone sour. Commander Lemmon had come out of the red pall and blocked the path. A comic figure showing a scraped knee through torn trousers. But there was nothing funny about the way he pointed his Browning at Rupert's left eye.

Rupert raised his left arm and found that his right just hung there.

'Your crotch is smouldering,' he said.

Swaying.

Taggart couldn't believe it. One moment DB101 was fifty yards ahead, then it wasn't. It took the sharp bend in Distaff Lane just seconds ahead of the Q-car, and instead of Taggart clearing the bend to find it making a right or left hand turn into Queen Victoria Street, there it was, vanished.

Taggart slewed to a halt to stare at bumper-to-bumper traffic brawling in both directions, Big Alphonse shrank away from Payne's revolver, and they all listened to Dillman calling the Flying Squad units away from Farthingale Place. Taggart swore and punched the wheel, thinking back the way he'd come.

Payne said, 'Bubble-up time, Alphonse. Or it's you and Rupert going down for twenty years of heavy bird without smelling a single sixpence.'

'Cunning armpits,' Taggart cursed. 'Cunning, cunning bastards.'

Alphonse thought of Rupert being scraped along thirty feet of wall before the Q-car dumped him on the cobbles like a sack of offal, and his own scrapes and bruises began to hurt in sympathy. Payne and this Taggart geezer weren't the usual run of CID bastards. Nobody was about to buy them with regular brown envelopes, and Alphonse knew they'd fillet him raw to put Mickey Raven in the dock. That was a sweaty old thought, but preferable to having Vito and Mimi jamming sawn-offs down his trouser if they thought he'd so much as winked at the heavy filth. There was nothing for it but to play dumb and swallow Her Majesty's porridge like a gent.

'Know nothing from nothing.' Alphonse lay along the backseat and appeared to lose interest.

'Your funeral.' Payne told the radio their position and status. Heard Dillman acknowledge between racking coughs, and got nothing but crackle when he asked where Commander Lemmon was. He had no way of knowing Mobile Two had caught fire and burned through Dillman's microphone cable.

Taggart mulled over a small image that had stayed in his mind. Something glimpsed as he cleared the bend in Distaff Lane. Two wet trails crossing a dry oblong of cobbles. Cut off by old posters on an older pair of gates. In the lee of an archway. Wet tyre stripes going nowhere.

'Tell Dillman to converge on the old bell foundry, Painful. And hold onto your breakfast.' Taggart found reverse with a hard snick of gears.

'Mobile Two, Mobile Two. Acknowledge.' Payne hunched forward as Taggart threw the Q-car backwards with spinning tyres. 'Mobile Two, come *in*, Dildo . . .'

Taggart breasted the gates to the old bell foundry and swung the wheel hard over with, 'Here goes nothing,' ready to reverse at full throttle.

'Wait for back-up, you—' Payne started to yell.

Taggart's rebel yell drowned him out until the impact choked him off. The doors gave, shedding splinters. Alphonse was rolled into the well between the seats with a bleat of shock. The lid of the boot sprang open to smash the rear window, showering the interior with pebbles of opaqued glass. Payne could see nothing, and Taggart drove on the tiny shivering image in his cracked wing mirror. What he saw made him wish he'd listened to Payne.

The rear doors of a silver chiller truck were being closed on the grey loom of DB101. Vito and Mimi Raphael threw the last bolts home as somebody who could have been Micky Raven stopped running to open the gates out into Victoria Mews. Reached instead for a stubby shotgun as Mimi and Vito raised their weapons, no more than fifteen feet away.

Taggart swung the wheel in a hard turn. Slammed the Q-car back into the side of the arch, using the rain-slick cobbles to bring the bonnet around. The Q-car slid sideways and jammed itself across the arch, blocking the Distaff Lane exit. Then Payne was saying he was an armed police officer as if he read from the manual, and Taggart saw Alphonse's head come up over the back seat to call his own name. The shotguns were le˜ elling, and Taggart tried to make himself small behind his door as he reached for his Webley and tried to push Payne down beside him. He was still trying, or thinking of trying to do all those things at once when his world exploded in hammers of flame and shot and flying glass.

The Q-car jumped on its suspension and Payne went out through the passenger door in a twisted sprawl, punched there by Taggart's push and a rake of shot. He lay on his back with his legs inside the car, his shoulder peppered with blood spots. He still held his Webley, and his thumb jerked

343

on the chequered grip as he stared up at the vault of the arch as if wondering where the sky had gone.

Taggart felt weary, and wondered where all the blood was coming from, confused by shock and deafness and the way Alphonse spat claret through a red hole in what was left of his face. Then Alphonse was kicking himself all over the car and thrashed out through the rear window to finger-paint his own blood over the boot and the crusted brick-work. Taggart's scalp burned, and there was a numbness spreading through his neck and shoulders. He hated the noise coming from whoever was yelling and was puzzled by the slowness of everything. He knew he had to reach Payne to give him some comfort, and he passed out trying to pat the upturned face.

Then there was just Alphonse trying to make sounds that weren't liquid grunts as he crawled towards Mimi and Vito who reloaded to finish the job, and Micky Raven telling them to close the gates into Distaff Lane as he ran to open the gates into Victoria Mews. To forget topping the filth, they were finished anyway.

Vito threw Mimi his sawn-off and went over the bonnet of the Q-car. Got his shoulder to the right-hand gate and fought twisted hinges to close it. The hinges squealed in the same high register as Big Alphonse, and Vito wished he'd shut up, pass out or just die. Vito wasn't panicked, he just wanted Alphonse to stop sounding like a gut-shot dog.

He got the first gate pushed closed. Hauled the left-hand gate away from the wall and felt it bind on the cobbles. Braced his shoulders to lift it free, and had it up off the ground with a double-handed lift when he was grabbed by the hair and told the hard chunk of metal digging at his right ear wasn't a penny whistle. The gate dropped to trap Vito's fingers, and he saw Rupert leaning on the rainpipe he was handcuffed to.

One glance at Lemmon's dirty face was enough to convince Vito to stay right where he was and hope he wouldn't

344

lose any fingers if Lemmon decided to kick the gate back open. The real problem was telling brother Mimi the score without him shooting through Vito to hit Lemmon, and Vito put his mind to that as his fingers turned bloodlessly whiter than white.

At least Alphonse had shut his clack and was lying quiet to spit blood bubbles up at the rain clouds.

Micky Raven threw his unfired sawn-off up into the cab of the chiller lorry as he passed. Vito and Mimi had done enough damage without him putting in his two pennyworth. Not that he was squeamish about triggering filth if it came to it. Harry Roberts had shot two, and fat Georgie Sewell had peppered one to death without going to the gallows, so no sweat there. Shooting lawmen earned no more bird than armed robbery, so why pull your punches in a tight spot?

Raven had more than two million in old and new readies, and it would take more than a couple of headstrong filth with baby shooters to stop him banking that little lot amongst the senoritas in Spain. Bringing that kind of loot back into the country when it had been laundered made Raven the undisputed Emperor of Whitechapel Road, and with the Chinese backing him, the Crosbys, Tates and Flynns could go back to selling clothes-pegs door-to-door like their gypsy relatives. Raven was up, and they were all the way down. Just Charlie Dance left to fit with concrete boots for a long downward swim somewhere off Foulness. A pleasure to come.

Raven cracked the gates to look out into Victoria Mews, listening for law waggons. A hot rock grew in his throat and his stomach turned solid. Two black rats sat aside their motorcycles with shotguns across their thighs. The one with sergeant's stripes and a military moustache beckoned with a crooked finger. Blew Raven a kiss and told him to come out. This time, Froggy and Matt weren't pointing rolled raincoats at him.

345

Raven slammed the gates and threw bolts. Stood back, expecting solid shot to come through at him at any second. Knew Charlie Dance was somewhere close. That Froggy and Matt only had to sit there until the heavy filth came in force, and Raven was up the Alamo without a coonskin cap. And more shooting would only bring the real filth faster. The only way out was into Distaff Lane, and that meant crashing through the Q-car when Vito had reopened the gates at that end of the yard.

Raven climbed into the cab of the chiller lorry and yelled to Mimi to get his brother moving, to go and help him for Chrissakes. But Mimi was yelling back, both sawn-offs pointed at the spot where Vito crouched with a fist in his hair and a gun growing out of the side of his face. Mimi seemed to shrink in the rain as he traded shouts with Lemmon's voice and Vito pleaded with his eyes, too proud to give voice to his fear. Then, unbelievably, Mimi laid both shotguns on the ground. Kicked them away and threw his arms above his head. Told Lemmon to take the pigging shooter out of Vito's ear, he was coming quietly, wasn't he?

Raven swarmed up into the cab and turned the key in the ignition. Thinking survival, his brain throbbed with the engine. The combined weight of the chiller lorry and DB101 would flatten the Q-car, turn the gates to matchwood, Lemmon and yellow Vito to pulp. Mimi too if he didn't jump. Taggart, Payne and Big Alphonse were excluded from his calculations, they'd already been worked the fickle phallus of fate.

Raven revved hard to warm the engine and ignored Mimi's frantic face in the big commercial side-mirror as it shouted at him to stop and think. He was crashing out with the money and five hostages, end of story.

Raven saw Mimi duck aside as he let the clutch out, and Lemmon's face came around the gate for a split second to give Vito Siamese heads. Raven stamped on the accelerator and held tight to the wheel. The silencer threw out black smoke and backfired a massive gunshot. The cab trembled as the engine died, and Raven found himself pumping unresponsive controls. Knew just as suddenly he was as finished as the lorry if he didn't move fast. He left the shotgun on the seat. Went out of the cab in a leap, hit running with the fire-escape only three paces away. Mimi was a wet blur to his left, coming out of a crouch with a mouth full of expletives. Raven was midstride, jumping for the chain when he was picked out of the air and thrown in a heap.

There was no sound, no pain. There was something wrong with his chest, and he couldn't bring himself to look at it. He looked up at Mimi and his smoking sawn-off instead. Knew then what had happened to him and hated it. Hated Mimi as Mimi spat down full into Raven's face. The spittle was warm and the ground was cold, and Raven gave himself a moment before retaliating. The fire-escape was a fret of red rust above him, and a face he knew looked down through it.

Raven blinked and the face was gone, but he knew what he'd seen. He ignored Mimi. Last moments were not to be wasted on a nobody. Not Micky Raven's last moments. Using the last of his strength, Micky Raven spat up at Charlie Dance and died hunched over himself, dribbling into his lap.

Mimi was still staring down at the body when the first Flying Squad mobiles arrived, and he heard police motor-cycles roar out of Victoria Mews as he was handcuffed and cautioned. He made no reply, it had all been said.

Albert Penslow was shredding print-outs in the windowless vault below Farthingale Place when the Flying Squad left to surround the old bell foundry. Penslow knew it was only a matter of time before he would be ordered to make a tally of the armoured car's contents under the supervision of police and Treasury officials. Penslow smiled at that thought in his weatherless basement, and fed a last item into the shredder. It went through like any other piece of paper and was turned into long fingers of gibberish, but without that vital list of concurrent serial numbers to match to the legally printed banknotes, all future referral would be to the list in the file on his desk. The fact that those numbers matched the forged notes aboard DB101 would make his revenge on the bank complete.

Penslow sat at his desk and waited. The internal phone rang at 11.15 a.m., and the MD told Penslow to prepare his staff to work through the evening and on into the small hours if necessary. There would be no exceptions. Knowing otherwise, Penslow suggested he and his people take an early luncheon, and was told to do what he thought best in the circumstances. The MD had every confidence, blah, blah, blah, and rang off without a goodbye.

Penslow issued precise instructions, put on his black homburg, silk scarf and worsted overcoat, and went out into the rain without hurry. For the first time in thirty years, he passed the pub he usually lunched in, called a cab on the corner of Milk Street, and was never seen again.

The man who boarded the liner at Southampton no longer had grey hair and was dressed in the latest word in Gucci and Pierre Cardin. A recent throat operation kept him mute, and he preferred to take his meals in his state room. There were always fivers pinned to the notes he left the stewards, and invariably meant the best service possible. When he disembarked at Lima, Peru, he was whisked away by the cultural attache of the South African embassy and installed in a villa manned by expatriate German staff. He was never happier.

CHAPTER TWELVE

Armchair Doris sat Commander Lemmon across from
Charlie Dance with a large Glenfiddich and a Perfectos Finos
before making herself scarce. The office had a tree decked
out with tinsel and lights, Christmas cards strung across the
walls, and imitation snow sprayed on the windows.

'Do I detect the hand of Doris in party mood?' Lemmon
said.

'Armchair,' Charlie agreed. 'I hid the paper hats.'

'You'll have heard about Fulham earning another kind
of paper hat.'

'After a head-to-head with you and your brave lads. Your
lot earned some heavy lumps, but Micky Raven's fitted with
brass handles. How's your war wound, Mr Lemmon?'

'Middling to fair. According to the quack, the hundred-
yard dash with a popped knee is for younger men.'

'Happens he's right. What are we drinking to? A quiet
Christmas and a peaceful New Year?'

'After a seasonal game of Question and Answer, maybe.
I ask – you answer. You know the rules.'

'Old hat.'

'The oldies are the goodies, Charlie. My favourite is still
Pin The Charge On The Villain.'

'Hard game to win, that. Means I have to play my joker.
Means my brief pops out of the legal cake to whack you
with a slapstick of heavy Latin. Let's play Off The Record
and Without Prejudice.'

'As always.'

'First choice every time,' Charlie smiled. 'We've both seen enough heavy and hard for one year.'

'Am I arguing? Am I coming at you with sixteen-ounce gloves for a three-rounder? Great Scott, I'm picking up your speech patterns.'

'Comes with the territory, don't it?'

'Safe old Soho, or are you about to take an interest in the East End?'

Charlie laughed aloud at that. 'And knock heads with the Tates, Crosbys and Flynns? No thanks.'

'You could just be saying that.'

'I could, but I ain't.'

'D'you want to convince me?'

'You want a refill?'

'In my own good time. Like you plan to move east.'

'Sing another song, your stylus is stuck.'

'The Whitechapel Road's only a spit and a jump from the City of London. And you know the City well.'

'Do I, Mr Lemmon?'

'Yes, Mr Dance, you do.'

'Your sixpence. Your breath.'

'You know the City well enough to have two of your very own black rats swanning around down there last Friday week. Directing traffic. Putting ideas into the head of a certain young copper on point-duty. Getting me out of a traffic-jam. That sort of thing.'

'Did I now?'

'D'you have shares in Tate & Lyle?'

'Not that I know of.'

'Really, I thought otherwise. Last Friday, some zealous shareholder pushed their sales up by one bag. Somebody who thought that the petrol tank of a certain chiller van had a sweet tooth. Spoiled it with most of a pound of best granulated. Now you have to admit that it takes a very keen shareholder to do that under the noses of three shotguns.'

350

'I wouldn't admit to nothing. This is your fairy tale, right?'

'I'd dearly like to meet that shareholder. Shake his hand.'

'I'd shake him warmly by the throat. Sounds a vandal to me.'

'Ordinarily, so should I. But there's a strange outcome. This shareholding vandal happened to save the lives of two of my brave lads. That chiller truck would have made them the jammy centre of a Q-car sandwich. I might even owe him my own life. But who can tell about such things?'

'Don't look at me.' Charlie looked convincingly puzzled.

'He most certainly saved Vito Raphael's neck, and Vito's going crazy trying to work out how he managed it. Vito knows that chiller was a perfect runner when he jumped out of the cab. Just as he knows full well that the late Mr Raven would have driven him down without a second thought. Just as Big Alphonse knows *he'd* have been past tense, instead of having his face rebuilt by experts. They've saved his eyesight, you know.'

'So I heard. But ain't all this *sub judice*? Not to be uttered until introduced into court as evidence? Why tell me?'

Lemmon chuckled through smoke.

'Now it's my turn to laugh. Who in their right mind would want to confuse a jury with extraneous nonsense? The average juror needs the direct and simple approach. Not a story that goes nowhere. No, all this is for Uncle Theo's scrapbook of unanswerable conundrums.'

'If you say so.'

'D'you know a man called Albert Penslow, Charlie?'

'Ventriloquist on Children's Hour, ain't he?'

'Play dumb, Einstein. Perhaps it's just as well Rupert Baer admits to knowing Penslow. After he'd seen what the Raphaels had done to Big Alphonse's face he felt obliged to write it all down and sign it with a big fat X.'

Charlie killed a long stub in a stream of thoughtful smoke.

'He's well dead if the Raphaels put the black spot on him.

351

You won't keep him long enough to give evidence as a prosecution witness.'

Lemmon turned his hat and sipped whisky.

'We've learned a lot these past three years. You see, Big Al himself tells the same tale, and we've got them both buried where nobody can get at them. You can pass that on if you wish.'

'Why so confident?'

'That's for you to work out.'

'You boasting, or just telling me?'

'You'll think of an answer.'

'Could be I will at that. Could be you figure the Raphaels don't have any friends left. Not even for ready cash.'

'What did I tell you? Clever Charlie. This is excellent whisky.'

'You know where the bottle is.'

Lemmon poured and sipped malt. Looked across at Charlie and smiled his avuncular smile.

'I'm looking forward to a long holiday now. My brave lads need to rest up for a few weeks, mend their broken heads in vinegar and brown paper. Then we'll be coming at you from all sides, Charlie. Business as usual.'

'I'll be here, Commander.'

'Did you hear old Pencils went down at the Bailey for fifteen years? His lawyer said he wouldn't live to do three fives, and the judge said he should do the best he could. The same judge gave that kid Rosie Bottoms a five stretch. I guess he should have listened to you, Charlie.'

'Can't say one way or the other. Never met the lad.'

'He tells it differently, but no matter. Major Gerry Fox drew two concurrent tens. That won't bring manly tears to your eyes, I know.'

'Nor yours, Theo. You've wanted him for a lot of years.'

Lemmon feigned shock with: 'What are you suggesting, you villain? I? An officer of the law? Given to personal vindictiveness? I am above such petty emotions. My heart is pure, and I wear a white hat to match my wings. I also *never* drink with villains or need to go to the lavatory. You should know better than to make such an unfounded allegation.'

'Forgot myself, didn't I?'

'Indeed you did, and you can make up for it.'

'Sure, so long as it doesn't involve cautions or handcuffs.'

'Not this time. This time, I charge you with an errand I cannot discharge myself. One that must be couched in secrecy and requires extreme discretion. There is no remuneration in it for you personally, so you are obliged to act the Christian for the good of your immortal soul, Charles Dance.'

'What the thump did Armchair put in your glass? Bottled Angelus?'

'Fine malt whisky, you recidivist, what else?'

'Words like that don't come out of my bottles, I know.'

'The Christmas spirit is upon me, that is all. Scrooge has seen the light. Will you, Tiny tim, run my simple errand, or not?'

'What is it? Yuletide cannabis for your mistress?'

'Just a package of modest proportions I want delivered to our elusive sugar vandal. It contains an item that belongs to an associate of his. An associate who is close to the said vandal. And since I can do nothing for the vandal himself by way of thanks, this oblique token will have to suffice. You'll note that it is gift-wrapped, but that doesn't mean he has to wait until Santa's Day to open it. Just so long as I am nowhere in the vicinity when he does so, no harm done. Is that understood?'

'Boiled down? Yeah.'

Charlie looked at the oblong parcel Lemmon laid on his blotter. Teased a nostril with a nail and poured himself another shot of good Irish whiskey. Watched Lemmon button his coat and set his trilby square. Noticed he had touched the package with his gloves on.

'At least it ain't ticking, Theo.'

'Not my style. When I feel your collar, I want your head in one piece.'

'Every man should have a fantasy, even the heavy filth.'

'Dreams are what we truly are, Charlie. Didn't you know that?'

'And reality is only the raw material for colouring them. Yeah, I know the theory.'

'You've been taking on Chinese culture, then.'

'It rubs off.'

Lemmon drained his glass and paused at the door.

'Make one of my dreams come true, Charlie. Take your naughty Chinese back to Hong Kong with you. Cho Sun *and* his nephew. Yes, I know all about them. And Charlie, leave them there?'

'My Christmas Box to the heavy filth,' Charlie said.

'I knew you had a better side. Seasons greetings, Mr Dance.'

'And robins on logs to you, Commander.'

Lemmon went away and Charlie listened to traffic purling around Piccadilly Circus as he stared at the package. The wallclock ticked and the tree lights blinked on and off with the plodding gaiety of electric policemen. He pulled the bow apart and ran a nail through the Sellotape holding the paper together. The box was cardboard and had forensic evidence seals. Inside was Vinnie Castle's Mauser. The barrel had been drilled out, and when Charlie pulled the trigger, a bright silk flag unfurled. 'BANG!' Charlie read aloud. He toasted the chair where Lemmon had sat. 'I owe you one,' he added thoughtfully.

Vinnie Castle carried his shopping bag through the casualty department of the University College Hospital, took the tunnel to the private wing, stripped off his streetclothes and found himself a wheelchair. Dressed in pyjamas and dressing-gown, and with his bag and clothes hidden under

354

the blanket over his lap, he wheeled himself into the lift with the confidence of a long-term patient. A male nurse pressed the button for him, and let him out on the floor closed to visitors. Vinnie rolled into the day room and found Bulstrode asleep in a chair. Dillman played solitaire with bandaged hands, Payne read the *Playboy* he'd propped on his arm-brace, and Taggart stalked a fly with a rolled *Daily Express*, his shaved head swathed in thick dressings. They looked like remand prisoners waiting for due process of law to release or incarcerate them.

'You lost, sunshine?' Taggart kept his eyes on the dozy winter fly. 'Nobody here but us chickens and this buzzing bastard.'

'Just wanted a close squint at real heroes. Never been close to so many before. You look just like your pictures inna papers. Any danger of an autograph? For my daughter, of course,' Vinnie said like an awed fan with enough grey cells to fill a thimble.

Taggart smeared the fly against the wall with: 'Gotcha.' The slap of the newspaper brought Bulstrode out of his doze to groan, and he blinked at the champagne Vinnie fished from his shopping bag.

'Very cold, very dry,' Vinnie said, finding tulip glasses and three more bottles. 'Krug '57. Chilled the way m'sieu adores.'

'Go away and come back when I'm awake,' said Bulstrode.

'Paper hats and caviar. Beluga, naturally,' Vinnie said.

'Naturally,' Bulstrode fed himself a Capstan and coughed it alight. 'This is a switch. You visiting me.'

'All comes full circle, Buller.'

Dillman showered his cards at the wall, and Payne let *Playboy* fall to the floor, swivelling his torso from the waist like Dorothy's Tin Man in Oz. Taggart forgot his dead fly and stripped foil from one of the magnums.

'Real shampoo,' Dillman said. 'Yummy.'

'Beats having the nurses sing carols at us,' Bulstrode coughed.

'Lovely threepennys, rotten voices,' said Payne.

The first cork sighed from the bottle and Taggart poured froth.

'Barbarian,' Dillman said, holding his glass with both hands. 'Don't bruise the grape as if it were bad Dublin porter, Tag.'

'That's rich, coming from a berk who let both his pleasure fingers get singed.' Taggart filled Bulstrode's glass with extravagant care. 'That ain't a whole smoked salmon, is it, Mr Castle?'

'And the brown bread's buttered and sliced thinner than Kleenex.'

'There is a Father Christmas, Virginia,' Dillman said, sipping.

'Thought you was out of the country, Vin?' Bulstrode said.

'Was. Got back yesterday. Go again day after tomorrow.'

'This ain't caviar. Tastes of fish eggs,' said Taggart, earning a scalding look from Dillman followed by a short, sharp lecture on the Baltic sturgeon.

'Well, if it's bloody Russian, no wonder it's fishy,' Taggart sniffed. Ever the rabid anti-communist, he preferred honest Scotch salmon.

'Since when were you into fight management, Vin?' Bulstrode said. 'Saw a squib about it in one of the sports sections, and I still don't believe it. You've got Trooper Wells on the string?'

'Business, is all,' Vinnie grinned. 'Drink up, you're still sober. There's another crate of this stuff down at the porter's lodge. Thought it might see you through being stuck here for the Christmas period.'

'Don't wriggle. What's the full strength of this Hong Kong lark? You and Charlie ain't playing an away game, are you?'

'Coincidence. Business. I told you.'

'Telling is one thing. Telling it straight is another.'

'Put your suspicion in your back pocket. Everybody's a believer at Christmas. Tradition, right?'

Bulstrode thought of Stannard's film and shuddered. Swallowed champagne and wished it was bitter from the wood.

'Mr Magoo's blind, but you ain't a cartoon like him, Vinnie. You sail off a high roof, you won't bounce.'

'That bang on the head's made you morbid. Get them bubbles down your scrag.'

'Be lucky then, you pillock.'

'Cheers,' Vinnie smiled. 'And you watch out for bags of silver swinging at you, eh?'

Bulstrode raised his glass.

'This is the only way to get seeing double. Definitely.'

'I've heard it said.' Vinnie clinked glasses. Pretended to need the toilet, and left the hospital without being challenged.

The hospital receptionist ushered Charlie into Ben Bunch's office, and Ben poured large measures of Irish over cracked ice as Charlie refused to settle.

'What's occurring, Ben?' Charlie just looked at the drink he was offered until Bunch sat it where Charlie could reach it if he wanted to.

'You no longer need the services of Mutton Jeff. Do I keep him here for Christmas, or let him go back to that filthy little room he squats in at King's Cross?'

'That mean what I think it means?'

'I found them gone this morning. How they got out of the secure section is beyond me, Charlie.'

Charlie wiped Bunch's nervous smile off with a dark look.

'Cho Sun could get out of anything if he put his mind to it.'

'He left you a note. I haven't read it.'

357

Charlie took the square of rice paper sealed with a blob of wax. The dragon chop imprint was as red as a chorus girl's thumbnail. Charlie opened the paper fold and read:

I will eat the quail's egg. Come share the yolk.

Charlie crushed the paper and smiled down at the drink. Raised the glass and toasted Bunch.

'Keep Mutton Jeff *if* he wants to stay. If not, there's a place fixed for him over at the Cromwell Road Hotel.'

'What are you doing for Christmas, Charlie?'

'Going on an egg diet, what else?'

'Not like you to indulge in such fads.'

'Surprise myself sometimes.' Charlie finished his Irish and went back to his car. Drove to London whistling, knowing he would share the yolk with Cho Sun. Maybe, he reasoned, it *was* all written down somewhere. There really *was* such a thing as Fate.

Lemmon found Wade the Treasury man waiting in the Command Room at West End Central. Gone was the sleek look. He had been chain-smoking and looked like the spectre at the feast. His handshake was clammy and boneless, and he could neither settle or come to the point. After some hums and hahs he sighed, 'I had no idea who to turn to, you see. I mean, should I really be here? Protocol apart, that is? What to do?'

'How can I help you, Mr Wade?'

'There's no avoiding an internal enquiry, of course. A discreet search for the culpable. It's me who qualifies, I'm perfect for it. There's no other course to take. Resignation, you see. Or early retirement. They might just go for that, don't you think?'

'It's usual,' Lemmon said as if he knew. 'Under the circumstances.'

'That is my fond hope, Commander.'

'I can see it would be.'

358

'I suppose I should have deputised – sent a junior to oversee the count and check of the recovered money. Not relied on IBI's records. They'd been falsified, you see. Not that I shouldn't still be held accountable by my masters, but it just might have eased my way.'

Lemmon knew all this muddy reasoning was a cockeyed attempt to expunge guilt. Wade had come to Lemmon's secular church to use it as a confessional. Hear me, Father Filth, for I have sinned . . .

'It was only later that I made my internal audit, and there it was.'

'Ah,' said Lemmon.

'The third check was absolutely conclusive.'

'I see.'

'Debden finally confirmed my suspicions.'

'Debden? Isn't that where all Treasury notes are printed under the highest possible security?'

Wade used a handkerchief on his neck and face. Sat and stood and sat again.

'Debden, yes. With their immaculate despatch notes, one was able to check the serial numbers against the Doyle & Brandt receipts, and those of IBI's we had used to make the first audit. I suppose Albert Penslow's absence should have made us all more careful.'

Lemmon leaned forward. Finally seeing a thread through the labyrinth. 'It should have,' he agreed.

'The entire consignment. My God. I suppose I could use the old standby. Health reasons.'

Lemmon didn't strangle Wade. He listened politely as Wade tore at his handkerchief with his teeth, counted off a couple of decades and said, 'The entire consignment was what?'

'Forged. All two million plus.' Wade looked surprised by Lemmon's slow-witted progress. 'Completely different numbers. The serial sequence followed the notes you gave me. Why else would I be here?'

Lemmon's knuckles cracked along with his pleasant expression.

'The notes I gave you? You can't mean the forgeries?'

'That's exactly what I mean.'

'DB101 carried forgeries?'

'It did. But when did the exchange take place? And how? Nobody could possibly have breached Debden's security.'

'You're sure of that, are you?'

'My dear fellow, are you quite mad?'

'Not this week, but I'm working on it. Am I to understand that the banknotes supplied by the Debden mint were exchanged for forgeries before the raid on the armoured vehicle?'

'Precisely.'

Lemmon stared. 'There was a robbery *before* the robbery?'

'There can be no other conclusion.'

'You couldn't be mistaken? An error in computing . . .'

'By the Bank of England? Hardly. The very idea is risible.'

'A monumental chuckle. Where are the forged notes now?'

Wade's laugh was shrill and abrupt.

'In circulation.'

Lemmon wished he had Charlie Dance's bottle of Glenfiddich to hand. He poured himself a phantom drink and felt his throat constrict. Saw headlines a mile high above his silly face. Perfect fodder for the Christmas newspapers. Technically, somebody had actually robbed the Bank of England. The Old Lady of Threadneedle Street herself. The gutter press would have a field day. Their laughter would be as hollow as Santa chuckling down two million chimneys. Ho, ho, bloody ho . . .

'You'll withdraw the notes from circulation, of course.'

'Impossible,' said Wade, tying knots in his shredded handkerchief.

'Impossible?'

'Any such attempt would end in chaos. Have you any notion just how many banknotes there *are* in circulation? As high as three billion in London alone. It would take all the staff of all the clearing banks a full fiscal year to check every banknote. And then it would prove fruitless. The forgeries will already have changed hands a dozen times, and the genuine notes could be anywhere from Ghana to Washington. And you can't expect the Royal Mint to admit to circulating forgeries. It is only two mill, after all. A drop in the bucket.'

'Plus,' said Lemmon. 'Let's not forget the plus.'

'Inconsequential, I assure you. We shall just have to rely on natural wastage to absorb the discrepancies.'

Lemmon neither knew or cared what *that* meant. He was completely out of his depth. 'I'm assured,' he lied.

'You've been very good to listen. Most kind.'

'My mission in life, Mr Wade. Are we then saying there *was* no robbery? No robbery before the attempt to steal the forgeries, that is? That the forgeries themselves are to be treated as genuine?'

'Not at all, technically. The Fraud Squad will have to find the source and act accordingly. Not our problem, Commander. But if the genuine money turns up, we shall have to bring charges under the relevant section of the existing currency regulations. Then again, that's a matter for our legal chaps, isn't it?'

'And no embarrassing headlines.'

Wade tutted. 'Perish the thought, Commander.'

'Contrary to good order in the mighty banking world, that it?'

'Exactly. I shall be disciplined, of course. Put out to grass with discretion, and that will be that. My masters will close ranks. They'll probably give me the Peachey Project. Somebody senior has to head that up.'

Lemmon felt strangled. 'Our Pencils is a *project*?'

'Didn't you know? We shall be spiriting him out of prison

361

some time in the New Year. Set him up in one of our secure facilities. He should prove invaluable. A rogue talent like his will help us to safeguard against all kinds of forgery. Bank documents, credit cards, printed currency itself. Who knows, if I get the post, it might well be a left-handed leg-up the ladder of promotion. It might even be an exciting challenge, what? Once I get used to being banished from the City itself.'

'Your resilience is remarkable, Mr Wade,' Lemmon said, his voice larded with heavy sarcasm.

'One does try one's modest best to look on the bright side. Goodbye, Commander.'

Lemmon shook the boneles hand and wiped his damp palm off on his blotter. The City boys took care of their own, and the rest of humanity could go hang, including Lemmon's squad. Bulstrode had concussion, and Dillman needed skin-grafts for his badly burned hands. Taggart's neck would forever be a moonscape of puckered craters, and there was every chance that Payne's smashed clavicle would set crooked. And all for a dustbin filled with play money.

Lemmon wished himself a Merry Christmas and went home to his Elizabeth, entertaining serious thoughts on early retirement himself.

'The Peachey Project,' he snarled, pouring his first evening drink. 'Elizabeth, listen to this for a silly game of . . .'

Vinnie scrubbed between yawns.

An afternoon nap had done nothing for him, and he hoped a long shower would pound some vitality back into his body. The round trip to Hong Kong and back had left him drained and listless, and the hard London cold was strange after the dry winter heat of the colony. Almost as if his home town was an alien city and he was a rootless nomad washed up in the Cromwell Road hotel by careless tides. He dug soap and wax out of his ears and wished he wasn't so damned tired all the time. The mirror told him he was thirty, but inside, he was older than mankind's forebears. He gave himself a smile and knew it only lived on the surface of his face. Fooled nobody, including himself.

Charlie had stuffed the suite with flowers to welcome him home, but Vinnie smelled mortality in their fragrance. The sweet odour of the remembrance chapel. The doctors had told him he'd feel this way on occasion, to take the small brown pills if it got too bad. But they only induced an outer chemical calm. Inside, where the real Vinnie lived, he was a silent screaming fist beating at the walls of depression behind a sloppy smile. Even lizards could grow new limbs, and what did they do but eat flies off the wall?

'Cockless and legless,' he told his reflection. 'What good are you? Charles Atlas you ain't. Any moppet with a bucket and spade can kick sand in your face, and you'd have to take a body-building course to lift a man's pint. Pitiful ain't in it.' That made him grin. It was fleeting and shallow, but it was by God genuine, and Vinnie tried it again. Liked it and kept it, and went out into the sitting room to find Charlie had made himself at home with a long Irish.

'Don't you ever knock?'

'And miss you talking to yourself in the mirror? No chance.'

'Everybody does it. Known fact.'

'Your weak gin's by your elbow. Cheers.'

Vinnie lounged on a couch and looked at Charlie at his sleepiest in a leather chair. That look meant his mind worked overtime on solving problems before others knew they existed. Playing poker hands before they were dealt. Wishing he had Charlie's lazy energy, Vinnie said, 'Cheers yourself. You want the bad news, or the bad news.'

'Not until the second drink.'

'Crow still tastes of crow, Charlie.'

'Then save it. There's a present from the heavy filth on the table. Merry whatevers from Uncle Theo.'

'Looks like my Mauser.'

' "Looks like" is right. Using it'd be like shooting rapids in a castrated canoe. You'd only get the red flag. I think he's trying to tell you something.'

'Or you, mister. That shrewd old copper does nothing without there's a reason for it. That's where you're alike. His Christmas presents come with brass handles. That shooter means he's sure he's closer to feeling your collar without bothering with the likes of me to do it, s'all.'

'Kiss mine, you cynic.' Charlie gave himself a stiffer second drink. 'Your mood's black enough to make you an honorary Brixton brother. Cheer yourself up, Vin, give me the bad news. Then we'll both go out and jump under a bus.'

Vinnie's grin was as weak as his drowned gin.

'I ain't that bad.'

'But you've been better, right?'

'You can be nice to me once in a while, you know. I won't fall apart. And don't give me that "famous last words" look, neither. I've got a medical condition, not a double-dose of self pity. You think I came haring back here for nothing? We got trouble of the worst kind, and I ain't having you walk in on it blind.'

'Then get started before we're both too old to do anything about it. You've got the stadium booked, the training camp running. Got the local bigwigs turning up in their penguin-suits and pearls. I've heard nothing but purrs from New York, so they ain't a problem. Chinese Cyril's done the business with the local Chinese, so we're golden with them. That leaves what? Troop? Hettie can't get the kind of wool she likes to keep her needles busy?'

'Don't bear's breath me, Chas. That side of it's fine. Except maybe that Chinese Cyril and Troop can't pass a restaurant without trying at least one dish of that heathen nosh. Their palates are in love. They do open a place when they get back, the menu'll be the size of a couple of telephone directories. They'll need a lorry load of woks and ducks, and a kitchen with the legroom of Wembley Stadium.'

'Trooper Wells ain't cutting down his roadwork? Nothing like that?'

'You know Troop. Everything's a laugh. But he's fit enough to handle the American fighter New York has matched him against. And this Sugar Boy Tatum – a Congo Billy Devon he ain't. We've run films of all Tatum's fights for Troop, and Troop figures he's a plodder. No flair. All heart and no science. The kind of hardhead who takes punishment and keeps on coming forward. The Las Vegas high rollers love that kind of dumb courage enough to have chartered a jet to bring them out to Hong Kong in strength, so our initial receipts are dollar-healthy.'

'So where's the trouble? That blond kid of Chappie's, that Tony Hackney?'

'No. Hackney idolises Troop, and he's working hard to look good in his bout. Troop's seeing the boy don't overtrain and leave it all in the gym. Showed the boy some naughty wrinkles too. Not to use, but to avoid.'

'So? So what?'

Vinnie sighed and gave himself a cigarette to turn in his knuckles.

'The bad news is Chappie August. He's got some scheme going with the New York bookies. Nothing I can pin down, but he's about to pull some flanker on Troop. Something in the ring, I dunno. Without tearing his arms off, could be we won't find out *what* until too late. The man's a sewer, Chas. One bitter bastard about something from the past. Blind as a worm about his own shortcomings, he blames anybody handy for what goes sour for him. Now it's Troop. Later, could be it's you.'

Charlie nodded with veiled eyes. Turned the Mauser with a finger and watched it spin to a halt.

'I've played cards with the man, remember?'

'That was facing him.'

'So long as Chinese Cyril ain't too busy stuffing his face with oriental delights to keep Chappie in his sights until I get there.'

'I thought you was . . .'

'Was what?'

'Staying in the background. Leaving the biz to me and Hatton. Hong Kong ain't the healthiest place for you to swan around in with what occurred between you and them people.'

'That ain't what you meant at all.'

'It's all getting handled. No need for you to take chances. You're worried about Troop, forget it. Cyril won't let nothing happen outside the ring. He's still got the ringcraft to take a man's head off if anybody even tries laying a finger there. And with the dollars we've been spreading around to grease palms, we've paid off the Tongs for all the protection going. No need for you to take chances, right?'

Charlie pointed a finger around his glass.

'You've gone all chalky, Vin. You think I'm horning in on your project. Think I'm taking the tiller. I ain't, right? I'll just be there, is all.'

'You ain't never *just* anywhere.'

'I'm taking Mrs Sadler to the fights. How bad?'

'Question is: which fights? Them in the ring, or them in the streets of Kowloon?'

'Now you've lost me.'

'Lost you nothing. Balls, Charlie. Bloody balls.'

'Language, Vincent.'

Vinnie shook ice from his drink without noticing. Lost the glass on a side table and lit himself a shaky Player. Lay back as if totally exhausted, all his strength in his voice.

'Don't snow Vinnie, Charlie. First you wasn't coming out there at all. Then it's a long weekend to see the fight. Now, suddenly you're planning to be in Hong Kong a good two weeks before Troop climbs into the ring to fanfares. That was always in your mind, right? To be there ducking and diving like it was Soho Square with palm trees. Well, there ain't no palm trees, just bauhinnias and banyans, right? You'll be the original innocent abroad, Charlie Dance, and they'll lift more than your wallet they get the chance. Why can't you do like always? Let the bastards come at you on your own turf. Where's the percentage in playing with their marked deck?'

'Still only fifty-two cards, Vinnie. Even if I did know what you're talking about. Call it a holiday outing for the firm. The lads need a break, and two weeks of suey and sunshine won't hurt.'

'A row of long-nosed skittles waiting to be knocked down, more like.' Vinnie's disgust made him tremble.

'You running the firm now, Vin?'

'Do this, and there won't be no firm to run.'

'You pays your money and you takes your choice.'

'Charlie shrugs, Charlie smiles, Charlie gets dead. No problem.'

'You're making me hungry. Get your leg on, we'll grab some nosebag at the Astor Club.'

'Stuff my leg, I'll have sandwiches sent up.'

'Get your leg on. I need your company, you need some fresh air.'

'Call Margot. She's got legs, and she's always hungry.'

'She's meeting us there. Your leg, Vin.'

'My leg, my leg. You bloody wear it, you're so keen on my leg.'

'I like walking you into places. Makes me proud. You wouldn't take that away from me, would you?'

'What are you up to, you cunning—?'

'Get your leg on and find out, eh?'

'No leg, no supper, that it?'

Charlie spread his palms with: 'Now would I?'

'If I knew *that* I'd be you.' Vinnie hopped into the

bedroom talking under his breath. Banged a drawer and the wardrobe doors. Bounced on the bed and made noises of discovery. Furious and then intrigued, he called Charlie to join him, holding up his artificial limb. 'What's all this hardware? Now I'm a walking arsenal?'

'Just something Horseface Flynn's armourer tooled up for me. A three-piece shooter as lightweight as he could make it. The butt and grip are plastic. Only the barrel's steel. Takes a clip of nine rounds of high-velocity ammo. Whole thing only weighs a couple of pounds. Like it?'

'What's to like? Couldn't get to it in a hurry, could I?'

'Not without practise. But handy for going through Customs, and I don't want you out there with nothing but your finger to point if there's trouble.'

'So that's it.'

'Have to see if you can walk with the extra weight, though.'

'Yeah,' Vinnie said. 'Hmmm . . .'

'I'll have a drink while I'm waiting. Take your time.'

'Anything else I should know?'

Charlie stopped in the doorway with a sleepy smile.

'There's a Derringer in your shoe. Sam the Spade wanted you to have it.'

'I'm supposed to believe that? My night for guns and lies and deceit.'

'And thirsts. I'll be by the whisky.'

Charlie closed the door and let his face sag. Vinnie was nothing but bones and courage, and Charlie hated seeing him waste away. He made a very stiff drink and tossed it down in one. Sober and melancholic.

A world without Vinnie Castle would be as dark as the meanest alley.

J.C. Hatton felt queasy just looking at the sampan Chinese Cyril whistled out of the darkness of Causeway Bay. The Royal Hong Kong Yacht Club on Kellet Island was a seaward jewel hovering in ink. Sky and sea were jet on velvet, and sleek yachts showed riding lights along the eastern mole of the typhoon shelter. Countless Chinese lanterns marked the floating village of junks crowding the main body of water inside the harbour, and their mirrored reflections were soft moons trailing shimmers of fire. Out in the northern strait, and below the glittering thread of Kowloon, ferries were gliding bugs of luminescence. All very beautiful, but the wafting smells of rot, fish and untreated effluent turned Hatton's stomach in very slow circles.

He entertained thoughts of cholera and amoebic dysentry instead of contemplating the promise of exotic culinary delights, and wished himself back at the hotel. Cyril and Trooper seemed oblivious to the stinking water. Like jolly schoolboys who had managed to winkle their favourite head teacher out of his classroom to join their adventure, they were only anxious to please the old duffer. They helped Hatton down the gangplank, and settled him under a stern awning where a lantern glowed over a table and chairs. The sampan-man took himself off to the bow, and his small and shapeless wife sculled the craft out into the darkness. Radios droned pop, and distant voices shouted in polyglot dialects whilst violins and an upright piano churned out 'Jingle Bells'.

Hatton hoped to be introduced to Szechuan or Tien-tsin cooking on a floating restaurant with an upper dining saloon far above the noisome water-line. Something on the lines of the *Queen Mary* would suit, preferably with efficient air-conditioning. All he could see was a light dusting of stars, serpents of reflected light, and the dark fret of many masts. The jangling strains of 'Lily of Laguna' dogged the sampan's blind course with eerie persistence, and Cyril decided it sounded like the *Titanic*'s orchestra going down for the third time. The woman stopped sculling and Hatton asked where the floating restaurant was.

'You're on it,' Trooper laughed. 'The nosh comes to us. Here's the first course now.'

The crab-seller's boat glided alongside, and the sampan-man's wife brought bowls and chopsticks from somewhere Hatton was convinced had to be unhygienic. Cyril peered across into steaming cauldrons of sea-food and bartered with busy fingers, and the result was a basket of boiled swimming crabs dumped in the middle of the table. Rice and sauces arrived, and Cyril and Trooper wiped their hot faces on napkins steeped in disinfectant. Hatton preferred to live with the mist of sweat on his top lip, picked at a claw, and wondered if the shellfish had been cooked in the water they rode on.

The beer-seller's sampan bumped in, and Trooper poured warm beer into cracked glasses as Cyril ordered battered fry from yet another sampan. The small flotilla floated in the glow of its own lamps, Trooper and Cyril ate with enthusiasm, and Hatton threw most of his food overboard uneaten. He sipped beer, hoping alcohol would protect his delicate constitution, and determined he'd summon a doctor the moment he returned to the hotel. Publicly, he professed enjoyment of the picaresque setting, horrified by the thought that he might need to relieve himself over the side in full sight of the sampan-man's wife.

Cyril and Trooper splashed the gunwhales with cheerful indifference when there were more than a dozen empty bottles on the table, but Hatton desisted. However inured the shapeless female may be to the sight of silver parabolas emerging from open flies, Hatton would never share his lavatorial requirements with the gentler sex. For the occidental English gentleman such base practises were fine for the lower order of heathen who knew no better; and that he noted sadly, included his two companions. Hatton bottled his urine with grim determination and a grimmer smile.

'You all right there, J.C.?' Cyril asked, shovelling abalone.

'Never better,' Hatton lied with clamped thighs.

Trooper kept eating with his elbows out, his bowl close to his mouth in the oriental fashion. Cyril uncrowned more beer and Cyril's complimentary belch had the crab-seller bowing and smiling with pleasure. The sampan-man's wife suckled an infant as if she were alone, and a fifth sampan moored up on the port bow. In the waist under a huge paper lantern were two violinists and a pianist dressed in shiny pyjamas. The upright piano had more scars than shine, and its ruched-satin front was threadbare between the empty candle holders. Requests were $5 each, and Trooper got them vamping and sawing through an eccentric version of 'A Bicycle Made For Two'. The old music-hall song turned the waters of the typhoon shelter into an adjunct of the Mile End Road, and Hatton crossed and recrossed his legs with rising discomfort. The untuned chords seemed to cut at Hatton's crotch, and there were waterfalls of pressure in his ears.

The tea and coffee boat arrived during 'My Old Dutch', and nobody but Hatton seemed in any hurry to leave. He was about ready to swim home with his knees tied together when yet another sampan came out of the darkness.

Hatton watched it close in as Cyril and Trooper sampled battered fry and the local cockles, humming the old songs as they chewed and swallowed what looked to Hatton like grey balls of perished inner-tube. Unlike the working sampans, this one was highly lacquered and the prow was gilded wood. The stern canopy was rich silk, and dragons reared on the lantern housings. The music boat shot off murdering a cockney air, the tea and coffee boat just wasn't there, and the crab-seller helped his oarsmen to put water between himself and his customers. The sampan-man's family disappeared under some rush mats in the bow, and all the other craft in the area seemed a very long way off. The radios went silent, and lights went out as the entire floating village darkened ship.

'If this is the cabaret,' Hatton said, holding himself. 'I for one abstain.'

Cyril's appetite died at first glance. The crew of the sampan were all in black. The man seated in the stern wore red robes and a skullcap. His white beard and moustaches were waxed, and his index fingers were long golden knives. He was too old to be given an exact age, but Cyril realised he was less than ten feet from the Sichuen Dragon himself, and *he* had lived through seven dragon years. That made him eighty-four years old, enough reason to venerate him without his great power in the colony.

'Say nothing. Do less,' Cyril whispered.

Trooper rolled his shoulders and watched Cyril watching the sampan, but Hatton had stood up with: 'No women aboard. How gratifying.'

'Christ, J.C.—'

Hatton shrugged Cyril's restraining hand away with dignity. Went across to the opposite rail and made water with his back turned. The tinkling gush went on and on, and Cyril knew the insult must end in their summary execution. He might hold the Killing Shadows off long enough to let Trooper slip away over the side and swim for the shore. For himself and Hatton there was nothing to be done but pray it would be over quickly, *if* Hatton ever stopped peeing. The man's bladder had the capacity of a city reservoir. The flow went on and on like the traditional water torture, became a persistent dribble, and began to peter out in small spurts. Hatton sighed and buttoned up. Sat down again and looked for conjurors and musical instruments, ready to be entertained.

The old Chinese in the stern asked something in Mandarin, and one of the men in black asked the question again in fast Cantonese. Cyril answered at length; was questioned some more, and turned to Hatton, his face glistening with perspiration.

'The Old One would know how old you are, J.C. And

before you come the old acid with, "None of the old tart's business", that's the actual Sichuen Dragon out there. Nobody ain't seen him in the fresh air for a lot of years. Him or his barge. And he can have you put to the question for a thousand days, he puts his mind to it. So, best to answer up bleeding snappy.'

Hatton used a napkin on his streaming face.

'With alacrity. I am seventy-eight years of age. But don't ever tell Charlie, or he'll put me out to grass the moment he knows.'

There was more musical Mandarin and harsh Cantonese, then Cyril's brand of London cockney.

'He wants to know what?' Hatton said. Askance with shock.

'What I said. How it is you have control over your bodily waters, as if your mind could dam the Pearl River? Does a water god live in your crutch? Make it long if you can't make it interesting. The Old One has no sense of the humorous, and he don't ask nothing without good reason.'

'Deep breathing and regular walks, tell him. Whisky and hot milk each night before retiring. A lot of ruffage in the diet. Absolutely no sugar or potatoes.'

Cyril went through more question and answer and said: 'Now he wants to know about women. Do you use your penis that way any more? Or is it dedicated like his to making grudging water at cockrow and at night's end? The Old One has women, but he dare not use them for fear they may silt up his internal waters like the mud that comes with the tides of the monsoon. Laugh, and we're dead.'

Hatton looked down his nose. Sniffed and wiped off his glasses.

'Not a subject for risible comment, young Cyril. Should you make old bones you'll see the wisdom of knowing what can and cannot be sniggered at, I assure you.'

'Lovely, tell your mum,' Trooper groaned. 'Tell the old face what he wants to hear, will you? I need a serious leak now, and I don't wanna die poor trying for one, right?'

'Hold your water,' Hatton said, the small revenge pleasing him more than it should have done. Through Cyril he told the Old One: 'We are autumn, you and I. Closer to winter than spring. Our tides run slowly but more surely. Not for us the flash floods of enthusiasm that plague the young and foolish . . .'

'Handsome,' Cyril murmured. 'He'll like that.'

'. . . Let them dart at women like hummingbirds. Sipping here, sipping there, never able to take the full draught that slakes the thirst entirely. Translate, Cyril.'

Cyril spoke, and Trooper turned a glass with glassier eyes.

'Go on, J.C. He's lapping it up.'

'But with great age comes greater discernment. We do not gulp down all the dishes to hand, spoiling our palates with too many tastes taken too close together. Rather, we enjoy one dish at a time. We take the woman of our choice when the sap rises with sure deliberation. When it is right to do so, enjoy it as if it were the last time, and savour the memory of it long afterwards. Much as we hold a favourite book we know off by heart. With no need to scan the pages, for the words themselves are engraved deep inside us. Such is the way of the intelligent man with many years weighing on him. I find this so, and it is a comfort to me.'

Hatton leaned back polishing his glasses. Idly listened to the exchange that followed as a clean breeze sprang up from the seaward side of the harbour to blow the odours ashore. He was hungry now, and would search out the restaurant recommended to him by a friend at the Foreign Office. The *deem-sum* was reputed to be the best that could be had in the whole of Hong Kong Island. There would be excellent *shau-shing*, a warm rice wine drank from delicate porcelain cups, and a modest portion of *chow-fan* to finish off with. No more experiments with hotheads like Cyril and Trooper that ended on leaky boats with strange old men asking for the meaning of life as if Hatton were some gypsy fortune-teller in a booth on Brighton Pier.

The silk bag was over Hatton's head before he knew what was happening. He was trussed and thrown over a hard shoulder, and he felt the sampan dip as he was passed across water to other hands. Then he heard Cyril explaining rapidly as his voice grew more distant. The Old One had taken a shine to Hatton. So much so, that he wanted his company until the bones of Ho Fatt were returned to him. It pleased the Old One to be host to a man of sagacity who could discuss matters of import to pass the time pleasantly. As an honoured guest who was also a hostage, Hatton would be treated with great respect.

'Bit of a holiday for you, J.C.,' Cyril bawled faintly.

Then there was just the inside of the hood and the sound of dipping sculls as the barge made for one of the islands in the Tathong Channel.

Drizzle and more drizzle.

A grey morning world beyond batting windscreen wipers.

Margot Sadler yawned into her glove and waited for Charlie to come back to the white Rolls. She had never been in dockland before, and quickly recognised she had missed nothing but ugliness. Her broken night monochromed the peninsula of old warehousing, docks and shabby terraces that was the Isle of Dogs, and she wished she hadn't insisted on coming along.

Jarred from sleep by her bedside phone, she'd grasped only one word in three Chinese Cyril gabbled through frying warbles of static, and it was all cockney Cantonese to her fuddled mind. Charlie took over and functioned without a millisecond of mental twilight. In sleep he was serene; awake he was Charlie. No grey areas for Mr Dance the Human Light Bulb. His dorsal muscles ridged as he listened, and Margot's stomach tightened with dread at talk of bones and hostages. The tiny dart of fear bloomed as she dressed, and had her chafing by the Rolls long before Charlie strolled outside and muttered about catching low tide on Limehouse Reach. Left in the car, Margot hunched over the heater, and Charlie walked to the foreshore at the end of Cuba Road where the West India Dock Pier ran out over the brown Thames water.

Margot fidgetted as time dragged.

She retied her headscarf and blushed her cheeks. Glossed her lips and fed an early cigarette between them. Smelled the river she could not see and stared out at dreary frontages and hoardings, slick grey roofs and riverside cranes jabbing muddy cloud. Lorries with wet tarps and hissing air-brakes rolled past in their own walls of spray. Men coming off shift drove battered saloons, rode bicycles under rain-capes or walked with their heads down. Working men drudging to retirement in soulless tower-block utopias where television ruled and the square-eyed man was king. No gardens for the green-fingered, no community centres for the socially-minded; only stranger-neighbours in identical concrete shells, too high above the earth to belong anywhere but in a limbo of overcast.

Margot crushed the dark vision out with her blue Sobranie. Lit one of black and gold that made her silver nails seem lifeless slivers of grey sky. As if the weather had seeped through the smoked glass to steal their pale fire. To busy her hands she played with the zipper of the fishing bag on the back seat. Felt the cold steel inside with her fingers and knew what she touched from shooting parties in childhood Surrey. One glance confirmed her tactile suspicions, and she looked out of the window so as not to look at the guns or her offensively tarnished nails.

Told herself she knew what Charlie was and could care less. he rebuilt more lives than he took. Her's for example, and that was worth more than a blind eye and simple gratitude. He accepted what was offered, and shared what he could have taken as tribute from a vassal. No faking it

376

with Charlie like she had with her husband and the other bores before him. If Margot felt no inner worth, why then should he? And not just in the physical sense, that natural conjunction flowed from all else he gave her. Or was it rather he made Margot see herself as whole without the need to play a part? Nothing spelled out, all tacit, and therefore somehow more profound and fulfilling to the born again Margot staring out at rain and drear with a knot of fear in her stomach.

A green Jaguar had parked by a coffee-stall. Four men lined the counter to watch the Rolls without seeming to. The man serving tea, pies and saveloys kept his back turned, as if afraid of their taint in front of his regulars. Customs men wore uniforms, and Margot was sure these strangers weren't plainclothed filth. They belonged to the area without being clock-watchers who worked double shifts for luxuries. Camelhair and barathea worn carelessly in the rain set them firmly apart, and their knowing faces were ungrained by dockyard toil. They left their cups in line and walked away down Cuba Street without paying, and Margot knew them to be the source of her fear without knowing how that could be. Instinct was enough, and she employed her mental prompt to put names to faces as if her funk was mere first-night nerves.

Flynns, Crosbys and Tates, she dredged from overheard snippets.

Mixed voices cued her memory.

Vinnie wheeled on a winter lawn and said: 'Chas knows the world's due for a serious spanking if them three firms ever got together. But that'd take a common enemy they hated more than each other. They're tribal, see. Blood-ties thicker than their heads.' Then his ice-cream smile.

'Naughty bastards all,' Nasty said from the grave.

A living Sodbonce, drunk and maudlin, confided: 'Them Tates just hates and hates. Even themselves. I should know, wasn't I cosied up to one of the Tate girls when I was a

377

young Jack The Lad? Till she all but brained me with house brick having one of her turns. She used to go out night-walking and never say where, even with her arm up her back. Come home filthy but happy and clean out the cooker. Then they found her inna canal with a sack of kittens she was drowning. Must have slipped and banged her crust somehow. There was the filth and the RSPCA looking out for a gang of fur bandits emptying Bethnal Green of moggies, and all along it was nutty Sylvia Tate relieving her feelings. Funny family all round, love.'

And a rare unsmiling Ollie Oliphant: 'Them Crosbys wanted your class wheels, *you'd* be the optional extra they'd heave out the window. Drive off well happy.'

Then from Pimlico: 'Common knowledge round all the manors them Flynns are gyppo headbangers. To them animals, talking's a sign of weakness. They grunt for beer, a woman, or a hot meat pie. Same difference to them. What comes in bottles, crusts or beds gets sucked, fucked, or chewed. And there ain't no nice way of saying *that*.'

'Fretting over that'll only give you worry lines, toffee nose,' Charlie had hushed her questions with.

Armchair Doris knew her own for what they were. 'The East End is nothing turf for nothing faces, darling. You stay West End and be thankful for it. My pisshead father had me over the kitchen table when I was ten. After that it was every Saturday night he got my mother drunk enough to get away with it. I was on the game at fifteen, and fucked my way to the West End before I turned sixteen. The old man sent my brothers to bring me back. Hated not having that money going into his pockets. Archie saw him off, and the brothers. The old man's dead and gorn, but the brothers have sons now, and all cut from the same rotten cloth.'

Margot couldn't remember if Armchair was a Tate or a Crosby. And did it matter now? Four to one against Charlie was the reality of the here and now, wasn't it?

Margot had the fishing bag. Watched her dead hands

assemble the sawn-off shotgun with its pump action and oily smell. The cartridges as red as stoplights. Thought of her own late father training her for summer shoots when beaters drove game onto the guns. The gay soar of plumage and soft plummets as shot tore beauty from the sky. Shooting for daddy through tears as surrogate for the son he never had. His good girl in tweeds who retched when the hung birds were served at table. Glad when death duties swallowed the estate and no more foxes were torn by hounds. Leaving it all behind for greasepaint and repertory in the provinces, exchanging the theatre of the absurd for the real thing.

She stepped out onto cobbles with the gun under her duster coat. Glad of sensible brogues, and ignoring the odd stare or two through hard drizzle. There were high gates and a weighbridge where lorries waited in line. Slipping past the inspectors was no problem, and she glimpsed four overcoats crossing a narrow-gauge track weedy from disuse. Her chest was tight and hot, yet her feet and breasts were as cold as stones. Hard nipples nudged her bra, made erect by the foreplay of fear that sent worms of heat through her liquid crotch. She thought of rape victims who admitted to arousal through terror, and knew her unfortunate sisters told it truly. She would write a cheque for the cause when she got home. If she got home.

The pier was a rainwashed apron where nobody danced or sang to entertain the orange boxes and driftwood beached on the foreshore of ochre sludge. Winter gales had brought seabirds inland from the mudflats of Foulness, and they walked the water's edge from habit, knowing there was no edible forage in the polluted mud. Just keeping up appearances until they wheeled off to the nearest council dump to squabble over refuse.

Margot followed a stone wall to old pilings and wooden stairs sagging down to the foreshore and the smell of sulphurous decay. There were footprints in the treacherous slime, and Margot trod warily as she descended. A thumping engine from across the river found an echo in her breast, and she couldn't distinguish it from her own heartbeat. She seemed to see too much and nothing at all, just glaring bits of detail that made no sensible whole. She thought of going back. Of plump eclairs in Fortnum's tearooms. Dainty sandwiches and well-bred shrieks of greeting. Saw waterlogged timbers and a drowned something lapped by dark water. Wanted to sit down to sob on a landing, but the voices coming off the brown strand kept her feet moving down.

Jeers without humour or good will. If Charlie was there, or said anything in response, Margot could not say. If she heard his voice it might steady her. She hoped that. Prayed even, and thought that a terribly weak thing to do. No better than a heathen Chinese becoming a rice Christian to fill his belly in exchange for parroted hymns. The voices were off to her left, and had to come from beneath the pier itself. On the last stair she paused, and saw the sliding marks go off in that direction. She thought their expensive shoes would be ruined and was glad. She stepped down gingerly, and promptly sat in ooze.

'Bother and blow,' she scolded.

Margot wanted to laugh at her self-control. Early training had her with a dry shotgun and a fouled bottom. Dear dead daddy would have applauded without helping her up. Clothes and dignity meant nothing during the hunt, only the size of the bag at the end of the day. The old bastard would have tramped off chuckling.

A fusillade of stones rattled in the pilings, bringing Margot's head up. Charlie was working his way down through cross-struts about twelve feet above the men on the strand. A well-aimed flint had opened a knuckle and bloodied his free hand. He held a decorated box, and his face gave nothing away as taunts and rocks flew at him.

'Looks what he is, don't he, Mitch?'

'Wassat, then?'

'Archie Ogle's monkey on a stick.'

That drew laughs, and the men around the tall one called Mitch showed Charlie the pickhandles they planned to use on his ribs and skull.

Margot buried an elbow in mud and got a knee under her. Went down in a sprawl to smear her chin with odorous mud. Told herself mudpacks were good for the complexion and tried again to rise. That put her into a long slide, but it got her *closer*.

A stone clattered away after a meaty thump.

'Right inna bread-basket. Good hit there, Chick,' Mitch told a man with a thick neck and a lot of teeth.

Margot knew she had to get closer still. She might pepper backsides with the sawn-off at thirty feet, but that might just annoy instead of hurting. She had to make a clean knockdown, and she made swimming motions to get traction. To hell with standing up.

And why doesn't Charlie duck? she asked herself. Fuming. She'd give him whatfor for playing macho man in front of these cretinous jackanapes. And why couldn't he see her? He had the elevation, surely? Margo slithered and kicked. Lost a brogue shoe in sucking mud and left it there.

'Shouldn't have come poaching, should you, cunty?'

'On our turf in that bloody white Roller. Them wheels stand out a sea-mile. Had to get a call about it, didn't we, *Mister* Dance?'

'Had to,' jeered a man with a lazy right eye. 'You was well clocked, you tart.'

Charlie nodded. Said 'That figured', and sidled to a crusted piling. Ducked a rock and looked for new footholds.

'You're well dead, you know that, Charlie?' Mitch patted his hair. The centre parting drizzle and exertion had disordered.

'Lot of hard road between saying and doing, Tate.' Charlie worked downward one-handed.

'*Mister* Tate to you, dead man.' Mitch Tate smile-sneered. Slipped a length of polished beech across an open palm.

Margot sobbed for breath. Found a bar of solid gravel under her, and freed a leg from a boggy patch. It came free with the stink of badly rotted eggs. Revolted, Margot wondered if she'd ever be clean again, and washed mud from her right hand in a small dark pool rainbowed by oil. *Even pollution can be pretty*, she thought. There were similar patterns on the barrel of the shotgun. Bright coloured pearls of rain and gun lubricant. The shot-silk hues of the pheasant she had shot for daddy. *Death and beauty. Christ.*

'Only six feet to go, Dance. I like a man who can take his lumps.'

'Ain't much of a man who needs three to hold his coat, Tate.'

'Shouldn't have earned yourself a rep as a tasty geezer then, should you?'

'Happens not.' Charlie sounded disinterested. Fatalistic.

The four men were in a semi-circle. Waiting. They had trampled Charlie's overcoat underfoot after searching the pockets, and Charlie looked lean and frail in his black sweater and trousers against the bulk of their thick overcoats.

'Don't hang it out, Charlie. You've give us all a good appetite for breakfast. You down and dirty followed by egg and bacon. Handsome.'

'What if he doubles through the pilings, Mitch?'

'Charlie Dance? Do a runner? Not him. Where's to run to anyhow?'

'Just let me whack him, thass all,' said lazy eye.

'Fucking swarm the bastard,' muttered the one with a thick neck.

Charlie hung off the lowest crosstree. Swung and dropped.

'Come on, come on,' somebody said.

Margot was upright in the classical shooting posture. She worked the pump-action to freeze further movement.

'I'll trouble you gentlemen to stand extremely still,' she said.

'Am I hearing things, or what?'

Nobody moved. Nobody turned.

'Hello, toffee nose,' Charlie said.

Mitch Tate grunted. Looked over his shoulder to stare at the muddy thing with the shiny shooter.

'What?' he questioned. 'Is that? Not a fucking tart.'

'And an excellent shot, Mr Tate,' Margot said.

'It is a bleeding female,' said the one with the thick neck.

'Watch Dance you three. This looks like one for me.' Tate turned fully to face Margot. 'Pointing ain't shooting, girl. You know that?'

Margot said nothing. She was cold again, and her breasts seemed swollen. Growing inward to stifle her lungs. The nipples inverted to nail her clogged throat. She was filled with semenal fluid. As if Charlie had discharged a thousand times, filling her with cream like a receptive eclair. It had seeped into the sponge of her brain. Blinded her eyes with sexual conjuctivitis. She had to stop inventing imagery. The trigger was thicker than her shrinking finger. Harder to pull than a ten-coach express train.

'Got yourself a bit of a shake on there, girl.'

Mitch Tate swung his stave. Moved it from hand to hand. Made the head sway like a poised cobra. Margot would see the tongue forking at her if she dared look closely. The man's face was closing in on her too. Flying glass had puckered one side of his wide mouth where a hurried shave had left a dark copse of stubble. His nose had deep pores and a tiny crescent scar on the bridge. His eyebrows were thick and sandy, yet his hair was black and slicked by rain and Brylcreem. The eyes were oddly unaligned. The left one was large and brown and heavily lashed. The right one was turned up at the corner in a lear. Made ugly by a white scar that pulled the thin lid to the corner of the socket. It had no lashes at all, so it stared with bald malice.

'Out of your class, ain't you, lady?'

'Stand . . .' Margot said through glue.

Mitch Tate ignored her words and concentrated on her eyes. Locked stares with vapid cornflower irises and got closer.

'You put the shooter down. Just like a nice Harrod's lady who's picked up the wrong umbrella, eh? Or Mitchy-boy's gonna have to slap it right out of your hands with his naughty big stick. And that could hurt. Then I'd have to hurt you serious for getting my wild up. And you ain't dragged-up rubbish who grew up with good hidings as a way of life. Not you, pet. You was gymslips and warm classrooms. Good big house, toffee accents and hunt balls. All that social toffee down there in lahdie land. Worst happened to you was having your old maid serve the tea a bit chilled, eh?'

Margot warned him to stay back without uttering a sound.

Her breasts had ballooned to grotesque proportions. Were buoyant enough to carry her away on the slightest breeze. She would sail out to sea and become a hazard to cross-Channel shipping until jealous gulls pecked her to ribbons and plunged her into cold green wastes . . .

Mitch Tate was almost close enough to use his stave on the silly bitch. He covered his next two steps with words.

'Yeah, always had it warm and cosy. Nice antiques, nice central heating. Carpets nobody ever walked on before. Nice stockbroker husband with nice manners . . .'

Mitch Tate swung at the shotgun at the precise moment he conjured Bastard Malcolm. The stave was a swollen penis boring at Margot's face. Then it splintered in smoke and shot, and the kick against Margot's shoulder hurled the stump and Mitch Tate away. Tate's shoulder tore out of its socket as Margot and her piece of foreshore reversed away from him. Shock sizzled to whiplash his neck as he flailed Chick and Badger aside like cardboard scarecrows. He hit and bounced and bawled agony. Felt it in his crotch like an electric hernia. Flopped in foul sludge below a sewage outfall and was washed by fouler waters. Then there was just lying there trying to see if his manhood was intact.

The blast that had bowled him away came back across the river. A chattering echo dimmed by the thump of a pile-driver at Cuckold's Point. Tate could stand the pain, but he didn't much like Charlie Dance standing over him. Tate looked away to see Donkey heaving Chick and Badger out of the slurry. The woman hadn't moved except to eject the spent cartridge and pump a new one into the chamber.

'Didn't think she had it in her,' he said.

'Must be you said the magic words, Mitch.'

'She ain't shot if off, has she, Chas? I gotta know that much.'

'You'll live.'

'But it's *there*, right?'

'It's there.'

'Two thousand volts going through it. Christ. Didn't think she'd do it. Look at me tasty tailoring. Ruined. You finishing this, Chas?'

'It is finished.'

Tate stared with mismatched eyes.

'I'll be coming back at you. Got to.'

Charlie sighed at the gulls.

'I won't be coming back, so where's the need?'

'We'd have done *you* permanent. Lost *you* inna tide.'

'*And* the lady?'

'Maybe spanked her and sent her home. Can't top a class tart, can you?'

'Not that one, no.'

Tate got a hand to his dislocated shoulder and kneaded torn muscle.

'Know that now, dunn I?'

Charlie scaled dried mud from the ornate box under his arm.

'This is a sorry chunk of turf to lose claret over. I walk, you live. Simple.'

Tate wanted to deny it was over, but he had to bite on the pain before he started to whimper. Charlie had gone anyway when he came back to himself, and the lads were looking for ways to get him off the strand before the tide turned. Could be he could boast about being triggered by a class tart. Might go down well over a good drink that . . .

Margot found herself back in the Rolls without a stitch on. There was no memory of leaving the wharf or Charlie hosing her down at a fire-hydrant sluice. She shivered and drew the car-blanket closer, glad of the smoked windows. She sniffed fingertips to see if the brilliant nightmare had any substance in reality. There was the merest trace of gun oil, the bonfire smell of smokeless powder. Proof positive.

'Hungry, toffee nose?' Charlie asked as he drove.

'Ravenous,' Margot lied. Realised it was true. 'But *not* eggs and bacon.' That particular breakfast dish would always remind her of blowing a fully-grown man twelve feet across smelly mud. She wished she had the religious conviction to ask for absolution as she snuggled.

Then she slept.

Smiling.

CHAPTER THIRTEEN

Chinese Cyril had a nervous stomach and a bouquet for Margot.

Kai Tak Airport was cooled by crisp winds blowing down from the nine hills of Kowloon, and a winter sun spiked the calm sea beyond the extended airstrip. Charlie's flight had landed and taxied to the terminal, and the first-class passengers were already in the Arrivals Hall with their baggage.

Cyril thought of bones and tribute and nosy Customs men and shivered. The sooner Charlie and Vinnie cleared Customs the better, then Cyril could dump his mounting troubles in their laps and get back to the serious business of eating. Trooper had Cyril sharing his roadwork each morning at early bright, and Cyril was trimmer than he had been in years, although he put that down to worry rather than to regular exercise. Mental stress got his gastric juices running the four-minute mile, and he had to work hard at keeping up with his huge appetite.

Cyril's stomach rumbled as a group of ex-patriate wives in silks and hats called each other 'dahling' and talked in carrying voices as if Victoria Regina still ruled an empire; as if Kowloon were leafy Park Lane, and they carried Britain's former glory wherever their husbands were posted. They were there to meet Humphrey or Justin or Cedric, men of the Colonial Office returning from sabbaticals or yet another FO conference in London. Supportive wives from Chelmsford or Braintree who enjoyed their status in the colony and dreamed of an England that never was or ever had been for women like them. Only on overseas service could they flesh out their fantasies as they clung to the skirts of power, being the 'ladies' they yearned to be for as long as they avoided a home posting where reality waited to hand them a rude awakening.

Cyril listened without wanting to as he craned to spot Charlie.

'Dahling, Ashley was quite ashen from overwork when he left. They do so put upon the poor dahling so terribly much.'

'It's the same for all of us, dahling. Dear Peregrine is a complete martyr to obligation. One is so cramped in our present quarters, but he won't *think* of complaining.'

'Dahling Dione, he has *you* to do that for him.'

'One can't merely be *mute*, Beryl.'

'One can and *does*, Elspeth. One soldiers on regardless. I do just hope Tarquin managed to wheedle that dahling gown out of my little woman in Knightsbridge. (Sniff) She's *quite* the lady now she has her own salon. My dears, such *odd* people have money nowadays.'

'Blame the war, dahling.'

'Mother – well, you know mother, Beryl – She blames *both* world wars. They threw up so many nouveau monied upstarts.'

'Don't tell *me*, my dearest dahling. One knows.'

'Look, there's Peregrine now. Gosh, he looks awfully *fit*.'

'Lucky boudoir. Lucky *you*.'

'Elspeth! How desperately . . . *basic*, my dear.'

'Why, Beryl, you're quite *pink* with joy.'

'Dione. Really . . .'

'Come off it, dahling. Being *coy* never pruned the roses.'

'Beast. Over here, Peregrine . . .'

'Cedric. Yoo*hooo* . . .'

'Ashley! Sweetie! How yummy, flowers . . .'

'Tarquin. *Dahling* . . .'

Cyril got his belly to the barrier as the wives whirled away with glad cries and a husband apiece. Saw the whole Dance firm troop through glass doors, and managed a furtive wave in a sudden attack of shyness. Charlie shook hands and Margot accepted the bouquet with a peck on the nose and, '*Dahling* Cyril. Tiger lilies, how *sweet*.'

Cyril giggled. Snorted muted laughter behind a plump hand.

'What's tickled your laughing bone?'

'Nothing, Chas. The cars are this way.'

Charlie took in bustle and strangeness, absorbed data as he strolled Margot through clots of noisy Chinese and their blaring transistors. The neat Hong Kong police in pressed khaki, the knots of tall Europeans in crumpled lightweights, their ladies in summer frocks or sheer *cheong-sams* that enhance the slender oriental figure and do nothing for the matron from Broadstairs.

'You're still hacking out the chuckles, Cyril.'

'Nerves. Good flight?'

'Silver service all the way. What nerves?'

'You don't know the half of it, Chas. I tell you—'

'These our cars?'

'These three, yeah. See, how it is, Chas—'

'In you go, Margot. See to Vinnie, Cyril. In the first car with us, right?'

'Yeah, right, Chas. See, how it is—'

'Now. Not next week.'

Charlie sat beside Margot in the first limousine and sniffed the scentless tiger lilies as Margot lit him a Sobranie. The Chinese chauffeurs bullied the baggage handlers until the cars were loaded, gave Cyril bare seconds to squeeze in beside Vinnie, and drove out of the airport like Fangios with a lot of lane changes.

Charlie nodded approval. Trailing vehicles would find it impossible to keep up without becoming visible. Whatever Cyril had burning on his tongue had to wait until the speeding motorcade reached the Peninsula Hotel. Holding on through the swerving ride without being toppled across Vinnie took all his concentration, and by the time Cyril had extricated himself and seen Vinnie up the marble steps, Charlie had Margot in the lobby. Then there was unfolding the wheelchair and tipping the drivers, and by the time Cyril had panted inside, Charlie had been escorted up to his suite by the manager.

Cyril took the stairs to the fifth floor, and reached the passage just as Charlie, Margot and Vinnie came out of the suite behind the manager, took the lift, and went up a further floor. Cyril took to the stairs again, and watched Charlie inspect the suite above the one he had rejected out of hand.

'What was wrong with it? Cyril asked Vinnie.

Vinnie shrugged. 'The wallpaper clashed with Margot's flowers.'

'You're kidding.'

'I'm kidding.'

'You know how much it cost me to reserve that suite? An arm and a ruddy leg. What's Chas up to?'

'Ask him, why don't you?'

'Chas? Chas, hold up,' Cyril called, but Charlie was already off down the corridor with the harassed manager and an amused Margot. Cyril caught something about the view from the seventh floor being the best in Kowloon before the lift doors closed, and he pounded up a further flight, sweating seriously. When he got to the suite, Charlie was nodding at the view and had the manager beaming. Margot was ordering champagne from room service, and the assistant manager came in with a stream of matching luggage that could have meant Margot planned to stay for a year and a day. Somebody took Margot's bouquet to arrange in a huge vase, and Charlie tipped every upturned palm. He presented the manager with a box of Havana Havanas that were unobtainable in the colony, slipped a slightly smaller box to the assistant manager, and ordered a dinner from a menu that could well have been published as a substantial coffee-table book. Cyril gave up. Found himself a glass of excellent champagne and a plate of canapes, and sank into an overstuffed armchair as Vinnie sauntered in with the slightest limp.

'This is arriving incognito, Vin?' Cyril asked around shrimp on a shell of rice cake.

'Just Chas being contrary, ain't it? Says one thing, does the other. There's a mob of sports reporters in.the grill room, all tanking it up on August Enterprises. Be flashbulbs popping like balloons when they get here to take publicity shots.'

Cyril stared mid-swallow. 'Of Chas?'

'And Chappie and Trooper.'

Cyril could see Aman Lee Fook opening his morning paper to hiss at Charlie's face. Crooking an olive finger for his Killing Shadows as he fondled Wind with an angry hand. The ornate suite with its rich mouldings and richer furnishings grew darker shadows that stuck in his throat, and Cyril pushed the food away.

'Suicide, Vin. I gotta talk to Chas. Private. He don't know—'

'Does he look anxious?'

'No, but—'

'Then why should you, son?'

'This is a bloody circus.'

Vinnie's easy smile went with a solemn wink.

'That's the fight game, Cyril. All hype and ballyhoo.'

'All right there, Cyril, Good, good.'

Charlie patted Cyril's head and kept walking the manager to the lobby door, giving precise directions as he went. A bellboy in a pillbox asked Cyril to sign for a pile of cables and telegrams, and lingered until Cyril paid him a handsome gratuity. Margot made an appointment with the hotel hairdresser, and sent somebody out for a particular shade of nail varnish to match her jade green evening dress. Cyril took another drink from a passing tray and sulked. Stared at full-sized cut-out photographs of Trooper Wells and Sugar Boy Tatum flanking the huge fireplace as a woman showed Margot swatches of material for the drapes around the stadium, and a designer in sincere corduroys waited to have his portfolio of advertising layouts approved. Vinnie opened the cables and telegrams and made notes in a black book, shouting pieces of news at Charlie as he took phone-calls and ordered gold chairs for the press conference.

Cyril gave himself wind taking champagne bubbles down too quickly. Chappie August bustled in with his big cigar, and Trooper brought Hettie into the suite with her bag of knitting. Porters arrived with chairs and began setting them out in the salon under the direction of the assistant manager. A buffet bar came into being, and more bouquets arrived to fill the suite with heady perfume. Cyril fielded more champagne and forced himself to nibble a second plate of canapes, a morose rock in a sea of confused activity. They had left him holding the shitty stick, and now they ignored him. It didn't seem to matter that the whole enterprise was built on sand now the local Tongs had upped their price for co-operation; that they could cause overnight chaos by starting lightning strikes at the arena, make even the food and drink vendors boycott the event. One word from them, and there wouldn't be a taxi or a rickshaw within a mile of the stadium. Not a single ticket would be sold, there would be no power or lights, and every road in or out would be closed for repairs or blocked by union demonstrators. And Charlie hadn't even *mentioned* J.C. Hatton.

Cyril's slow fuse began to smoulder close to the powder. It wasn't as if Charlie hadn't been told about Chappie August's naughty deal with the New York bookies neither. Vinnie must have nailed that point home harder than hard, yet here was Charlie glad-handing the bastard like they were kissing cousins. Press photographers took them shaking hands, giving victory signs, or smiling with Trooper

392

between them. They even had Margot in some of the shots, and what she had to do with anything was beyond Cyril's ken. And there was Vinnie grinning through wreaths of smoke as if the whole flaming charade was funnier than casting Oliver Hardy as the Jade Emperor in a *Noh* play. And where was the rest of the firm? Pim, Ollie, Froggy and Matt? Cyril got onto the switchboard to be told they all had 'Do Not Disturb' signs on their doors.

Certain he'd been sold Tower Bridge, Cyril guzzled champagne in a bombardment of flashbulbs. Wanted the room to turn to vapour as alcohol wrapped him in a protective glass shell. Where the colours were muted and sounds were nothing but a tidal wash on distant sands. He fielded another drink and paused midsip. Charlie held an ornate box for the cameras as Trooper used it as a rest to write a substantial cheque for local charities. A box that had borne Cyril through the turbulent waters of Limehouse Reach.

Cyril set the glass down on a skimming tray. Wiped crumbs from his mouth and began to chuckle deep in his stomach. So that was what The Supreme Snake and the Sichuen Dragon would see in the early editions of the *South China Morning Post* and the *Hong Kong Shih Pao*. Charlie in the colony, ready to exchange Ho Fatt's bones for Hatton.

'That Charlie, a box of monkeys,' Cyril hardeyed Chappie August, wishing he knew what Charlie had in store for him when the time came.

Vinnie read Cyril's mind with: 'Now ain't the time to wander down *that* road. Get the reporters shuffled back to the Grill Room and stay with them until you get a call. Charlie wants to go visit a few faces before he puts the evening nosebag on.'

'Now? Tonight?'

'You handed him the shitty stick, son.'

Cyril blinked and his stomach churned. Charlie's roller-coaster was going downhill too fast for his linear mind.

Hoping he wouldn't be spun off on the faster bends, Cyril ushered his charges from the suite. Doing instead of thinking. It was easier.

Charlie smoked a hotel cigarette in quiet disorder.

The suite was empty of everything but old smoke and furniture, and he moved a comfortable armchair to face the windows. Killed the overhead lights and stood a standard lamp by the armchair. Put an ashtray and cigarettes within reach, and accustomed his eyes to the gloom. Vinnie and the lads were resting by order, and Margot was having her ends crimped, or whatever it was women had done to themselves in beauty salons. She would come back happy, so what did it matter that he thought the whole racket was a conspiracy to turn all women into plastic dolls out of a toyshop window?

Humming to himself, Charlie opened the French windows and stood on the rococo balcony. Leaned on the carved balustrade to take the evening air. Serpents of neon undulated along Salisbury Road, and the Golden Mile was an argumentative brawl of primary light. The spiced dusk still held the day's heat despite wind bowling in from the waterfront, heavy with ozone and kelp.

Charlie flicked his glowing butt away, and watched it spiral down into traffic. It struck in a shower of sparks before a taxi mashed it flat, and Charlie went back inside to build himself a weak Irish to wait with. The funerary box glowed in the lamplight, and Charlie opened the lid to check the carefully knotted folds of brocade. The Derringer and spare ammunition was in a plastic bag taped inside the lid, and Charlie dropped the whole thing into his jacket pocket. Sat in the armchair with a fresh cigarette, he watched the breeze from the Lammas Strait stir the curtains at either side of the open windows.

He had taken the top inch from his drink when he sensed what could not be seen. A something on the balcony. A smudge dark against the darker night. Charlie blew a small blue smoke ring and stayed seated. Hummed a while and said: 'Waste of time God inventing doors.'

The curtains swirled and went quiet. A taxi made a U-turn to collect a fare from the hotel foyer in a squeal of rubber, and a food hawker yelled, 'Aiwa' as he cycled past. Then Cho Sun was in the room, his face as black as his pyjamas.

Charlie toasted him. Said, 'May my hearth gods smile on your exalted presence in my humble rooms. I could do no more than come two floors closer to your perch on the roof.'

'Your Cantonese is as atrocious as this unharmonious decor,' Cho Sun grunted.

'You were at the airport.' It wasn't a question.

'Somebody was there. You entered like the wind of a sick elephant. A man with everything to hide *should* be visible.'

'Glad you approved.' Charlie wondered if the lemonade vendor with pebble glasses had been Joe Yellow. 'Your sodding Sichuen Dragon grabbed old J.C., Cho. With your help, I plan to get him back.'

Cho Sun listened to the sounds of the night and the hotel. Bowed fluidly at the waist and sat on the carpet with his back to a leather footstool. Toyed with a tuft of carpet.

'My help is yours, *if* you can stay alive.'

'Well, I do have something the old Dragon wants.'

Cho Sun's smile was an ugly pucker in old vellum.

'Ha, I saw the bones when I served you champagne.'

Charlie thought *Did you, by Christ?* and said nothing.

'He wants my head as much as your boiled bones, Char-lee.'

'As much as Fook wants mine?'

'Fook? He is nothing – bad wind soiling a midden.'

'Happens I don't agree.'

'Then you must deal with him before anything else.'

'Wanna tell me how?'

'There are many "hows", Char-lee. One chooses the most

expedient. Your arrival here will have puzzled him, made him cautious. He knows from experience that you are not a stupid man, yet your coming here at all is the height of foolishness. An act of total folly. You have even brought your minions with you. And to his eyes, they are the lowest form of life. He sees them as he sees the local street gangs. Mere Hill Tribesmen, to be used for money and discarded. Nothing more than cheap hatchet men, yet you honour them as equals. Yes, Fook will be puzzled.'

'So, he's wrong-footed. Question is: For how long?'

'Hours. Days. No longer.'

Charlie swallowed watered Irish and smoke. Exhaled through a nostril and asked casually, 'Is he here in Kowloon?'

'No, Hong Kong Island.'

'Then I'll go there.'

'But that is what he will expect. No, Char-lee, you must start here. Shake the edge of his world. Not the centre.'

'Could be I was thinking just that.'

'Of course, it is logical.' Cho Sun was dismissive. Seeing the obvious had no merit. He listened to the night, his nose flared like an old and bald badger. Ignored his sight in favour of his other senses.

'Cho?' Charlie jogged softly.

'Merely movement in the corridor. Of no concern.'

'Tonight soon enough?'

Cho Sun flowed toward the balcony and tested the darkness.

'That would be . . . unexpected. Since Fook already thinks you crazy, be crazy. Crudity and speed would work at this point. Not after. There is a pimp here in Kowloon. A poor thing of no value. But he is a White Paper Fan in the coils of the Snake, even though he slithers in the dung of prostitution as a cover for his dealings on behalf of the man Fook. This Liang Quing surrounds himself with men who steal young girls from the mainland. Some of his older and richer clients believe that lying with untouched girl

396

children help them to live longer. When these girls have lost their bloom, Quing's men seed the mouth of the Pearl River with their rotting remains. I think that man is an ideal target to direct your first madness at.'

Charlie agreed in a cloud of smoke.

'There's the small problem of getting out of here. Unseen.'

'There is a laundry truck that serves this hotel. The boys who run the truck serve me. They are my worthless nephews, and have learned to be clever behind stupid faces.'

'And I find this Liang Quing where?'

'Tsim Sha Tsui. The waterfront. Use your halfy-halfy to find the way.'

'Cyril?'

'Of course. He has been dealing with Fook's people all along. They *own* the entertainment industry here. But I think you know that already. The halfy-halfy Cyril does not. For a blind man he has avoided snakebite well. Luck or cunning, would you say?'

Charlie sat with lidded eyes.

'He's been aching to get something off his chest. Maybe now I'll let him.'

Cho Sun barked a laugh. 'To confirm your own suspicions. Ha, as always, you make your own joss, good or bad.'

'This don't get me to the Sichuen Dragon, Cho.'

'True. For that Exalted One, you must look in the Clouds of Heaven, and the Middens of Hell.'

'That the name of some cabaret bar, or you being obtuse? Spit it out plain for Charlie, Cho.'

Cho Sun thrust his hand into the southern darkness.

'Out there, Char-lee. In the thousand Islands that are few and many. Countable yet numberless. Most are bare rocks without water or vegetation, and the sea currents run fast, cold and deep. They are bad joss, for they are haunted by ghosts and devils.'

397

'Invented by mandarins to frighten peasants,' Charlie snorted.

'Once, maybe. But not since the dark dwarves of Nippon came to conquer China and throw the British out. They knew what to do with Chinese mouths too numerous to feed or waste bullets on. They ferried them out to the islands in their thousands. Marooned them there to die of thirst and malnutrition if they didn't drown trying to swim back to the mainland. Flesh-eating birds nobody had seen before came to feed on the putrid meat until the Nipponese dwarves used their precious petrol to burn the dead where they lay. Even today, the Hoklo fishermen avoid the islands. They still hear the cries of the unhonoured dead in the still of night. Or in daylight, when the monsoon winds make the bones sing. But the Suchuen Dragon has no fear of the dead. His place is protected by the night sounds, and he is secure. That is where your old money man is, Char-lee, out there.'

'You know which island, Cho.'

'Such a matter is for another time. If you live, Char-lee.'

The ugly smile showed in the spill of lamplight and Charlie found himself alone. Cho Sun climbed towards the roof, and Charlie had four hours to fill before taking Margot to dinner.

He circled LAUNDRY SERVICE on five sheets printed with hotel services, and had a bellboy deliver them to five separate rooms. Told the desk to give him an alarm call after a three-hour nap, called Cyril in the Grill Room and told him to be at the service entrance in ten minutes.

'It always comes down to pimps,' he said softly, turning off the standard lamp.

Ten minutes dragged to thirty.

Cyril pretended to read the fire regulations on a notice board as he waited for Charlie to show. A woman in blue pyjamas offloaded flowers from a handcart; a baker brought fresh bread rolls still hot from the oven; and an old laundry truck blocked the service bay as two delivery boys trundled baskets of clean linen to the lift. Cyril flattened himself against the wall to let them pass, and the smell of hot food made his stomach rumble.

Two more minutes crawled by. Broken cockroaches seeking dark corners to die in.

The service lift sighed open, and the laundry boys pushed their baskets of dirty laundry out into the corridor. Cyril ran a finger down the fire regulations with his back turned, muttering under his breath. A basket slammed into the back of his knees, and he turned in a crouch prompted by pure reaction. Glimpsed a grinning laundry boy as his lapels were grabbed. Let himself go with the hard pull, ready to use knee and elbow in the clinch, and found himself tumbled into a laundry basket. An arm circled his throat, and the wicker lid slammed closed with a creak. In slatted light and stale sheets, Cyril found himself staring at Charlie. Charlie blocked a reflex punch to the chest and flicked a finger at Cyril's top lip.

'Put your fists away. Know a better way of getting out?'

'You flaming box of monkeys.'

'Shut it.'

The basket went up a ramp and was banged against other baskets. Doors slammed, gears clashed, and the truck toiled out into Salisbury Road. Charlie raised the wicker lid and hauled Cyril out after him. The laundry boys giggled as they split their bribe so that Cyril could see, trading ribald remarks in Cantonese.

Cyril got his necktie back into his collar.

'What the thump did you tell these guttersnipes, Chas?'

'Ducking out on the wife for naughties, ain't I? They'll drop us at the waterfront.'

'Waffor, for Chrissakes?'

'Naughties, what else?'

Cyril sagged on the lip of a basket.

'Got any idea what they're *saying*?'

'One word in ten.'

'Just as well you ain't sensitive. You, my old Chas, are a monster fuck-fuck with a penis where your head oughtta be. They figure you'll make ten whores walk crooked, and maybe make halfy-halfy Chinee-long-nose babies. Unclean offspring the bad yellow of sour mustard seeds. Means they take you for a fool.'

Charlie sat on a heap of linen.

'Being underestimated gives you an edge, Cyril son. Don't knock it.'

'I think they're right, as it happens. You won't listen, so you don't know nothing. Bulling in here without knowing the bloody starting prices and runners is stupid.'

'That right?'

'That's damned right. You think a few dollars has bought these kids? Wrong. The minute they drop us off, they'll run to the nearest White Paper Fan. Tell him about the barmy long-nose Brit the whole bloody colony knows is worth more dead than alive. The words out on you, Chas. From the minute you landed. We're all marked, and once they've sucked us dry of cash, that's us finished. Dead.'

'That right? Well, well . . .'

'You *are* barmy.'

'Happens you're right. Only they want the cash first, right?'

'Yeah, but—'

'So these kids bubble up to the local mobster. Tell him we're running the streets. He passes that on to the man above him, and that gets passed all the way up to the Perfume Master, and on to the face who controls him. Right?'

'Bloody right. S'what I'm saying.'

'All the way up to the Sichuen Dragon? To the Supreme Snake?'

'Yes. And—'

400

'And that, Cyril, gives us what we need. Time.'

'To do what? Make our wills?'

'To buy more time. Nobody'll lay a glove until one of the top faces gives the word. That, my son, is our edge.'

'Some edge. They bleed us dry, then cut our throats. Lovely.'

Charlie punched the linen into a ball to cushion his buttocks.

'Question is: how much money, Cyril?'

Cyril's thumb trembled as he ticked off points on his fingers.

'First the gate receipts. Know how much they want? Thirty bloody per cent. Gross, mind you, not net.'

'Give it to 'em. Chappie can afford it.'

Cyril let that ride, knowing it was one of the ways Charlie meant to punish August.

'Not so fast. Know what else they want? Ten cents on every Hong Kong dollar in side bets.'

'House stakes. Fine.'

Cyril groaned and lurched with a lane change.

'And a good bet on the winner? Odds in their favour?'

Charlie said nothing with unreadable eyes.

'Yes, Charlie. Like they expect a certain somebody to take a dive. Like it has to be Troop who hits the canvas because the fat money only gets earned if the ref raises Tatum's glove.'

'Greedy, ain't they?'

'Greedy ain't in it, Chas. They figure they've got Trooper by the short and curlies 'cause they've got *you* by the pubics.'

'Greedy *and* confident.'

'Don't you get it, Chas? They're feudal. They see you as just another warlord. Almost a king. If they disgrace your champion in public, that ain't his face in the mud, it's *yours*. After that, you ain't worth wiping off their shoes. Humiliation in public *is* a kind of death. They'll have you chopped off at the knees by the lowest Hill Tribe in Hong Kong. The hatchet men of some . . . *pimp*. And they *are* the lowest of the low.'

Charlie nodded with cold eyes.

'They ain't so different to us then, are they?'

'No, as it happens.'

'Bad joss all round.'

Cyril wiped beads of sweat from the bridge of his nose.

'You're saying that, Chas, but I don't see you *believing* it.'

'Happens I don't.'

Cyril tried pleading.

'Let's turn this heap around. Go back to the hotel. Think of ways to have it away on our toes. There's a flight—'

Charlie's cold hand clamped Cyril's hot mouth.

'Ain't you forgetting something, Cyril? Some*body*? You think I'd sit at home waiting for a special delivery? Old Hatton's head in a box? No, old son. Oh blimey no.'

Cyril's jowls grew crimson finger marks when Charlie gave him his face back. He shuddered and wished he had Charlie's speed and stamina. The eyes were just grey stones in a dead face, yet the mouth smiled. *It* smiled, but the rest of the face did nothing. The smiling mouth even had words to bite off.

'They want me to grovel like you want me to grovel, that it, Cyril?'

'Them, yeah. Me, no.'

'Better grovel, then. My way.'

'Wassat mean? What?'

'Means you take me to the last face you got an ultimatum from. We show him what an empty face I am. Something he can maybe relate to.'

'He ain't nobody, Chas. Just a go-between—'

'You been dealing too far down the ladder, Cyril? Or is this face being modest? Name this modest face for me.'

'He uses Liang Quing when he deals with me. I dunno if that's his real—'

'But I do, and it is.'

'You do?' Cyril asked. Thought, *How?*'

'Another pimp, right?'

'He runs a place . . . I suppose so, yeah.'

'A pimp. And you ate his crow like a good little minion. Nice one, Cyril. Just as well I'm after some naughties then, eh?'

'You? You want a ficky-fick? You?'

'I got glands,' Charlie said.

The laundry truck bumped left through high wire gates and made hard turns through old Victorian godowns and modern warehousing. Ground to a halt between two buildings under construction, and one of Cho Sun's nephews ran to open the rear doors.

'I give you much satisfaction, sir? You call Pak Wo for much heavenly fuck-fuck you don't see what you want in this low place. My uncle is a great man, sir. Has a place with youngest girls in all Kowloon.'

Charlie just walked Cyril away.

'I too have an uncle with girls, sir,' called the driver.

Charlie guided Cyril around a corner into heavy pedestrian traffic and yelling hawkers. Wove through the crowds like a dancer who knew where he was going.

'Point the way, Cyril.'

'You're going right. Only a spit and a jump away. The place with the green parrot. Look, Chas, you can't just walk in there. He knows me, and he'll know something ain't kosher right off.'

'Not with you pimping for me, he won't.'

'You ain't making sense. When did you ever pay for it?'

'Now. Tonight. I wanna live a thousand years, don't I?'

Cyril stopped to stare.

'You want . . .'

'I want. And I'm a drunk with a hard on, see?'

Charlie's legs got rubbery. He draped an arm over Cyril's shoulder and began to croon in a dreary monotone.

'Sing up, Cyril son. Where's these twelve-year-old virgins you promised me?'

Cyril supported Charlie's weight.

Groaned through a few bars of an old song.

Charlie's fingers were steel pins in his deltoid.

Ollie came out of his doze when the printed sheet came under the door. He turned it over in his hands and saw the circled words: LAUNDRY SERVICE. Tore the sheet across and dropped it in a waste basket. Got his feet into his shoes, laced them up and checked his watch. 6.02 p.m. local time. Less than four hours before Charlie ate in public opposite Margot. Ollie armed himself with the lead sash-weight he had carefully removed from the bathroom window casement. Fed it into two pairs of socks, tied off the ends and swung it against his palm with a satisfying slap. It would curdle brains used right.

Down in the lobby, Ollie went through the motions of ordering chauffeured limousines from the Chinese desk clerk. They discussed rates as Ollie checked out the lobby, and Ollie spotted a couple of likely lads who didn't belong; a thin Oriental tucked behind a copy of that morning's *Shih Pao*, and a chunky Chinese in a smooth suit that hung all wrong. There had to be others, and flushing them out was the name of the game. Ollie turned back to the desk and made a hash of converting sterling into Hong Kong dollars to make the desk clerk smile to hide exasperation.

Vinnie showed first. He crossed the lobby and had the doorman whistle him up a cab, gave the address of a curio shop in the Golden Mile and had himself driven away. The Chinese in the smooth suit took a taxi in the same direction. Ollie asked if a weekly hire got him a cheaper rate, one eye on his watch.

Matt and Froggy left the lift in mid-argument, and stopped close to Ollie without noticing him, too intent on driving their points home. When they decided they couldn't agree on which cabaret to patronise together, they flagged separate cabs and sped off in different directions. The thin Oriental came out from behind his newspaper to use one of the lobby phones. When he'd talked and listened, and listened some more, he bowed to the phone and pushed out through the revolving doors to flag a saloon parked without lights on the opposite side of the road. It U-turned to drop a man beside the thin Oriental, and roared off after Matt's taxi. The thin Oriental bundled the man into the last taxi in the hotel rank, sent if off after Froggy, and stayed outside to surveille Ollie without the possibility of eye-contact. He knew his trade, but was clearly uncomfortable functioning without back-up. Time and geography were suddenly working against him.

Ollie asked for hotel matches to light a Capstan. Peeled a cuff from his watch in a show of impatience. The desk clerk rummaged for a list of authorised rates that would undoubtedly include a kickback for himself, and Ollie played drum riffs on the mahogany counter with thick fingers. The thin Oriental was wondering whether he should re-enter the lobby to overhear what Ollie might be saying to the desk clerk, and Ollie began to fret about Pimlico's whereabouts. He was cutting things a little fine.

Ollie grunted and let the desk clerk get transcendental about the excellence of the vehicles available for honoured guests. He spotted Pimlico coming up the front steps from the street with an unfurled tourist map. Ollie pinched off a grin and nodded at the desk clerk. Trust Pim to be different. Pimlico got his map untangled and stopped the wind from folding it all wrong. Showed it to the thin Oriental and asked directions. The thin Oriental showed polite interest and went pale as he traced a route with a long finger. His mouth opened to expel air that had gone solid in his throat. He clutched at Pimlico who helped him to kneel very slowly.

Ollie scratched his crotch. Pim's fist couldn't have travelled more than three short inches.

The thin Oriental took the tourist map down to the ground with him, tearing it in two. Pimlico used the tattered remnant to attract the doorman's attention as the thin Oriental fell on his side to vomit weakly. Pimlico backed away as though disgusted by drooled bile, and was edged aside by the gathering crowd of hotel staff and rubbernecking tourists. Pimlico waved to a non-existent friend, ran down the steps to the street, and was swallowed by the night.

Ollie told the desk clerk to have three limousines ready to drive up into the New Territories at eight sharp the following morning, and sauntered outside for some air. The doorman had the thin Oriental covered with a blanket, and the hotel doctor checked pulse and heart rate. Ollie tutted in sympathy and walked past slowly. Pimlico had walked to the corner and crossed the road without anybody on his tail. The thin Oriental's back-up would arrive just too late. Ollie followed Pim, and they hailed a cab three hundred yards along Salisbury Road.

When the driver had circled the block several times, Ollie had him park on the west side of the Peninsula Hotel near the service entrance. The driver had no grumbles. All he saw was the money they promised him, and if they wanted him to park all night, that would suit him just fine. He dozed under his peaked cap for half an hour, and awoke to find three more long-nosed men climbing in to settle beside Ollie and Pim.

'Any sweat, Vin?' Ollie asked.

Vinnie patted the brass Buddha he carried.

'Nope. Bought this fellow to bring us luck. Went straight out through the back of the curio shop, and had it way back here in another sherbert. My tail must still be sitting there if he ain't blown his brains out.'

Matt rubbed the Buddha's oval stomach.

'I rolled out of my cab on a left-hand turn. My cabbie was still kissing his money when he took off with my Chink after him. They'll be doing a tour of Mongkok around now.'

'You?' Ollie asked Froggy.

'About the same. Left my tails searching one of them big tenement blocks. Led 'em up to the roof and left 'em counting the socks in about ten miles of washing. Even managed to bring the same cab back. Spoiled him with a wad of dough, and said he should pick me up at a bar in the Golden Mile in about an hour.'

Ollie checked his watch.

'Charlie'll be moving about now. Let's just hope we got the opposition looking in all the wrong places.'

Pimlico chewed a cinnamon dragee.

'My geezer went down like a bleeding horse,' he said.

'Nice hook, that.' Ollie watched a laundry truck flash its lights and pull out from the hotel service bay. 'Right, driver, get in behind that truck. Don't lose him, and don't get too cosy with his exhaust neither. Savvy, old son?'

Vinnie laid more large bills in the driver's lap.

'That enough rice?'

'Most splendid, heavenly sir. I will drive like the sun chariot.'

'Slower is better,' Ollie grunted.

'I have honour of being most-most patient driver in all Kowloon, great sirs. The oh so unclean vehicle we follow goes to the waterfront. You seek pleasure there?'

'Oh blimey yeah,' Vinnie said, quoting Charlie.

'May Buddha and the Christian Jesus grant you erections that abide a thousand lifetimes, honoured men.'

'Awkward playing snooker,' Matt said. 'On them cushion shots.'

There was laughter in the cab, but it was taut and unamused.

Cyril walked Charlie into a wall of sound and heat.

The Tropicana Bar heaved with negro sailors on liberty from an American carrier, and a live combo sprayed decibels to drown out a jukebox crooning romantic songs in fountains of coloured lights. The long bar was shoulder-to-shoulder with happy sailors, and the neon parrots around the walls gave the dark faces a green cast. Mixed-blood hostesses sipped $5 shots of Coca Cola from liqueur glasses, and allowed themselves to be pawed with their usual indifference. Any jolly jack with ideas of romance had come to the wrong place, he might enter the body, but the mind flew elsewhere, untouched by emotional blandishments.

Cyril found a booth away from the dance floor, and signalled drinks from the bar. Charlie sprawled where he was sat. Slapped a palm against the underside of the table to fix the Derringer securely, and lolled with dull eyes and a sloppy grin.

'The Savoy Grill this ain't,' he muttered.

'Hold the clack, Chas. We're being looked at.'

Cyril watched Momma-san weave towards them carrying her usual glass of medicinal whisky. A big and flaccid woman from Macao, she had a Portuguese complexion and the high Slavic cheekbones of her Tanka mother. Her small and slanted eyes were black buttons of mistrust, and she moved her heavy body with surprising grace. She sat facing Charlie, her hip brushing Cyril's thigh, and ordered a drink on Cyril's tab without invitation, $11 worth of cold tea from her private bottle behind the bar.

'Long-long time don't see, old green monkey,' she said.

'Long-long,' Cyril agreed.

'I send girls when they free. Black Yankees spend much-much dollar, but girls think they lose "face" sitting with them.'

'You think we're here for pleasure, gross one?'

'No back room tonight. So, yes. You say different?'

'It may be you can't supply what is required.'

'Say fuck-fuck who?' The big woman stared at Charlie. 'This man who?'

'That he is with me is enough, gross one of too many years.'

'Him plenty fuck-fuck. Not too old to see that.'

'But plenty-plenty rich enough for special service from back room.'

'Ha! You say! My girls $130 for walk-out. No profit in that for me. No profit for man in back room.'

'There is profit. For the right walk-out girl.' Cyril shut up until the drinks were served and the barman was back behind the bar. 'This man fuck-fuck generous when it comes to his pleasure.'

Momma-san toyed with her cold tea and soda.

'Big-big talk only noise. Cheap-fuck-nothing, old ape. All men talk rich-rich until droop after fuck-fuck. Then only got small dollars in shoe. More holes in foot-covers than dollar.'

Cyril managed a laugh, and stopped Charlie laying his face on the table.

'This one has no holes in *his* socks, gross one.'

'My girls only sixteen-seventeen. Eight pounds English money for all-night jinky-jink. Let this man pick one of them. Leave me to take real dollar from Yankee sailors.'

Charlie came out of his stupor to leer. Fumbled high denomination notes from a pocket and laid them on the table with his fist over them.

'Girl,' he slurred. 'Young . . .'

Momma-san looked at the money. Licked a fleshy lower lip.

'He get throat opened for carrying that much in Kowloon. This man? He crazy-bastard-mad-crazy?'

'Crazy,' said Cyril. 'And you be fuck-fuck glad he is. This man makes money a gift to you. He wants a fresh purse between young thighs. Not many-fucked saddles like your cheap-cheap walk-out whores.'

Momma-san wanted the money. Enough to mist her upper lip.

'It is . . . much to ask,' she said.

'It is much money,' said Cyril.

Charlie swayed and belched. Talked at Cyril through bubbles of wind.

'Tellis whore t'get . . . *pimp*. Now . . . other pimps . . . bars . . . right?'

Cyril put his glass on the money when Charlie fell back.

'This fortune is nothing to this man. Be quick, gross one. If you would have this money for yourself. I only have to lift my drink, and it is yours. Enough to keep your stinking brood of illegitimate relatives in rice for half a year. Think how much red paper you could burn to bring luck in the New Year. How many mercies you could buy from the goddess Kuan Ying.'

'Old monkey talk like . . . devil.'

'Then pick up the money. Go to the man in the back room. Walk away and be rich. Burn my malignance away with red paper dragons. My influence could not survive the flames.'

'True,' said Momma-san.

'Do it now, or do nothing. Well?'

Momma-san lifted Cyril's glass, and the money went into her skirt. She stood and jerked her head at Cyril.

'He stays here. You come alone.'

'No. To leave him here would cause him great displeasure. Now his mind is addled, but tomorrow he would remember the slight.'

Momma-san clicked fingers.

'My girls will protect his heavenly person, green ape.'

'And keep their deft fingers out of his pockets?'

Momma-san sneered her impatience.

'Knowing I bite off thieving fingers and spit them into their faces? Ha, they will be honest.'

Cyril nodded. 'I choose to believe you. Bring the whores.'

'One question first: why does this man seek what is young and not within the law of the British *jing cha*?'

Cyril's frayed nerves helped feign a show of temper.

'You mention the *police*? You plan to take this man's money and entrap him with the *jing cha*? Give back the dollars.'

Momma-san raised a hand in placation.

'Softly, I ask only to understand.'

'This man is not old, but he would put off joining the heavenly departed by pleasuring himself with a girl-child. Catering for such tastes is the main business of the man in the back room.'

Momma-san slid from the booth.

'Say nothing more to me. Say it to *him*.'

'Of course.'

Cyril followed Momma-san through dancing sailors and loud music, wanting to urinate very badly. He stole a last glance at Charlie, and saw him being fondled by three girls as a cover for frisking him. Nobody was missing a trick tonight, and Cyril's bladder protested at the thought of what waited for him in the back room.

Vinnie's artificial limb made him anchor man.

He and the brass Buddha had a tired whore and three Australian sailors for company at the coffee stall across the street from the Tropicana Bar. Vinnie's missing foot itched, his stump throbbed. He'd fed a sandwich to begging children, refused offers of gold Cartier watches with bubble-gum jewels and rubber-band movements, glass diamonds in rolled-gold settings, and sipped cold coffee as he waited for Ollie and the lads to report back to him.

The whore touched Vinnie's sleeve with her small bosom raised.

'You want girl, mister? You give maybe cigarette?'

'I give cigarette,' Vinnie lit two and passed one across.

'Just few-few dollar. We make jiggy-jig?' The whore

might have been twenty, but her eyes were older than the granite hills. Her dress was creased, and she couldn't afford stockings.

'Not with me, Lotus Blossom. Try these blokes.'

The whore sad-eyed the Australians.

'Cheap-cheap sailors take. Don't pay.'

'You should get protection. Like the girls inside.' Vinnie jerked his chin at the Tropicana, and the girl followed his glance.

'You fuck-fuck crazy, mister. They bad. Very bad people. I once be there. Too many times too sick to work. They say go, no pay. I go,' the whore trickled sighing smoke through a plump rosebud mouth.

'Too bad.' Vinnie swivelled to watch the street through the hawkers, bicycles and street traders. Pimlico came out of a door in the building next to the Tropicana to cut the air with the flat of his hand. Signalled a blank. He'd sat through an old porn movie to find a vantage point above the side door to the bar.

'Damn,' Vinnie emptied his cup in the gutter and ordered a refill. Bought the tired whore a coffee and a sandwich on impulse. The defeat in her face reminded him of the girls back home. The lazy-smart ones when the dreams of being rich left them poor and cold and sick and unwanted in midnight alleys. The Chinese still exposed unwanted girl children on hillsides, and who was to say this whore hadn't been sold to a brothel before she was five years old.

'Bit of a soft touch, ain't you, sport?' one of the sailors asked as he and his mates moved away.

Vinnie said nothing. The two floors above the Tropicana had balconies hung with washing, and there were no lights showing at the shuttered windows. Froggy had checked out the rear of the building, and found a kitchen that serviced the restaurants on either side. There was no way through into the bar or the rooms above. Had there been, Froggy would have ferreted them out. He had a nose for such things.

412

'Twenny dollar. I clean. Room clean.'

Vinnie refused. She wanted thirty shillings sterling, the price of a hundred Player's. *Christ.*

'Want for nothing, huh? For cigarette,' the whore said.

Vinnie just looked at her. Something in his eyes made tacit contact. She offered to return the sandwich, and smiled when Vinnie pushed it back at her.

'Lose more than leg, huh? Face see-all like thin Buddha. Big sick-sick do that to people.'

'Buddhas are fat, lady.'

'Only outside,' the whore demolished her sandwich with small bites. 'Inside thin. Like high air where mountains ive.'

Ollie pushed in and took a stool. Ordered what looked ike a hot dog in a floury bun and bit its head off. Said with a full mouth, 'We'll have to do a full frontal with the Eighth Army. No way in down the side alley. One door, barred solid. Take more'n a docker's boot to stove that sod in. All creek and no paddle.' He chewed gloomily.

Vinnie watched green neon parrots flick on and off. On and off. The whore watched him watching as she dabbed at crumbs with her tongue. Two stocky Chinese emerged from the alley to watch the street. One stared at the tired whore with recognition, said something with a coarse laugh, and dug wax from a thickened ear.

'Bad people,' said the tired whore.

Ollie raised an eyebrow.

'She used to work there,' Vinnie said.

'She *says* she worked there,' Ollie grunted, as Matt and Froggy drifted out of racks of clothes to stand near the two Chinese. Pimlico joined them, and showed off a kimona he thought he'd buy for somebody.

The whore sneered at Ollie for Vinnie's benefit.

'Him *look* like fat Buddha, mister. No air inside. All in bad mouth.'

'You could be right,' Vinnie agreed. 'Finish your coffee.'

The whore slid from her stool onto thin legs and thinner stilettos. 'I go.'

'How much, sweetheart?' Ollie asked with suddenness.

'You? You much-much heavy. Thirty dollar, half-hour.'

'And for this?' Ollie crackled a folded $100 bill.

The whore hesitated. Clutched a small bag sewn with bright glass beads. Looked across at the flickering parrot and back at Vinnie.

'Why you stare alla time there?'

'He gets backache doing it in alleys,' Ollie said for effect.

'Him don't do it. Face too . . . clean.'

'A plaster saint, ain't you, Vin?'

'Why you stare, mister?'

'He never had no toys as a kid, dearie,' Ollie said. 'Had to play with his—'

'Not fat man tell. You tell.'

'Tell the lady, Vin.'

Vinnie plucked Ollie's note from his fingers. Eased down from his stool and took the whore's arm. Tucked the bill into her silly handbag and snapped it closed.

'Let's take a walk, shall we?' he said.

The two stocky Chinese had seen all they wanted, and had gone back into the alley. Vinnie started the whore walking, needing a lucky break if he was to help Charlie.

The narrow passage had smelled of foetid air and dirt.

The back room was thick with joss fumes and stale humanity, and a fast game of mah jong went on at a table in a corner. Cyril was held by two men smelling of fish and lentils, and a third man jammed a revolver into Cyril's spine. Cyril stared at Liang Quing and watched him eat noisily.

Liang Quing wore a crumpled white sharkskin suit, and his cerise and veridian suede shoes matched his silk shirt and tie. His socks were dayglo pink, and his sallow face shone with moisture. His bleak eyes had the same dull sheen as his overoiled hair, and he ate fish from a twist of paper without manners.

'Nobody called you here, halfy-halfy,' he said. 'Nobody *wants* you here, yet here you are. I spit on you, and the gross whore who took your stinking bribe.'

Cyril his his feelings as the gun bored deeper into the flesh of his middle back.

'You spit too readily at a friend who brings you easy profit, Liang Quing.'

'Your foul mouth dirties my name, halfy-halfy. Do *not* use it again.'

'You refuse a friend's business, nameless one?'

Liang Quing crossed a knee and spat flakes of boiled fish.

'You no friend. You nothing.'

Cyril braced his thigh muscles. Rolled his shoulders. Worked the nervous kinks from his body, ready to move fast if he needed to. Said: 'And "nothing" takes three men and a gun to render it harmless? This is a puzzle, nameless one.'

'You are the running dog of the long-nosed one. Running with sores and messages. That *is* nothing.'

'And you are a fool who prefers insults to profits.'

Liang Quing crushed the twist of paper. Listened to a man who came in to whisper, and showed Cyril more contempt.

'This man you bring for heavenly pleasure with a rare pearl is a fuck-fuck drunk. What then, does that make you, halfy-halfy?'

'His man,' Cyril said.

'My unclean whores had fondled this man. He has money. Money that is mine for the small effort of rolling him in the gutter.'

'You could try,' Cyril's laugh was a soft sneer.

Liang Quing threw the twist of greasy paper into Cyril's face.

'Who is this man? Who?'

'A man seeking the ultimate pleasure. I told you.'

'And you fear him more than you fear *us*?'

Cyril refused to think about that. Humiliation had to stop somewhere, and he let the words flow like combination punches.

'As you should fear him, *pimp*. This man agrees to all the paltry demands you parroted for the faceless ones above you. He laughs at their small greed, as he would laugh at you, were you worthy of his notice. If he prefers the mists of alcohol to the fogs of opium, that is his choice.'

Liang Quing worried a thumbnail with small grey teeth. Stroked an ugly suede shoe with a greasy hand. Cyril's round face told him nothing, which in itself was alarming. In the previous negotiations his face had been an open scroll, now it was as closed as a walled garden. The halfy-halfy mouse of a few days before had become a mongrel with bared teeth, despite the gun in his back. Fear pushed him forward at Liang, when he should be shrinking away. This drunken man must be something more than a rich pervert seeking illegal and expensive sex with a girl child.

'He pay $20,000 Hong Kong, this man?'

'If this unspoiled pearl is as tranquil as the Queen of Heaven, Lik Mak Leung herself. For such a quiet maid he would gladly pay the paltry sum you extort.'

'Sooo,' said Liang. 'Sooo . . .'

Cyril stepped back into the gun. Swung a shoulder and elbow into a hard gut. Heard lungs empty in a brawl of breath as the revolver hit the bare boards. Kicked the gun away to spin to a halt under Liang's chair, and heaved the two insignificant limpets off his powerful arms like a swollen bullfrog. The gunman kneeled to gape, and the furious limpets flailed away into watchful crouches, stayed by Liang's signal. Liang himself stood to tremble with anger and indecision.

'You dare . . . *this*?'

Cyril dared without knowing why.

416

'And more, you mindless fuck-fuck pimp. I have offered he harmony of agreement to the T'ang's demands – *you* hrow wretched insults back like morning-stars. The Perfume Master will show his displeasure, hooded insect. Your unguarded mouth has dug your grave in the man-roves. Even these dogs know that much. Ha, if you were worthy of being a true White Paper Fan, you would have nown about the man I brought here for diversion.'

'This man is *that* man?' Liang could not believe it.

'Look deeply into the faces of your own dogs, Liang Quing. See the answer that is there. And *there*. And even *here*, where this mongrel tries not to spill his rice. They will pass your arrogant stupidity on to the right ears, and hen . . .' Cyril drew a snake in the air and turned its coils nto a fist. 'So stupid,' he sighed.

The mah jong tiles stopped their clatter. Liang Quing's ace was raw abalone. Bass chords thumped through the brown walls, and a singsong girl mooed too close to a microphone.

Liang Quing rubbed his loose mouth. He had lost much ace by insulting the halfy-halfy messenger without thought. The man was as great as the message he carried, and the message was more valuable than Liang's fragment of the greater tapestry that was the great brotherhood of the snake. To Liang, the powers above were faceless and without form. Cold voices on the telephone. Omnipotent.

Liang forced himself to bow low three times. To smile with pleasant hatred at the halfy-halfy Cyril as he sat in Liang's chair to lounge comfortably.

'This man *is* that man,' Liang admitted aloud.

'And untouchable. You said the price of the pearl was vhat?'

Liang tried to match Cyril's surface calm.

'The pearl I have in mind is beyond price. I can only offer t as a present to this man. I beg you to accept this gift on his behalf.'

417

'For the sake of harmony, I will. Now you must see enlightenment, Liang Quing. Find the courage to use th talky-listen machine. Have your fingers make five circle to bring your words to a certain house on Hong Kon Island. Words you hope would please the Supreme Snak himself. You force me to use his name in public, becaus you haven't the mind to understand the subtle birdsong o Mandarin thought. For you, all must be spelled out in crud dialect.'

Liang murmured his thanks. The halfy-halfy was pre dicting Liang's moves before he made them. Laughing a his loss of face without cracking a smile. Cyril had raise a finger to wag and then point.

'You are as see-through as glass, pimp. You think tha maybe this man's humble compliance with the will of th T'ang makes his life shorter. Shorter maybe than the nigh itself. You hope that he may be sent to join his ancestor during the act of heavenly intercourse, as would be fittin for a person of his great importance. You even pray tha you may be the cutting edge of the Supreme Snake's wil It burns through the bones of your skull.'

Liang almost shrugged, thinking fast.

'This is strange talk for a man who would surely die wit his master, should such an order come.'

'Realistic, not strange. If such is written . . .' Cyri achieved the shrug Liang had fudged. His heart thumpe hard enough to bang out through his shirtfront. There wer seven men in the room with Liang, and any one of then was capable of murdering by order.

Liang saw the ex-wrestler through a lifting veil.

'You are more Chinese than long-nose. I honour you fo that.'

Cyril favoured him with a jaded glare.

'You are still a pimp, and the man is impatient. You wil bring the pearl here. Send these jackals for her.'

'Difficult, but it shall be as you say,' Liang knew he coul

418

control events better inside his own building. There was an upper room that could be made ready, and the further expense of hiring a garden of wind-chimes and songbirds would be avoided. Spite made him add: 'You know the girl-child must die once she has served her purpose? The potency of the act would be nullified without her death. Most sad.'

Cyril kept his face bland as his stomach convulsed.

'This man will take that matter into his own hands. His way of making certain he is not cheated. Savvy, pimp?'

'All is most clear, honoured one,' Liang hid surprise. *What kind of a man was this drunken long-nose?* he wondered. To kill such a man would bring Liang great kudos within the coils of the snake. Wipe out his most recent and regrettable mistakes. And two bodies in a sack were as easy to dump in the Pearl River as one. *Or would it be three?* Liang worked Cyril's weight out in his mind as the halfy-halfy finalised the arrangements for the upper chamber.

'There will be Irish whiskey and iced water. Fresh blooms. No weapon will be needed, this man will despatch the pearl with his own hands.'

Liang was dizzy with delight. The honour of killing such a man grew in his mind like the shining heart of the Forbidden City.

'It is already done,' he said.

Cyril rose and handed Liang the revolver from under the chair.

'Now take me back to this man. I must sooth his impatience with the great purity of this chaste pearl.'

Liang saw no harm in that concession. They were both unarmed. He gave orders in swift Kuoyo, knowing the halfy-halfy did not speak or understand the national language of the mainland.

Everything was a weapon if used properly.

Vinnie left the tired whore in her room and walked back the way he had come. Found a long arcade full of dark

corners and racks of cheap clothes lit by kerosene lamps
and sent the shop-boy to fetch Ollie from the coffee stall.
Pimlico drifted in with Matt who said Froggy would be
along when he'd seen to something.

'Seen to bloody what?'

'Dunno, Vin. You know Frog, free spirit, ain't he?'

'I'll give him "free".'

Ollie bulked in to say, 'What's free? Not Vinnie's lady
love, I know. Or does that secret smile mean different,
Mister Castle?'

'Means she earned her hundred.'

'Her hundred? My hundred. Wassat in real money, Vin?'

'About twelve quid. Charlie's twelve quid.'

'Yeah, still runs to about a pound a minute. Hope she
was bloody worth it.'

'She blew in my ear.'

Ollie crossed his eyes and screwed a finger into a dimple.

'So you're easily pleased. So there's a secret passage right
to the bloody treasure. Spill it, Vin. Charlie and Cyril are
still banged-up innat parrot's poxhole.'

'Yeah, talking to a face called Liang Quing. A pimp.
Except he's a pimp with a difference. This one negotiated
the stadium for the fight – and the gambling skim for the
local Chinks. He ain't just a three-tart string, he's got
himself a small private army in there. Trades in young
virgins for the carriage trade, and dumps 'em like kittens
inna sack when . . . well, I don't have to spell it out, right?'

'Y'do to me,' said Matt.

Pimlico said he'd heard of the like and let Matt stew in
ignorance with, 'Ask Frog, you moron. Go on, Pim.'

'Only two ways in and out. The side door in the alley,
and through the bar itself. That's it.'

'Cuts down the options,' Ollie growled.

'Means them inside are as stuck for alternatives as us,
right, Vin.'

'Yeah, Pim. I figure we put two in the alley, and three

of us mix it up at the bar. Get that jumping with pissed-off matelots of a negro persuasion, and hope it's enough to flush the bastards.'

Ollie fingered an embroidered piece of tat.

'The daddy-question is: who fancies the alley? They send out for help, it'll be the heavy mob that comes skipping up to take our heads off at the hips. You can look hard all you like, chaps, but I don't want none of us getting it hard and nasty like Soddy and Nasty.'

'Fair comment,' Pim fed himself a scented dragee. 'I'll take the alley. You with me, Vin?'

'Wait up,' Ollie blurted. 'Vin ain't Nureyev no more.'

'And means he can't outdance humpty sailors with chairs and bottles, right?'

'I say Vin's out,' said Ollie.

'And Vin says he's in,' said Vinnie. 'Shut it, Ollie, I mean it. You handle the bar with Matt and Frog. The special cocktail trick oughtta do it. Lighter fluid and hipflasks, you know the form.'

'Ought to, I invented it,' Ollie had to grin as Matt caught on.

'We worked that one Christmas in Southend, right, Ollie? Bang, bleeding whoosh,' said Matt. 'Worked a dream.'

'Forget Memory Lane,' Vinnie snapped. 'Just do it up brown.'

Ollie laid a gentle paw on his shoulder.

'Ease up there, Vin. Gotta laugh when it's this grim, right?'

'I miss something?' Froggy said, sidling in.

'Only everything, you pillock. Where've *you* been?'

'Doing the phones, what else?'

'What?'

Froggy looked around the semi-circle of hard faces.

'The public phones. Done every one within walking distance. Cut the wires right under the coinbox where it don't show. Then I done the poles around the Tropicana.

Y'know you can buy acid right over the counter here? Even sulphuric? Wrapped them connector things in cotton wool and bandage, and dripped acid over 'em. See, if I'd cut the wires staight off, they'd have come down all over the traffic and give the game away. Take a bit of time, but it'll do the business. What're you all grinning at?'

Vinnie pinched Froggy's cheek.

'You, you life-saver. What a team?'

'Frog,' said Matt through muted laughter, 'what's drowning kittens gotta do with tarts and carriages? Vin said . . .'

The firm walked away from him with their shopping lists memorised, laughing out excesses of adrenalin.

Liang Quing dialled, watching Charlie and Cyril through a trick mirror in the backbar. The line hummed as the sea-cable connected Liang to a stone house on the outskirts of Victoria, and Charlie missed his mouth with a slop of whisky. The girls mopped him dry with a bar-towel and laughed behind their palms. He was fuck-fuck drunk all right.

'Yes?' said the telephone.

'My fan is paper. My number is four,' Liang whispered.

'Wait.'

'With humility.'

A cold male voice said, 'Unfurl your fan, Four.'

'The halfy-halfy has brought the long-nose's compliance, Lord. He has also brought the long-nosed taipan with him. This man is much-much drunk, and his stated pleasure is an untouched pearl. I have sent for such merchandise to please the barbarian, Lord. I now ask to be of further service.'

'This man is truly intoxicated?'

'My humble vigilant eyes confirm this.'

'And he is alone?'

'But for the halfy-halfy, yes, Lord.'

'There are no others?'

'Others? My low bar *is* for others, Lord. But others of his kind are not in evidence, no.'

'That means nothing. Less than your life.'

'Yours is the wisdom—'

'Silence. Your foolish words deny what others have told us.'

'The error must be theirs. He is here.'

'Describe this man.'

'Long in the leg. Hair black. Eyes like old winter cloud. I have not heard his voice, but the halfy-halfy ordered the dark whisky of the Irish.'

The line bubbled submarine interference and washed itself clear.

'If you spoke, Lord, the talky-listen devils stole your words,' Liang said with apology.

The telephone breathed for a long moment, and Liang's sweat dripped into the mouthpiece.

'Where is this man to be pleasured?'

'In my own poor upper quarters, Lord. There is only one side door, and the one staircase. To leave, he would have to fly away above the heads of my seven guardians of tranquillity.'

'You make much of small—'

Interference spat. Gobbled what might have been said.

'Lord, forgive my deafness . . .'

'. . . Men will come . . . you . . . act blind so . . . not see . . . arrive or leave . . . nothing . . .'

'Lord?'

The telephone was a dead plastic shape in Liang's hand. He jigggled the tines and heard nothing but the sound from the bar. Slammed the receiver down on the cradle and mimed a punch at the wall. The half-heard directive had been whole enough for Liang to see himself through the eyes of those who looked down at him. Not worthy to be trusted with a simple assassination. An whoremastering cur to be thrown favours like bones. If men were being sent

423

from Hong Kong, they must be Killing Shadows. The Supreme Snake had decided not to wait to take revenge on the man Dance during the boxing tournament. He had offered himself for death in his drunken ignorance, even the halfy-halfy had seen that with the Chinese part of his mind, knowing true fate for what it was. Inevitable.

Liang Quing smoothed his face and hair, wiped his teeth on his sleeve and returned to the back room. The specialists would fail the Supreme Snake by arriving too late, whereas Liang Quing would not. The long-nosed drunk would die from a single thrust at the very pinnacle of perfect bliss.

It was written.

Aman Lee Fook held the extension telephone long after it had died during the Perfume Master's final orders to the fourth fan in Kowloon. Sea devils had swallowed the directive somewhere in the Lammas Strait, and the will of the snake lay somewhere in the deep waters. Fook hardly noticed Wind take the instrument from him and replace it in the japanned cabinet where it lived, for there was much to puzzle over.

The man Dance was at the Tropicana Bar, yet still slept jet-lag away at the Peninsula Hotel. In less than an hour, Dance's minions had scattered the Dragon tong's watching ones across Kowloon, and could not be anywhere within the city. The halfy-halfy Cyril had somehow spirited Dance out of the hotel to guide him to the only visible link in the chain of command, and nothing was as it should be. Even Liang Quing had expressed himself with bold strangeness through the frying rice of the cable connection, and more importance must be given to his bald impertinence than to his words. This odd request to be of further service was a new and surprising thing, coming as it had from a perfect subservient who did just what was required without question or selfish embroidery. Liang Quing had somehow been changed, and only his motivation was obscure.

424

Or was it?

Aman Lee Fook allowed sudden insight to furrow his brow. Saw what was obvious. Ambition to be more to the T'ang had caused the fool Liang Quing to forget his allotted station. The desire for kudos had prompted his offer of service; had turned the great wheel of inevitability to destroy what was truly harmonious. Liang Quing had become a danger to the brotherhood, and there was only the question of what form his new madness would take. Burning a red paper stork to placate the goddess of luck would not serve to forestall what was about to happen.

Aman Lee Fook stood. Called for street clothes. Even now the men despatched by the Perfume Master would be boarding the ferry to practise invisibility amongst the other passengers. They would arrive in Tsim Sha Tsui to witness . . . what? The Supreme Snake must see for himself. There was no other choice. Merely disturbing Fook meant Liang Quing and his so-called guardians of tranquillity had set themselves on the dark road to destruction.

But at whose hands?

Fook looked down at his own hands as Wind stripped off the golden fingers he wore in the peace of contemplation under the bohinnia trees of his private garden.

Mine, he prayed. *Mine.*

CHAPTER FOURTEEN

The hostesses melted away when Liang Quing brought two guardians to the booth. He smiled his grey smile of false humility and said, 'All is ready. I offer the poor hospitality of my establishment to this man who honours us with his divine presence.'

Charlie belched and leaned over the table, one arm dangling close to the floor. The two men with Liang looked hard and capable, and made Liang seem slight in his ill-fitting white suit. The music brawled, and Charlie supported his chin on a crooked forearm, doing his best to look about as useful as a rubber banana.

'Well,' he slurred, 'Genghis Khan hisself.'

'I do not understand the worthy one's words,' Liang lied.

'He likes your face,' Cyril lied back.

'I am overjoyed. If you will both follow me?'

Charlie touched the Derringer tapped under the table.

'Not Cyril, Genghis. He stays here.'

Liang could not fathom the long-nose's use of the Great Khan's name in regard to himself. It was a compliment or an attempt at alcoholic humour. Either way, it was best ignored with smooth tact. He said, 'Your man would enjoy greater comfort away from these crude sailors. You must allow me to insist.'

'He allows no such thing,' said Cyril. 'If I am ordered to remain in this booth, I stay.'

'Fat but loyal,' Charlie said, picking at the tape.

Liang's eyes glittered and veiled.

'Then my men must guard his person. On that I do insist.'

'No fluff outta my navel,' said Charlie. 'S'long as they're drinking men.'

'Cup for cup,' Liang's loose mouth showed all his grey teeth. 'Warmed wine will add speed and cunning to their slow-witted . . . conversation?'

Cyril knew a phoney euphemism when he heard one, and he ignored the silent hatred of the man he had disarmed so easily. The second guardian was one of the limpets he had shrugged off, and keeping those two busy left Charlie with five more of the bastards to handle alone. He calmly asked Charlie if he was ready to take his pleasure.

'Born ready, Cyril son,' Charlie had the Derringer tucked into a sock and lightly taped to his calf. The clever little whores had been thorough around his ankles when they dabbed whisky away. He swayed upright into a shallow, nodding bow. 'Lead on, Genghis.'

Momma-san was busy seeing a drunk into the street, and the jukebox wailed syrupy violins as the combo jammed a popular song with crass enthusiasm. Negroes spun and twisted on the dance floor, alive to their own inner rhythms. Outclassed by hips and feet born in Memphis or Little Rock, a couple of hostesses jerked on the spot. Charlie followed Liang Quing with solemn care, and somehow crossed the dance floor without being knocked over.

Liang bowed Charlie through a tatty bead curtain, and the door beyond closed to cut down the noise. Only the thumping bass followed them past two more guardians and the mah jong game in the back room. They climbed a flight of wooden stairs, and the decor changed on the first landing. Flock wallpaper covered the lumpy walls, and there was cheap hessian underfoot. Framed sepia portraits of ancient Chinese patriarchs hung in an alcove lit by a small hanging lamp. Fretted wood formed a latticed surround on the turn in the stairs, and the walls glowed with rich green silk

427

hangings. The lamps were bronze and crystal, and the stairs and the passage beyond were carpeted in thick and expensive felts of many subtle shades, simulating the blue and white Sky Road to the Heavenly Gate. An old woman in a black kimona kneeled to exchange Charlie's shoes for silk slippers, backed away and bent double, and beckoned him forward.

'I leave you here,' Liang said.

Charlie hooked a grubby white lapel to bring Liang close. The man's pores leaked stink, as though he ate prawn fertiliser by the sackful.

'Lord?' Liang's look killed with dead eyes.

Charlie patted the pocked and hollow face. Weaved gently.

'If Aman Lee Fook was my host, Genghis, he'd pour my first drink himself. Serve it to me in my bath. And show me the pearl personal, not leave it to some old woman.'

'If that is your pleasure, high one.'

'Oh blimey yeah,' Charlie bared his white teeth.

Jolted, Liang Quing kicked off his ugly shoes and edged his feet into slippers. Not only did the long-nose know the strict laws of hospitality, he dared mention aloud the name that was never spoken in Kowloon. The family name of the man who occupied the celestial chair of power. The tall long-nose had even looked upon the face Liang had never seen; and who knew, he might drop further indiscretions of use to a humble White Paper Fan? Liang told the old woman to lead the way, and smiled hatred at the long-nose's back until his face ached.

Charlie paused at the portal to the upper chamber. Shook his head as though to clear his mind of alcohol. He could have been thrown back to the feudal empire of the Ch'in dynasty. Candlelight swayed along the black hardwood ceiling beams. The wooden floor had been beeswaxed to a deep golden sheen, and the black silk wall hangings sewn with bowers of cherry blossom backed delicate screens of gilded wood. Fine jade pieces stood on low pedestals, and

428

there were sprays of orchids in small porcelain bowls on finely carved ebony tables. The bathroom was in an alcove of olivewood and sea-grass matting, and scented water steamed in a sunken wooden tub. The bottle of Irish whiskey was on a lacquered tray beside a low brocaded couch, a brash alien, jarring the harmonious juxtaposition of shape and texture almost as much as Liang Quing's shabby modern clothes. The old woman was just a moving shadow that threw no shadows of its own.

Charlie nodded at the room's visual perfection. Only its corrupt smell made it less than it should have been. Freshly smouldering joss could not mask the lingering cloy of cooked opium pellets, for many of the old ones used the pipe to make their dreams of regained youth more dreamlike. It was no great trick for Charlie to see the old woman bring old ones from the opium mat to cover a drugged pearl, and bringing about physical conjunction with deft practice. Easing the way with oils or the knife when necessary. A screaming pearl merely spoke of an old one's virility. Compliant silence meant a pearl offered up hymen and life with heavenly consent. The pearl's final drugged drink made her part of the dream of immortality, already beyond life; so, where was the suffering in that?

Charlie forced himself to feel nothing.

Liang stripped the foil cap from the Jameson's and added iced water to a generous measure. Charlie padded into the bathroom and threw his jacket at the old woman to fold and lay in a niche. Liang set the drink on a tile by the bath as Charlie's shirt came off. Saw the scar winding across Charlie's shoulder and sucked his teeth. A dragon with opened jaws, it pointed a ridged tongue at the base of the long-nose's neck, the perfect point to plunge the knife. The omen stole Liang's breath, and he forgot to smile when Charlie stared at him. Distracted, Liang did not see Charlie tape the Derringer under the slatted bench before stepping down into the bath.

'Tell me about my pearl,' Charlie said, reaching for the tall Irish.

Liang smiled then, there was more in the glass than whisky and water.

The changing cubicle smelled of raw denim and cheap dye.

Vinnie assembled the rifle in the semi-darkness whilst Pim kept the proprietor from ducking his head around the curtain to see if his shoddy goods gave satisfaction. The ammunition clip snapped home, and Vinnie passed Pim a pair of jeans to haggle over. Vinnie used the time that took to get his artificial leg and trousers back on, worrying about Pim relying on nothing but his fists. It was Pim's choice, and as he'd said: 'Me and shooters don't mix. Let's just see how a pair of cobbles germans stand up to all that Chinky prancing and dancing'.

Vinnie remembered a time when he'd have felt the same way. He stroked the stock of the weapon he'd test-fired on Foulness Marshes, and knew it to be accurate with little recoil, even using his doctored ammunition. Steel splinters suspended in the wax he'd poured into the heads of the hollowpoint loads gave each round the impact and spread of a shotgun load. His first shot had blown a hole in a birch sapling, his second had blown the trunk apart. It ought to be edge enough, even for a one-legged man with the punching power of an unweaned toddler.

'You fit, Sampson?' Pim handed a shopping bag through the curtain for Vinnie to feed the rifle into. Only the narrow stock stood proud, and Vinnie fed it up his sleeve as he followed Pim through the racks to the open front of the arcade.

Their appearance in the street was the signal for Ollie, Matt and Froggy to wander into the Tropicana Bar, with Ollie carrying the brass buddha like a tourist's trophy. Vinnie and Pim lounged at the entrance to the side alley behind a knot of chatting sailors.

We're here, Charlie, Vinnie thought. Waiting.

Liang Quing saw the drug hit, and wondered if he'd got the dose right.

Charlie heard birdsong in the embroidered cherry blossom, and wondered how that could be. Liang Quing told of the pearl's abduction from a Shum Chun village with flinty echoes in his voice, and Charlie watched the sallow face melt upwards into the oily hair. Reform and do it again. The green knots in the olivewood were mouths miming the pimp's words, and the scented water was pink undulant glue holding his limbs together. The old woman was a gnarled stick wrapped in flowing ebony, and her face was a wizened fruit with simian eyes. The bony hands spread on her lap grew leaves where her nails had been, and it was crazy she didn't notice.

Charlie knew he was Charlie for as long as he could hold onto the core of himself. His thoughts were peeling away in spinning rings. Spiralling downward and inward through tunnels of rushing blood, they banged through the great aorta and, oxygenated by the heart's huge pump, sped away in crimson boils of anarchy.

The glass in his left hand held the answer to something important. Somthing bad had come from the glass. Hidden by the tastes of misted peat, it had become the enemy within. He made that thought a fist in his mind, and swam back through his skin to wallow in thickening pink water. Closed his eyes to the giddy winds whirling across his face and scalp as jagged sadness welled, and manic laughter was another madness to be fought. He must not lie in St Anne's Court again. Must not see the small figure kick and block, stun and paralyse. This time it would be his identity that was shattered, his wholeness routed.

Charlie linked mindfist to body and sent a command.

Charlie's left hand jerked at the wrist to sink the glass in foaming pink glue. Came up with the glass awash with

431

suds and adulterated amber liquid. That small victory prompted his voice to join in the charade that was so difficult. It sounded natural. Just lazy enough, as the left hand offered Liang Quing the glass for a refill.

Knowing and thinking were in two hemispheres of consciousness, divorced by birdsong from the tapestry. He, Charlie, needed to know the enemy within. To name the thing eroding his mindfist. Not Heroin. Not cocaine. They made the surreal real. Had the swollen ego soar to copulate with dwarf suns to sire moons. Had the mind fall into the whorls of the thumb where all the colours of the universe gathered in endless rainbows. The enemy was Acid. Bastard Acid. Acid turned mind-magic to dripping horror, turned dream to nightmare. What had been nameless was known and could be fought.

The old woman was an old woman. The pimp was a pimp.

The Chinese in white took his melting face away to the bottle near the whiter couch, and Charlie made his long legs bend at the knee. Made his floaty feet find purchase on the drowned baseboard of the tub. His buttocks tightened, and there was animal strength in the taut thighs. The right hand opened and closed under the watery glue, and Charlie let the old woman's hands grow leaves. Charlie's made fists.

He extended himself beyond the bathroom. Made the unseen birds his friends to stop them changing into unspeakable things. Liang Quing gave flinty orders to two men who brought something small and cuddly to tie down across the white couch. There might have been a small cry, but it was lost in birdsong. The olivewood mouths just gaped in the walls, and Charlie knew they were ashamed to give voice to what had been brought for his pleasure.

Charlie and his mindfist stood with a shudder of ecstatic moral hatred. Felt cold water burst over his swimming head as the old woman rinsed him off. A million beaded pearls hung in the air. Exploded cascades of frozen water droplets, each one precious and in need of comfort. More water slammed into his back, and towels dried him with rasps of animal breathing. If Charlie turned, he would confront what pursued him out of the well of fear all people haunt themselves with.

Charlie flew with tiny flocks of wings through cherry blossom. Hummed counterpoint to birdsong with crystal pitch that matched the sane voice of his mindfist.

His knotted arms went into wide sleeves, and a kimono was loosely tied around his narrow, tensed waist. The bathroom matting cut at his feet like spurred wheels until he strode the satin floor. The melting smile of Liang Quing rippled with his vibrant cerise shirt. He handed Charlie's left hand a second glass of enemy, and stood aside to show Charlie the pearl tied across the couch.

Looking turned the mindfist to black ice.

The naked pearl was spreadeagled on her back. The hair was coarse and black, the fringe chopped square across a round forehead. The eyes were black almonds in fine-grained skin. The tiny mouth had been lightly painted. The small olive body was hairless, and the prepubertal mammaries were no more than pink buds. Silk ropes spread the slender arms and held the thin thighs apart. A hard pillow under the buttocks thrust the tiny hips forward, slightly parting the lips of the girl-child's mons veneris.

Charlie tasted adrenalin and sulphur.

Liang Quing talked on. Saying the traditionally obscene things he would say to old ones who needed such stimulation. Then he was leaving with the old woman, and the men who had been there had moved off down the blue and white cloud passage.

'If you require more, use the bellpull, honoured one. All will be made available . . .'

Charlie swayed without moving. A last weakness that left him drained of all but one singing emotion. A nightingale soared in song, and bitterns honked from reeds in the ebony walls. The blacker eyes of the girl-child were vague marbles lost in drugged stupor.

'One thing . . .'

Charlie really swayed. Found the pimp's shoulder with a shaking hand. Dug fingers deep in sinew, and his left fist took Liang Quing in the stomach before the glass of drugged whiskey hit the floor. Drove deep as Charlie punched through him at the wall beyond. Fish and bile erupted from the rippling mouth as it widened in shock, and a slipper skipped away as the pimp's feet left the floor. Charlie's deltoid took the shock with a muscular laugh. His fist felt tissue impact and turn liquid.

Liang Quing was still trying to fall when Charlie's left smashed nose and septum flat. The right fist crossed to bat the body away, and Charlie was turning in the slowest slow motion as the old woman hobbled towards the door, making a thin sound in her throat. Slower than the electrified madness that was Charlie, she got a hand to the portal frame before he was on her. A thousand dead pearls sang with the hooked palm that snapped her head back and aside. The cords in the thin neck burst as the face went slack, and there was the thin crack of a breaking pencil. The woman slid in a heap, and a dead hand brushed a jade bell to the floor. It chimed as it rolled, the sound that had preceded an unmarried daughter in the palace of a long-dead emperor.

The very air was trying to eat Charlie's face as he remembered to breath. There was blood and gobbets of fish on his forearm, and he wiped it off on something silk as he sensed the men coming back along the Sky Road to the Heavenly Gate.

The bathroom was way off in mists that fogged the inside of Charlie's mindfist. He got his bare feet padding, and the slatted bench was as long as a rainwashed pier running out of brown Thames water. There were men growing from river mud to snag his slow ankles, and Charlie kicked out at nothing before he fell. The falling went on a long time, and angry adrenalin fought gravity and the grasping hands of men far away in the East End of London. Mitch Tate crowed from the knots of olivewood with too many mouths and no face at all. Charlie's shoulder hit the floor and skidded him to the lip of the tub. The pink glue was diluted blood too close to his face, and he mewed sick nonsense as he backed away from it.

The floor vibrated to warn him of fleet shoefalls, and Charlie ignored the splinters growing from the bench to rip his scrabbling hands. The blood was not his. The smeared fish ate through the kimono and into his flesh. Charlie touched tape and plastic. He tore at it, scattering huge brass shells. The thing from the bag fell into his bloody palm, and had the double snout of a steel dragon. Charlie slammed his hands at the floor, flipped himself into a high roll no sober athelete could have achieved. The black ceiling beams spun past his bawling mouth as he faced himself away from the bathroom. A foot crashed where his gut had been, and a magnified leg came at him like a swung tree. The steel dragon barked flame at it. Tore a hole in a turning groin, hurling it down a tunnel lined with cherry blossom and candle flicker. It flopped and thrashed, and Charlie would not let himself hear the ruined thing roar like the fall of a winter weir. There was too much water in his world, and something else was swimming through it to kill him. It had a man's face, but Charlie knew it had come out of the deep well of fear. He shot it in the mouth. Watched the head disintegrate into red streamers and thick clots of brain matter.

Charlie was on his back. Something had smashed into his chest. Had weakened his mindfist. A kick of the emperor's horse had broken bones in his front. He shot the pain away with the empty gun, and heard the click several times before it registered. The birds no longer sang, and Mitch Tate had taken his thousand mouths home with him.

Something dripped with slow persistence, and Charlie

435

heard his face liquify to run from the bones of his skull. It was puddling on the edge of the pink pool. That brought darkness in a swirl, and the mindfist refused to accept the delusion.

Charlie tried not to unravel completely.

A woman waited to dine with him.

Something small and helpless needed help.

And Charlie needed the brass teeth of the steel dragon.

He searched the floor on hands and knees, making his wet eyes see only what was truly there.

Ollie had an elbow and the brass buddha on the bar.

Froggy and Matt had toured the booths and the dance floor, and located Cyril with his two Chinese guardians. Passing him without a sign of recognition, they paused at the jukebox to load it with coins, and Matt poured lighter fluid from a hipflask into the coin slot. Froggy wandered off to check out the lavatories at the rear of the place, and joined Matt down the bar from Ollie to drink beer from a tankard. By drinking with his little finger extended, he told Ollie he'd doctored the toilet cisterns with sodium pellets. Jammed above the ballcock and water line, they would be tumbled into the cistern the next time the toilets were flushed.

Ollie bought large Jim Beams for the sailors around him, and introduced them to his buddha, the Great Poobah of Magical Power.

'Juss some ol' tin gewgaw is all,' said a mulatto from Tulsa. 'Where you getting off wiv all this shoot, man?'

'The Poobah is forged from the finest brass, sunshine,' Ollie told him. 'Rub his tummy for luck. If he's inna good mood, he'll tell your fortune.'

'Where's this dude comin' from?' asked a big PO with shoulders.

'Outta space, outta mind,' said a thin stoker from San Luis Rey. 'Flim-flam, you hear?'

Ollie looked hurt. 'Boys, have I asked you for a brass farthing? Just spreading Christmastide joy, ain't I?'

'Ain't that some Whitey carnival?' asked the PO. 'Don't think that festa ever reached our neck o' the boondocks.'

'Could be I mebbee heard of it,' grinned the mulatto. 'And if this dude say he make the brass man spit golden eagles for an itty-bitty side bet o' fi' dollars, well, damned iffen he won't.'

Ollie laughed and threw notes on the bar.

'OK, sceptics. This two hundred dollars says my brass friend *will* tell your fortunes. And, hear this, it won't cost you fellows a red centime. Of course, he don't, you fellows get to split the money.'

'For nothin'?'

'Absolutely gratis.'

'You see anything wrong with this, Red?' the big PO asked the stoker.

'Not so far, Milton my man. One time, down there in Subic Bay, I seen a guy pour two pints of good mash bourbon into a pint bottle. And I seen him pour it back out as well. Now that *was* impossible, but I seen it wiv these here eyeballs.'

'I seen sim'lar,' the mulatto said.

'Best go for it, bro,' the big PO nudged Ollie gently. 'Me'n the bros'll be happy to see some wonderment, or split your dough atween us.'

Ollie shot his cuffs and stood away from the bar.

'Firstly, we employ the good services of the barman. At no time will my hands touch the Great Poobah. You get the barman to stand old Poobah on the backbar with a nice space around him. I concentrate, see, and when I give the signal, the barman pours a glass of straight tapwater into the Great Poobah's smiling mouth.'

'Then what?'

'Then, Milton, it is Milton? Then, Milton, you will see and hear the true wonders of the Orient.'

'It goes wrong, what then?'

'You handsome men of the world pick up the money and have yourself a time. Me, I curse the fates and fade away, leaving the Great Poobah in your custody.'

'Gotta be a whole somethin' wrong with this,' said the stoker.

'Like say *what*, man?'

'Only one way to find out, boys.'

'Hell, I wanna see how he does this,' the mulatto called the barman and told him what he needed him to do.

'No time for dumb-dumb business,' the barman sniffed. 'Many thirst, many drink. No time, no time.'

Ollie skimmed a $100 bill at the barman.

'You *made* of that stuff, bro?' asked Milton the PO.

'What thirsts, barmy?' Ollie asked.

The barman's grin showed a gold incisor.

'Got maybe one minute, hey?'

Ollie took three measured paces from the bar and put his hands over his eyes. Squinted to see Froggy filling his empty tankard with lighter fluid. Matt was doing the same thing with his pint sleeper, and when they stood their glasses back on the bar, they adjusted their lighters to maximum flame.

'Oh mighty Poobah,' Ollie intoned. 'Show the man Milton his future path with your inner-eye of all-seeing knowledge. Lift the veil, and when the pure water lubricates your divine throat . . . speak.'

'Now?' said Milton the PO.

'Do 'er, man,' said the mulatto.

'Yo,' said Milton.

The barman trickled water into the brass mouth. Stood there for a moment, and flinched when the brass buddha gurgled. He jumped away when the buddha hopped from the backbar into the well with a muffled boom. Grey chemical vapour rose in a pungent cloud, and a sharp explosion drove the buddha's head through the ceiling. Brass shrapnel smashed bottles, and the well of the bar went

438

up in a white sear of sodium flare. The barman jumped the bar when parabolas of choking fumes shot at him, and Ollie sank to his knees in mock terror.

'I have angered the gods,' he wailed, and rolled into a foetal ball.

'Mother*fucker*,' breathed Milton the PO. He scooped the money from the bar and made for the street with the mulatto and the stoker crowding his broad back.

Froggy shrieked unmanly falsetto when a long spit of flame climbed from his tankard. He knocked it away from him, and a rolling wave of burning petrol ate its way along the bartop. Momma-san came out of the crowd to take Froggy by the collar, and he fell into her arms to scream like a woman. She clamped his mouth and raised a fist to knock him cold. The building shook, and the toilet door burst open to decant choking sailors amongst the dancers. Oily grey cloud burst out behind them, and a ruptured pipe sprayed water over the combo until the self-closer swung the door shut. Momma-san dropped Froggy and threw the barman back over the bar, screaming orders he wasn't listening to. The toilet door was sucked open and banged closed in a series of fast explosions, and the dancers scattered.

Matt's burning drink hit the jukebox, and it disappeared in a storm of shorting circuits and a spreading rosette of liquid glare. Some stuffed parrots hanging over the dance floor caught alight and dropped to the floor to spread blazing flock across the front of the small stage. The combo dropped their instruments and jumped for the exit. Momma-san was ahead of them. She threw her bulk at the bottle-neck in the doorway, and bored a dozen sailors into the street ahead of her.

Froggy dusted his suit off and ignored the barman rolling back over the bar with his hair alight. Two men had emerged from a door behind a bead curtain. They took one look at the flames and panic, and went back the way they had come. Froggy went after them, playing the hysteric like a champion.

Ollie was bowled over twice before he used a wall to pull himself to his feet. Froggy had ducked off somewhere, and Matt was in a corner under a couple of hostesses who wouldn't let go of him. If he was trying to extricate himself, he was taking his own good time about it, and Ollie bawled at him without being heard. The mindless bastard was brushing invisible sparks from a wriggling rump and a jiggling bosom. Ollie kicked Matt in the thigh as he went past, jerking him out of his sexual reverie. The smoke was thickening, and the records in the jukebox threw out toxic fumes as they melted into black glop.

Ollie freed the lead sashweight from his waistband as he worked his way through overturned chairs to the booths. A big Chinese had Cyril in a headlock as he tried to drag him away, and Cyril kept a second guardian off with a flurry of desperate kicks. The second man was pulling a gun to gutshoot Cyril, and Ollie threw the sashweight with the whole of his sixteen stone behind it. The five-pound pig of lead went home with the solid thud of a punched pillow, and the second guardian backflipped with a smashed face. His head bounced off a bench, and he spread his limbs like a decked prizefighter. The gun shot a hole in the skirting and spun on the spot.

Ollie drove a fist into a kidney and kicked the back of a knee. Cyril fell with the first guardian under him, winding the man enough to be released. Cyril batted the jaw behind him with the back of his skull. Rolled upright, and drop-kicked the man's throat. That finished it, and Cyril fell on his hands and knees to wheeze at the floor before giving Ollie a dreary grin through tears of exhaustion.

'Where'd you come from?' he managed through sobs for breath.

'From a Christmas cracker with a motto and party hat,' Ollie got to the revolver before it stopped spinning. Checked the load and snapped it closed. 'Where is he, Cyril? Where's Chas?'

'Upstairs. Through . . . there . . .'

Cyril pointed a groggy arm as the remains of a bead curtain fell away from a burning door. Smoke rose in sullen banks to reduce the bright fire to dull smudges of orange, rolling around the booths in choking veils of poisonous stench.

'Then he's well fucked. And us, we stays here,' Matt coughed, voicing what they all realised.

Ollie didn't even have the breath to swear.

The mindfist listened as Charlie worked.

His feet had sensed the buck of sodium-torn plumbing, but the explosions could have been echoes from the bark of the steel dragon. It had killed, and could again, the bodies proved it. The thuds from below the satin floor could be the enemy deluding him. The others were coming up the stairs, violating the purity of the Sky Road with street shoes because of their haste. Charlie could hear them breathe as they came. He had to be ready for them.

The old woman lay on the white couch where Charlie had flopped her, and Charlie arranged what had been Liang Quing over her in an obscene embrace. Then he scrubbed at his tingling forearms, wondering if he'd been bitten. The silk ropes had snaked up his arms when he severed them with the long knife from Liang Quing's scabbard. The pimp had no more use for it now, but it looked well growing from his neck.

Charlie lifted the pearl gently. She weighed nothing as she lay against his shoulder, yet there was pain where her legs dangled against his ribs. Another delusion, and Charlie ignored the pulsing agony to please the mindfist. It was his only friend now the birds had gone. Somebody used Charlie's tear ducts to weep, and he tried not to mind as he made for the blue and white passage.

441

Charlie stood beside the portal with his back to the wall. He could smell them coming through smoke that mingled with the mist behind his wet eyes. The mindfist cut off the wracking sobs with an impatient command, and Charlie held his breath to hear what the mindfist heard. There were screams and cries from outside, hooting traffic, and the dull roar of a gathering crowd. The smoke drifting through the portal bit his nostrils and stung his eyes, and he blinked it away. *They* were sending the smoke to flush him, and he sneered at the delusion. A leather sole caught at the nap of the padded felt, and Charlie left the steel dragon to point itself towards the sound. It would know when to bark.

The pearl snuggled sleepily, and her breath was warm on his neck. Charlie nuzzled coarse black hair and waited and waited.

Soon, said the mindfist. *Patience, Char-lee.*

Charlie fought stomach cramps and the burning splinters in his chest for the sake of the sleeping pearl.

Wreathed in veils of brown smoke, Froggy found himself in a browner passage. Two Chinese were running for the stairs at the far end, and made the turn as a third man bored from a back room carrying a heavy kitchen cleaver. The men on the stairs shouted Cantonese at the man with the cleaver, and he yelled pigeon at Froggy. Froggy held his crotch like a frightened child and babbled back. The men on the stairs hesitated as Froggy slid down the wall, flinching away from the cleaver threatening him. When Froggy whined and drummed his heels on the floor, they came towards him with ugly expressions.

'It's burning,' Froggy screamed. 'Burning, burning, burning . . .'

Hauled up by the three angry men, Froggy scrabbled at their faces with frightened hands. Got a thumb into an eye and heeled blood from a nose. Dropped on his back, he kicked kneecaps like a demented fool until a hard kick took him in the pit of the stomach. Froggy's keening rose in pitch as his head spun with nausea. Still screaming, 'Burning, burning,' he was lifted bodily, hauled down the passage, and thrown through a door somebody unbolted.

Froggy smelled night air as his chin lost dermis on gravel and stone. He was face down in the side alley, and he eeled backwards to jam a leg in the closing door. The heavy jamb slammed against his thigh, impacting muscle, and Froggy opened his mouth as wide as it would go. Nothing emerged but a trail of spittle, and his bladder betrayed him. The door was opening a fraction to release his leg, and a shadow kicking up gravel as it sprinted, threw itself bodily at the door. Shuddering on its hinges, the door opened to spill Pimlico inside, and he stamped on Froggy's ankle in passing. Froggy held on long enough to jacknife back into the passage, and passed out watching Pimlico use his fists like bludgeons. He did not hear the snap of a high-powered rifle, or see the man with the cleaver lose an eye and the back of his skull.

Pimlico hit the door and the door mashed somebody behind it. He popped a knuckle on a cheekbone and smothered a knife thrust between arm and rib. Set himself square, and head-butted the knifeman between the eyes. The knife sliced as it withdrew, scoring Pimlico's lateral muscles, but the Chinese took the man who'd been behind the door down with him. They sprawled on the staircase in a jammed tangle, and Pimlico feinted to draw the one with the cleaver in at him.

Vinnie's rifle cracked from outside. The guardian's head changed shape as an eye burst, and the cleaver bit the floor between Froggy's thighs. The guardian took his jerking body down the passage and collapsed in a heap.

Pimlico grinned as the third man got himself out from under the unconscious one on the stairs, and changed his comical expression with a hard hook to the jaw. Fear must have absorbed the pain. The man just shook his head and leapt the bannister, landed on the balls of his feet, and was through the alley door like a greyhound out of trap three. There was a light crunch of gravel, and he was gone.

Pimlico listened for Vinnie's rifle and heard nothing but vague crowd-noise. He caught his breath in the stairwell, and felt pain where the knife had scored his ribs. When he raised his arm to look at his wound, the knife fell at his feet. Pimlico kicked it away, and decided Froggy could stay where he was for the time being. There was no blood, and he looked peaceful enough. A good man with a shooter, Froggy was useless with his fists, and it must have taken all his courage and some for him to bang through that bar door with nothing but his thumb in his fist.

Pimlico patted Froggy's face and climbed the stairs to the upper floors. The walls were already hot to the touch, and smoke was streaming over the dead man in the lower passage like sullen strands of marsh gas. There was no time for the old softly-softly.

Pimlico passed the niche of sepia portraits, and gave the blue and white passage a silent whistle as he snagged a toe in uneven felt carpet. Candle shimmer lit the fretted portal, and he could hear hubbub in the street below; the distant chiming impatience of a fire engine stalled in traffic. He wanted to move faster, but caution prevailed, and he kept to the wall as he peered in at the guardians sprawled in their own blood trails. They were the wrong size and shape to be Charlie, so where was he?

Only one way to find out, he told himself.

Pimlico steeled himself to cross the portal and froze. Felt his neck hair bristle as he picked up the low keen of weeping, the steady click of metal on metal. The metallic sound meant nothing, but that inhuman keen took him back to nights in the high-security wing of Durham Prison. To lying awake whilst hard men tore at the silence with the deep fear that came with sleep. Men who could take no more steel doors, locked cages and solitary confinement, barred

444

walkways slung with suicide netting. Crying out through heavy soporific medication that drugged the waking mind and released the childlike funk of the vulnerable inner core. The sound of the naked soul wanting mother and comfort and home.

'Charlie?' Pimlico whispered.

The sound choked to silence. Resumed after a long heartbeat as a soft mewing. Pimlico made himself confront what was there in the shifting shadows.

Charlie held a Derringer and a naked child. His silver kimono was spattered with vomit and blood, and his lost face was bled veal. His jaws ground together to bite off the sounds in his throat, and his brimming eyes were as empty as an evacuated cell. The Derringer pointing at Pimlico clicked off shots like a mechanical pulse, and Charlie's limbs shook with drugged ague.

Pimlico offered his hand as though to a child lost in darkness.

'Pim's here, Chas,' he said softly. 'We're going home.'

He took the Derringer and held the cold hand, feeling the forefinger jerking off shots against his palm. Led the way down lamplit stairs that were hot underfoot, talking in quiet undertones to the automaton he led to safety. Wanting to kill, and hoping somebody would give him the excuse.

Rusty bolts were drawn and the side door shuddered open. The dark alley grew an oblong of yellow light as Froggy was thrown out, and Pimlico bored in. Surprised by his own surprise, Vinnie trapped the doorway in his crosshairs. There was a confused milling in the scope, and the houndstooth check of Pimlico's back shielded his opponents from effective backing fire.

Vinnie took shallow sips of air to still his aim and waited.

Froggy rolled all the way back into the passage and braced a leg to keep the door open. His head smacked back into the architrave when Pimlico trod on him, and Froggy showed his backteeth in a silent gape of protest. Pimlico smothered a knife darting to gut him, drove his forehead into a face, and followed through with solid punches. Vinnie caught the gleam of light-slick on a cleaver as Pimlico feinted aside, and the face of a Chinese taking breath to make his swing effective filled the scope. Vinnie expelled air and squeezed off a snapshot. His shoulder took recoil, an eyeball exploded in the scope, and the guardian staggered away to collapse out of sight. Froggy had gone limp, and Pimlico mixed it with two men he had driven up a flight of stairs. Froggy's rubber leg was scraped aside, and the heavy door started to close.

Vinnie stole a glance at the main street. The snap of his rifle had gone unheard by the brawling crowds and honking traffic. Men and hostesses streamed from the Tropicana Club, and the neon parrots went out as fire ate the circuits. There was just noise and confusion under thin tungsten street lights, and a street vendor was knocked over his handlebars with his tray of baked fish. Men fell with him, and his bicycle disappeared under rolling bodies. Vinnie thought he saw Ollie and Cyril dusting themselves off as they cleared their lungs of smoke inhalation, but the sudden sound of running feet jerked him back into the alley. A man had broken from the doorway, and Vinnie glimpsed a sprinting figure in the last spill of light from the closing door. The alley went dark, and Vinnie was alone with night shadows, the rifle and indecision.

Vinnie shook himself, thinking of Charlie to clear his mind. Crouched clumsily to scoop up the ejected brass casing, and dropped it into his pocket. The fire was licking out of the front of the Tropicana Club, and banks of sepia smoke drifted over the crowd. The fish-seller called on his gods to witness the misfortune of a buckled front wheel and ruined wares, and people crowded the balconies across the street where nothing but lines of washing had hung only moments before.

Vinnie held the rifle at high port and took comfort from the wall at his back. His missing foot needed a serious scratch, and there was too much sticky sweat in his eye sockets. Killing for the first time would become meaningless if Charlie was lost. If Charlie got out safely, the nightmares would never come.

A police whistle shrilled, and part of the crowd opened to let three small and neat Chinese police officers through. They had their truncheons drawn, and one with a stripe and a loud-hailer gave orders in Cantonese and heavily accented English. The mob swilled and shifted without thinning, and the insistent ringing of a fire bell came from some way off. A constable shrugged off the complaints of the fish-peddler, and used his truncheon on the sides of motor vehicles to get them moving. A truck and a battered Ford Popular passed the mouth of the alley, and Vinnie found himself staring at a black limousine with smoked windows. A rear window was wound down a crack, and the narrowed eyes watching the club burn seemed familiar. *Were* familiar.

Vinnie flicked sweat from his forehead. Thumbed at a sweating socket and nestled the rifle into his shoulder. The eyes sprang at him through the crosshairs, and Vinnie knew he had a clear shot at Aman Lee Fook. It was him. No doubt about it, no doubt at all.

Vinnie licked a mouth that was suddenly salt.

Fook spoke to a constable and was answered with quiet respect. The neat little Chinese copper didn't use his truncheon to hurry the limousine on its way. Instead, he bowed to listen and answer with a show of civility, his truncheon behind his back.

Vinnie's mind boiled and froze in fast overlaps of nausea and exhilaration. Firing was just something the finger did, as reflex as a sneeze. The stock bit his shoulder, and he smelled the bloom of smokeless power. If there was a report he didn't hear it. The smoked window grew a ragged star,

447

and glass chips scaled away. The eyes stared back, yet there was no hole in the window, only the star-shaped scar.

Vinnie fired again. Higher and to the right. Saw the eyes jump open as the window wound closed. The limousine was moving off in tyre-squeal, and the constable had dropped into a crouch. Was lying flat and calling a warning to his fellow officers. The limousine bounced the fish-peddler away with his bicycle. The crowd surged, and the limousine was gone. The fish-seller scrambled to his feet to kick his bicycle, and a ball of flame burst through the shuttered balcony above his head. The blast of heat had him scurrying away with the breaking crowd, and Vinnie felt the wash of heat as the shimmer drove the people down the street in rising panic.

Vinnie shivered with emotional reaction. Burned his fingers picking up the shell casings. Blew on his hand as instant mental replay showed his second bullet drive Fook the width of the back seat. Knew he must have hit Fook high in the chest below the left shoulder, maybe even hit the big pulmonary artery itself. The bastard could be bleeding to death right then for all Vinnie knew, and he wondered how he ought to feel about that. There was nothing but an odd flatness, the need to slake his thirst with something cold and clean and refreshing. Something to cut the acrid taste of his dry mouth.

The alley was strobed by guttering orange light, and the abandoned bicycle spun a buckled front wheel between its front forks. The air was filled with burning splinters, and breathing was a ragged thing that made his chest ache. Vinnie broke the rifle down and fed the sections into the gaudy plastic carrier bag. His good leg jerked in spasm, and he felt sympathetic nerve-pain in his artificial limb. If he pinched the unfeeling thigh he thought he would feel pain there. The notion made him try a smile that died stillborn.

A Chinese woman and a shop boy threw buckets of water over the frontage of the clothing emporium. The wood and brick steamed, and Vinnie retreated from the growing heat. The side door had opened to let grey ghosts into the alley, and Vinnie looked into the vacant face that was Charlie's. The child he held like a lifeline to sanity. Pimlico gave Vinnie Charlie's hand to hold, and Vinnie had trouble breathing.

'Here's Vinnie, Chas,' Pimlico said. 'It's all right now, just fine . . .'

The cold forefinger stabbed Vinnie's palm, and Charlie's dead eyes saw nothing outside himself. Pimlico had Froggy over his shoulder, and he pushed Vinnie to start him walking. Vinnie led Charlie down the alley away from the fire, and wondered who comforted whom. The heat on his back wouldn't take the chill away, and he shivered uncontrollably as the shadows swallowed them.

The mindfist and the friendly shadows with known faces guided Charlie through mean alleys, and the tender weight in the crook of his arm kept him going. His mind twisted and turned with the narrows he was led through, and the seeing part of him linked him to the pain of another in the back of a speeding saloon. There had been the massive shock of being punched flat by a hot fist, and now there was lying on leather upholstery as somebody tried to staunch the blood from a huge exit wound. The mindfist took pleasure from the other's pain, and the walking Charlie gripped the hand that had sent the lead fist tearing through tissue to punch shards of splintered shoulder blade out of the other's back. If the other man sensed Charlie's presence he gave no sign.

There was stumbling across a building lot and being helped into the back of Cho Sun's nephews' laundry truck. Being sat on a wicker basket as the other one was jogged by fast turns through the docks. The known faces in the laundry truck compared their experiences with sombre deliberation. Their voices blurred the contact in Charlie's mind, and he crushed the friendly hand until it used

Vinnie's voice to order silence. The chatter grumbled and died, and Charlie lay in the other's congealing blood as the saloon was swung aboard the ferry to Victoria. There was a wash of melancholy at the thought of dying over water that would sever for ever the contact with his ancestors. Hemp ropes were cast off to disturb the midship swirl as bronze screws churned the ferry away from the quay. Engine vibration shook the saloon on its suspension to jar the other's hold on consciousness. Voices buzzed anxiety and clinical calm. A hypodermic plunged through dermis to take his torn body away, leaving his mind to float in peace. Charlie and the other one were almost indivisible now, and they knew the other one *would* last until landfall. The will was there. The body might die when the water was left behind, but the mindlink to the other's ancestors joined him to the dawn of everything. Birth and death were mere punctuations in the endless continuum of tribal being. Knowing that gave comfort and strength.

Somebody swabbed Charlie's face and tried to take the pearl.

Charlie snarled and became unmoving stone as the other mind skimmed across the Lammas Strait to the lights of Victoria. The snarl lasted until the hotel was reached, and died in the steel womb of an elevator rising seven floors. An impassive Charlie padded down empty corridors ushered by shadow friends he could no longer relate to.

There was a shadowed suite he had been in before, and an elegant woman with a mannish voice. She sent the others away without fuss, and allowed Charlie to select a bed good enough for the pearl to rest upon. He lay beside the child to guard her sleep, and caught the bump of a saloon hitting a jetty and speeding through night hills of granite. There was the sweep of headlights on high and castellated stone walls, and people running to tend the body the mind had decided to discard. It was a poor thing that others could cherish if they chose to. It no longer mattered in the great scheme of things. There was a red blanket and a stretcher. Being lifted and carried into conditioned air where gowned figures waited to work miracles. A mask clamping over the labouring mouth, and a brief sear of wonder before the mindlink died in a reducing ball of spin.

Charlie's body softened and slept, and the hooked forefinger curled inside a loose fist.

Margot sat in a chair to keep vigil without complaint. It was enough that he had come back to her.

CHAPTER FIFTEEN

Charlie came back to the timeless dusk of drawn curtains and the nimble click of knitting needles. They had tied him down to stop him hurting himself, and he couldn't scratch his itching nose. There was a vague memory of being haunted by night things from the pit, and his mouth was raw from biting itself. Phlegm bugs had bred in his pores and clogged his nostrils with jellied spawn. Brueghelesque nightmares had lit charnal fires in the walls where the dead copulated with shapeless saurians and ate rotting young hatched from clutches of black eggs. Drowning in swamp-stench, he had been eaten alive countless times and been reborn in middens of foul defecation that screamed . . .

Hetty Wells knitted in a chair near the bedroom door. A plump shadow with busy fingers, she purled and plained without the need for a light.

Charlie coughed. Croaked. 'You'll ruin your eyes, Het.'

Hetty counted off a row and said, 'You're back with us, then?' She could have been scolding a straying tom cat.

'Where's . . . toffee nose?'

'Sleeping. You've given us a time, you know. Margot needed to rest, bless her. She's a good girl, that one.'

Charlie searched the wallpaper for ugliness and found nothing but flowers. The floor was just hotel carpet, and no slithering things twined around the ceiling light, waiting to drop on his face.

'I smell like last week's washing.'

'Smelled worse. Nursed my old father through his last

illness. Had to burn all the bedroom furniture and scrub through with lye before we got the smell of him out of the house. Can't grow roses without manure.'

'Got any smokes, Het?'

'Don't use 'em. And you'd blow your bum off lighting one. Lie easy, Charlie.'

'Some nurse you are.'

'More of a minder, ain't I? You sound like you're making sense, but you've done that before. Don't last though. You start playing up, I've to give you a shot in the thigh. You want that?'

'Been a trial, have I? How long, Het?'

'This is the third day.'

Charlie reared against his bonds. Mumbled about getting up and slipped off into foggy twilight. When he came back, it was true night, and Hetty was Trooper reading a boxing magazine in lamplight.

'Where's . . . the pearl?'

'In the oyster. Evening, Chas,' Tropper smiled. 'We got the cover of *Boxing News*, see?'

'I've already had the runaround from your missus. Don't you start.'

'Hettie said you sounded like yourself again. How you feeling?'

'Like sweating you up over three rounds. Fancy it?'

'Why not? If the doc says you can give it a go.'

'What doctor?'

'The tame one we got out at the training camp. Flew in special and comes in regular. Knows his stuff too. Says you're more horse than man. Reckons you got the constitution of a brewer's dray.'

'Then he's a bloody quack.'

'Stopped you doing yourself all kinds of mischief. You been right outta your swede, Chas. Lucky to be alive. Luckier to be sane. We said you wasn't sane before you was drugged stupid, so there ain't no way of knowing for sure.'

453

'Have you got any smokes?'

'Athelete like me? Nope.'

'Then go find somebody who has.'

'Doc says not.'

'Who is this flaming doctor?'

'Vinnie got him over. Name of Bunch. Ben Bunch. Good lad as it happens.'

Charlie let his soggy head hit the pillow. It was too heavy for his wasted neck. Then it was later, and there were other people in the room. Margot sponged him down and Ben Bunch listened to his chest. Charlie leered up at him.

'It against the Hippocratic Oath to give my nose a good scratch, Doctor Sir?'

'Do it yourself. Nothing holding you back, is there?'

Charlie raised a hand to his face and looked at it.

'Nice to have it back.'

'Scratch away then. Good therapy, self-help.'

'And go for a walk? Buy an evening paper?'

Bunch poked his glasses back to the bridge of his nose.

'There's the door. Try it.'

'Meaning you think I can't.'

'Uhuh.'

Charlie frowned at Margot.

'And don't *you* give me no arguments.'

'Not I, you wilful cretin,' she said.

Charlie swung his legs to the floor and followed through with his face. Then he was back on the bed with a spinning head that saw double. Trooper had lifted him like a badly stuffed doll and laid him out like a corpse.

'All I need are pennies for my eyes,' Charlie croaked.

Margo said she'd look in her purse.

'Only ever hit one woman in my life, you could be the second,' Charlie muttered wearily. 'How long, Ben?'

'Before you're up to woman beating? I know a good rest home in Scotland that might have you walking a slow mile after three months.'

454

'Be serious, will you?'

'That is serious, you clown. You want it straight, or with bedside embroidery?'

'I only water my whisky, Ben.'

'Now you water your water, my friend. Booze is out. You're massively dehydrated, and you came within an ace of liver collapse. Your kidneys are shot, and your heart has taken a pasting. From now on, Mr Dance, you're an invalid, if you want to live, that is.'

'Don't waste your soft words on me, you smooth bastard.'

Bunch's eyes held none of their usual laughter when he put Charlie's middle finger to the pulse in his right wrist.

'Feel that? More a bongo rhythm than a pulse. You strain over the lavatory pan too hard you could have a coronary. Laugh too loud at an Andy Capp and you could have a stroke. Take a sip of Irish, and that's you hyperventing to catch your breath. That serious enough for you?'

'If I was a horse you'd shoot me, that it?'

'Wouldn't put you out to stud. And that's out too.'

Charlie swore under his breath and made weak fists as Bunch droned on about special diets and vitamins, talking across at Margot as if Charlie was nothing more than a number on his hospital call sheet. A patient, no longer a man.

Charlie trembled a finger at Trooper.

'Roadwork. Six sharp tomorrow morning, right?'

'Thass up to the doc there, Chas.'

'He says "no",' Bunch primed a hypodermic from a vial. 'This is the last sedative I can give you, Charlie. Opiate derivatives have nasty side-effects. You'll sleep the clock round.'

The needle went home and lassitude crept through Charlie's chest, dulling the pain in his cracked ribs.

'A last smoke at least, Ben,' he yawned.

'You'd be better off sucking carbon monoxide from a car exhaust. From now on, you and the weed are divorced.'

Charlie's eyes lost focus. Bunch was pink fuzz with tinted glasses, Margot was an angular smear of dark taffeta, and Trooper was a square loom against blobs of flowered wallpaper.

'Roadwork . . . t'morraaah . . . Troop . . .'

'Sure, Charlie, yeah . . .'

'He talks a good fight,' Margot's laugh was vibrant with scorn and caring.

Charlie watched the wriggles behind his eyelids as the three blurs let themsleves out, taking the light with them. He counted off a yawny ten seconds and forced himself into a roll that flopped him on the floor like a soft marionette. He crawled across acres of tufted carpet to the door. Opening it a crack took both hands, and picking up the conversation from the main saloon made his ears pound. Margot was trying not to be tearful, and Trooper mixed her a gin and french with comforting noises. Bunch thanked Trooper for a weak Irish and said things were not really as bad as he had painted them. Charlie had to believe he was sicker than he really was or the hardheaded clown would be up and tearing telephone directories in half to prove his bloody manhood. He was a sick boy, but nothing that couldn't be cured with a week or two's bed rest, no booze or ciggies, and a balanced diet full of vitamins and fibre. There were grateful noises from Margot as Charlie let the door close.

Getting back to the bed took a dreary fortnight, and climbing between the sheets a lifetime more. Charlie glared at the invisible ceiling, a hand to his chest to feel the strong bump of his heart. There were five short days to the boxing tournament if he lost tomorrow to drugged sleep. Time was running out like eggtimer sand.

Charlie's temples ballooned, and he felt the brush of another mine in another bed across the Lammas Strait, holding on as he was holding on. Then it was gone, and a small Chinese girl walked him through a twilight garden without telling him her name. That was annoying, and

456

Charlie's need to know sent her running off through tinkling fountains, and left him lying in warm grass that smelled of Margot's fragrance. It was very pleasant.

'Overslept, didn't I? Sorry, ain't I?'

'That an apology, you sorry sod?'

'I reckon, Ollie mate,' Matt took Ollie's chair at the head of the stairs and stared the length of the hotel corridor to the lift. With Froggy on the landing below, they had the seventh floor of the Peninsula Hotel covered as best they could. 'Ciggie, Ollie?'

'Nah. Smoked myself stupid watching nothing. A last good drink, and it's beddy-byes for this kiddy.'

'Have one for me. What's the story on Chas?'

'Bunch reckons he's over the worst, but he won't be kicking elbows for a bit. Up to us now, ain't it?'

'Waiting for a bunch of Happi Coats to do us a proper mischief is a funny old way to spend Christmas Eve, thass all I know, Ollie. I just wish they would come and get it over with. Waitin's a right bastard,' Matt patted the new Colt Savage in the shoulder holster he'd softened with saddle soap. He and Froggy were happier wearing shooters, and were chuffed to buttercups that Vinnie had shelled out an arm and a leg to some dealer in Tsim Sha Tsui for two handguns. They both thought it strange Ollie and Pim preferred to go unarmed, and hadn't turned a hair when Cyril adopted the old Webley Ollie had brought out of the Troubadour Club.

'Nod off, you'll wake up a bit dead, right?'

'No danger of that, Ollie old cock. That Charlie's carried us long enough, and you oughtta let me show you how to use one of these things.'

'Not bleeding likely. I like my tootsies where they are. 'Night, Matt.'

'Be lucky. And while you're supping ale, think of me counting rampant stags inna bleeding wallpaper.'

Ollie left Matt leaking smoke and took the stairs to the Grill Room. He refused another cigarette from a bored Froggy on his landing, and met Vinnie at the bar.

'Beer or a short?'

'Beer *and* a chaser. This hanging about is cornholing the lads, Vin. Better when they was *doing* something.'

'Just how lucky d'you think we'd be a second time?'

'Ten-nil down at half-time. Wouldn't make it past the lobby.'

'So, shut your face and drink your drink.'

Ollie drained his pint and released wind behind a hand.

'Didn't touch the sides. Same again here, barmy. You really think they'll come at us head-on, Vin?'

'No, as it happens, I don't. Charlie got it well right. They'll spank us at the stadium somehow.'

'Now ain't *that* something to look forward to.'

'Without Charlie just being there, my bottle's squeaking like boxing boots in a resin box. I could play tunes just flexing my bum muscles.'

'Fear and brains go hand in hand, don't they? Only doorknobs and kerbstones feel nothing. Me, I got a hammer banging in my gut. Nagging like a mother-in-law 'cause I forgot to do something stupid and important: like feed the papers and cancel the cat.'

Vinnie's laugh was a short melody.

'My goosebumps are bigger than Miss World's three-pennies,' he said into his drink. 'If I was Charlie, I'd handle this like a champion, but Charlie I ain't.'

'Charlie ain't even Charlie right now.'

'But you fellahs are still *you*, right? You ain't crumbling like an old wedding cake. Look at Pim. He'd just spit and set himself if the Golden Hoardes was riding down on him. Just zips his mind up in an ice-cube and does the business. Matt's so thick he'd still be scratching his dandruff if you fed him his head. But he'd do the business without a shrug. Froggy gets his underwear wet, but he'd rather die than let Chas know he didn't have the spit to whistle. No, he'd die looking for a pat on the bonce from Chas, and go all the way down smiling. Christ, even Cyril has balls like a carthorse when he's on the bloody spot. Me, I crumble like halva on grannie's fork.'

'And me?' Ollie asked.

'You're better than the others. You show your dimples and drive like a bastard angel — grin when it's over like it's all been a soppy game of soldiers. Your grey cells never stop working no matter what, right? Don't dissolve like sugar in tea like mine do.'

'What are you looking for, Vin? A medal? A slapped wrist? They may have shot your real balls off, old son, but you grew another set in your head. You'll do in my book. This is the old midnight blues talking through whisky, s'all.'

'Just want to be fair. To let you know . . . how it is with me. Y'know?'

Ollie sank his chaser and drank more beer. Caught sight of a thin Oriental in the mirrored backbar and set his pint down very slowly. Eased a buttock off his stool and said: 'Clock this face coming up astern. He's definitely one of the runners and riders. Last time I seen him, our Pim was whacking nine bells of hell outta his waistcoat.'

'Got him. He a talker or a goer?'

'Stuffed if I know. Gonna find out, ain't we? He's set his nose in our direction,' Ollie's spine kicked out sudden sweat as he turned to face the approaching man.

'Two more inna doorway,' Vinnie said.

'Cheer me up do,' Ollie grumbled, edging his bulk sideways to shield Vinnie.

Vinnie gave himself space with a cluck of anger.

'You wanna shake hands, or just kiss my teddah,' he joked.

'Think your head grew *two* sets of testicles,' Ollie said.

'Talking's well different to doing, ain't it?'

'Yeah . . .'

The thin Oriental halted three feet away. Bobbed his head and looked at Ollie and Vinnie with a face as blank as a bar of yellow soap. Vinnie saw the barman slide away down the bar and duck through a hatch. The other customers melted away, and the two Happi Coats just stood in the doorway like mean bookends. The bar of the Grill Room seemed to have lost its air and heat, and the Christmas tree lights blinked out unreadable semaphore.

'You've found us, we're listening,' Ollie was ready to break teeth with his pint mug. Smother a rush with his bulk to give Vinnie some sort of a chance.

The thin Oriental nodded at Ollie and used stilted English.

'You are fat-fat who drive fast-fast. He is the hopping one. Ears of taipan Dance. This is so, hai?'

'And you'd want what?' Vinnie hated his new appellation.

'I of family Chang. Have words. Instructions. I tell. You do.'

'Who from? Flaming Fook?'

Chang looked puzzled. Held up a hand to show a huge ruby in a gold setting.

'I wear dragon ring. I serve Old Dragon. You see?'

Ollie felt and sounded drowned.

'Not many we don't. Vin, you thinking what I'm thinking?'

'Like we ran the wrong tong all over Kowloon? Yeah. We see the ring, Mr Chang.'

'Not mister. Just servant. Just Chang.'

'Right then, Chang. Spit it out or swallow it,' Ollie grunted.

'Spit mean talk?'

Ollie gave that a silent nod. He felt like a dragooned extra in a grand guignol pantomime hammered out in Braille for the deaf. A dangerous nonsense writ large in blood.

Chang said, 'Tomorrow. Jesus baby's birthday bay, hai? No moon tomorrow night. This good omen. Very good. You go to Hong Kong. To typhoon shelter when dark come. Take bones of Ho Fatt with. Boat come from sea. Take honoured bones to final purification in fire. You bring chair of wheels. We see you have for tired leg of hopping one. This for old money man to ride. We don't hurt old money man. He hurt self. He hurt self here in body. In heart, hai?'

Ollie hefted his pint and took a long draught.

'You can't be saying old J.C's had a coronary? A heart attack.'

'Hai, here in top of body. Him work too hard the body. You savvy?'

Vinnie scrubbed at a mouth that didn't sweat. Pulled his lower lip away from his teeth with a light pop.

'Working hard? Old J.C.? Bloody how? He cuts the crossword out of *The Times* so he don't have to lift the whole bloody newspaper. The man never exercises. What the hell have you done to him?'

'Only kindness.'

'Kindness, you yellow get? Kindness?'

'Easy, Vin. Them Happi Coats in back of Chang don't like the shouting stakes one bit.'

'Easy nothing. I smell a lie here.'

Chang raised a hand of long and bony fingers.

'Wearing dragon ring, I. Cannot lie wearing ring. I only tell true things about old money man's heart. Too much good-good. Too much the big jig-jig, hai?'

'He saying what I *think* he's saying, Vin?'

'Can't be.'

'I ain't got the words to ask.'

Vinnie felt his scrotum tighten and itch like his missing foot.

'You saying the old man's been well at it? Er, sexually?'

Chang bit on the elusive word, and a gold tooth winked in his thin mouth.

'Sexing. Hai. Jig-jig. Old Dragon much happy about making good water through manhood thing. Old money

461

man teach this. Old Dragon make clear water flow any time he wish now. Him reward old money man with young palace girls. Old money man like much-much too much. Him like man who eat all time. Hurt heart from too much chopsticks in sleeping rooms with young girls. Think him much-much young and hurt heart. Much sorry for old money man.'

'The scrofulous old bastard,' Ollie bellowed.

'Please?' said Chang.

'The greedy old tosspot.'

'Not understand laughing at hopping one,' said Chang.

'What's so sodding funny, Vin?'

'It's that or cry, Ollie.'

'Bloody cry, you dipstick? I'll feed him his raddled old dick in two slices of Mother's Pride. We bring the whole Dance firm half round the sodding globe to save his sorry old hide, and what's bloody mastermind doing? Only bonking the arse off baby biddies just old enough to be his great-great grand daughters, that's all. Putting it to 'em hot and hard and sideways, up and down and around and sodding upside down. Am I hearing this, or what?'

Chang's eyes narrowed to hide their creamy whites.

'You do what Dragon command, hai?'

'Yeah, yeah, yeah. We'll bring a wheelchair to carry away what's left of the old tart.' Ollie banged the bar with his empty glass. 'Where's that bleeding barman? This calls for a serious drink. What's your poison, Chang?'

'You offer poison? I have offend?'

'Not you – him. That bloody J-sodding-C. Explain to the man, hopping one, I'm well out of the game.'

Vinnie chose his words with care as Ollie manned the pumps to pull pints with a lot of froth. Ollie was stabbing the optic to serve Chang a decent double when two shots from a revolver echoed in the Stairwell.

Margot came out of sleep running.

Her hand found light switches on the way to Charlie's

room, and she almost fell over Matt as he came up out of a crouch to pull her down behind him. Froggy called from the passage, and Margot bit Matt's hand to make him let go of her. She got to Charlie's bedroom and threw herself inside with Matt cursing and Froggy shouting negatives at a sleepy Cyril and a growling Pimlico. Charlie just lay on his back with closed eyes, and Margot could see the big vein in his neck bump with life. He smiled in his sleep when she laid a hand to his heart and muttered something only he understood. Ollie and Vinnie were at the door of the suite asking questions, and Matt swore on in vicious undertones as he let them inside.

'Who's bloody trigger happy?' Matt was affronted. 'Come in to get a gargle of water, didn't I? Eh, eh? Was giving meself a nice little vodka when this shadow made for the window. Hadn't put the lights on, had I? Didn't want to disturb no one, right? Then up gets this bloke and does a hotsman for the balcony like I wasn't bloody there. Got him framed in the window and let him have a couple inna back. But he ain't there no more. Like he melted inna carpet or something. Then there's Margot banging about the place and getting inna way, snappin' on lights and blinding me. Time I gets to the window there's nothing but night out there. Nothing. I couldn't miss at that distance, but I bloody did.'

'Or he came outta the Stolichnaya bottle,' Pimlico said. 'Anybody checked on Chas?'

'Margot's with him. She'd be doing her pieces if he was got at,' Ollie said.

'Nothing came outta that vodka but vodka,' Matt said hotly. Shaken and angry. 'When did I ever see what ain't there, Frog? Ain't got the imagination, right?'

'No arguing with that,' Froggy told Pim. 'We gonna bite lumps out of each other, or sort out what happened? Me and Matt's just soldiers, up to Vin and Ollie to do some thinking with Chas well out of the game.'

'Just so long as Matt's sure,' Vinnie said.

'As certain-sure as my balls turned to marbles when that geezer come out of nowhere, Vin. The man was there. Little like a thin kid, but he *moved* adult, y'know?'

'That convinces the fluff outta my navel. You, Ollie?'

'Likewise,' Ollie swished curtains aside and touched a new furrow in the stone balustrade. The scrape was about waist-height, and Matt usually hit what he pointed at. There were no blood spots, but a strand of black cotton had snagged on one of the cornice stones. Ollie picked it out and let it sail away on the breeze, knowing Matt hadn't shot at shadows. He closed the windows and drew the curtains. 'Somebody get Margot organised. We're out of here, *now*.'

'Where to?' Pim poured large shorts for the company.

'Nowhere else, is there? The training camp. Keep all our faces in one place. Stay forted up till we go to the stadium. Reckon that's what Chas'd do, *if* he was doing. Right, Vin?'

'Gets my vote. I'll see to Margot,' Vinnie went to Charlie's bedroom and leaned in the doorway. 'You heard, love?'

Margot stroked Charlie's hair off his forehead. Nodded. 'Somebody was here. Smell it, Vincent?'

Vinnie located a musk that wasn't Charlie's odour or Margot's perfume. A vague something that was different and masculine. Somebody had been closeted with Charlie and hadn't laid a glove. That thought jarred, made no sense. If there was an answer, it was inside Charlie's head, and would stay locked up there until he was willing or able to enlighten.

'Yes, you smell him,' Margot said. 'From here on in, I don't leave Charlie's side.'

Vinnie tried smiling and couldn't. Margot looked at him without seeing him. Forming tangibles from shadows to fight in her mind.

'So long as he's asleep, maybe,' Vinnie said. 'Awake, he ain't so easy to . . .' There was no way he could finish the sentence. He was talking to dead air and a closed mind.

'I'll know that smell again,' Margot said. 'Oh yes, I'll know it, and this time I won't hesitate.' Her right index finger curled around an invisible trigger and she sighted down her arm at the wall behind Vinnie's head. 'We'll be along, my dear. You go ahead . . .'

Vinnie said something unmemorable and went off to soothe the night manager. Glad to have something to occupy his mind, he converted gunshots into knocking plumbing to forget the expression on Margot's face. When he had closed the door on the night manager, Ollie had a last question to drop before the limousines arrived.

'Do we do the business for J.C. tomorrow night, or what?'

'He's one of ours, ain't he?'

'Saying it don't make it sensible, Vin.'

'Nor it don't, but you wanna tell Charlie different?' Ollie's smile had shallow dimples.

'You had to use the one argument there ain't no answer to.'

'Wouldn't Charlie?' Vinnie asked, making for the lift.

Joe Yellow smelled the gunfire he could not hear.

He had made himself small behind the Christmas tree, and when the dragons and the long-noses left the bar, he took the service lift to the top floor of the hotel. He passed the staff bedrooms unseen, and slipped through the emergency door to climb to the unused attics under the mansard roof. At the top of an unlit flight of stairs he ducked through an inspection hatch beside the elevator housing and locked it behind him. His uncle Cho Sun sat on a thin mattress under a bare bulb hooked to the rafters, binding his right hand with a scrap of white muslin.

Joe Yellow's fingers asked Cho Sun if he had been hit.

'It is nothing. The one called Matt shot a shadow. My hand was slow and got burned.'

You saw that the taipan Dance lives as I said?

'I saw this and heard more. And you, green wand? You learned what?'

465

This hotel uniform made me invisible, and I was a shadow behind the tree of Jesus lights when the Dragon sent Chang to make talk with the fat one and the one-legged person. Chang wore the red ring of light to make his words true. This makes him one of the Council of Seven now, I think. Chang made the fat one angry over the health of the old money man the Dragon holds hostage. But the one-legged one laughed strangely because the old money man has hurt his heart bedding young pearls. They have agreed to meet the Dragon's barge at the typhoon shelter tomorrow night. The exchange will be at the dark of the moon. Chang and the long-noses would have drunk together, but the shooting took their thirst. It is as you hoped, Uncle?

'Hope is a dream you would make real merely by wishing it. What will happen will happen. Only from reality can one forge dreams into truths. You see?'

Only in the light of your wisdom, Uncle.

Cho Sun stripped off his black hood and wiped his forehead. Untied his cotton jacket to let his chest cool by evaporation. His body smelled like sun-spoiled butter, rank and sweet, and he thought it would be pleasant to bathe in hot water. Now that the long-noses were leaving the hotel, he could use the facilities they abandoned. Deliberately showing himself to Matt had been a risk worth taking, and it had been amusing to cling to the face of the building as the fat one touched the bullet scar in the balcony a mere arm's length below him. The word that the long-noses had left Kowloon for the training camp in the New Territories would soon spread, and nobody would watch the hotel with them gone. Cho Sun could stay where he was, close to Hay's Wharf and the ferry that would take him across to the typhoon shelter on Hong Kong Island.

'Your mouth quivers with yawns, Nephew,' he said. 'Sleep now. I will wake you at sunrise.'

Joe Yellow stripped to shorts and singlet and zipped himself into a kapok sleeping bag, asleep the moment his

466

head touched his pillow of newspaper. Cho Sun lifted the pebble glasses from Joe's nose, laid them on a packing case within reach, and made certain his nephew's ears were shielded from draughts. He did not see his actions as an act of kindness, merely those of a master ensuring his servant was not made useless by sickness. Emotion was for women and children.

Cho Sun turned off the dim overhead light. Allowed the dark to free his mind to concentrate on the great board game he played to survive. Checking Charlie's respiration and heart rate whilst he slept had made Cho Sun remove his pawn from the board. Charlie's mental aura had shrunk to the size of a child's knuckle when Cho Sun laid hands to his temples. The skin had been oily with the seep of sweat tainted by mind drugs, and the bumping heart was as slow and sure as a plodding oxen. Charlie would be strong again, but not soon enough to take a hand in what had to be done the following night. For that great task, Cho Sun had to act alone.

Cho Sun had smelled the woman sleeping in her room down the hall when he had whispered in Charlie's ear. Had picked up the snap of Matt's lighter in the passage, and the soft scent of the pearl in the cot beside Margot's bed. Why Charlie had saved a worthless village girl was a great puzzle to Cho Sun, and he had managed to hide his surprise when his laundry-boy nephews had told him about it. For their sake he had explained it as an act of cleverness they were too foolish to understand, and wonder over it himself in privacy. Only Joe Yellow had shown no curiosity, and that was only because of his blind loyalty to his uncle. If explanations were necessary, Cho Sun would supply them, it was as simple as that.

Cho Sun shrugged the conundrum away.

The Sichuen Dragon and the Council of Seven would come by barge to make the exchange with all due ritual. Would keep faith with the dead more readily than they

467

honoured their commitments to the living. Had they not posted Cho Sun as a dishonoured fugitive rather than hear the truth? There could be no loyalty without honour, and without honour, Cho Sun was as good as dead already. All that was left was the act of dying itself, and Cho Sun had chosen his path to the final door with due deliberation. Dying itself was nothing, but the manner of dying was of paramount importance. He must die causing death, there was no other way for the true shadow warrior.

The very moment Ho Fatt's bones were burned to ash, sending his spirit to his ancestors, the Dragon would unleash his young dragons on Kowloon. They would destroy what was left of the Snake Tong in the city before returning to Hong Kong Island to sever the head from the dying coils. With the Snake Tong weakened by Aman Lee Fook's recent purge, the old Dragon and his advisers must believe themselves invulnerable.

The thought disgusted Cho Sun. Only a senile fool would order such a move at this black phase of the moon. It was a dark time of strange stars and comets, and a moon in shadow would not alter the influence of unseen heavenly bodies that shaped man's destiny. The lessons were there in history, in the soothsayers' almanacs, and should not be ignored. The dark solstice had seen the death of the Great Khan and the Greek who conquered India, and their empires had died with them. Herod the Jew had been eaten by an internal crab for ordering the death of innocents to save his throne. The king had died and the Jesus child had lived, just as it was written. Cho Sun saw what the Sichuen Dragon would not.

Joe Yellow shifted in his sleep, and the lift mechanism dropped a cage between floors. Mice moved along the joists, and a car slammed doors in the street. Cho Sun heard these things without being distracted by them, planning his coming moves with infinite care. He found his long bundle of weapons in the darkness. Loosened the drawstrings and

468

unrolled the layers of stiffened cloth. His knowing fingers brushed the throwing knives in their pouches, the poisoned morning-stars in their pockets. The folding composite bow in its leather sling, the short bullet-headed arrows in their oiled quiver. The old sword that had snapped across a dying ancestor's knee had its own bamboo scabbard. Now only two feet long, its point had been reforged and given a new curving point five decades before Cho Sun had been born. Passed on to Cho Sun by his father, it was now his, and could only be used to kill those worthy enough to feel its bite. Cho Sun had never used it throughout his long career, but he had carried it often as a talisman.

Was it to be blooded at the dark of the moon? he wondered.

His father had told him the sword would know. Would come alive in his hand, and Cho Sun would not be surprised if that proved to be true. He folded his weapons away and sat in the lotus position. Made himself one with the black waters he would have to swim through to reach the dragon barge. Testing the currents and the cold undertow, he swam in his mind with only cold starlight to see him emerge as a liquid shadow to climb the painted stern. The single factor those fools around the Sichuen Dragon would not have calculated for.

Cho Sun's hand burned to remind him he was only a man.

And he smiled his ugly smile.

Content.

Night had reclaimed Repulse Bay, and the transistors and jukeboxes were silent. The day-trippers were back in Wanchai, Aberdeen or Victoria, and seabirds had colonised the rocks at the sea's edge. The kerosene lamps of fishing boats formed a feeble constellation in the East Lamma Channel, and gentle rollers bobbed the diving rafts on a dark and undulant swell. The phosphorescent ghosts of fish haunted the shallows, and hissing surf left a thick scum amongst the weed and litter along the tidal strand.

On a thick finger of granite hooking seaward to form the northern wall of the bay, the castle of the Yu family spread its curtain walls and squat turrets in the yellow glow of tinted floods. Built between the wars as a pretentious private house, it awaited the assault of a medieval army that would never come to brave boiled oil poured from its overhanging bastions as they deployed trebuchets and mangolins to breach the thick stone walls. Inside those walls, the gardens were laid out in the Italian style around a swimming pool that glowed in the dark like a slab of brilliant jade. What had been built as a folly was now a fortress protecting the patient in an oxygen tent deep in the cellars.

He was awake now, and he lay on his side in the recovery position inside a plastic cocoon. Pure oxygen kept his mind sharp, and to free him of pain, the medical staff had resorted to the ancient art of acupuncture. The long silver needles in his ear-lobes, neck, stomach and groin, seemed to hum as they worked their magic on agonised nerve-endings. He could talk if he wished, but he had nothing to say to the nurses or to Wind who had fallen asleep keeping vigil at his side. Her devotion was touching, and exceeded anything he would normally have demanded of her. So much so, that he had doubled her severance dowry, and specified that she was free to marry by choice. Wind would make fat boy sons that bore his family name, and her chosen husband would honour that marriage clause upon pain of death. Playing madam in a house of pillows was not for Wind, and even if he did die, his wishes would live on in his irrevocable will.

He closed his eyes and licked his dry mouth. Sipped from the invalid cup set near his face and tasted limes. The clock on the wall swept past midnight, and one of his shadows waited to speak to him through the two-way microphone that had been rigged to keep him free of outside germs. He raised a hand and the shadow whispered his message.

Aman Lee Fook listened and gave concise orders. The shadow bowed and left, and Fook watched Wind sleep in her chair. The Sichuen Dragon was leaving his island to meet with the long-noses before coming against the Snake Tong. The head of the Snake felt his coils open out to embrace the typhoon shelter, ready to close with crushing force. The long-noses could witness the event and report back to Dance without harm coming to them. Their defeat would come when the dark solstice gave way to the new moon.

In five short days Aman Lee Fook would witness the humiliation and death of Charlie Dance in person. He had precisely one hundred and seventeen hours in which to grow strong enough to take his seat at the stadium in Victoria, even if that vanity cost him his life. Savouring that thought, the Supreme Snake slipped into dreamless sleep as a sudden gale swept across Repulse Bay to throw white breakers against the granite cliffs.

'You'd be who?' Charlie yawned.

Squinting for focus, he turned the hovering cream blob into the face of a serious little girl. She hugged a doll almost as big as she was, and her new smock seemed very blue in the lateral evening light. She stood on one leg and stared at Charlie's nose as if it were big enough to bite her. Her pigtails had fat silk bows, and one of them brushed Charlie's unshaven cheek as she leaned in to say something halting in Hakka dialect. That done, she took two quick steps away and looked over her shoulder for reassurance.

'She thanks you for her doll, and wishes you a Merry Christmas,' said a mannish voice.

'Welcome, ain't she?'

Charlie found Margot near an iron heater with a grumbling stovepipe. The bare room grew around her, and the wooden walls had a thin coat of flat white emulsion over pink primer that bled through in patches like the sunset tinting the uncurtained windows. A medicine ball thumped outside and plimsolls ran on gravel as somebody yelled for more speed.

Charlie gave the girl a solemn wink and got a foot to the floor without needing to hold on to the brass bedhead. The girl skipped away to bury most of her face in Margot's skirts, and a single almond eye watched Charlie articulate his second leg to the floor.

'Know where I was two Christmasses back?' Charlie said, making the floorboards hold still in nailed rows. 'Brixton nick. Counting tiles on the cell wall. All this place needs is some ripe prison graffiti, and it'd be home from bleeding home. Do I get given some clothes to cover myself, or does the kid get to grow up sooner than she should?'

Margot tossed a dressing gown across with, 'Here, grouch. There's a shower and a razor down the hall. There's grey in your beard, did you know that?'

'From being around women too much.'

'His bad temper means he's feeling better, Mai Ling.'

'And means I get to be nagged in two languages. What a life.'

Charlie fumbled with sleeves and a silk cord. Got his long feet into slippers. A still, small voice whispered in his head. Gone before he made sense of the words. The ceiling bore down like oppressive cloud, and the knotholes in the floorboards tried to make swearing mouths until he stamped one closed. He was through with that giddy old nonsense, and he wished Margot would lose the anxiety in her silly precious face. The undercoated door waited for him to open it, and somebody ran past whistling an off-key carol.

'Where's Vinnie?'

'Somewhere around.'

'And Cyril? Ollie?'

'Here too, just as Pim, Trooper and Hettie and Matt and Froggy are. They're all here, Charlie. Now bathe, will you?'

Charlie winked at the solemn almond eye peering from folds of skirt.

'Mai Ling, huh?'

'Do you need help getting to the shower?'

472

'Not this side of whenever, no. Pretty thing, ain't she?'

'Very.'

Charlie rubbed his unshaven jaw and made his palm tingle.

'Something ain't right,' he mumbled into his hand.

'Ben said you'd suffer anxiety attacks.'

'Small beer for a paranoiac, Margot love. Nothing fits where it should. That's sense, not bloody anxiety.'

'Nothing a good wallow in suds won't cure.'

'Why don't I believe that?'

For some reason Charlie remembered Big Charlie his dad taking him to the public baths with soap and towel on Friday nights. Banging on the partition to get the man to send more hot water down the pipe. Wanting his full threepence worth even if he was only a kid. Standing up for his rights like Big Charlie said he should. And the flood of hot water that almost scalded, and playing submarines with the soap until Big Charlie hooked him out for a fish supper at the pie and eel shop. How just being clean all over was a big weekly event when you lived in a cold water house. Seeing his hair plastered down around his ears in the steamy pie shop mirrors through the big gold lettering advertising hot sixpenny meals for the discerning public. Scoffing jellied eels or pie and liquor with all the crusty bread you could wolf. The damp towel rolled up on the wooden bench beside a goose-pimpled thigh, and Big Charlie saying he didn't know where a skinny railing of a kid could tuck it all. Ruffling his son's damp locks and called for more hot sweet tea from the urn.

Charlie found tears on his cheeks for some unfathomable reason, and he hid them with a sleeve.

'You could whistle them up, then?'

'Sorry?' Margot said.

'Vinnie and them. And they'd come running, right?'

'This is a very large complex, Charlie, and I've told them to leave you alone until . . .'

'You're lying, Margot.'

'Am I, my big, brave self-confessed paranoiac?'

'Not many you ain't.'

'If you say so.'

Charlie's eyes refused to stop leaking. He took himself out of the spartan room to find the shower, unwilling to meet Margot's pinched look. His scalp crawled as if his hair follicles were boring insects, and his face had started to melt again. If he wiped his cheeks they'd come off on his sleeve. That was arrant nonsense, and he ignored the sound of dripping flesh until it went away.

The bathroom was untiled and unpainted. The shower stall was a hardboard partition nailed to sawn studding, and the pipes shook when he ran water. He stood under the hot, shuddering stream and used a nailbrush to tone up his shoulder muscles. Scrubbed his pectorals red and lathered his dirty hair with a great glop of liquid shampoo. The suds ran grey through his fingers, and he smelled opium wash away with the second rinse.

The bordello room came back in washes of black silk and cherry blossom, and the killings were a slow ballet in his mind. He hummed an old music hall song to jumble the images with cockney lyrics, and felt again the pain he had shared with Aman Lee Fook. Felt the huge hole Vinnie's slug had torn through bone and sinew, and once again lay in stupor at the Peninsula Hotel with the whispering in his mind. Recalled every syllable and understood them. Knew Margot's lies for what they were without knowing how, and heard a car draw away from the parking lot. Knew Vinnie and Cyril and Ollie would not come if he called. He was mute anyway, and his tongue writhed in his mouth with a life of its own.

A sharp stomach cramp folded him in two. He knocked his head against the partition. Fell to his knees to watch snakes of suds vortex down the soakaway. A poisonous hissing came through his own clenched teeth, and Margot was asking if he was all right through the locked door.

'Handsome,' Charlie called out. Made his mouth frame the convoluted words of another old song. 'I painted her, I painted her, up her belly down her back, in every hole in every crack. I painted her, down in Drury Lane, and I painted her old tomato, over and over again . . .'

'It's just as well the child doesn't have much English.'

'Prudish cow.'

'Don't drown, you barbarian bastard.'

'Nice talk, ducks.'

Margot went away on high heels.

Charlie huddled under the spray as the whispered words came back to him in Cho Sun's dry crumble of a voice. Shook from head to foot as the full import of the words hammered his slack mind. Charlie's teeth ground and chattered, and he bit his tongue as it probed his lips. The blood tasted of salt and bile, and he was just a sprawl of disjointed latex over rubber bones as Big Charlie sang with rum on his breath and sobbed over an empty bottle. Charlie the boy told his father to be a man as Charlie the man told Cho Sun he was a fool to seek death as if his fate was already written on some celestial scroll. Big Charlie and Cho Sun were somehow the same; the warrior and the drunk seeking the end because they'd built that final door in their mad heads.

'You write the rules,' Charlie mumbled. 'You, not them. Whoever *they* may be. You. Us. Bloody Christmas.'

He had rolled out onto the cold linoleum floor. Trailing suds like a huge pink slug, he heard the bubbles pop like smallarms fire. The cramps hit harder. A burning bite across his rigid stomach muscles. He floundered with his legs thrashing weakly. There was a singing moment of agony, then the pain exploded as he ripped off a foul stream of ripe stomach gas. The growl and flutter ended, and he was as wonderfully empty as an inflated paper bag.

Then he was vomiting up long ropes of white fluid into

475

the shower. Long viscous strands ran from his mouth and nose as he voided the congestion from his upper respiratory tract. He burned with heat and shivered with cold, and the convulsions lessened as he spat and hawked and let nature take its course. He heard Margot outside the door again, saying his clothes were on the bed and she was taking the girl off to bed. She would be back in a few minutes. Charlie told her she was a mother to him and lay under the shower to let cold water do its magical work. When she had gone, he got the clothes from the bedroom and made the long walk back with his shoulder to the wall.

He leaned on the handbasin and the shaving mirror was cool against his forehead as he fed a new blade into the Gillette. That took forever and no time at all. His breathing settled and his heart stopped banging in his chest. He spread shaving foam with his fingertips and dared his reflected eyes to lose focus. Some solid food and hot sweet tea would make his stomach behave. Everything else was delusion and fear set free from the pit by bloody LSD. A cigarette would blow his head off at the neck and an Irish would have him puking like a sick tourist on the Isle of Wight ferry. No thanks, just keep it simple.

'I told you drugs were bad news, Archie,' he told the mirror. 'Take a good long look, Arch, I'm living proof. And it ends here, old son. Right here.'

And Charlie shaved and dressed. Hummed as he climbed out through the bathroom window with night coming on. Dropped onto bald grass with violent red wriggles pulsing in his peripheral vision and walked toward a big Nissen hut where cars were parked in rows. Found an unlocked Daimler that smelled of Chappie August's cigars and had keys in the ignition. Let air out of the interior to stop himself gagging on the bitter stink and took deep breaths to keep the clog out of his throat. Some laughing black thing thought he should give it all up, and Charlie snarled at it. Silently.

A heel cracked gravel in the dusk behind him, and he turned in a crouch to see the bore of a revolver eyeing him at nose-height. Margot pointed it, her face sculpted chalk in a thin amber spill of tungsten bulbs.

'My hero,' she said with dull sarcasm. 'If I can outguess you, what chance have you got out there against them?'

Charlie felt the night thicken and waver. Sought answers and a witty reply with black laughter tickling his mind. And came up empty.

CHAPTER SIXTEEN

Charlie patted himself for cigarettes he didn't have and couldn't smoke. Margot's eyes were chips of flat cornflower nothing, and her mouth seemed to have cried itself to death. A big vein throbbed in her lean throat, bumping in and out of a shadowed hollow like a misplaced heart. Charlie should have been angry enough to hit her there, and wondered where that emotion was hiding now he needed it.

Margot sneered his own dialogue at him.

'If you were a used-car, I wouldn't get sixpence for the tyres.'

'Stop talking and say something.'

'Would you listen? Your ears are as dead as your brain.'

'I have to go, Margot,' Charlie wondered if she understood.

'Not alone, you don't. You have a choice, Charlie. I drive, or you're crippled.'

'What?'

'A bullet in the thigh should slow you all the way down.'

'That's saying something?'

'Call it, Charlie. Heads or thighs.'

'You're getting the one-liners in, ain't you?'

Charlie swayed and saw the gun didn't. If he fell down she'd let him, her point proven beyond doubt. She might even laugh as he was carried back to bed by men with fast fists and slow words. He knew female resolve when he saw it, and he didn't have the saliva to spit.'

'Well, you hardhead?'

'You and your doubled-headed coin,' Charlie sighed.

478

He walked around the car and got himself sprawled in the passenger seat. Watched his hands jerk in his lap as Margot slammed in beside him. The Daimler came alive with a muted growl, and the revolver was heavy when she threw it across at him.'

'Prize at the cokernut shy, was it?'

'Don't thank me for stealing it. Or the spare ammunition in my purse. Matt will have to sleep with his thumb under his pillow tonight. You do realise you wouldn't have found your way to Tsim Sha Tsui alone.'

'Ain't nothing simpler than pointing the motor south.'

'If you like being up to your hubcaps in stagnant paddy fields or oyster beds.'

Margot leaned on the horn until a Chinese gatekeeper unlocked chains and padlocks. Her mouth as closed as her face, Margot went through the opening with a coat of paint to spare. Took a sharp bend in high gear, and Charlie saw the blur of dry stone walls and shacks beyond. The sad eyes and stark ribs of a chained dog, and pinched his chin to stop it dripping in his lap.'

'So, what else don't I know?'

'Apart from everything?'

'Use your mouth sensible for once.'

'Hah!' Margot barked. 'Hah!'

Charlie swallowed an expletive and felt the first stir or adrenalin in his lower gut.

There were bald tors beyond the heads, and low headlands running into what had to be a lake or an inlet. The rest of the night was just starlight and the distant yellow loom of Kowloon coming and going between dark hills of scrub.

'Driving silent means you want a fat sorry with butter and jam and the crusts cut off, that it?'

Margot said nothing. Drove with her chin out. Exasperated, Charlie wished his fists would harden enough to hit her. They shook around the revolver and did nothing worthwhile. Margot overtook an army lorry full of Gurkhas, then a Ferret armoured car. Used a short straight to drive on full heads and make a long swing through a village of wood and tarpaper shacks that smelled of unwashed and unseen humanity. Took the Daimler through a shallow valley of marching pylons and army huts, and unravelled the winding road with skilful cornering.

Charlie decided to grumble for effect.

'You ain't you without all that fast bunny, toffee nose.'

Silence.

'You ain't even anybody I recognise.'

'Then I'm Catherine of Aragon.'

'She lost her head at Tower Hill.'

'As I lost mine over you. We were both foolish.'

'Were, eh? That mean you're over me and it's finished?'

'Quite over you.'

'And nobody loves poor Charlie no more.'

'It was a temporary aberration, I assure you. The cure is complete. I am more than happy to drive you to the water's edge for the pleasure of watching you jump straight into the deep end. And drown.'

'And if I decide to swim?'

'You're having trouble just sitting upright. Swim indeed.'

'Then I'll hold my breath and walk under water. Come up in Macao for a nice plate of winkles. How's that?'

'Stupid.'

'As stupid as all that salt running down your face? You cry any more and you'll rust.'

'Nonsense. You're seeing things. Ben said you would.'

'Like the car won't stay on its own side the road? Like your face is under a waterfall? Things like that?'

'That's you. Talking. Distracting me.'

'You wanna go back?'

'I want *us* to go back.'

When we're washed up? Finished?'

'Yes. No. Bastard.'

The Daimler tried to stand on its nose. Threw Charlie

480

against the dash and slewed to a halt on a soft shoulder. The engine ticked over and the night turned peaceful outside the car. Margot's small fist took Charlie in the neck and skidded a diamond ring across his ear. Turned on the fire in his mind. Made his body into tensed stone. Then Margot made frogmouths and beat at him as though demented. And Charlie held her close long after the army vehicles overtook them, a column of khaki dinosaurs with growling stomachs.

Later still, Charlie asked who had taken the ferry to Hong Kong.

'Vinne, Ollie and Cyril. And they took Ben Bunch with them. To give Hatton medical attention.'

Charlie blew Margot's hair from his face. Stared through the windscreen at diamond starlight above the sodium smear of the city. Thought about missing the ferry. Waiting for the black laughter that didn't come.

The capital of Hong Kong Island wore the night face of a glittering whore. Victoria hid her crusted and pitted complexion behind chasing bulbs and hard neon, seducing by night those she repelled by day. Dingy bars became dark caves of promise, their slim hostesses exotic sirens in darker booths. Seedy establishments were transformed into charming dining rooms by muted lamplight and wondrous culinary smells. Speakers blatted Mozart and Beatles and Stones into the streets, duelling for the senses like loud seas in tidal conflict. Tuneless tunes overamplified to feedback and fuzz brawled in contrapunction with the rude persistence of Joshua's brazen trumpets. Bellowing for profit, Victoria killed silence with noise to drive off the evil spirits who came in silence to steal honest profits.

The Royal Navy had doubled its shore patrols to keep the cork in the festive bottle, and army jeeps stiff with MPs waited for the cork to pop. The neat Hong Kong police directed traffic in white gloves under their tin pagodas; or walked in pairs, taking statements from voluble Chinese

481

witnesses after the long-nosed offenders had been taken into military custody. Early trouble had been smothered, and the brigs and cells waited for a midnight crop of unmanned sailors and soldiery fuddled by local brews and Christmas on foreign service. There would be the belligerent and bloody, the battered and bemused. Drunks that sang or had lost to faster boots and fists. The maudlin and homesick aching for home and drizzle and Chatham beer. Missing their women and mother's dumplings. Punching other drunken heads to relive the misery of separation from their nearest and dearest; their pubs and mates, their claustrophobic home communities. Perversely missing the very things they had enlisted to get away from.

The watched pot simmered to a slow boil as the equally insular Chinese counted profits and looked the other way when the brawlers brawled and the whistles brought the redcaps. They wanted no trouble, no questions. And above all, no police. To them, the police were an anathema imposed by the long-nosed Colonial Office. As alien to the Chinese community as talking crystal blobs from Alpha Centauri. And police investigations interfered with the prime objective of amassing wealth, an intolerable imposition.

The long-nosed Europeans had come like a sudden strong wind, and would just as promptly blow away again at some unspecified future date. There had been many such conquering winds before, yet the Chinese remained true to themselves, untouched and unchanged. As abiding as the earth itself, they clung to their traditional ways, paid tribute and 'squeeze' to the bribable and powerful, kept 'face' by honouring their debts at the end of each lunar year, and reared sons to carry on the traditions of centuries.

It was The Way, and they followed The Way gladly.

The acquisition of wealth could only be a good thing. Swelling the family coffers with gold brought the only true happiness they recognised, and for the Chinese to wish neighbours and friends rich in worldly goods with '*Kung hei fatt choy'* summed up their all-consuming passion for Chinese Mammon, the only true god of the colony.

Many thought that sympathy for the cause of mainland communism was laudable, but it was much better to be a rich communist than a poor one. A poor comrade who could not send gifts of money and burned rice to relatives on the communist mainland during famines lost 'face' with his peers, and that pragmatic view made any conflict between communism and rampant capitalism obsolete. There could be no lasting merit in any political ideology that required a man to go hungry with only rags to his back like some low mendicant priest. Better to have a fat bank account and a fatter wife, sturdy children and the 'face' that extreme wealth brought a man. Gold teeth were better that no teeth at all, yes? And to the click of the abacus, the crash of hot woks, Victoria raked in the money with both hands. End of argument.

Only on the waterfront of the Causeway Bay District was the mad tempo missing. The typhoon shelter showed few riding lights and little activity. Hokka fishermen had landed their catches early, and a fine nose for trouble kept them below decks with hushed children and dimmed lamps. Nobody plied boats for hire and the usual persistent crowd of rickshaw boys were conspiciously absent. No taxis cruised for fares, and the flat newness of Victoria recreation ground was deserted when three London long-noses wheeled a fourth across new grass turfs. The previous night's wind had gentled into quartering scurries, yet the water blanket inside the moles rolled in oily motion, slapped hulls and creaked timbers with lazy strength. A channel buoy tolled on the swell, and a naval frigate hoop-hooped on its way out past Green Island.

'This where Chang said?' Vinnie braked his chair at the water's edge.

'About, I reckon.' Ollie peered at dark seaward nothing beyond the dark huddle of junks. 'They'll find us.'

'So long as it ain't sudden-sudden,' Vinnie said.

Cyril nodded with a grunt. Sweating in dry night heat.

Ben Bunch looked around sadly, a disappointed tourist with nothing to add. Poor night vision made him timid and distrustful of his senses, and food eaten by candlelight tasted like boiled broth of polystyrene. All he could see was his luminous watch and the red and green pulses of port and starboard lights reflected in the sea. Had he known the truth of the situation he would have acted very differently. Only confidence based on massive ignorance stopped him dropping in a dead faint, for he believed that Hatton had been taken ill whilst staying with friends on one of the outer islands. Not that the others were much better off, none of them saw or heard the dark figures gathering in the darkness behind them.

'There's a light,' Ollie said, jerking his chin at the harbour entrance. 'Hop outta the chair, Vin.'

Vinnie eased himself upright, the rifle hidden under his travelling blanket, and stared at the low shape of the dragon barge coming through the gap in the breakwater. Missing Charlie as his heart missed a couple of beats.

Beside him, Cyril held the casket of bones, a white gown of mourning over his street clothes, his mind empty of the fluid Cantonese he needed to recall.

'Off and running,' Ollie murmured like a relaxed uncle waiting to host a children's party, too much adrenalin giving his mouth a coppery taste.

And the creak of fifty oars came closer and closer.

Cho Sun was just another shadow in the night. He picked his way through the elegant huddle of old Jardine Matheson godowns and sprinted along the long stone causeway to Kellett Island, ready to hide in the sea if a car should come along. None did, and there were no pedestrians. The Royal Hong Kong Yacht Club was in darkness when he crossed the dinghy park and got into the trees on the seaward side of the building.

Cho Sun lingered there to steady his breathing and to moisten his mouth from a strong bottle of rice wine. Listened to the whispering sea and the long breakers idling along the northern skirt of the typhoon shelter. To the boats riding at anchor, the trees bowing their upper branches in the toying breeze. Smiled his ugly smile because he was ready for his final trial of strength. Flexed his fingers to keep them supple for the work to come. Then he made his way along the mole to lie beneath the starboard leading light, careful not to show himself in the intermittent spill of green light. He lay motionless for an hour. For two. Memorised the location of every yacht and junk, each unused mooring buoy. Watched the changing mood of the sea surface, the whorls and eddies marking undertows and cross-currents. Turned the blanket of water into a gridded and three-dimensional chess board the size of an aquarium in his mind. Seeing himself as one of the pawns. Heard the squeak of an unoiled chairwheel coming across the flat nothingness of the recreation ground. Sensed young snakes padding across the grass and out of the dark godowns to form a semi-circular perimeter with the four long-noses at the centre of their advance. He heard the flat slap of feathering oars out in the Harbour Channel and a warship sound its klaxon near Green Island. A boat dog bark before a kick shut him up.

Cho Sun drew on his inner core and went into the harbour without a sound. Went deep with long strokes and kicks, using the first curl of undertow to speed his forward motion. He dribbled air to keep negative buoyancy as he made for a mooring buoy he had marked out in his mind. Three minutes of hard swimming brought him to the sinker and anchor chain, and he rose up along it, trailing out the last of his air to keep the killing pressure bubbles out of his body. His head broke the surface, and he hung in the water filling his lungs for a second dive as he relocated the barge. It came towards him on his port quarter with dipping oars, and Cho Sun pulled himself down to two fathoms before swimming under water to cross its course.

He was almost too accurate on his fast swim through the dark waters. He made for the surface in a controlled curve and came up right under the prow. The long and gilded dragon's snout scraped his ribs and snagged in his tunic. Cho Sun relaxed his muscles, draped an arm over the shining prow, and freed himself. Checked that his light weight had not altered the trim of the barge to alert the dragons above to his sudden presence, nerve endings and senses extended as sensitive filaments. Found himself below the forward lookout, and could have hooked him overboard with two fingers to his nostrils. Heard the lookout grunt to keep the coxwain on course, and quelled the desire to jab a killing phoenix into the extended throat. Sank instead, and let the skimming keel run over him as he trod water. Knew the bubbles he trailed would be lost in the measured chop of the oar blades. Racing his metabolism to keep the cold from biting into his muscles.

The stern came up fast, and Cho Sun fought the swirling wake, eeling upward to dig three fingers into the carved fret of the ornamental chine. Hung there with his head submerged, husbanding his air as he became one with the barge. Laid a hand to the rudder, feeling through it to the tiller bar; through the tiller bar to make contact with the coxwain himself. Felt how the man stood, the pressure he used to guide the barge, forming a ring of contact that linked him to the man, the barge, and the sea he hung in. Knew how the coxwain distributed his weight and in which direction he faced, watching the lookout in the stern.

Cho Sun blew used air through a tight grin. Used the trident hold to lift himself bodily from the water until his toes found purchase on the carved chine. Got his free hand to the deep scales of the dragon's tail curving inboard over the pilot deck to support the canopy over the dragon throne. Went up and over the gunwhale to take the coxwain from behind with soundless efficiency. Killed his brain with a knuckle to the base of his skull. Smothered his last exhalation of breath and lowered him over the side like a soft doll. Had the tiller bar on the correct trim without a pause, and took the stance of the dead coxwain with balletic grace. Apologised to the man's ancestors as was only fitting, and responded to the lookout's signals with the surface of his mind. Prepared himself for death if it was written. For the upward road to the Dragon Throne if the dark stars willed it. Whatever the outcome, Cho Sun, the last true Shadow Warrior, would be remembered for centuries.

Cho Sun's blood sang.

Long tapers lit the bow lamps as the shore closed; a line of wooden pontoons bobbing and sawing against a raw concrete apron, and Cho Sun saw Chinese Cyril in white robes on the towpath. The bones of Ho Fatt resting on the wheelchair. The doctor, the fat man and the one-legged one in a line behind him. He sensed the snakes he could not see, but they were there, they were coming. . . .

Cho Sun eased the tiller to port. The starboard oars were shipped, and the barge turned broadside on as the port oars backstroked and dragged. Dragons dropped ashore with fore and aft warps, and the barge settled against cork fenders to gently wallow on swell. A gangplank was run out, and Cho Sun heard Chang ask the Sichuen Dragon for permission to proceed. If there was a response it was a silent gesture, and Chang gave orders as the lamplighter reached the stern deck.

Cho Sun turned away to lash off the tiller as the lamplighter put his taper to the stern lamps, bathing Cho Sun in sudden golden light, showing up the telltale pool of water around Cho Sun's feet. Cho Sun spun about with a darting blow. His left palm smashed the lamplighter's nose and drove the septum bone up into the man's frontal lobes. Letting the body fall where it would, Cho Sun drew his short sword. Felt it come alive in his hand as he cut through the canopy behind the Dragon Throne.

487

Stepping through the slashed silk, Cho Sun faced the Sichuen Dragon. And paused. Stared. Saw the great lie in the clouded eyes and the slack and drooling mouth. The frozen left side of the parchment features. The paralysis of a massive heart attack that had turned the Sichuen Dragon into the puppet of the Council of Seven. Using the shell of an old and noble man for their own ends. Thieves who would steal his power and his good name to start a tong war that could only destroy. The kidnapping of the long-nosed money man had been a clever fiction to keep the Sichuen Dragon alive. A clever lie based on the eccentricity of age.

Cho Sun's anger seemed to rouse the old man from stupor. The milky eyes flickered and squirmed and focused. Recognised Cho Sun and glowed with pleasure. Saddened and hardened. Passed on silent commands. Passed the throne to Cho Sun. And the right of retribution to a true son of the Dragon T'ang.

'I hear, father,' Cho Sun kissed the knobby unfeeling hand.

The milky eyes clouded and closed. At peace.

Cho Sun became a shadow behind the throne. Watched Hatton's stretcher being lifted ashore, knowing him to be drugged. Saw the bones handed to the man Chang with ceremonial words and bows, the rest of the Council of Seven standing in a semicircle on the pontoon behind him. Using his perfect mimicry, Cho Sun projected the reedy voice of the Sichuen Dragon the length of the barge. The death sentence for treason as was only fitting. Naming himself as heir to the throne as was ordained. Then he went back over the side and swam away.

Margot parked outside the tenements facing the Victoria recreation ground. Followed Charlie across the road, and was lifted over the low perimeter fence like a girl scrumping apples from an orchard. She had watched the Charlie she knew disappear on the short ferry ride, becoming the cold stranger she had often wondered about and never met. Gone were the lazy eyes and lazier smile, the laughing drawl and the easy walk. The grace of movement was still there, but more catlike and controlled. More flowing and deadly, the face washed of expression. And when he spoke, the words were bare, without inflection.

Carrying her high heels and holding Charlie's hand, she kept pace with his fast lope across dewless and spongy turfs. Felt the complete metamorphosis through his cool, dry palm. The power in him tingling up her arm like a static charge. The wonder in her became overwhelming sexual curiosity, and she needed to know what it would be like to feel that raw energy inside her. Her thighs goosefleshed as an internal shudder dried the roof of her mouth, and she would have sprawled headlong if Charlie hadn't supported her.

They moved down an avenue of saplings, crossed gravel paths and the worn oblong of a cricket pitch, passed low buildings that might have been groundsmans' huts. The raw harbour smell was directly ahead, and Margot heard the mutter of voices. She was about to tell Charlie where she thought they were when Charlie flowed to a halt and whirled her against a tree caged in wire. Bore her to the ground and lay across her, simulating intercourse as he muttered cold endearments against her startled cheek.

Margot saw Charlie's skull outlined in starlight. Then another hole in the infinite glitter. The darker shape of a hooded man with pale smudges for eyes, staring down at them with distaste before moving on with a jerk of his arm. Then another and another passed, dismissing the copulating Europeans as rutting mongrels. For a wild run of moments Margot wanted to scream protests of innocence and run for the car, to find Charlie really erect and turn pumping mime to wonderful liquid fact. Did nothing but tremble as Charlie growled to hold her still. With the purr of Blake's Tyger vibrating through her supine breasts, Margot yearned for endless climaxes right there on the burned grass. Fear in a picaresque setting made her wanton, and she marvelled at her complete lack of self-control. More attuned to gutter carnality than the still small voice of childhood puritanism. Dizzy with need, it took her a while to realise Charlie had risen to leave her.

'Poo,' she said as Charlie told her to stay low. To stay put.

Then Charlie was running swiftly away, and she was alone on dark grass smelling of parched hay. Quite alone with fear and her shoes for company. She turned her stiletto heels into weapons and stood there in stockinged feet. Lost.

Charlie sprinted easily for thirty yards. Came up on a crouching snake and toe-punted him behind the ear. Knocked him into a forward roll and ran over him when he flopped. Back-heeled the rising chin and made sure with the long barrel of Matt's Savage. Turned the body to search it for weapons and found a cleaver in the grass. Was reaching for it when he sensed others converging on him.

Charlie angled away and sidled into a half-circle. Panned the Savage for targets and wiped spangles away from his eyes. Felt the ground roar through his ankles as his stomach side-slipped and lurched. Teetered and felt the heavy revolver drag his stringy arm down. Let it fall and waited for them to swamp him.

A weir roared in his ears and there was a hot paste he couldn't swallow away. It was wrong and stupid and needed puzzling over. The barge had swung in against the pontoons, a distant jiggle of fat paper lamps and oars that wouldn't hold still. Three white Cyrils jogged apart and melted into a soft whole as he bowed to other men in silk gowns. Charlie counted seven of them before they too became blurs. The towpath twisted out of the horizontal into the almost perpendicular, and Charlie had slumped onto one knee in a clumsy genuflection, his head hanging. The Savage was there if his stupid hand wanted to pick it up, but it lingered too long and it was snatched casually away.

There was a greedy red mouth in Charlie's chest, swallowing his air. Getting to his feet was a slow and laboured thing, and he found himself swaying in a circle of hooded men. He measured off a punch. Swung his fist at the nearest face and swung himself around in a vortex of nausea until he was caught from behind in a double armlock. The neck blow he expected didn't come. Hands in his hair made Charlie look up at a snake he might have met with Fook in London, but he couldn't be sure. Of that or anything. Sucking air to feed oxygen to his dull brain was all there was. The snake was telling him things about himself that should have turned him to an earthworm in the grass.

Charlie might have found that funny, but his laugh was just a weak drone between clenched teeth sipping air around a coated tongue. The bastards had him and that was probably all there was to that. To anything. The night was scratched with white lightning like a scored negative, and he heard the crack of a high heel on a hooded head. Margot was squirming and being held until she heeled a crotch and scrabbled over to hold herself against Charlie. She still held a shoe and whatever she murmured in comfort sounded nice. Charlie told her so as his head revolved and cleared. Revolved and cleared.

A speech in Mandarin came from the barge and seemed to interest the snakes. Cyril was translating it for the lads, and the seven dragons on the towpath shouted in angry dismay. Making an unmanly commotion about being condemned to death as traitors to the dragon tong. A dreary little tableau of panic and recrimination that rose in pitch as the barge pushed off, abandoning the Council of Seven to the rival snakes. Vinnie showed the world his rifle, Ben Bunch tended Hatton in the wheelchair, and Cyril and Ollie argued together as the barge glided away into deeper water. Watching just as Charlie and Margot watched. Knowing more about it all than poor Charlie Dance with his useless lungs and melted brain.

The Council of Seven had scattered every whichway, and the head snake who had insulted Charlie sent men to bring them down. Charlie was irritated by the cowardice of the first dragon the snakes caught and killed on the towpath, glad when he gurgled and died and made a splash in the water. The following wails and screams were just repetition, and Charlie yawned for air through it all. Uninvolved. Detached. He coughed bile on the grass and Margot wiped his mouth off with a dinky little handkerchief. Put smelling salts to his nose and jerked him aware. The pressure on his neck and arms was suffocating, but he bridged his shoulders against the pain to show the bastards he still had some pride. He even cooed at Margot in reassurance as she massaged his heart and kept the sweat out of his eyes.

The snakes dragged a last man in robes across to the circle and threw him down to grovel. His legs thrashed like thin sticks as fear made him falsetto. He promised the snakes riches in exchange for his worthless life. Dragon tong secrets. Anything to live. It was the thin dragon Chang, and he talked through hard slaps to the face. Talked on as he was told to act the man. Talked and talked until a cleaver eviscerated him. Spat blood until a cleaver chopped through his skinny neck. His head made a thump on the turf and there was a kind of silence that Margot mewed into.

Charlie knew it was his turn, and he defied the night with a stone face, wishing he had the words to comfort Margot. All he had in his mouth was scummy mucus too curded to spit at the bastards. Somebody threw Margot's lost shoe down near her foot, and the men behind Charlie let him go with a push. He went down on stiff forearms and tried to look the head dragon in the face, but the barge was gone, the snakes had gone, and there was just Chang's headless body as mute testimony to what had gone before.

Charlie was hate and humiliation and useless limbs. He shook his heavy head, smelled Margot's rose perfume, blood and rotting kelp. They had given him back his gun, and he had just enough strength to hold the bloody thing. He got it into a pocket and took a stab at standing like a man. Made it with Margot's help and heard the wheelchair squeak as it was wheeled towards them with Ben Bunch pushing the handles. Heard Margot call to Ollie and Vinnie and Cyril like a superior cub mistress. Grinned like a decked boxer to show he was still game, and shrugged Margot away before he had to be his own man whatever it cost.

'That's mother's little soldier,' Margot said. Understanding.

'Charlie? Christ, *Charlie*?'

Vinnie took Charlie's arm as if he had the strength to help.

'It's me,' Charlie shrugged him off too. Gave Cyril an acid look because he still held the box of bones. 'That goes in the sea. Now, you tart.'

'I'll do it,' Ollie hurled the box way out into the harbour. Fed himself a Capstan and a long draught of smoke. 'Left us standing here like little boys. Don't get it.'

'Wasn't our turn, was it?' Charlie rolled his shoulders. Asked Bunch how Hatton was.

'Swimming in the same stuff they pumped into you. Heart attack my Aunt Fanny's gluteous maximus. Would somebody like to explain all this to me?'

''No,' said Charlie.

Lights began to show in the floating city of junks, and a bold dog woke up a lot of others with long coughing barks. A transistor radio came on halfway through 'White Christmas', and Bing Crosby groaned syrup across Causeway Bay.

'We stay here,' Ollie said, 'we'll have to explain that mess to a lot of Tall John Law.' He jerked his thumb at Chang's body.

'That gets it said.'

Charlie led Margot away with the others trailing after. Strolling and deadly.

CHAPTER SEVENTEEN

Amber fire haloed the nine dragons of Kowloon and silvered an airliner dropping into Kai Tak. Taimosham mountain brooded under a crown of enamelled light to the north, and the valley around the Jubilee Reservoir lay in dawn shades of dull iron and copper. An early kingfisher swooped out over the dark waters as feet pounded along a shadowed path to labour up a sharp incline into the first cut of rose light. The first man reached a spur of rock where wild myrtle and bracken made a fragrant carpet. Ran on the spot with a high, pumping action, and crouched on his hams to wait for his running partner to catch up. Windmilled his arms and watched Charlie cover the last few yards before sinking down to huff breath at the lightening sky.

'Too many ciggies, Chas,' Trooper Wells said.

Charlie just lay there with a heaving chest.

'But better than yesterday. Ain't many can keep up with me over five miles.'

Charlie groaned and massaged his stomach.

'And you ain't got that green look no more. Chas Dance, the killer cabbage. Terror of all the lettuces.'

'Have your fun, Champ,' Charlie huffed.

'Beats crying, son.'

'That gets my vote.'

'Tuck your knees up. Might help.'

'What knees? Lost them a mile back. Been running on my hipbones.'

'Listen to sad, sick and sorry for himself.'

'Don't write me off just yet.'

'Still three miles to go.'

'Yeah? You wouldn't be the first fighter who left all his stamina on the gym floor. Overtrained himself into a knockout first round.'

'You ain't talking to some rookie mauler, you know.'

'Just save some for Tatum tonight.'

Trooper laughed. Broke off some bracken to chew.

'Wonder if you can cook with this stuff?'

Charlie rolled up on an elbow to point a finger.

'Belly, belly, belly. You quit roadwork you'll blow up the size of Cyril. Have to call your restaurant "The Tweedle Dum".'

'Not me. Too many glands. Tonight I give Tatum a boxing lesson, then that's me and the fight game divorced. Trade leather gloves for kitchen gloves. The good life, Charlie.'

A shaft of pearl light made Trooper squint as it cut through the broken rim of the valley to scale the reservoir with shimmer. Charlie studied the seamed and humorous face with its wide mouth and cleft chin. The simian eyebrows and cropped black curls. The one thickened ear and the dark stubble on the heavy jaws.

'You worried about which way it goes tonight, Troop?'

'Always nice to go out on a clean win.'

'That how it'll be?'

'Well, he's got the reach and the weight, but I'll jolt him hard from the bell. Get inside them long arms and hammer him through to the fifth. Waltz him into over-confidence in the sixth, and nail him in the seventh. Teddah, Sugar Boy Tatum.'

'That's your prediction, is it?'

'I reckon. Always some surprises though, eh?'

'Yours or Tatum's?'

'Who knows? that's the surprise, ain't it?'

'You walk away with twenty thou clear, whatever happens, Troop.'

'The fans'll get value for money. So'll you.'

'Who's saying diff?'

'You maybe. Think I don't know how much I owe you for straightening out Chappie's books? Cutting out all them promotor's expenses that used to whittle my purse down to not a lot? You want kisses and thanks?'

'Just you doing what you do best.'

'You selling me a bridge, Chas?'

'Why ask that?'

'With you looking at me with a face like a smacked arse? You've got your breath back. Use it sensible. Clear the air.'

'Sugar Boy Tatum's a strong boy. And the wise money's on your swede hitting the canvas. You've got the crowd's affection, but you ain't got the bookies' vote for a strollover.'

Trooper spat green paste. Used the back of a heavy hand on his mouth. Looked wary.

'Always the way, ain't it? The clever money waiting for old Trooper to go down and stay down. Or you saying diff? Straight hooks, Chas. No naughty kidney punches in the clinch.'

'I'm in your corner, Troop. Are you?'

'So, that's it. You figure old Troop's taking a dive for readies the taxman don't get to know about.'

'Ain't *saying*, Troop. Just asking.'

'Smoke without fire? Horse feathers.'

'Come off it, Troop. There's just you, me, and all that water. Nobody else. I want it straight, is all.'

'You wanna stand up and say that?'

'And get decked without an answer? Forget it.'

Trooper danced out of his crouch. Angry chocolate flecks in his hazel eyes.

'This is Troop, not Chappie-bloody-August you're mouthing off at. Take it back or put 'em up.'

'When you can talk me down? Give me an honest "no"?'

'Yeah? What's words but punches you can't block? Stand

up, you yellow get. Let's have your face where I can smack it.'

'How's that sensible, Troop? Maybe crack a knuckle and have to fight Tatum with one paw? All I want is your word. Nothing more.'

Trooper was close to shouting.

'And what's my word worth if I have done a naughty deal with the bookies? Spit on a kerb, right? You think August didn't have his usual mutter about long odds? A few crafty grand on Tatum for me under the table if I got the staggers around round five, eh? If I was to turn my toes up inna sixth? And I thought you was different from them other blackheads. Well diff, but you ain't. Bent is bent, Charlie, and that's you too, ain't it? So bent you can only smell your own backside. You ain't worth hitting.'

'Are you?'

'Get the wax outta your ears, Dance. Or do I knock it out?'

'And hear what? You frying a greasy breakfast you can't swallow?'

'Bloody stand up.'

'Bloody calm down.'

'Just put your chin here.'

'Give me yes or no. Then you can take your best poke at me, right? But make it a goodun, Troop. This ain't no cosy square ring with seconds and a ref. This is the cobbles, my turf, my advantage. Think on.'

Trooper stared. Swallowed.

'You would give me a go?'

'Ain't but one of us would walk away.'

'And to what, that it? You'd cancel the whole bloody shooting match. No fight, no purse, no nothing.'

Charlie's grin was as tight as a hurt boxer's.

'For the principal, not the money, yeah.'

'You'd be paying off for ten years.'

'Happens I can afford to.'

497

'Fuck you, Charlie. Fucking fuck you.'

'That means what?'

Trooper looked angry and tearful. Groaned deep in his throat and batted the air with his fists. Shadow-boxed the searing dawn light. Threw killing punches at the first fingers of true sunlight. Kept up the furious combat until he had control. Bowed over a granite boulder to rip it from the earth. Hurled it out over the reservoir, and watched it spread golden rings across the placid pewter surface. Let his shoulders sag and showed Charlie his broad back. Speaking raggedly.

'You think I didn't think hard about throwing the towel for a fat backhander? Who wouldn't? I'm a fighter, not a moral crusader. With dough in your bin you can afford to be fucking noble. You think I don't know how many grands have been screwed outta my purses over the years? First thing Hatton did was do the sums for me. These fists are all I got. Ain't no bloody mincing accountant with a soft office arse and phoney letters after my john henry. I'm bloody Trooper Wells. Almost a hasbeen. Ain't no smooth J.C. Hatton. Ain't no whoring Chappie August.'

Charlie scratched a prickling eye and kept his face blank.

Trooper finally turned to face him. On the ropes but still game. A fighter with nothing but ringcraft and fading strength to his name.

'Then we're both in the same corner, Troop.'

'Could I face my Hettie otherwise? Chappie August can't bribe me, but you can ruin me. That's about the size of it, ain't it?'

Charlie rose like a lazy cat. Stood there with his arms hanging. Unsmiling.

'Take your best shot, Champ. You earned it.'

'You think I won't?'

'You think I care?'

Trooper closed on Charlie. Stood chest to chest, and their breath mingled in the cool, dry morning air.

'I ain't kow-towing, Charlie. Ain't kissing arse.'

'Who asked you?'

'This stinks.'

'You're right.'

'What're we talking here? Integrity or dough?'

'Both, as it happens.'

'Make sense, will you. You've had me swearing like a kid with the arse outta his trousers. Hettie gets to know, she'll have me gabbling Hail Marys till Easter.'

'Sixty grand in cash should get her smiling.'

'For a dive, that it?'

'For a win, Champ. For the pleasure of seeing Chappie August drain out through his underwear.'

'Clean, Chas. It's gotta be Marquess of Queensbury.'

'It's gotta be in the fifth.'

'I'm a fighter, not a bloody Churchill tank.'

'You're Trooper Wells. The best.'

'Once, maybe.'

'No maybe about it. Tatum goes in the fifth.'

Trooper looked wise and laid a finger to Charlie's deltoid.

'This ain't just to put August down. There's something bigger at stake here, right?'

'What could there be?'

'Your neck is what. You figure to get hit by them Chinese monkeys right there at ringside. Right about the time I'm supposed to go down to the New York favourite. You think I don't know you're in a war? Think I don't know how these Hong Kong Chinese think? I'm your "face", Chas. I go down, you go with me. Then they do the real business on Charlie Dance.'

'That gets it said.'

'In spades with gold edges, Chas. Micky Raven was a mate of mine, but you done him to keep the Smoke clean and free of them Triads. I ain't holding a grudge for that, I just want you to know I know, is all. Wasn't for you, Cyril'd be catsmeat long ago, right? Raven or the Chinks would have done him down. I owe you more than money, and you'll get paid off in the fifth tonight. OK?'

'That'll maybe give me the time I need.'

'I'll do her, Chas. And it ain't the dough.'

'You think I don't know that?'

'There's been hard words, Chas . . .'

Charlie ducked around Trooper and began jogging away.

'Three miles to go. Save your breath,' he called over his shoulder.

When the men had gone a bulbul marked his territory with his distinctive call. A vixen crept to lap at the water's edge before going to earth to sleep beside her cubs, and the day grew bright and warm.

The noon-day gun slopped coffee into Margot's saucer as startled pigeons circled the Victoria sports arena.

'And *I'm* highly-strung?' sniffed the precious designer in pale corduroys. 'Sauce for the goose, Mrs Sadler dear.'

Margot's look was hotter than his burned-orange cravat.

'Direct your effete impertinence where it might do some good,' she told him. 'Get those impossible workmen of yours to hang those blue drapes properly. They're more creased than your silly face.'

'Calm yourself, dear lady. They have yet to be ironed and battened. Kindly allow a professional to ply his trade.'

'Show me one and I will.'

'There is really no need to be offensive—'

'There's every need. Look at these shrivelled stalks. I contracted for fresh white blooms, not the leavings of a Chinese funeral. How can I seat His Excellency the Governor next to these dead offerings?'

'The real floral displays stay refrigerated until the heat of the day is spent. If you must go through the change of life, kindly have your hot flushes in the privacy of your own cauldron, there's a dear.'

'How *dare* you!'

500

'And how dare *you*? Shall it be pax with little fingers, or do we scream in front of the coolies? Heavens knows what the Chinese think of us already.'

Margot sat in a blue and gold chair and grinned.

'You're a bitch, but you're right.'

'I'm the one who should be screaming with rage. It's in the small print of my contract. Jonathan Brierley has a royal blue fit to match the decor. Is mollified by client, "She-who-must-be-obeyed". Sniffs, flounces, and does a won-drous job by the eleventh hour. Is rewarded by smiles and gratitude and a handsome cheque. Exits left so as not to be involved in gladiatorial combat between the muscular and sweaty. Why don't you come down off the chandelier and tell dear Jonathan what's up, love? I had you pegged as cool, calm and collected.'

'Change of climate perhaps.'

'And Jonathan believes you . . . liar.'

'That makes you astute – and far too nosy.'

'But discretion itself. And I rustle up the best coffee this scruffy colony can offer. Alcoholically enhanced to bring the roses back to your cheeks. Yes?'

'Life-saver.'

'Back in a trice, madam.'

Margot watched the designer sidle off through carpenters and electricians. Looked at the banked tiers of empty seats with Charlie's eyes and shuddered. Visualised the arena full and floodlit, a perfect killing ground for a determined assassin with a telescopic sight. The VIP stand where she sat was open on three sides, and she felt very exposed and vulnerable as she checked the seating plan. Rather she *tried* to check it, her hand shaking the typewritten names into a blur.

Workmen swarmed everywhere, and the midday sun beat down on the oval of grass around the blue and white ring with its neat rows of ringside seats. Saws and hammers ripped and banged, and any faint-hearted pessimist worth

501

his salt would know with dread certainty that nothing could be ready in time for the opening fanfares.

Margot decided she knew differently. She relaxed and sat back to enjoy the winter sunlight on her closed lids. She and the effeminate Jonathan had everything under control. The noisy activity around her became a comforting symphony of progress without anarchy, and the seating plan slid from her lap to glide to the ground three tiers below her. A Chinese in pebble glasses picked it up and committed it to memory as his uncle Cho Sun had taught him. Silently returned the list to the chair beside Margot, and went off to be bellowed at by an harassed foreman. An hour later, he drew the plan in the dust of a tenement roof overlooking the arena.

It serves, Uncle? his fingers asked.

The deckle-edged and engraved card read:

Mr CHARLES DANCE
Requests The Pleasure Of The Company Of
AMAN LEE FOOK ESQUIRE & GUEST
At An Exhibition Tournament Of 12 Rounds
'TROOPER' WELLS (GB) V
'SUGAR BOY' TATUM (USA)
Plus Full Supporting Bill Of Mixed Weight Bouts
Entrance 'A' VIP STAND. 7.30 p.m. 31st December 1965
Black Tie. Running Buffet In The Directors' Bar
AN AUGUST ENTERPRISES PROMOTION

Aman Lee Fook lifted it from the lacquered tray Wind held out for him, and noticed the tremble in her hand. The little finch knew what it meant to her lord and to herself, and she was afraid. Fook dismissed her and allowed the Perfume Master and his council of White Paper Fans to approach his couch. They bowed and waited for him to allow them to speak. He knew what their collective advice would be, and he was impatient with the long jaws they hid behind impassive masks. The funeral fires of the old Sichuen Dragon had lit up the sea approaches to the island in the Tathong Channel, and all the unhonoured dead had wailed with the winds at his passing. Too many honoured ears had heard the spectral voices for the phenomenon to be dismissed as a manifestation of ignorant superstition. The dark solstice had marked the old Dragon's passing with a black moon as the most sage of soothsayers had predicted; just as they had unanimously foretold the named heir to the Dragon Throne would be a dishonoured renegade. All this had come true, and any shadow over the House of the Supreme Snake had been burned away by the sun of reason. The luck of the Dragon was now vested in Cho Sun, and the Dragon T'ang could do nothing until he ascended the throne after a long period of purification. The headless Dragon would therefore sleep, and all the other great houses were safe for the foreseeable future. There was no need for low spirits.

Aman Lee Fook told the Perfume Master to speak. Leaned back into cloud pillows sewn with Sky Dragons to listen with half an ear to a set speech he would know by heart. Saving his strength and cunning for more important matters. Found the words were all wrong, and sat forward to have them repeated. There had been a new reading of bones and smoke from burning prayer scrolls, the ancient craft of finding sign in the entrails of sacred carp. A long tooth had been found in the fish's belly, a tooth that only grew from the snout of the narwhale. The carp had been unscarred, and the tooth had come by magic from a sea-creature into the vitals of a freshwater fish. The meaning was clear. A foreign long-nose lived in the body of the Snake T'ang, and to cut him out would kill the host, just as the knife had killed the carp. He who raised a hand against the long-nosed Dance would perish, destroying his T'ang along with him.

Fook kept his face immobile with an effort. Asked, 'But is the carp truly the House of the Snake?' Dared the Perfume Master to hesitate when he replied.

'There is a mark on the narwhal tooth. It coils like the snake. Yet . . . and yet . . . it could be a dragon. It is here for you to see, Lord.'

Fook leaned over the ivory thing lying on a silk square. The writhe of nicotine shading was both snake and dragon. Was both rampant and defiant, and there was a clean white scar where the beast's heart would be.

'You see, Lord, the omen is doubly true. Doubly strange.'

Fook made his interpretation a decree.

'This omen has been shown to us, not to the dragons. Therefore, it is we who are favoured with the fore-knowledge. I see a dragon rearing from a mortal wound here. Our brotherhood will not touch the man Dance, but I will witness what must be. Make the arrangements, Perfume Master, then take these others with you when you withdraw. You have my permission to do so now.'

Fook ignored their retreat from his room. He had read the omen correctly, and was driven by a calm curiosity that suffocated the pain from his half-healed wound. He and the engraved card would go to the arena and witness what must unfold.

Charlie bought himself a long Canada Dry over ice on the noon ferry to Victoria, and allowed Chappie August to spot him from the other end of the crowded bar. Sucked into the company, Charlie was introduced to Carmine Domino and Casey Pollard from New York. To a man from Detroit with the unlikely name of Doll Gardenia, and to Sugar Boy Tatum himself.

'Good luck tonight,' Charlie told him.

'No offence there, but it ain't needed,' Tatum drawled. A head taller than Trooper Wells, he had a strong brown neck, ropey arms and thick wrists. The fine features of a mixed-blood Mestizo from the Caribbean, and a lilting Islands accent.

Charlie liked him with a smile.

'That confidence of yours wouldn't come from the odds these characters are laying on you, would it?' he asked. Looked for flaws in the boxer's veneer.

'It all comes down to the one thing, Mr Dance – me and your boy in the ring. It's these gents that's gambling, not Sugar Boy. I seen all I needed to see at the weigh-in this morning. When me and Trooper Wells shook hands. I'll retire him tonight.'

'You ain't the first to think Troop's a walk-over.'

Chappie August slapped shoulders nervously.

'No confidence, no fight, Charlie. A fighter's gotta believe in himself, right?'

Charlie looked at Tatum as he sneered at August.

'They have to with you around, Chappie. The day you climb through the ropes is the day I'll buy that bridge in your brochure.'

'That friendly?' Doll Gardenia asked Domino and Pollard.

'Charlie's just kidding,' August said uneasily. 'A great kidder, our Chas.'

'I'm kidding,' Charlie lied. 'How much have you laid out on a win in the blue corner, Chappie?'

'Me? Nothing. I'm the promotor. I'm neutral.'

'We're both promoting here, Chappie. And I ain't neutral.'

'No law against it, Chas. You be partial. Just keep this nice and friendly, eh? The press have ears, and they'd love to see a rift in the camp.'

Charlie smiled his most meaningless smile.

'Let's give 'em something to headline that might sell more tickets. The promotors having an up-and-downer with our American chums as seconds, and Mr Tatum there acting as referee. Yeah, you give me the finger and wobble your chins, and I give you a poke in the cigar. Whaddaya say, partner?'

505

'Kid, kid, kid,' August eased a long cigar between his lips. Moistened his mouth with a coated tongue and tried a sick parody of a smile.

'Say,' said Gardenia, 'some clowning like that could make the evening specials here. Might even get it on the wires to New York.'

'Forget it, Doll,' Domino grunted. 'We're already sell-out. Who needs birdsville looney tunes? Right, Casey?'

'All locked in,' Pollard agreed.

Charlie stared over his boring drink.

'A closed book already? You Yanks work well different from the Smoke bookies. Ain't a single track or horse parlour at home I can't get a late bet down – right up to starter's orders. Where d'your punters go for a bet on the tapes – Wall Street?'

Domino's Latin complexion burned dark plum.

'Is this guy for real, August? Now we know why you kept him outta our hair. You, Dance, we're talking a sell-out on the seat's for the fight, not flying bets. You wanna flap something more than your smart mouth, get it said up front. Me and Casey here'll be glad to see the colour of your dough.'

'Money's honey,' Pollard said. 'You got – we want.'

Charlie showed pained surprise.

'Got it well wrong, did I? Didn't mean to hit no nerves.'

'What a kidder,' said August.

Domino goaded Charlie with, 'You gotta couple of hot bucks, Dance?'

Charlie winked at Tatum and flagged the barman.

'Wouldn't waste your time with my small stuff. Let me buy you fellows a drink and forget it.'

'Ain't a bet too big, or a wager too small,' Domino said around a fresh Camel.

Charlie asked August the current odds.

Eh? Oh, evens on Sugar Boy. 3-1 on Trooper Wells.'

'Tight book,' Charlie ordered drinks and left himself out of the round. 'The locals are betting combinations across the board. Love a crazy bet, the Chinese.'

'And you?' Gardenia asked, tasting a whisky sour.

'Depends what's offered, Doll.'

'Intrigue us with a suggestion.'

Charlie paid the barman and looked thoughtful.

'How about no bout on the card goes the distance? Give me odds of 5-1 on that, and I'll lay out $100 Hong Kong for openers. Too small for you?'

'Covered,' Domino snapped.

'That's cash, right?' Charlie handed a new banknote across.

'Cash,' Domino agreed. Crumpled it in a fist.

'And let's say Trooper Wells wins inside the distance for something bigger. Two-fifty. No offence, Mr Tatum.'

'It's your money, Mr Dance.'

'That's sterling,' Charlie told Domino and Pollard.

'Two hundred and fifty sterling. Covered.'

'Yards,' said Charlie.

'Say what?' Gardenia's jowls and drink shook.

Charlie looked around the circle of meaty faces.

'You do say "yards" for thousands, right? That's two hundred and fifty thousand pounds on Trooper to win inside ten rounds. At 3-1.'

Tatum looked at Charlie as if they had been thrown into the ring together for a catchweight five rounder. Bared teeth and gum in a biting grin. Swayed on the balls of his feet as the ferry cut the wash of an outgoing liner. Said, 'Half a million dollars? Hoo-eee!'

'Quit the kidding, Chas,' August turned grey and flaccid around the mouth.

'You ever know me to kid on a bet, Chappie?'

August swallowed air with what he might have said. Muttered, 'No', very quietly.

'Half a mill in cash?' Gardenia laughed. 'Come *on*!'

'Too big?' Charlie asked. Sipped tasteless ginger ale like peaty Irish whiskey.

507

Domino seemed to have too much neck for his tight collar. Pollard calculated odds with a distant expression, and Gardenia scowled at August as if betrayed by a fat mouse with a rat's appetite.

'What's going on here?' he asked.

'That's me in the resin box with more than my shoes squeaking,' August said. Ashen. 'Come *on*, Chas. That's more than the whole stable's worth if we sold our boys off as prime steak. This ain't the Gardens in New York. This is here. Now.'

'Going somewhere, Chappie?'

'Out of my tiny mind, is all.'

'Mind if I watch?' Charlie asked.

'Kidder,' August mourned. 'This ain't nothing to do with me, fellahs. Straight up it ain't.'

'Dance is your partner, pal,' Domino growled at August. 'And here he is squirting cider in my ear from a sealed deck of bicycles. Like it I don't.'

August protested with, 'You think I ain't surprised? Look at me, I'm on my back.'

'OK, Dance,' Domino said. 'What's the gag?'

'Chappie does the gags, Carmine. You want the bet or not?'

'I want answers. We all do. A straight deal turns into a war? Where are you mothers coming from?' Domino's flush was an unhealthy mottled plum. 'You start talking Fort Knox right here inna middle of the ocean, when the deal is set? Sewn up tighter than a Don's mouth?'

'What deal would that be, Domino?' Charlie asked.

'Ask your goddamned partner there.'

'So, I'm asking. Well, Chappie?'

'Ain't just this boat you're rocking, Chas,' August bleated. 'It's the whole Pacific Fleet. This is business. Business, not just playing promoters in this stupid armpit of Empire. There's stuff I can't spell out here. Not now. And after this, maybe never.'

'You can count on that,' said Gardenia. Close to spitting.

'Uhuh,' said Pollard.

Domino just knuckled his mouth and looked mean.

Charlie's hard smile was a fissure in stone before it faded.

'Yeah,' he said. 'There had to be something sweet between you three beauties and the fat man with the green cigar. A nice little deal that leaves me out inna cold with nothing but my toes to count. I talk money, and you all bellyache like I nicked the milk you birds had your beaks in. Like this boxing tournament is just a taster for some great event stupid Charlie knows nothing about. Like this is the start of the yellow brick road you guys are gonna dance Sugar Boy Tatum down. Not to Oz, no. But to the build up to the bigger money. The chance of a shot at a bigger title, maybe even the title itself. Greasing here, greasing there, then the fat shot at Madison Square Gardens.'

'You fishing or turding?' Domino said through white knuckles pressed to his upper lip.

'Not here, Carmine,' August pleaded. 'Please, Chas?'

Charlie ignored him. Turned to Tatum.

'Whatever they sold you, son, check the warranty for rust.'

Tatum nodded. Looked thoughtful.

'Never hurt to listen, Mr Dance,' he said.

'You're making a big mistake, Sugar,' Gardenia said. 'This guy's nothing. A cheap hoodlum. A nebish. Only thing cheaper than his mouth is his suit.'

'You through?' Charlie said.

'One of us is, Dance. One of us is . . .'

Charlie put his drink aside. Snapped fingers to bring Matt and Froggy out of the crowd. Stood easily until Pimlico handed him a leather suitcase and a thick manilla envelope. Laid the suitcase on the bar and slapped the manilla against August's chest.

'That's your future in there, Chappie. As of right now, all you own of August Enterprises are the debts. Seems the

509

expenses of this baby tournament came out of your share of the profits. And once you've paid off the local tongs, ain't a bean left for you. See, I've lodged Troop's end of the purse with the bank. Comes out at a round sixty grand. You owed him forty yards from past naughties, and I've had to clear the decks to stay kosher with the Inland Revenue. The same goes for Mr Tatum's dough. You want your percentage, Gardenia, you get Sugar Boy to write you a cheque.'

Domino was beyond bluster. Pollard said nothing, and Gardenia was seeing Charlie for the first time. August was stunned and speechless. The bemused Tatum was the only one with a healthy colour.

'Only thing I'm buying from you tonight, Mr Tatum,' Charlie said, 'is for you to fight your way and not their's. If Gardenia don't want your management no more, have him give me a price I can live with. Your choice.'

'Not so fast,' Gardenia said. 'He's tied to me womb to tomb. An unbreakable contract. Forget it.'

Charlie looked sleepy. Shrugged.

'Come off it, Gardenia. We ain't talking principle, we're talking money. And don't you like the long green, eh? Ain't no new thing to find a good young fighter and bring him on too fast. Hype him to the public and put him up against a real champion before he's ready. That's about when the fighter wakes up to find out it's all over. He's finished and usually broke. Owes Uncle Sam what he can't pay. You people have run with the big bucks to pastures new, and he's left to shine shoes or sell pencils. Just another Bowery bum left to rot whilst you people find yourself another tasty hopeful and do it all over again. Like Chappie said, it's business.'

'Morals from an alley cat? Shoot,' Gardenia said with disgust.

Charlie singled him out with a steady finger.

'You mentioned ironclad contracts. Read the bastards. You deal with this kiddy from here on in, not the green

510

cigar. It's all there in the fine print. You and me, womb to tomb, like you said.'

'We'll take that under advisement,' Domino muttered.

'The silent partners ain't so silent, eh? Where you going, Chappie?'

'Air . . . need air . . .'

'And a nice pressurised seat to foreign parts? Leave others to clean up your mess? Not this time. Stay with Chappie, Matt. See he don't fall overboard or nothing. Want that cigar at the ringside for the cameras tonight. And after, Chappie gets to go over the gate receipts with some unsmiling Chinese gentlemen who want their dues. Ain't all beer and skittles being a promoter.'

'It don't end here, Dance,' Domino promised, his colour bad.

'That gets it said, Carmine. We just got married, too soon for divorce, right?'

Domino made fists and looked down at them.

'Madison Square Gardens ain't this Chink fairyland, Dance,' he said. 'We'll own the fiddler at that barndance. You hearing this?'

'Big talk for a man who wouldn't cover my modest wager.'

'That was just talk,' Pollard threw in.

'Mine or your's?'

'Who carries that kind of money around?'

'Show him, Pim,' Charlie said.

Pimlico shouldered into the bar and opened the leather case. Left the lid up and stood aside. The mint notes were as green as the sea rolling past the portholes, and light refracted from the hissing wake danced in the drinks on the bar.

'Well?' Charlie said. Waiting.

'Holy Mother of God,' Gardenia said. 'The fucking fruitcake's loaded for bear.'

'Covered,' said Domino, hating Charlie with his eyes.

511

'Carmine?' said Pollard. 'You know what you're doing here?'

'You wanna walk away, Casey? Walk!'

'Covered,' Pollard choked.

Charlie smiled coldly at Tatum.

'Seems they believe in you, son,' he said.

'Or something,' Tatum said with a thick tongue.

Charlie told Pim to get a receipt and went on deck to watch the ferry dock. Humming.

A light breeze cracked the lines of washing into dance on the roof of the tenement block where Cho Sun squatted behind his bow. Lashed off to a tripod and the parapet, it was as secure as he could make it. The Victoria arena spread out below his vantage point, and the scurrying workmen were dark ants in the afternoon sunlight, too far off to have individual features. The VIP stand could be cupped in his two palms, and the blue and gold seats wavered in heat haze. An accurate double-shot would be difficult in daylight, and virtually impossible at night, even with the aid of powerful floodlights. And firing arrows with poisoned trident heads over such a distance had only ever been attempted in practice, never for a professional kill. Cho Sun needed markers to zero in on, and he patiently waited for his nephews to supply them.

Cho Sun had spent the night in contemplation of his dilemma, struggling between opposing loyalties. As the Named Heir of the Sichuen Dragon he was obliged to discharge his adopted father's will before ascending the throne, and paramount were the most solemn debts of honour. The order to assassinate Dance and Fook had not been rescinded, and as the Chosen Son of the Dragon Throne, Cho Sun's personal loyalties were now of secondary importance. He must make the double kill and expunge all personal guilt through prayer and purification. The road had been chosen for him, and he must follow it.

512

Cho Sun came alert and shaded his eyes. Two pinpoints of light glittered in the VIP stand, shards of mirrored glass catching the sun to mark the seats Dance and the Supreme Snake would occupy.

Cho Sun aligned his crossbow and marked off the two points on the ivory radius in the bow's shank. Calculated for elevation and windage, and marked the deviation on the beaded plumbline hanging from the tripod. The lights winked out, and Cho Sun made precise scratches in the concrete to mark the position of the tripod before breaking it down. He would erect the weapon again when the time came. Until then he would sleep. Nobody would notice another derelict taking his rest where he could.

A defiant Chappie August found Charlie on the podium where Pathé, Movietone and Gaumont-British were setting up their cameras. August waved a seating plan and gobbled furious filth until Froggy and Matt got him into an armlock. He hacked at ankles, missed his footing, and went down on his face to break his cigar against the turf. A stills cameraman took a flash picture with his Speed Graphic, and August would have gone for him if he'd had the wind and the use of his pinioned arms. Hauled to his feet and held, August spat the mashed cigar out with a fresh stream of oaths. His face was a livid crimson, and there were green roundels of chlorophyll on the knees of his light grey suit.

Charlie whispered, and the photographer opened his camera to ruin the exposure, preferring the chance of the big exclusive Charlie had hinted at. The photographer wandered off, and Charlie asked August what had got up his silly nose.

'The press wants a story. I'll give the bastards a story,' August raved. 'How you've fucked me in New York. How you've nicked my firm out from under me without a sou to my name. How my good name of thirty years standing has been swiped by a greedy overcoat. They'll fucking love printing that. Make bloody headlines from Fleet Street to Honolulu, that.'

'That it?'

'Only bloody starters. Tip of the ice-bloody-berg!'

'Then get it said.'

'You may be a lot of clever things, Charlie Dance, but an Archie Ogle you ain't never gonna be. He *knew* men did Archie. He never took *everything* from a man. Always left him *something*. His bit of pride and *somewhere* to go. I'm still Chappie August, mister. Not some nebish face. I got a public image, and whadda *you* do to Chappie August? Shove me down in the orchestra stalls. Not even at ringside, when I should be kinging it inna VIP stand with the bloody toffs. Where I bleeding belong. I've shook hands with royalty, cunt. With lords and ladies and bloody barons. I know the form with those jumped-up monkeys, right? And you've tucked me up right outta the limelight. Well, fuck you, Charlie Dance. Fuck you *and* the rickshaw you rode in on. I ain²t standing for it.'

'I can see how you wouldn't.'

'Don't soft-soap my corns, I—'

'Nobody's arguing, Chappie.'

'Flannel.'

'It's yours, right? You wanna handshake the lahdies, go for it. Do the honours, I don't want none of it. Never did.'

'That's butter on parsnips − what?'

'You want my seat, have it. Have another one for your cigar, I don't give a monkey's.'

'You, you . . . You mean it?'

'He means it,' Matt said, applying pressure.

'Yeah,' Froggy said, applying more. 'Listen to the man.'

'It's your show, Chappie. Make what you want of it. I'm here to see the fights, is all. Have your press conference, I should care less.'

'But I thought . . .'

'Let him go, chaps. He's a busy man.'

August staggered and winced. Circled an arm. Straightened.

'I don't get it,' he said.

'You front, I'll do the business, right?'

'But New York, what about New York?'

'They've got four months to calm down. That's if they can cover my bet. They don't, and I win, different story, ain't it?'

August nodded dumbly. Asked, 'I'm still on the firm?'

'So long as you earn your corn you'll get wages, yeah.'

'But, Chas, I thought . . .'

'Your mouth moved with your brain in neutral. Flap your tongue at me again, and you'll be another Joe Yellow.'

'Who?'

'Do something about yourself if you don't wanna scare crows away from the governor. A change of suit and a fresh cigar should do it. Teddah, Chappie.'

'Yeah,' August went away talking to himself.

'That's him finger-tamed,' Froggy said.

Charlie nodded vaguely. Watched two lights wink from the centre of the VIP stand. Followed their probable line of sight and stared up at the three four-storey buildings overlooking the arena. Picked the most likely roof to see twin reflections on the parapet. Looked back to where Margot and the designer gossiped over laced coffees. The lights had gone, but he knew which seats they had shone from. He thought of calling August back, of warning Margot. Picked up the crumpled seating plan August had dropped to check out what he was already half-certain of. Confirmed it and stared into space. Heard the voice of the Sichuen Dragon naming Cho Sun as his heir.

'And all bets are off,' he said. 'New runners and riders.'

'You all right, Chas? Gone a funny old colour.'

'Oh blimey yeah,' said Charlie.

His stomach suddenly liquid.

CHAPTER EIGHTEEN

Flashbulbs exploded like manic glow worms as the Governor of Hong Kong and Lady Grant took their places in the VIP stand to polite Chinese applause. Chappie August presented a huge bouquet to her ladyship with his green cigar in place, and everybody but Aman Lee Fook stood for the National Anthem played by the massed regimental bands. Climbing to his seat had been an ordeal for Fook, and he was glad to let the pain show when the main lights dimmed and darkness became his friend. Wind had a phial of liquid opiate should he need it, and he stayed her hands with a squeeze of his own, unwilling to cloud his senses with drugs.

The boxing ring grew into a bright square as six spot-lighted buglers played a fanfare, and the MC announced the first bout. The capacity crowd roared as the flyweights entered the ring with their seconds and the referee, and a kind of hush fell when the bell rang for the start of round one.

In his dressing room under the western stand, Trooper Wells read well-wishers' telegrams to Hettie whilst Cyril loosened the fighter's knotted back muscles; and down the hall, Sugar Boy Tatum emptied his mind of discord as he was oiled and pummelled by his personal masseur. Both men readying themselves in their own way for what they knew to be the most important bout of their lives to date. For Tatum, it was a passport to bigger things; to Wells, it was the final farewell to the sport that had made him the most popular boxer in post-war Britain.

Barred from Tatum's dressing room by the temperamental boxer, Doll Gardenia kept company with large whisky sours in the Directors' Bar, and toyed with baseball park figures for his piece of Tatum's contract. There were plenty of hungry South Americans Gardenia could buy with Dance's money; hard young Hispanics with no more ambition than to fight their way out of the poverty of the California pea fields.

Down at ringside, Carmine Domino and Clay Pollard took late bets from their Las Vegas party without need of a written book, laying-off skilfully with the local Chinese to balance out their massive wager with Charlie Dance. Breaking even was the name of their game, and at the back of their minds was the sweet revenge they would work at Madison Square Gardens when the time came. On their home turf. In New York. Even Stephen in the Big Apple. Working hard, they sweated on a shortfall of $300,000 that could only become clear profit if Wells hit the canvas and Tatum's glove was raised. If nervous laughs and perspiration were big bucks, they were already millionaires when the British flyweight went down to a left hook in the third round.

In the control booth behind the scoreboard at the eastern end of the arena, Vinnie Castle sat with the chief electrician, Chou Wing Ping. Connected by telephone to both ringside and the boxers' dressing rooms, Vinnie and Mr Ping could control the arena lighting with split-second timing. An assistant worked the spot that tracked with the boxers emerging from the western tunnel, and the spot could be swivelled to light any point of the arena should it become necessary. From the little Charlie had told him, Vinnie knew it would, and he had practised assiduously most of the evening, ready to elbow the assistant aside if Charlie's call came. Nothing would happen before the interval, and Vinnie tried to enjoy the tournament, one eye on the big electric clock above the control panel.

Margot sat rigidly between Fook and August, and thought of a thousand delicious ways to wither their vines as she leaned forward now and then to amuse Lady Grant with mild anecdotes about the British boxers on the bill. Charlie had told Margot about the change in seating plan just as the Governor and Lady Grant reached the receiving line, and left Margot to it. Patted her rump like a prize mare and wandered off to exchange chill pleasantries with Fook before quite disappearing. Furious and sick with worry, Margot kept her resentment alive so as not to think about what Charlie was up to.

Margot despised August's brashness. Hated Fook's patrician coldness, and wished she had two hatpins. One to deflate August, and a poisoned one to pay Fook out for Sam the Spade. Oh, Charlie hadn't spelled it out in so many words, but he had the knack of not saying things with a grunt and a sleepy look. Even an occasional 'Oh blimey yeah' covered myriad subtleties she had now learned to decipher.

A featherweight contest ended in a points win for the British boy, and Margot busied herself with telling Lady Grant about the lightweight entering the ring for the third bout before August could get a word in. When Margot put her mind to it, she could cut out any social misfit with the skill of a surgeon. August had the face of a diseased polyp anyway, and she killed his conversation with a light barrage of upper class repartee.

August fumed and Fook fought pain, and the lightweight contest ended in the sixth with a cut eye for the American.

Matt and Froggy found the men they were looking for in the north stand at the start of the fourth bout. Froggy planted a watch on one, and Pimlico's wallet on the second as Matt did the bump and apology bit. When the two men were certain Charlie was not in the VIP stand with Fook, they started for the nearest exit where Pimlico chatted with three policemen. Pimlico took the cue from Froggy, and had the two men stopped and searched for his stolen property. To the men's surprise, the items turned up in their pockets, and after a brief struggle at the turnstiles, Cho Sun's nephews were arrested thirty yards from their laundry truck. Pimlico went to the police station to prefer charges, and Matt and Froggy reported to Charlie at ringside before resuming their search for Joe Yellow.

Charlie told them they'd done well. Palmed Matt's revolver, and sent Ollie to get the best odds he could on Tony Stepney winning the middleweight contest inside the distance. Saw him get 2-1 from a Chinese bookie with silver teeth, and sat back to fidget through the bout. Heady and tense, he could have killed for a cigarette and a fair swallow of Irish. Might well have done if they'd been offered.

The American fighter was a hard puncher who only knew how to go forward to trade punishment, and Charlie was glad to see that Tony Stepney boxed clever for two rounds, letting his opponent come to him. In the third, he opened up a little, and had the crowd on its feet with rapid combinations that confused without rocking. Scoring points without lathering himself or mixing it. The fourth saw the American make his power play of crowding and leaning to swamp Stepney's nicer ringcraft. Brawling tenacity pinned Stepney in the corner twice before he regained the centre to dance in. The bell saved the American from a complete loss of temper, and he came out for the fifth with blood in his eye.

Stepney traded body blows and grinding heads for the opening seconds, then stood off to speed-deliver stinging lefts to the temple and nose. Never there when the counters came bludgeoning in, a foil darting at a cudgel. A milling right caught Stepney on the bell, and he spat blood out with his gumshield back in his corner. Charlie was reminded of Stepney's last fight at the Albert Hall, and he hoped the boy would keep his distance to pick his man off. Ollie was of the same mind, and Charlie let him do the shouting for

519

both of them through the sixth, a round that coasted without spark.

In the seventh, Stepney let himself get crowded into the red corner, and took some mauling to the body before he eeled away. He caught the American with a sweet cross that showered sweat and spit over the ropes, weaved away from a brawling counter attack, and picked his man off with straight lefts and crossing rights that slammed his opponent back on his heels. A last hook travelled five inches at most. The American went down in a heap to foul Stepney's legs, stumbling Stepney forward to burn himself on the ropes. Thinking on his feet, Stepney got to a neutral corner, and the referee was at the count of nine before the American bulled to his feet to be saved by the bell.

Charlie went through his pockets for cigarettes. Found his hand around the gun and forced his fingers into a cat's-cradle. Locked his knuckles together and laced his hands around a raised knee to watch Domino and Pollard work the Las Vegas crowd like the experts they were.

Time crawled like a paraplegic with broken fingers until the bell for the eighth.

There was some holding, boring and crude punching in the clinches. The referee parted the boxers three times, was coming in to do it again when it was suddenly over. The American was on his face with jerking legs, and Stepney was back in the same neutral corner. The referee got to ten and held up Stepney's arm. Unsighted, Ollie and Charlie had missed the punch that finished it. Ollie was yelling on his feet, and Charlie left him there, using the confused excitement to slip away.

Martial music crashed over the Tannoy as the main floods came on for the interval before the main bout, and Margot and August escorted the Governor and Lady Grant to the Directors' Bar. Fook stayed where he was, and watched Charlie climb the sloping aisle towards him. Waved off the

520

Killing Shadows he had stationed in the stands on either side, and blanked the pain from his face, glad that Wind had mopped his brow in the previous darkness.

'This European way of boxing is crude,' he said. 'But your last man fought well.'

'Could be we all do, when there's something to fight for.'

'There are always two meanings to your words, Char-lee. And now is no different. Let us hope the man Wells knows he has much to fight for.'

'He knows, Aman. And win or lose, he'll fight like a gentleman. The pity is, you and me don't have that choice.'

'A tiger without stripes is still a tiger.'

'All cats are grey in the dark, and young pearls lose their shine for old men with the lights out. You can wrap anything up in pretty words. Don't make the mouth that says them any cleaner.'

'Or the oyster a millionaire.'

'Oysters ain't men, don't know right from wrong, do they? You and me do. Or should. This ain't a good place for you to be, Aman. Walk away, and let what happens happen.'

'A threat?'

'Advice. From a friend,' Charlie's spine felt as wide as a highway billboard. As vulnerable as a snowdrop in a rockslide.

'You? A friend? Lie to yourself if you must. Do not lie to me.'

Charlie looked and felt bitter. He was talking to a closed mind with his back turned on an assassin's bullet.

And for what? he asked himself. *The stupid ideal of fair play? Who can afford that luxury dealing with a bastard who'd kill kids with poisoned white powder for profit?* 'The Judas goat traps the Judas goat,' he said.

'That is an admission of guilt? You want absolution?'

Charlie blinked a red mist away. Kept his hands in his pockets.

'No, just words, ain't they? Sounds. Meaningless mutter. That's all we've ever traded, you and me.'

'But there has been stimulation between us. And now all that can be learned, has been learned. Except for the final lesson that proves the inevitability of what must be. You will learn that last lesson tonight.'

'Yeah, the last brick in the wall. Teddah, Aman.'

Fook watched Charlie stroll away with placid objectivity. The contemplation of triumph had eased the pain to a background nag, and a lesser man would have been grateful.

Ollie was collecting from the Chinese bookie when Froggy came panting up looking for Charlie.

'You know Chas, Frog. He was here, then he wasn't.'

Froggy swore and cast around. Saw Charlie coming and plunged towards him. 'We got him surrounded, Chas. Me and Matt.'

'Who?'

'Joe thingy. The little yellow git with the pebble glasses. Had his binoculars on you and Fook in the VIP stand. Only stayed outta the way in the first half, didn't he? Locked himself in the men's lavs under the South Stand, right? But we had him spotted. I mean, nobody sits on the thunderbox through four bouts without dropping his trousers, right? We just left him there till he come out in the interval. Watching him clocking you through his bins, and followed him back to the same lav. He's in there now, with Matt on the door.'

'You left Matt there? Without a shooter?'

'Matt ain't no Tinkerbell. And this geezer ain't more'n five foot and a fag paper.'

Charlie was already striding away. Under the stand he broke into a run with Froggy working hard to keep up until they reached the toilet block. Apart from a group of soldiers making for one of the upper bars, the wide corridor was empty.

'Here? You left him here?'

'Right here. Maybe the little git went trotting, and Matt done a hotsmans after him.'

'Ain't likely, is it?'

'Matt ain't a runner, no.'

Charlie kicked the outer door open. Dived through on the swing into the hiss of automatic flushing. A Chinese at the long urinal buttoned up and left without washing his hands, and there were just tiles and cubicles and handbasins smelling of over-perfumed liquid soap. Charlie slammed cubicles open until he came to a locked one. Looked under the door to see Matt sprawled against the pan with a blue-black egg growing on his forehead. Splintered the lock and knelt to feel for a pulse. Found it bumping under the skin of a slack wrist.

'How, Chas? He didn't look to have the strength to punch porridge. Let alone have Matt over like bloody Humpty Dump—'

'Shut it! How short was this face?'

'Short. Your size without the legs. Wouldn't have come up to your dicky bow tie. More of a monkey than a man. Y'know, ugly.'

'Young?'

'Not young, Chas. Youngish. More your old but preserved.'

'Then Matt's lucky to be alive. Joe Yellow it wasn't.'

'Bloody who then? You didn't say to look for nobody else. Just them laundry boys and the little git with bottle-top bins.'

'I know it.'

'We inna deep shit, Chas?'

'Never deeper, Frog.'

Froggy cocked an ear. The fanfare for the big fight echoed down the tunnels and off the hard, tiled surfaces. The crowd sounded like a thudding sea.

'Who's loose out there, Chas? I mean, Troop's climbing inna ring right now. Is that who he's after?'

Charlie made sure Matt hadn't swallowed his tongue. Laid his head to one side to keep his throat open, stood and looked down at Froggy.

'Get the ambulance boys to Matt. That's first. Then get to Vinnie. The minute there's a knock-down or a decision in that ring, I want a spotlight on the roof of the middle building behind this South Stand. You got that?'

'For what? For why?'

'So I can wave to you, right?'

'Not without me and Pim behind you, you ain't.'

'You wanna sleep beside Matt?'

'First the ambulance, then Vinnie. You got it, Chas.'

'That's my Frog.'

'Yeah, that's me all right. Never the fucking prince . . .'

Trooper heard Cyril say it was time to go. Hettie pecked his cheek over her knitting, and Trooper started the long walk to the ring flanked by his seconds and Tommy Badell the trainer. Badell's talk was just buzz. A fanfare fluttered brass wings in the concrete tunnel with the bass roar of the crowd, and pushing through the security cordon into the open arena was like emerging into a wild carnival. His back was slapped, hot faces wished him luck. The lucky red silk dressing gown was the teasing skin of a woman against his flexing muscles, and lazy worms of heat writhed in his testicles. The boardwalk was springy underfoot, and the ring came up as a floodlit raft in a black sea of sound.

He was through the ropes and raising his arms to the unseen crowd. Dancing to show off his Lonsdale belt. Showing his taped hands and the soles of his boots to the referee. Facing Tatum with the referee saying what referees always say. The gloves were on and snug over the bandages, and he pulled on the corner ropes until the bell turned him for his last professional fight.

Tatum was no longer a shadow he had watched on film. A target with his own peculiarities of style and defence. A long reach and a right that must be made to miss. This was the man himself, not some brown doll he had theorised about in training.

There was block and counter. Duck and weave and feint. Put out a jab to see the speed of reaction. The first impact of leather on rib. The first jolt of contact through the gloves. Making Tatum real, his punches more real. A scrappy showing of punch and counter-punch. Testing, probing, using the ring. Circle, attack. Stand toe to toe and break off. Give and take and measure, and the bell again.

Back in the corner with Tommy Badell giving out pithy analysis in abrupt cockney. Looking past Tommy at the brown man with the long reach and fast feet. The man himself, not the chemical robot the trainer saw. And being annoyed by the long-legged girls showing the round cards to the crowd and swaying around where he had to fight the good fight. All that dumb ballyhoo and balderdash before the gumshield was back in his mouth and he was back out there on the hard canvas, doing the business only he knew how to do. Him and Tatum alone, all the rest was shadow and noise. Forget the animal faces in the ringside seats, the glib mouths at the radio microphones, the cameras getting it all recorded on film as if Trooper Wells was already history. See only the man. Keep him off until all that jerky testing and mauling became fluid control.

Shape telling punches that score points. Show the clever brown boy what real combination punches mean inside the guard. Roll with his long rights and avoid grinding foreheads. Give him the clumsy shuffle and rock him with that sweet hook rising from the navel. Sting his nose and eyes with light left crosses to cover you putting a low shoulder behind a digging snap to the solar plexus. Feel the wall of muscle give. Get away from his long counter punches to where you *were*. Go in on his open right side and work on his ribs some more.

Then slam.

Stupid.

Take a good solid shot to the pectoral above the heart because you had it coming. A jolter to the gut that sings up into your ears. Smooth out of that stumble, champ you chump. Grin for air behind your gumshield and circle away on the balls of your feet as if there ain't no more than a ton of lead in your calves. Cover and counter and get them lungs working smooth.

Another bell already, and dropping your arms like anchors. Let them see you're tired and maybe wonder if you ain't acting. Keep them guessing. Walk to the stool and slump for water and towelling and the words of Tommy Badell. Him knowing the good and the bad, knowing the mistakes you made without feeling the hurt they caused. Breathe deep and forget the bloody swaying hips and nipples thumbing silk from heavy jiggles of ripeness. Forget how you could do both them girls some wicked damage if you wasn't so busy right now.

There were flaws in Tatum's defence. In your own, as always. He knew you knew about his, and you know he's got yours sussed. Just don't let him work you a sucker punch because you're slow getting off from working in close. He can punch, that boy, and he's clean on the breaks. Watch his head, though. He drops it with his chin and bores with it in the clinches. Got to watch that like Tommy Badell's saying. *Was* saying, because the bell has ducked him out of the ring. Now there's just you and Sugar Boy Tatum for the third round.

Move it, Trooper my son. Go to work . . .

Charlie left the arena by the south gate and found himself in a tree-lined avenue, blocked at either end by police detour signs. The Tannoys overlapped out of phase, turning the MC's amplified bawl into any language but English. Charlie climbed a railed wall and dropped into a small public garden where the trees baffled the noise. Walked across grass to the side of the first four-storey building fronting the avenue. The lit and empty offices sold marine insurance during the day, and the rear of the building had meaner windows and a steel security door fitted with automatic alarms. Charlie found a basement door on a corner. Leaned in to make it yaw sluggishly open, fighting a stiff self-closer. Pushed it wide to look down rough cement stairs. Heard the chatter of night cleaners going to work. Women's voices cut off by a closing elevator door. No shadows moving in the passage below. No sound, no movement.

Charlie went swiftly down the stairs. Turned a sharp corner and traded blank stares with a man in a glass cubicle. He had a sandwich up to his mouth, and his security cap was on a hook behind his head. Keys and a whistle lay on his desk, and he reached for an alarm bell on the wall as Charlie drove a hard one to the point of his chin. The man rolled his eyes, sank low in his chair and let his arm drop. The sandwich fell apart beside the keys, and Charlie jammed the cap over the blank face. Hoped he was the kind of Chinese who thought all long-noses looked the same, and left him there.

Charlie took the keys and let himself through a security door to the emergency stairs. Climbed fast, listening hard. Heard nothing but vacuums, female chatter and Chinese music on portable radios. Reached the upper door, banged the bar open and stepped out onto a flat roof. Let the door close to without locking itself.

Probed the night for another presence and felt nothing.

Mistrusted his senses and was assaulted by a wall of sound rising from the arena. Made a crouching run to the front of the building and looked over the parapet. The boxing ring was a bright square in an oval of monochrome. Two manikins fought it out toe to toe until a third manikin separated them. The ringside seats showed as dark shapes against thin red veins of carpet nailed to boardwalks. Cigarettes twinkled here and there in the tiered seats, and the VIP stand was a hard slab of darkness. Charlie tried to feel nothing for the people sitting there. Tore his eyes from the ring at the end of the second round and put his mind to the business in hand. He worked around the parapet to peer over at the roof of the adjacent building.

Apart from the loom of an elevator housing, the roof was as flat as the one Charlie kneeled on. There was no light to show him any details, and a regiment of Scots Guards could have been bivouaced there for all he knew. The gap between the buildings was a good fourteen feet wide, and the drop to the street was sheer. An Olympic champion might have jumped it, but not Charlie Dance. The police cars parked below were die-cast toys, and looking down gave him vertigo.

'You ain't ahead of the game on this one,' he told himself. 'Old Cho Sun's holding all the aces and holdout cards. What to do, Charlie son? Go back down to the street – see if you can find a way into that block from the street? Even if you did, that clever bastard would've made damned sure getting up there was no doddle.'

Thinking of man-traps and other delights, Charlie explored the roof of the insurance building, and barked his shin against a dark loom of fretted metal. Risked putting a penlight on it, and grinned. Blessed the good old insurance boys for foresight. Thinking of fire hazards or earthquakes, they had installed an extending fire ladder. All he had to do was wind it out to its fullest extent, and it would run across the fourteen foot gap and reach the opposite roof.

'Who says there ain't a God?'

Charlie set to work sorting out the mechanics. Too dry-mouthed to hum. One clank of metal and he'd be walking into the spider's parlour. The bell for round four brought an animal roar from the arena.

'Make this your round, Sugar,' a Las Vegan yelled.

You got it, brother.

Tatum danced out to meet Wells. Let him bore right in with that odd styless style. Smothered hooking body blows with a smooth grapple. Pushed him off before a clinch. Drove a glove square to the heart, ducked a returning feint and blocked a headshot with a shoulder. Felt the heat of impact in the bunched deltoid, knowing it would have turned his head around if it had hit the button. The man was strong and resilient. Had years of craft in his head, but he could be worn down and beaten. The man was thirty-six fighting twenty-six. And the game old dude wore that extra decade like a shroud.

Dance, Sugar, be a phantom. Watching that sidling attack of his. The way he got in under your guard with that crabbing shuffle. How he went under your longer reach for punishing close-work with you still hitting air. Punch and go past the mother. Have him off-balance and sorting his feet out. Swing and pivot. Pop him as he goes past. Slam that jaw without making it a rabbit-punch to the neck.

Clean, Sugar, clean.

Turn again and drive a heavy one. Feel it go home with all your weight behind it. Hook one to the ribcage. Make his legs tire as he works hard to refill his lungs. Another loop to the head to make him bob aside with his chin way out. Duck him onto this rising whistler. Slam. Feel cartilage give as you spread his nose with a mother of a cross. Nail another to his mouth. Spread his busted lips away from his gumshield. Watch him go down like a gutshot bull. Less than a minute into round four and there he is kneeling on canvas. Looking around like he missed the Greyhound to the big bucks.

Get to the neutral corner for the count.

Hear the Las Vegans yell numbers with each drop of the ref's arm. Count yourself. Five and six and seven and . . . shit! The mother's up! Counting off the ref's fingers and telling his name and address. Woozy, yeah, but not out yet. Taking a compulsory standing count with eyes like haunted puddles of mud. You've hurt him deep, Sugar, but do you move in and go for a fast finish? Risk him getting in a lucky pop? No, smooth as cream, boy. Outbox him to take the round and take the hard shot if it feels right. Move to the centre on the referee's signal.

Go to work, Sugar, go to work . . .

Margot stood when Trooper went down. Forgot she was a lady who never made noises like that in public. Or in private, for that matter. Smoothed her face and skirt and sat sedately. Stole a glance at August to see if he leered at her loss of dignity. Saw that he hadn't eyes for her. He was glued to the ring with a foul smirk of unholy satisfaction on his pulpy face. Eyes as pink as a farrowing sow's, he enjoyed seeing Trooper down. Jerking her head aside, Margot saw that Fook had a similar expression on his sweating yellow face. Realised she was sandwiched by polarised hatred.

Lady Grant's coo of surprise was hardly genteel.

'How magnificent! He's up, my dear. He's up!'

The Governor drily admitted he had noticed, and Chappie was bolt upright in his seat.

'Nervous, Mr August?' Margot asked sweetly.

'Of . . . *what*?'

August swabbed his face. Lost his handkerchief like a guilty secret, murdering Margot with a sideways glance.

'Why, of losing if Mr Wells doesn't, of course. Avarice before loyalty. All those hot little pennies you want to make into pounds.'

August's whisper was bronchial with fury.

'Keep your snotty snout outta my truffles, lady.'

'Gladly,' Margot purred. 'How *awful* it must be to be *you*.'

'You pretentious mare. If I was Charlie . . .'

'The man and not his breakfast? Not this time around on the wheel of Nirvana, you cuckoo.'

'Laugh, you bitch. The night's only half over . . .'

August choked on phlegm and shut his mouth. Watched Trooper survive any way he could until the bell sent him back to his corner. It was going to be a long night for everybody, not just Chappie August. For bastard Charlie. For that ungrateful traitor Wells. For the bitching bitch he sat beside.

Every bastard had his day. And Chappie August would have his.

Working in the dark had been painfully slow, even with the tiny penlight between his teeth. Some security-conscious clown had fitted a retaining chain to the drive wheel that kept the drive ratchet from engaging the gearing mechanism. A typical example of the bureaucratic mind: supply one escape device and lock it against misuse by unauthorised personnel. Minutes were lost until Charlie found the right keys on the security man's ring. Released the locking cotter pin and drew the chain out of its housing a link at a time, wondering how hysterical secretaries would have coped with fire singeing their corsets.

Wouldn't have, would they? Was this the third or fourth round coming up?

Charlie decided it was later than he thought, erring on the side of caution. Heard the distant timekeeper's bell cause a roaring upswell of anticipation, and slammed the motor into drive. The leading edge of the extending ladder crept out into space in jerking inches. Clanked like shunting rolling stock, the electric motor humming and adenoidal. The forward motion became a regular creep, and feet became yards.

His nerves screaming, Charlie locked the lever off and swung over the rail onto the frail bridge. Thought it better to meet Cho Sun midway than sit on his thumbs.

'What's the round? Who's the Queen of England? What's Hettie knitting?'

Tommy Baddell's educated fingers reset dislodged cartilage so Trooper could breathe through one nostril. Forced packing up into the right side of Trooper's nose. Made him breathe over a bottle of pungent salts and numbed his mashed nose with novocaine. Dabbed coagulant on his split lower lip. All the time talking, talking . . .

'Fifth round. Elizabeth. A cardigan.'

'Good, Champ, handsome. Box him so he comes to you. Save your legs. Get your head into his chest and cannonball him. Take his wind.'

Trooper inflated and deflated his chest. The laughs were over, and he had to reach deep in the barrel for reserves he'd never needed before. Tatum was the target, but Chappie August was the enemy. That sly bastard had worked a real flanker. This Tatum was lightning on a stick. Not the eager kid August had promoted to Trooper as a tasty crowd-pleaser. He was class with reach and style and stamina. He was three Congo Billy Devons. A bloody octopus with four pairs of gloves, a punch in every one. Could punch right or left hand. No one-armed tanker him. There were rough edges, sure, but this ain't ten years ago when I could have sponged up his good hits and punched out his lights with a smile. Laugh at the bruises on my hide and have a knees-up at the party after the knockdown as fresh as a morning daisy. Give my Het a seeing-to in bed with the dawn coming up at the window . . .

'Get that stuff outta my nose, Tommy.'

'But Champ—'

'What are we, fairground three-rounders? Out.'

''Kay, Troop. But box clever, eh? He's . . .'

Trooper was already off his stool and angling off to show Tatum his right side. Chin in, and his left arm down. Snuffing up the blood and tasting salt as he swallowed what seemed like gallons of the stuff. Pasted August's shitty face over Tatum's clean features. Gave Tatum the gumshield grin of a hurt man to bring him on into the frail web of an old pro's deceit. Took two rockers on the forehead and gave ground like a tired man with nothing holding him up but dumb courage. A lace skated a sideburn in a close miss, and Trooper rolled into the ropes to cover. Headed the careless chin to jerk Tatum's head away. Dug some hard rights and lefts into an open midriff. Poked a short stinger to the angle of the brown jaw. Got Tatum turned to bounce on the ropes near the red corner and got the windmill going, taking wind from lung and stomach, hurting those long lateral muscles where good punches were born. Killing them in the cradle. Punching the money out of August's wallet. The smile from his flabby face. Doing the business on a better man . . .

Not better, younger.

Let Tatum get off the ropes and find himself some room. Follow him around like a hungry old dog. Take a breather yourself, you need it more than Tatum does. But he ain't got so many arms now. You cut off three or four of the murdering pistons.

Let Tatum come again. Keep that chin right in and let him skate punches off your head and shoulders. Absorb what he's handing out and keep him off your face. Take it on the gloves or let him hit air. Keep those tired old heels off the canvas for the old bob and weave. Draw him right on into a sizzler off the floor. Rock him and dance aside. Come at him from the left side and let that swing of his punch holes in the night. Bore in on his laterals. Bang out chords on his ribs like a pub piano. Keep in there and turn his torso to mush.

Hear the crowd change its tune as the old class came back for the swan song. Howling morons at a bear-bait. Fold Tatum up like a busted deckchair and lay him on the sand for the tide to wash away. Stand off and watch him trying hard to work out what planet he's on. Forget the bawlers outside the ropes. It's the quiet fans Trooper Wells fights for, for all the Charlies who know what it's really all about.

Measure him as he flails out at where you ought to be. Smack that jaw up at the stars and watch him keel all the way over to bang the canvas like a sleeping sentry.

Walk away to that safe neutral corner like it was all in a day's work. Think of that neat little blue bank book Charlie sent Hettie. All them sexy little zeroes behind that fat six. Pretend you don't need to lie down beside Tatum and let the ref hold your rubber arm up for the morons to scream at. Let Cyril carry you round the ring and get sweat all over his suit. Let it really be over so I can get back to Hettie and a shower. Pop a champagne cork with Charlie . . .

The ladder yawed under Charlie's weight. Sudden vertigo was a claw in his mind, a sick vacuum in his gut. The void came up at him as he lost balance, and the fretted metal plates under his feet were no more substantial than cheese holes in black paper. Jerked off his feet, there was air between all his fingers until he found the safety rail with a slapping palm. He hung on with the marrow draining from his legs, wryly telling himself that this was a fine time to find he had no head for heights. Made himself stand up to stop the damned ladder from grinding to a halt.

Opened his eyes to will the closing roof closer. Bit his tongue when the leading edge nudged concrete. Had his teeth set on edge when the whole ladder shuddered. Contact cut in a servo-motor, triggered a grapple, and turned a section of folding steps down to slot neatly over the parapet. Locked off the ladder and made it rigid.

Charlie took a step forward and wasn't plunged to the ground. Kept his eyes locked on the roof and stepped down onto the blessing of solid ground. Put a hand to the lovely brick of the elevator housing, and followed his fingers around the corner. Found himself facing the high glass pitch of a central skylight that he must scale to reach the other side of the flat roof. Stepped up onto the low sill and laid a ginger knee against a metal upright between dirty panes of wired glass. Felt it flex, and hurriedly spread his weight for the climb. Thought of falling through bayonets of shattered glass to hit concrete hardness at the bottom of a central stairwell. Crawled upward across strutting bars inch by inch until his leading hand hooked over the pitch. Hauled himself up to lay along the crest, and remembered to breathe for the first time this century.

Heard his heart pound hard enough to blow his earlobes off. Looked down at the unlit expanse of roof, the man and his archaic weapon outlined against the lights of Victoria. Saw him make final adjustments to the elevation of a curving bar on a heavy tripod. Fit a long-stemmed trident into the central channel of what had to be a crossbow. Saw the shoulders narrow as the chest snuggled into the stock. Shouted to break the bastard's concentration, to turn him away from the shot, unwilling to backshoot him.

Began the long slide down the far side of the skylight, his jacket rucking under his armpits. Felt his heels jar on the jutting concrete sill. Pitched forward, fighting his jacket to find Matt's revolver. Got it levelled and supported between both hands. Called Cho Sun by name. Earned silence as the bowstring hummed, flicking the trident away. Called louder as a second trident was fitted and the bow swung to a new setting.

Fired then. Put two shots into the base of the man's spine. Saw the head snap up and rear on a thin neck as the hips were driven forward against the parapet. The trident fired wild as the crossbow swung where it would. The hooded man wouldn't drop, had a gun in his left hand, and Charlie snapped a shot into the turning torso. Threw the man back across the parapet with his head turning to see where the punches came from. Fired on the run to pulp his hooded face. Put his last two rounds into the chest, hurling the body out into the dark beyond the roof. Trod on glass as he craned to see the body hit the road. Drew his foot back from

shattered lenses and two halves of a hornrimmed frame, and
saw Joe Yellow burst apart across the sprung bonnet of a
police car.

Stood there sapped of energy. Understood why the deaf
man hadn't heard his yells. Heard the crowd chanting
Trooper's name, and knew the fight had gone in his favour.
Knew he had somehow lost count of the rounds, and
knew without any shadow of a doubt that he had been
outmanoeuvred. Cho Sun must have signalled Joe Yellow's
shots from inside the arena. Assassinating Fook and Charlie
by remote control being his peculiar way of keeping faith
with a former friend whilst fulfilling his duty.

'A bloody fine distinction, Cho,' Charlie told the night.

The gun shook in his hand, and he reloaded it without
thinking. Dropped it into his pocket when a spotlight swept
the roof. Realised Froggy was only following orders, and
stood to show himself, gratified when the spot blinked off.
A crowd was gathering about the body, and the police were
taking an interest in the roof where Charlie stood. The
sooner he got away from there to lose himself in the crowds
leaving the arena, the better.

Moving was an effort. He went slowly back to the skylight
and started to climb. Hauled himself up the dusty glacier
as lights came on in the offices below. Slid down the far
side and wearily made his way around the elevator housing.

Stepping out onto the fire escape took all his waning will-
power, and he staggered along it like a three-bottle drunk.
There were shouts in the street, but he dared not look down
to see if he was the centre of attention. It was all so far away
and nothing to do with him. He had reached the middle
of the ladder when he was rocked off his feet. He fell badly
and numbed an elbow. Took skin off a knee and may have
banged his head. There was nausea and confusion and being
swung through space. Charlie held the rail with both hands
and tried to control his stomach. Knew the ladder had
somehow detached itself when he heard the servo-motor

536

whine. There was a sickening lurch when something banged down on the swinging end.

Charlie looked back along the ladder as it contracted towards him. Saw a small figure crouched there. Recognised Cho Sun, and forced himself upright.

Margot stood and cheered and waved her programme. Wished she had someone to kiss, no longer giving a hoot for what people thought. The Governor and Lady Grant had also risen to applaud Trooper Wells' gallantry, and Chappie August's swearing monotone as he stayed hunched in his seat was both silly and amusing. He could stew in Hades for all Margot cared, for Trooper had despatched Tatum like a gentleman. Without clumsiness or brutish fury. With perfect shots to the body and chin, and no sign of the mauling and sloppy ringcraft of the previous two rounds. Margot understood there really was an art to boxing now, and she planned to have Charlie take her to all the best tournaments from now on.

The vicious hum of a large insect brushed her hair, and Margot turned to glance at Fook. His lips parted for breath, he clutched at his chest and the feathered end of a thin wand. Looked with shock at something far beyond the floodlight gantries, beyond the veil of night itself. Said something that had his pretty escort starting from her chair to cover the arrow with her evening stole. She brought men in dark suits swarming from the tiered seats to surround Fook, gave Margot a warning look to remain silent, and went away as the men carried Fook from the stand. Jostled aside, Margot let her programme flutter to the ground. Saw the group turn into the tunnel and disappear unnoticed by anybody but her. The standing ovation for Trooper Wells was a great swell of noise that blanketed her shock. A spotlight swept the buildings overlooking the arena, and for a moment, a distant figure showed in the disc of glare. Made a cutting motion with both arms and winked out with the light.

The Tannoy played tinny elevator music as the crowd began to drift towards the exits. Margot found herself making small talk to the Governor and Lady Grant. Walked away with them through the tunnel to the Directors' Bar. Offered hospitality like an automaton and promised His Excellency he could congratulate Trooper in person. And all that time she knew it had been Charlie on that roof, Charlie on that roof . . .

Come back to me, Charlie . . .

Charlie talked and backed away. Saying anything to get a response.

'Where were you, Cho? Not in the arena, eh? On the floor below the roof? Watching the fight through binoculars?'

Cho Sun advanced slowly. Careful not to trap a foot between the closing floor plates. A silent wraith in black cotton.

Charlie fought fear with fear. Lumped vertigo and Cho Sun together to give his fear a single point of focus.

'Yeah, you just had to lean outta the window. Wave to poor old Joe, and have him do your dirty work for you. Keep my blood off your precious hands. Some Shadow Warrior you are. Getting the poor deaf bastard dead on account of you got squeamish.'

Cho Sun was in the air. Rose high in a forward roll. His leading foot drilled Charlie in the forehead. Slammed him onto his back. Sailed over the prone Charlie to land on the rail with balletic grace. Teetered there and stepped down, waiting for Charlie to be drawn towards him.

Charlie had two stomachs and three sets of eyes. Saw overlaps of everything through a crashing headache. Let his weak legs scrabble about as one arm hooked itself over the rail. Turned himself to face the multiple blur that was Cho Sun. Forced himself to laugh and point a shaking finger.

'You kill me, and we're both finished. Should have

consulted the stars before you tried this kill, my old cockalorum. You hear me?'

Cho Sun moved again. Drove Charlie's feet out from under him with a kick. Flipped over Charlie as he fell. Landed and flipped backwards. Back where he had been before with three light hops. Left Charlie to sort up from down, left from right. Watched him suck air like an asthmatic.

Charlie drooled puke. Felt for the revolver and found it had snagged in torn lining. Hadn't the strength or wit to draw it, and found that funny. Coughed and laughed and coughed some more. Heard himself goad Cho Sun with the reedy voice of a geriatric.

'You can't put things right now, can you? Me and Fook can't die together whatever you do. So finish it. Like a man. Don't peck me to death like a pissed-off sparrow. Look me inna face and do it. Or ain't you got the balls, you eunuch? Come on. Walk up and do it face to face. It's just you and me, right? Now you've run outta nephews.'

Charlie didn't see Cho Sun move. He just wasn't there any more. His chest ignited in a bloom of cold fire. His sight vapourised in a huge rosette of white lightning. There was blood in his throat. Too many teeth in his mouth to close around his swollen tongue. He was hurting meat hung out to dry over a thin metal rail, and the real world was a long way down. One smeary eye was still open, and several Cho Sun's flickered at the wrong end of a kaleidoscope. Coming for Charlie without a word. A short sword spinning patterns of light in his right hand.

'The death of a thousand cuts, eh, Cho? Better than the death of a thousand yawns. Come on, you woman. Don't get blood on your frock.'

The sword stopped its shining motion, and Cho Sun kissed the blade. Charlie felt the revolver jump in his hand. Blow a hole in his pocket. Heard the metallic wang of a ricochet as the bullet went through Cho Sun to scale paint from the rail behind him. Saw all the Cho Suns come together and stand still with the sword raised. Saw the man's eyes for the first time, and wondered why they had whites all around the pupils. Heard himself mumble nonsense about stars and inevitability as his finger depressed a tongue of metal inside torn material. Heard the bark of a night fox as it bit a hole in Cho Sun's chest. Saw bits of black cotton blow away from an exit wound. Saw Cho Sun stiffen and try to step back as a metal plate closed on an ankle, and kept closing with the sound of flesh compressing against bone. Saw the hood suck in against an opening mouth that remained silent.

Then Cho Sun pivoted on the trapped foot. Wrenched himself away, and one legging had a ragged end and no foot. The sword had gone away somewhere, and there was a foot in a soft shoe being mangled between metal plates. It made little sense to Charlie. Cho Sun was hopping away using the rail to support himself, and singing to himself as he sprinkled black blood as a trail for Charlie to follow.

Charlie got his legs moving. Fell over a coping and rolled on a roof, wanting Cho Sun to wait for him. Lay there until his body began to articulate, and followed the wet trail and the sound of chanting and dragging. Found Cho Sun talking to the night as he swayed on the rear parapet. Thought to make the man's end cleaner with a close shot, and watched Cho Sun dive away from him still singing. Heard the crash of glass somewhere below, and took his time finding the courage to lean over and look down. Saw a street and a broken canopy over the forecourt of what might have been a restaurant. Had no idea that Cho Sun had smashed down into a thirty foot aquarium to spread crimson streamers amongst darting fantails. Grinning his ugly grin at hysterical diners through a glass wall.

Charlie pushed himself away from the edge of the roof. Let his legs do their best with flights of stairs as cleaners gossiped and hummed along with their Hoovers and transistors. Pushed out into the wonders of ground-level living where men comforted women as they streamed from a building with a smashed canopy. Turned a couple of corners and walked against the tide of people leaving the arena. Loved them all in spite of being jostled. Loved being called a drunk by passing soldiers and their girlfriends. Heard a taxi pull in and a familiar voice call his name, tell him to wait for Chrissakes. Ignored it and kept walking. Letting his knowing legs get him somewhere to someone.

Pimlico paid off the taxi and found Charlie working a turnstyle the wrong way. Took him away down a tunnel where it was dark and quiet and safe. Cleaned him up in the deserted showers and dressed him in street clothes Charlie had left in Trooper's dressing room. Took him to the liquor store behind the Directors' Bar and let him fall apart with a cigarette and a slug of Irish to the sounds of celebration braying through the wall. Lost the gun down a drain, and walked Charlie to where Margot played hostess with a face like bleached chalk. Watched them embrace like lost kids with the whole firm crowding around, and went off to find the New York bookies in their corner. Tapped Domino on the shoulder and held Pollard by the bicep.

'You owe the man money, gents,' he told them.

'You'll take cash?' Domino said.

'Oh blimey yeah,' said Pimlico.

THE END

The Smoke
by Tom Barling

When a Maltese assassin buries Archie Ogle, London's 'Godfather', under a collapsed building, thirty years of peace are swept away as the old gangland loyalties end in a bitter struggle for supremacy.

Now everybody wants a piece of the action. Eyetie Antoni dreams of a Mafia empire in the West End. The Troys from Bethnel Green want Archie's Mayfair casinos while the Harolds want to destroy the Troys' control of the East End. The Tonnas from Toronto want Archie's international money laundry, the Triads see London as the drugs capital of Europe, and a shadowy City financier plans to forge his own organisation from the shambles.

Only one man — Charlie Dance, professional villain and Archie's top gun — stands in the way of all of them. Divided by greed and the brutal lust for power, they are united in one common aim — KILL CHARLIE DANCE!

THE SMOKE
sweeps from climax to climax: across the battle-scarred map of London, through the drug networks of Asia to a final explosive confrontation in the diamond fields of South Africa where Charlie Dance makes a last desperate stand.

0552 125040

God is an Executioner
by Tom Barling

IN A WORLD WITHOUT MERCY . . .
Matthew Pepper thought he'd left the horror and corruption of
Vietnam behind and that only his nightmares stood between him
and contentment. But a ruthless gang of terrorists explodes into
his new life and kidnaps his wife and son, leaving no trace of
them. And it is only then that Pepper's nightmares really begin.

Faced with a hostile police force that believes him guilty of
murder, Pepper's only thought (and hope) is to track down those
responsible. And Pepper can do it — because Pepper is a lethal
killing machine, his skills honed in the murderous tunnels of
Vietnam.

But someone has gone to a lot of trouble to set Pepper up,
someone out of his past, now dangerously close to the heart of
Washington. Someone who has to get Pepper before Pepper can
get him.

**For the first chilling confrontation to the final devastating
climax,
GOD IS AN EXECUTIONER
is Tom Barling writing
at his raw and ferocious best.**

0552 128139

A SELECTED LIST OF FINE TITLES
AVAILABLE FROM CORGI BOOKS

THE PRICES SHOWN BELOW WERE CORRECT AT THE TIME OF
GOING TO PRESS. HOWEVER TRANSWORLD PUBLISHERS RESERVE
THE RIGHT TO SHOW NEW RETAIL PRICES ON COVERS WHICH MAY
DIFFER FROM THOSE PREVIOUSLY ADVERTISED IN THE TEXT OR
ELSEWHERE.

*All Corgi/Bantam Books are available at your bookshop or newsagent, or can be ordered from the
following address:*

Corgi/Bantam Books,
Cash Sales Department,
P.O. Box 11, Falmouth, Cornwall TR10 9EN

Please send a cheque or postal order (no currency) and allow 60p for postage and packing for the
first book plus 25p for the second book and 15p for each additional book ordered up to a
maximum charge of £1.90 in UK.

B.F.P.O. customers please allow 60p for the first book, 25p for the second book plus 15p per copy
for the next 7 books, thereafter 9p per book.

Overseas customers, including Eire, please allow £1.25 for postage and packing for the first book,
75p for the second book, and 28p for each subsequent title ordered.